MY NAME IS MARTHA BROWN

Nicola Thorne's perceptive storytelling skills have won her an army of fans, and she is the author of many well-known novels. South African born, she came to England when she was a child and was educated at a convent school and the London School of Economics. She worked for many years in publishing before becoming a full-time writer. A Londoner for most of her adult life, she has now made her home in Dorset where she became fascinated by the mysterious life and tragic death of Martha Brown.

By the Same Author

A WOMAN LIKE US
THE PERFECT WIFE AND MOTHER
THE DAUGHTERS OF THE HOUSE
WHERE THE RIVERS MEET
AFFAIRS OF LOVE
THE ENCHANTRESS SAGA
CHAMPAGNE
PRIDE OF PLACE
SWIFT FLOWS THE RIVER
BIRD OF PASSAGE
THE RECTOR'S DAUGHTER
CHAMPAGNE GOLD
A WIND IN SUMMER
SILK
PROFIT AND LOSS
TROPHY WIFE
REPOSSESSION
WORLDS APART
OLD MONEY
IN THIS QUIET EARTH
THE GOOD SAMARITAN
PAST LOVE
A FAMILY AFFAIR
A TIME OF HOPE
CLASS REUNION
IN TIME OF WAR

The Askham Chronicles
NEVER SUCH INNOCENCE
YESTERDAY'S PROMISES
BRIGHT MORNING
A PLACE IN THE SUN

My Name is
Martha Brown

NICOLA THORNE

HarperCollinsPublishers

HarperCollins*Publishers*
77–85 Fulham Palace Road,
Hammersmith, London W6 8JB

www.**fire**and**water**.com

This paperback edition 2000
1 3 5 7 9 8 6 4 2

First published in Great Britain by
HarperCollins*Publishers* 2000

Although this work is a work of fiction,
it is based on real historical events surrounding the public hanging
of Martha Brown in Dorset in 1856 and, therefore, some of the characters
portrayed therein are based on the real people involved in the incident.
However, any resemblance to any persons, living or dead, who are
unconnected with the incident is entirely coincidental.

ISBN 0 00 651365 4

Typeset in Perpetua by
Palimpsest Book Production Limited,
Polmont, Stirlingshire

Printed and bound in Great Britain by
Omnia Books Limited, Glasgow

This book is dedicated, with affection and admiration for their tenacity, to 'the team' whose lives, like mine, have for so long revolved around Martha:

Nick, Angela and Graham

Contents

Part I

WAYS OF ESCAPE

1831–9

A Marriage in
Powerstock

Chapter One

May 1831

There must be a way of escape, Martha Clark thought wearily, leaning her head against the warm brown flank of the cow, momentarily resting from her labour. The heavy wooden pail beneath the cow's udders was half full and soon her brothers would be along to take it to the dairy house by the side of the farm.

It was late afternoon and the fields about her were bathed in a golden light, the trees and hedgerows covered with the fine green gossamer of spring, the frothy white blossom of blackthorn.

Martha was a country girl who had grown up in this land, largely indifferent to its beauty as she had toiled from an early age on the farm. If she had dreams they were not about the glories of the Dorset countryside but about the harsh demands that its care, the nurture of its beasts and crops, made on her daily life. Her dreams were of being other than what she was: someone who could read and write, live in a nice, neat house, consort with educated people, maybe even have a servant, her own cow and hens and a pig or two.

There was no end to her speculation as to what she might be were her father not a dairyman, and her life not that of a dairymaid who milked cows and helped her mother in the dairy from early morning until nightfall, to eke out their meagre existence.

There were rich farmers in the district who, though not gentry, sent their boys to be educated and their daughters to learn the piano. They sat in the best pews at church and looked down their noses at the rest of the congregation. Why, even their servants were better off than the families who worked on the land to feed them.

Martha grasped the teat of her cow, Prudence, and gently, deftly continued with her task until the pail was nearly full and she sat back, wiping her brow, and looking at her sister Mary who, a few yards away, was still earnestly engaged in milking. On the other side Ann had finished and was carefully wiping the teats of her cow. Ann's milk pail would be fuller than those of her sisters. She was diligent, a hard worker, whereas Mary was rather slow and Martha, well Martha was a dreamer, unhappy with her lot.

Martha was convinced that, somehow, she had been changed at birth, whisked out of a great house to a lowly farm dwelling. She'd had this fixed in her mind for a very long time. She was not like the others; she didn't even look like them. She was of different stock.

As the church clock struck six the brothers, Tom and Charles, appeared over the brow of the hill. Ann stood up and gave her cow a friendly pat and it trotted off to resume its grazing. As the sun began to sink, shadows lengthened across the meadow. Mary was still hard at work, her lips pursed in concentration, her brow

4

furrowed. Martha wiped Prudence's teats with a clean cloth and then she too stood up and indicated the heavy pails of foaming, creamy milk.

'You can take Ann's and mine, Tom. Charlie can wait for Mary's because she's slow.' Martha, though younger than her two sisters, always gave the orders in a firm, authoritative voice.

'Right!' Tom, seventeen, a tall dark-haired lad of few words, hooked the pails to the yoke, and slowly, grimacing, the veins bulging on his forehead, lifted the heavy yoke onto his shoulders.

'Father said Mary has to leave if she hasn't finished. Mother wants the milk for butter making and it has to be set tonight.'

As Mary sat back, little Charles, ten years old and small for his age, lifted the heavy pail and, with a grunt, tottered after his brother, moving the pail from one hand to the other as he tried to keep up.

The sisters stood watching and, as Martha stooped to pick up her milking stool, she looked at her sisters, passing her forearm wearily across her brow.

'I'm so tired,' she said. 'I *wish* there was another way.'

'Another way of what?' Ann asked, smiling, because she already knew the answer. Who didn't know about Martha and her dreams?

'You *know* what I mean. There must be another way of living. A better way. Other people do. Why can't we?'

Ann stood considering Martha. The eldest sister, Ann was as practical as she was diligent. She was used to Martha's dreams, the fantasies she wove about her birth: that, somehow, she had been spirited away from a castle to a croft. Yet one endured Martha's stories because they were amusing. She had a gift. Lying in their beds at night, listening to her, it was possible to believe in that enchanted world far away from the daily grind.

'What other people?'

'Folks with money, you know. Mr Walbridge's daughter has music lessons and never does a hand's turn in the farm.'

'Ideas beyond your station,' Ann grunted. 'You always have had, Martha. Maybe you should marry Mr Bearn.'

'But he's so old. He's as old as Father, well almost.'

'He's a lot younger than Father, though I must say he doesn't look it.'

'Anyway,' Martha concluded with a note of finality, 'he never asked me. No reason why he should.'

She skipped ahead of her sisters because she was taller and stronger than them, lithe and athletic. Her tiredness soon wore off. They plodded behind her carrying their stools, across the succulent green grass interspersed with buttercups, past the frothy blackthorn and catkins in the hedgerows.

As they descended the hill she could see Mr Bearn's house by the river below the church, a large house with sprawling buildings surrounded by an orchard full of apple and cherry blossom.

Mr Bearn was a man of a certain standing in the community who had extensive property and lands which he rented from the Earl of Darlington. He kept cattle in the fields above Powerstock, butchered them himself and sold the meat in Dorchester and Bridport from where it was often taken by boat to London.

He had an orchard full of fine apples from which he

made cider, and he also brewed beer from hops grown in the fields.

Mr Bearn had been the subject of some discussion in the family: ever since the Clarks had recently returned to Powerstock to try their luck, he had asked Martha's occasional help in looking after his orphaned children, his young wife having died in childbirth. He had a boy, James, and a girl, Eliza, named after his late wife.

He always asked for Martha, never for Mary or Ann. Her sisters teased her that it was because he liked her, and Martha knew this was true. He definitely sought her company, he set out to please her and had promised to teach her to read and write. There was something pleasing about Mr Bearn, also an understated flirtatiousness, not obtrusive or rude, almost a gallantry. Nothing to which one could possibly take exception.

Despite his profession as a publican and butcher he was shy, almost gentlemanly. He was self-taught and had a shelf of books. But the idea of marriage to Mr Bearn was not something she entertained. For one thing he was too old and, for another, his daughter Eliza was a thorn in Martha's side. She could never have lived with her.

But more important, there was someone else who had captured her fancy, her passion, if not yet her heart: Josiah Symes who worked for Mr Bearn in the slaughterhouse and looked after the cattle. They were the same age. They liked to be together, to exchange, when alone, hot, passionate kisses while Josiah put his hand inside her bodice and frenziedly squeezed her breasts.

It was a very physical thing. Josiah had no ambition except perhaps that of the moment: getting Martha to go that final step which, so far, she had refused to do. She was too afraid of her mother, also called Martha, who, as she and her sisters now approached the house, was standing in the doorway of the creamery where she churned the butter and made the cheese, hands on her hips, a familiar expression of disapproval on her face.

'You've been a long time,' her mother chided. 'I expected you to get the supper, Ann, and there's a lot for you to do in the house, Mary. Oh, and Mr Bearn sent to ask if you would look after the children, Martha, while he goes to a meeting at the vicarage. Hurry now. I expected you back before this. You dawdle in the fields, you girls.'

Nothing pleased Mrs Clark very much. She was a sour, rather grim woman, always complaining, always scolding, finding fault, particularly with her younger daughter. Martha and her mother did not get on.

'But I haven't had nothing to eat, Mother,' Martha said querulously.

'You'll find something at Mr Bearn's, I daresay. I told Josiah you hadn't had your supper.'

'Oh, *Josiah* came did he?' Mary looked archly at her sister.

'And you be careful with that young man,' her mother rounded on her. 'He has no money and no honourable intentions. If he puts you in the family way, your father will have you out of here, and you'll find yourself in the poorhouse before you know it.'

'Mother, you wouldn't put *Martha* in the poorhouse would you?' Mary looked with mock horror at her mother.

'I wouldn't have her here with a bastard and she knows it. I wouldn't know where to put my face. But

I tell you one thing, Josiah Symes is in no position to provide for her. So you take care, my girl. Now, be on your way or Mr Bearn will be annoyed.'

Martha, angered by her mother's taunts, hurried to the room which she shared with her older sisters and with the youngest, Elizabeth, who was a delicate child of eleven and did only light work about the farm. She helped her mother with the butter and cheese, collected the eggs and was her father's favourite. In his eyes Elizabeth could do no wrong.

Martha unfastened her black pinafore, straightened her dress and removed the clogs she wore for milking, putting on her one pair of good shoes to which she gave a quick polish with her sleeve. She took off the scarf that had kept her dark curls out of her eyes and ran a brush through them. Then she hurried downstairs, out of the door, taking care to avoid her mother. She crossed the yard, treading carefully past the pigsty, and walked swiftly along the lane that ran down to the church which stood on a hill dominating the village and serving as a gathering point as well as a place of refuge and worship.

It was in a state of disrepair as, indeed, was the whole village of Powerstock, whose narrow lanes ran with mud in the winter. Many of its cottages needed rethatching and some of the inhabitants were so slovenly that piles of filth stood before their doors, a dire stench rising up from them.

All roads seemed to end in Powerstock. Yet, despite its poverty, it was a small, pretty village attractively set in a wooded hilly part of West Dorset between Beaminster and Bridport.

Martha had lived all her life in this area, bounded on

the west by the Marshood Vale, where she had been born, and to the east by the great pre-historic mound of Eggardon Hill, beyond which she had never been. Among her dreams of bettering herself was getting the chance to travel in far-off places, to shake the dust of her native county off her feet.

Her father, as a dairyman with a large family, had moved frequently during her childhood seeking greener pastures, but he had not always been successful. He seemed dogged by bad luck. The gradual enclosure of the common fields had reduced the number of small farmers from whom he could hire cows and the dairy house. The bigger farmers, who could afford to buy the land, had grown even wealthier and employed their own dairymen and, as John Clark had an independent streak and liked to work for himself, opportunities had grown fewer as the small farmers went out of business.

The farmer he was renting a few cows and a mean house from now was teetering on the brink. It was difficult to make a living from the small quantities of cheese and butter his wife was able to make or the milk he could sell from his cart.

It had been a weary business moving house every year or so to another place, usually nearby, with Mrs Clark nearly always pregnant and the burden of looking after the young children and working in the fields falling to the older ones. Some people, most she supposed, considered it their birthright: but Martha was sure that if one tried, struggled, maybe, one could get away, achieve something better.

Martha turned right by the church and walked down the hill until she came to the large house by the river, Meadways, where Bernard Bearn lived with his two young children, one of whom was awaiting her expectantly.

'You're late. Father already went to the vicarage,' Eliza said accusingly. 'James is in the orchard with Josiah.' She looked slyly up at Martha. 'You like Josiah, don't you?'

'Not particularly,' Martha said in an offhand manner. 'Did you have something to eat?'

'There's cold beef and bread in the larder. Father said to help yourself.'

As Martha went into the larder Eliza followed her and then leaned against the kitchen table, chin propped on her hands, as Martha returned with a huge side of beef and cut herself some slices, laying them on a plate.

Eliza was a tall, languid, attractive child who looked much older than her years. Her mother had died giving birth to her brother so Eliza had been deprived of that special maternal love, though her father, who adored her, did what he could to make up for it. She had to grow up early to become the woman of the house. She was bright and alert and could already read at eight, whereas Martha couldn't even sign her name. Indeed, Eliza seemed to regard Martha as a servant paid to look after her, whose family were definitely inferior.

Whereas James was lovable Eliza was cold, critical, censorious. Martha never felt comfortable in her presence.

'What did you do today?' she asked.

'I went with Father to Bridport. He was taking a cart of meat for the ship. He bought me a new dress. Would you like to see it?' Eliza's bored expression vanished.

Martha nodded and Eliza ran out of the room to return a few moments later with the dress over her arm and a new bonnet on her head. She held the dress against her and pirouetted round. It was, indeed, very pretty: made of blue muslin with a pattern of forget-me-nots and cornflowers, a gathered bodice and gigot sleeves.

'Ann Walbridge has one like it,' she said, referring to her friend who was the daughter of one of the district's most prosperous farmers. 'Ann is going to study piano in Bridport and Father says I may go with her.'

Martha swallowed. Eliza was always talking about her friendship with the Walbridges, of whom there were many in Powerstock, some more affluent than others. They were prominent on the parish councils, the manorial court, the Poor Law Commission and other worthy bodies. Under the scrutiny of Eliza, Martha finished her meal and took the plate to the sink wondering how best to while away the rest of the evening with a youthful charge who never wanted to go to bed.

At the sound of a commotion outside the kitchen door she looked up and saw James running across the yard with Josiah Symes close behind. They pulled up just outside the door and there ensued a friendly scuffle at the end of which Josiah triumphantly wrenched the ball from James, which he had been clutching tightly to his chest with both arms, and began to retrace his footsteps across the yard. Hurriedly wiping her hands on a cloth, Martha went to the door and called after him: 'That will do, Josiah. It's time young Master James was in bed.'

She reached out and pulled James in by the scruff of his neck while he wriggled and panted in an effort to get away from her, at the same time giving voice to loud squeals which stopped when Martha had him inside.

'That's enough now,' she said sharply. 'Your father

will want you in bed by the time he comes home.' She looked over at Eliza. 'And *you*, missy.'

Eliza gazed at her, her expression stubborn. 'I am a year older than James.'

'I don't care how old you are. It's time for bed.'

She turned to see Josiah Symes leaning against the doorpost, a sly expression on his face. He tossed the ball to James.

'Best do as Martha says. Don't want your pa to give you a walloping.'

'You run up to bed now, and I'll come and say goodnight,' Martha promised, giving James a little push towards the door. 'And you too,' she said to Eliza.

'I suppose you want to be alone with *him*,' Eliza gestured meaningfully towards Josiah.

'I'll thank you not to be cheeky, and Josiah is about to go home, aren't you, Josiah?'

'Bernard said I could have something to eat,' Josiah looked hungrily at the side of beef still on the kitchen table. 'Said there was some beer in the larder too.'

'Oh well!' Martha shrugged and then once more pointed towards the door. 'Do as I tell you, Eliza. You know Mrs Gill was much stricter than me. If you don't behave yourself, maybe she'll come back.'

Mrs Gill from Netherbury had been a particularly strict disciplinarian, unpopular with both children, and their father had reluctantly agreed to send her away on condition the children behaved themselves and did as they were told.

The mention of Mrs Gill's name was enough to send Eliza scurrying out of the room, by which time Josiah had emerged from the larder with a jug of beer which he had drawn from the barrel.

13

'Brewed this myself,' he said, holding the jug towards Martha. 'Could you do with a drop?'

Martha smiled at him and, going over to a shelf, selected two glasses and put them on the table in front of him.

'Shall I cut you some beef?' she asked in a soft voice, her manner towards him changing.

'I'd prefer a kiss.' Sensing the change, he poured the foaming beer into their glasses.

Martha looked anxiously towards the door.

'Mind what you say. For all I know that little miss has her ear pressed to the door.'

'Oh she's all right.' Josiah handed Martha her glass but she was now busy laying slices of beef on a plate in front of her.

'She doesn't like me.' Martha pointed towards a chair and handed him his plate.

'She's not exactly fond of anyone except her pa.'

'*And* the Walbridges.'

'Oh, she's fond of them, and the Walburtons, and the vicar and his wife. Anyone who is anyone in the village is a friend of Miss Eliza. They say that Bernard is anxious to find her a new mother.' His gaze lingered on Martha.

'Why do you look at me?' Martha put the glass to her lips and slumped provocatively in a chair, facing Josiah.

'You know he likes you, Martha.'

'He is as old as my father.'

Josiah shook his head. 'No matter how old he is, he's rich. He could give you a good life. It's what you want, isn't it?'

Martha looked across at him, her expression unfathomable. '*Why* are you saying all this to me, Josiah?'

'Well, isn't it what you want? The good life? You're always talking about wanting something different. Bernard could give you that.'

Although his tone was sarcastic Martha finished her beer, rose from the table and went over to the sink where she began to wash out her glass, her expression resolute. That was that, then. His kisses meant nothing. She had been warned they didn't. Ann had warned her because she too had dallied with Josiah Symes, and so had a lot of the girls in the village. Josiah was tall and fair, his hair bleached by the sun from the long hours spent in the fields in summer. All the girls fancied him.

'You don't mind if I marry an old man?'

As Martha felt his presence behind her, she slowly turned to face him, her head level with his chest. He put his arms around her and, pinioning her against the kitchen sink, stuck his knee in her crotch, beginning to kiss her violently, his hand sliding under her bodice and grasping her breast. She felt that surge of raw desire Josiah always aroused in her, an abandonment as she threw her head back and let him kiss her neck, her cheeks, finally her lips in a bruising embrace.

'What time is the old man back?' he said breathlessly, trying to lower her to the floor.

'Oh no!' She shuddered. 'Not *here*. I wouldn't dare. That Eliza might be listening to everything.' She hastily rearranged her dress, hurried over to the door and gently opened it.

But there was no one outside and the hallway was in darkness.

'You're a tease, Martha Clark,' Josiah said, tenderly feeling his crotch. 'You lead a man on, always making excuses. You'll do me a terrible injury.'

Martha, her composure restored, returned to the chair by the kitchen table and sat heavily upon it.

'My mother says she'll send me to the poorhouse if I get in the family way. She says you can't offer me nothing.'

'Oh she said that, did she?' Josiah, disgruntled, rose from the floor and leaned sulkily against the sink.

'Everyone knows you have a reputation, Josiah,' Martha said severely. 'A reputation and no money.'

'I'm going to go farming with my cousins, John and Robert. There's a farm coming up in the Purbecks. I'll have plenty of money then.'

'The Purbecks! But that's the other side of the county.'

'Why don't you come with me, Martha? We could be wed here. We'd have a good life.'

He went over to her and attempted to kiss her, but she moved sharply away.

'Don't kiss me, Josiah. I feel confused.'

'I'm making a proposal, Martha.'

'I know that,' she muttered, rising from the chair. 'I don't know what to say. I'd better go and see that the children are in bed.' She looked over at the clock on the mantelpiece above the grate. 'Mr Bearn will be very vexed if he finds you here.'

'Then when will you let me know, Martha? I mean it.'

'I don't know that I want to go all the way to Purbeck. I'll miss my family. It's so far.'

'Will you think about it, Martha?' his tone wheedling, 'I need to find a wife. You'd do as well as anybody.'

'Oh *thank* you,' she said, feeling stung, pointing towards the door.

*   *   *

Later that night Martha thought of Josiah's hot kisses, his strong body, the hard thing that had pressed against her as they'd kissed so passionately by the sink, her burning response. It had nearly happened several times, but always she drew back. She was afraid. Too many girls in the village had babies out of wedlock, were disowned by their families and ended up in Beaminster Poorhouse. They were a disgrace, a shame. It was said that Bernard's first wife's mother had been no better than she should be, and that Elizabeth Bearn had been born out of wedlock, her mother's stigma attaching itself to her.

Appearances meant a lot to Martha. She knew she was nice looking, with her gleaming black curls and olive skin, her dark brown eyes, her neat trim figure, taller than the average woman. She wanted to keep herself nice inside as well as out, to be respectable, to raise her standing in the world.

And Josiah had never mentioned love. It was as though he was choosing a suitable cow. She'd do as well as anybody. The passionate kisses, the feelings of desire, would wane. She'd be a wife, a housemaid, a breeding machine, like her mother. She'd grow sour like her, carping, critical. The dreamer Martha wanted romance in her life rather than a business arrangement.

Besides, what chance would she have of bettering herself on a remote farm? It would be a life of drudgery, much as she had now. Perhaps worse.

'What's the matter?' Ann whispered, as Martha turned restlessly in her bed. 'Why can't you sleep? Did Mr Bearn say something?'

'No,' Martha whispered back. 'It was Josiah who said something.'

'What did he say?'

'He said we should marry. He's going to farm with his cousins in the Purbecks.'

There was a long pause. 'And what did you say?'

'I didn't say anything. I didn't feel it was like he loved me. He just wanted a wife to save him looking for one there.'

'You know he doesn't love you. He doesn't love anybody. There is only one thing he wants. You know what that is. They say he has Mary Place in the family way. That's all he's interested in.'

'Mary Place!' Martha was shocked. She was the rather plain daughter of a butcher in Netherbury and well over thirty.

'They say that's why he's going away, to avoid a bastardy order. Mary's father says he'll kill him.'

'Mary Place.' Martha couldn't believe it. 'Maybe it's not true.'

'I think it is true. They were seen together. You wouldn't have thought it because she is so old. Frankly, Martha, I would keep a wide berth of Josiah Symes. No good can come of it. I know him. Believe me.'

She spoke so feelingly that Martha turned to her. 'Did you ever . . . you know . . . with him.'

There was another long silence. Then:

'No I never. I was too frightened of Mother.'

'I was frightened, too.'

'Thank God for that.' Ann gave a sigh of relief and patted her sister on the shoulder. 'Put Josiah out of your mind. Try and get some sleep.'

Chapter Two

September 1831

The young man working in the orchard picking up the rotten apples from the ground and putting them in a wheelbarrow had a look of Josiah: tall, thin, with fair, sunbleached hair. But it was not he. His name was Ezekiel Burridge, he was Josiah Symes's replacement and he came from Symondsbury. Martha sighed and, as she turned from the window, she saw that Mr Bearn had entered and was standing in a corner of the room gazing at her.

'Do you miss him?'

'Who?' Martha said defensively.

'Josiah. *I* do. He was a very good worker.' Mr Bearn had some books under his arm and moved over to the table where he took a seat.

'I don't miss him at all,' Martha sniffed. 'Why should I?'

'I thought . . . well I understood . . .'

'There was nothing to understand. He was just someone I knew.'

'I see.' Mr Bearn appeared to consider what she said. 'Eliza thought . . .'

'I don't know why you prefer the word of a young girl over mine, Mr Bearn,' Martha said sharply.

'I don't *prefer it*, but she is very observant. She told me she thought you would miss Josiah when he left so suddenly.'

'Eliza is wrong.' Martha moved a hand to cover her hot cheek.

She lied. She did miss him. It was the manner of his going that irked. He hadn't even said goodbye or returned to ask whether she would marry him or not. His abrupt departure had made tongues wag that the story about Mary Place was true. Yet, months later, Mary Place was still walking about Netherbury with her stomach as flat as a pancake.

'Well that's that then.' Mr Bearn appeared unconvinced but spread the books he had been carrying in front of him. 'I thought we might do a little reading, Martha,' he said, consulting the timepiece that was tucked in a pocket of his waistcoat. 'We have an hour or so before Eliza returns. Would you like that?'

'Yes, Mr Bearn,' Martha nodded docilely and went and sat next to him at the table.

Reading and writing. So important but so difficult to learn, she thought, watching him effortlessly cover a sheet of paper with bold, flowing strokes from his pen frequently dipped in ink.

'How are you coming on with your writing, Martha?' Mr Bearn enquired.

She hung her head.

'Can you show me?'

He put a piece of paper in front of Martha and handed her his pen. She felt her heart thudding painfully in her chest. She bent her head, grasped the pen, pursed her lips and looked at the paper. Very carefully she began the upward stroke of the 'M'. Then she stopped.

'Down again,' Mr Bearn said encouragingly and he gently put his hand over hers and guided it until she had jerkily finished the name Martha.

'There,' he exclaimed triumphantly, as if the completion of the task gave him much pleasure, and removed his hand.

'But you did it all,' she felt defeated and dismayed.

'Then you do it.'

Once again the upward stroke of the 'M'. Then, painfully, the downward stroke. Then up again. This time the triumphant smile was hers.

'Well done, Martha!' Mr Bearn's hand gently closed over hers again and stayed there.

'Martha, there is something I want to ask you,' he said, looking intently at her. 'I realise you will want to talk to your parents about it, and it is something you must consider carefully.' He let go of her hand and stood up, thumbs in the pocket of his waistcoat, and stared intently out of the window. He was a tall, strong-looking man in his breeches and white shirt, open at the neck with a handkerchief tied round it. He'd been working with Ezekiel in the orchard and the line above the handkerchief was red and continued so upward, while below it was white.

Mr Bearn had black hair heavily streaked with grey, a strong yet kindly face with well-defined features, and a firm rather humourless mouth, a hint of sternness in it. In repose his expression was usually solemn as though the cares of life weighed heavily upon him. He was a sad man, seldom given to laughter and one felt that he had never recovered from the death of his wife whose grave he regularly visited.

He was also a man given to prolonged silences and Martha regarded him carefully now as he gazed out of the window thoughtfully sucking his lower lip. 'Martha,' he said, turning, 'you know I have had a series of housekeepers since my dear wife died. None of them have proved really satisfactory. Mrs Green, who went home last week to nurse her mother, will not be returning. I wondered, Martha, if it is a position that might appeal to you? You know me by now, you know the workings of the house, and the children like you.'

'Like me!' Martha gasped. 'Eliza does *not* like me.'

'Oh yes she does,' Mr Bearn smiled indulgently. 'She pretends she does not like you because she is a little madam. She likes to tease. Anyway, she prefers you to Mrs Green or Mrs Gale, and James likes you very much. I realise of course that your mother and father will miss the work you do for them but, on the other hand, I will pay you a wage as well as free board and lodging.'

'You mean I will *live* here!' Martha exclaimed.

'Of course. Occasionally I am away for days when I go to market or to London or Bristol to seek new outlets for my products. I make a very fine cider which I think would do well in the taverns there. You will have your own room. You have to share one with your sisters, I believe?'

Martha nodded. Her own room!

'What do you think, Martha?'

'I think I'll have to ask my mother and father.' Martha's eyes were troubled. 'I don't know what they'll say.'

*   *   *

'That man is an impudent rogue,' Mrs Clark exclaimed wrathfully. 'Who does he think we are?'

'Some very respectable women have held the position, Mother.'

'Yes, but they were much older women, Martha, considerably older than you. A girl of nearly twenty and him nearer forty! Your reputation will be ruined and, believe me, it is not hard to lose a reputation in these parts. No respectable man would look at you. You would be used goods.'

'I don't know what you mean, Mother.' Martha gazed at her feet.

'You do know what I mean, Martha.' Her mother came over to her and stamped her foot. 'Don't you be impertinent. You're no fool, so don't pretend to be one. Besides, why does he want a young woman like you living there? There are plenty of older people for the position, whose reputation no one cares about.' She turned to her husband. 'Well, John, what do you think?'

John Clark sat at the table peacefully smoking his pipe, looking as though he was not paying much attention to the proceedings, his mind elsewhere, his wife's hysterics as usual passing over him. At the age of fifty-three he was a good-looking man, slim and strong with a weather-beaten face and a mass of thick dark hair. It was said in the village that he still had an eye for the women, but his wife gave him little opportunity to indulge it, even if he dared. Mrs Clark was the head of the household in everything but name. John Clark was easy-going, indulgent with his children. But his wife ruled the roost.

John Clark removed his pipe and, leaning towards

the cold grate, knocked it on the side. Then he looked at the two Marthas and shrugged.

'Don't know what to say.'

'But you must have *something* to say.' His wife goaded him. 'Don't you care about your daughter's reputation?'

'Bernard is well thought of. I don't think he'd take advantage . . .'

'Never mind whether he would or not. It's what people think that matters.'

'And you say they'd think worse of our Martha?'

'Yes I do, with no other servants in the house.'

'The money would be useful.'

'Five shillings a week,' Martha said and beside her Mary's eyes grew round as she echoed:

'Five shillings! Whatever would you do with such a sum?'

'I would save for a new dress, and the rest I would put aside for . . .' she paused and looked speculatively at her sister, 'for when I go away.'

'Go where for heaven's sake?' her mother asked sharply.

In the background, listening to the conversation but saying little, Ann smiled.

Martha's escape fund: that's where the money would go.

Mrs Clark stood at the gate of the field leading to Meadways, hesitating. Should she go in or continue down the road and across the bridge, ostensibly to see a friend who lived on the other side of the river?

All night she had thought about her plan without mentioning it to a soul, certainly not her husband or Martha, the matter of whose future they had left unresolved when, after tears and raised voices, they had finally crawled into bed. Nor had it been referred to in the morning, which seemed to come round all too quickly, and the children were about their various tasks in the dairy and on the farm.

Young William, who showed some aptitude for scholarship, took private lessons from the curate. Little Elizabeth would have liked to have some lessons too, but in her mother's opinion there was no place in a woman's life for learning. No need for it at all.

Mrs Clark leaned over the gate looking at the house which she had never been in. It was a substantial dwelling, a farmhouse with a barn and outbuildings, a house for slaughtering cattle and a place for storing carcases, a large garden at back and front, and an orchard beyond. The property was on a slope bounded at the top by a wall which backed onto the Three Horse Shoes public house, and the river at the bottom. Prettily situated in a dip it was possible to see from the house the bold outline of Eggardon Hill and the remains, to the south, of Powerstock Castle.

Mrs Clark nodded with approval, thinking to herself how nice it would be to have Martha installed as mistress of such a place. It would get a troublesome daughter out of her hair as well, someone with an iron will, opinionated and argumentative, someone who led while her sisters followed, with whom she had never seen eye to eye.

The Bearns and the Clarks knew one another, having come from the same village, Netherbury, a few miles distant, but the Bearns, who farmed, were slightly further up the social scale than the Clarks, who were mere labourers. To be a butcher or a farmer, a publican, a cordwainer or a carter was to be numbered among the skilled, while the term 'labourer' covered just about everything.

Her husband had been a labourer on her father's farm until, maybe as an inducement to marry her, to get one of his four daughters off his hands, Richard Hussey had given him enough money to rent some cows and set himself up as a dairyman.

Martha Clark was a determined woman, not lacking in courage, but it seemed a bit much, even to her, to march up to the door of Bernard Bearn, a man she hardly knew, and, well, take him to task.

At the last moment her nerve failed her and she was about to continue down the road when, hearing a sound behind her, she turned and saw a cart full of hay driven by Ezekiel Burridge who hailed her with his long whip.

'Good morning, Mrs Clark.'

'Good morning, Ezekiel,' she said.

'Are you looking for Martha, Mrs Clark?'

'Martha is in the dairy.' Suddenly her courage revived. 'As a matter of fact I came hoping for a word with Mr Bearn. Is he about?'

'It's his day for doing his accounts,' Ezekiel said, jumping down from the cart and walking across to open the heavy gate, swinging it back for her to pass through.

'After you, Mrs Clark.'

'Why thank you, Ezekiel.'

As he passed through she closed the gate after him, fastening the catch. The cart trundled towards the barn by the side of the house, Martha following on behind.

'I'll tell Mr Bearn you're here,' Ezekiel said as he dismounted, tethered the horse and, crossing the yard, disappeared through the back door.

Martha walked round to the front of the house which was covered with roses whose full, fragrant pink blooms were now past their best. Autumn was in the air. Around her the leaves fluttered gently down from the trees.

The front door opened and Mr Bearn appeared and beckoned to her.

'Do come in, Mrs Clark. I hope I haven't kept you waiting?'

Martha shook her head and hurried up the path, pausing to wipe her feet on the mat just inside the door.

'There's a lot of mud on the road,' she said apologetically.

'I'm afraid we're going to have a bad winter,' Mr Bearn said, closing the door. 'I feel it in my bones.'

She waited for him to lead the way and followed him along the hall into a pleasant parlour overlooking the orchard. Everything about it seemed to gleam and shine: the floorboards, the heavy walnut sideboard and table on which there were papers – obviously the accounts he'd been working on – and the black grate in which a fire roared.

She settled into a chintz-covered easy chair and looked about her.

'What a nice place you have here, Mr Bearn.'

'Thank you,' he said, settling opposite her. 'I think so.'

'Have you been here long?'

'The house was in the family of my late wife. We came here after our marriage.' Mr Bearn gave a deep sigh. 'Alas, she died here, too, giving birth to our son James. It's a sad thing for a man to be alone with two children.' He sighed heavily once again.

'Very sad.' Martha lowered her eyes in sympathy.

'And how do you like Powerstock, Mrs Clark?'

Martha made a face. Never a beauty, she had become, by her mid forties, a stern-faced woman whose sepulchral appearance was not helped by her habit of wearing black, maybe in mourning for the babies she herself had lost in twenty years of almost relentless childbearing. Her chalk-white face and tight little grey curls framed by a black bonnet made her seem much older than her years.

'We have lived here before, Mr Bearn. Our daughter Elizabeth was born here. We have, of course, moved around as farmers have given up land, which they farmed but could not afford to buy, because of the enclosures. Times have been hard.'

Martha leaned forward in her chair. 'It's not what I am used to, Mr Bearn. I was born a Hussey and was brought up to better things.'

'Oh, you were a Hussey?' Mr Bearn looked impressed. 'I did not realise that. Of course I know the Husseys. Robert Hussey . . .'

'Is my cousin. He farms four hundred acres.' Martha leaned even closer towards him. 'I married beneath me, you know. It's no secret. My husband, John, although a good man, was a labourer working on my father's farm. Everyone at the time said . . .' she faltered, 'well, you know how it is. He was handsome and I was headstrong. I will not criticise my husband except to say that he has little idea of business. He is too easy-going, too trusting. I learned how to manage the hard way. I try and make

28

the most of things, and my cheese and butter are the best value in the district.'

'So I hear, Mrs Clark.' Mr Bearn smiled amiably. 'But let us come to what I suspect is the reason for your visit. Martha told you about my offer?'

Mrs Clark's expression became grim. She drew a deep breath.

'Oh yes, she told me. We had a family council about the matter. It is appreciated, but I'm afraid there is not the least chance of her accepting it.'

'Oh dear.' Mr Bearn, looking abashed, sat back. 'I'm very sorry to hear that. May I know why?'

'Her reputation, Mr Bearn,' Martha said censoriously. '*Surely* you thought of that?'

'I don't really understand.' Mr Bearn continued to look perplexed.

'Come now, Mr Bearn. A young girl, not quite twenty, living in the same house as a man of,' she paused and looked at him speculatively, 'I suppose forty years? What will people think?'

'Think?' Mr Bearn's confusion seemed to deepen. 'But she works here already.'

'That's quite a different matter isn't it? People about during the day, Ezekiel at work in the slaughterhouse and the orchard.' She looked innocently around her. 'I suppose you have a woman to clean?'

'Well, my housekeeper usually takes care of that.'

'Oh does she? As well as the cooking, bread-baking and looking after the children, and yourself of course? Quite a tall order.'

'No one ever queried it.'

'I suppose they were glad of a roof over their heads. Anyway, that is not the point. My Martha is quite used to hard work, but her reputation is another thing. Once lost it can never be regained. Don't you agree?'

Bernard Bearn perplexedly scratched his forehead. 'It's something I never gave a thought to. My intentions were entirely innocent. However, I suppose you're right.'

'That's settled then.' Martha stood up. 'I am sorry to be the bearer of bad tidings, but my husband and I are quite adamant about it.'

Mr Bearn reluctantly got to his feet.

'But I hope Martha will continue to help out from time to time. That doesn't change does it?'

Mrs Clark, lips tightly pursed, shook her head.

'Oh no. *That* is quite out of the question.'

Mr Bearn's jaw dropped. 'But . . .'

'I think there is already some gossip in the village. It is known that you like Martha.'

'Oh but I do. She is a very engaging young woman. I was teaching her to read and write. Surely . . .'

'There is no need, in my opinion, for a woman to be able to read and write. My daughters are skilled dairymaids and scholarship does not help them to churn butter better or handle a pair of curd knives with the skill necessary to cut the junket when making cheese. My son, William, is taking lessons from the curate. I have no objection to that if William wishes to better himself, but for women it is a waste of time.'

Martha looked towards the orchard, and gave a deep sigh. 'I am sorry to be the bearer of bad news. I earnestly hope you will soon find an *older* woman more suited to the position you are offering. Good day, Mr Bearn.'

As Martha walked towards the door Mr Bearn hurried to waylay her.

'Please Mrs Clark. Before you go, listen to me.' Beads of perspiration had appeared on his forehead which he mopped away with a large white handkerchief. 'I am extremely *loth* to lose Martha. As you say I have become fond of her, extremely so, in fact, but of course there is nothing in the least untoward in my relationship with her. That has been conducted with the utmost propriety. You can be sure of that. I . . .'

He hesitated. Martha looked at him gimlet-eyed feeling, now that she was somehow able to see into the tortuous workings of his mind, that her audacious, even risky plan had worked.

'I wonder if Martha would agree to *marry* me, Mrs Clark?'

'*Marriage*!' Martha cried, feigning astonishment. 'I don't see how . . .'

'I know I am a lot older than she is, but I can provide for her.' Mr Bearn's words fell over themselves. 'She will have a nice home. I will get someone to help her with the cleaning. She will live well. Meat every day. I may, in addition, be able to help Mr Clark find a better job if things now seem insecure for you.'

Martha still appeared unimpressed.

'At least put it to her,' Mr Bearn pleaded. 'Sound her out. If she is not too opposed to it she would make me very happy. And you can be sure that I will do everything in my power to make her happy . . .'

Ezekiel, summoned from the barn to open the gate for Mrs Clark a few moments later, wondered at the sprightliness of her step as she went back up the hill to her home, almost running as if she had some exciting news.

Some weeks before the wedding Mr Bearn had sent Martha into Bridport together with her mother and sister with money to buy a new dress, shoes and bonnet. It was the first new dress Martha had ever had, having previously to exist on cast-offs from the older sisters, all their clothes being made at home and much altered and patched in the process of being passed on. First Ann, then Mary and then her. As for a new bonnet and shoes . . . such luxuries were unheard of.

The dress was made of green velvet with a low, round waist, a close fitting bodice buttoned up to a high collar made of white fur. Her bonnet was of green moiré trimmed inside with white fur, and her cloak of rich green velvet was lined with silk. Her shoes were of soft black kid, quite the finest she had ever had. And everything was brand new. It was almost worth getting married for.

Ann had done her hair the night before, washing and cutting her shiny black curls so that they framed the sides of the bonnet and, though she was a shade pale, it seemed to enhance rather than diminish her natural beauty.

Not to be outdone, Mrs Clark wore her best dress of black bombazine, normally reserved for christenings and funerals, and a felt black bonnet with scalloped edges. Ann wore a simple dress of pale blue and also a cloak and new bonnet, everything paid for by Mr Bearn.

But in the early hours of the night before, the new clothes had been forgotten. Martha had lain in bed clutching Ann's hand and weeping silently into her pillow while Ann did her best to reassure her that Mr Bearn, despite his age, was a good man, a nice, kindly man who would look after her and improve her status in life, something, after all, that she'd always wanted. She would have her own home, he'd promised her a servant. She would be independent of her mother, the frequent and unjustified chastisements that so ruined the day. Martha had wanted to flee that night, but Ann would not let her, pointing out that, anyway, instead of finding freedom she would perish with cold.

So on that cold day in December, two days after Christmas, as she climbed the hill to the church with her family in close attendance, young Martha Clark was shivering not so much from cold as from fear. She felt she was marrying a man she scarcely knew one whit better than when she had first worked for him.

Once his proposal had been accepted the decorous courtship had been conducted in the presence of her family in the kitchen of the dairy house when Mr Bearn came to visit. He would sit there chatting mainly with her father while she listened, or brought tea and cake and clotted cream, or a jug of beer if the men preferred it. She would sit silently watching him – she could never think of him as Bernard – and occasionally he would look at her and give her a kindly, rather avuncular smile.

Her mother had assured her that *she* had hardly known her father, and that's how most people got married; but they had respected each other more as they got to know each other better, and sometimes love came, but not to expect it. She didn't say whether or not she had ever loved John Clark.

The path to the church was thronged with the people of Powerstock who considered that Martha had done quite well for herself, had bettered herself. They peered curiously at the bride and there were many gasps of admiration at her transformation, but Martha didn't see or hear them. Deafened by the sounds of the bells summoning her to her marriage she tried not to think about what she was doing.

Flanked by her family, the numerous Clarks and the Husseys, chattering with excitement and still scarcely recovered from Christmas festivities, who had come from the surrounding villages, she arrived at the porch. Dramatically, at some hidden signal, the bells stopped, and immediately the organ inside the church commenced a rousing anthem. Martha put her arm through her father's and, Ann following close behind, they walked solemnly down the aisle between packed pews to where Mr Bearn stood stiffly to attention in a black suit and with his hair well brushed and his whiskers neatly combed. As she arrived he turned and held out his hand towards her. But Martha ignored him, keeping her eyes on the ground as the curate, Mr Brewster, began the solemn service of marriage.

Afterwards she never remembered saying 'I will' or hearing Bernard say it either. All too soon she found herself in the vestry, a married woman, with the curate inviting her to sign the register under Bernard's name.

Mr Brewster handed her a pen, Bernard looked at her encouragingly. They had rehearsed this moment. She took the pen, gripped it tightly in her hand, leaned forward, but she found that she was unable to focus on the page or remember how to start the upward stroke of the initial letter of her name. She looked at the page and she looked at the pen. Bernard leaned forward as if to put his hand over hers, but she shook her head.

'Can't,' she said in a small voice.

'Make your mark,' Mr Brewster whispered loudly and

Martha made a slash on the page that could have been the beginnings of the 'M' if only she had been able to think straight. Then Mr Brewster wrote carefully over it 'the mark of Martha Clark'. As he did so Martha, stealing a surreptitious glance at Mr Bearn, thought he looked disappointed.

Ann also made her mark, but William, to the evident approval of his teacher, wrote his name and, as he was under age, a friend of Bernard's, George Donn, signed the register too.

Bernard then took Martha by the hand, kissed her cheek and they emerged into the sanctuary as the organ broke into a voluntary, and walked back down the aisle as man and wife.

Martha had never been in a hotel before, never had a meal served to her at table or drunk wine – never tasted wine – never been alone with a man like this: her husband.

She had thought she would not be able to eat, but when she saw the rich fare set before her she realised she was hungry. They had reached the hotel at nightfall having slipped away from the Three Horse Shoes while the wedding party was in full swing. The following day there would be many a sore head. Outside Ezekiel had been waiting with the cart which carried the hay and animal carcasses to market. It smelt strongly of straw and dried blood and Martha sat hunched between Ezekiel and Mr Bearn, well wrapped up in her cloak, glad of the cold air on her hot cheeks during the miles that separated Bridport from Powerstock, a distance made longer by the number of steep hills and winding, narrow lanes.

Mr Bearn – she still couldn't think of him as Bernard

— was obviously known at The Bull Inn and the landlord had personally conducted them to their room where the sight of the large four-poster bed startled her.

When the landlord had gone Bernard sat on the bed, patted it and she sat beside him. He put an arm round her and they had their first kiss. His skin was leathery and prickly and it was nothing like the moist kisses she had enjoyed with Josiah Symes. Nor did she long to open herself to him as she had to Josiah. Quite the reverse.

It seemed an awful indication of what was to come. Bernard had wanted to linger, maybe go further. He stroked her hair and put his hand under her skirt. His breathing became heavier and the veins started to swell on his neck. Martha crossed her legs tightly.

'You are afraid, aren't you?' he asked, not unkindly.

'A little,' she'd said sliding off the bed and, going over to her carefully packed bag and looking for her hairbrush, she sat down at the dressing table and began to brush her hair while behind her Bernard, still sitting on the bed, gazed at her.

To her relief he'd said, 'You must be hungry,' and they went downstairs to dinner.

'Did you come here with your first wife?' Martha asked, looking at him. It was the first time she'd initiated a conversation, and Bernard felt encouraged that the good food and wine was doing its job and that it would eventually make her more receptive to him when they returned to the bedroom.

'Oh no,' he assured her, 'I had not the means then that I have now.'

He laid down his knife and fork and slid a hand across the table towards her. 'This is a very special treat just for you, my dear Martha.'

His gaze embarrassed her. Her eyes strayed to the broad band of her wedding ring. She was married. There was nothing now she could do about it.

Bernard looked around at the other diners in the cheerful dining room with a great fire leaping up the chimney and waiters hurrying about carrying trays groaning with food. There were merchants, citizens of the town, travellers, some with wives, some without; but none of them appeared to be paying any attention to the newly married couple, so he put a finger under Martha's chin and compelled her to look at him.

'I know you don't love me, Martha, as I most surely love you. Today you looked so beautiful as you came towards me in the church I couldn't believe how lucky I was. I want to do all I can to love you, protect you, make you happy. Do you understand?'

'Yes, thank you,' Martha said, nearly adding, 'Mr Bearn', but remembering just in time. The name 'Bernard' still came awkwardly, so she didn't call him anything.

'Martha, tell me this, did you ever kiss Josiah Symes?'

Unprepared as she was for it, the question startled her.

'No I never did.'

'Never?'

'Never!' She shook her head emphatically.

'Do you promise?'

'Yes I promise.'

'Not any man?' His expression was sceptical. He removed his finger from her chin and sat back.

'Not any man.' She shook her head again.

'I find that hard to believe.'

'My mother would never have allowed it.' She looked

earnestly at him. 'You see I was frightened of my ma.'

'Oh *that* I can believe.' Bernard smiled with obvious relief. 'Then I am the first?'

'Yes,' she said and started to tremble.

She should have known it would be over so quickly. After all, she had seen enough animals coupling in the fields: bulls mounting cows, dogs over bitches, stallions covering mares. It only took a few seconds. But somehow she had thought that with humans it would be different. Josiah Symes's kisses had been so tender, long and passionate. They had made you want to give yourself, as he'd wanted, as she'd wanted, if only there hadn't been that overpowering vision of her mother's wrath and the prospect of the poorhouse.

Maybe her husband had had too much wine? As soon as they were back in the bedroom he kissed her clumsily, started fumbling with her dress until she removed it herself for fear of him tearing it. After that he stripped off her underthings quite roughly and then as they tumbled onto the bed he got on top of her and straight into her and she felt she was being torn apart.

After feeling elegant all evening with the candlelight and the red wine gleaming in tall glasses it seemed awful that the day should have ended like this with soiled sheets, a pain between her legs, an ache in her belly, and a feeling of self-disgust that she couldn't altogether explain.

After all it wasn't her fault.

The snores of Bernard lying beside her suddenly stopped. His large hand, calloused with work on the land

and slaughtering animals, began to caress her breasts. She stiffened.

'I'm sorry,' he mumbled. 'I was clumsy. It wasn't very nice for you. It's a long time since I've been with a woman.'

Still, you would have thought he'd remember something, or have learned a little tenderness.

Martha felt shame. Shame and anger, a sense of unworthiness. There was also a feeling, somehow, of being rejected.

This was no way of escape. She had merely exchanged one prison for another.

Chapter Three

May 1832

Martha climbed up the hill clutching a large basket of damp washing. Half way up she paused, looking behind her to where Eliza Bearn toiled with an identical load; only Eliza, as usual, was making heavy work of it, stopping every few seconds, moaning about her lot. She very much objected to having to do anything as mundane as housework, but the more she objected, the more determined Martha became that she should do as she was told. Eliza customarily pointed out that the Walbridge or the Walburton girls didn't have to do the washing or help with the housework whereupon Martha retorted that she wasn't a Walbridge or a Walburton, however much she would like to behave like one. As it was Eliza went once a week to Bridport for music lessons with the Walbridge girls, and twice a week to reading and writing lessons with Mr Brewster.

In Martha's opinion, however, it did Eliza no harm to learn the housewifely arts and already, in the few short months of her marriage, she had had many an argument with her husband on the subject.

'Come on, Eliza,' Martha cried. 'We won't get the washing dry at this rate.' She looked anxiously at the sky with its lowering clouds and intermittent sunshine on a blustery May day.

'I shouldn't have to do it,' Eliza complained, puffing in an exaggerated manner. 'That should be for Joanna.'

'Joanna has enough to do. She has the floors to clean and all the grates to black.' Joanna, still in the boiler house finishing the rest of the laundry, was the servant promised by Bernard, a pleasant girl and a willing workhorse. She was fourteen years of age and greatly patronised by Eliza who tried also to use her as a lady's maid.

Martha reached the washing line and started to hang out the clothes and sheets while Eliza finally caught up with her, dumped the basket on the ground and turned to make her way down again.

'Oh no you *don't*!' Martha called out sharply after her. 'You can help me hang the washing.'

'Do it yourself!' Eliza retorted. 'You're nothing but a servant here. That's why my father married you.'

Martha raised a hand with the intention of slapping Eliza across the face but the girl dodged the blow and ran down the hill calling: 'Servant, servant, servant.'

Martha suddenly experienced a feeling of extreme fatigue and sank onto the pile of wet clothes in the basket running her hand wearily across her brow.

She had, indeed, exchanged one prison for another. Married life was not easy. Being a wife was hard but being a stepmother was particularly difficult. James was no trouble at all. He was warm and loving and seemed pleased to have a permanent feminine presence in the house, a woman young enough to be playful with him.

41

They responded well to each other. Martha was already fond of him and could see the time when she would come to regard him as her own child.

But Eliza? Never. Eliza watched her all the time as if hoping to catch her out. She was forever peering round corners or peeping out of windows. Yet whenever Martha called her to do something, Eliza was never to be found. Sometimes, Martha thought, Eliza actually hated her and she knew that she often lurked outside the bedroom door when Martha was inside with her father, doubtless with her ear pressed closely to the wood.

With a deep sigh Martha rose and completed the hanging of the cumbersome washing on the line by herself. It was not such an onerous task, and yet this feeling of exhaustion worried her. Everything seemed an effort. It was strange, not at all like her, someone who was used to being busy from morning until night, milking cows twice a day, doing housework and then spending the rest of her full day in the dairy house helping to make the cheese and the butter.

Her task finished, she gathered up both empty baskets and slowly began to make her way back down the hill towards the house. She saw a familiar figure sauntering casually through the orchard who, when he saw her, stopped and waved. Martha stood dumbstruck. She dropped the laundry baskets and slowly walked towards him.

'Josiah Symes!' she exclaimed. 'Where did you come from?'

'Visiting my father,' Josiah said.

'Have you gone to your cousins in Purbeck?'

'Not yet. There are some formalities to settle. It's a grand place, Martha.' Josiah stooped as if to try and kiss her cheek but Martha quickly turned her head away.

'Oh, I forgot,' he said with a slight sneer. 'You're a married woman.'

'That's right, I am.'

'Happy are you, Martha,' Josiah jerked his head in the direction of the house, 'with the old man?'

'I am very happy thank you, and he is *not* an old man.'

'To me he's an old man. Is he here today?'

'He's gone to Bridport with the meat.'

'You should have come with me when I asked you, Martha. You'd really like it in Purbeck. It's not far from the sea.'

'You never asked me again. You never even came to say goodbye.'

'Would the answer have been any different?' He gave a sly smile and moved towards her but, again, she sidestepped him.

'I can't say.' She pushed the hair back from her brow. 'Anyway, it never happened.'

'And is Bernard a good husband?'

'Very!' Martha nodded emphatically.

'Glad to hear it. And does he pleasure you well?' His gaze was insinuating.

'Don't be cheeky, Josiah Symes,' she snapped angrily, eyes blazing.

'They say you did well for yourself.'

'Is that a sin? I still work hard.'

'I s'pose not.'

Josiah suddenly grasped her by the waist and pulled her to the shelter of a tree.

'A kiss for old time's sake, Martha?'

She looked into his roguish eyes, at his warm red lips and she suddenly had an overwhelming memory of those kisses. A vivid memory that tormented her. Momentarily, as his face moved nearer to hers, she was tempted. She could already feel her body reacting to his.

He grasped her arms pinioning her tightly to the tree. With all the force she could command Martha pushed him away and, reaching up, slapped him hard across the cheek. As he staggered back, clutching his face in astonishment, she fled through the orchard, grabbed the baskets she'd left in the garden and ran down to the house.

As she reached it, breathlessly, suddenly she stopped as if aware of a presence. Knowing instinctively what she would see, she looked up and there, as she expected, was Eliza gazing enigmatically down at her through an upstairs window.

Martha hailed her sisters as, in the late sunshine, she walked across the field towards them. It was a beautiful evening in May and, as she'd walked up the lane between banks of red campion and tall cow parsley, she was reminded that it was just about this time a year ago when the relationship with Bernard became an issue and she started to think of him as a future husband.

From this distance that seemed a golden time, a carefree existence in the company of her sisters. What had made her then so dissatisfied, discontented, always wanting something other than what she had, looking for ways of escape? It was something in her nature that made her restless, as she was restless now. Never contented with her lot. She often wondered why she hadn't the placidity of Mary, or the resignation of Ann.

Would that she could be that simple girl now, back with her family again.

Seeing her approaching, Ann's pale face lit up with pleasure. She jumped up, stepping over her nearly full pail, and, energetically wiping her hands on her apron, went over to greet her sister.

'We miss you,' she said with a smile. 'The work load has doubled without you.'

'Nonsense. If you want any help you can always ask me. I was thinking of those happy days as I came along. I wish I was back here together with you.'

Martha, out of breath from her climb up the hill, sank onto Ann's stool by Prudence, the cow who was Martha's old favourite, and greeted her affectionately. Seeing her wistful expression Ann looked at her with concern.

'You didn't think so then.'

'I know,' Martha gazed steadfastly at the ground. 'I was silly.'

'Are you all right? You look very pale.'

'The climb tired me.'

'It didn't used to.'

'Mother used to get tired, you remember?' Martha looked knowingly at her sister who flopped down beside her.

'A baby?'

'Mother got very tired and we never knew why until it was obvious.'

Ann put her hand on her sister's.

'Is Bernard pleased?'

'I haven't told him yet.'

'You *must* be pleased.' Ann put her arm round Martha's shoulder.

Martha shook her head. 'I think of Mother and all those years of babies, the funerals too.'

'Oh, you mustn't think of funerals.'

Intrigued by the behaviour of her sisters Mary left her cow and came over to them.

'Is something wrong?'

'Martha's expecting.'

'Oh!' No flicker of pleasure lit up Mary's grave expression as though she shared Martha's foreboding. She had never been as close to her sister as Ann, but she, too, sank down beside her now, though without touching. Mary had Ann's reserve, though none of her warmth. Of the four girls she was most like their mother in temperament. She was overtly critical, quick to find fault and slow to forgive.

However, she sympathised with Martha. Pregnancy in rural communities wasn't always a matter for rejoicing. It was often a long and difficult time during which the woman had to keep on working, taking to her bed at the last minute and getting up as soon as she could, the newborn baby often accompanying her to the fields or to her place of work. Then, as Martha said, birth was all too frequently followed by death and, although it was the natural course of things, it was still a matter of grief when a young life was so cruelly snuffed out.

The three were sitting there in thoughtful silence when they were assailed by an unexpected sound and, looking up, saw their mother standing on the brow of the hill gazing scathingly at them.

'What's this?' she cried, wagging a finger, 'wasting time again? I might have known it was you, Martha, causing trouble as usual. Have you nothing better to do?'

'I came to see my sisters, Mother,' Martha said frostily, rising awkwardly to her feet.

'Martha's expecting,' Mary cried, putting a hand on her sister's flat stomach as if to emphasise the point.

'Huh! That's no excuse for wasting time. Now you get back to your work.' She gestured to the elder daughters. 'I want to talk to Martha. I was told she was here.'

'What is it you want, Mother?' Even Martha was surprised by her mother's apparent indifference to the prospect of a first grandchild.

Her mother drew her away from the others and began walking with her across the fields.

'Albert Hunt wants to sell up. He says he can't make ends meet. He can get a good price for the cattle and with what he gets he wants to move in with his daughter in Bridport.'

'So, what will happen to you?'

'You may well ask,' Mrs Clark sniffed. 'Your husband *did* say he would help us when he was so anxious to marry you.'

'In that case I'm sure he won't go back on his word.' Martha bit her lip.

'I wondered if *you'd* ask him? It may sound better coming from you. Maybe now that he's to become a father again he will have more sense of responsibility towards his in-laws.' Martha looked keenly at her daughter. 'Though some people *do* say Mr Bearn isn't very clever with money.'

'I don't know why they should say that,' Martha said defensively.

'They say he over-extends himself, anxious to make

an impression. He would like to be into this and that to do with the village, you know, a member of the vestry and so on. People don't quite trust him.'

'People will say anything,' Martha said angrily. 'I think that is a cruel and uninformed thing to say, Mother. Mr Bearn is very generous with me, and his son and daughter lack for nothing.'

'Let's hope he'll be as generous to your child.' Her mother threw her a dark look and continued purposefully on her way down the hill without even a farewell.

Martha stood for a while watching her, trying to fight back the old familiar feeling of resentment, remembering quite vividly now why she was so anxious at one time to be gone from home.

Then she slowly wended her way back to her sisters.

'What did Mother want?' Ann looked up from the task to which she had hastily returned, the pail beside her now almost full.

'She says Mr Hunt is going to sell the animals and leave the farm. She wants Bernard to help them. And yet she only had unkind things to say about my husband.'

'What kind of things?'

'Says he can't manage money.'

'Then why should he help them?'

'Because Mother said he promised to when he asked to marry me.'

'Did you know that?'

'No.'

'Maybe that's why Mother was so anxious that you should marry Mr Bearn?'

Martha looked thoughtful. 'Maybe it was. I might have known that Mother would have another motive.

I thought it was just to get rid of me. Well, I'd best be getting back.'

'Will you tell him about the child? Maybe that will make him happy. By the way,' Ann looked sideways at Martha, 'Josiah Symes is back.'

'I know.'

'Oh, how do you know?' Ann looked abashed.

'I saw him.' Martha's expression remained impassive.

'He came to see *you*?'

'He came to see my husband.'

'Oh!'

Martha thought she saw relief on Ann's face. She had a feeling that her sister wanted to tell her something and waited patiently for her to speak.

Suddenly Ann blurted out: 'Josiah has asked me if I want to go to Purbeck.'

'And what did you say?'

'I said Mother and Father couldn't do without me now that you were wed.'

'That shouldn't stop you if you thought you could find happiness with Josiah,' Martha said earnestly. 'But *could* you, Ann? You know what he's like.'

'I know his reputation well enough, but much of it is malicious. Mary Place was never with child; that was a wicked lie. Remember, I'm twenty-five, Martha. Who knows if I'll find a husband if I wait too long? You forget about that, and Josiah would have preferred you. I know he'd have preferred you because you are prettier than me. I don't know why he wants me at all because a lot of girls set their caps at him.' After a short pause she whispered sadly: 'Maybe he thinks I'd be a good worker on the farm.'

'I'm sure there's more to it than that.' Martha looked intently at her sister. 'But do you love him?'

Ann boldly returned her gaze: 'Did you love Mr Bearn?'

'You know I didn't, nor do I now. It's something I regret.' Martha looked across at the sun beginning its descent in a cloudless sky. 'I must go back. I have to prepare the evening meal.'

On her way back down the hill Martha ruminated on the fact that Ann hadn't answered her question. Did she love Josiah Symes? To be an unmarried woman in a rural community was not only a disadvantage: it was a stigma. Martha knew it was because Ann thought she was plain, like her mother, and everyone said, though not aloud, that grandfather Hussey had paid John Clark to marry her, set him up as a dairyman rather than a labourer.

Martha knew that Ann lacked self-confidence though in her eyes Ann was beautiful, because she was her favourite. Bypassing Mary, they had shared confidences since they were children. She was also strong, sensible and honest. She was hardworking and methodical and she would, indeed, make a very good farmer's wife.

Martha also knew that Ann wanted to be married, as she herself had not, except as a way of escape; but then she was five years younger than her sister and she had never had any difficulty attracting admiring male glances. The problem had been to keep them at bay.

So why, then, had she agreed to marry Bernard Bearn?

Too late, now that she was having his child, to question her decision.

Bernard looked sadly at his young wife. He was so

proud of her, loved her so much yet he knew he was clumsy and rough with her. He had difficulty expressing himself, showing emotions. She made him feel awkward, and although he did his best to try and please her she was reserved with him, remote. The more he tried, the worse it got. He was also jealous of her and when she went out, even to the village, he tormented himself with thoughts of what she might be doing or who she might be seeing on the way. He thought every man must desire her as much as he himself did.

He was watching her now for any tell-tale signs. She said she had been visiting her family, and as she put her bonnet on the table and shook her curls free he went over and helped her out of her coat. He would have liked to have kissed her neck, but it wasn't a gesture that came naturally to him. Anyway, she would probably have misunderstood it. He knew that she resented his embraces, even that he disgusted her. It was awful to want someone so much who found you repulsive.

'How was the family, dear?' he asked.

'They're all right. I saw Mother, Mary and Ann. Mother had a message for me to give you.'

'Oh, what was that?'

Martha looked at him steadily: 'She said you offered to help if they got into difficulties.'

'Oh!'

'Well, Mr Hunt wants to sell up, so there will be no place for the dairy.'

'And what does your mother expect me to do?'

Martha's gaze became openly contemptuous. 'Did you *buy* me then, Bernard, from my parents? Did you pay good money for me?'

'I certainly did not,' Bernard said heatedly. 'Not a penny changed hands.'

'Then why did you offer to help them?'

Bernard shrugged. 'If I recall it right your mother spoke of difficult circumstances in farming and I said – and this had nothing to do with my marrying you – that maybe, if such an eventuality occurred, I might be able to help. I would do that for my in-laws, naturally.'

He looked at her appealingly, lowering his voice:

'You know I loved you, Martha, and I *do*. I would do anything in the world to please you and make you love me.' But despite his good intentions, jealousy began to overwhelm him again and his voice rose. 'Yet I hear that you were *flirting* with Josiah Symes the other day. That hurts me very much. I feel I can't trust you as a wife.'

'I was *not* flirting,' Martha said indignantly. 'This gossip comes from Eliza, of course.'

'She saw you in the orchard with him.'

'Josiah was coming to see you. I told him you had gone to Bridport with a cart of meat. I couldn't ignore him, could I? Turn my back on him? Anyway,' she paused briefly, 'Josiah is interested in my sister Ann. He wants to marry her and take her to the Purbecks where he is to farm. He has no interest in me nor I in him.'

'In that case I wish he would go to Purbeck and stay there!' Bernard said angrily. 'I'd be glad to see the back of him.'

'I thought he was your kinsman?'

'He's a distant relation. Very distant. By marriage. That doesn't mean I have to like him, because I know he liked you. I could tell it by his manner, see it in his eyes.' Bernard's own eyes glowed enviously.

'Your jealousy does you no good service, Bernard,'

Martha said coldly. 'And you could try and stop your daughter telling tales. She causes nothing but mischief. She lurks about spying on me. She is lazy and gives herself the airs and graces of a lady. She do *twist* things so . . .' Martha paused and then burst out, 'I tell you, she hates me, Bernard, and really sometimes I wish . . .' Martha paused again, this time more dramatically, kneading her handkerchief in her clenched palm, 'I . . . I wish I'd never married you and that is the truth. I wish I'd stayed at home with my mother and father, my sisters and brothers. Oh how I *wish* I could undo what I have done. And now,' she looked at him wildly, clutching her belly, 'I am to have a child. And this can only tie me to you more because no one will want me now.'

She threw herself down on the chair and, leaning across the table, broke down and wept.

After a few seconds she felt the pressure of a hand on her shoulder and, looking up, found Bernard gazing down at her.

'Our child?' he enquired, his expression curiously timid.

'Of course it's our child!' she said, clawing at his hand to try and unfasten his fingers. 'I suppose you think it's *Josiah Symes's* child or any Tom, Dick or Harry who happened to be passing! Do you think I'm a whore? You don't trust me, Bernard, and yet you have every reason to trust me. I never lay with a man before I married you, and you knew it. You knew what pain you caused me, and still do because you know not how to love a woman. I feel it's very strange that I have a child inside me because I wonder how it got there. Nature is cruel if a child can be conceived with violence instead of love.'

She put her elbows on the table and resumed her weeping while Bernard stood gazing helplessly down at her. Then he sat beside her and put his hand on her back ignoring her attempts to wriggle away from him.

'Martha, clumsy as I may be, the child was conceived with love. My love. I do love you, but I am a man unused to expressing my feelings. If it is my child . . .'

'Of course it is your child!' She rounded on him again, her despair and anger now almost out of control. 'How many more times do I have to tell you that, you bumpkin? What sort of simpleton are you really, Bernard Bearn? Even if I did lie with Josiah Symes which, as God is my judge, I never have, he went away in the summer and has only just got back.'

She rose and stamped her foot on the floor.

'There now! Please get it into your poisoned, jealous mind that Josiah Symes is nothing to me nor I to him. This is *your* child and you are responsible for it.'

'And when will it be born?'

'Around Christmas.'

And putting both hands on her back in an attempt to ease the dull ache, she looked wearily at the clock on the wall as if wishing that time would fly and she could be delivered of her burden.

Thrilled at the prospect of becoming a father again and desperately keen to ingratiate himself with his wife by helping her family, Bernard Bearn lost no time in hurrying to see Albert Hunt, an old man whose wife had recently died and whose children had moved away from the area. He wanted to live out his days by the sea with his daughter who was married to a fisherman in Bridport. He had grown maize, potatoes and corn and let out his cows and dairy, but he had little interest in keeping the farm viable, and spent his days drinking in the Three Horse Shoes with his cronies. He would roll home at night, fall over the gate and pass out, sometimes being found stiff and cold in the same position in the morning. Consequently his neglected crops withered and died and, due to his slipshod methods, his soil was poor.

Farmer Hunt was reluctantly prised out of the Three Horse Shoes and taken on a tour of his property by Bernard Bearn who was deeply anxious, at the same time, not to be seen by his in-laws.

But what he was shown depressed him: wilting crops, untilled soil, decrepit and ill-cared-for farm buildings, everywhere evidence of neglect. The only signs of prosperity were the well-fed cows and fat pigs grazing contentedly in the fields, thanks to the care and diligence of John Clark and his family.

Bernard sat in a rickety chair in the kitchen contemplating the rheumy features of Farmer Hunt who, even now, was attempting to drown his sorrows in a tankard of beer. As he raised the foaming brew to his lips he looked over at his guest: 'Be ye sure ye won't join me, Bernard?'

Bernard shook his head, his brow deeply furrowed in thought.

'You have much neglected your land and property, Albert,' he said after a while. 'I had not realised it was so bad. It will cost a lot of money to put it to rights. The house,' he looked around at the grimy walls, blackened stove and soot-covered cupboards, table and chairs, 'is in a shocking state. Who has to pay for repairs?'

Albert Hunt's lower lip shook tremulously.

'You, I suppose?' Bernard said.

Albert nodded. The property, like much in Powerstock, was owned by the Earl of Darlington and rented out by tenant farmers.

'His lordship's agent won't be too pleased when he sees all this neglect.'

Albert, made maudlin by drink, wiped a bleary eye.

'I am a poor man, Bernard. I cannot afford to do anything.'

'If I become a copyholder you mustn't expect anything for it.'

'You, become a copyholder?' Albert looked dumbfounded. 'I thought you wanted this for the Clarks?'

'I will hold it for the Clarks. John cannot afford the rent. I will be responsible for all these repairs, tilling the land and sowing fresh seed. I hear the dairy house is also in poor condition.'

'I am an old man,' Albert sorrowfully stroked his stubbled chin. 'My wife has died. My children all gone. They will have to keep me or I shall end up in Beaminster Poorhouse. Never did I think, at the end of my days I should have so little to show for my life . . .'

And letting his chin sink upon his chest he began to sob very quietly, an eerie whimpering sound like an animal in distress.

Chapter Four

August 1832

The village was still in darkness as Ann Clark stole away from the dairy house, past the slumbering dogs, the sleepy cats tired out after a night's hunting, towards the lane that ran past Hunt's farm on the outskirts of Powerstock.

She carried only a bundle in which, besides a few personal belongings, was the dress she had worn for Martha's wedding and which she hoped to wear for her own. Her only sorrow was that her beloved sister would not be there for it, nor had she confided to her her plans.

Almost sick with nerves she halted by the side of the road, drew breath and watched the dawn breaking in the eastern sky: first there was a long streak of grey, then gold, then pink until the whole horizon burst into a gorgeous kaleidoscope of merging colours. Ann had never been a person to pay much attention to the beauties of nature, but this particular dawn struck her and was to remain in her memory.

A few minutes later she heard the sound of a horse

and cart and, as wan sunlight began to flood the valley, it emerged through the morning mist with Josiah Symes holding the reins, a cheerful, easy self-confident expression on his handsome features as he halted in front of her and bent towards her.

Then her doubts vanished. She knew she was doing the right thing and, with a smile, threw her bundle into the back of the cart and climbed up beside him.

Immediately he flicked his whip over the broad back of the horse and it trundled off towards Eggardon Hill.

'Did anyone see you?' Josiah asked, looking down at her. Ann shook her head. She felt too emotional, too confused to speak. She had also hoped his reception of her would help to allay her many misgivings, but there was no smile to match hers, no welcoming kiss or gesture of affection. His demeanour was simply that of a man giving someone, even perhaps a stranger, a lift.

As the cart passed King's Farm she impulsively glanced back, but all she could see was the tower of the church, nothing of the village itself. Resolutely she turned away again and set her eyes steadfastly on the road before her.

It was difficult to know why she had agreed to elope when she would have liked a wedding such as Martha had had, in the church, surrounded by relations and friends. The hectic weeks that Josiah had courted her had been full of secrecy, subterfuge and lies.

Why? It was a question she couldn't answer. Whenever she asked Josiah why he was so secretive, he replied simply that it was for the best. Too many people would oppose their marriage. It was best to run away and then tell them about it afterwards. But *who* would oppose their marriage, she wanted to know? Her father would be glad to have her off his hands. Josiah, who in any case was a man given to few words, wouldn't say.

It was not in her nature to behave like this. She was sensible, responsible, reserved, as the eldest girl in the family, one used to looking after the younger ones, shouldering heavy burdens.

It was to do, she knew, with the weakness of the flesh: the desire for bodily union. She wasn't even sure it was love. She only knew that when he had caressed her, pressed her body against his, felt her breasts and covered her face with kisses while they had lain in the warm hay in Albert Hunt's barn she had wanted him more than anything in the world and would do all she could to get him. Not that she yielded completely. As her sister had been, she, too, was afraid of her mother and there always came a point in their cavorting when she held back and, red in the face, he was forced to hold back too.

She had had qualms, many qualms about what she was now doing, but she kept them to herself not even sharing them with Martha. All she knew was that it had to do with her age, with her circumstances and, above all, with wanting Josiah and that ultimate moment of physical union.

Beneath her veneer of caution and prudery she, like Martha, was a deeply physical, passionate woman.

They made good time on the journey up and down the hills leading to Dorchester which they reached by mid afternoon. Ann had never been so far and looked about her with wonder at the tall buildings, the handsome churches, the horses and carriages thronging the main street, the pedestrians dressed in fine clothes. They stopped at an inn outside the town for bread and cheese and ale and to feed and water the horse, and then they set off again, taking the low road that would lead eventually to the sea.

'Will we get there by dark?' Ann asked anxiously.

'Oh no,' Josiah smiled. 'We're lodging for the night with a friend of mine who has a farm along the way.'

'Oh!' Ann, who had little idea of the distance between Powerstock and their destination, felt a flicker of apprehension. 'Is he expecting us?'

'No, but we'll be welcome. Don't worry,' and for the first time that day he turned to her and kissed her cheek. Then he gave her a broad wink.

Her apprehension turned to alarm.

It was almost dusk when they turned off the road, up a narrow track, crossed a neat farmyard and stopped before a house the door of which opened immediately and a man and woman came out to see who the visitors were.

'Why,' the man cried with obvious pleasure, 'it's Josiah Symes.' He went up to greet him while his wife, remaining in the background, looked curiously at Ann.

'I wondered if we could have a bed for the night?' Josiah said, jumping down. 'We're on our way to Steeple to join my cousins, John and Robert.'

'Of course, there's plenty of room.' The man, whose name was Matthew, turned enquiringly to Ann.

'This is my wife Ann,' Josiah said. 'We just got wed.'

'Well, congratulations.' The woman, wreathed in smiles, approached Ann who sat on the box hoping that the flush that stole over her cheeks could not be seen in the half light.

'There, my love,' Josiah said with uncharacteristic

tenderness, reaching up for her with his strong arms. As she stood up he clasped her round the waist and carried her in his arms towards the house. Delighted, Matthew and his wife stood by.

'You should have let us know you were coming,' the wife said. 'We have very little in the house to eat.'

'Some bread and cheese is all we need.'

'Oh, we have more than that.' Matthew's wife bustled past them.

Josiah lowered Ann to the ground while Matthew got her bundle from the back of the cart and followed them into the house.

The bedroom into which they were shown was small with whitewashed walls, a large double bed and a chest with a jug and basin on the top. Matthew didn't close the door but, chatting amiably, waited to escort them downstairs where his wife, whose name was Phoebe, was busy laying food upon the kitchen table.

Matthew and Phoebe were a couple perhaps in their late forties, who proved kind and admirable hosts not at all put out by the arrival of unexpected guests. Maybe because of their isolation, they seemed glad to welcome them. They were full of chatter about people whom they knew in common with the Symes cousins, about his family, and the farm in Steeple.

'Do tell us about the wedding.' Phoebe, eyes shining, leaned forward.

'Oh it was a very quiet affair,' Josiah said. 'Ann's mother was not well.'

'Oh I'm sorry.' Phoebe was all concern. 'Not *too* ill, I hope?'

Josiah made a face while Ann who, sick with nerves, had scarcely spoken, now hastened to reassure her and by asking questions about their own family changed the subject as soon as she could. It appeared they had two children in their twenties, and a boy in his late teens who helped them on the farm. The two elder children had left home; the girl was married with her own small family, the elder son apprenticed in Wareham to a blacksmith.

Everything about them exuded a sort of quiet, orderly prosperity and Ann contrasted the warm comfortable house, the clean and tidy yard, the obvious air of well-being with the decrepit farmhouse of Albert Hunt, the tumbledown outbuildings. She was, however, very tired. Her day had begun well before dawn and she could not stop yawning. As soon as the meal was finished Phoebe said:

'You two will want to get off to bed,' and maybe a sense of modesty made her turn her back on them and walk towards the door.

Nervously Ann wished them goodnight as Matthew handed her a candle and stood at the bottom, another in his hand to guide them as they climbed the stairs.

Once inside the bedroom Ann carefully placed the candle on the chest by the wash-basin. Then, as Josiah busied himself at the back of the room, she looked carefully at herself in the mirror over the wash-stand, noting her high forehead, her eyes — perhaps too widely spaced — her short upturned nose, her thin, rather forbidding mouth and wondered how it was, how it could possibly be, that Josiah had preferred her to all the pretty women who would so gladly have had him?

She then went over to the bed and sat down, sighing heavily, eyes downcast on to the bare wooden floor. Now that the moment was upon her she felt frightened.

'Well?' Josiah said, standing in front of her.

'Why did you tell them we were wed?' Ann looked timorously up at him.

'But we *are*, my love, in the sight of God. Or soon will be.' He gave her a suggestive smile.

'You did lie to them, Josiah. I felt ashamed.'

'You would have felt more ashamed if I had not,' he said and, his eyes gazing intently into hers, he began to unfasten the buttons of her bodice, gently easing it away from her body until her top half was quite bare.

Then with the skill and familiarity of the practised seducer, he kissed her breasts, his tongue lingering on each red nipple until she felt such an overwhelming desire for him, such a sense of abandonment that all doubts fled. Tears were banished as he removed the rest of her clothes and went over to the chest to blow out the candle.

Stretched out on the bed, shivering with cold as well as apprehension, she lay in the dark listening to his quick breathing, the sounds of him undressing. But when he lay beside her, the feeling of warmth, almost of heat returned. The thought of yielding at last was delightful. She turned eagerly to him, tentatively exploring his body, relishing the sensation of body hair, of bare skin, knowing that the moment for mere kissing and fumbling was well and truly past.

Blackmanston Farm was in a valley between the Purbeck Hills and the sea. It was a very beautiful spot but so remote that those living and working on the farm formed their own small community self-sufficient in food and the necessities of life. The main farmhouse was still undergoing repairs after the last tenant had left, the owners being the Cavell family who lived in Smedmore House overlooking Kimmeridge Bay.

The brothers John and Robert Symes were very different from their distant cousin, the Symes clan being numerous in Dorset. Originally hailing from the Powerstock area Robert was only twenty-one, John some five years older. They were sombre, hardworking, ambitious men of few words, dedicated to the task of making good. They cannot have been unaware of Josiah's reputation but had agreed to take him on because, as well as being a kinsman, he was strong, able and willing to work for a pittance. Whether they summed up the situation between Ann and Josiah cannot be known, and Josiah was too ashamed or sheepish to explain, but they immediately cast a damper on any amorous activity, or aspirations to respectability on Ann's part, by putting Josiah to sleep above the cowshed while she was given a room below the eaves of the farmhouse. Spartan and cold it was sparsely furnished with a narrow iron bedstead, a rickety chair and a chest of drawers that leaned sideways on three legs.

But, more importantly both were made to work extremely hard and Ann's duties were immediately made clear. She was there to work, to look after the men; to act as a skivvy, a maid, a housekeeper and her duties were long and arduous.

Both Robert and John Symes were churchgoers, almost Puritan in temperament and it was clear that they regarded Ann not as a woman, a source of carnal temptation, but as a vital extra pair of hands.

Besides looking after the animals, milking and tilling the fields, there was a great deal for all to do on the farm which was in some state of disrepair and neglect

– though not as bad as Albert Hunt's – and working from early morning until late at night Ann had little chance to question, certainly not to bemoan her lot. The fact was that, once they were installed at Blackmanston, Josiah virtually ignored her except to wriggle into her bed whenever he could escape the vigilant eye of his cousins, and to fend off any questions she asked him about their future.

There was little talk between them, certainly no mention of a wedding.

It was a very unsatisfactory state of affairs indeed, not the dream that Ann had once expected, and she had a great deal of time to repent of her impetuosity and her shortsightedness when she had known all too well the character of the man she had run off with.

Ann had been used to hard work, but the work she had at Blackmanston was even harder. She was expected to cook, clean and wash for the three men and two labourers who lived in a nearby cottage, as well as a boy who looked after the pigs. In addition she was also required to help out in the dairy because of her experience as a dairymaid.

She had no free time at all and the only moment of the day she could be said to enjoy was in the evening when she milked the cows. Walking across the fields, carrying her pail and stool, always reminded her of home, of her dear sister Martha whom she missed so much, and that simple family life that now, in retrospect, seemed like a golden time. She had never been scolded by her mother as Martha had. She had been regarded as a rock; the steady, reliable eldest girl in the family. Why then had she uprooted herself? Except for a single letter to say where she was and that she was well, she had made no contact. Certainly no reply from them, not even from Martha.

Two months after her arrival, as the days were beginning to draw in, Ann sat milking her cow, her head leaning wearily against its flank as she alternately squeezed the soft teats and then released the pressure. Aware of a shadow over her she looked up and saw Josiah who had come to help with the milking.

'All right?' he asked.

She didn't reply but, lowering her head, went steadily on with her task.

Josiah squatted on his stool beside her.

'Anything the matter?'

'You know what's the matter, Josiah Symes. When are we to be wed?'

Josiah sucked on a blade of grass clenched between his teeth.

'We are wed in the sight of God. Well and truly by now.'

'God!' she exclaimed. 'I didn't know you believed in Him.'

'Why do you say that?' He looked at her curiously.

'Because you don't behave like a man who believes in his Maker. We are living in sin.'

'*You* as much as *me*,' he said slyly.

'I came here thinking we were to be married. Now I think you never meant that at all. You got me here to . . . to be a housekeeper,' she looked at her clogged feet, 'and to bed me.'

'Well, you like it well enough, don't you?' he said jeeringly. 'I don't notice no protest on your part. A hot little wench you are, just like your sister . . .'

'Like my *sister*!' Ann gazed at him aghast. 'You mean . . .'

'You know what I mean.' Lazily Josiah got up and smiled down at her, not a kindly smile. 'You women are all the same. Well, I tell you, I'm not for marriage, Ann. I mean not real marriage in a church. It suits me as it is.'

'Then why didn't you *say*?'

'Why should I say? That way I'd never get a woman.'

'So do you promise marriage to everyone?'

'Not everyone; some,' he said. 'The more fools they if they take me seriously.' He looked at her contemptuously. 'Maybe you should go and find an old man, like your sister, if it's marriage rather than hot-blooded loving that you want.' He paused. 'Besides, the brothers would never want me as a married man with a wife to keep and children, should they come along. They'd soon send me on my way and then we'd all be without a home or a bite to eat.'

He turned away and walked towards one of the cows waiting with full udders, whistling a tune as though he had not a care in the world.

Ann paused as she came up the hill and looked with foreboding at the buildings that comprised Albert Hunt's farm and the dairy house beside it. Above were the fields where she and her sisters had milked the cows. She wondered what had happened to them since. Mary would not have been able to cope alone and her mother would have resented having to resume that onerous task after all these years.

The thought of her behaviour was enough really to make her hang her head in shame. She, the eldest sister of whom so much had been expected by way of example. And now here she was having to fling herself on their mercy. Ann faltered and turned to look back the way she had come. But it was cold, a keen November wind biting through her cloak. She was inadequately shod and the leather soles of her shoes flapped on the ground as she walked. She was desperately tired. It was a week since she had left Blackmanston Farm, again like a fugitive by nightfall, running across the fields with her bundle, her precious dress which she had never, after all, worn for that wedding.

Kindly carters had given her lifts, but she had walked a good deal of the way and, with only a little money that she had saved from her meagre wages, she had hardly eaten. At night she took shelter in farm buildings on the way, dreading discovery by the farmer, but she was always gone before daylight. In Dorchester she used her remaining few shillings to take the coach to Bridport and now here she was, nearly home.

She swayed momentarily, feeling faint and nauseous and she knew that there could be no question of turning back. As she approached the farmhouse she realised it was empty. Farmer Hunt must have gone. Would her father now take it over, helped by Bernard? The thought of Bernard brought memories of Martha flooding back, the one person she would be really glad to see. But what would Martha's reaction be on seeing her? After all, she had excluded her from her plans to elope. If the others didn't forgive her, would Martha?

All in all it seemed that she could not expect a friendly welcome from any member of her family and, indeed, this was all she deserved.

Did not the Bible say that as you sowed so should you reap?

Ann completed the last few yards, her toes so cold from the holes in her shoes, for she wore no stockings, that she could scarcely feel them. She stood hesitantly at the back door of the dairy house and then, very cautiously, she pushed it open.

It was four in the afternoon, nearly dark and her mother was standing over the fire with a pot in her hands. Mary was at the kitchen sink washing vegetables and Elizabeth was sitting at a table writing.

As the door opened the three of them turned, Martha Clark still stirring, and when they saw Ann three mouths simultaneously sagged open in surprise. Overcome once more by nausea and intense fatigue, Ann slumped in a chair by the kitchen table letting her precious bundle with the crushed blue dress in it fall to the floor.

'Well,' Martha Clark said at last, her tone scathing. 'Well, I never . . .'

'Ann isn't well, Mother.' Elizabeth hastily crossed to her sister looking at her with concern.

'Could you give me some water to drink?' Ann gasped, looking up, trying to smile, touched by the expression on Elizabeth's face, anxious to reassure her. After all, she had let her down too.

Mary immediately poured some water from a jug by the sink into a cup and took it over to her sister who drank thirstily.

'Thank you,' she said, handing Mary her cup.

Martha, still with the pot in her hand, hadn't moved from her stance in front of the fire, but she took everything in: her daughter's fatigue, her dishevelled appearance, her evident despair.

'So you've come home then,' she said tartly.

Ann nodded.

'And are you wed?' Martha examined her daughter's hands. 'No ring I see.' As Ann shook her head her mother snorted, 'I thought not. Did he throw you out, you good for nothing?'

Ann shook her head again and suddenly overcome by nausea she rushed to the kitchen sink where she was violently sick. Mary tenderly rubbed her back, as if trying to help. Elizabeth got a cloth, but Martha, grim-faced, remained where she was as if she had made up her own mind about her daughter's condition.

'I suppose you're expecting?' she said as Ann was helped back to her chair where she sat, eyes closed, breathing heavily. 'Why else would you come home?' Taking the spoon out of the pot, which she had put back on the fire, and shaking it at her daughter, she continued, 'There is no place for you here in your condition. The village has already made up its mind about a woman who runs off with a man who already has a reputation. You didn't think about us, did you, your family? You were expecting already, I suppose, when you left?'

'I was not.' Ann shook her head.

'I must say you don't look far gone.' Martha Clark, who had had so many children, expertly eyed her daughter's stomach.

Again Ann shook her head, incapable of saying anything.

'Lost your tongue, have you?' Martha said sharply. 'Well you'd best be gone before your father comes back.'

'But, Mother, where can she go?' Mary protested. 'You can't throw her out. It's bitterly cold outside.'

'You hold your tongue,' Mrs Clark snapped. 'I'll decide what goes on here.'

'I think you should let Ann stay the night at least,' Mary said defiantly. 'It is her home.'

'One she walked out of.' Mrs Clark glared at her daughter. 'I told you to hold your tongue.'

The door opened and John Clark appeared, shaking the rain off his head and rubbing his hands as if glad to be indoors. When he looked he saw four pairs of startled eyes regarding him and then he observed his eldest daughter slumped dejectedly in a chair. He went over to her his face suddenly alive with joy.

'Ann, you have come back!' he cried and, although he had never shown much emotion as a father, he looked as though he was about to embrace her when Martha intervened.

'She's with child by that man. *That's* why she's here. What do you think of *that*?'

John paused and stared at Ann.

'Is it true?'

Ann, still yet to speak, nodded.

'She's lost her tongue,' Martha said. 'The cat's got it.'

'Shush, Mother,' John retorted. 'Let her talk.'

'She's got nothing to say. Not a word out of her.'

'I think she should go upstairs to rest,' Mary said firmly, going over to take Ann's arm.

'I've told her to get out.' Martha jerked her head towards the door.

'You can't put her out on a night like this.'

'Well, first thing tomorrow,' and Martha turned her attention again to the pot simmering away on the fire. 'If she stays *I* go, and I haven't done anything wrong,' she said, gazing fiercely at her husband.

*   *   *

Bernard Bearn looked round the shell of the farmhouse which he was restoring so that his in-laws could run not only the dairy but the farm as well. He knew he was taking on an awful lot. Ever since he had become a copyholder — that is, he had taken on the lease from the estate of the owner, the Earl of Darlington — he had been aware of an extra burden, one he could not really afford. But so anxious was he to please Martha that he went ahead. To try and win her love and, above all, respect, he would do anything. He was a man almost pathetically anxious to please.

Bernard Bearn had come from a family of comfortable farming stock but they were not wealthy by the standards of some farmers in the area: members of the Hussey, Walbridge and Walburton families. He was of limited means and yet he kept taking on different projects in the hope of increasing his wealth. He rented a number of fields and outbuildings from the estate of the Earl, including his own substantial dwelling, the slaughter-house and outbuildings attached, and the orchard from which he made his cider. Had he stuck to one thing, or even two, Bernard might have fared better; but he thought his much desired goal of becoming a rich man lay in diversity and in this he was, perhaps, over-optimistic.

He was up early to look at the progress on Hunt's farm and found many things done to his dissatisfaction. John Clark and his sons undertook a number of tasks, but they were busy with the dairy and the cattle — they were short of helpers since Martha and Ann had left — and Bernard had to employ labour to carry out the main repairs. Now that the winter had set in, it was becoming an urgent necessity to repair the cracks in the walls, the holes in the roof letting in the rain.

With a feeling of increasing dejection he walked round inspecting what had been done and, more importantly, listing in his mind what yet needed to be done, and how much it might cost. He was half way through his inspection when John Clark came in and apologised for being late, his manner agitated, like that of a man in some kind of emotional distress.

'The fact is,' he said, mopping his brow, 'we have been up half the night.'

'Is something wrong?' Bernard enquired solicitously.

'Well,' John hesitated, 'the fact is my daughter Ann has returned . . .'

'Oh surely that is *good* news,' Bernard exclaimed then, as he saw his father-in-law's face, 'or is it not?'

'My daughter is expecting a child. She is not married. My wife says she won't have her in the house and I'm at my wits' end.'

'I'm very sorry to hear that,' Bernard murmured. He hadn't known Ann very well but what little he knew he liked, and he knew how much Martha had missed her. 'Then what is to become of Ann?'

'Unless someone else will take her . . .' John hesitated again, 'and we have no money to offer for board, I'm afraid it will be the Beaminster Poorhouse.'

'But that's a terrible state of affairs,' Bernard said, appalled. 'My wife would be very distressed to hear that. The poorhouse is not a pleasant place, or so I'm told.'

'I know, but what else can I do? That is unless . . . I don't suppose that . . .' and John Clark looked hopefully across at Bernard Bearn.

*　　*　　*

73

Martha Bearn's baby was nearly due and time seemed to hang heavily on her as she did her best to find a comfortable position either standing, sitting or lying down. She had had an easy pregnancy but it had seemed a long one. Despite her husband's professed affection and concern for her she felt more isolated from him than ever. He appeared not to understand women, or womanly things. He was brash and awkward and she knew also that he was very much afraid of the outcome of the pregnancy, as his first wife had died in childbirth. He seemed to try and avoid her as much as he could, and never attempted to touch her in bed, for which she was grateful.

Martha knew he was not an unkind man. Sometimes her own attitude towards him made her feel guilty. She should have tried to temper her resentment, be more sympathetic to the burdens he had to carry. She knew that he overreached himself financially, that, in helping her parents, he was trying to please her. But it was so difficult. He was, she realised, simply insensitive. He really wanted a woman to cook and clean, to go to bed with and bear his children. The normal things that a wife was expected to do. It was a bonus if she was young and pretty as well, except that in Bernard's case he was profoundly jealous and flew into a rage if she so much as looked at another man.

She supposed that, in time, she would simply sink into the apathy about her marriage that affected most wives. In the lonely months of her pregnancy Martha found herself thinking a lot about the first Mrs Bearn and wondering what sort of person she had been. Her sister, Sarah Crocker, was a friend and came often to the house, but she gave little away about the first marriage beyond saying how devastated Bernard had been when Elizabeth Bearn died.

Martha, feeling particularly oppressed and heavy that morning, occupied herself with some darning, sitting close to the fire because it was so cold. Joanna was doing out the grates and lighting the fires in the rest of the house. Eliza was staying with friends in Bridport and James was at his lessons in the vicarage. Martha realised that she should endeavour to be calm and serene about the approaching birth, but all she could think of was what might go wrong and of the grave up the hill in the churchyard where Elizabeth Bearn lay, dead at only twenty-two.

As the clock on the mantelpiece struck ten she heard the sound of the front door opening and noises in the hall. Surprised, she looked up as she had not expected her husband home so soon.

She put her sewing to one side and sat back, her hands folded on her stomach, gazing expectantly at the door. Slowly it opened and there on the threshold stood her sister Ann.

Chapter Five

December 1832

Following morning service on Christmas Day the son of Bernard and Martha was christened William, after her brother who had been best man at her wedding. Young William born a few days before was a fine sturdy child and his mother held him proudly in her arms as the vicar, the Reverend Cookson, poured water on the child's forehead and pronounced him a member of the community of Christ.

Gathered around the font were the Clarks and the Husseys, a few members of Bernard's family, including his daughter Eliza who stood sulkily by her father's side, having already made up her mind to hate the baby. Her brother James's angelic treble voice boosted the choir.

After the ceremony the christening party went across to the Three Horse Shoes for a round of celebratory drinks, but Martha went home with William, where Ann was waiting to greet them. Martha was tired and it was time for the baby's feed.

It was almost a year to the day since her marriage, and Martha's emotions had been mixed as she stood at the font while William was christened. It had been a turbulent year, in many ways an unhappy one; yet one in which she'd grown up. She'd also become a mother which compensated for the trials of being a wife with all that wifely duties meant.

She loved William as soon as she saw him. Indeed she thought she had loved him all along from the first slight movement in her belly to his first cry as he slid out of her.

She had reflected deeply on the words of the lesson in church a few Sundays ago, and thought that she had now put aside childish things and, in one brief year, become a woman.

She wanted now not only to be a good mother but a good wife to Bernard too.

Ann had not come to the christening. She never went out except occasionally after nightfall when she would not be seen, and then it was only to walk down the field to the river or through the orchard, really just to get a breath of air. Ann was a changed woman too, changed and saddened. She felt she would never trust a man again, and how she would cope with a child without the support of her family she didn't know. It was too much to expect that Martha and Bernard would give her and a child a permanent home.

Ann greeted them at the door, tenderly relieved Martha of the baby and took him to the fire.

'It's raw outside.' Martha held out her hands to warm by the fire. 'You should be glad you weren't there,' and then, realising she had been tactless, she crouched by Ann's side. 'I'm sorry. That was a silly thing to say.'

'I'm glad I wasn't there,' Ann said stubbornly, 'to be gawped at by everyone in the church. But I'm sorry I missed the little angel's christening,' and she held him closely to her breast perhaps feeling the movements of the baby inside her.

Ann had helped bring William into the world, as Martha's contractions had started in the middle of the night and labour had progressed so rapidly that there was no time to send for Agnes Legg, the nurse, who had arrived after the baby was born. But Ann was an experienced midwife: even at a young age she had helped to bring some of her brothers and sisters into the world, holding her mother's hand or stuffing a rag into her mouth to stifle her screams when the pain got too bad.

Childbirth was terrifying, but it was a fear that vanished as soon as a lusty infant was produced, the cord was cut and it was laid in its mother's arms. Then there was relief all round, smiles appeared and, then, at that late stage the nurse would arrive, the baby was cooed over, bathed and swaddled and introduced to its father before being laid in a crib or drawer, or even a box, whatever happened to be at hand.

Martha settled herself comfortably in a chair, put up her feet and undid her bodice as Ann put the baby to her breast and he settled down contentedly to feed.

It was a very thrilling, satisfying experience, Martha thought, to feel that little mouth tugging at her nipple. She could never have imagined feeling so special as her devotion to the baby grew. Somehow the tensions and discomfort of the past months had vanished in these few days and she now felt complete, and at rest.

She looked affectionately at Ann sitting by the fire, head bowed, put out a hand and touched it.

'Thank you,' she said, 'I don't know what I'd do without you.'

'Or I without *you*.' Ann reached up and took her hand. 'Thank you for being so nice to me, and Bernard was so good.'

'He *is* good,' Martha affirmed. Bernard had been so happy and relieved to see her safely delivered, and the child well with all ten fingers and toes, that he couldn't do enough.

She recalled, too, the day that Bernard had walked in with Ann, having told her mother and father that he would take her and give her a home. For good measure he had also given Martha Clark an opinion, not couched in gentle words, about her attitude to her daughter. He had not stayed to see if they had any effect – but observing her indignant face he thought not – and had told Ann to get her things while he waited for her outside. From then on Martha's attitude to Bernard had changed. She had known he was a good man, an upright man, and she saw clearly now this side of him.

He was supposed to care about what people thought, to be anxious for the good opinion of others, to toady up to those in authority – or such was her mother's cruel opinion of him – but he didn't seem to care what people thought in the village about him offering a home to his sister-in-law. Bernard grew in stature in her estimation and his tenderness and concern when William was born, his gratitude for her safe delivery, was touching in its simplicity and sincerity.

Martha felt that in a way she couldn't quite explain – it was emotional rather than physical, in the heart not in the head – she had begun to love Bernard and value him for what he was.

She became gentler with him. It was, she knew, all part of the business of growing up.

Late in the afternoon the remnants of the jolly christening party tumbled out of the Three Horse Shoes together with a number of inebriated Christmas revellers who had not been in church, but had tagged along. There was much jovial chat on the forecourt outside, exchanges of good wishes, back slapping, more congratulations to the new father. Bernard, in great good humour, responded in kind. He was in fact well out of pocket for the number of drinks he had bought in the course of the day.

But then it was Christmas and the christening of his newly born son. Was it not a time for a man to rejoice, to live for the day and give little care for the morrow?

'I tell you what,' he said slapping John Clark convivially on the back as the partygoers dispersed, 'why don't we go and have a look at the repairs to the house? William Smith and his son have done a good job repairing the thatch.'

The Clarks seemed hesitant.

'Maybe we could see it another day?' John Clark looked shiftily at his wife. 'We have to milk the cows.'

'It won't take long.' Bernard put an arm round John's shoulder. 'I should think, anyway, you'll be very eager to move in. William Smith says there's a leak in your roof too! That will have to be seen to by and by.'

Whereupon Bernard set off at a brisk pace ahead of the Clarks who followed with a show of reluctance which Bernard didn't seem to notice.

It was nearly dark and as Bernard flung open the door it was rather difficult to make out the interior.

'Maybe we should see it in the morning?' John suggested.

'No, no, there's enough light.' Bernard left the door wide open and strode confidently into the main room. 'The carpenters and masons have nearly finished. I tell you the work has been done to a high standard.' Bernard looked about him, not concealing his satisfaction. 'What do you think, John?'

'Mmm,' John mumbled.

'Go on,' Martha said, giving her husband a sharp poke, 'tell him.'

John shuffled his feet, looking at his toes, and Martha dug him in the ribs again saying this time more loudly, 'Go on, *tell* him, John.'

'Tell me what?' Bernard looked bemused.

John continued to study the ground.

'Well if you won't tell him I shall.' Martha folded her arms and gazed steely-eyed at her son-in-law. 'The fact *is*, Bernard, we're not staying. We shan't need the house after all.'

'You're . . . I *beg* your pardon?'

'We're going to my cousin Robert's farm in Pilsdon. He has need of a dairyman and the accommodation is good.' Martha gave a derisive sniff and looked about her. 'Better than this.'

'But you said . . .'

'*We* said nothing,' John stammered, clearly embarrassed by his wife's ungracious tone. 'It was you as did all the talking, Bernard.'

'Didn't give us a chance to get a word in.' Martha sounded aggrieved.

'As if *that's* likely!' Bernard said angrily. 'I've never known *you* lost for words, Martha Clark. Do you mean before I did all this you had *already* thought of moving?'

'No, not 'xactly,' John studied his fingers. 'We didn't know what we were going to do, and that's the truth.' He looked at Bernard placatingly and, once again, Bernard despised his father-in-law for his weakness, remembering how reluctant he was to stand up for his daughter Ann against his wife who was quite willing to commit her to the poorhouse.

'But you asked me to repair this place for you.'

'No,' Martha corrected him, 'it was *you* as suggested it, Bernard.'

Bernard began to splutter, recalling that she was half right. 'I only suggested it when you said you were going to be thrown out. I did it for Martha who asked me to help you. *You* pleaded with her. Do you think I could afford to do all this?' Bernard gestured around him. 'To bring it up to such a high standard? It is good for another fifty years.'

'Then you shouldn't have difficulty getting rid of it,' Martha said smugly.

'But it's not my property,' Bernard roared, rapidly losing his temper. '*You* know that. I have been doing repairs Lord Darlington should have done, but declined to. I did them for *you*, my parents-in-law, so that you would have a bigger property, a farm . . . I did it for my wife who wanted to advance you. For her father to be a farmer instead of a dairyman.'

'John didn't *want* to be advanced,' Martha said sulkily, 'nor did he want the responsibility. He isn't capable. Albert Hunt let the farm run down. John knows about dairying but not about farming. He don't know much 'bout crops and such. Just cows.'

'Then he should have said so.' Bernard threw his arms in the air in a paroxysm of exasperation. 'Look,' he paused, 'I'll help you. I know something about farming. I grow my own maize and wheat, the barley for my beer.'

'Then you should take it over, Bernard,' Martha said, as though she was addressing a child. 'It has all been very well done. It's just that we don't want to live in it.' She paused, her expression spiteful. 'After all, you have only yourself to blame. You gave Ann a home, and that caused so much talk in the neighbourhood we had to hang our heads in shame.'

'How do you mean it "caused talk"?'

'She should have been sent away in secret. People would have been no wiser if she'd gone as soon as she came home. But *you* gave her a home, as if to say you approved of her behaviour. So everyone knew how she was led up the garden path by Josiah Symes, and left in the family way by him. People have been ignoring us in the street. Today the Walbridges and the Peaches left the church before the christening. I felt so humiliated when they walked out. You could see how we stood on our own in the Three Horse Shoes, how shunned we were.'

'I saw nothing of the sort. You're imagining it. People haven't been ignoring *me*.'

'But she's not *your* daughter, Bernard. The shame is on us not you. As soon as you took her in we knew we'd have to leave.'

'Then you should have told me.' Bernard, so angry by this time, believing he was following a trail of falsehoods, could hardly suppress his rage.

'Nothing was settled,' John Clark murmured, obviously deeply ashamed of himself. 'We didn't know where we were going to go. It was only last week Robert Hussey told us about the vacancy in Pilsdon. We settled it today with him.'

'Oh, did you?' Bernard roared. 'While I was in the same room buying you all drinks.' He leaned against one of the newly rendered walls and put his face in his hands. 'God knows how I'll ever recoup the money I spent on this property. It may well reduce me to penury.'

The Clark family left Powerstock in the first week of March, their departure having been delayed because of problems with the property in Pilsdon. Once Mrs Clark had inspected it she found that it wasn't quite as satisfactory as she'd expected, certainly no better than the dairy house in Powerstock and a good deal worse than the farmhouse that Bernard had so carefully restored.

On the morning of their departure Martha went up to say goodbye, taking William with her, but Bernard stayed behind. Ann hadn't seen her parents since the day Bernard had given her shelter.

Bernard had not been able to let the farm because the dairy house and cheese loft were in poor states of repair and he could not afford to touch them, having over-extended himself. In desperation he decided to try and make good his losses and farm the land for which he was paying a high rent. However, the soil was in such bad condition, Albert Hunt having had little interest towards the end of his farming life in soil preservation and the rotation of crops. Thus Bernard was obliged to leave most of the land fallow as the sowing season had passed.

He was not joking when he said it had brought him

to the verge of penury and this was at a time when he was trying to enhance his status in the community by attempting to become an overseer of the poor, a member of the church vestry.

Bernard longed to be a man of some consequence, a respectable man with a lovely young wife and three handsome children. But in a close-knit, class-conscious community such as this, to be accepted was not an easy matter.

Martha found the cart well laden when she got to the dairy house, the contents balanced on top of a motley collection of furniture, chattels and half a dozen noisy hens loudly complaining in their basket. Memories came back to her of similar journeys made throughout the years, usually with a baby in a crib, and her feelings towards her parents softened. Theirs had been a hard life, fortune never quite seemed to favour them and in her heart she wished her family well and hoped that one day their endless journeys might be over.

She ran impulsively over to the door as her mother emerged laden to the eyeballs with bundles of clothes.

'Ah, Martha,' she said sarcastically, 'have you come to make sure you're rid of us?'

Martha felt hurt. No matter how hard she tried she could never get it right. There was always that sense of agitation, of misunderstanding. The harsh word, the unexpected reaction. Martha lifted baby William onto her shoulder.

'I'm sorry that you're going.'

'Huh!' Martha Clark sniffed. '*That's* hypocrisy for you. You won't miss us at all. Glad to see the back of us I reckon.' She paused and wagged an accusing finger at her. 'It's *your* fault that we're going, you realise that, don't you? But for you we would be snug in the farmhouse repaired for us by your husband, by all accounts at vast expense. Don't think we enjoy going from pillar to post. Haven't we done enough travelling? And now we have to throw ourselves on the mercy of cousin Robert who always did think himself and his family a cut above the rest of us.'

'Stop your grumbling now,' John Clark attempted to stem the flow before it became a torrent and pushed her up onto the seat of the cart. Mary was already sitting there with Elizabeth, and behind her, squashed in among the goods and chattels, was Charles while Tom and William had gone on ahead with another cart. Elizabeth, pale and frail, looked sadly at her elder sister.

'I wish you were coming with us, Martha,' she said impulsively. 'I *wish* you had never gone.'

Martha reached for the young girl's hand.

'I'll visit. I'll visit often.' She felt close to tears herself as she realised what a wrench it would be, particularly from her father and siblings.

'Don't you believe it. She'll forget all about us,' Martha Clark scoffed, but suddenly her husband held up his hand and said sharply, 'That's enough, Martha. Cease your wittering.'

And while she sat, taken aback by his outburst, he went over to his daughter, took her hand and kissed the baby's head.

'You'll always be welcome. There will always be a bed for you, a place at table.' He paused. 'Maybe we shouldn't have gone, but your mother was such a trial about Ann and what she thought people thought that I got tired of listening to it, so we had to take the chance when it came.'

'I know, Father.' Martha smiled bravely and put a hand on his arm. 'Don't worry about it.'

'We did treat your husband bad; but,' John lowered his voice, 'I can't stand up to your mother. Never could.' Nor could he now as his wife bawled from the seat on the cart.

'John! Do you want to get there by nightfall?' Then the sight of Martha's face, or perhaps the fact that she and her father stood so close together, seemed to infuriate her. 'Don't let me see that smug smile on your face, Martha Bearn. *You've* nothing to be proud of. Ann should have gone to the poorhouse and no one would have known, none any the wiser. *That's* the only place she was fit for. You made us a laughing stock by taking her in. They laugh at us not you, the one who gave her a home. Is that fair? You are a scheming, stubborn . . .' Martha Clark stopped, choking on her words as if she couldn't find enough with which to express her bitterness.

'Mother,' Martha protested, 'how can you talk like that to your daughter? You *know* it's not true.'

But by now Martha Clark seemed, perhaps through weariness and disappointment, out of control. 'You're no daughter of mine,' she shrieked. 'Don't think you are. No daughter of mine . . .'

'How do you mean I'm no daughter of yours?' Martha asked bewilderedly.

Her mother raised her arm pointing a finger at her husband, whose expression had dramatically changed to one of alarm.

'Ask your father,' she screamed, whereupon John Clark, suddenly turning his back on his daughter, scuttled across to the cart and jumped onto the seat next to his shrewish wife. Then, with a flick of the whip, he sent it bowling down the lane to the accompaniment of a chorus of squawking, protesting hens as if they were reluctant to say goodbye to the only place they had ever known as home, and fearful of an uncertain future.

May 1833

Martha thought how good it was to have her sister with her now that the family had dispersed, her mother still grumbling about the discomfort of the quarters provided for them by cousin Robert at Pilsdon. (But that was no surprise as it was practically impossible to satisfy Martha Clark about anything. She must have come into the world complaining.)

It wasn't that she'd seen a lot of the family after she was married, even less after Ann came to live with them, but it was knowing they were there.

Even her mother's constant nagging seemed to diminish in retrospect so that to her surprise Martha missed her. Despite her bad temper she retained an affection for her mother that was hard to explain. But more than her mother she missed her sweet, weak father who if he did not always stand up for her was never known to scold and to whom she had always been especially close. Many a time they had seemed as conspirators against the woman who plagued both their lives.

A couple of months after their departure, when the trees were in blossom and it was possible to think that winter was finally over, Martha and Ann sat together by the fire in the front parlour. Ann's time had nearly come and Martha felt an instinctive pity for her as she shifted about in her chair trying to find a comfortable position.

Over in the slaughterhouse Bernard and Ezekiel were dealing with the latest batch of cattle destined for the market. The sound of them bellowing under the knife always distressed Martha. It was something she had still not got used to and, even more, the mournful expressions of resignation as the cows and sheep were led into that dreadful place. Occasionally one escaped and scampered frantically round the yard looking for refuge, but soon it was hauled back with great savagery by one of the men and its throat slit even before it was through the door.

Bernard and Ezekiel, however, always despatched their business with almost grotesque cheerfulness, helped down by tankards of ale from the beer-house next door, and in no time the carcasses were dealt with and loaded onto the cart to be taken to market in Bridport. But all day long after the slaughter a seemingly endless trickle of blood wended its way across the yard to be absorbed by the soil in the field and, ultimately, the river, and the whole place was filled with the stench of death.

'I wish they didn't kill the cattle so near,' Ann said as if putting words to Martha's thoughts, her hands covering her ears to muffle the sound.

'It will soon be over,' Martha said. 'Anyway, it gives us a nice piece of steak for our dinner.'

Ann nodded, but her expression was morose. She looked up at Martha who was embroidering a romper suit for baby William.

'I wish I had your confidence, Martha, also your security.'

Martha lowered her sewing. 'Why do you say that?'

'Because I often wonder what will become of me and what I shall do with the baby after it is born.'

'You have a home here as long as you wish.' Martha put out a comforting hand.

'I don't think it's fair to Bernard. I know he is kept off the vestry because of me.'

It was true that, whatever its protestations about Christian charity, the church was noticeably strict towards those who transgressed its laws. It had as little time for women who got themselves into trouble as Mrs Clark, and those who harboured them were thought to be not much better. The poorhouse with its miserable conditions and harsh regime was definitely the best place for such people.

There had always been a doubt in the minds of some of the village elders about Bernard Bearn, a man not native to Powerstock. His first wife had been the daughter of a woman called Betty Mawson who had enjoyed a reputation for notoriety in the district, having had three children out of wedlock before she married the father of the last two, Samuel Wrixon. Elizabeth Mawson, the first born, had never been quite sure who her father was and the stigma seemed to continue even after she had made a respectable marriage and borne legitimate children.

'Bernard is more concerned about you than the vestry,' Martha assured her.

'He is a good and kind man.'

Martha nodded. 'I feel I am beginning to value Bernard more and more. He has qualities I didn't know about when I married him.'

'Would you say you loved him, then?'

Martha put her head on one side. 'You asked me that before, you remember, when we were talking about Josiah Symes.'

'You didn't answer.'

'I do love him now in several ways, but not in an intimate way, do you understand what I mean? Without that aspect of our life I would be quite happy.'

Ann nodded her understanding. Such matters were too delicate even for sisters to talk about.

'Josiah Symes now,' Martha went on, 'he *was* an attractive man. I would feel differently about him, yet his character is nothing like as good as Bernard's.'

'His character is rotten,' Ann said savagely.

'He would have done the same to me if I'd gone off with him. He would have treated me exactly as he treated you. But you, at least, knew a deep passion which I never had with Bernard, and certainly not with Josiah Symes because we kissed, no more. I do not love Bernard in that physical way.'

Feeling that she'd said enough Martha paused for a moment and looked at Ann.

'I often wonder what Mother meant by saying that I was no daughter of hers. It puzzled me.'

'Oh, you know Mother. I expect she meant that you didn't behave as she would like you to.'

'I think she meant more than that. Because she said, "Ask your father." Father wouldn't look at me but hurried to the cart and drove off. You know, Ann,' Martha's expression was thoughtful, 'I often *did* wonder about my origins. You know that I do not physically resemble the rest of you? I wonder if I was a changeling.'

It was the old familiar story. Ann smiled. 'You used to joke about it when we were small. I never knew if you meant it.'

'Seriously, perhaps Mother did mean it?'

Ann sat quietly for a while gazing into the fire. 'It's the sort of thing people say when they're angry. But there is something, Martha, I never told you.' She paused again and stared deep into her sister's eyes.

'Go on,' Martha encouraged her, aware of a strange sensation that was partly excitement, partly foreboding.

'Well, when I was about five Mother was pregnant, as usual, but I know there was a great commotion when the baby was born and I seem to remember we thought it had died.'

'You never told me this before,' Martha said, astonished.

'I know, but it lodged in my mind. You see, after a few days there *was* a baby, large as life and it was big for a new baby but, of course, we asked no questions because we were very young. I never thought of it from that day to this. So,' Ann paused, 'maybe you *will* only get the truth from our mother and father.'

The tension in the room, the moment when the sisters stared wonderingly at each other, was broken as the door opened and Eliza came in, a bored expression on her face.

'Oh, I do *wish* they'd stop killing the cattle,' she said. 'It's so horrible.'

'It will soon be over. I wonder you're not used to it by now.' Martha looked at the clock. 'Do you not have your lesson with Mr Webber this morning, Eliza?'

Mr Webber was the schoolmaster who had set up a schoolroom in his house where he taught local children with his wife. As yet only a few villagers had taken advantage of this as few could afford it.

'Mrs Webber is not well. There will be no lessons

today or tomorrow.' Eliza slumped on the floor in front of the fire, her chin cupped in her hands.

'Why don't you have one or two of your friends to tea?' Martha said brightly. 'Ann Walbridge or one of the Peach girls, or maybe both? Would you like that? I'll ask Joanna to make them a cake.'

Eliza didn't even raise her eyes from the fire. 'No thank you.'

'But why not? You go and visit them and yet you never ask them here.' Martha looked curiously at her. She might have known it would be hard to please her stepdaughter. She only had to suggest a thing for Eliza either not to want to do it, or to do something different.

'How can I ask them,' Eliza looked pointedly at Ann, 'with *her* here?'

'I'll soon be gone,' Ann felt herself colour, 'and then you can ask anyone you want.'

'I think that's a *very* rude thing to say,' Martha said, getting up. 'Say you're sorry.'

'But I'm not, and it's true. Everyone in the village talks about her and the fact that you and my father have her living here. They don't know how you can do it, and nor do I.'

Struggling to control herself, Martha crossed to the door and threw it open making a sweeping gesture with her arm.

'I think you'd better go to your room.'

'Well I shan't. I have as much right here as you have – more right. I was born here but you came as a servant. People say my father should have known better than to marry you.' Eliza put her hands to her ears. 'And as for the cattle bellowing outside do you

93

think anyone would want to send their well-brought-up children here?'

'The Walbridges are farmers too,' Martha said, gritting her teeth.

'Yes, but they don't slaughter the animals in the backyard. Father sends me for piano lessons and to be taught reading and writing, but what chance do I have in a house where there is blood all over the yard and people like you and,' she pointed to Ann, '*her*. I think it's disgusting, and Ann Walbridge agrees with me.'

'*And* I think *you're* disgusting,' Ann exclaimed, making a feeble attempt to get to her feet but, failing miserably, sank back into her chair. 'You're a horrible, mean, disgusting little girl. Martha is worth *ten* of you, and yet you do nothing but upset her. You are rude to her, you are even rude to your father. I really pity Martha having someone like you as a stepdaughter.'

With an exclamation Eliza rose to her feet and, rushing across to Ann, raised her hand to strike her. Only Martha, anticipating her action, got to Ann before her. She seized Eliza's arm and twisted it until her stepdaughter cried out in pain. She then dragged her across the room and bundled her into the passage outside before slamming the door. Then she leaned against it, breathing heavily.

'I hate her,' she said. 'I really do.'

'Oh, you shouldn't have done that.'

'I could have killed her. I could.'

'Maybe you hurt her?'

'I hope so.'

Ann looked anxious. 'You'd better go and see.'

'I don't care if I did hurt her. And if Bernard is angry with me I shall tell him she attempted to strike you.'

Martha paused and looked anxiously at her sister. 'Oh Ann, what is it? Are you all right?'

Ann, grimacing with pain, had suddenly doubled up. 'I think my labour has started,' she gasped. 'Would you help me to my bed?'

Agnes Legg, the nurse, looked anxiously at her patient while Martha, a lamp in her hand, hovered by her side. Mrs Legg had her sleeves rolled up and then, once more, she put her arm into the birth passage but she soon withdrew it and shook her head.

'I can feel a leg, not a head,' she said. 'The baby is in the breech position. We must send for the doctor.'

'But the nearest doctor is in Beaminster.'

'Then you must get him quick. I can do no more,' her voice dropped, 'or you will lose both mother and baby.'

Bernard waiting anxiously outside the door was told the bad news. Ezekiel had stayed to help and, although it was late at night, he was told to take the horse and ride as quickly as he could to the town and fetch the doctor.

Nurse Legg, exhausted, left about midnight and Martha sat by her sister who seemed to lapse in and out of consciousness with pain and exhaustion, pressing her hand, murmuring words of comfort and occasionally applying cold compresses fetched by Joanna. Downstairs Bernard paced about reliving the agonies of his first wife's last confinement.

The hours seemed to pass very slowly and Ann's struggles were dreadful to see as her belly heaved with the efforts of the stricken infant within her to escape into the world.

Finally at dawn there was the clatter of horses' hooves

outside, voices were heard in the hall, footsteps running up the stairs and the doctor entered the room and, immediately going over to the patient, felt her pulse.

'Plenty of hot water,' he commanded, 'buckets, dishes.' He looked at Martha. 'Why was I not called before?'

'Mrs Legg did all she could.'

The doctor opened his black portmanteau and took out a fearsome looking pair of forceps which he laid on the bed while he removed his jacket and donned his black rubber apron. Then gently issuing commands to the semi-conscious Ann he inserted the heavy instruments and began to try and extricate the infant lodged so firmly inside.

Martha could hardly bear to look but, after a while, the doctor laid aside his forceps and putting both hands inside the luckless mother pulled with all his might as though he was in a tug of war.

Ann screamed. Martha seized her hand and, in a rush, the baby was born, one foot caught up. It lay on the bloody sheet quite inert, like a stranded fish and, like a stranded fish, suddenly gave a gasp and was still.

The doctor tried resuscitation but to no avail.

The struggle for the infant to live had proved too much.

Chapter Six

November 1834
The Reverend George Cookson, vicar of Powerstock, took his parish duties very seriously. He was a strict, orthodox churchman, but devoted to his flock and concerned about the less well off, of whom there were many. This part of Dorset was predominantly rural and there was no industry to take those who, because of economic hardship, had to leave their work on the land. Consequently there were many who depended on poor rate relief but, since the passing of The Poor Law Amendment Act earlier in the year, the plan was to send the destitute of the parish to the workhouse rather than support them in their own homes.

Powerstock was not a wealthy parish. Its roads, such as they were, were in poor condition, many of the cottages were run down and in need of repair, the children ran shoeless in the street. Many farms such as Albert Hunt's had closed down and others were closing, while the roads were full of mournful flocks of animals either being taken to slaughter or to the market as their owners could not afford to keep them.

The church, too, was in a dilapidated state and badly in need of repair, but the vicar dared not request the substantial sum needed for rebuilding while so many of his parishioners lived in poverty.

Powerstock numbered about a thousand souls, almost all of whom were churchgoers and known personally to Mr Cookson. Every Sunday the church was almost full, the young men sitting on the church wall waiting until the last bell had tolled to troop in and all sit together.

Bernard and Martha Bearn were regular churchgoers and now that Ann had left they were always greeted by the vicar with more cordiality than when they had harboured a woman of fallen virtue, and their family enquired after. The vicar was of the school which thought that although their sins could be forgiven sinners must be punished and their behaviour should not be condoned. By harbouring Ann, Bernard and Martha had condoned her sin and, in the vicar's opinion, it would have been better for her immortal soul for her to be incarcerated in a proper house of correction.

In February 1834 Martha and Bernard had become the parents of another son, Thomas. Mr Cookson was also a family man with five daughters, one just a couple of months older than Thomas.

After the normal civilities were exchanged after church one Sunday early in the autumn the vicar asked Bernard if he would step along to the house on his way home as he had something to discuss with him.

Bernard told James and Eliza to go along with Martha and waited for the vicar to finish greeting his parishioners. He then walked with him to the vicarage, Mrs Cookson in front shepherding her brood, some of whom were friends of Eliza's.

'I have also asked Thomas Walbridge to join us,' the vicar said, entering the gate which his wife had left open.

The vicarage was a large house close to the church and also in need of repair. It was dark and rather cold inside and Bernard was glad when the vicar took him into his study, where there was a warm fire, and offered him a glass of sherry which he drank with his back to the flames, warming his behind. They were soon joined by Thomas Walbridge who farmed one of the largest farms in the area.

The Walbridges represented the sort of yeoman farmer that Bernard aspired to be. They were rich and successful, owning or renting much of the land in Powerstock. Like the Husseys they were a large, closely knit clan with many members scattered in the locality. They had elegant homes, wives who, though accomplished housekeepers, were not expected to do rough work, and children of both sexes who went to school. Ann, Thomas Walbridge's daughter, was the friend with whom Eliza attended piano lessons.

The Walbridges for the most part were pillars of the community, and in many ways they kept it going. Bernard always felt that whatever the Walbridges did they would fall on their feet, success would come their way. It was galling when a person like himself had worked so hard all his life and yet had not achieved quite that success, a degree of riches as well as respectability which seemed to come so easily the way of people like the Walbridges. Somehow they seemed born to it.

Bernard was now forty-two and he felt that he had a lot of catching up to do.

Once the newcomer had a glass of sherry in his hands

and tried to edge Bernard a little to one side, so that he too could warm his backside, the vicar came to the point of the meeting.

'I have asked you here, Mr Bearn, to sound you out as to whether or not you would be willing to act as a churchwarden. The rest of the vestry, of whom Mr Walbridge is a member, have suggested your name.'

'Why,' Bernard, though thrilled to the marrow, tried not to sound too eager, 'I am of course honoured to be asked.'

'We have not asked you before,' the vicar coughed discreetly. 'I think you know why, but now that your sister-in-law is settled at a farm in Netherbury . . .'

The vicar's words hung ominously in the air and Thomas Walbridge's gaze wandered over to the window. 'One of course *admired* your sense of Christian charity towards this unfortunate woman,' Mr Cookson proceeded in unctuous tones, 'but at the same time we also had to think of the effect on the local population if a man seeming to condone such behaviour was a church functionary. I hope you understand.'

Bernard understood only too well. He felt a sudden stab of anger at the hypocrisy of people who, supposedly, took Christ as their model.

However here was a step up, the chance he had always wanted to be a man of consequence in Powerstock, a member of the vestry, maybe one day an overseer of the poor, a person of respectability. It would not do to be too outspoken.

'My sister-in-law was taken advantage of,' he said, 'she thought she was about to be married.'

'Let's not discuss the whys and wherefores,' the vicar noisily cleared his throat. 'The matter is finished.' He looked across at Thomas Walbridge. 'I'm sure we're delighted to have Mr Bearn's agreement?'

'Delighted,' Thomas said.

After chatting about procedures, the next meeting of the vestry, the state of the church and the necessity of repairs being made soon if it was not to fall down, the vicar saw his guests to the door and, after saying goodbye, they made their way together along the road past the church and stood at the crossroads.

'You must bring your wife to dinner,' Thomas said amiably. 'I don't think she and my wife have met. After the next vestry meeting we'll arrange a date.'

'My wife would like that,' Bernard said. 'And it's very kind of you to let my daughter go along with yours to piano lessons. She's coming on very well.'

'I'm glad to hear that. She's a delightful little girl. I think Ann rather envies her her skills at the piano.'

Thomas paused, stroking his chin. 'Oh by the way,' he made it sound like an afterthought, just as they were about to part, 'we have some land to sell, a few acres we have no need of. Would you by any chance . . .'

'I'd be delighted to consider it,' Bernard said smiling insincerely, a sudden weight descending on his heart. He might have known there would be a catch.

Martha hadn't sat at such a fine table since she and Bernard had eaten at The Bull in Bridport during their honeymoon. She had felt nervous about the evening. The Walbridges were only remotely known to her and, although she had seen her at church, she had never actually met Mrs Walbridge, who was a handsome woman in her mid fifties. Martha suspected that she and Mr Walbridge had married late in life. They had a boy, Robert, and a girl called Ann. Also at the dinner party was their nephew William and his fiancée, a Netherbury girl who knew the Clarks.

Martha had on her best dress for the evening, her wedding dress with a few alterations, which she had only worn since for the baptisms of her children. Bernard, in order to try and impress his host and hostess, had wanted to buy her a new one but she said it was a waste of money when she used it so little. Now she was sorry she hadn't.

There was an air of finery about the Walbridge women which made Martha feel out of place and awkward. There was an assurance, a sophistication that she was quite unused to as a countrywoman, and knew she lacked. They spoke more nicely than she did, their Dorset accents not as heavy as hers. Often people visiting from another county had difficulty making out what the real Dorset folk said, even claimed it was a foreign language; but sometimes Martha felt she couldn't understand *them*.

One thing she knew for certain was that she was prettier than the Netherbury girl. She was also younger. She had washed her hair and her black curls shone; her skin was so good that it glowed. She knew her figure was trim and supple and her height gave her an advantage over others.

She imagined she got envious glances from William's fiancée, but she could have been wrong.

She tried to enjoy the evening, she had set out to. She was so pleased that Bernard was to be a churchwarden, maybe soon an overseer of the poor authorised to dispense the Poor Law in the area. He wanted to be a prominent member of the parish and, through him, she would be prominent too. But there were limitations, she thought as she looked around the highly polished table with its gleaming candles and sparkling silverware. Where on earth did folk get these ideas from! She supposed they read about them in magazines because she was sure that Mrs Walbridge could read.

Though a good cook she didn't think she could ever produce meals in such elegant surroundings as this, she wouldn't know how, where to start but, yes, she had always wanted to better herself, and this was definitely a step in the right direction.

The Walbridges had two servants who waited on them at dinner, simple wholesome fare cooked by Mrs Walbridge who, whatever Martha's opinion, had no pretensions to be other than a plain, sturdy farmer's wife whose husband happened to have made a lot of money.

Mrs Walbridge kept on giving her friendly glances as if to try and put her at ease, but Martha felt so awkward. Bernard was right about the dress, which was now three years old, even if it had been little worn.

Bernard might have taught her to sign her name, but she knew nothing about entertaining or being entertained by society, people like the Walbridges who kept a good table and shopped regularly in Bridport and Dorchester. Surely their dresses were new and had come from one of those towns? She had never been to Dorchester in her life. Martha had this terribly familiar feeling that, somehow, she did not fit into this society, or any society. She was an outsider and life, in some strange way, had made her an outcast. She feared that she would not be the adornment Bernard wanted her to be, but would inevitably fail him.

The conversation was also above her head. She felt

woefully ignorant. They were talking about farming prices and new methods which they felt would result in fresh riots, such as had occurred in the county for several years now. Agricultural workers were having to form themselves into unions to better their conditions and increase their wages. The extent of militancy varied in Dorset – there had been more in the north than in the south and west – but the fate of seven men from the Dorset village of Tolpuddle had caused a national outcry when they were tried and sentenced to deportation in Australia.

In Thomas Walbridge's opinion – and he was a very opinionated man – this had been a good thing as it would stifle dissent which would not be good for the wellbeing of the community. Bernard and William seemed to agree. In fact Bernard appeared anxious to agree with everything Thomas Walbridge said. Didn't Bernard have *any* opinions of his own at all? Martha wondered.

The talk then turned logically to the new Poor Law and the effect that it would have on rural communities. Here Martha was better informed. She knew little about farm prices and nothing about new methods, but she did know about poverty. She pricked up her ears.

Again, in Thomas Walbridge's opinion, it would be a good thing to force paupers into the workhouse, rather than keep them in the community. They couldn't look after themselves or their children and their houses were dirty and ill cared for with rubbish piled up outside. All this was a danger to health as well as a sight for sore eyes. Powerstock would be a better place if some of the paupers were sent off to Beaminster, out of the way. They were no asset to society. Rather the reverse. 'After all, the object of the workhouse is as a place of *correction*. Sometimes people seem to forget that.'

'You mean that the people have only themselves to blame?' Martha spoke timorously for the first time since they'd sat down.

'Well, of course,' Mrs Walbridge looked at her in astonishment, not quite so kindly this time. 'They don't work hard enough. If they did they wouldn't be where they were.'

'My family worked very hard,' Martha insisted firmly. 'They worked their fingers to the bone.'

'But they never went to the workhouse, my dear,' Bernard intervened, anxious not to offend. 'Nor near it.'

'They were *very* near it at times. That's why we had to move about so often, take anything that came, rather than go to the workhouse or be a burden on the parish. I tell you poverty has nothing to do with hard work, and I do know what I'm talking about.'

Martha, her face flushed — which made her even prettier — looked about her. Remembering how she and her sisters had dreaded being sent to the poorhouse she felt more confidence in herself than at any time that evening. She had everyone's attention, no doubt of that. 'Well, obviously none of you know what it's like to be poor, not to have enough to eat or the wherewithal to feed your children. I do. I feared the workhouse several times when my father was out of work. We all did.'

'Hush, Martha.' Bernard looked at her furiously. 'You don't know what you're talking about.'

'But Bernard, I *do* know what I'm talking about,' Martha insisted. 'I know much more about the poor than you do, or any of these people here. My parents . . .'

'But the fear kept your parents out of the workhouse, didn't it, Mrs Bearn?' Thomas Walbridge attempted a forced joviality as if to hide his embarrassment at being contradicted by a woman. 'It wouldn't do to make these places more comfortable, or they would be rushing in and we would all be paying huge amounts to accommodate the poor.'

'I think we should abandon this subject and leave the gentlemen to their discussion,' Mrs Walbridge said firmly, rising and signalling to her future daughter-in-law. Then she extended a hand to Martha: 'Mrs Bearn, would you like to come with us?'

There was no concealing Bernard's annoyance when they got home.

'Speaking out like that, Martha! In front of those people too! Whatever got into you?'

'Because they didn't know what they were talking about,' she replied indignantly. '*And* they made me feel so small. I didn't like the Walbridges and I don't want to go there again.'

'I don't think you'll be asked, my dear, have no fears about that! And just when I am about to become a churchwarden and, perhaps, one day even an overseer of the poor. No thanks to you now if I don't. I've just bought a parcel of land I don't want and can't afford in order to increase their good opinion of me.'

'*What* opinion?' Martha said hotly. 'That you are a rich man? Why does their opinion matter to you so much? I think you're a foolish man, Bernard. You overtax yourself. Don't you owe enough money already? You say you can't pay the Glebe farm for pressing your apples, so you can make no more cider; you have debts everywhere.

What will happen when the Walbridges, or the vicar, get to hear about *that*, if they don't know already? They'll think you a fool and take advantage of you.'

'You know nothing about this, Martha.' Bernard looked furiously at her. 'I know what I'm doing. The Walbridges wanted to get rid of that land and I did them a favour. One day they will do *me* a favour. You never know when such people will be useful.'

'I think you're a fool,' Martha said shortly and she went upstairs to take off her fine dress, sad that the evening had been so disastrous, and wondering when she would have the chance to wear it again.

On the landing outside the children's room Martha paused. Then she gently turned the handle and, holding her candle high, peeped in.

William now had his own little bed. Thomas slept in a cot, and both were fast asleep. In a truckle-bed in a corner Joanna, the maid, was fast asleep too. She had her own room in the loft but when the parents were out, which was not often, she slept with the two younger children.

Martha was always uncomfortable leaving Eliza alone with them, not because she thought she'd do them harm, though she wouldn't put that past her she was so jealous, but for fear that she might neglect them.

Martha held the candle over the cot and looked at sleeping Thomas. He was such a bubbly, cuddly, contented baby with a loving disposition. He was the sort of baby you always wanted to hug. She stifled the impulse to do so again, but reached down to make sure that the covers were over him because the room was so cold. He lay on his back, arms outstretched, little fists curled, a blissful expression on his face and, as she touched him, he moved in his sleep and gave a little sigh. She kissed him lightly before moving over to William who lay curled up like a ball.

She covered him up too and as she did he opened his eyes wide, as if she had frightened him, so she sat on the bed and took him in her arms to comfort him. He clung to her for a little while as she hugged him tightly until she could feel his body growing heavier and knew he was asleep. She laid him gently down and covered him with the blanket before she rose and tip-toed out of the room.

Her heart felt very full. Her anger had evaporated. It was thanks to Bernard that she had these two beautiful children. She felt gratitude to him and also a sense of love, enhanced by the fact that they were a family. The arrival of William and Thomas, the fulfilment of motherhood, had done much to settle her, to steady her, to ease her discontent. She was now happier than she had ever been with her lot in life.

Also, Bernard, while not neglecting his elder children, adored his new family.

Martha realised so well how much she had to be thankful for: a more stable – despite Bernard's misadventures – and secure life than her parents had ever had and a man who, while he did not excite her, plainly adored her and took care of her.

It was in a better, more sanguine and peaceful frame of mind that Martha returned to her room and prepared for bed.

By the time Bernard came up Martha was in bed, but she knew sleep was far away. He said nothing as he undressed, put on his nightshirt, blew out the candle and climbed into bed beside her. He lay on his back, his hands under his head.

'I'm sorry,' he said. 'You were quite right. I was too mealy-mouthed. I should have defended you. Those people know nothing about hardship, and when they see it around them they think such folk should be put away.'

'I was thinking too of Ann.'

'I knew you were.' He put out a hand and touched her. 'I was thinking of her too.'

'But maybe I did speak out of turn, Bernard,' Martha said with uncharacteristic humility. 'I was too hasty. I didn't want to make you ashamed of me.'

Bernard gripped her hand tightly. 'No, you did right.'

'Fact is, we are not like those people, and we never will be.'

'No. I realised that tonight after you'd gone, and I sat thinking downstairs. They called my former mother-in-law a whore in the village, and the Walbridges would *never* have asked my Elizabeth to dinner, I'm sure of that.'

'I don't know why you care so much about their opinion.' She turned and looked at him through the inky blackness.

'I want to improve myself, Martha, for you and my children.'

'But that makes you buy things you can't afford, like that land. You can't *buy* a good opinion, Bernard. You will be found out. What these people think matters too much to you.'

'I want it for you too. Believe me, Martha, I love you. You looked beautiful tonight. I was so proud you were my wife. Really proud. That's what matters. You and my darling children.'

'It *is* all that matters, but you won't change, Bernard.' Martha, suddenly feeling older and wiser than her husband, sadly shook her head. 'As long as you let people like the vicar and the Walbridges patronise you, as long as you want their approval, you'll never change. You should tell them you don't want that land. Stand up to them.'

'I've already told them I'd have it.'

'Then how do you come to have the money if you can't pay the Glebe farm?' Martha began to feel really angry because she'd done without a new dress partly because she knew Bernard had debts.

'There's a money lender in Bridport I've used before. He charges a lot of interest but I think I'll be able to make the land pay. If not, I'll sell it to someone else.'

Bernard endeavoured to sound cheerful but in the dark Martha thought it sounded awfully hollow.

'We are happy, Martha, aren't we?' he whispered after a while. 'You do love me a little?'

'I love you quite a lot,' she said, patting his hand. 'I know that you're a good man, with a very kind heart, but you're a foolish one too. You exasperate me, Bernard Bearn.'

Emboldened by her tenderness his hand stole up her leg and under her warm flannel nightgown.

Martha closed her eyes in resignation.

This, after all, was the price of love, the only way that he really wanted, the way she could thank him for what he'd tried to do for her ungrateful parents – which, in fact, had started his spiral of debt – and what he'd done for Ann.

A good, kind man but a deeply misguided one.

*   *   *

Sarah Crocker, Bernard's sister-in-law, was a warm friendly woman whose husband George worked as a dairyman at a farm in Witherstone, a hamlet just outside Powerstock. Bernard had been a witness at their wedding. They had a son, also called George, who was five and a baby, Sam, a couple of months older than Thomas.

Sarah had become Martha's best friend since her sister Ann had left to work as a dairymaid on a farm in Netherbury. She found her warm and sympathetic, a discreet and valued confidante, maybe because she knew Bernard as well as anyone since her sister had been married to him.

Martha liked to talk to her about Bernard's first wife, a woman tragically cut off in her prime. It was clear that Bernard had had a great deal of affection for her too, proved perhaps by the fact that he had been in no great hurry to marry again.

A few days after the dinner party Sarah came visiting with George and the baby. Her husband had brought some sheep to be slaughtered and, as he helped Bernard and Ezekiel in the slaughterhouse, the two women sat in the parlour chatting.

It was a bitterly cold January day, with a keen eastern wind blowing, the sort that seemed to cut through your skin, and they sat close up to the fire with the babies on a rug between them. George and William, well wrapped up, ran about in the orchard outside where their mothers could keep an eye on them.

'George is a little grizzly,' Sarah said. 'I think he caught a cold. We won't stay long.' She looked across at Martha. 'I hear Bernard is now a churchwarden?'

Martha nodded and told her about the dinner party they'd had with the Walbridges.

'A step up then,' Sarah said a little enviously. 'Bernard will be pleased. He was always ambitious. You will soon look down your noses at the likes of us poor folk.'

'I will *never* look down on you,' Martha retorted indignantly. 'I can tell you I *never* want to be like the Walbridges. You're the only friend I've got now that Ann has gone.'

'Is Ann happy where she is?'

'As happy as a woman can be away from her family and having lost her little baby.' Martha sighed thinking of the tiny body lying in an unmarked grave in the churchyard. 'She didn't want the baby at first, but in the end she did.'

'Just as well.' Sarah was a brisk, practical woman. 'She can now make a new start.' She stopped as George came running in crying, and wiping his nose.

'Whatever is the matter?' Sarah asked anxiously, putting a hand on his head as he leaned against her.

'Don't feel well,' little George sobbed, his tear-stained face flushed. Sarah felt his brow.

'He's very hot,' she said to Martha. 'I'd best see if my husband has finished and get him to take us home. They say there's measles about.'

'Oh I do hope not,' Martha cried in alarm seeing her to the door.

But there was, and within a few days poor little George Crocker, only five years old, was dead.

Sitting round the lunch table in the Husseys' dining room in their Pilsdon farm Martha was reminded of dinner at the Walbridges' where, despite her once cherished desire to better herself, she had formed a dislike for polite society. There was the same sham air of elegance and respectability in the Hussey dining room with the table all nicely laid with a lace cloth and plenty of good country fare to eat, vegetables grown on the farm, a choice of pork or lamb, a luxury even in the Bearn household. However, though Cousin Robert who was a widower wore a suit for the main midday meal, his younger sons were all in their working clothes, their boots having been left at the back door. The women present wore dresses of similar finery to the Walbridge ladies while Mrs Clark, Mary and Elizabeth had come straight from the dairy and still wore their aprons, having left their clogs outside the door beside the men's boots.

Eliza Bearn was delighted to discover a family that so resembled the Walbridge, Peach and Cookson families in Powerstock, and sat chatting eagerly with the younger girls who were also, she discovered, taking piano lessons and never did a day's turn on the farm if they could help it.

The meal over, John Clark and Bernard had gone to discuss some family business taking James with them, and baby Thomas sat on Martha's knee where he was greatly admired by his new relations who had never seen him. This was the first visit of the Bearns to Pilsdon since the Clarks had left, as it was some distance from Powerstock.

Martha Bearn had never been close to the Hussey cousins. There were so many of them scattered all over the area. She knew they rather looked down on her father and had induced in her mother this deep and unnecessary sense of inferiority, which was probably what had made Mrs Clark a woman of such a mean and cantankerous disposition.

Consequently she was always prickly and uneasy in their company and after the meal she was anxious to get away so that she could have a moan to her daughter in the privacy of the dairy house. Eliza Bearn gladly accepted her new-found friends' invitation to stay behind, but they all came to the door of the farmhouse to wave, impressed by Martha Bearn's seeming affluence, her dress and cloak and the obvious affection of her husband, even if he was much older.

'Thank goodness that's over,' Mrs Clark sniffed, drawing her daughter into the kitchen. She stopped short, looking accusingly at Martha.

'I see you've got your best dress on. The one you wore for your wedding.'

'I've got another one now, Mother,' Martha said. 'This is my second best.'

Martha Clark sniffed disapprovingly. 'Oh, I see. A fine lady now, are we?'

Martha swallowed a retort, 'Don't be spiteful, Mother. We don't see you so much and I want it to be a nice day.'

'I see.' Mrs Clark thought for a moment and then with seeming calculation pointed to a hole in the roof through which the sky could clearly be seen. 'You can see how we've been let down by Cousin Robert. The place needs doing up and he don't want to do it. I think John is having a word about it with Bernard.'

'About what?' Martha peered uneasily at the roof, as well as the general state of disrepair and squalor around her. The back door hung on its hinges and hens were openly scavenging on the kitchen floor, while one seemed to have made its nest in an open cupboard.

'To see if he could let him have some money or,' she

looked slyly at Martha, 'maybe let us have the house he repaired in Powerstock.' She sighed deeply. 'I wish we'd never left. We were much better off there. Do you know that was the first meal we've been invited to since we came here? They have such airs and graces I can't stand it. The men are no better than the women when they dress up in their finery and entertain. Oh, we're not invited to their smart suppers I can tell you.' Martha Clark put a hand to her eyes as if prepared to shed tears, probably in the hope it would soften her daughter. 'I wish we'd stayed with you and Bernard. We made a great mistake coming here.'

Martha sat uneasily next to Bernard on the way home clasping the sleeping Thomas tightly in her arms. Behind them sat James and Eliza who had been invited to stay the night with her new friends, but had not been allowed to by her father who did not want to have the bother of going all that way to pick her up again. So she sulked in the back, which was not an unusual event.

'I'm sorry Mother is so unhappy with Cousin Robert,' Martha said, looking at Bernard who seemed rather grumpy. 'What did Father want?'

'The usual thing. Money. I said I couldn't give it him. He wants to rent some cows from Robert and do up the dairy house which, as you saw, is falling down and I said that was the landlord's job. Besides I told him, I couldn't afford it.'

'Oh you shouldn't have said *that*!' Martha exclaimed.

'Why not?'

'Mother thinks we have money.'

'Well we haven't, at least not enough to give away.'

'She would like to think we had so that she can boast

to the Husseys.' Martha sighed. 'I feel sorry for Mother. She never seems to have much luck. Father is only a labourer now on the farm working for Cousin Robert because he owns the cows. He sells the milk, cheese and butter himself so that Father gets nothing. Father could not afford the rent for the cows or the dairy house. Mother says he's being used by Robert and they are thinking of moving on again. I know I've said unkind things about Mother but I pity her, the family too. Mary looks quite pinched. My sister Elizabeth has lost weight and is snubbed by her better-off cousins,' she lowered her voice so that Eliza, sitting behind, who had been such a success with the Hussey girls, couldn't hear her.

'My dear,' Bernard touched her arm, 'we have enough problems without worrying about your family. Your father asked me if the house in Powerstock was still available. I told him I had to hand it back to the landlord and lost all the money I spent on it. I was angry that he had the cheek to ask me. I tell you, Martha, even if I could afford it I wouldn't attempt to help your family again. They are grateful for nothing, and that's the truth.'

Martha didn't feel like arguing and remained silent for the rest of the way. When they got back it was almost dark and Martha was worried that there was no glimmer of light in the house. She hurried indoors, lighting lamps and candles on the way and calling to Joanna.

Thomas still in her arms, she ran up the stairs and opened the door of the boys' room where she found Joanna asleep on the bed next to William who had been left at home because in the morning he seemed out of sorts. A feeling of relief swept over her as she hastily put Thomas in his cot and shook the sleeping servant.

'Joanna!' she hissed. 'What is this? Don't you know the time?'

Joanna's eyes opened wide and her hand flew to her mouth.

'I'm sorry, mum,' she said wearily, 'but oi've had such a time with little William since you left. I think he's terrible sick, mum, covered in spots.'

The doctor, summoned quickly from Beaminster, diagnosed a severe case of measles complicated by pneumonia.

Watched over night and day by Martha and Bernard, William lingered a week, by which time it was clear that he had passed the infection onto his brother.

By the time William died in his stricken mother's arms Thomas was very ill indeed.

Martha had not the strength to go to William's funeral and, after a short service, his little coffin, carried into the churchyard by his father, was placed next to Ann's stillborn baby just as snow began falling. By the time Bernard and the few mourners who had gathered left the churchyard the grave was completely covered over, impeding the work of the gravediggers.

At first Thomas seemed to get better. Martha never left his side, slept with him and, under her tender ministrations, he appeared well on the way to recovery.

But one night as she was lying by his side he became restless and, roused from a slumber that was almost drugged she was so tired, she felt how his little body burned against hers. Every time she touched him he screamed with pain, and at dawn Bernard was sent again for the doctor.

While he was gone Martha got down on her knees by

the side of the bed and prayed as she had never prayed before that God would spare her darling, her remaining child, just a year old.

The doctor, arriving with Bernard some time later, immediately examined the baby. First of all he produced an instrument from his bag with which he looked very carefully into each of the little child's ears. He tried to lift his head and found that his neck was stiff. He then raised one leg at a time only with difficulty, and when he had completed his examination his expression was very grave.

'I think he has contracted an infection of the ear that is affecting the brain and causing the pain.'

'Will he get better?' Martha demanded almost demented now with worry.

'His condition *is* extremely serious,' the doctor said. 'The only treatment there is, I'm afraid, is to pray. He will either die or he will get better.'

And with those cheerless words, and after pocketing his fee, the good doctor left.

That night, however, Thomas's condition worsened. He was very sick and screamed the whole night, clutching his head in pain.

Martha, sobbing by his side, didn't know how God could let a little child, an innocent who had never hurt anyone, suffer so much. As the doctor had suggested, she went down on her knees and stormed heaven with her prayers. Bernard and Joanna went up and down the stairs with compresses but, shortly after dawn, the screaming grew weaker and Thomas lapsed into unconsciousness.

He remained so for the rest of the day gradually turning paler, becoming less restless, visibly slipping away.

To his parents, clinging together in their grief, it seemed as though the life was literally draining out of him.

So at nightfall, peaceful at last, free from pain, baby Thomas died.

Strangely at that moment there was a flutter outside, from the eaves over the window, and a bird, a pigeon or a crow who had settled for the night, suddenly took fright and flew away.

'Martha, it is the soul of our little one going to heaven,' Bernard said piously, pointing out of the window in the direction of the disappearing bird. But Martha didn't look up; her face remained fastened on the features, so peaceful now, of the dead child.

'There is no God, Bernard. If I ever believed in one, I don't now.'

Martha herself carried the small, plain coffin up the hill, as if she couldn't bear to be parted from Thomas. She clutched it to her as she had clutched him all the way back from Pilsdon only a few weeks before, tightly, not wanting to let go.

The Reverend Cookson, a man used to burials of the young, of which there had been quite a few due to the outbreak of measles, thought he had scarcely seen a more grief-stricken couple as Bernard and Martha followed him to the graveyard. Martha still carried the coffin which she was so reluctant to let go of that Bernard had to prise her fingers away, gently so as not to hurt her and, as it was put into the grave, he hung onto her in case she should try and follow it.

And for a long, long time they remained like that despite the biting wind, while the mourners drifted

119

away and the gravediggers completed their melancholy task.

For days Martha was inconsolable. She sat dressed in black in the parlour and wouldn't move, not even to go to bed.

In the end Bernard feared for her own life, as well as her reason, and begged her to take some nourishment. Kneeling by her side he petitioned her to listen to him and, at last, she put a hand on his head and stroked it gently.

'I know you feel it as much as I do,' she said, laying his head on her lap, 'but I can't help myself.'

'Why is God so cruel?' he said, beginning to sob. 'Just when we were so happy?'

'There is no God if you ask me, Bernard,' Martha said in a strong vibrant voice. 'Despite what the vicar said about their young souls going straight to heaven I would much prefer that they had been left on this earth with us.'

'We can have other children, Martha,' Bernard wheedled, his eyes still streaming with tears. He looked pitifully up at her face, at her features rigid and stern, a woman keeping herself strictly under control. She had not shed a tear since the funeral, but just sat staring in front of her or, occasionally, out of the window.

'There will be no more children, Bernard,' Martha said in a strange, almost sepulchral, tone of voice. 'We must live as brother and sister because I cannot bear to go through all this ever again.'

Then she looked dispassionately down at him. 'I will now take a little soup. Please ask Joanna to fetch me some.'

Chapter Seven

Martha stood at the window of the room that had belonged to her little boys and, as far as she was concerned, still did. She could feel both their presences every time she looked at the bed or the cot, tucked away in the corner, and she kept everything in the room exactly where it had been. They had not gone away. They were there.

To be nearer to them she had her own bed made up in the room and she now slept there every night.

Outside the leaves on the trees were slowly turning to the browns, russets and reds of autumn, tumbling gently onto the ground. The orchard was full of apples, some overripe, and bore a neglected look because Bernard, on account of his debts to the Glebe farm, no longer made cider, but fed his apples to the pigs or let them rot in great piles in the yard.

It was six months since Martha's babies had died and for most of the time she lived in a dream, a dream that always saw them returning to her, a dream where she woke in the morning and looked over expecting to find them safely tucked up in their beds.

Sometimes she thought that by living in the past like this, or hoping for something she knew could never happen, she was losing her mind. She knew that Bernard worried about her, poor man, as if he had not enough worries with a falling income and a pile of debts, which he tried to conceal because of his hard-won position in the community. This very minute he was downstairs talking to Lord Darlington's agent about his arrears in paying the rent.

Martha knew that children very often died in infancy, as some of her mother's had, but still this did not make it more easy to bear. She realised now how much they suffered while having to make the pretence of struggling on, soon to become pregnant with another. She wondered how many women survived but, maybe, losing one at a time was easier than losing two within the same number of weeks.

Or maybe, as she suspected, she was more sensitive than most women she knew and for this reason it was harder for her to overcome the grief that bit so savagely, so deeply into her.

Behind her the door swung open and, thinking it was Bernard come to report on the visit, she turned, but it was James looking shyly round the door and when she beckoned to him he crept in and came towards her.

James was a very shy, timid, clever little boy to whom Martha had become excessively attached since the deaths of Thomas and William. Not that he had taken their place — nothing could do that — but it was as though she had a third son, one who had survived. She loved him very much because his nature was so sweet and gentle, not at all like his sister's.

He was not very tall, fine-boned with fair skin and hair the colour of golden corn. In fact he had the beauty that Eliza should have had. It wasn't that she was ugly, or even plain, but she had not the startling, almost feminine good looks of James. It is often said, with some justification, that boys take after their mothers and girls their fathers. If so, Bernard's first wife must have been very beautiful, which was what Martha had always been told. Eliza definitely resembled her father in that her hair and eyes were brown and her features strong with a large nose, a firm chin and a prominent brow.

In an even world Eliza should have been the man and James the girl.

'When are you going to put all the toys away?' James asked, looking round at the teddies on the bed, the coloured blocks on the floor, the wooden rocking horse in the corner.

'Never,' Martha said, going to sit on William's bed and patting the place beside her so that James could join her. 'I want this room to be as it was when my darlings died.' She put her arm round his shoulders and pressed him tightly to her.

'Ezekiel did see a white rabbit in the churchyard yesterday,' James said with a note of awe in his voice. 'He ran all the way home he was so scared.'

'Nonsense!' Martha said sharply. 'That's a silly superstition that you must take no notice of.' But even as she spoke, trying to calm the boy's fears, she herself felt as though a shiver had run down her spine.

A white rabbit seen in Powerstock churchyard was supposed to presage a death.

'Ezekiel said someone in the village saw the rabbit before Thomas died, but didn't want to let on.'

'I don't believe such tales,' Martha turned to him, 'and nor must you. It is no good your father trying to turn you into a scholar if you listen to stupid village talk like that. You know, James,' she took his face between her hands and looked solemnly into his eyes, 'you are very precious to me now that Thomas and William have gone. I want you to think of me as your mother – not to love your own less – but to love me too.'

'Oh I *do* love you.' James gazed with equal frankness at her, his own big blue eyes round like saucers. 'I love you much better than my sister Eliza.'

Martha let go his hand and, rising, went to the window where she could see Eliza, for once in her life, doing a bit of work, gathering up the apples that had fallen in the orchard and putting them in her apron. She was not carrying out her task with much diligence, but the fact that she was doing anything at all was remarkable. She must have been ordered to by her father whose patience she sometimes tried as much as she did Martha's.

Martha sighed. She would be very glad indeed when Eliza, now thirteen, was old enough either to marry or to leave home for some kind of work. The latter seemed unlikely as long as she had her head filled with tales from the Walbridge or the Peach girls whose parents would never have dreamt of them doing anything but marrying well or, God forbid, settling down at home to look after their parents.

As Powerstock was so near the sea netmaking or 'breeding' was a common domestic industry among the women in the village, many of whom did it in order to make a little extra money. They would sell their nets in Bridport and come home with a new bonnet or shawl or, occasionally when they had saved enough, a new dress.

Although her skills were as a dairymaid Martha had learned 'breeding' from the village women in the years she'd been married to Bernard. She found it restful and, since the children had died and she had no knitting or mending, and fewer clothes to make, it had become a solace to her. Sometimes she would go with the women over the hill to Bridport to sell her nets and return home with the same feeling of satisfaction over some new purchase as they had. Or she might tuck the money into Bernard's drawer as a gift to help towards expenses. He never acknowledged it, but she knew he knew where it had come from.

But even the relatively gentle art of 'breeding' was below Eliza who could turn her hand to nothing except playing the piano and gossiping with her friends. She always rejected Martha's offer to teach her.

'Would you like to go for a walk?' Martha turned and looked at James. 'Stretch your legs? It's a nice day.'

James jumped up from the bed expressing his enthusiasm and Martha also rose to smooth her hair in the mirror and look for a shawl to put over her shoulders.

The Earl of Darlington's agent, George Harwell, looked with some exasperation at Bernard who, as usual, had gone through a long list of excuses as to why he was late paying his rent.

'Yes I know times are bad, Mr Bearn,' the agent said in a tired voice, 'but you have an uncommon amount of land, and maybe you don't make the best of it. After all you wanted it in the first place. No one forced it on you.' Mr Harwell tried to look reasonable.

'Make the best of it!' Bernard cried angrily. 'I work my fingers to the bone night and day and look,' he gestured towards the ceiling, 'this place is in a bad state of repair. The walls are falling down, the thatch leaks, yet his lordship refuses to do anything about it.'

'You're withholding your rent then?' the agent enquired frostily. 'In that case I think we may have a case for repossessing some of your property . . .'

'I am *not* withholding my rent at all,' Bernard spluttered. 'I am just remarking that repairs that should have been done are outstanding.'

'When you are up to date with your rent I think we may be able to do something about the state of the house. But I notice the yard and outbuildings are also in bad condition. I'm afraid there is a very pervasive and distasteful odour when one approaches the yard, particularly in the vicinity of the slaughterhouse, which some of the neighbours are complaining about. When the wind is in a certain direction it can be most offensive. I also noticed apples piled up in the orchard which seemed to me to be rotten. Do you no longer make cider? That should provide you with a good source of income.'

'When I can,' Bernard mumbled. Then, in the tremulous tone of one seeking sympathy, 'You know this year I lost two of my children. It has been a very bad year for me and my poor wife. It was hard for us to get over such a loss.'

'I am very sorry about that,' the agent said in a manner which suggested the contrary, 'but children, alas, do die, with great frequency I'm afraid, in these sorry times, and business is business, Mr Bearn.'

He looked at Bernard with an air of brisk expectancy.

'I can certainly pay you something on account,' Bernard whined, 'there is no problem about that, and the rest by quarter-day.'

Mr Harwell seemed satisfied. 'In that case I shall suggest to his lordship that when the arrears are cleared we shall do something about repairs to the property. Ah . . .' Mr Harwell looked up as Martha entered, clasping James by the hand. 'Good day, Mrs Bearn.'

'Good day,' Martha nodded. 'Have you completed your business?'

'Just about,' Bernard said with forced cheerfulness, going to the drawer of his bureau and extracting a bundle of notes which, after counting them, he handed to his visitor. 'I think you'll find that in order. Seventy pounds and fifteen shillings. The balance to follow.'

Mr Harwell checked the money and nodded.

'I thought we might go for a walk with James,' Martha said to Bernard as the agent tucked the money into his portmanteau.

'No, I must go up to the wood and see how the tree felling is going,' Bernard glanced surreptitiously at Mr Harwell, now preparing to leave, 'so that I can pay off my arrears.'

'Well,' Mr Harwell put on his hat. 'That seems quite satisfactory.' His expression seemed more sympathetic now. 'Don't think you are unique, Mr Bearn, you're not.'

'I know I'm not,' Bernard said shortly, 'and it would do his lordship no harm if he were to remember that we are not all as wealthy as he is.'

'His lordship is well aware of that. He knows that times are hard and the village, like many villages, is suffering from low wages and poor productivity. However, we all have a crust to earn.'

'Good day, Mr Harwell,' Martha said, abruptly moving to the door and opening it, anxious for him to be gone. 'Be careful as you make your way across the yard. Bernard was slaughtering all morning.'

'So I saw,' George Harwell said with some distaste. 'I assure you I'll watch my step very carefully indeed.'

'I do detest that man,' Martha said, watching him as he made his way fastidiously across the field towards the gate. 'Why is it that people like that are always nasty?'

'Rent collectors are a breed. They have a job to do,' Bernard said philosophically, closing the drawer. 'And so have I.'

'Must you go to the wood?'

'Yes I must.'

'Then maybe we can all walk with you? It's a nice day and it will do us good.'

Going to the window Martha opened it and called out to Eliza who was still apathetically carrying out her task in the orchard. 'Eliza! We're going to go for a walk.'

'I don't want to,' Eliza retorted, eyes scanning the ground. Martha was about to close the window when Bernard came over and shouted through it.

'Eliza, do as you're told for once in your life!'

Docilely she bowed her head and, deliberately dropping all the apples she had collected into her apron on the ground, she came running into the house.

Eliza was in awe of her father. She knew he loved

her, doted on her but all the same she respected him in a way she did not respect or like her stepmother. She and Martha had never got on and she knew why Martha resented her. She, in turn, deeply resented Martha who had taken the place of a woman whom, it was true, she had never known but who had also usurped her father's affections.

Things had never been the same as they were before Martha came to live with them, which was why Eliza constantly goaded and demeaned her by referring to her as a servant and ignoring everything she told her to do.

Eliza went immediately up to her room to fetch her shawl and change her shoes to a stouter pair.

When she came downstairs James was skipping around on the lawn, anxious to be gone. It was a fine, blustery day with clouds scudding across the sky.

'Race you!' Eliza cried suddenly and set across the field towards the bridge across the river, with James tearing after her. On the far side was the coppice where Ezekiel was already at work chopping down trees.

Martha stood with Bernard in the garden watching them.

'I do hope they'll be all right,' she said.

'Of *course* they'll be all right,' Bernard looked at her with amusement. 'They're only going for a walk, and we'll be right behind them.' He took her arm companionably as they followed the route the children had taken, chatting and walking at a slower pace.

Eliza had always been jealous of her brother James: his looks, his temperament, the fact that everyone loved him. She taunted and teased him whenever she could, losing no opportunity to belittle him. When she and

James were alone with their father before he'd married Martha she felt that she was in her mother's place. She was possessive and protective, as a mother can be, but without a mother's warmth and love. She was forever scolding James and telling tales about him to her father whenever she could.

But it did little good. James was so adorable. He was even nice to her, regardless of what she did to him, like a dog who, although repeatedly beaten by its master, keeps licking his hand.

This day Eliza was in an evil temper. Ann Walbridge had gone off to the music lesson at Bridport with the Cookson girls and had told Eliza that there was no room in the pony cart for her, because another Cookson girl now wanted to learn music too. Not even bothering to ask how Eliza would get there the five of them had gone off, leaving Eliza to fend for herself as best she could.

Eliza was angry and humiliated, because she always thought it came down to who her father was and what he did but, more importantly, who her stepmother was and what *she* had been.

Bernard couldn't spare Ezekiel because he was chopping wood, and couldn't take her himself because Lord Darlington's agent was due. So Eliza had sulked and gone collecting rotten apples which she put in a pile just under Martha's bedroom window where it would cause a good stink.

Eliza looked back and saw James running across the bridge, flapping his arms in his eagerness to catch up with her. In the background, strolling slowly across the field, were her father and Martha deep in conversation. This alone was unusual because since the two boys had died they had grown apart, seldom spending time together, or even conversing. She knew they no longer shared a bedroom, which had made her very happy. She hoped her father would get rid of Martha altogether and marry someone else or, better still, not marry at all. She would soon be quite capable of running her father's house.

Eliza ran faster up the hill, easily outpacing James, towards the coppice where Ezekiel, stripped to the waist, was busy chopping a tree. He was a strong, muscular youth not much older than herself, seventeen or so, but she never had much to do with him because she thought he was a little soft in the head. She stood watching him wield the large axe with some admiration, watching how his muscles rippled and strained, turning abruptly as James caught up with her.

'See, you couldn't do that,' she said, pointing to Ezekiel as James stood breathlessly by her side.

'I could,' James said, sounding, nevertheless, a little uncertain.

'Go on then.' Eliza pushed him forward, but James stood his ground.

'No, I can't,' he said after a while. 'Not now. But I will when I'm as big as Ezekiel.'

'Ezekiel is soft in the head,' Eliza said scathingly. 'So are *you*.'

'I am not soft in the head!' James protested.

'*And* a weakling,' Eliza scoffed.

'I'm *not*. I'll show you.' James looked up at the great oak under which they stood and saw that the lowest branch was just above his head. He jumped and held onto it then made his way hand over hand along the branch, fearful that at any moment it might give way.

Clasping the tree-trunk he levered himself onto the branch and, panting heavily, looked up and his head swam. He knew he had no head for heights, but when he lowered his gaze there was Eliza just below, with that familiar sneer on her face. It was always the same: 'You can't do it, James. You're not old enough, or clever enough, or big enough,' always something like that to make him feel small.

It was the same now.

'Cowardy custard,' she sang. 'I know you can't stand heights.'

'Can't I?' James retorted and, taking a deep breath, holding fast to the trunk of the tree, he began his perilous ascent branch by branch until he had almost reached the top. When he looked down again it seemed a long way to the bottom; the branches of the trees swayed from side to side and made him feel dizzy. The sunlight kept appearing and disappearing through the leaves. His head spun and Eliza, so far below, cupped her hands to her mouth and called.

'Go on, right to the top, cry baby.'

James looked up and the sky seemed to tilt, his heart pounded and his hands, tightly clasping the trunk of the tree, were clammy.

On the ground Ezekiel had seen what was happening and, ceasing his task, came over and stood by Eliza.

'James don't like heights,' he said.

'I know.' Eliza gave him a cool glance. 'He's an awful little baby. It's time he became a man.' She looked approvingly at his sweaty, naked torso and cupped her hands, calling again, and then she and Ezekiel watched as the body, which seemed quite tiny, now recommenced its upwards climb.

'Little baby,' she shouted, 'too scared to reach the top.'

Ezekiel, looking at her with alarm, put down his axe.

'He might do hisself an injury,' he said. 'Oi best go after he.'

'No you don't!' Eliza caught hold of his arm. 'He's got to learn some time. He's got to grow up.'

She raised her eyes and, driven on by a sense of devilment she couldn't quite explain, she started to shout at him again despite seeing his white face peering helplessly down at her.

'To the *top*,' she ordered, 'to the *top*. Baby. Baby James. Baby boy . . .'

Suddenly James swayed. He sat on the branch, gingerly lowered a foot and appeared to be attempting to climb down again. Ezekiel, looking seriously alarmed, began hurriedly to climb up the tree, shinning up the trunk like a monkey.

'I'm coming, Jamie,' he cried. 'Hang on.'

But James stood up, looked down, swayed, and then, unhampered by the branches, dropped through the air like a stone landing with a mighty thud at the feet of Eliza who stood gaping down at him.

Witnessing the whole scene from the beginning Martha and Bernard had run as fast as they could up the hill to the top arriving just as James began his fall. As he landed on the ground Martha let out a piercing scream and, hurrying across to him, knelt by his side and placed his head tenderly on her lap.

'He can't be dead,' she said to Bernard, who knelt beside her, her voice sounding relieved. 'See, his eyes are wide open.'

She smiled down at the boy and caressed his cheek, but Bernard was staring at the ominous trickle of blood from James's nostrils, from either side of his mouth, and at the staring eyes focused on nothing.

Martha mopped at the blood and gently pinched his cheek.

'Jamie,' she cooed, 'Jamie, speak to Martha. Say something to me, Jamie. Please.'

At that moment Eliza turned and fled through the wood clasping her head in her hands.

Martha took no notice of her but looked anxiously at Bernard.

'He *is* all right, isn't he, Bernard? He will live?'

As Bernard failed to answer, Ezekiel, who had jumped off the tree, slowly shook his head.

'He be dead, Mrs Bearn. I seed dead people before and they had their eyes open, just like he.' He pointed down at the little corpse. The tears ran slowly down Bernard's cheeks as he, too, shook his head.

'Oh no,' Martha said, 'no. He *can't* be dead.' She looked bewilderedly at the boy's face. 'Jamie?' she pleaded again. 'Jamie, speak to Martha.'

'Her taunted him,' Ezekiel angrily pointed the way Eliza had gone. 'He didn't want to climb that tree.'

'Of course he didn't want to go,' Martha said in a strange, bitter tone of voice and, gently laying Jamie's head on the ground, stood up and dusted her hands. 'He hated heights.'

Then with a resolute, almost fearsome expression she pulled up her skirt and began to run like the wind in the direction Eliza had taken until she came to the edge of the wood. In front of her were open fields across to Nettlecombe but no sign of the running girl. Martha, breathless, paused, looked round and then saw her half hidden by a bush.

'Come out,' she said. 'I want to teach thee something.'

Eliza put up her hands protectively as Martha bore down on her.

'I didn't mean . . .' she began. 'I thought he'd come down.'

'You *did* mean it.' Suddenly Martha reached down and, catching hold of Eliza by the hair, dragged her to her feet. 'You *wanted* to kill him and you *have*. You selfish, senseless, *wicked* little girl.'

'And *you're* a hateful, spiteful *horrible* woman,' Eliza retorted. 'You're unnatural. You deserved to lose your children, and I'm glad you did. Now you've lost Jamie and you've got *no one*. I hate you, Martha. I hate you. I'm glad they're gone and I'm glad *he's* gone.'

Still holding tightly onto her hair Martha hit her across the face. She slapped her hard this way and that with real force, with real feeling.

Eliza started to scream, struggling, twisting and turning but unable to break away. She hit out at Martha, catching her in the chest and a fight broke out with both women falling to the ground, Martha still grimly hanging onto Eliza's hair, and Eliza screaming even louder like a stuck pig.

Martha seized a stout piece of wood that lay on the ground and was about to bring it crashing down on Eliza's head when she was seized from behind, roughly dragged to her feet, and half choked by the strength of the grip on her collar.

'*What* do you think you're doing, woman?' Bernard roared. 'Do you want to kill my daughter too? Do you want me to have no children left, Martha? Not one?'

Martha, as if she had been in a trance, suddenly came

135

to her senses. 'Didn't mean it,' she said in a weary voice, shaking her head abjectly. Stricken, overcome with remorse, a feeling of enormous guilt and confusion, she looked down at Eliza who was sitting up and rubbing her head but appeared otherwise unharmed.

'Sorry,' she mumbled. 'Sorry, Eliza.' But Eliza ignored her, her expression set as if in stone.

Martha reached out towards Bernard, attempting to lay her head on his shoulder, but he brusquely repulsed her and shook his finger threateningly at her.

'I never saw such a carry on. Never in my life did I see a woman so violently attempt to strike another. I tell you if you don't curb that vile temper, my good woman, one day you'll kill somebody. You'll do them real harm and you'll swing for it, Martha. Believe me, one day, as God is my witness, you will.'

Chapter Eight

July 1837

Martha stood looking round the bedroom and then went over to the window and flung it open. A fly which had been buzzing despairingly against the glass made a rapid escape and flew away out across the orchard where the trees were heavy with apples.

It was a breathlessly hot summer's day and the room was stuffy. Martha wondered how the fly had got in. She hardly ever went into the babies' room now, just occasionally to air it and dust and have a few moments of quiet reflection about what might have been: William and Thomas growing into fine, strapping lads, as Bernard must have been when he was younger, and as her own brothers, after whom they were named, were now. Maybe their vigour and youth would have helped reverse their father's fortune and save his land. He would have had something to work for; now he had nothing except an unhappy old age.

They would have had children, making her a grandmother, and how she loved babies! But that would never happen now. And there was that other heartache, dear little James who had left them nearly two years ago. He would have been the scholar. Perhaps a clerk, even a clergyman. Despite her lack of religious belief Martha still had a superstitious respect for the cloth.

Then, as usual when she had these sad thoughts, Martha began to weep and thought about the one who got away: Eliza, strong and robust and perfectly useless. Eliza had fled to the shelter of her Aunt Sarah Crocker's home after James's death, and had remained there ever since, promulgating largely invented, scandalous and untrue stories about her stepmother.

Even in this room, facing away from the yard, Martha could hear the cries of animals in distress, imagine she could smell the blood as Bernard plied his trade with his customary relish preparing a batch of carcasses to take to Bridport for shipment to London. Sometimes their pitiful screams seemed to go round and round in her head from morning until night.

Martha wondered how much unnecessary suffering Bernard caused the poor creatures as he despatched them, because he was such a clumsy man. He'd been an inept lover, hurting her a great deal. He was always dropping things, falling over things, breaking this and that. How expert was he with a knife?

Martha could look on Bernard now with neither love nor affection. Since the terrible year when all three boys died, their marriage had returned to the state it was at the beginning: a state of strangeness, of mutual misunderstanding and lack of comprehension. Only now Bernard was affected by it as much as she was. He seemed as indifferent to her as she was to him. Joanna had been got rid of for economic reasons. But Martha was a good housekeeper, diligent and industrious, and she only missed Joanna's company and, maybe a little, the status of having a servant. This all seemed a symptom of their decline. She did all the washing, cooking, blacking and scrubbing herself. She washed out the yard, the great smelly vats of discarded offal. She worked tirelessly from morning until night when she and Bernard would have a solitary meal facing each other but hardly ever speaking. There no longer seemed anything to say.

She made her nets. She visited the poor and took them food, especially a young crippled woman who lived nearby whom she had saved from being sent to the workhouse. Bernard, as an overseer of the poor, was able to ensure that some relief went directly to her.

After the deaths of the children Martha never allowed herself a moment's repose until she sank exhausted into her bed at night. Then she was up at first light to feed the hens and milk the two cows they now kept in the field in front of the house, the rest of the stock, other than those wanted for beef, having been sold.

The sounds of slaughter ceased and Martha stepped back from the window. They would now be stripping the carcasses and putting them on the cart for transport to Bridport. Helping Bernard today was his brother-in-law by his first marriage, Samuel Wrixon. Samuel was an engaging rollicking young man, the same age as Martha, with a liking for drink that frequently got him into trouble. However, he was no wastrel but an industrious hardworking farmer with a farm on the outskirts of the village and a pretty wife and several children. Whereas Bernard, despite all his efforts, was a failure, Martha knew instinctively that Samuel, who never seemed to have to try very hard, to whom all things came easily, would be a success.

It was a long time since she'd been into the bedroom where both her sons had died. In time memory faded, grew less keen. One didn't love them less but missed them less, didn't think of them all the time. She had got used to living without them and then felt guilty when she remembered them again. Martha had long since put away the toys, the rocking horse had been sold, the little baby knick-knacks disposed of. The house was like a great, rattling shell, a barren, cheerless place.

'Martha!' Bernard called abruptly from the yard. 'Are you there?'

'Coming,' Martha called and, shutting the door behind her, went quickly downstairs.

'Sam and I are going to take the meat to Bridport,' Bernard said, as she entered the kitchen, wiping his bloody hands on a piece of rag. 'We'd like something to eat before we go.'

Martha smiled at Sam who acknowledged her.

'Morning, Sam.'

'Morning, Martha.'

'How are your wife and the children?'

'Very well.'

'That's good,' Martha nodded at him approvingly. She liked Sam, with his open, honest face, his uncomplicated personality. He was a stocky, good-looking man, musclebound, with head and shoulders like a bull and a mane of thick black hair. She should have married someone like Sam Wrixon instead of a clumsy old man like Bernard Bearn. She would wager that Sam kept his wife very happy and contented in bed as the number of children they had seemed to testify.

Martha went into the larder for some beef and cheese and then back into the kitchen to cut bread and pour them some more ale, though doubtless they had had plenty already. The little butter they had she made herself from the cream from the cows. They bought as little as they could. She was a thrifty housewife and her skills as a dairymaid helped her to save money. On the cart in front of the window the bleeding, headless carcasses were all that was left of the animals she'd seen only the day before grazing so peacefully in the fields. Suddenly her eyes filled with tears. It seemed a cruel fate, so undeserved, just as the children's fate was undeserved. They, like the poor animals, were innocents, had harmed nobody.

'What ails thee, Martha?' Samuel asked as she approached the table.

'I got something in my eye,' Martha said, wiping it after she'd put the victuals on the table. 'A fly or something. You'd better get off as soon as you can. In this hot weather those carcasses will soon rot.'

'We'll be spending the night in Bridport,' Bernard said, looking knowingly at Samuel, 'and returning tomorrow.'

And drinking too much and visiting the brothel, Martha supposed. But she didn't say anything and didn't care.

Bernard and Samuel hurriedly finished their meal and, after harnessing the horse to the cart, set out leaving a trail of blood in their wake. Watching them Martha wrinkled her nose with distaste and then set out to swab down the yard and get rid of all the blood, the offal and unsightly parts that remained in the slaughterhouse, covered with flies and already beginning to smell. That task finished she sat down to her 'breeding' taking a seat in the garden looking out onto the orchard and, for once, she experienced one of those rare moments of peace, almost happiness, such as these days she seldom had.

Bernard and Samuel had always got on well despite the age difference. Samuel had been a good deal younger than his sister. They liked bawdy talk, drinking ale and whoring when they spent the night in town. Bernard felt half his age in the company of Samuel, whereas these days Martha made him feel old. He had accepted their sleeping arrangements (she now had her bed in Eliza's old room) largely because, since the death of the boys, his desire for his wife seemed to have gone. Though Martha was as comely as she had ever been he preferred the company of whores, women who asked for nothing but money and knew how to make a man feel happy and important, not clumsy and insecure.

It was even hotter than the day before as Bernard and Samuel made their way over the hills towards Bridport hoping to get there by late afternoon. However, they were half way up a steep hill, the poor tired horse making heavy weather of pulling an overloaded cart in the heat, when it stumbled and almost fell. Samuel jumped off the cart in alarm and went over to the horse which appeared distressed.

'This nag is too old for this job, Bernard,' he said with a worried frown. 'Thee should have bought another.'

'Too late now,' Bernard said impatiently and made to flick his whip over the back of the horse while Samuel shook his head.

'She won't make it. Her shoe's half off and she's gone lame. We'll have to leave her here and go back and get another.'

'Then we'll never make it today,' Bernard said crossly, 'and I've got a lot of money wrapped up in that meat.'

Leaving the horse in an adjacent field and the cart on the side of the road, half hidden by trees, the men made their way, footsore and weary, back to Powerstock. After a night's sleep they proceeded back the way they had come the previous day with a fresh, younger horse from Samuel's farm. The meat was where they had left it, the horse safe in the field and, leaving it a bundle of hay they had brought with them, they harnessed the fresh horse to the cart and set off again with the sun still beating down.

'That meat's beginning to smell,' Samuel said after a while, sniffing the air when they were half way to their destination.

'It can't be, it's freshly killed, you know that,' Bernard said angrily, but he suspected Samuel was right. There was an unpleasant odour wafting from the cart behind him and the carcasses were almost alive with flies. He flicked the whip across the back of the horse trying to get it to go faster, and by early afternoon they were at the market in Bridport where Bernard planned to sell his meat.

It was thronged with buyers and sellers from all parts of the county and Bernard made his way to his customary wholesaler, a man called Richard Snagg who, on seeing him, hailed him and came over.

'I expected you yesterday, Bernard.'

'The horse went lame, had to go back for another,' Bernard explained, jumping down from the cart. 'I've a fine load of freshly killed carcasses here for you, Dick.'

But Richard Snagg was making his way slowly round

the cart putting his nose close to the pile of carcasses, some hanging limply over the side.

'This meat has gone bad, Bernard,' he said with a look of disgust, backing away. 'It can't be freshly killed.'

'I tell you it was killed yesterday, as God is my witness,' Bernard insisted, beads of sweat beginning to break out on his brow. 'Samuel will tell you, he helped me.'

'Well, it's not fresh now,' Richard Snagg briskly shook his head. 'Can't take it, I'm afraid.'

'But you *must* take it,' Bernard insisted. 'You ordered it. I have all my money tied up in this. I have no beef cattle left at all.'

'I can't take bad meat. I can't sell bad meat. You must have left it too long in the sun when you went back for the horse. If it's beginning to turn today you can imagine what it will be like by the time it gets to London. I'll get nothing for it. Not a penny. Sorry, Bernard.'

Richard Snagg turned peremptorily away to inspect the carcasses of another hopeful vendor, and Bernard was left staring at Samuel Wrixon, an expression of despair on his face, and rage in his heart.

'It will have to go into the sea, Bernard,' Samuel said cheerfully. 'No good to anyone. We better take it now before it goes even more rotten and we'll have all the flies in Bridport after 'un. I told you it smelt. We should never have left it on the road. We should have borrowed a horse from a nearby farm and got here yesterday.'

With no money to spend on whores and drinking, or with which to pay Sam for his labour, Bernard made his way home after tipping his worthless load right into the sea. However, just before they got to Powerstock they came across a party of haymakers who hailed them from their cart and invited them to join them at the Three Horse Shoes rather than go straight home.

'I haven't any money, not a penny.' Bernard turned to Sam who said he would take the horse back to his farm and fetch some.

'Don't worry about it, Bernard,' he said, patting his brother-in-law on the arm. 'You can owe it to me. I know you'll make good.'

But Bernard wasn't so sure. The money he'd hoped to make from his cart of meat should have been enough to set him up for weeks, help to pay some of his debts and buy fresh stock. Now all hope of that was gone.

The thought of facing Martha with this disastrous tale was too much for him so he agreed, if a little reluctantly, and joined the revellers at the inn.

At midnight Bernard, Samuel and a company of fellow inebriates spilled out into the road outside the Three Horse Shoes. Bernard was so drunk he could hardly see. He kept on falling over and as his companions, with cries of raucous laughter, tried to right him he fell down again. Samuel, who could hold his liquor, tried to put him over his shoulder, but Bernard began to be aggressive and said he could make his own way home.

'You better not let Martha see you like that,' Samuel, who knew – as did the whole village – about her assault on Eliza, said. 'You know what a temper she's got. She'll flay you alive. You'd far better to come along home with me.'

Samuel put his arm under Bernard's shoulder and half dragged, half carried him along the road; but just in front of the school house Bernard protested he could go no further and was violently sick in the middle of the street.

Alerted by the noise the schoolmaster came to his window, opened it and demanded to know who was outside.

Bernard and Samuel immediately relapsed into drunken giggles and Bernard started to crawl in an exaggerated manner along the road, whereupon the schoolmaster's front door was flung open and he stood there in his long white nightshirt brandishing a blunderbuss menacingly to right and left.

'Oh don't shoot he! Don't shoot he!' Samuel cried in mock alarm. 'It is only Bernard Bearn and myself, Mr Webber, going home after a night of fun.'

'Fun,' Bernard repeated. 'Just a bit of fun,' slurring his words so badly that the meaning was scarcely intelligible except to him.

'Mr Bearn,' Mr Webber said shocked. 'I am most surprised to see you in this state. Astounded in fact.'

'And I'm surprised and astounded to see *you*, you silly old fool, in *that* state,' Bernard shouted at him, perfectly clearly this time. 'Go back to bed along of Mrs Webber and block your big ears.'

'Don't worry, Mr Webber,' Samuel said, anxious to placate the schoolmaster. 'He's had a little bit too much to drink and I'm taking him home to sleep it off.' And with that, watched by the outraged schoolmaster, he dragged Bernard, practically unconscious by now, the rest of the way home.

Bernard, wearing his best suit, hair and whiskers neatly combed, stood before the vicar in his parlour like a disgraced schoolboy. Mr Cookson gazed at him censoriously, mouth pursed, hands behind his back.

'You do know what this is about, Mr Bearn?'

'I have an idea,' Bernard cleared his throat. 'It is about an incident the other night when I had had a little too much to drink and misbehaved in the village street.'

'Exactly,' the vicar nodded. 'So I am charged by certain people, shocked and dismayed by your behaviour, to talk to you about it. I believe it has even come to the ears of Lord Darlington himself.'

Bernard shuffled his feet and gazed at the floor. 'I think I can offer you an explanation for my behaviour, about which I am very sorry.'

Bernard halted uncertainly and the vicar said: 'Proceed.'

'I had been to Bridport with a cart of meat to sell. I desperately needed the money because I had slaughtered all my stock. But, owing to the particular hot weather, the meat went bad before I could sell it and I had to tip it all into the sea.' Bernard shook his head sadly, tears welling up in his eyes. 'I came back without a penny to my name.'

'I see.' Mr Cookson put the tips of his fingers neatly together, and appeared to ponder. He was not sitting and he had not asked Bernard to sit. Both men stood on the mat in front of the grate but, on this occasion, unlike the last one in this room, no sherry had been offered.

'It is still no way for an elder of the parish to behave, Mr Bearn, however unfortunate the circumstances.'

'I know it and I be truly sorry, Vicar.' Bernard humbly bowed his head. 'Truly, truly sorry I be.'

'You were *extremely* rude to Mr Webber. Called him a fool. A "silly old fool", I understand. This is no way to talk to the schoolmaster.'

'It is not. I will apologise to Mr Webber and hope that he will overlook this incident.' Bernard's features crumpled. 'It has not been an easy time for me or my wife. I think you know that, Vicar.'

'I understand all this, Mr Bearn.' The vicar relaxed a little and indicated a chair which Bernard thankfully took while Mr Cookson sat opposite him. 'I think everyone in the parish has a certain sympathy for you, knowing not only about your domestic difficulties, the loss of your children, but your er . . .' Mr Cookson loudly cleared his throat, 'financial concerns as well. However . . . however, Bernard,' he said, relapsing into informality, 'I am sure that you must realise you are in no position to act as an overseer of the poor being, I understand – and what you say confirms this – very nearly a pauper yourself.'

'But that doesn't mean,' Bernard interrupted indignantly, 'that I would *ever* touch a penny of parish funds. Never.'

'I don't for a moment imagine you would. The thought never crossed my mind, or the minds of any of your peers. However, such a position in the community is one of great responsibility. Consequently there has been an informal meeting on this subject and I am asked by your fellow overseers to ask for your resignation. It is very painful for them to do this, which is why they have given the unhappy task to me. I am also sorry to say, Bernard, that, on behalf of the church authorities, I think you would be well advised to offer your resignation as churchwarden as well.'

'But I have done nothing wrong.' Bernard leapt up from his chair. 'I have done *nothing* wrong.'

Mr Cookson rose too. 'You have disgraced yourself in a public place by appearing very drunk, and verbally assaulting a worthy member of this community. That is certainly no way for a member of the vestry to behave, whatever the circumstances. For that reason alone, I am compelled to ask for your resignation. Besides,' the vicar gnawed his lip, 'your wife has not been inside this church since your son James was buried. That is not a very good example either, and nor are stories put about by your daughter concerning her behaviour, her undisciplined temper . . .'

'My wife is a *very* good woman,' Bernard thundered. 'She has been an exemplary wife and mother. It is true she and my daughter did not get on, but Eliza has no right to spread untrue stories about her. Eliza was jealous of Martha. She resented her taking the place of her mother. She was also very careless over letting my son climb a high tree when she knew he had a fear of heights. She goaded him on, frightening the poor little fellow. Anyway,' once more Bernard cast his eyes on the ground, 'Martha no longer believes in God. After our babies died she became devoted to James, more so than before.' He raised his eyes and looked at the vicar. 'Her simple Christian faith has been destroyed by these tragic events. You can't blame her, can you? Fortune has dealt us a series of grievous blows.'

'God is all goodness,' Mr Cookson intoned, piously raising his eyes heavenwards. 'Perfection. Man is not.'

July 1839

'You've grown very thin, Martha,' her mother said with a disapproving sniff. 'Isn't Bernard looking after you?'

Martha did look pinched and pale. She had on a rather drab bonnet and the black dress of mourning she had worn ever since the children died. She looked much older than her twenty-eight years and Ann, who had not seen her for several months, and who was also on a duty visit to their parents, despite her mother's treatment of her, was shocked.

But of course Mrs Clark would not be shocked. She would just be critical. They never expected anything else.

They were alone in the house, John and his sons being in the fields and Elizabeth in the dairy. Mary had married a cordwainer and lived some distance away on the coast.

'I hope you're not still grieving for those children, Martha,' her mother went on with scarcely a pause for breath. 'You should have got down and had some more as I did. No use mooning about. If you have a dozen or so always a few survive, enough to help on the farm and keep you in your old age. That's what children are for, although,' she sighed deeply, 'I don't know that your father and I will be as lucky. We've had a hard enough life as it is.' She paused and studied her daughter's impassive, expressionless face. 'Bernard's having a hard time, I hear, making ends meet.'

'How came you to hear that, Mother?' Martha looked sharply at her.

'Oh I hear these things. News travels.'

'I suppose you heard that I asked Cousin Robert if there would be any work for us here?'

'And the answer was "no" I understand,' Martha Clark said with an air of triumph, 'as I knew it would be. You should have asked me first.'

'I wouldn't ask you anything, Mother.' Martha Clark stood up. 'Certainly not a favour. I'd know better.'

She made as if to go to the door but Ann held her back.

'Don't go. You know Mother's bark is worse than her bite. Isn't it, Mother?' Ann, who had grown bolder since she was no longer continually under her mother's sway, looked at her, a restraining hand still on Martha's arm. 'Are things really so bad?'

'Bernard hasn't been well,' Martha said. 'The last few years have been bad for him. The doctor says he has congestion of the lungs. Sometimes he can hardly get up the stairs to bed.'

'Then he couldn't do very much work could he?' Mrs Clark said unsympathetically. 'Cousin Robert would want people who can do a proper day's work on the farm.'

'Bernard can work when his lungs clear,' Martha said defiantly. 'And they do. He is better in summer than winter. He is very good with numbers and can do accounts. He has helped Mr Walbridge in the management of his farm.'

'Oh I see. Brains,' Martha said derisively. 'Well, we have no need of them here.'

'I thought Cousin Robert might make use of Bernard's clerical skills, as Mr Walbridge does? I could help out in the dairy. I hear it's doing well. But I know you're short, with Mary married. Anyway,' Martha shook her head, 'Robert said there is no work of that kind, so we must look elsewhere.'

'Well there's nothing for you here,' Martha Clark said brusquely. 'There's no room with us. Not an inch of space to spare.' She sat down and mopped her face with the hem of her skirt. 'Really, Martha, when I helped arrange your marriage it was in the hope that you would better yourself. I thought Bernard would provide for you and look after you. Of course I did hear he was not very clever with money. I told you that, but I thought he would make out with all the land he had. It surprises me he can do Mr Walbridge's accounts.'

'He is very *good* with money,' Martha said defensively. 'He has been unlucky. He worked hard but he took on too much; tried to do too many things. But he is a good, kindly man and does not deserve the blow that fate has struck him. He doesn't deserve to lose all his land and . . .' she paused, 'maybe the house.'

'In that case, it looks like the poorhouse for you,' Mrs Clark said maliciously. 'What a come-down.'

'Mother doesn't change, does she?' Martha said bitterly as she and Ann walked to the farm gate where Bernard was waiting for her with the cart, having not cared to bear the brunt of his mother-in-law's sarcasm. 'Not much sense of Christian charity *there*.'

'Mother is afraid that they might lose what little they have. Cousin Robert isn't very generous. They didn't want me to work here either — because they haven't really forgiven me — although Robert did ask me to. Anyway,' Ann paused and gave a shy smile. 'I'm glad I didn't.' A certain coyness in her tone made Martha look up.

'Oh?' she said encouragingly.

'Well there *is* a man,' Ann's cheeks went pink. 'He's very nice. He's a cowman at the farm. His name is John. John Record.'

'Oh Ann, I'm so glad,' Martha joyously clasped her sister's arm.

But Ann shuffled her feet. 'The thing is . . . well, he is much younger than me. Ten years younger. He's only twenty-three.'

'Well, I don't think that matters. Look how much older than me Bernard is.'

'Yes, but with a man and a woman it's different. The other way round . . . well, you know what I mean.'

'I don't see ten years makes much difference . . . providing he loves you and you love him.'

Sensing some doubt in her voice Martha looked questioningly at her elder sister.

Ann hesitated. 'I do *like* him. Love,' she put a hand to her chin, 'I don't know. He is very silent, doesn't say much. Doesn't say anything really unless he has to; but he does have a regard for me. You see, Martha, I'm getting old. If I don't wed now then I might never have another chance and grow into an old spinster woman whom nobody wants.'

'I will always want you, Ann.' Martha's hand closed tightly over hers.

'And I you . . . and Martha,' Ann said urgently, glancing across at Bernard, 'if things get really bad, and you lose your home, there will always be a roof over your head with me wherever I am. Never doubt that.'

The sisters continued their walk towards the gate where Bernard sat slumped in the driving seat, head on his chest as if he was dozing. 'He does look ill,' Ann murmured. 'Not himself at all.'

'It's all the worry, the pain of losing the children. Then Eliza is now a worry to him.'

'Eliza?' Ann looked surprised. 'I thought she was with Sarah Crocker?'

'Well, she is at the moment but Bernard doesn't know how long Sarah will keep her. Eliza, always so nice and well behaved, has taken a liking to the young men who shift around her as if she was a bitch on heat. Just like her grandmother, everyone says. Sarah says she's a responsibility and doesn't know how long she can put up with her. Can't talk any sense to her and she's a bad example to her children. It's all a great worry to my husband . . . and she doesn't listen to him either.'

Reaching the cart the two sisters briefly embraced and Martha clambered up beside Bernard.

'No luck with your mother?' Bernard asked gruffly.

Martha shook her head.

'No luck with Robert either, mean old scrounger,' Bernard said. 'He's plenty of money. They do say he's one of the richest farmers in the district with fields of flax as well as maize and wheat, and enough cows to supply the whole of Dorset with milk.'

Martha's hand stole into his.

'Never mind,' she said. 'We'll manage.'

Bernard, pleased with the unexpected gesture, returned the pressure of her hand. It was a long time since there had been any sense of closeness between them and he felt warmed by it. He flicked his whip over the back of the horse who failed to respond. It was tired and old and the next stage for it would be the knacker's yard, but not yet.

The cart needed new wheels and a plank was missing from the bottom, but Bernard no longer carried meat, as he had never replaced his beef stock. He grew potatoes in one of his fields and maize in another and, with the help of Martha's assiduous netmaking, they just eked out a living. Meat was a rarity now but there was a little cheese and butter from the few cows, and eggs and chickens from the hens, and Martha managed to sell some of the surplus to the 'higgler', who peddled wares to sell in the markets of Dorchester and Weymouth.

'I've failed you, Martha,' Bernard said morosely. 'No wonder your family despises me.'

'I don't care about them and *I* don't despise you.' She looked at him fondly aware, as he was, of this unexpected newly found intimacy. 'And *that's* the main thing. You're a good man and you couldn't help what happened. You should have married a woman with money and not one with no education and with a temper bad enough to drive your only daughter away. God knows how many times I've rued the day that happened.'

'I wouldn't have married anyone else,' Bernard said loyally. 'Your temper may get the better of you at times and you never tried to be a scholar, but Eliza deserved what she got. Without her James would still be alive, I know that.'

'I was *truly* sorry that I lost my temper with Eliza that day,' Martha said contritely. 'I was *truly* sorry and humbled. I frightened myself by the violence of my emotions; but Eliza had always managed to get under my skin. It wasn't the first time I hit her, or tried to. Something about her really riled me. Maybe it was just as well that she went away, or she might have come to some harm.'

'Not from you, Martha.' Bernard sidled his arm round her waist. 'You're the gentlest, kindest person I ever knew and when I spoke to you that day the way I did, I spoke in haste. You would never harm a soul. Not you.'

But Martha didn't tell him how much her violence worried her. At the time, she had no idea what she was doing, like someone who had temporarily gone out of her mind.

* * *

William Walbridge was now married, the father of three small children. He and his wife lived in some comfort on a farm where William, though still young, seemed all set to emulate his father and be a success and a rich man.

Bernard had contacted Thomas about disposing of his land but it was William who came, eager to look round and, perhaps, to snap up a bargain.

What he saw, however, filled him with dismay, and his face was grave as they returned to the house and the kitchen where Martha was preparing a meal.

'Would you have some tea and apple cake?' she asked politely but William shook his head.

'You can say what you like in front of Martha,' Bernard said. 'I have no secrets from her.'

'Well, to be blunt, you have let everything run down, Bernard. The house is badly in need of repairs. The ground has been neglected and your last crop of potatoes I believe failed?'

Bernard didn't answer. It was a cold December and he was wheezing. He'd hardly been able to climb the hill to show William the extent of his land. His whole attitude was that of a defeated man.

'I shall have to negotiate with the Earl about the rent because you pay a lot of money for what you have. And using it so badly it is no wonder that you got into difficulties. You've nothing much to sell either, have you, Bernard?'

Again Bernard morosely shook his head.

'If I can't get help from my own family or Martha's, it will be the workhouse for us.'

'Over my dead body,' Martha said firmly. 'I'd rather sleep in a field.'

* * *

A few days before Christmas Martha went round Meadways for the last time, alone, opening doors, peering into rooms to make sure they were all empty.

She lingered in the babies' room, surprised to discover that it meant nothing to her now. Four years, four bad years, had taken their toll and one did, after all, forget.

Maybe the dead children were better off, where they were.

Yet if they had lived would Bernard have made just that extra effort to husband his resources, to care for his land, to make wiser judgments, to be a better citizen?

Would they now be in the sorry pass they'd come to if Bernard hadn't lost all his family in one year? For not only the boys but Eliza too had been lost to him.

Martha thought she would never know. The little room, bare and cold, held no memories for her now. No memories of soft, childish bodies, warm kisses, hugs and the times when she'd sung them to sleep. If she tried she could remember all too well the pain of their deaths, but those black thoughts were banished as soon as they came.

She left all the doors open and went downstairs to where Bernard was finishing putting their few possessions in the cart. Most of the furniture had been sold but some went with them: a bed, a chair and a chest of drawers, not much from a well-furnished house once the property of a prosperous man. Martha recalled how the house had gleamed and shone when she first went there as a bride; the fine linen, the silver with which, perhaps, her husband had hoped to entertain.

They had had their own servant and a life of prosperity, perhaps of aspiration, beckoned.

But Bernard should have married a clever woman like Ann Walbridge, not an ignorant dairymaid like herself who had failed to realise her dreams, perhaps because she was incapable of doing so. The Walbridges had never invited them again after the dinner party, and she had never returned the invitation because she would not have known how to entertain such people, even had she wanted to.

He said he'd failed her, but in many ways she felt she'd failed Bernard. Despite her ambition she had remained a simple country woman able to sign her name and write a little, read a few words, but she'd never progressed very far, never applied herself. Maybe if she had, she would have helped him escape the near bankruptcy his unsuccessful ventures had landed him in, the fact they had to leave their home and start again. Easier, perhaps, for her than her husband.

Martha went out into the yard where Bernard was running a rope round the goods in the cart, sticking the inevitable basket with a few hens on top. It seemed like a family tradition to travel that way. Grim as the spectacle was, reminding her of a way of life she thought she had left forever, she nevertheless chuckled. Ezekiel, who had not worked for them for months because there had been nothing left to do, and nothing to pay him with, had come in to help and remarked on her good humour.

'Nice to see you smile, Mrs Bearn.'

'I spent years moving around this way with my family when they moved about each clearing day. We usually travelled with a few hens and, occasionally, a cow roped to the back of the cart plodding on behind.'

'Are you ready, Martha?' Bernard, edgy, had not wanted to return to the house and stood blowing into his hands because it was a raw day.

'I'm ready,' she said, glancing round the yard.

It was many months since the slaughterhouse had resounded to the screams of animals, or the beer-house smelt of barley. The hay loft was also empty as were the barn, the laundry and the dairy house where she made her butter and cheese.

She'd milked the cows that morning for the last time and given them a farewell pat. William Walbridge was going to take them over, and also the remaining hens and geese.

She wondered what he'd make of the place? Do with it all? It would cost a lot of money to restore it.

Martha returned to the kitchen to fetch her basket and after she'd put on her bonnet and shawl she took one final look round. But it all seemed now like an empty shell, not like home any more.

Bernard called out for her to hurry or it would be dark when they got to Netherbury.

One final look and Martha shut the kitchen door and hurried over to join him. She climbed up on the box and took his hand, a gesture that had become more regular of late. Since the days of their departure approached, he had grown more morose and leaned more heavily on her. He was a sad, disillusioned old man but she had married him, and now he needed her.

In a way she found that she needed Bernard too.

'I'm glad I've got you, Martha,' he grunted as the cart wobbled unsteadily across the field pulled by the same tired old horse, and Ezekiel ran ahead to open the gate.

As they passed through they waved to him and he waved back, called out 'good luck'. He was the only one in the whole village who had come to see them off.

That, in itself, seemed to say everything about their life in Powerstock.

Chapter Nine

January 1841

Martha's eyes flew open and remained fixed on the black beam in the ceiling close by from which was suspended a rope with a noose at the end.

She had a terrible sensation of choking, and her hand flew to her throat. She lay there panting, gasping for breath, as the dream gradually receded and, in the dim light of dawn, she saw that the rope hanging from the beam was the one used by John Record to tether his cows. She'd seen it dozens of times before.

Beside her, Bernard stirred. 'What is it, Martha?' he asked.

'I felt I was being strangled.' She still had her hands on her throat, could feel the rapid beat of the pulse in her neck.

'No one's trying to strangle you, my dear.' He lay back as the action of waking had started him coughing. 'I think it's because you see me choking so often when I have a fit of coughing.'

'Probably.' Martha looked across at him anxiously. 'How do you feel this morning?'

But Bernard couldn't answer for coughing which seemed to provide her with the answer.

In the spring Ann had married John Record and they continued to live at Long's Farm, where the Bearns joined them after being witnesses at their marriage. After leaving Powerstock they had stayed for a while with Bernard's mother in Netherbury. But she did not make them feel welcome and they were glad when Ann kept her promise and offered them a roof, however temporary, over their heads.

This roof was a long room over the cowshed which they shared with John and Ann. It was divided by a blanket thrown over one of the beams and afforded little privacy for either couple. Bernard had not had a good winter and coughed incessantly. He was able to do little on the farm to pay for his keep other than help the bailiff with his accounts. Martha joined Ann in the dairy and worked doubly hard to try and make up for Bernard, because they were fed as well as kept.

It was a very hard time for both of them, having no money, no possessions and no home. Martha was sure that it added to Bernard's chest problems because so much of the time he was depressed and lay on the bed covered with a blanket.

Martha knew they couldn't stay indefinitely with John and Ann, who was now pregnant. They were not happy with their position in the farm, the lack of opportunities for betterment, their cramped quarters over the cowshed pervaded with the stench of cowdung, and they were looking for somewhere else.

Martha got up and, peeping round the blanket that curtained them off, saw that Ann and John were both up. They would be preparing to milk the cows. In the freezing cold she poured water from a jug into the basin on the rickety chest of drawers they had brought with them and sluiced her face. Then she hastily dressed, anxious not to be late.

She looked down at Bernard who lay shivering with the blanket pulled over his shoulder.

'Don't get up just yet,' she said, stooping to cover him. Then on impulse she kissed his cheek and he reached for her hand and held it tight.

In the cowshed all was hurry and bustle as the dairy-maids set up their stools to milk the cows and the cowmen hurried from one to another with their wooden pails and yokes. It was a large, prosperous farm covering some five hundred acres. Farmer Long was not often seen on the farm but left its management largely to his bailiff.

Starting from humble origins as a labourer Tom Long had shown skill and acumen in, first, managing and then buying the farm from a man on whom fortune had failed to smile, being guilty of a number of mistakes and foolish investments, rather in the manner of Bernard Bearn.

Tom Long's wife and children were much too gentrified to be seen on the farm. Mrs Long enjoyed the sea air of Weymouth or Bournemouth, and the refined company there, and the Longs frequently rented a house in either resort for the summer months. The Long boys went to Sherborne School and had already turned up their noses at the idea of being farmers. The two misses Long went to an academy for young ladies in Bournemouth and hardly ever came home at all.

John Clark had known Tom Long since they were youths together, and it was through this connection that Ann had been employed, not that it did her much good. She never saw Tom Long and if she had he would probably not have known who, among the dozen or so dairymaids he employed, she was. She was very fortunate that she was able to live with her husband in a room over the cowshed rather than in a dormitory with the other girls, only seeing John at rare intervals during the working day and seldom alone.

Ann was already at work when Martha hurried into the milking shed, tying her apron and collecting her stool to milk her cow. They exchanged smiles but said nothing and Martha worked assiduously until her task was finished and she went into the kitchen to have her breakfast, some of which she would smuggle up to Bernard.

Bernard's condition worried Martha. Their misfortune had brought them much closer together than she would ever have imagined a year or so ago. His sadness and vulnerability moved her and made her the stronger partner. He seemed incapable of making any decisions and left everything to her. She wished this strength, this knowledge had come to her earlier and she might have been able to prevent some of the many mistakes he had made, stopped him drinking too much. It was not only once that it happened. As he went downhill he had spent more time at the Three Horse Shoes than at his work.

He was positively childlike now in his need of her, so she fussed over him and cosseted him. Ironically, he was now like her child, and she worried about him as she had about her poor lost children.

Martha had a piece of bread and cup of milk and stuffed some of the bread in her apron pocket. On the way out she would take a cup full of fresh milk from a pail in the milking shed, and that would be his breakfast.

Ann and Martha said little at breakfast. Ann looked tired; there were large circles under her eyes and Martha felt guilty that Bernard's coughing was keeping her awake.

'We shall soon be gone from here,' she said to Ann in a whisper so that those close by wouldn't hear. 'I thought we would try and get to the seaside and seek work there. It might help Bernard's chest. I know you can't sleep for him coughing.'

'No, I can't sleep for the baby moving,' Ann said. 'And the bailiff has also told me there will be no room for us here when the child is born. We shall have to move. We want to move anyway.' She looked anxiously at Martha. 'Maybe if you go to the coast we can all go together and look for something there?'

Martha clasped her hand under the table.

'Maybe,' she whispered, trying to hide her dejection.

That dreaded insecurity she had had as a child had returned to haunt her again.

Later in the morning Martha was working in the creamery where the milk to be used for making butter was poured into large setting dishes and left overnight until the cream had separated from the milk. Martha had begun the delicate task of skimming the cream from the milk with the skimmer before covering it with muslin and leaving it to ripen. Further along Ann was washing out the churners, which had churned yesterday's cream into butter, with salt water to prevent the butter sticking to the sides.

All these tasks they had done for years, and their experience was appreciated by the less skilful, or those who were still learning.

Other dairymaids were draining the whey from the churned butter, which would be given to the pigs, and then washing the butter in cold water before putting it in flat-bottomed troughs called 'butterworkers' to remove the excess. Still further along finished butter was being shaped by thin wooden butter pats.

The atmosphere in the dairy was friendly and good-humoured though, as Martha and Ann were older than most of the other women who worked, and also married, they remained rather apart. As sisters who stuck close together no new friendships had been formed.

Martha had just finished filling the setting dishes and started to cover them with muslin, where they would remain for forty-eight hours, when she heard her name called and looked up to see the bailiff, Joseph Hatton, standing at the door holding in his hand an envelope which he pointed at her.

Martha wiped her hands on a clean cloth and went over to him.

'Yes, Mr Hatton?'

'Is Bernard about, Martha? I haven't seen him this morning. I've got a letter for him.'

'A letter!' Martha exclaimed, taking the envelope. 'I'll go and look for him.' She was reluctant to let the bailiff know that, most probably, Bernard was still in bed.

'Oh, and Martha,' the bailiff said as she followed him out of the dairy house into the yard, 'you know that the Records won't be staying here after the birth? I'm afraid the room over the cowshed won't be available for much longer.'

'That's all right,' Martha said, 'we'll be moving on too.'

'Oh, I see. Well that's a pity, Martha, because your

work is appreciated here, but we need to convert the room over the cowshed into a dormitory to sleep more people. We're very crowded in the house. You're welcome to stay there, but Bernard will have to find somewhere else to live.'

'You think I wish to be separated from my husband?' Martha said tartly. 'No thank you.'

'It's just that Bernard,' the bailiff tried to explain, 'well, there's not much for him to do. There's not much call for an older man. He's just an extra mouth to feed. I wanted to let you know.'

Hatton looked embarrassed and Martha thought he probably had his instructions from Tom Long who was a hard man.

'We'd be leaving anyway,' Martha said curtly. 'The conditions in that room are fit only for cows, not human beings. You'll never get rid of the awful stench no matter how hard you try, and it sickens me to the stomach. You can tell *that* to Mr Long.'

Martha flounced off towards the cowshed and the bailiff stood looking after her, reflecting that, although Martha Bearn was a good worker, she had a temper and was thus a potential cause of trouble, of dissension among the workers, because of her outspoken views about conditions on the farm. He thought of the trouble that dissatisfied labourers had caused a few years before up and down the county, though at Long's Farm they had escaped fairly easily because of the subservience of its employees and the fact that Tom Long wouldn't tolerate trouble. She was a fine spirited young woman and he admired her devotion to her ailing husband, but one didn't want too many Marthas among the docile workforce causing unrest.

Martha ran across the yard and up the outside stairs to the top wondering what was in the letter, and reflecting on what the bailiff had told her: virtually giving them notice to quit when Ann's baby was born.

Joseph Hatton was not an unkind man. He was merely carrying out his master's orders, typical of his breed. Just as well they wanted to go anyway.

Martha found Bernard still lying on the bed, the breakfast she had brought him untouched by his side.

'You have a letter!' she cried, her eyes gleaming with excitement. 'I wonder what it means?'

Bernard took the envelope from her and studied the writing on the outside.

Then, watched by Martha who could scarcely contain herself, he extracted a single sheet of paper and slowly began to read, his brow puckering in the effort of concentration.

'It's from Sarah Crocker,' he announced. 'It's about Eliza.'

'Oh!' Martha's sense of elation evaporated. Nothing about Eliza could ever be good news.

Bernard seemed to have difficulty reading the letter and turned the page towards the light which entered through a single narrow window. 'She says Eliza has gone,' he announced after a long pause during which he seemed unable to digest the information. 'She's gone to London.'

'London!' Martha exclaimed. Then again 'London?'

'Yes, London,' Bernard seemed scarcely able to understand what had happened either.

'Does she know anyone in London?' Martha was confused.

'No.' Once more Bernard consulted the letter and

looked at Martha again. 'Not that I know. She went in a cart with Ezekiel. He said he'd take her to the railway station at Southampton.'

There was a fresh pause during which Bernard carefully re-read the letter, and then he swung his legs over the bed and sat on the side staring at the floor.

'I must go after her, Martha.'

'Oh no you won't!' Martha said, putting a restraining hand on his arm.

'Yes, I must.' He regarded her with a dazed expression. 'She's my daughter. I can't have her loose in London. She'll get hurt.'

'But you'll never know where to find her. London is a huge city, bigger than Bridport, bigger even than Dorchester. Don't be silly, Bernard.'

'I am not being silly,' Bernard said in the stubborn tone of voice Martha knew only too well. Gone, it had seemed in an instant was the air of childish dependence, and he was once more a man in command of himself. 'Eliza is my only child and I must go after her. I will begin to search at the railway terminus in London and go on from there. She has not been gone long and she doesn't know London either. She won't be too far away.'

'But *why* did she go?'

Bernard shook his head. 'Sarah doesn't say. She said she had no control over Eliza. In fact she seems, from her letter, glad to have seen the back of her.' Bernard shook his head mournfully. 'My poor daughter. My poor, poor daughter. I should never have left her. I should have remembered my promise to her mother to look after her. I made her that promise on her deathbed.'

His expression now became distraught and tears trickled down his cheeks. 'What will happen to her in

London if I don't save her? She will fall into prostitution, all kinds of vice.'

'But you don't know where to *look*, where to *start*. You say "at the railway terminus" but she could have gone anywhere. Besides, Bernard, you're not well, you're a sick man. You're in no condition to go, especially at this time of the year.' Martha began to feel thoroughly annoyed with him and started to pace the room. 'You are in no state to go *anywhere*, Bernard. If you feel you must go then I shall go with you.'

'Oh no, Martha,' Bernard said firmly. 'If Eliza sees you she'll run a mile.'

Yet again Martha experienced the sense of humiliation caused by the memory of her violence towards Eliza, the trouble which had arisen from it. It showed how one rash action could result in untold consequences, how careful one had to be.

'You don't have the money for such a journey,' she added, thinking that this objection might count more.

'I have a little put by,' Bernard said mysteriously, 'for an emergency such as this. As soon as I find Eliza I shall be back.'

The tears stopped as abruptly as they had started and, once more in control, he looked at his wife. 'I shall bring Eliza back with me and we shall have to start all over again, Martha. It's no use your objecting because it is what I intend to do!'

But Martha raised no objection. This threat didn't bother her because she knew that the chances of Bernard finding his daughter in a place the size of London were about the same as of finding a needle in a haystack.

Once having made up his mind Bernard seemed like

a man transformed. His step quickened and his cough was not so persistent. He was a man with a mission. He prevailed upon Joseph Hatton to let John Record take him to Dorchester from where he would get the coach to the new railway station near Southampton, the end of the line.

The idea of adventure seemed to excite him, but Martha was full of foreboding about the wisdom of letting him go.

The morning that he was due to leave she woke with her choking sensation again, a feeling of panic and apprehension that took some time to settle. She felt for Bernard in the bed beside her and, already awake, he clasped her hand.

'I don't feel I'm going to see you again,' she whispered, turning to him and stroking his face, a face that was gnarled, prematurely old and covered with stubble. For all that she realised now how very dear he was to her, how precious.

'You are going to see me, never fear,' Bernard said in a tone full of resolution. 'When I come back we'll start a new life. You and Eliza will be reconciled, you'll see, she'll have learned a lesson, and we'll go somewhere new and begin afresh. You are still a young woman, Martha, and you have all your life ahead of you.'

'I'm so afraid,' she murmured, resting her head on his chest, 'so afraid. I don't know what I'd do without you.'

Now it was Bernard who felt protective towards her, in charge again. He gently stroked her head and kissed her cheek and, slowly, the panic and apprehension receded and she began to feel a little of his optimism creeping into her. A fresh start? Maybe.

By the time John Record brought the cart around, Bernard was neatly dressed, had shaved his stubble, combed his hair and Martha had packed a bag for him which also contained bread, cheese and some fresh butter she had churned herself.

Before stepping up into the cart, he kissed her tenderly regardless of the few people who stood about gawping.

'I will soon be back, Martha,' he promised.

'Take care,' she said, smiling bravely to conceal her agitation. 'Don't be gone long, Bernard Bearn.' She leaned forward and whispered in his ear, 'You are my man, and I shall miss you.'

'Those are the best words I ever heard,' Bernard whispered back. 'Well worth coming home for.'

'I should have gone with him,' Martha murmured to Ann who had silently approached and stood by her side to watch the cart disappear down the lane. 'He is not fit.' She shook her head violently and said again as if to herself, 'Not fit, not fit.' Suddenly distraught she made as if to move, and then stifled an impulse to run after him. 'I don't think I'll ever see him again.' She looked wildly at Ann who, as if sensing her intention, had taken hold of her arm. 'I should never have let him go.'

'Bernard was not a man to be stopped,' Ann said grimly and, not relinquishing her grip, she began leading her sister towards the dairy house where work awaited them. 'You have nothing to reproach yourself for, Martha. Nothing.'

John Record was indeed a silent man. He was not someone Bernard felt he knew at all well, even though they had been sharing the same room for several months.

He never remembered having a conversation of any length with John who was very thin, tall and wiry with an angular face, prominent cheekbones and a large Adam's apple. Bernard thought it might have been because he was so much older, but John was silent with everyone, even his wife.

So, for the first part of the journey John was typically silent, and so was Bernard because, once they were out of sight of the farm, he had severe misgivings about what he was doing and he wished, after all, that he had brought Martha with him.

Where *was* he going to look for Eliza, and what would he do if he found her? He knew, as Martha did, that it was most unlikely she would wish to return with him. She was too wilful for that.

Bernard was on the verge of asking John to turn back but, at the last moment, he realised how foolish he would feel, even more foolish and inadequate than he had felt in recent years, as his fortunes and his health had declined to the extent that he relied with almost childlike subservience on his wife. His action in deciding to go and look for his daughter had restored some of his pride, reactivated feelings of manliness, of being in control, long dormant.

For a long time now he had been the mere shadow of the man he once was. Somehow, finding Eliza presented a challenge — also he was longing to see a railway train. This gave him a boyish sense of excitement. Not only seeing one, but *going* on one.

'I wonder if the railway will come to these parts?' he said companionably to John Record after they had travelled in silence for a few miles.

John shrugged.

'Do you know, I am quite excited at the thought of seeing a train? I can't quite imagine what it looks like, can you?'

John shook his head.

'I mean, imagine that one day we will no longer be dependent on horse and cart. The train will change our lives completely. Can you believe that?'

Bernard wondered just what would excite this strangely reticent man and relapsed into silence again.

By the time they got to Dorchester it was afternoon and John had some purchases to make on behalf of the farm.

'Good luck then,' he said, with his customary economy, accompanied by the most fleeting of smiles, as Bernard got rather stiffly off the cart and walked round it to collect his bag. Briefly giving Bernard the chance to take it off the cart John flicked the tip of his whip across the horse's back and, without another glance, trotted away up High West Street. Bernard stood dejectedly watching him, feeling alone and rather afraid.

He'd been to Dorchester several times, but now the size of the town greatly alarmed him, the question of making his way, where to get the coach and, as it was late afternoon, where to stay the night.

Had John Record been a different sort of man, someone a person could ask favours of, even communicate with, he might have confided to him his fears and asked his help.

But John Record would probably have despised Bernard for his timidity and, anyway, by now he was well out of sight. Too late to return to Marshwood, even had he wanted to.

Somehow Bernard got through the rest of the day

and evening, his confidence diminishing with every hour. He found where the coach left for Southampton the following day and at what time. But the cost rather staggered him and he realised that the money he had brought with him might well not be enough to take him as far as London, never mind keep him once he got there. By dint of asking around he managed to find a lodging place for threepence but he had no bed, only a rough blanket on the floor, and he had to share a room with two other men who were the worse for drink. After eating some of the bread and cheese Martha had packed for him he lay down on the floor on his coat, his head on his bag, the blanket over him, and went to sleep.

But he soon woke and spent half the night awake coughing until one of his fellow inmates threatened to throw him out.

For the rest of the night Bernard sat bolt upright, melancholy and wide awake until, with the coming of dawn, and already feeling far from well, he crept out to await the departure of the Southampton coach.

It seemed a long journey with a stop for a change of horses and food at an inn. Bernard had a pint of ale which made him feel sick, and he realised he was probably weak from hunger and exhaustion. It seemed an awful long time since he had left Martha and the comfort — for so it now appeared in retrospect — of Long's Farm, and heartily he wished he was back.

He rode outside the coach to save money, shivering all the way because it was so cold and wet, the wind biting through his thin coat.

By the time they got to their destination he was

scarcely able to get down from the coach and one of the passengers looked at him with concern.

'Are you all right, old man?'

'I'm all right,' Bernard said grumpily, 'and I am *not* an old man. I am not yet fifty,' and he turned away, staggering slightly, as he made his way blindly up a street, not even feeling strong enough to ask the way to the railway station.

Old man indeed!

Bernard walked on, without the slightest idea where he was going or in what direction, until it was dark. He knew he was feverish and he coughed incessantly spitting up great globules of yellow phlegm. A worrying pain, that he had had before, renewed itself on one side of his chest, crossing to the other, disappeared, and then returned again, only twice as bad.

He had to stop to get his breath and rest several times and, finally, he was unable to rise at all. As darkness fell, he spread himself on the wet ground and sobbed.

Bernard woke up in a strange bed in a strange place with a woman bending over him. She was grey-haired and worn, though with a kindly face, and was wiping his brow, and holding a cup to his lips. He was so parched he drank greedily before falling back on the bed exhausted by the effort.

'There,' the woman said, wiping his brow again. 'I shouldn't think you've eaten for days.'

'Martha,' Bernard murmured, looking beseechingly at the woman, 'can you get Martha?'

'Martha?' the woman replied. 'You have cried out her name for days.'

'Martha's my wife. I should never have come. I should

never have left her. She told me not to go.' Bernard began to weep and the pain in his chest made him catch his breath so sharply that he nearly passed out.

'Where did you come from, old man?' the woman asked gently.

'I am not an old man,' Bernard managed to gasp. 'I am not yet fifty.'

'I'm sorry. You were in a bad state when you were brought in here. We didn't think you'd last the night.'

'Where is "here"?' Bernard stammered, after a fresh bout of coughing.

'You're in the workhouse. They thought you were a tramp.'

Bernard lay back and closed his eyes. 'So, it has come to this at last,' he murmured brokenly.

'What is your name? Can you remember?' the woman asked, producing a pencil and paper from her pocket.

'Bernard Bearn.'

'Bernard Barnes,' she wrote down carefully, having, with some difficulty, interpreted his rich Dorset accent. 'And where is Martha, your wife?'

'At Long's Farm, Marshwood, Dorset.'

Bernard took a deep, rasping breath and, the tears continuing to stream down his cheeks, he looked pitifully up at the woman, seeing only kindly concern on her face. Feverishly he clutched her hand.

'If anything . . .' he paused, continuing to breathe painfully, 'if anything should happen to me, please be sure Martha knows . . . and tell her I'm sorry. Tell her . . .' he reached for the woman's arm and feebly pulled her closer because by now he was only capable of mouthing the words: 'Tell her I love her. I always have.'

Chapter Ten

March 1841

Martha in her black dress and bonnet, which concealed
her dark curls and part of her face, looked in deepest
mourning, the very picture of stricken widowhood, as
she sat facing Sarah Crocker who was studying the paper
Martha had given her. It was the death certificate of one
Bernard Barnes, who had died on 13 February. His age
was given as forty-nine and his occupation that of
labourer. The cause of death was pneumonia.

Sarah studied the document for some time and then
looked up.

'It says his name was Barnes,' she said.

Martha shrugged. 'I suppose they couldn't make
out too clearly what Bernard said. You know how
some foreigners say they can't understand what we
say. Besides,' Martha bowed her head, aware that she
was close to tears, 'it *was* Bernard. They sent on his
clothes, the little bag I packed for him. No doubt that
it was Bernard, buried in a pauper's grave . . .' She put
her face in her hands and Sarah rose to comfort her.

Martha looked up at her abjectly. 'If only I had the

means to bring him home to Powerstock to lie beside your sister and his children, but I have not . . .'

The pressure of a sympathetic hand on her shoulder was too much for Martha who began to weep openly, her head pressed hard against Sarah's thigh.

Sarah let her cry, mechanically patting her back and saying softly: 'There, there. There, there.'

It was difficult, looking at this bowed, crumpled figure, to recall the pretty young woman who had married Bernard on that day after Christmas ten years before. And how happy Bernard had been, released after eight years as a widower.

Martha had made him happy, at least until the death of the children in that fateful year of 1835. After that the relationship between them seemed to sour, but, from what Martha had told her, the tragedy of their impoverishment and departure from Powerstock seemed to have drawn them together again.

'You don't know how I feel, Sarah,' Martha sobbed. 'I don't think I did right by him. I realised too late what a good man he was. I should never have let him go.' She raised a stricken face to her friend. 'It was plain he was too ill. But nothing would keep him back. I wanted to go with him but he would not let me.'

'You couldn't stop him if he was determined.' Sarah smiled bleakly down at her. 'Bernard could be stubborn.'

'Latterly he was like a baby.' Martha blew her nose and attempted to dry her eyes. 'So dependent on me, but when he got your letter he rose from his bed like a man possessed. He was determined to go after Eliza and fetch her back. I knew he never would.' Martha buried her head again. 'You see,' once again she looked appealingly at Sarah, 'I knew he would not come back. I could feel it in my bones. He was too ill, too frail. I will reproach myself for the rest of my life that I didn't stop him. John Record took him to Dorchester. I should have stopped John. Ann should have stopped John, but my poor sister is married to a man who never says a word. Not even "I love you". He would certainly not have listened to either of us.'

'You did all you could.'

'I failed Bernard in another respect,' Martha went on as though she couldn't stop reproaching herself. 'I didn't do right by him. I denied him relations for many years.' She faltered. 'I was frightened of having more children after what happened to my little ones.'

'You did well to be afraid,' Sarah, who had also lost children, said comfortingly. 'I am frightened too.'

They impulsively joined hands, looking at each other as though each could, in her mind's eye, see the tiny coffins buried in the churchyard.

Sarah Crocker, the sister of Bernard's first wife, was a brisk cheerful woman, not normally given to introspection or moralising.

She had missed Martha since she left and it was a terrible shock to her when Martha had appeared on the doorstep of the farm just outside Powerstock that morning, having been dropped off by a carter who had brought her by various byways to Witherstone Farm where George Crocker was a dairyman. They were fortunate in having a cottage some distance from the farm where they kept their own chickens and a few pigs which, as well as the produce from a large garden, helped to keep them independent.

They were not far from Sarah's brother, Samuel

Wrixon, who had prospered even more since the incident when Bernard had offended the schoolmaster. Sarah was a loyal wife and if she hoped that her husband would show a little more enterprise and make some effort to advance himself in the world she kept it to herself, remembering what had happened to Bernard Bearn who had had such great expectations which he failed to fulfil. And here now was his widow, a woman showing signs of weariness and premature ageing, someone who looked forty rather than thirty, a woman very near the end of her tether.

'Were you on your way to somewhere, Martha?' she enquired kindly, but Martha shook her head.

'I wanted to see you.' She put a hand in the pocket of her dress and drew forth a piece of paper which she carefully unfolded, smoothing it on her lap before handing it to Sarah.

'Here. This was enclosed with the death certificate. I wanted you to read it to me rather than some stranger because I think it may contain some information about Bernard. That's why I came here.'

Sarah peered at the letter and, finding it hard to read, took it to the table where she attempted to smooth it again as it had been crumpled up in Martha's pocket. Then she took a pair of spectacles from the mantelpiece, put them on her nose and studied the letter again. Finally she nodded and gazed at Martha who was watching her apprehensively.

'It *is* about Bernard,' she said quietly. 'Do you want me to read it to you?'

'Please.' Martha joined her hands and leaned eagerly forward.

'It is from the superintendent of the workhouse.'

Sarah cleared her throat. 'It is dated about a month ago.'

'I received it some weeks back along with the certificate,' Martha said. 'Ann could not read, nor could John, and we didn't want to ask the bailiff in case it contained something we would not wish him to hear.'

'Dear Mrs Barnes,' [Sarah began]

'I am sorry to tell you that your husband, Bernard Barnes, died in this institution on 13 February and was buried two days later in the churchyard.

He was found collapsed in the street and was brought in here as, from his condition, he was thought to be a vagrant. He was feverish and delirious for several days so we knew nothing about him. Fortunately, he recovered enough to tell us his name and some details before he expired, the cause of death being pneumonia.

He was cared for by a kind woman, an inmate of this institution, to whom he uttered his last words which she wanted me to pass on to you.

He said to tell you that he was sorry and that he loved you and always had.

These were his exact words as repeated to me.

Mr Barnes's effects are being sent on to you by separate courier.

I am sorry to give you this sad news.

Yours sincerely,

Theodore Weller, Superintendent.'

By the time Sarah finished her reading Martha was in tears again and this time Sarah joined her. The two women sat side by side, sobbing openly into their handkerchiefs.

'He was such a good man,' Martha repeated. 'And he loved me. I never appreciated him enough. I . . . I don't know what will become of me now. I never thought all those years ago when I was young and ambitious, too ambitious, to better myself, to be somebody, that I would end up being nobody, worse than before, with no money, no husband or children and nowhere to live.'

'You must stay with us,' Sarah insisted, recovering herself. 'You must stay as long as you want. Bernard's wife will always have a home with us, dear Martha.'

But Martha didn't want to stay in Powerstock. It was not congenial to her. It had too many bad memories and she avoided the village and meeting the people there, none of whom had come to say goodbye when they left on that sad December day.

Nor did she want them to know that Bernard had died in a workhouse, that she was a pauper herself and dependent on the goodwill and the charity of others.

But news soon got around that Martha was back and, doubtless, also, the circumstances of Bernard's death. Sarah was not a gossip and nor was her husband, but there were other workers on the farm who knew Martha and there was no reason at all why they should keep this information to themselves.

One or two of the women she had made nets with, and with whom she had trudged on foot the many miles to Bridport and back to sell them, came to see her but there was no sign of the vicar or any member of the Walbridge, Peach or Walburton families who must secretly have thanked God that their daughters had escaped the fate of Eliza who had been the talk of the village before she ran off with Ezekiel. It was presumed they were still together because he had not returned to his home. Martha could just imagine what was being said among those tongue waggers with which most small communities abound:

'Fancy Eliza, with all her airs and graces, going off with a man she considered half stupid.'

That's what they would say and, unfortunately, they would be right. But Martha took no satisfaction in Eliza's downfall because it had been the certain cause of Bernard's death.

Martha did what she could to help Sarah in the house, but she avoided the farm and farm work while once again she planned, as she had in the past, ways of escape.

But for the time being none came.

One day just before dusk she made her way by the fields, avoiding the lanes, to Powerstock and stood for some time looking out over Meadways and the land that had once been theirs. The house nestled in the valley by the river and on one side was the orchard and on the other the outbuildings where Bernard had once brewed beer, made cider and cheerfully slaughtered animals. It all seemed deserted now, no cattle roamed in the field, there were no chickens pecking in the yard, no smoke rising from the chimney, no lamps to be seen in the house.

Empty.

A lump came into Martha's throat as she thought of her babies who had been born there, of Ann's baby born dead, of the pain but joy of childbirth and of the many happy times she had had until that year when they all died and everything changed. If she had been a good wife, a tolerant and understanding wife, she would have helped Bernard more; she would not have refused him marital relations – a right, after all, that he could have demanded but did not – and they would have had more children as her mother had, as Sarah Crocker had.

All sensible women made the best of their losses and went on. Why had she, Martha Bearn, been so different? Ignorance? Stupidity? Stubbornness? She wasn't sure. She only knew she had failed to bring out the best in a man who had never intentionally treated her harshly and who had said at the end that he loved her.

Maybe they would still be there if things had gone differently. Maybe, on the other hand, they would not and she and Bernard would have been left, as her parents had been, travelling round the countryside with a cart full of children and no home and nothing to eat.

Martha turned sadly away and, as darkness had now fallen, she followed the road back to the farm but, before she did, she took one last look at the house remembering how it had been in happier days.

She felt now as she trudged wearily back to Witherstone that happiness had eluded her forever.

When Martha got back the candles were alight in the cottage and the welcome smell of food greeted her as she entered the kitchen. Removing her shawl she tossed it over the back of the chair and straightened her dress.

She then realised there was someone else in the room other than Sarah, who stood by the cooking range stirring a pot over the hot flames. A man sat, legs crossed, in the corner watching her. He was smoking a pipe and the other hand held a tankard of ale.

'You will know John Symes,' Sarah said, turning slightly from her task in the direction of the visitor.

'Hello Martha,' John said, not moving from his comfortable position.

'Hello, John,' Martha said briefly and began to make her way across the room to go upstairs.

'I am here to visit my father,' John Symes said. 'He is not well.'

'I am sorry to hear that,' Martha said politely, moving across the room.

'I was sorry to hear about your troubles,' John went on. 'Also about the death of Bernard. It is a sad tale.'

'It is.' Martha had little desire to converse with Josiah Symes's cousin and, with the ghost of a smile, prepared to pass by and leave the room.

'Supper in half an hour,' Sarah called after her.

Martha was irritated with her reaction to the appearance of John Symes. After all, he had done her no wrong. She had been brusque, almost rude and Sarah would wonder why.

More and more she felt it was time she left this place, but for where she had no idea. Ann and John Record had gone to Uplyme in Devon to visit Clark and Hussey relations and investigate the possibility of work there, which was why she had been given notice to leave Long's Farm.

She had not been sorry to go, but after two months of the Crocker hospitality she had a feeling her welcome was wearing thin, and it was time to move on.

But where? That was the question.

To her surprise, and somewhat to her dismay, when she came downstairs for supper John Symes was seated with the rest of the family round the table and the only vacant seat was one next to him.

Martha sidled into it and began eating her soup,

listening to George and John chat about farming matters. Gradually she began to feel more relaxed, less threatened by his presence. After supper she usually put the younger children to bed, giving Sarah and George the chance to have some time to themselves. It was one of the small ways with which she could repay their hospitality.

However, this evening Sarah rose as soon as the last mouthful had disappeared and announced that she would put the children to bed herself while George went round the farm to see that all was well before retiring for the night.

Rather mystified, Martha looked across at Sarah and rose too, but as she did John Symes turned to her, saying:

'I would like a word with you, Martha, if you have the time.'

'A word?' Martha abruptly sat down again as Sarah, aided by her eldest daughter, began swiftly to clear away the dishes. After they were stacked in the sink she called to her other children who obediently followed her out of the room.

John Symes was a man of about thirty-six years of age, not nearly as good-looking or attractive as his cousin, and of a serious, even dour mien. His expression was lugubrious, even as he looked at Martha who felt increasingly uncomfortable in his presence.

'I will come straight to the point, Martha,' John said, as the door shut behind the last of the children. 'I am in need of a housekeeper at Blackmanston Farm. Ann Simpson, who worked for us, has gone back to her home. She was in her fifties and had not been well.

'Sarah told me something of your circumstances and

it occurred to me that this is a position that might interest you. Board, lodging all found, and five shillings a week.' He sat back with a magnanimous expression on his face.

'No, thank you,' Martha said, rising from her chair. 'I couldn't possibly consider it.'

'But why not?' John paused. 'If it is your sister Ann you're thinking about, I must tell you I do not hold it against her that she left us without notice. I mean, I would not employ her again but that is no reason not to employ you, of whom I have heard nothing but good.'

'It is too far, too remote, even worse than this place,' Martha said, pushing the chair firmly under the table. 'Goodnight.'

And without waiting for an answer she went up to her room under the eaves and lay, completely exhausted, on the bed where, eventually, she fell asleep without even removing her clothes.

The following morning Martha noticed a change in Sarah's manner. Instead of greeting her with her customary friendliness she ignored her when she sat down to breakfast, talked solely to the children and not to her, and then left all the clearing up for her to do while she went upstairs to see to the children's needs and her household duties. Usually they laughed and chatted in the morning, sharing chores, but today the atmosphere was glacial.

Martha washed the breakfast dishes, dried and put them away, scoured the pots, swept the kitchen and then went out to sweep the yard when Sarah came back, still not speaking to her, and began cutting vegetables for dinner which was shared by many of the farm labourers.

Martha finished cleaning the yard and returned to the kitchen for a pail with which to sluice it. Sarah's back remained turned to her, but there was a certain ferocity with which she hacked at the vegetables and threw them into a pot.

'Did I do something wrong?' Martha asked eventually.

'No.' Swish, swish went the knife slicing through some fine-looking leeks, Sarah's mouth resolutely pursed. Obviously she was in a lather about something.

'Your manner towards me has changed.'

'Well then, Martha,' Sarah despatched her last leek, spun round and pointed her knife at Martha. 'It is not that we mind having you here but you always said you did not want to stay.'

'Oh, you want me to go? I see,' Martha said stiffly. 'Very well, I'll go.'

'No, I do not *want* you to go, but you always said you would have to go some time. You do not like living in Powerstock because it reminds you too much of the past.'

'That's true,' Martha acknowledged.

'And now you have an opportunity to go and you do not take it.' The tone of Sarah's voice rose sharply.

'Oh I *see*.' Martha, light dawning, sank into a chair. 'I see. John Symes has been talking to you . . .'

'Has offered you a *very* good position. When would you get another one like it? *Where* would you get another like it? Did you ever think of that? As it is we have to feed you . . .'

'I'll leave today,' Martha cried, jumping up. 'I am very, very sorry that I have abused your hospitality.'

'Martha!' Sarah threw down the knife and, crossing

the floor, grasped her by the arm. 'Please don't be stupid. I don't *mind* having you here at all. I enjoy your company, but occasionally George does grumble about an extra mouth to feed and the children have to double up in that small room. I know you help in the house and with the children, but I can see you're restless, not happy . . .'

'Nor would I be at Blackmanston Farm,' Martha said firmly.

'How do you know?'

'My sister was there and she didn't like it.'

'There was a good reason for your sister not to like it if I remember,' Sarah said with an edge to her voice. 'You have no reason to imitate *her*.'

So, Bernard had told her who the father of Ann's baby was. Martha wondered how many other people had known too. She felt her cheeks beginning to burn.

'John is very keen to have you,' Sarah went on. 'He knows you are a good worker. I spoke of you very highly.'

'Oh, thank you,' Martha didn't hide her sarcasm. 'I still do not want to go to Blackmanston Farm, but I will leave here within a day or two. I promise you that.'

'Then where *will* you go?' Sarah, eyes blazing, caught her by the arm. 'Will you become a vagrant too? Martha, if you are not very careful, very very careful, you will end up in the same sort of place as poor Bernard, and once you are there, like him, there will be no way of leaving except in a wooden box.'

A few days later, just after sunrise, Martha stole into the cemetery, a mission she had avoided all the time she had been in Powerstock.

But now, upon her departure, she knew in her bones that she would never again return to a place about which she had so many mixed feelings, where she had known joy and sorrow in equal measure, her hopes and ambitions rise, only to be crushed.

For a while she had difficulty in remembering where the graves were, among so many, and then she came upon them, the larger cross over the grave of the first Mrs Bearn and her son, the smaller one marking her own babies.

Tears already pricking the backs of her eyes at the sadness of the moment, Martha knelt in the grass wet with dew, and tenderly traced with her fingers the names on the cross as though she would etch them forever on her soul:

William
beloved son of
Bernard and Martha Bearn
1832—1835

and his brother
Thomas
1834—1835

She rose and, kissing the cross, moved to the larger one next to it and, in the same way, traced out the name of James whom, in the end, she had loved as much as the others.

Then she stood up and looked across the churchyard over the village of Powerstock, now bathed in the gentle, golden light of early morning. It was a fine May day and in the tall grass the buttercups and cow parsley mingled with the clover and daisies already resounding to the soft, melodious hum of bees.

The sun cast a mellow glow on the roofs of the houses she had known so well for more than half her life, on the fat contented cattle grazing in the lush fields, and beyond them the tree-covered hills which she had crossed so often in her walks to the sea to sell her nets in the company of a group of happy, gossiping women.

Now she would be crossing them for the last time.

Turning once again to gaze on the graves she blew each a kiss and then, shy of being observed, went quickly to the gate of the churchyard where John Symes was patiently awaiting her, his horse munching from its nosebag, the cart filled with goods and provisions bought for his remote farm.

Without a smile she got up beside him, with all that she possessed in the world tied up in a small bundle by her side. Yet another chapter in her life had begun.

As they came over the brow of the hill at the approach to the small hamlet of Steeple, which was their destination, the spectacular view made Martha catch her breath and John Symes drew the cart to a halt and looked at her.

'Nice, eh?'

'It's lovely.' Martha broke into a smile, the first one he had seen since they left Powerstock. Dressed in her widow's weeds with her black bonnet obscuring her fine black curls he could not believe she was only thirty. She looked much older – forty or even forty-five.

He remembered what a bonny girl she was when he had first known her in Powerstock. She must have been in her mid teens, and it was whispered by the village gossips that she was too pretty to be Martha Clark's daughter. Her appearance, when he saw her again, had shocked him. It was terrible what misfortune could do to a woman.

'That's Kimmeridge Bay,' John pointed towards the sea with his whip. 'You can walk there from the farm, and yonder.' He looked over to the west. 'Just out of sight is Tyneham village. It's a pretty walk on a fine day, and Warbarrow Bay beyond. Up there,' he pointed directly in front of him, 'is Smedmore House where the Cavells live who own my farm.'

'Are they nice people?' Martha asked.

John nodded. 'Gentry. We don't see too much of them as long as we pay the rent which we do, regularly. Yes, they'm good landlords. Better than some.' He looked at her again. 'You'll be happy here, Martha. You'll be able to forget the past.'

Martha's smile disappeared and she looked ahead of her, as yet unconvinced that anything would ever change.

Here, too, the land, barren during the winter, began to yield up its goodness, the tender young shoots of maize and corn, barley and oats. The fields they passed were golden with rape, the hedgerows white with blackthorn, a profusion of tiny white or pink flowers on the hawthorn trees from which came the thrilling songs of thrush and blackbird. Buttercups, cow parsley and pink campion bobbed up among the tall grass at the sides of the narrow lanes down which the cart slowly wended its way. They had stopped overnight at lodgings, but the horse still seemed tired at the end of another warm day.

Once at the bottom of the hill they left the road and bounced along a narrow track towards the farmhouse enabling Martha to take stock of her future home. It was a well-proportioned dwelling with outbuildings and a row of cottages next to it.

The cows were being brought in for milking, a welcoming, familiar sight which gladdened Martha's heart.

Normality was returning after all.

As he helped Martha down from the cart John stopped for a few words with the cowman while Martha gazed about her, pleased with what she saw. It seemed a well-ordered, well-stocked farm and the fat cows being led to the milking shed looked nourished and contented. Hens ran clucking agitatedly about the yard while a flock of geese scurried nervously by. A couple of dogs ran up to greet them, barking, and a friendly tabby cat rubbed its back against the pump before going to investigate an interesting sound in the corner of the yard.

As the cowman followed his cows into the shed John led her indoors, straight into the kitchen which was a typical farm kitchen with flagstones, a large range in which a welcoming fire roared, and polished pots and pans hanging from the ceiling together with some fat sides of ham.

'The cowman's wife has been looking after the house after Ann left,' John said, turning to Martha. 'She has left everything in good order for you.'

'Have you no other help?' Martha looked surprised. 'Am I to look after this all by myself?'

'Did you expect a maid, Martha?' John looked down at her, smiling. 'We are not the Cavells, you know. We have to watch our pennies. The cowman's wife is very obliging and I'm sure will help you on washing day, and other times if you need her. Now let me show you to your room.'

John took up her bag and led her through a stone-flagged corridor, up a flight of stairs, then along the landing and up a narrower flight to an attic room which had an iron bed, a chest of drawers, a tallboy with a washing basin and jug and a wooden chair with a cane back. There was no mirror, maybe to discourage vanity, and one picture on the wall of a girl with a garland in her hair looking soulfully at a lamb which she held tightly in her arms. There was a small rush mat on the wooden floor. The window was uncurtained, and from it was a view of the hills.

'No sight of the sea,' Martha said, wistfully, looking out. 'I hoped there would be. I love the sea.'

'The sea is just beyond the hills.'

John, perhaps from a sense of decorum, had only stepped a few paces into the room and now seemed anxious to be gone.

'Come downstairs when you're ready, Martha. You can then prepare our supper. Doubtless you'll be hungry yourself.'

After John had gone, Martha, glad of a few moments to herself, looked round the bare room. Despite its simplicity it had an air of calm, but whatever its drawbacks it was a hundred times better than the evil-smelling room over the cowshed at Long's Farm where daylight hardly ever seemed to penetrate and where, even covered with blankets, they shivered with cold all night.

Martha took off her bonnet and shook out her curls. She was glad she couldn't see herself because she felt weary. The strain of the last few days and the long journey from Powerstock – literally crossing the county from west to east – had taken its toll.

However, in time she would embellish the room with, perhaps, another picture or two and a mirror. She would have nothing on which to spend her five shillings a week, so a few little luxuries wouldn't come amiss. She had two good black dresses, one that she was wearing now, and the other in her bag with two chemises and a pair of best shoes made for her by the Powerstock shoemaker, Mr Read, when she was able to afford such things.

Martha sat down on the bed and spread her fingers out on her lap.

She already felt at home in the room. It would be her home, her refuge, for she didn't know how long. Maybe forever. She was beginning to relish the fact that she was purged of all possessions. And so, alone in the world, she could begin again. It was, she supposed, like being reborn. She was being given a second chance.

Martha brushed her hair, poured some water from the jug on the stand into the basin and sluiced her hands and face. Refreshed, she made her way downstairs, along the stone-flagged corridor, into the kitchen.

There an unwelcome surprise, but one she should have expected, awaited her. Standing in front of the range lighting his pipe was Josiah Symes.

He eyed her speculatively as she came in.

'So, Martha! My cousin has just told me the news that you are to be the new housekeeper. Welcome to Blackmanston Farm.'

'Thank you,' she said coldly. 'Can you tell me where the provisions are for supper?'

'Is that all you have to say to me, Martha?' Josiah threw his spill into the fire and puffed at his pipe.

'For the moment.'

'I have done nothing to offend you, Martha.'

'It was not *me* you offended, but my sister . . .'

At that moment John Symes came in, and put some papers down on the table.

'The milking yield is good,' he remarked to his cousin. 'Ah, you and Martha have become reacquainted I see. I had forgotten that Josiah used to work for Bernard.' He turned to her with a pleasant expression on his face.

'That was a long time ago,' Martha said, firmly setting a loaf of bread on the table together with a dish of butter. 'The past is much best forgotten.'

'If you say so, Martha,' John said with a twinkle in his eye. Obviously he was very pleased with his new acquisition and could detect no undertones in the situation. 'I must say I am looking forward to your cooking which I hear is very good. My brother Robert will be delighted you are here.'

And he rubbed his hands together in a gesture of eager anticipation.

Martha, accustomed to changes in her life, soon got used to the routine of Blackmanston Farm which was as well run as she had expected. The brothers and their cousin worked with a surprising degree of harmony, each in charge of his separate sphere in the farm.

John was the farm manager. Generally speaking he was in charge and gave the orders. Robert went about his business quietly, had little to say but was clever and interested in new methods of farming, new techniques in the use of machinery. This was why the farm thrived, mainly because of the skill and dedication of the bachelor brothers.

Martha had known Josiah Symes was a good worker when he put his mind to it, but the extent of his efficiency surprised her. He had indeed come a long way since he worked for Bernard in Powerstock. He was the head stockman, in charge of the cattle, the sheep and the dairy.

Josiah seemed slightly in awe of the brothers, had little in common with them and tended not to socialise but to go off by himself in what little free time he had.

By the time she had breakfast ready for the men, they had each been in the fields or with the cattle for a couple of hours. Sometimes the shepherd, the cowman and one or two boys came to eat with them but, usually, they ate in their cottages, looked after by their wives.

In the course of her first week Martha met them all. They seemed nice, simple people but she didn't expect to strike up any new friendships, and the farm was in an extremely isolated position. Occasionally the men went out to the public house two miles down the road, sometimes taking their wives, but Martha had no inclination to go anywhere except across the fields, in the little spare time she had, for a view of the sea and some fresh salty air which she drew deep into her lungs.

One day, about a week after her arrival she went upstairs in mid afternoon to clean her room which she had neglected while doing the housework elsewhere.

She was busy with her brush and pan when there was a tap at the door and the handle slowly turned.

'Who is it?' she called sharply but the door was already open and Josiah Symes stood on the threshold.

'What is it you want, Josiah?' she asked, flushing with annoyance. 'Is something wrong with your room?'

Josiah put his finger to his mouth in a conspiratorial gesture and gently closed the door.

'I wanted a quiet word with you, Martha,' he said,

coming towards her with a smile on his face, familiar to Martha from the past, of unmistakable lechery. 'You know . . . old times.'

Martha's hand shot out in a warning gesture. 'Don't come a step nearer, Josiah Symes. I want nothing to do with you.'

'But I thought . . .' Josiah halted looking surprised.

'You thought *what*?'

'I thought well, now that you was a widow, like, we could maybe resume our old relationship.'

'You are a *fool*,' Martha laughed sarcastically. 'Do you imagine for one moment that I would take up with you again after what you did to my sister?'

'I did nothing to your sister,' Josiah protested indignantly, ''cept lie with her. And she enjoyed it. Don't let her tell you she didn't.'

'She told me that she came here expecting to marry you.' Martha's voice rose heatedly. 'Instead, she was used as a slave and abused.'

'She was *not* a slave! She never was that. She was paid, like you, and what she did she did willingly. She was certainly not abused. As for marriage . . .' Josiah paused and carefully examined his nails, 'I 'baint the marrying kind, Martha, that's for sure. Never was. I 'spect, like my cousins, I shall remain a bachelor 'til the end of my days.'

'I see. Well, you misled Ann and in my book she was badly treated.'

'She was not badly treated. She left of her own accord.'

'She was with child,' Martha said furiously, stamping her foot. 'Now what do you think of *that*, Josiah Symes?'

Josiah leaned back against the wall, the shock on his face clearly unfeigned.

'With *child*? She never told me.'

'Quite. And what would you have done if she had? Sent her to the workhouse, I expect.'

'I would have married her.' Josiah's distress appeared genuine. 'As God is my witness. I had no idea of her condition, Martha, none at all. I would have married her and given it a name . . .' He paused. 'What happened to the baby?'

'It died. It was stillborn, luckily for her and for you because I don't suppose you would have made a good husband or father.'

'Martha, that is not fair.'

'It *is* fair. Ann is married now to a good man who treats her properly, and will soon give birth to a child in wedlock, which is how it should be.'

Josiah began to walk towards her again, his hand once more outstretched, the smile on his face intended to disarm.

He was still a handsome man, tall and muscular, who wore his years well as, she believed, did she. They were both unattached and she could recall even after all these years the warmth of his kisses, quite unlike any she ever had from Bernard. Momentarily, perhaps from a simple human need to be loved, she weakened, looked across at him; but then suddenly her desire seemed base, her thoughts treacherous, unworthy of her and disloyal to Bernard, and she prepared to rebuff him.

Mistaking her signals, misinterpreting the expressions flitting so swiftly across her face, Josiah said in a wheedling tone: 'Let's make up, Martha. Let's be friends. For you know we had good times. Here we can be of comfort to each other . . .'

As he came close to her she could feel his hot breath on her cheeks, and he made a sudden grab for her. But, too quick for him, Martha stepped back and slapped him hard on the face.

'There, Josiah Symes. I have done that to you before and I will do it again, have no doubt of that. Now get out of this room and stay out, and stay well away from me. I tell you that if you ever *dare* make advances to me again, or suggestions of any kind, I'll tell your cousins just what sort of man you are. If you ask me, even from the little I know of them, being, as they are, such devout churchmen and believing powerfully in the wickedness of the flesh and the sanctity of the marriage vows, they'll throw you out right on your neck and that will be the end of you. And, believe me, I won't try and save you, not a jot. I'll be laughing.'

Interlude

THE YEARS BETWEEN

1841–51

Blackmanston Farm

For ten years Martha Bearn worked diligently as house-keeper to the Symes brothers at Blackmanston Farm. They were, on the whole, contented years devoid of incident, governed by the routine of the farm which in turn obeyed the immutable laws of the seasons. The Isle of Purbeck, where Steeple was situated, was blessed with a temperate climate devoid of extremes of cold and heat.

The even tenor of her life contrasted sharply with the ups and downs of her years in Powerstock. As opposed to those eventful times, absolutely nothing happened in Purbeck except that farm cottages changed hands occasionally as labourers came and went, children were born, animals were bought and sold for slaughter. More stock and land were acquired as the Symes brothers increased in prosperity, although Martha's wages did not.

But she had little need for money, and she was queen of her domain; someone to be looked up to and respected, deferred to and consulted, a person of some importance in her own right. Martha seldom went far from the farm except to visit the sea which she grew to love more and more; as it seemed to represent freedom – a way of escape such as she had always sought but never found, and she knew now that she never would. She would stand on the cliffs at Kimmeridge looking across the Channel and imagine far-off places full of exotic sights such as she had never seen or could even visualise.

Although still not a believer Martha went every Sunday to the pretty little church across the field walking just behind the Symes brothers and ahead of the inhabitants of the cottages, all employees on the farm, who were required to attend Divine Service. Her position in the little procession, which never varied, emphasised her status in the community, not equal to the brothers but more important than anyone else.

Martha never formed any close friendships in all these years. She was not unfriendly but she didn't encourage intimacy or speculation about her past. She was a woman who kept to herself, whom few people could say they knew. A mysterious woman, some felt, who revealed little about herself. In her way too she was just as strict a disciplinarian as John Symes, extending her influence over the labourers and their families by insisting on exacting standards of order and cleanliness. She was a person the men looked up to and the women were a little afraid of.

Although personally austere, Martha was a kindly woman, one to whom people turned in trouble or if children were sick. There was none better to nurse them through the night, lowering a fever with cold compresses or reducing a swelling with a hot poultice; no one quite like Martha to comfort a woman in labour and assist in the safe delivery of a child.

Martha never talked about her own children, but the more observant mothers knew she must have got her knowledge, her maternal concern and nursing skills, from experience.

Martha supposed that she would spend the rest of her life at Blackmanston Farm, or until such time as the Symes brothers decided she was too old to be of further use, as they had with her predecessor. What would she do then? However, she gave little thought to the future but lived in the present.

Once or twice in those ten years Ann visited her with her daughter, Mary-Ann, and gave news of herself and their parents, their sisters and brothers.

But Martha had little desire to see them. She felt that, in their eyes, her life had been a failure. Despite her importance in this tiny community she had come down in the world, and she wished to be spared their recriminations, although she gave as a reason her work and, in an effort to emphasise her status, the fact that without her the farm would fall apart.

It was not true but it served as an excuse because, in truth, she didn't want to leave the place which was now her home. As well as her little room, now pretty with curtains, a fresh bedspread and pictures on the walls, a mirror over the chest containing the wash-basin and jug, she had a little garden of her own where she grew flowers. In the summer she would select a shady patch under a tree and sit there, contented and at peace, admiring the beauties of her surroundings until duty called again and it was time to go in and prepare another meal.

Josiah Symes never attempted to touch her again or initiate any other form of intimacy. Rather like his cousins, he became increasingly insular, taciturn, parsimonious and, like everyone at the farm, went early to bed. Fridays and Saturdays he went to the public house and came back very late, very drunk. The brothers didn't approve but Josiah had proved his value tenfold and, in a spirit of Christian forgiveness, they tolerated this particular weakness.

Although his hair grew thin on top, he never lost his rugged good looks. Unlike Robert and John he eschewed religion and didn't attend church. It seemed that his status as family allowed him to absent himself from the Sunday parade required of everyone else.

Perhaps the reason was because there were times when he disappeared for days and it was rumoured that he went to Wareham or even as far away as Poole. What he did in those places was unrecorded but he always returned seeming much the worse for wear with unsteady gait and bloodshot eyes. After a good night's sleep however he was his normal self and one would never have known what he did when he went on these mysterious trips though one could certainly guess.

Whenever Martha went to Wareham or Swanage it was a big occasion and one on which she would spend some of her accumulated wages on a picture for her room or on her embroidery silks, never very much. Twice in the ten years she bought a new black dress, only after one, much worn and patched and with a shiny seat, was almost reluctantly thrown away as though it had become a friend.

In those years, not unhappy ones, Martha became a creature of habit, set in her ways. It seemed, as she entered her fortieth year, that nothing would ever intervene to disturb the steady pace of her contented and tranquil country life.

Part II
A Man to Die For

1851–6

Birdsmoorgate

Chapter Eleven

March 1851

John Symes finished going through his post, putting the bills on one side, what correspondence he had on another. He was a careful, meticulous man and each paper was itemised and the bills would later be transferred to a ledger, when paid, and the letters answered, if necessary. As he worked, Martha cleared the dishes from the breakfast table and took them over to the sink to begin washing up.

Like much else at the farm this routine seldom varied. They all rose early. John and Robert began their work on the farm, instructed the men about their jobs. Martha fed the hens and lit the fire in the kitchen, fetching in the logs herself. She then prepared breakfast for the boys, of whom there were three now living and working on the farm. Usually when they had finished, or just before, John and Robert, followed by Josiah, would appear, but would usually eat in silence or exchange merely a few words. Sometimes Martha sat with them and had a cup of tea, and then Robert and Josiah went off while John inspected the post which had by that time arrived.

Usually there was quite a lot of it. The well-managed farm had expanded and prospered in the years since Martha became housekeeper and, in addition to the boys, there were five men, their wives and families, and four hundred acres to manage, part-dairy, part-arable.

It was by now quite a sizeable enterprise serviced by a small, hardworking workforce.

The bachelor brothers were much respected by those who worked for them but considered a little eccentric, mainly because they were not married. John Symes was now forty-five and Robert the same age as Martha.

When Martha first arrived there had been a lot of gossip and speculation about her among those there at the time, because she was such a good-looking woman. Bets were placed that one of the brothers, or their cousin Josiah, would soon take this personable widow for a bride. But the speculators were wrong and, in time, everyone grew accustomed to the curious ménage in the farmhouse; three unmarried men and a woman all of whom, most certainly, slept at night in their respective beds.

All the time she was there not a shred of scandal attached itself to Martha. Her status as a widow, symbolised by her black dress, was greatly respected and anyone, any newcomer, who hinted at anything different would be immediately put in their place.

Martha finished clearing the table and gazed at John who was poring over a letter just received.

'It's time I had a maid, you know, John. Someone to help me in the house.'

'I'll get to thinking about it,' John muttered, not raising his eyes from the letter.

'I'm getting on, you know,' Martha said grumpily,

going across to the sink and, rolling up her sleeves, she began to wash the stack of dishes.

'Nonsense.' John looked up at her in surprise. 'You're a young woman.'

'"Young woman" no more. Forty this year.'

'Really? I'd never have thought it,' John said, and went back to his letter.

'I'm quite serious, John,' Martha said with asperity. 'You expect a lot of me and I give good service. My wages have not risen for years and yet the farm grows in prosperity. It may be that one day I'll just take myself off, and then what would you do?'

John looked at her with concern.

'Oh Martha, you must *never* do that. We'd be lost without you. I promise I will consider the matter of additional help.'

'Well, see you do.' Martha returned to her task with a satisfied smile, feeling that she had made her point and made it well.

Between the two there was an easy camaraderie, rather as though they were brother and sister. It was not exactly friendship, but nor was it the relationship of master and servant. They would discuss matters to do with the workings of the farm — staff problems, provisions, any emergencies, sickness and so on — but little else. They would normally eat together in the evening but after she'd cleared the supper dishes the men would go about their business and Martha would sit in the kitchen, close to the range in winter, or outside the back door in hot weather and sew before going early to bed.

'Anyway, at last I've got some good news,' John said, waving the letter he'd been reading. 'We are to have a new dairyman. He writes, or someone writes on his behalf, to say he will be here next week. His name is Robert Brown.'

'Robert Brown.' Martha raised her head and looked thoughtfully out of the window. 'I think I know him. Is he from Marshwood?'

'Originally, yes.'

'He had a young family, if I remember, a boy and a girl.'

'Well, they're not so young now.'

'No, I suppose not.' Martha went on with her work.

'His wife Frances could maybe help you in the house.' John came over to her. 'Don't think I don't appreciate what you do, Martha.' He looked for a moment as though he was going to make some small physical gesture of appreciation – touch her arm or put a hand on her shoulder – but at the last moment decided against it. He returned to the table and got his papers together, preparing to take them to the small office he had next to the kitchen. 'The Browns will be here next week. Maybe you'd prepare the dairyman's cottage for their arrival?'

'Children too?' Martha enquired.

'If you can still call them children, yes.'

Martha was glad they were getting a new dairyman, and it would be nice to have some help in the house. She couldn't remember the Browns very well, nor was she sure it was the same family, but John Symes kept his connections with West Dorset and had recently been there on a visit, so it was possible.

The dairyman's cottage was one of three next to the

farmhouse. The previous occupant had left a few weeks before with his family to take up another position on the Isle of Purbeck. Purbeck wasn't exactly an island. It was a large chunk of land that jutted out to sea, but it was always called 'The Isle', and the Purbeck marble quarried there was celebrated throughout the world for its high quality.

After she finished her chores Martha spent the morning vigorously sweeping out the dairyman's cottage, cleaning and blacking the grate. But everything had been left in good condition by the previous occupants, the dairyman's wife being particularly houseproud, so there was little for Martha to do.

It was a fine, blustery spring day and she threw open the windows and then took the curtains down to wash them and the white counterpanes from the beds. She wondered where the children would sleep? She still thought of them as children, though, as John said, they must be nearly grown up by now.

There had, if she was thinking of the same family, been a dark-haired, impish little boy always into mischief and a pretty but docile and more conventional girl a year or two younger. Well, it would be nice to have some new people about, especially ones she thought she knew and who knew her parents and might have some news of them.

Gathering up the laundry, Martha made her way across the yard to the wash house where she looked with some dismay at the amount of washing that waited to be tackled. How had she managed to cope with all this, and all the cooking and cleaning for ten years? Were it not for the comfort of the place and the conditions she enjoyed it would be like slavery.

Well, if John kept his promise she would soon have some help, and what a relief that would be.

Truly she felt she was indeed getting old.

A week later, Martha finished hanging out the most recent batch of washing and stood for a while watching the sheets and shirts, cloths, counterpanes, socks, nightshirts and other assorted garments flap wildly in the wind. April had come in with much rain and this was one of the few days when it promised to be dry, at least until dinner time. Then there would be a rush to get it all in before it started to pour.

Martha picked up her basket and stood for a minute gazing at the landscape, the hills beyond dotted with sheep peacefully grazing, the land sloughing off the torpor of winter and the trees beginning to show signs of spring. Already the birds were flying about all day long, their beaks stuffed with grass and twigs to build their nests.

It was a very beautiful part of the world, Martha thought, not for the first time, and she was filled momentarily with a feeling of contentment as she wandered back, her basket clasped beneath her arms, a sense that she had indeed found a measure of peace and tranquillity in this place so far from her home.

When she got back to the yard she saw a cart outside the dairyman's cottage piled high with belongings. As she gazed at it a young man emerged from the cottage and began to unfasten the straps over the cart. He was tall and well built with thick long brown hair reaching to his shoulders. He appeared muscular and strong as he lifted a table onto his back, as though it was as light as a feather, and went into the cottage with it. There was no one else in sight. They were probably inspecting the interior of their new home, Martha thought, as she put the laundry basket back in the wash house and went into the kitchen, passing John Symes who stood at the door of his little office filling his pipe.

'I see the Browns have come,' Martha said.

'Yes.' John moved across to the window and looked out into the yard.

'Who's that good-looking young man?' Martha indicated the youth emerging again from the house.

John looked at her with amusement.

'Oh, you find him good-looking do you, Martha? Well that's their son, John Brown.'

'Oh really?' She appeared surprised. 'I would never have recognised him. I thought he was much younger.' As if she was a little embarrassed she turned away into the kitchen and began her preparations for dinner.

'I'll let them settle down before I go and see them,' she called to John.

'No, come over with me now,' John beckoned to her. 'See if they remember you.'

Reluctantly, Martha undid her apron, smoothed her hair and ran her hands down her dress. She didn't know why but she felt a little nervous, not usually the case with new staff. Perhaps it was the association with her past, which for so long she had managed to put behind her, that unsettled her.

However, John Symes had already started towards the cottage and she followed in his wake just as the young man came out again and tugged at a bundle of bed linen which was still partly secured with a rope.

He nodded at her but said nothing as he half staggered, this time with a much greater load, into the house.

Following behind him Martha found a small congregation in the living room all chattering at once.

'You remember Martha Bearn don't you?' John Symes put out his hand to draw her into the group. 'She's our housekeeper.'

'They remember me best as Martha Clark.' Martha smiled shyly. 'Many years ago.'

Robert had been looking at her with surprise. 'Why, I do remember you, Martha. I didn't realise we should find you here.'

'We saw your mother and father not long ago,' Frances Brown put in. 'They never mentioned you.'

'Maybe they had forgotten I exist.' Martha laughed as if she was trying to make light of the gaffe. 'I have been here ten years. How did you find my parents?'

'Your mother looks very frail,' Robert said doubtfully. 'Your father is ailing too.'

'Maybe you should pay them a visit, Martha,' John Symes looked at her.

'One of these days,' she replied offhandedly and turned to the two young girls who were staring at her with interest. 'And these are your daughters? I remember you only had one.'

'This is Christiana,' Robert drew the elder one forward. 'And this is our Bess. The baby.' Her father looked at her with affection and Bess smiled shyly at Martha.

'But you will remember John,' Robert pointed to the young man struggling with yet another large load. 'I'm afraid we're leaving him to do all the work. Never mind: he has broad shoulders.'

'So I see.' Martha acknowledged the young man with a nod of her head. 'I had not realised the children were so grown up.'

Close up Martha thought John Brown even better looking than from a distance. He had a wisp of a beard following his jawline and a moustache that looked like soft down. His deeply set, almond-shaped eyes were of an intense golden brown and long lashes swept his cheeks, almost like a woman's.

Aware of her appraisal he gave a half smile, a little like a swagger and she glimpsed a row of beautifully even, strong teeth.

'You won't remember me, John.'

'No, Mrs Bearn,' he said politely, his Dorset accent heavily pronounced.

'I played with you when you were a little boy, and Christiana.' She turned to the elder girl who had the same colouring as her brother, together with high cheekbones, a pretty mouth and a direct, rather disconcerting stare. 'Little Bess, of course, I never met.' She bent to touch the little girl of about ten who darted shyly behind her mother's back.

'They are all handsome children,' she said admiringly. 'You must be proud.' Then she turned briskly to Frances. 'We'll leave you now. You will have a lot to do. Let me know if you need anything. There is plenty of bread, milk, bacon, and cheese which we make in our own dairy.'

'I'll show you round this afternoon, Robert.' John adopted a practical tone. 'After you've had time to settle down. You can start work with the milking.'

'Christiana, run along with Mrs Bearn and get some provisions for our dinner.' Frances looked across at Martha with a weary smile. 'We haven't eaten since we set out from Owermoigne, and that was before dawn.'

*　　*　　*

The Browns settled in well and proved a useful addition to the community. Robert was an experienced dairyman, helped by his daughter Christiana, while Bess, who was actually eleven, went to the local school.

At first Frances demurred about helping Martha in the house but in the end agreed to do certain hours for an extra shilling a week, a useful addition to the family income of seven shillings.

It was from Frances that the children had got their good looks. She was in her mid forties, a handsome woman with wavy brown hair, strong features and the robust complexion of a countrywoman. She gave the impression of being a prickly, rather difficult, person whereas by contrast Robert Brown was a jovial, warm-hearted man with an easy-going manner. He was not handsome, his features blunt and nondescript, his head partly bald. But what he lost in looks he made up for by being good-natured, a hard worker who took pride in his job. Frances was clearly the dominating influence in the household, rather as Mrs Clark had been in hers.

John Brown already had experience as a shepherd and was put to help Josiah Symes in looking after the sheep.

So the spring passed and by early summer the Browns were fully integrated into the busy life of Blackmanston Farm. The inhabitants of the farmhouse didn't alter their routine. There was little socialising with the Browns and life continued to run its even course as it had for so many years past.

June 1851

Martha was proud of her little garden, tucked round the side of the house, in which she thriftily grew plants from seeds she had collected the previous summer. From May onwards she had a variety of colours which spanned the months until late autumn: roses, foxgloves and hollyhocks, delphiniums, lupins, poppies, scabious, dahlias, antirrhinum, sweet-smelling phlox mingling with bright blue agapanthus, bushes of purple-headed lavender and white, heavy-scented orange-blossom. To one side stood a mature magnolia tree, long predating Martha, with its delicate pink waxy flowers fully in bloom.

It was a bewitching medley of colours and smells, which had taken her years to accomplish, to reach the sort of perfection she desired.

In the summer Martha passed as much of her spare time as she could in her garden, time that she might normally have spent sewing or resting in her bedroom. Her main recreation was taken between the hours of three and five in the afternoon, after serving dinner to the brothers, the boys and unmarried men who worked on the farm, and before cooking supper, sometimes for the same number of people.

This routine hardly ever varied day in and day out, week in and week out, year by year.

Martha seldom had a complete day off, but then she didn't expect it. All her life she had been used to work except, maybe, in the few days before her babies had been born when Bernard had been indulgent towards her and made Joanna do all the work.

Today she had finished her inspection of her plants, had dead-headed where necessary and, conscious of an exceptional feeling of peace and serenity, she sat down in her chair to absorb the best of the day's sun, head back, eyes closed, attuned to the sharp singing of the birds, the distant, somnolent drone of busy bees. A shadow crossed the sun and Martha, opening her eyes, saw John Brown gazing down at her.

'Nice little spot you have here, Mrs Bearn,' he said conversationally.

'Yes, I think so.' Martha shaded her eyes, suddenly powerfully aware of his physical proximity. He was, she decided, exceptionally good-looking, striking in a way that none of the other men were, although perhaps more closely resembling the youthful Josiah Symes in personal magnetism.

'How are you getting on, John?'

'Very well,' John said, continuing to look at her, idly chomping at a blade of grass in the corner of his mouth.

'You like it here, do you?'

'As well as I like anywhere, though it do be awful remote.'

'Yes, it is very far away from anywhere. I suppose you miss the friends you had in Marshwood? Maybe the girls?' She looked at him a little archly.

John mumbled something non-committal and continued to look at her in a way that Martha found disconcerting, not to say suggestive. Although he had been around for three months they had scarcely spoken, never really come across each other despite the fact that his mother helped her most mornings in the main house.

It was perhaps because of that that the Browns tended to keep themselves to themselves, going quietly and diligently about their business, Frances with her in the house, Robert and Christiana in the dairy, and John in the fields minding his sheep. A strange, rather detached young man, she nevertheless found herself thinking about him from time to time, as though he had invaded her mind. Somehow, in a way she couldn't quite fathom, he seemed out of place, restless and anxious to be gone.

Without waiting to be asked, John sat down on the grass beside her, leaning back, propped on his hands, ankles crossed, eyes closed to the sun.

It suddenly felt very right and comforting to have him here by her side and she smiled down at him.

'I expect you're tired. Haymaking is hard work.'

John nodded and looked up at her.

'How long have you been here, Mrs Bearn?'

Martha squinted towards the sky as if calculating.

'Oh, ten years.'

'As long as that?' John thoughtfully digested the information.

'Yes, a long time.'

'And Mr Bearn . . . where is he?'

'Mr Bearn's dead.'

'Ah. I thought you was a widow. Mother didn't seem to know.'

Martha looked surprised. Frances did know, they had talked about the demise of Mr Bearn and also, eventually, about the deaths of her children, information which she had chosen, for some reason, not to pass on to her son.

'Will you stay here long, do you think?' Martha enquired.

'I'll move on some time soon. It's time I started my own life.'

'Yes, I suppose so.' As she had imagined, he was restless here, probably missing the girls as there were few available in these parts. Martha looked at the sun and decided it was time she started preparing the supper. Rather reluctantly, because she was enjoying his company, she rose from her seat and as she did John leapt to his feet and took her hand, helping her up.

His touch was firm, the effect instantly sensual. From the way he clasped her hand and looked at her she thought for a moment that he was going to lean down and attempt to kiss her, but he changed his mind, perhaps deterred by her expression. She knew what a formidable aspect she presented to people — deliberately so as to preserve her privacy.

Their hands fell to their sides and Martha turned and hurried ahead of him aware of a feeling of confusion, of emotions gone strangely haywire.

This wouldn't do at all, and she said no more that day to John Brown.

And yet that night Martha tossed restlessly in her bed, haunted by a pair of dark almond-shaped eyes, by the vision of a male torso naked to the waist such as she had seen from a distance as he worked in the fields. His back was like no other back, straight and strong; his chest, when he turned, covered with soft, silky hair like his beard.

She slept fitfully, and when she awoke her hands were round her throat and she was gasping for breath, her heart drumming painfully in her chest. It was a sensation she hadn't had for many years and she lay staring up at the ceiling, conscious of a feeling of dread combined, at the same time, with a warm sense of erotic pleasure as if she had made love in her sleep.

Finally she rose from her bed, threw off her chemise and washed herself from head to foot in cold water as though to drown her unwholesome thoughts, her feelings of sexual desire. She dried herself and dressed in her usual black, vigorously brushed her hair and descended the stairs to prepare breakfast which she served in her usual way and at the usual time. At nine she started the housework, annoyed that Frances Brown had not yet made an appearance.

But as she felt in need of hard physical work she got down to scrubbing the flagstones of the kitchen and the hall as hard as she could until it was time to think about dinner, though, during haymaking, the midday meal was served at supper time as the men ate in the fields, so she began cutting up the meat and peeling the potatoes.

Soon afterwards Frances Brown arrived looking flustered, dressed not for working but in her best with a bonnet on her head. Martha leaned against the kitchen table and stared at her.

'Well, what hour of the morning do you call this, Frances?'

Frances Brown's hand flew guiltily to her mouth. 'Oh Martha, I forgot to tell you yesterday, but Robert is to go to Wareham to get some feed and asked me to go with him. I hope you don't mind. I should have said . . . oh, and Martha, would you take the men their dinner in the fields? I promise I'll make it up to you.'

'I think you might have told me,' Martha said grumpily, 'but, all right.' She returned to her task. 'You can get some flour from the miller while you're in Wareham.'

'Anything else, Martha?' Frances, in common with everyone else, was a little afraid of the housekeeper and anxious to please.

'No. Have a nice time,' Martha added magnanimously.

'Oh I *will*, Martha, thank you and I promise I'll make it up . . .'

Martha waved Frances away as if she was annoying her. After she put her mutton stew in a large pot to simmer slowly over the range she prepared the fare for the men in the fields, making up little bundles with bread, cheese and an apple which she put in a basket, and a flagon of beer which she carried in her other hand. And thus loaded she set off, quite glad to escape from the gloomy kitchen into the sun on such a nice day.

Haymaking was in full swing, the men, bare to the waist, scything the long grass with which the animals would be fed in winter. As they saw her they put down their implements and, wiping the sweat from their faces with the backs of their hands, came eagerly towards her, grasping the beer she offered and sharing it among them, taking long thirsty gulps as the flagon passed from one to another.

'Where's John?' Martha asked, looking around.

'E's gone to look for stray sheep. One or two were missing when he counted them this morning.' James Giles, one of the workers, pointed across to the fields beyond the church. 'Shall I run along with his dinner, Mrs Bearn?'

'No, I'll take it to him,' Martha said, offhandedly. 'Drink your fill and then give it to me.'

The men passed round the flagon again until Martha thought there would be hardly any left, so she snatched it from them saying gaily: 'Leave a little for poor John.'

'"Poor John",' Emanuel Rideout mimicked, giving

her a knowing look. 'Work here's too hard for he, if you asks *me*, Mrs Bearn.'

Martha said nothing, but as the men sat down to eat she walked past them across the fields to where, behind the church, a flock of sheep was contentedly grazing in the noon sun.

But of John Brown there was no sign. Suppressing a feeling of disappointment Martha was about to lay down the basket and flagon by the wall in the hope that he would find it when she saw movement in the long grass. Looking down, she found John Brown, bare to the waist, stretched out and gazing up at her in surprise, rather bleary-eyed as if he had just woken from sleep.

'Oh!' she cried, startled.

'Sorry to frighten you, Mrs Bearn.' John sat up slowly, rubbing the sleep from his eyes. 'The heat made me feel tired . . .'

'And did you find your lost sheep?' Martha asked tartly, as though she disapproved of such laziness when those about him were working.

Momentarily John looked puzzled. 'Oh, I see. That was just an excuse. I haven't lost no sheep but my arms ached with scything.'

'Not used to it, I expect.' Martha held the flagon out to him. 'I saved you some beer. The men didn't want to part with it.'

''Spect not,' John put it to his lips and drank thirstily. Then he wiped his mouth and held it out to her.

'You want some?'

'No thank you.' Martha carefully averted her eyes from his body, half naked, just as it had appeared in her dream. 'I must get back now.'

'Stay awhile,' John said in a pleading tone. 'It is

so nice and restful here, just like your garden, Mrs Bearn.'

'I like my garden better,' Martha said firmly. 'I must return to my work.' But, as she turned, a hand caught at her ankle and held onto it.

'I said stay awhile,' John insisted. 'It's lovely here in the sunshine.'

'Please take your hand off my ankle,' Martha commanded. 'You're taking a great liberty with me.'

'Then why did you come instead of my mother? It was to see me, wasn't it?'

'It certainly was *not*,' Martha said indignantly. 'It never entered my head that you would be here alone. Your mother asked me because she's gone with your father to Wareham.'

'Honestly?' John still held onto her ankle. 'You didn't want to see me?'

'Honestly!'

'I fancied you'd taken a liking to me, Mrs Bearn. I seed it in your eyes.'

'I am old enough to be your mother,' Martha said sharply. 'Remember that.'

'I wish you were. No, I don't,' he corrected himself. 'I wish you were my lover.'

With a swift movement he caught her arm and pulled her down beside him. She fell quite clumsily but without hurting herself. John immediately put one arm around her, both to imprison and to cushion her, threw the other tightly across her body, and then he kissed her hard and long until her lips felt sore. Supposing her to be acquiescent he began to unbutton her dress, slipping in his hand to grasp her breast.

Summoning all her strength, Martha struggled to

an upright position and slapped him hard in the face. Astonished, he let go and, taking advantage of his confusion, she got awkwardly to her feet and hurriedly rearranged her clothing, buttoning up her dress and smoothing her hair which was also in disarray.

As he lay confounded on the grass she leaned down and smacked him again, this time harder.

'Don't you *dare*,' she said, 'try that again.' Then she seized her basket, grabbed the empty flagon and ran across the fields, his furious words resounding in her ears. 'You can't escape me, Mrs Bearn. I know thee want me and I want thee, and I'll have thee yet!'

Chapter Twelve

The more Martha avoided John Brown the more she felt drawn to him, especially as the memory of that long, harsh, but deeply sensuous, kiss reminded her of the distant embraces of Josiah Symes, reawakening memories of her passionate youth. She would watch for him out of the kitchen window or from the corner of her bedroom, and quickly step back if she felt he had seen her. Her mind, once so peaceful, was now in a frenzy of indecision, of wanting and not wanting, of desire and rejection. Above all, she seemed to have abandoned the common sense and decorum which had been her mark as the respected, and respectable, housekeeper at Blackmanston Farm.

Sometimes when her back was turned she imagined she heard John's step behind her, his eyes boring into her, but when she looked round he was not there.

Occasionally they did encounter each other – in the yard or the fields or walking along the path – and would exchange glances but not speak. One day he came into the kitchen to talk urgently to his mother – something secret not meant for her ears – and it was an agony knowing that he was so near, yet so far away.

For several days Martha didn't see him at all. It was after his conversation, conducted in whispers, with his mother, and in a panic she thought he'd gone away. When she was in a chatty mood Frances always spoke of him being restless in such a quiet place, but Martha didn't dare betray her interest in her helper's son. Instead, a feeling of depression descended on her which only lifted when she saw him again cross the yard. Immediately her spirits soared and a sense of elation carried her through the rest of the day.

So this curious game continued until one hot afternoon in mid July when Martha went into the dairy for some fresh milk, that in the kitchen having soured. The dairy was empty and so cool that she was inclined to linger and, as she poured milk from the churn into the jug, she thought of her young days as a dairymaid; and as often happens, those times seemed happy ones when in retrospect, in fact, they were not always so. There was the continual war with her mother, the perpetual moving about the country, the lack of security, the longing to get away. There was . . .

Suddenly she felt a hand lightly caress her buttocks then slip round her waist. She turned angrily and saw John gazing down at her with those limpid brown eyes, so adoringly that, instead of beating him on the chest, her knuckles already clenched, as she intended, she hesitated. Then, as his other arm came round she felt her body, so long disciplined and restrained, relax, go limp, and she sank into his arms. This time the long warm kiss was a mutual one. Finally, guiltily, she pushed him gently away but he pulled her to him again.

229

'Don't be silly,' he murmured.

'This can't go on. I'm so afraid,' Martha said, glancing towards the door. 'At any moment someone might come in.'

'Then, when?' He looked at her appealingly. 'When?'

'Come, if you can, to my room tonight,' she said, and put a hand on his chest. 'But be careful.'

And then she fled, leaving the jug full of fresh milk behind.

Martha lay in her bed watching the door in the light of the moon. She hoped he wouldn't come. It would be an act of unpardonable folly. Stupidity. Once it had begun how would it end? She slipped out of bed and put the chair against the door. What had got into her in the dairy she didn't know. Well, she did. Lust. Desire.

John Brown had been quite right. She wanted him as much as he wanted her. In her middle age she was considering behaving in a way that she would frown on in a younger woman. Maybe that was why: because she was middle-aged and life had gone by so quickly.

Anyway, now he couldn't get in. Tomorrow she would explain why. She would suggest that, after all, he should go away and leave her free from temptation, from ruining her reputation, perhaps losing her job. For heaven knew what would happen if the churchgoing Symes brothers found out.

The door handle suddenly turned, the chair wobbled but held. Martha watched it spellbound. The handle turned again. There was a pause. Now he might go away . . .

Suddenly she flew out of bed, moved the chair, opened the door and saw John about to steal down the stairs. He turned back and she put a finger to her lips, stood aside to let him in.

'Did anyone see you?' she whispered.

He shook his head, then looked at the chair standing by the door.

'This is madness,' Martha said.

He reached out for her. 'I know.'

He drew her into his arms and they kissed again. He reached for the hem of her nightgown and drew it up over her head, throwing it on the floor. He caressed her body as she stood before him and then he kissed her breasts tenderly and lowered her gently onto the bed.

As their bodies met, there was an intensity of warmth and love, tenderness, sweetness yet rawness that was unlike anything she had ever known in her life.

In the middle of their lovemaking he paused.

'Should I finish outside, Martha?'

'Oh no,' she cried, 'I am too old to have a child.' She drew him even closer to her until the explosion came, engulfing them both.

Now there was no turning back.

They lay in the moonlight, naked, bodies entwined. John seemed to be asleep but Martha was too excited to close her eyes. He lay with his head resting on his arm and she let her fingers run gently through his hair, giving his face little kisses, wanting him to start again.

When he awoke he kissed her tenderly and the expression on his face was curiously humble.

'Thank you,' he said.

Martha didn't reply but smiled. To thank him would be meaningless. She felt at that moment that she owed him the world.

'Tell me, Martha,' he whispered. 'How old are you?'

'How old do you think?'

'I have no idea.'

'Nearly as old as your mother.'

'It doesn't matter. I don't care how old you are. You're a wonderful looking woman. When I first saw you I fancied you, you know.'

'All that time back?' she asked skittishly.

'Immediately. I could tell you were scared.'

'Not scared,' she said indignantly. 'Just cautious. You know what people say.'

'People will never know.'

'You must be very, very careful.'

'Don't worry. As I was coming past the old man's door I heard him snoring away.'

Martha smiled to herself.

The 'old man', Robert Symes, was the same age as her.

The summer passed in a whirl of emotion alternating between ecstasy and misery. The ecstasy of lying in his arms, the misery of not knowing the future.

Violent sexual images haunted her during the day, erotic manifestations of their tempestuous lovelife.

Every night Martha lay waiting for John and every night, without fail, he did not disappoint her. He came silently up the stairs, past the snoring Robert's door and up the narrow flight that led to her bedroom. She was ready for him and the rest of the night, almost until dawn, was spent in a frenzy of lovemaking.

It made for a very tired Martha, who had to get up

an hour or two later and sometimes she saw John Symes looking at her with concern.

'Are you taking enough care of yourself, Martha?' he asked one September day when Martha, half asleep, sat at the kitchen table peeling potatoes.

'Oh yes, I think so,' she said without looking up.

'Maybe you should have more help?'

'I have enough help, thank you, John.'

'Have you seen John Brown?' Symes asked suddenly and Martha, thinking he was a mind-reader, nearly dropped her knife.

'No . . . no. Why do you ask?'

'Because when I want him I can never find him. He's a lazy good-for-nothing. Spends his day skiving.'

'Oh, I don't think so,' Martha said defensively. 'I thought him a good worker.'

'You thought wrong. We had several cases of foot-rot in the sheep which he never even noticed. I could lose my flock that way.'

'Maybe it's due to inexperience?'

'Maybe it's due to laziness, you mean,' he retorted. 'I don't know why you try and defend him, Martha.'

'Then you should have a word with him, John.'

'I will, or tell him to look for work elsewhere.'

Later, in the intimacy of her bedroom, Martha said:

'You should take more care when you go to sleep in the fields. John is dissatisfied with you.'

'And *I'm* dissatisfied with him,' John said petulantly. 'Really, Martha, I would like to be gone from this place.'

'Oh, don't say that.' She flung her arm tightly round him. 'What would I do?'

'You could come with me.'

She was silent for a while before replying.

'You didn't really mean that, John.'

'Why not?'

'Because . . . I am old enough to be your mother. You will tire of me and want someone younger, children . . .'

'I will never tire of you, Martha.' He wound his arms around her. 'Never. But Martha,' he whispered, nuzzling her cheek, 'there is a favour I want to ask of you.'

'Oh? What is that?'

'You're too pretty to be wearing black all the time. It makes you look old. Why do you do it?'

'I do it in memory of my husband and children.'

'But, my love, they have been gone a long time.' His arms around her tightened. 'For me, for the new life we have together, will you go into Wareham one day and buy yourself a new pretty dress? Something colourful. Please?'

'I'll think about it,' Martha said a little teasingly and, although she was nagged by a feeling of disloyalty, it also seemed to her a signal of liberation from the sadness of her past life.

A few days later Martha cadged a lift from John Symes to Wareham and returned with a pretty dress of blue fustian with a close-fitting bodice, a plain skirt and long sleeves with deep cuffs. When she took her apron off in the evening she wore over her bodice a pretty fichu of muslin edged with lace.

Martha's transformation immediately became the talk of everyone on the farm. Not only did she look prettier, and younger, but far less formidable. However, the housekeeper was still capable of inspiring awe around her, and no one but her lover dared comment on it for fear she would turn on them and tell them to mind their own business.

Early in October Martha was feeding the hens in the yard when a young man on a horse approached and stopped beside her.

'Do you know where the Brown family lives?'

'Over there,' Martha said, pointing to the middle cottage.

'Thank you.' The young man smiled at her. 'Are they at home do you know? My name is Richard Damon. Frances Brown is my aunt.'

At that moment Frances herself appeared at the door of the cottage and came running over to greet her nephew who jumped down from his horse and embraced her.

'Richard!' Frances cried with pleasure. 'What brings you here, my boy?'

'I came for a visit, Aunt.'

'Nothing wrong?' she asked anxiously.

'Nothing,' he smiled reassuringly.

'But you're not living near here, are you?'

'No. I had some business to do in Wareham and took the fancy to pay my favourite aunt a visit.'

'Well I'm glad you did.' As she hooked her arm through his, she turned towards Martha. 'This is the housekeeper, Mrs Bearn.'

'How do you do, Mrs Bearn?' Richard said politely.

'How do you do?' Martha replied.

'Your cousin John will be glad to see you,' Frances

said as they walked away. 'He finds it awful lonely in these parts.'

That night John didn't come to Martha's room, nor for many nights after. He offered no explanation but she frequently saw him about with his cousin and at night she thought they went to the inn or maybe as far as Corfe.

Richard Damon's presence agitated Martha. She experienced the first pangs of jealousy she had had since the affair began. Even though she knew it wouldn't last, the fear was there that John would soon go away and leave her. What was more natural than that he should be led astray by his cousin, maybe out in the village looking for girls?

Now she was unable to sleep, not as a consequence of lovemaking but from jealousy, and all the old doubt and insecurity returned at the thought of losing him.

Finally one morning she turned to Frances Brown who was blacking the grate before lighting the fire and enquired casually:

'How long is your nephew staying?'

'Not long,' Frances replied. 'A few days. He has a sweetheart to go back to,' she added disapprovingly, 'and she won't like him being gone long. For John it's different.'

'How do you mean "different"?' Martha asked.

'Well, he's not attached. He can do what he likes with the girls.'

Martha kept her head bowed so that Frances should not see the expression on her face, but Frances was watching her keenly.

'I seed you making eyes at John, you know, Martha.'

'That's not true,' Martha said, stamping her foot.

'But I seed you. Every time he passes the window your face lights up.'

'You think I'd be interested in a man so much younger than me . . . or he in me? Why, you say he goes with the girls.'

'I don't *say* he goes with the girls,' Frances said in a malicious tone of voice. 'I don't know what he does except that sometimes he's out all night. The fact is my son is restless. I think he may well go back to the Marshwood Vale with his cousin and leave here altogether.' She paused and looked meaningfully at Martha. 'Perhaps a good thing, Martha, don't you think?'

But Martha didn't reply and went out into the yard to scatter corn for the hens.

Whatever the cause, the fact was that the visit of Richard Damon, the cousin from the Marshwood Vale, marked a turning point in the relationship between John Brown and Martha Bearn. Matters that had been simmering were brought to a head, and the reasons were not difficult to see.

John Brown was very restless, he was out of favour with John Symes and he was anxious to be gone.

The night following the departure of his cousin, John came to Martha's room and slipped silently into bed beside her. Martha felt withdrawn, resentful, prickly and not in a mood for lovemaking.

She acquiesced however until it became obvious that John was not at his best either. At length he lay on his back, head on his arms and sighed deeply.

'Can't make it. Sorry.'

'Is it that you've been with another woman?' Martha said accusingly.

'Oh, that's what you think?'

'Your mother . . .'

'My mother doesn't know anything.'

'She said . . . she hinted that you and Richard went to look for girls.'

'My mother doesn't like you,' John said. 'She'd say that to upset you.'

'I know. She told me I was making eyes at you.'

John laughed softly and his mood seemed to change. He put his arm round her and drew her closer.

'It's just that Richard set me thinking.'

'He's made you restless, I can tell.'

'I was restless before. More so now. Richard said that in Birdsmoorgate in the Marshwood Vale there is a little house with a shop. That's what set me thinking.'

Martha didn't reply and the touch of his hand, the feel of his skin next to hers filled her with deep sorrow.

'I knew I would lose you,' she said. 'I knew that one day you'd leave me.'

'But I don't want to leave you, Martha,' he whispered. 'I want you to go with me. Wouldn't you like a little shop?'

Such was the surprise, the shock, that Martha thought her heart would stop beating.

'You mean to take me with you?'

'Yes.'

'But how can I leave here where I am so safe and secure?'

'You'll be safe and secure with me.' There was another pause, this time a longer one. John turned to her, studying her face in the little light that came from outside. 'Have you got any money, Martha?'

'Money?' She looked at him uncomprehendingly.

'For the shop?'

'Oh, I see. Well yes,' she sounded wary, 'I have a little put by.'

'That's good.' John gave a sigh of relief and squeezed her hand. 'All we have to decide now is when we go.'

'We can't just "go",' Martha objected.

'Why ever not?'

'Because . . . I am a respectable woman. I can't just go off with you and lose my reputation, you must know that. I am respectable and I always have been. If you want my money, you must marry me, John. Before we go anywhere we must be wed. Besides . . .' she paused, 'you do love me, John, don't you?'

'Of course I do.'

'Or are you worried about what people might say about marrying a much older woman?'

'Of course I'm not.' His tone was robust, but she thought his voice sounded strained.

After a while he got out of bed and dressed without making love to her. Then he let himself out of the room as silently as he had entered it.

After he'd gone Martha lay for a long time staring into the inky-black darkness illuminated from time to time by the moon emerging from between the clouds. It was a clear night and she wondered what the winter would bring. This winter and all subsequent winters would, she knew, if she remained here at Blackmanston Farm, vary very little. One winter would be just like all the others, past and to come. They would be cold, sometimes the roads might be closed because of snow.

There would be drifts in the fields and, inevitably, animals lost. Then spring would come and the cycle of the seasons would begin all over again. She would grow old along with Robert and John and she would never know what she had missed.

But to throw in her lot with a much younger man? Was it wise? Did he love her, really love her or had he realised that his particular way of escape lay through her money, what little money she had saved over the years from her wages, lying in a tin under her mattress?

Martha tossed the question around in her mind all night but by dawn she was no nearer reaching a firm decision.

Martha went down the stairs, fastening her apron, already a little late for the preparations for breakfast. To her surprise Josiah Symes was stoking the fire in the kitchen having got down before her and lit it, an event indeed because he was someone who never expected to have to raise a hand to help in the house.

'I'm a little late this morning, Josiah,' she said, hastening across to the larder.

'*And* I know why,' Josiah said gravely as she stood by the door.

'Oh, and why is that?' Her tone deliberately casual she opened the larder door to emerge a second or two later with the ham and eggs, bread and cheese needed for breakfast, together with a string of fat sausages that the butcher in Corfe had made from Blackmanston Farm meat.

'I saw John Brown coming out of your room in the early hours of this morning.'

'Oh, did you? Noseying around were you?'

'No.' His tone was dignified. 'I had gone to relieve myself. I had no doubt about it and, for that matter, it wasn't the first time.'

'So you snooped, I suppose?' In her irritation Martha began vigorously cutting the ham and putting large slices into the frying pan. Her manner was calm but her mind was in turmoil.

All her mental gymnastics the night before had been futile. Whatever happened now her future clearly was not at Blackmanston Farm.

'I'm going to tell my cousins, Martha, that you are fornicating with this young man. It is my Christian duty, and I have no doubt what they will do.'

'*That* should give you satisfaction!' she said, looking at him scornfully. 'Peeping Tom.'

'I am not a peeping Tom but immorality of that nature cannot be tolerated in this household.'

'In that case,' Martha, beside herself with anger, marched up to him, her large kitchen knife tucked purposefully under her arm. 'I shall also tell John about you and what you did to my sister. Fornication indeed! Fornication *and* treachery.'

'But . . . but,' Josiah spluttered, 'that happened years ago.'

'No matter,' Martha said firmly. 'The fact is that it happened. I shall tell them that you slunk up to the room where I am now and that you left her with child. Then I daresay we shall find ourselves on the same path away from Blackmanston Farm.' And with a look of undeniable satisfaction on her face Martha returned to the table and resumed her preparations for breakfast leaving Josiah to fume silently.

'So?' She looked up after a while. 'Is it a bargain?'

She waited for him to reply but as he remained silent she continued: 'Anyway, we are to be wed. John wants to marry me.'

'I don't believe it,' Josiah gasped. 'Why should he want to marry a woman twice his age?'

Martha stared at him defiantly.

'Because he loves me.'

'If you believe that, Martha Bearn, you're a fool. Why should a young, good-looking man with everything before him want to tie himself for life to a barren old woman like you?' Josiah paused and smiled as if an amusing thought had struck him. 'Why, he must be after your money. I 'spect you've some put by.'

Martha experienced a sudden, overpowering sense of anger that left her shaking. She clenched the knife in her hand, feeling its power beneath her palm. Slightly nauseous, struggling to control her wildest impulses, she carefully put the knife down on the table wiping her sweaty palm on her apron. All the time her eyes were on Josiah Symes who, however, did not flinch.

'Do you take that back, Josiah?' she demanded, but he was not deterred.

'I can think of no other reason, Martha, why . . .' he began jauntily, stopping abruptly as Martha's hand made contact with his cheek, and she slapped him not twice but three times, for good measure, hard across the face. His hands went up to protect his cheeks as he staggered back, peering at her through his fingers as though unable to believe what had happened.

'My God, Martha, you never learn, do you? I thought the years would bring you wisdom and control but they haven't. Instead you've shown yourself in your true colours.' Then he hurried from the room leaving

Martha once again wishing she could undo what she had done.

Despite all the commotion, her regret at her precipitate action, Martha managed sufficiently to pull herself together to cook the breakfast to which everyone came as usual, though Josiah well after the others. His face was flushed and he avoided her eyes, as she avoided his. However, she did not sit down to drink tea with the men at the breakfast table but got on with the washing up and after they left was about to clean the floor when Frances Brown stole sulkily into the kitchen.

'You're late again, Frances,' Martha said crisply. 'It won't do, I'm afraid.'

'Don't you speak to me like that,' Frances said, eyeing her malevolently. 'Child-stealer!'

'I *beg* your pardon?' Martha drew herself to her full height. 'Did I hear you properly?'

'You heard me properly right enough,' Frances hissed. 'I nearly fainted when I heard from John this morning that you were to marry. I knew you were making eyes at him and you denied it.'

'Why not deny it,' Martha said with a sparkle, 'when he was my lover already?'

The remark appeared to infuriate Frances. 'You're a shameless whore,' she shouted. 'When I think how everyone respects you. *I* don't, of course. I know the truth, what kind of person you really are. Tricked my boy into marrying you. Yet you must know he's only after your money.'

'That's not true,' Martha said furiously. 'John loves me for who I am and what I am.'

'You can try and deceive yourself for as long as you

like,' Frances sneered. 'The truth is he's so keen to get away and when he's spent all your money, because he hasn't a penny of his own, he'll leave you and go off with someone more his own age. Just you see . . .'

Martha felt like slapping her, but she clenched her fists tight against her side and took deep breaths in an effort to control herself. One outburst that day was quite enough. It would never do to hit her future mother-in-law, however provoked, so it was with a sense of relief that she saw John coming across the yard and, in a moment he appeared at the doorway and stood listening to his mother's tirade, the fury on his face plain to see. He rushed across the room and took her roughly by the arm shaking her until she stopped.

'Now Mother, I won't have you talking like that to Martha. She doesn't deserve it and what you say is not true. She certainly did *not* steal me. I stole her. I loved her from the beginning. As for only wanting her money, it is a very evil thing you suggest. We'll have a little business of our own and our own house. You should be happy for me, Mother, that I found such a fine woman with whom I can settle down.'

'"Happy" for you,' Frances jeered, throwing the mop she had in her hands down on the floor. 'I *pity* you, and don't come running back to me when things go wrong.' She then turned sharply on her heels and ran out of the door while Martha turned her eyes a little anxiously on John.

'Take no notice of Mother,' John said, stroking the damp curls away from her forehead and kissing her brow. 'In no time we shall be gone from here and will never come back.'

'May it be soon,' Martha said fervently, trying to fight against the fear and apprehension which had insidiously begun to creep upon her.

Just supposing everyone was right and she was wrong?

On the evening of that same day Frances Brown sat huddled in a corner of the kitchen in her cottage, her face a picture of grief. Next to her sat Robert aimlessly poking at the fire while on the far side were Christiana and her boyfriend Thomas Barnes, a dairyman from a farm in East Stoke. Also present at the family conference was Sarah Brown, Robert's sister who was paying them a visit.

'There's no doubt Martha set her cap at poor John,' Frances wailed shaking her head. 'He didn't have a chance. The day I saw her walking in with that fancy new blue dress — so unsuitable at her age — after wearing mourning all these years, I knew she was after my boy.' She gazed mournfully round the room. 'I seed her following him around with her eyes. I tell you no good can come from it . . .'

'There, there, Frances,' Josiah said, attempting to cheer her up but having little hope of success. Frances was a woman of lugubrious disposition who enjoyed a good moan. 'You shouldn't be bitter.'

'But I *am* bitter,' Frances insisted fiercely. 'Of course I'm bitter. Who wants an old woman for a daughter-in-law?'

'That's not fair to Martha,' Robert protested. 'She doesn't look her age.'

'Who wants to be *fair* to Martha?' Frances scoffed. 'Was she fair to us? Was she honest about her intentions to ensnare a younger man? She'll never have children.

How can she make him happy? What else can you expect with that age difference?'

Sarah Brown was a woman of a practical turn of mind who normally got on with her sister-in-law but now found herself disagreeing with her.

'I don't know Mrs Bearn,' she said. 'But I must tell you, Frances, that from what I've seen she strikes me as a pleasant, sensible woman . . .'

'You never complained about her before.' Christiana seemed to agree with her aunt.

'That's because I didn't then know she was going to snatch my son away from me. But when I began to suspect such goings on I kept my eyes on her . . . and I seed . . . and I knew.'

'Mother,' Christiana pleaded, 'John wanted to go. He's never been happy as a shepherd in Steeple.'

'True,' Robert, who hated tension in the family, said soothingly. 'I know that John Symes is not very happy with our John. He neglects his duties. Richard Damon unsettled him too much.'

'More like that woman unsettled him,' Frances sniffed. 'Not enough young girls here in these parts. But he still didn't need to think he had to marry her. If you ask me, she insisted. She ensnared him with her money. I can't see John ever doing it on his own. Oh, how I would give anything for him to be free of her . . .'

Frances put her head in her hands and wept.

January 1852
John Symes sat across the room from Martha, his expression solemn.

'Are you sure you're doing the right thing, Martha?'

'I'm quite sure, John,' Martha nodded vigorously.

'The Browns don't think so.'

'Frances Brown doesn't think so, but she has always been very possessive of my John. Kept him tied to her apron strings.'

John Symes raised an eyebrow. 'Perhaps *you* will do likewise, Martha?'

'I certainly shall not,' Martha said hotly. 'I shall be a wife, not a mother. It is not *all* the family who disapprove of me. Sarah Brown, a woman I scarcely know, has been quite kindly disposed towards me and Tom Barnes will be a witness at our wedding. Robert Brown, though afraid of his wife, still smiles at me when she's not about.' Martha paused and then gave a heartfelt sigh. 'Don't think I would not like the approval of the family but it is what is between John and me that matters.' She looked affectionately towards him. 'Anyway, I have been here a long time, John. Maybe it's good to have a change.'

'We shall miss you very much.' John opened a drawer and withdrew from it an envelope which he put into her hand. 'There is something in there to help you start your married life. I know we never paid you very much, but you have had a comfortable life here and as you were never extravagant I expect you have a bit put by.'

'Why, thank you, John.' Martha beamed with pleasure, tucking the envelope into the pocket of her dress and, seeing the gesture, John Symes thought again how attractive Martha had become since she had discarded her black for the colour blue. There was a lightness in her step and a ready smile instead of her previously rather grim, set features.

It was amazing what love could do for a woman.

'I won't hide it from you that I find John Brown a young man reluctant to work. I think he's an idler. I hope he won't disappoint you, Martha.'

'Oh, John won't disappoint me,' Martha said, getting up. 'I have no fears on that score. Once we have our own little shop –' she took the envelope out of her pocket and waved it at him – 'and thank you for this gift, John – we shall be as happy as two peas in a pod.'

Martha made her way from John's office, through the kitchen and along the flagstoned hall towards her room. It was time to start packing. The licence had been obtained and they were off to Wareham in two days' time.

Reaching her room she stood for a few moments reflectively looking through the small window up at the bright starlit sky. She recalled the day she had arrived and been shown to this room by John Symes.

She placed her candle on her dressing table and looked around. Then it had been bare and stark, now she had made it cosy and comfortable.

She would miss it. It was a little den, a love nest too. Here she had known peace and also nights of tumultuous passion such as she had never experienced in her life. Now, instead of being deserted, she was to be married to a man she loved and who loved her, she was sure of that. A whole new life was starting for her. Yet it was with a mixture of sadness as well as joy that she began putting her few possessions together to prepare for her departure.

She was sure that John would not come this night, but soon they would be together forever.

* * *

Martha Bearn and John Anthony Brown were married in the register office in Wareham on 24 January 1852. The witnesses were Thomas Barnes and Sarah Brown and on this occasion Martha, having practised long and hard, signed her name without difficulty. As she finished her task the thought flew through her mind how proud Bernard would have been of her.

After the brief ceremony the couple, the witnesses, and Christiana, who had defied her mother to go along, went to a nearby public house for a few drinks. Then, in a borrowed cart, the newly-weds, well wrapped against the biting cold, set off together to start life afresh in Birdsmoorgate, a small village in the heart of the beautiful Marshwood Vale.

Chapter Thirteen

September 1852

Martha looked with satisfaction around her little shop, now stocked with a variety of supplies such as might be needed by the local community, the isolated hamlets and farms in the locality. Their inhabitants would come the few miles to Birdsmoorgate for necessities such as tea, sugar, flour, potatoes, root vegetables and, occasionally, a few luxuries such as jam or honey.

It had taken eight months and nearly all of her money to furnish the shop with goods and also the house, which was small but cosy and in tolerably good condition when they arrived there following their marriage in January. It had been a happy time building a home as well as a little business, exciting in a way Martha had never expected, and also demanding. But they worked hard during the day and went to bed early. Their lovemaking seemed even better than at the farm where they always had to worry about noise or whether John had been seen entering or leaving her bedroom.

All that uncertainty and anxiety was over and all those who had prophesied disaster had been proved wrong.

The house was entered through the shop and had a main room, a kitchen and up the stairs two bedrooms. It was not as big as Meadways but it was snug and warm and above all, it was theirs, the home of Mr and Mrs John Brown. Martha had such joy and pride in this.

However Birdsmoorgate was not the place she would have chosen to live in. Because of its situation on an escarpment almost within sight of the sea, it had a sort of grandeur, but nothing of the beauty of Powerstock or the peace and remoteness of Steeple. It consisted of a number of houses on the main road to Broadwindsor and a junction where the road, with more houses, led south-west to Marshwood, where John had been born, and north-east to Blackdown where those who worshipped went to church, Birdsmoorgate not having one of its own. The village was a cold place, bleak in winter, the houses continually buffeted by winds blowing in from the sea. Martha had at first been keen to make friends, to be a useful part of the small community, but the villagers seemed to keep her at arm's length, regarding her with suspicion, a curiosity on account of her age and that of her husband.

She hoped that as time passed this would change, she would become accepted, and the shop was a good opportunity to make this happen. She was always welcoming and helpful, and slowly attitudes had improved.

Her appearance was always pleasing. To her natural good looks, her olive skin, brown eyes and gleaming dark curls, was added a good dress sense. She dressed neatly – usually in black as she considered it more businesslike – always with a white apron over her dress and white cuffs to protect her sleeves. She looked the cool, capable woman she had learned to become, but some continued to resent her and thought her uppity.

John's cousin, Richard Damon, lived about a hundred yards away on the other side of the village. His wife-to-be, Susan, was much younger than Martha but she went out of her way to be kind and helpful to her and a sort of friendship had sprung up between the two women.

Over the past months Martha had endeavoured to keep her head, as well as a pleasant smile on her face, and to ignore the snubs and rude innuendos when they came her way.

One problem however that did not go away was the neighbours who lived almost opposite: William Davis, his wife Mary and a small son. William Davis was a carpenter, thirty years older than his wife who was twenty-seven, a pretty woman with golden hair and a flirtatious manner. Martha had gathered in a very short time that Mrs Davis had a reputation in the neighbourhood for liking the company of other men.

She too kept a shop but without the range of goods that Martha had, or any of her skill in selling them, and she had to take in washing to help with the family income.

Mary used to come and peer into the window of Martha's shop and then when she saw Martha looking at her she would run away. Martha was sure it was just to annoy her and she took a dislike to Mary Davis which seemed to be mutual. But Martha was too busy, and too happy, to mind too much about any of the neighbours, or Mary Davis in particular. She perceived her as a nuisance rather than as a threat.

She had her John and she loved him. And, despite all the gossip and innuendos, she knew he loved her.

Today she had a special reason for rejoicing and she bustled about her shop making up bundles of goods for John to take to people who had ordered them. John spent the morning in the shop and the afternoon delivering. Sometimes he was away for more than the amount of time it should have taken to deliver a few items up and down the road and Martha suspected he dropped by at the Rose and Crown because he always returned in good humour.

This particular day John came back late in the afternoon after his errands, a little breathless from his exertions.

'Now, I have things here for Harriet Knight,' Martha pointed to a pile and then indicated another. 'These are for Mrs Sampson. While you're that way, dear, you can take some flour and a sack of potatoes to the Rose and Crown. Mrs Staunton sent down a boy . . .'

'Then why didn't he take them back?' John demanded truculently.

'Because he was only a *small* boy and the potatoes are very heavy.' Martha looked at him in surprise.

'Martha,' John sat on the sack of potatoes and folded his arms. 'All this fetching and carrying is very hard for me.'

'But you're a fine strong man, my John,' Martha said, and she went over to him throwing her arms round his neck, and gazed adoringly into his eyes. 'I have some very special news.'

'What news?' John asked.

'I am going to have a baby.'

'What? How?' John pushed her gently away and struck his brow with amazement. 'I thought you told me you couldn't?'

'I thought I couldn't too. But,' she patted her trim stomach, 'I'm fairly sure.' Noticing his expression she looked at him anxiously. 'You *are* pleased, John, aren't you?'

'Well . . .' John scratched his head as though she had presented him with a problem rather than a present. 'The fact *is*, Martha, I was going to ask you if you had any money left to buy a cart and now you tell me we are to be parents.'

Martha's face fell. 'I thought you'd be pleased, John, and all you can say is that you would prefer a cart.' Martha's tone betrayed her disappointment.

'Don't try and muddle me, Martha,' John said tetchily. 'I don't mean that at all. I'd be pleased to have a child, hoping, of course that it is a boy, but I sorely need a cart. It would help me so much to deliver our goods and increase trade. I could take things over to Pilsdon or Blackdown.' His expression suddenly became boyish, eager.

'Well,' Martha turned thoughtfully away. 'Maybe we can afford a cart *and* a baby. I will have to consider. The truth is we are not yet making enough from the shop to pay our way.'

'With a cart we will, Martha,' John said eagerly.

'But a cart has to have a horse. We need a horse as well.'

'That follows,' John nodded gravely. 'I think I can get a good horse cheaply from George Fooks who lives in Blackdown. He knows of a nag and maybe a cart as well.'

John had the excited expression of a little boy and Martha's spirits sank. She knew she wouldn't have the heart to refuse him. Of course he was very young, maybe too young to be a father. But the deed was done. There was no undoing it and she went across to the door to fasten it as it was time to close. Somehow the joy had gone out of the day.

As she went over to the door she saw Mary Davis gazing in at the window.

'That woman again!' she said wrathfully. 'Always peering in at the window. I don't know what she wants. Sometimes she strikes me as simple-minded.'

'Oh, I don't think she's simple-minded. Maybe she wants to buy something,' John said with a friendly smile in the direction of Mrs Davis who looked as though she was once again about to take flight. 'Can I help you, Mrs Davis?' he said, going to the door. 'Is there something you want?'

'I was just looking, Mr Brown,' she replied, gazing over his shoulder at Martha who was staring at her with a stony expression. 'I do hope you don't mind. What a nice display you have. My shop isn't doing so well since you came. I have to take in washing to help out.'

'You should get a better range of goods,' Martha said. 'You should pay more attention to your stock.'

'Or follow our example,' John continued to smile at her, much to Martha's irritation, 'and offer to deliver.'

'Oh, I can't *deliver*.' Mary adopted a plaintive little girl's voice which Martha found irritating as it was aimed solely at John. 'My husband is too old and my son too young.'

'I may buy a cart,' John said eagerly, 'and then perhaps I'll be able to help you out.'

'Oh, that's *very* kind of you, Mr Brown.' Mary gave him a flirtatious smile. 'So kind of you to be so helpful.'

She then tossed her head at Martha and walked back across the road to her house.

'Well, you didn't have to be so nice to her,' Martha snorted, fastening the door. 'She'll be in and out the whole time.'

'I think you have to get on with your neighbours,' John said. 'You have to make an effort. She's a nice little woman with an old husband. You must know how it feels.'

'I didn't go round making eyes at all the men,' Martha said crossly. 'I didn't get a reputation like Mary Davis, I can tell you. And if you go on making such an effort to please her she'll mistake your meaning. Now, take those goods up the road and when you return I'll have your supper ready.'

And Martha, recognising a sharp pang of jealousy, and angry with herself because of it, went through the shop door into the house without waiting for his reply.

John Brown got his cart and horse because Martha could refuse him nothing. And it was true that it did help with the business. For a time their trade noticeably increased whereas it was also noticeable that Mary Davis hardly did any and there was talk of her shop having to close.

Despite Martha's success it was hardly the way to further her popularity in such a small place, to put someone out of business who had been there before her, and such had not been her intention. She didn't think Mary Davis was a serious shopkeeper, because most of the time her shop was closed and she was off somewhere without her husband who gloomily got on with his own trade as a carpenter, either out on jobs or in the shed behind his house.

However, John was so happy with his new cart and horse that he seemed to pay little attention to Mary Davis. He did however spend more time away from the shop than in it and he began to do jobs for other people, carrying timber or poles for them or anything they wanted. Sometimes he was away all day and Martha was frustrated lest none of the groceries get delivered at all, or she might have to struggle up the road with them herself.

Maybe a horse and cart had after all not been such a good idea? However, Martha tried to maintain her optimism and got on with her work. She had plenty to do.

About a month after the cart and horse arrived – paid for out of her dwindling funds – on a chilly November day Martha was weighing flour in her shop for Harriet Knight who lived next to the field where John kept his horse. Mrs Knight was a widow who, knowing everyone in the village and everything that went on in it, was one of the prime sources of gossip. She was a keen-eyed, sharp-faced woman who always wore a black bonnet, even indoors, and widow's weeds which had nothing of the elegance of the black dresses Martha had worn for so many years. She was among those who had held back from Martha and maybe helped to spread untrue stories about her.

Consequently, on the rare times she came into the shop Martha went out of her way to be pleasant to her in the hope that she would change her mind about her and encourage others to do so too.

Mrs Knight was watching her critically, as if to be sure that the weighing was accurate and she was not being short-changed.

'There,' Martha said, patting the bag, 'that is just over the pound, but I won't charge you any more.'

Mrs Knight, pursing her lips, permitted herself the flicker of a smile.

'That's nice of you, Mrs Brown.' Then, after a pause, 'Settling down well at last, are you?'

'Oh, very well. We like it here. My husband keeps very busy with his carter's business.'

'I don't see him in the shop so much. I like your husband. He's friendly to everyone.'

'I hope you don't consider *me* unfriendly, Mrs Knight,' Martha looked at her anxiously. 'I really do try hard to please.'

Mrs Knight considered her thoughtfully for a moment. 'Not at all, Mrs Brown. But you are so much older than your husband and he has such youthful charm. I hope he makes a success of his carter's business.'

Martha momentarily clenched her teeth so as not to respond to Mrs Knight's unkind jibe with a retort she might subsequently regret. 'There's a demand for his services,' she said after a pause. 'He not only carries wood. He chops it too when he can be prevailed upon.' Her expression broke into a soft smile. 'You're right. He is charming and that helps with his business. I think he didn't really like being a shopkeeper. As a shepherd he was used to the outdoors. Oh!' Martha suddenly gasped, doubled up and clasped her stomach.

'Are you all right, Mrs Brown?' Mrs Knight asked anxiously.

'No, I don't think I'm all right,' Martha murmured, her face creased with pain. 'You see, I'm carrying a child and . . .' The dreadful spasm came again and Martha recognised it as the sharp pain of labour. 'Excuse me,

Mrs Knight, but I must go to my bedroom. If you don't mind I'll close the door.'

'I'll go fetch your husband,' Mrs Knight said with an air of real urgency. 'Have you any idea where he may be? The horse is still in the field next to my house.'

'You could try the Rose and Crown,' Martha said, wincing with pain. 'That would be very nice of you.'

She barely managed to make the door, usher out a flustered Mrs Knight, get to her bedroom before a rush of blood streamed from beneath her dress and she lay in agony on the floor. In between contractions she crawled round the room looking for towels with which to try and staunch the blood. This went on late into the afternoon, the sky darkened and night came and still there was no sign of her husband.

Finally it was finished and she managed to crawl downstairs and fetch a bucket and some rags with which she made an attempt to clean up the room. But the effort exhausted her and she collapsed on her bed sweating profusely, only relieved now that it was all over. She fell into an exhausted sleep and was awoken by the sound of heavy footsteps on the stairs. John burst through the door and then stopped abruptly, looking at her inert form in the bed, at the bloodstained sheets and rags, the bucket with its grim contents in the corner.

'My God!' he cried, staggering slightly. 'It looks like someone has been murdered here. Whatever happened?'

'I lost the baby, John.' Martha turned wearily to him and held out her hand longing to be comforted, taken into his arms. However he ignored her, screwing up his nose with distaste.

'You'll have to clear all this up, Martha. It's disgusting. A sight to sicken any man. Have it all done before I return.' And he turned his back on her and went unsteadily down the stairs.

Martha suspected he'd been drinking, probably all afternoon. She buried her head in her pillow and gave herself up to a torrent of weeping not only for her lost baby but because she felt in her heart that her fairy-tale love affair was over.

From the time of the miscarriage John Brown's attitude towards Martha changed and he began to neglect her. Instead of giving her the loving comfort and sympathy she craved, he remained completely indifferent to her plight – the physical and emotional shock of losing a much-wanted child. It was as though she was a beast in the field rather than a sensitive, rather vulnerable woman, for all the care he took of her, expecting her to be at work in the shop the very next day and refusing to talk about her ordeal, or explain why he hadn't come sooner, as Mrs Knight had found him where Martha thought he would be.

Now he seldom worked in the shop. He was often away for a day or two, or more, without telling her. He came home late at night, usually drunk. But there were two sides of John. He was popular in the village because people considered him so pleasant, willing and cheerful. He also quoted good rates for the use of his cart so he was given plenty of work. He had a set of cronies he used to meet at the Rose and Crown or other public houses in the area. He wasn't a drunk by definition, but he liked to drink, certainly more than Martha, who was very abstemious, thought was good for him. Remembering so vividly the heyday of their love and romance, the intensity of their passion,

Martha couldn't believe it was over and hoped that this was just a phase of restlessness on the part of a young man shackled to an older woman, who now could never give him a child. The doctor who had examined Martha after her ordeal told her she would never be able to carry one again.

Yet for one who, at one time, had seemed so tender and loving, so concerned, she couldn't properly account for his neglect of her, this abrupt change in a man she thought she knew as well as loved. And she still loved him. Tall and strong with his long thick hair he was the most handsome man in the village, so better to keep up the pretence that all was well instead of betraying by her expression and behaviour that all was not.

Mrs Knight, of course, had soon spread the news that Martha had lost a baby and there seemed to be a degree of sympathy for her, as well as surprise that someone of her age had managed to conceive.

So she would smile at the customers and, as for John, she left him as best as she could to his own devices without nagging or asking him questions, hoping against hope that of his own will and in his own good time he would return, emotionally at least, to her.

Chapter Fourteen

August 1853

So time passed in Birdsmoorgate and the best season of all, summer, finally arrived after what had seemed to Martha a depressing winter, the coast hit repeatedly by strong gales which seemed to gather momentum as they travelled over the sea.

She stocked up with groceries, introducing one or two new lines, and she sometimes put flowers in a bucket for sale outside the door together with fruit and vegetables.

It was possible, almost, to forget a neglectful husband in the joy of activity, being busy in and about the house and garden. For her love of gardening continued in her own garden at the back of the house. She was especially busy in the shop, though now she almost always had to make her own deliveries. It was, after all, the purpose for which the cart had been bought, but now John conducted most of his business elsewhere, though he had an erratic and somewhat vicious horse who had been badly trained and didn't always do what was expected of him. Still, it had come cheaply.

*   *   *

It had been a very hot day and Martha decided she would have no more customers and it was time to close. As she went to the door she saw a woman standing outside. A stranger with a child in her arms.

The outline was somehow familiar and as she stood in the doorway Martha peered at her more closely.

'Why, it's Eliza. It *is* Eliza, isn't it?'

'Yes, Martha.' Bernard's daughter gave a shy, awkward smile. 'I didn't think you'd recognise me.'

'I hardly did,' Martha said, coming forward. 'What are you doing standing there?' She made a broad gesture towards the shop with a sweep of her hand. 'Come in.'

Nervously looking about her, with faltering steps, clasping the baby tightly to her, Eliza walked ahead of Martha turning to watch her as she shut and locked the door.

'I didn't know if you'd welcome me, Martha,' she said as Martha finished her task, and took a brisk look round to assure herself that all was well for the night, before leading the way into the house.

'Why shouldn't I welcome you?' Martha looked at her appraisingly and, particularly, at the infant in her arms who looked no more than twelve or so months old. 'Here, let me take the baby. Is it a boy or a girl?'

'A boy,' Eliza said shyly. 'Seth.'

'Seth,' Martha nodded, and took the child in her arms. 'Yours?'

Eliza nodded, avoiding Martha's eyes.

'I suppose there's no father on the scene?' Martha saw that the baby was well cared for, though with perhaps too many clothes for a hot summer's day, so she gently

263

unloosened his woolly jacket, a gesture which made the infant wake up. However, instead of crying he gazed at her with interest, his expression alert and intelligent and suddenly he chuckled putting out a chubby hand to touch her nose which made Martha too break into a smile. He was indeed extremely winsome. She cuddled him closer relishing the feel of a child against her breast again.

'Well,' Martha said as Eliza remained silent. 'Seth Bearn is it?'

Eliza nodded.

'You can tell me about all that later. Sit down, girl, you look weary to death.'

'I am,' Eliza admitted.

'And hungry too?'

Eliza nodded.

Martha began to bustle round the kitchen making preparations for supper.

'Where did you come from?'

'Powerstock.'

'Powerstock?' Martha looked surprised. 'Were you living there?'

Eliza shook her head.

'I went to see Sarah Crocker, but she wouldn't even let me in. She said I was a bad influence on the children and I should go to the workhouse where they would give me and the baby shelter. She told me Father had died and you were married again. I asked where I could find you, knowing . . .' Eliza faltered, 'that you were a kind person, and she told me. Someone gave me a ride in a cart and,' Eliza gestured helplessly, 'here I am.'

'So I see. And what do you expect of me, Eliza?' Suddenly, despite her pitiful plight, and remembering the past, Martha's attitude towards her stepdaughter hardened.

'Somewhere to leave the baby while I look for work. I am fit and able to work. I cannot leave him in the workhouse. Sarah told me all about how my father set off to look for me all those years ago.'

'I blame you for the death of your father,' Martha rounded on Eliza for whom, after all, she had never felt any affection. Why should she now? 'Do you expect me to help you still, knowing that? Why should I behave any differently from Sarah Crocker?'

'You can't say *I* killed him,' Eliza protested, reminding Martha of how stubborn and wilful a child she had been.

'I do say you killed him,' Martha snapped. 'He was not a well man. He had bronchitis all winter, coughing his heart out. When Sarah wrote that you were gone to London he upped and left at once, and he got no further than Southampton.' Martha paused momentarily, overcome with grief, recalling what a good, kind man Bernard had been. However, seeing the unexpectedly contrite expression on Eliza's face, she quickly recovered. 'It's no use going over all that now, I suppose. It happened a long time ago.' She attempted a brave smile. 'Best let bygones be bygones.'

Looking at her drawn features, her ill-fitting shabby clothes, her down-at-heel shoes Martha's heart was unexpectedly filled with pity for someone she had never liked but who now looked completely worn out, her looks gone, older than her years – for she could only be about thirty – thin, ill nourished and forlorn.

'You'll have to tell me what happened to you, Eliza, how you reached this path.' Martha looked up at the sound of the outer door opening and closing. 'But here is my husband John, I think, and he'll want his supper.'

John Brown came in, pausing briefly on the threshold and frowning when he saw Eliza and the baby whom she now had again in her arms.

'This is Eliza, Bernard's girl,' Martha said, 'and her child, Seth.'

'Bernard's girl?' John stared at her. 'His daughter?'

'I never mentioned her because she left home many years ago. Now she has turned up here because she had nowhere else to go.'

'Well, there'd be no room for her here.' John sat down on a chair to unfasten his bootlaces. 'We have no room for a woman and a child.'

'It's not permanent,' Martha said quickly. 'Just until she finds work.'

'What sort of work?' John finished removing his boots, shook them and gazed up at her.

'Anything,' Eliza said. 'I can do anything.'

'Can you drive a horse and cart?'

Eliza, abashed, shook her head.

'Then you can't do everything,' John concluded with a note of triumph. 'Can she, Martha?'

'Why do you want her to drive a horse and cart, John?' Martha asked suspiciously.

'So's she can help me with my work.'

'Very nice it would look you riding around with a strange young woman next to you,' Martha said contemptuously.

'I'd say she was your daughter, which she is. Stepdaughter, Martha, ain't she?'

'Don't be silly.' Martha, beginning to feel alarmed,

as well as annoyed, finished slicing potatoes over the broth and ladled it into plates. 'Now pull up a chair for Eliza and let's start eating. She looks as though she hasn't had a meal in weeks.'

'She does that.' John seemed now to have changed his attitude and was studying Eliza with interest. 'Maybe given it all to the child. He looks well enough.'

After supper John, as usual, went up to the Rose and Crown and Eliza helped Martha make up a bed in the spare room. Then they went downstairs to wash the dishes and tidy up before sitting by the back door to enjoy the evening air. Martha felt ill at ease in Eliza's presence. She didn't know what to do about her and she wished she hadn't come. But the appealing little baby, so bright and happy, seemed to bring some life to the house and Martha wished she could devise some way for him to stay.

But she didn't want Eliza around. In some indefinable way her presence spelt danger.

'How did you get yourself into this trouble?' Martha asked eventually as they sat breathing in the scents of summer as the sun sank below the horizon.

But Eliza wasn't vouchsafing anything and remained silent, her eyes half closed as if she were tired. Little Seth had been put in the bed upstairs and his mother looked as though her only wish was to join him.

'What happened after you arrived in London?' Martha prompted her again.

Eliza shook herself and sat up.

'I went to work for a family in the City of London. He was a rich merchant.'

'As a maid?'

'As a scullery maid,' Eliza said bitterly. 'It wasn't as I'd hoped.'

'What happened to Ezekiel?'

Eliza laughed. 'Oh, he didn't last long in London. He came back as soon as he could, tail between his legs! He had his horse and cart stolen, no money. London is full of thieves. The streets were not paved with gold for him, nor me.' Eliza sighed. 'I often wished I had been reconciled with my father, not so hasty in my attitude towards you, but . . .' she shrugged, 'there it was. You had a nasty temper, Martha.'

'*And* you!' Martha retorted. 'Headstrong. You were a headstrong girl with ideas above your station, put into your silly head by the misses Walbridge, Cookson and the like. I don't know what harm they did you, but you began to go off the rails when you were in Powerstock. Your father, upset by the stories he heard about you . . .'

Eliza's eyes flashed angrily.

'Put there by rumour-mongers . . .'

'Who were proved right when you went away with Ezekiel.'

'*Nothing* happened between Ezekiel and me.' Eliza's tone became haughty. 'I wouldn't demean myself. After all, he used to be our servant.'

'Like me,' Martha said quietly.

'It was you who suggested that bygones should be bygones,' Eliza said after a while. 'I am content that that should be so.'

'I'll ask you no more questions, if you prefer it that way except – who was the baby's father?'

'He was the son of the people I worked for.'

'As a scullery maid?' Martha asked in astonishment.

'No. I'd moved on. By that time I was a lady's maid to some prosperous folk who lived in Mayfair which is a smart part of London. Their son, Edward, promised to marry me.'

'The old story.' Martha looked at her with compassion. 'I suppose they threw you out?'

'Oh no. They never knew. Edward provided lodgings for me, and I left, saying I was going home. Edward gave me some money and used to come and see me right up to . . .' Eliza paused and, as she struggled for words, Martha observed her eyes glistening with tears. 'He never came to see me or the baby after he was born. He sent me enough money for me to go home. He suggested I should seek reconciliation with my father. He said he was going to marry someone his parents approved of. He was his father's heir and if he married me he would be a pauper.'

Martha gave a disbelieving sniff. 'He wanted to be rid of you.'

'I think Edward loved me,' Eliza said staunchly. 'He did right by me. A lot of men would have thrown me out. He gave me enough money, a generous sum, but I had most of it stolen in the coach on the way home. I think even now if I asked him he would help me, but I shan't. I have my pride.'

'Pig-headed,' Martha exclaimed, looking at her and feeling, for the first time, just a glimmer of admiration, even affection for this doughty survivor, like herself. 'And what do we do about you now, I wonder?'

John came home soon after midnight. Martha had sat up waiting for him, the candle burning low beside the bed. He was surprised to see her still awake and she was similarly surprised to observe that he wasn't drunk — well, not as much as usual. Sometimes he fell in through the door and spent the night on the floor.

'Can't sleep?' he asked, sitting on the bed to take off his boots.

'Can't sleep for thinking about Eliza and the poor baby,' Martha replied. 'He's a dear little thing. Could we,' she paused, 'could we keep him do you think, John?'

John eased his boots off and lay on the bed.

'And do what with Eliza?'

'You were joking about her working for you weren't you?' she asked anxiously.

'Of course I was! I don't want a petticoat messing up my business. I don't see why she came home in the first place,' he finished grumpily.

'She didn't know her father was dead. Although we never really got on I do feel some responsibility for her. She has family living in Long Bredy, relations of Bernard. She seems quite anxious to go there.'

'Then why doesn't she go and take the baby?' John finished undressing, got into bed and, yawning, pulled the bedclothes up to his face.

'I think she wants to see how she will be received. It would only be for a few weeks, John. I mean for us to look after the baby.'

'She could help you in the shop,' John said as an afterthought. 'You're always saying you miss me.'

It was an idea that Martha didn't take to. There was something threatening about the very idea of having Eliza around despite her loneliness after her own, recent, tragedy.

Nevertheless John appeared keen on the idea and Eliza

stayed and, for a while, it worked out. She seemed anxious to make amends for her past and was a diligent and conscientious worker. She weighed out the butter and flour, the potatoes and corn and did all the local deliveries. She even helped in the house, blacking the grates and sweeping the floors, dusting the shelves in the shop and rearranging the goods on display. A far cry from the Eliza of old.

With good food, plenty of rest and a steady routine she lost her pinched expression and her looks returned. She was a rather fine, slightly buxom woman, not beautiful but pleasing enough with her chestnut hair, pale complexion and lustrous brown eyes. Martha gave her two of her old dresses which Eliza altered to fit her, edging one of them with lace and taking them both up because she was shorter than Martha.

It was obvious that John liked having Eliza, some-one nearer his own age, around. The atmosphere was friendly rather than flirtatious, as Martha had at first feared – as though they were brother and sister. What was more important, however, was that for some reason relations between husband and wife improved so much that Martha toyed with the idea of offering Eliza a permanent home and helping to bring up the baby.

September 1853

With September came a change in the weather, and the winds blowing in from the sea grew keener. Martha didn't relish the winter in this bleak place, but here she was and here she would remain for the foreseeable future. But somehow this future now seemed more tolerable because of baby Seth on whom she doted and whom she had come increasingly to regard as her own.

Eliza was a good, if not overfond, mother. She did all she could for her baby, looked after him well, but she didn't seem to dote on him or love him in the way that Martha had loved her children. It was true she could have abandoned him long ago, or left him in a workhouse, but the fact that she did not seemed to indicate some degree of affection, which was not hard to believe, because he was such a winsome child, with a mop of brown curls, large brown eyes, pink cheeks and an infectious smile.

Perhaps it was that Eliza felt resentful about the way the poor little thing had arrived on this earth, that made her seem a little distanced from the child. Perhaps the more she brooded the more unfair it seemed. However, Eliza's loss was Martha's gain and she spent an increasing amount of time with Seth while Eliza seemed perfectly happy running the shop.

In a way it was a very good arrangement. John, too, seemed happier and spent more time at home and not so much with his cronies at the Rose and Crown, the Cross Keys or The George in Beaminster.

Martha stood at the counter while Harriet Knight took a final look round the shop to see if she'd forgotten anything. Then she shook her head, returned to the counter while Martha finished laboriously totting up the amount Mrs Knight owed. Martha had made strides with her reading and writing because it was essential to be at least partly literate, as well as numerate, if you were to run a shop.

'That will be two shillings and fivepence,' she said, looking up as she completed the bill. Mrs Knight grimaced and started groping about in her purse.

'The cost of things is terrible,' she grumbled, 'and me

a widow with children to feed. The government don't seem to care about the poor. Sometimes I wonder how I shall make ends meet.'

Martha managed a sympathetic expression.

'How are you keeping, Mrs Brown?' Mrs Knight looked at her with that knowing expression of one privy to information that others may not have. After all, had she not been present when Martha Brown's miscarriage began, and did not the whole village know how reluctant her husband had been to return home when Mrs Knight went to summon him, preferring to spend the rest of the day at the Rose and Crown? If anything gave an indication of the state of the Browns' marriage surely that was it?

'I'm keeping very well, thank you, Mrs Knight.' Martha began to tuck the goods into Mrs Knight's basket. 'Will you take this or shall I ask Eliza to run across with it?'

'Where *is* Eliza?' Mrs Knight asked, curiously looking round.

'She's out on an errand.'

'*Often* out on errands isn't she?' The tone of Mrs Knight's voice changed subtly.

'How do you mean?' Martha looked up.

'Well, that is to say she does go on a *lot* of errands.'

'We do quite a lot of deliveries . . .' Martha paused, knowing there was more to come.

Mrs Knight appeared to hesitate, looked towards the door so as to make sure that it was firmly shut and then, leaning across the counter, lowered her voice.

'I don't want to speak out of turn, Mrs Brown, but if I was you I would keep an eye on that young lady . . .'

Martha was aware of that awful feeling of dread that

had somehow seemed to lie just under the surface, like some hidden monster always threatening to raise its ugly head, ever since Eliza had come to live with them. Eliza had had a reputation in Powerstock; she had had a child out of wedlock in London. Why ever should Eliza have been expected to change her spots? How foolish of Martha to have given her a home which was also shared by a handsome young man.

'I don't know what you mean, Mrs Knight. Is there something that I should know?'

Mrs Knight drew herself up, an expression of virtuous outrage dominating her prim features.

'If I had been *you*, Mrs Brown, I should not have given that young woman a roof over the same head as my husband, especially as he is so much younger than you. Now,' Mrs Knight reached out for the basket and tested its weight on her arm, 'I have said enough. I just felt it a neighbourly thing to do to warn you, that's all. I hope you won't take it amiss.'

'Have you *seen* anything? Do you *know* anything? Or is it just a suspicion? Just idle gossip?' Martha didn't want the truth, yet she knew she had to have it.

'Oh it's not *gossip*, Mrs Brown!' Mrs Knight said indignantly. 'Don't forget Mr Brown keeps his horse in the field next to me. I see a lot of comings and goings . . .'

'*With* my husband and Eliza?' Martha spoke firmly yet falteringly.

'There. I've said enough.' Mrs Knight's face now registered the kind of satisfaction that the true gossip, the true mischief-maker, feels at a job well done, at someone's happiness or peace of mind shattered.

'You can draw your own conclusions, but if I were

you and I wanted my marriage to remain intact I would give that young woman her marching orders . . . and soon, before you have another mouth to feed.'

Martha spent the rest of the day in a mood of extreme agitation, almost frenzy. She even went across to the field where John kept his horse but, of course, it was not there. And Eliza, who had only a few errands to make, had not returned either.

Martha kept the baby in the shop so that she could see to him but he had just begun to toddle and she could not let her eyes wander for a moment or he was into something or had fallen over something else. Finally she locked the shop and went into the house taking Seth with her. It was mid afternoon and Eliza had been away since late morning. John, as far as she knew, as far as she could trust anything he said, had gone to Beaminster to deliver some poles. Normally his friend George Fooks, who lived in Blackdown, went with him.

On an impulse she decided that she would walk the two miles or so to Blackdown to see if George was there. She would ask Ellen Davis, wife of the builder, Joseph Davis, who lived opposite her and who had young children of her own, if she would look after Seth. This way she would be able to avoid the road in case John came back, and walk more quickly across the fields.

Martha was in the act of putting on her hat when she heard a tapping on the shop door and, quickly taking the pin out of her hat and throwing it on a chair, she went into the shop and saw Eliza peering through the window in an attitude that reminded her of Mary Davis.

Martha unlocked and flung open the door, confronting Eliza with an expression of undisguised rage.

'And where have you been?' she demanded.

Eliza looked bewildered.

'I had to go all the way . . .'

'You had *three* calls to make . . .' As Eliza walked past her Martha seized her by the collar of her dress and half propelled, half dragged her through the shop into the house. 'It should have taken you *half* an hour. Instead you've been away *four* hours. Now,' Martha thrust her into a chair and stood over her, 'can you explain yourself?'

The colour of Eliza's cheeks, the way she tried to avoid her eyes, told Martha all she wanted to know. She leaned over the chair confronting Eliza.

'You have been with HIM, haven't you?'

'I er . . .' Eliza looked truly terrified and curled herself almost into a ball at the back of the chair.

'With *my* husband . . .' As Martha raised a hand Eliza threw her arms protectively across her face.

Suddenly the vision of years ago, of James falling out of the tree and of herself chasing after Eliza and nearly killing her swam before Martha's eyes.

She knew now that if she started to attack her, such was the rage in her heart, Eliza would have little life left by the time she had finished. Shaken, she was only too aware of the strength of her emotions, the violence of her actions. The awful feeling of choking seized her again and, making a superhuman effort to control herself, she lowered her hand and stood upright while Eliza remained cowering behind her protective shield.

'Get out,' Martha said, pointing to the door. 'Take

your things and get out. If you're still here when John comes back by God I'll kill you.'

She stood aside while Eliza crawled out of the chair and made a dash for the stairs.

'And you can leave your baby,' Martha shouted after her. 'I will take good care of him. Besides the fact that I love him as my own, he is my late husband's grandchild. If you ever manage to reform and can prove it to me without doubt, you may have him back.'

A minute or two later Eliza appeared at the top of the stairs having very quickly tied her few possessions into a manageable bundle.

'Don't think I don't love my baby, because I do. But I know you love him and I trust you to look after him. But as soon as I am able, Martha, you can be sure I'll have him back.'

She went to the door and when there was a safe distance between herself and Martha shouted: 'As for you — cradle-snatcher! What use do you think your husband has of *you*? A barren old woman with a sharp tongue and a dreadful temper . . . mark my words you won't keep him for long! He's got a roving eye . . .'

And before Martha could get near her Eliza fled through the shop and began running along the street in the direction of Beaminster.

By the time John got back Martha had calmed down. Indeed she had even regretted a little her precipitate action. Maybe a warning would have sufficed? As usual she had been overhasty. Wouldn't her temper be the undoing of her? However she had now fed the baby, crooned him to sleep and prepared

277

a meal of meat and potatoes which she set before her husband who then noticed there were only two places laid.

'Where's Eliza?' he asked, looking round.

'Gone,' Martha said, taking her place opposite him.

'Gone where?'

'God knows.'

'You mean she's just *gone*?' John's expression was one of incredulity.

'Yes.'

'Did she take the baby?'

'She left him with me.' Calmly Martha began to eat her meal.

John got up and paced the room, stood at the foot of the stairs and looked up.

'I can't believe she's gone.' Then, looking threateningly across at his wife, 'You didn't harm her, did you, Martha?'

'Of course not.' Martha looked across at him. 'Why should I harm her, John?'

John slumped at the table again.

'Should I harm her because you were carrying on with her? Is that what you mean?' Martha went on, her tone deceptively silky.

'That's a lie,' John shouted, jumping up.

'It is *not* a lie. It is the truth,' Martha thundered, also leaping to her feet. 'You were carrying on with my stepdaughter under my very nose and everyone in the village knew about it . . .'

'Just gossip . . .' John began to falter.

'*Not* gossip. The truth.' Martha banged at the table. 'But what should *I* expect from a man with eyes for every skirt he sees? Who flirts with Mary Davis every time she appears in the street . . . or did before Eliza came on the scene. And blind I was to it.' She struck her head as though for a fool.

'Well what do you expect?' Appearing to recover himself John rose and towered over Martha, his expression malevolent. 'What do you expect when I am married to an *old* woman who can't give me a child, who is losing her looks, her passion, yet is so possessive? Sometimes I feel I'm in a prison . . .'

Martha ran up to him and began pummelling his chest with her clenched fists.

'Not true,' she cried. 'Not true. I have not lost my passion. I love you, John. Despite everything, I want you. I love you, and I believe that you love me. I can't believe all that was between us has gone. I refuse to believe it. I don't want anyone to come between us. *Please*, John, let things be as they were. Please, please, please.' She ceased pummelling him and threw herself against him, her head on his chest giving vent to loud hysterical sobs.

John took hold of both her arms and twisted them cruelly behind her back. As she cried out with pain he hurled her onto the floor and as she lay there he seized a heavy thonged whip that hung over the mantelpiece and began to whip her until blood poured from the cuts he had made and it seemed that there was hardly any life left in her.

And as she lay there, only half conscious, whimpering like a dog, he carefully placed the whip in position again, smoothed his hair, dusted down his clothes and went over to the door pausing at the threshold and gazing down at her, his expression one of utter fury and contempt.

'There. Let that be a lesson to you. Don't think you're the only one with a vicious temper, Mrs Brown!'

Then, leaving her alone in darkness, he turned on his heels and went to keep his usual rendezvous at the Rose and Crown.

Chapter Fifteen

September 1854

Swathed in blankets, though it was not cold, Mrs Clark sat bolt upright in her chair. She refused to lie down, fearing that death would claim her and, despite her infirmity, the pain she endured, she did not wish to die. She had rather expected that her husband, who was two years older than she, would predecease her, but no, he hung on too, sitting in a corner not far away from her, also huddled in blankets, smoking a foul-smelling pipe which he only took out of his mouth in order to cough.

As Martha entered the dark room in the little cottage in Marshalsea, where her parents lived, her mother looked up and stared at her mournfully.

'Come to see me before I die have you, Martha?'

'Oh no, Mother.' Martha leaned down to take her mother's hand but she found that she kept it firmly under her blanket, so she straightened up, again with that familiar feeling of rejection, of rebuttal. No matter how old one got it still seemed to recur: the memory of childhood, of the lack of a mother's love.

'Don't tell lies,' her mother growled. 'You know you've hardly ever visited me since you came to Birdsmoorgate. I expect I owe this visit to the fact that you never expect to see me again.'

In the corner her father snorted.

'Leave Martha be. She does you a kindness and you won't accept it without bickering.'

Martha backed away and, putting the basket she had brought on the table began unpacking it. 'I brought a few groceries for you and Father, Mother. Some sugar, flour, butter and tea . . .'

'Tea!' Mrs Clark exclaimed. 'A long time since we had any tea.' She looked over to where her daughter-in-law, Sophia, hovered in the background. 'Did you hear that, Sophia? Tea.'

'Yes, Mother. Very kind of Martha.'

'Kind!' Mrs Clark retorted. 'Nothing very kind about visiting your mother every blue moon with a few gifts. A daughter's duty, I'd call it.'

She looked across at Martha who was watching her patiently determined not to react because she knew she was a very sick woman and, indeed, near death.

'Make us a cup of tea then,' Mrs Clark commanded her daughter-in-law. 'No, better wait until Martha has gone and there will be all the more for us.'

'It's quite all right, Mother.' Sophia looked embarrassed. 'There's plenty to spare if I make a large pot.' She looked at the other goodies Martha had left on the table. 'There's a cake too!' Sophia, her brother Charles's wife, smiled at her sister-in-law who wondered how on earth they all fitted together in this humble dwelling, especially as their daughter had to be accommodated too. The previous year they had lost three children, all daughters, within six months of one another, a tragedy which, at the time, reminded Martha, who attended the funerals, of her own loss.

'Ann is with me, Mother,' Martha said, pointing to the doorway where Ann hovered. 'Come all the way from Stoke Abbott.'

'"All the way",' Martha Clark mimicked. 'She's as bad as you. If it wasn't for Charles and Sophia your father and I would die of neglect. When I think of all the children I've had and now, at the end of my life, I am reduced to this . . .' She looked round the sparsely furnished room and tears slowly trickled down her face.

'There, there, Mother.' Sophia, robustly cheerful despite the tragedies in her life, placed a cup of tea by her mother-in-law's side. 'You drink that up and you'll feel better.' She turned to Martha and smiled. 'We always keep the kettle boiling on the hob just in case.'

'I shall make sure you have a supply of tea,' Martha said humbly. 'You make me feel ashamed. You must ask me for anything you want.'

'Oh a *rich* daughter have we?' her mother jeered. 'Pity she didn't put a little of her money our way before we nearly starved to death. Gave it all to that young husband I expect.'

'Oh do hush, Mother!' John Clark said grumpily from his corner. 'No wonder our daughters don't come and visit us when all you do is grumble at them.'

'If it was not for Charles and Sophia,' Martha Clark continued obstinately, 'I don't know what would become of us, and that's flat.' She looked up as Ann joined Martha, also refusing the cup of tea offered by Sophia.

'Came to see how you were, Mother.' Ann stooped

to peck the withered cheek which had been reluctantly presented to her, a privilege denied to Martha.

'They think I'm dying,' Mrs Clark announced. 'But I'll defeat them. As long as I sit up, I'll be all right. Once you lie down you're as good as dead, and I never was one to give in, was I, Martha?'

'No.'

Despite herself Martha's eyes filled with tears. There was something touching, indeed noble about this proud, tough old woman who had survived so many disasters: a life of poverty, of continual childbearing and perpetual moving seeking work that was hard to find. She should have made more of an effort to understand her mother. But then that was the story of her life. Regrets, regrets. She'd felt the same about Bernard when it was too late. Sometimes she felt the same about John.

'If it wasn't for Charles we'd be in the workhouse,' Mrs Clark continued to rub salt in the wound. 'And he can scarce afford to give us a penny. A very good son is Charles, and Sophia a treasure.' Martha Clark looked with approval at her daughter-in-law who lowered her head in embarrassment.

'Mother, I'd like a word with you and Father in private.' Martha glanced across at her sister and Sophia who immediately and tactfully removed themselves from the room while Mrs Clark, who seemed to be enjoying something of a revival in health, looked on with bright, curious eyes.

When they had gone Martha drew up a chair and sat as close as she could to her mother while her father watched from the corner.

'What is it you want to know?' her mother asked.

'A long time ago when you left Powerstock you hinted I might not be your daughter.'

'Oh, I can't remember *that*! Can you, John?' Martha Clark exclaimed, looking across at her husband.

'You said that I was no daughter of yours, and when I asked you what you meant you said I should ask my father.'

'Well, perhaps you *should* ask your father.' Mrs Clark's eyes glinted mysteriously as she looked across at her husband to whom Martha now turned.

'Father?' she prompted.

Since a seizure her father saw and heard little and remained relatively detached from the world, his only comfort being in tobacco and, perhaps, drink, a commodity in short supply in a poor household. But this time her father seemed quite able to comprehend what was going on and shook his head several times.

Martha edged her chair towards him. 'What are you trying to tell me, Father?'

'I'm trying to say,' her father said slowly, so slowly that the words seemed to take an eternity to emerge, 'I'm trying to *say* that it's best not to talk about the past except . . .' he looked up at her and gave her a tremulous smile, 'that I can assure you that you *are* my daughter.'

To these words of apparent wisdom Mrs Clark slowly nodded agreement.

'Just accept what is, what you know about, Martha, and don't ask so many questions. You always did and it has done you no good at all.'

The sick woman paused and then held up her head to her daughter, reaching out to take her hand. 'You know, Martha, you may think I be a bad-tempered old woman, impatient and sometimes foul-mouthed. I confess I may have been all these things in my time. We haven't always got on. Maybe I was unfair to you,' she paused to look fondly over to her husband nodding in the corner, 'to John, maybe to you all. As my end approaches I ask forgiveness, and that when I'm gone you will all pray for my soul. Though I never had much to do with religion in my life except for the formalities, I do believe that there be a God and that we live on, hopefully in a better world. Now,' she paused for a moment, slightly breathless, 'I am very tired and before you go you may give me a kiss.'

And Martha fancied, as she felt that soft withered cheek against hers, that, for one of the rare times in her life, she and her mother – if she was her mother, but now it didn't matter – were at one.

Martha felt a sense of sadness as she sat beside Ann who had travelled from Stoke Abbott in a pony and cart, picking her up on the way. Although they were close, the sisters saw little of each other, Martha busy in her shop and Ann helping her husband on the farm where they now lived and worked. It was the news that their mother was dying that brought them together for the first time in more than a year.

'I don't think they'll be with us long, do you?'

'Perhaps not Mother. Sophia told me, while we were out of the room, that she made a special effort for today.'

'And I should have made an effort to see them more often,' Martha said guiltily. 'Mother and I became very fond for a few moments. I'm glad I could bring them some groceries. I should have realised how hard things were, I'm selfish.'

'Oh, you're not selfish!' Ann touched her hand and looked into her eyes. 'Far from it. I never knew a less selfish person and if Mother chooses to be nasty to you every time she sees you, why should you bother?'

'I wanted to ask them today the truth about my origins. You remember we spoke about it?'

Ann nodded. 'I wondered about that. Did you get anywhere?'

'Father said I should let the past rest, but that I was his daughter.'

'And what did Mother say?'

'She said I should accept things as they are. I suppose she's right.' Martha looked over to where, in the distance, the houses of Birdsmoorgate could be seen straddling the hill.

'I shall always wonder, though. It was a strange thing for him to say.'

As they approached the crossroads where Ann was to drop Martha off she stopped the cart and looked closely at her sister.

'Martha, you don't look well, you don't look happy and . . .' she glanced down at Martha's arm which was partly exposed, 'how did you get those marks on your arm?' As Martha didn't reply she went on: 'Does John beat you?'

'Does it look like it?' Martha glanced at the scar, then at her sister.

'To me it looks like a whip mark.'

Martha pulled her sleeve down over the scar as though to expunge the memory. 'It was a long time ago, last winter, after Eliza, Bernard's daughter, left. He was so angry he took a whip to me. I thought I was dying and had to stay for two days in my bed.'

'Why was he so upset about Eliza?' Ann asked. 'Was he carrying on with her?'

'I should never have married such a young man,' Martha evaded the question. 'What could I expect but that he would look at every pretty young girl he saw?'

'Does he still beat you?'

'Occasionally, but not with the whip. People say I have a temper, but he is worse, with a very violent and cruel streak, especially in drink. I think he was quite afraid of what he'd done when he whipped me. I had to close the shop. People talked and John wants to be liked by the villagers. They see a very nice side of him, and there *is* a very nice side. He is very popular, especially with ladies,' Martha laughed mirthlessly. 'I try not to mind, not to listen to gossip, but then Eliza came along and there were rumours about her. Strong enough to believe.' Pursing her lips tightly Martha was silent for a moment. 'I believed them and I gave Eliza her marching orders. That's when he beat me, so it shows that the gossips were right.'

Martha sighed deeply. 'You see, I love my husband and I wish he loved me, but, truthfully I think he wanted me for my money. I didn't have much, but a little to help stock the shop and buy him a horse and cart. Now he is tired of me, restless and bored. My ageing body interests him only a little. What money I earn from the shop we live on, what money he earns he spends on drink.' Martha smiled wanly.

'But then, you see, I have my little Seth. He is my consolation. I adore him. Nothing makes up for losing my children but, in some ways, he makes up for what

I have to endure with John. I think John, too, likes the little fellow. He plays with him and is good humoured with him when he is about. No doubt but that John would have liked children. All is not gloom.'

Ann took her sister's hand and held onto it tightly. 'It is true, women's lot is not a happy one. My John is as silent as the tomb and I have to make my own life, my own entertainment. Do nothing rash. Look, as sisters let's try and meet more often. Now that I can drive the cart John will let me have it from time to time.'

'That would be nice.' Martha embraced her sister warmly and before she stepped down outside the Rose and Crown clung to her for a few moments. 'I wish that too.'

Not long after the visit of Martha and Ann, Mrs Clark died in her sleep. She was seventy-six years of age and with her passing Martha felt an affection for her that she had rarely felt in life; whether or not she was her mother didn't matter. And, as is often the case with friends or relatives after a death, her main regret was that she had not done more to see her and perhaps help to ease her path through a long and difficult life.

It was also true that Martha missed her sister. She missed all her family. Even, for a while, she missed her mother and the knowledge that she was there no longer was somehow upsetting in a strange and unexpected way. She made sure that she visited her father more regularly. She took them groceries and tobacco and, occasionally when she could afford it, a bottle of whisky. She never again raised the matter of her parentage. Some things it was better not to know.

* * *

Martha, in the lonely isolation of Birdsmoorgate, would have liked more friends but she didn't miss them because for most of her life she had been surrounded by people rather than friends, and she had plenty of people coming into the shop. Apart from Ann she had never made a true friend in her life though, given the chance, she would have liked to.

Normally the presence of a young child would have provided an introduction to other mothers with young children, but the population of Birdsmoorgate largely consisted of older people and here she was an anomaly: an older mother with a young child, so she didn't really fit in anywhere.

She liked Susan Damon, now Richard's wife, though she was ten years her junior. The Damons were childless but Susan was desperate to have a child and took a great interest in Seth. She would come and play with him and often looked after him if Martha had errands to run.

If she had a friend, Martha regarded Susan as that friend; certainly a sort of bond had sprung up between the two women and the two couples got on and would occasionally share a meal together. Richard was one of John's regular cronies at the Rose and Crown.

Her many years at Blackmanston Farm had accustomed Martha to solitude, to a life of her own until John Brown had invaded it.

But she didn't regret her marriage to John, even if it had not quite provided her with the way of escape she had hoped for. Indeed, during the year following her mother's death their life together seemed to settle down, assuming a more even tenor than the high with which it had started and the low of the time he whipped her, which she thought had frightened even him.

However, she was wary of John and the occasional beatings she received when he came home drunk, even if they were usually relieved with vigorous lovemaking afterwards.

Martha, who was a sensible woman, was not sensible or rational about John. She knew that it was foolish to love a man who could treat her with such cruelty and indifference at one moment, at others with passion. But then common sense told her that it was not the outpourings of love she was experiencing, but that he was using her rather as Bernard had, as a receptacle for his lust.

But, only a fool would expect love to last forever.

January 1856
Martha sat in front of the fire, her chin resting on the top of Seth's head as she swayed backwards and forwards crooning to him. Seth was a bronchial child and his weakness worried her. Every time he breathed in, his little chest rattled like an old man's, the wheezing reminding her of poor Bernard in his last days. She hugged Seth even closer because of the dreadful fear of losing him.

Night was falling and it was bitterly cold. Martha hated the dark, the way the days closed in. January seemed to her the worst time of all. The wind roared perpetually across the ridge, and she could visualise the boiling sea and imagine the ships tossing about like corks and the sailors in fear of their lives.

She sat even closer to the fire and, clasping Seth carefully, leaned forward to poke the flames, trying to make them go even higher. Then, hearing footsteps coming through the shop, she straightened up prepared to rise as John made his appearance. He was always hungry for his supper.

'Does the child still ail, Martha?' he asked, pausing at the doorway.

Martha nodded. 'I am quite worried about him.' She leaned back, looking anxiously at the red face which contorted whenever he tried to catch his breath. 'Of course, my husband was bronchial and maybe his grandchild takes after him.'

'Why do you say "my husband" like that, Martha?' John asked, standing in front of her, although he was looking directly at the child.

'Because he was my husband.'

'Yes. "Was". Not "is". *I* am your husband now, Martha.'

'I know that, John,' Martha said docilely, feeling some apprehension because his mood seemed so strange and she couldn't be sure whether or not he'd been drinking. He was known as a man who could hold his liquor and sometimes the effects were not apparent until it was too late.

'I often think,' John went on, reaching out to take Seth in his arms, 'that you care more for the child than you do for me.'

'You know that's not true, John.' She watched anxiously as John lifted the child and, holding him close, seemed carefully to study his face.

'Please don't harm him, John,' she blurted out before she could stop herself.

'Of *course* I'm not going to harm him!' John's face clouded with anger as he looked down at her. 'How *dare* you say that? I am very fond of the little fellow.

You know that, Martha. I would never harm him. Now, Martha, are you going to put him to bed and get me some supper?'

'Of course, John,' Martha said, jumping up. Uneasily she took Seth from John's arms and hurried up the stairs to put him to bed.

But when she came down again her brow was still furrowed and John watched her as she hurried back and forth from the stove to the table with the supper she had prepared.

'Are you still anxious about him, Martha?'

'Yes. I recall what happened to my own babies. They went very quickly.'

'Then I will go tomorrow to Beaminster and fetch the doctor for you,' he said magnanimously.

'Oh, that is very *kind* of you, John,' Martha exclaimed, her face alight with gratitude.

'But I *am* kind.' John looked with satisfaction at the meal she put in front of him. 'I don't think you give me credit for the good things I do.'

Martha was silent as she sat down opposite her husband and lifted her knife and fork. She felt now that John's mood was rather ominous. He seemed to be baiting her and she looked instinctively over to the wall where the whip hung, vowing that at some stage she would take it down and get rid of it.

'You know it's not true, John.' She turned her gaze to him. 'Of course I love you, but do you love *me*? You told me not long ago I was too old.'

'Well, you know how it is with you, Martha.' John shifted the food around on his plate. 'Sometimes you can seem very superior.'

Martha looked at him with astonishment.

'I didn't mean that, John.'

'You may not mean it, but you make me feel somehow lower than you and it makes me say unkind things.'

'We must try not to hurt each other, John.' There was a note of pleading in Martha's voice as she put her hand out towards him across the table.

That night in bed it was as it had been the very first time when they had come together at Blackmanston Farm.

'I wish you were always like this,' she said, stroking him tenderly, 'gentle and warm and loving.'

'It's the kind of person I really am, Martha. You must do more to understand me.' He had his arms wrapped completely round her, their bodies together and she felt the ecstasy of knowing that he and she were one.

'If only it could always be like this, John.'

'It will be, Martha,' he said, and then, a little wistfully, 'if only we could have had a child.'

There it was, the feeling of foreboding again.

'We have little Seth,' Martha said timidly. 'You like him, don't you?'

'Yes I do. Besides,' he went on, trying to sound reasonable, 'when I married you, you told me we couldn't have children. It is a pity, though, you couldn't keep the one you lost.'

'A great pity,' she agreed, feeling that all this was leading up to something.

'Martha,' his arm tightened round her. 'Do you have any money?'

Even though she had been expecting something, the question shocked her.

'Well, I have a little.'

'Have you none saved from Blackmanston Farm?' His tone was querulous.

'That went a long time ago! Also the money John Symes gave me. What do you need money for, John?'

'I would like a new horse. Mine is so vicious. I fear that one day he might kill somebody.'

Martha, anxious to please, to prolong this loving and romantic mood, thought for a few minutes.

'John, what do you spend your money on? You never give me any.'

'I have expenses.' His tone now became peevish, wheedling. 'I have my horse to feed. A complete set of new shoes the other week. One of my wheels broke . . .'

She noticed that in the litany he produced he never mentioned drink. Did he spend it, perhaps, on women too?

'Well, I will do what I can,' she said. 'I will try and find the money to buy you a new horse, John. It will take some time, but I will find it.'

'I knew you would,' he said, kissing her cheek before contentedly nestling down beside her.

And she thought: if only love didn't have to be bought and paid for.

Paid for dearly.

Chapter Sixteen

April 1856
William Staunton, who kept the Rose and Crown, and his wife were an elderly couple who usually had their goods delivered. Martha was always anxious to keep such good customers happy and she would frequently go up herself with their order, popping it in at the back door and having a word with Mrs Staunton. Despite being in her seventies this good lady still did all the cooking as well as occasionally serving at the bar where John Brown was a well-known customer. Martha herself never drank in the pub – considering it unladylike – though Mary Davis frequently did.

Martha had not been much bothered by Mary Davis in recent months. Days, sometimes weeks, used to go by without her seeing her. However, Susan Damon's brother Francis Turner had just moved in next door to the Browns where he practised his trade as a butcher. Although he was a nice enough man with a pleasant wife, Mary Davis was now, to Martha's irritation, much more in evidence as, probably out of boredom or simple curiosity, she had taken a liking to Mrs Turner. She was frequently to be seen crossing the road in order to offer them assistance in settling in, or simply to pass the day with her new friend. Or maybe she had another reason, for, invariably, on her way there or back she would glance in at the Browns' shop window and if she saw Martha she would give her a provocative little wave.

In Martha's opinion Mary Davis was a silly, flighty woman with not enough to do despite having an elderly husband, a young son to take care of, and, supposedly, a shop to run, and the washing that she did for various people in the locality, sometimes fetching it herself. One would have thought there was plenty to keep Mary Davis from running back and forth but after the Turners moved in that is exactly what she did. Backwards and forwards like someone with too much time on their hands.

Occasionally she and John would bump into each other when he was returning home and stop for a chat outside the door of the shop.

Of course, ostensibly, there was nothing at all wrong with that. There was no harm in being friendly with the neighbours, but Martha saw the suggestive way that Mary stood when she talked to John, somehow thrusting out her trim bosom like a signal of her availability and fluttering her eyelashes, swinging her full hips and gesturing excitedly with her hands. Maybe she did it precisely to annoy Martha, knowing she was watching, and John always came into the shop with a smile on his face as if he found Mary's company entertaining and what she had to say amusing.

For some reason Martha had Mary Davis on her mind that day as she went up with groceries for the Rose and Crown and, as usual, passed the time of day with Mrs Staunton who had no need to ask after John because she saw him nearly every day. But she always asked after Seth, and Martha never tired of talking about him.

She never lingered because she had so much to do, and after delivering her goods and passing the time of day briefly with the landlady she stepped back from the door and was making her way round to the front of the pub when, happening to glance up the road that ran towards Painsdown, she saw her husband's cart just on the brow of the hill, empty, with the horse tied to a tree contentedly munching his nosebag, as if he was there for a long stay.

Sensing something was amiss Martha was about to walk towards it when Mary Davis emerged from the trees by the side of the road with a spring in her step and a smile on her face, that self-satisfied, sensuous expression which Martha knew so well. Once clear of the wood she stopped and looked behind her as though she was waiting for someone.

Within a moment of being seen Martha quickly retraced her steps to the back door of the public house and stayed there while she decided what to do. Finally, puzzled, Mrs Staunton appeared at the door and asked her if she had forgotten something. Flustered, Martha replied that she wondered if there was anything else Mrs Staunton wanted and Mrs Staunton, with an odd expression on her face, replied that there wasn't.

When Martha, still flustered, returned to the road there was no sign either of the cart or Mary Davis. For a moment Martha even wondered if she had imagined the whole thing, but she knew she hadn't.

Momentarily she was tempted to climb the hill to see if the cart was still in sight, but the road wound upwards through the trees and it would soon be lost to view.

As she walked slowly down the hill Martha experienced a variety of intense emotions of which the predominant one, after doubt, despair and suspicion, was jealousy.

All those apparently chance encounters outside the shop, the little smile on John's face, the flirtatiousness of Mary, began to mean something.

Perhaps it should have before?

As she crossed the road, Harriet Knight appeared at her garden gate and waved to her. Harriet really seemed to have very little to do except watch out for passers-by, most of whom she would try and accost in order to tempt them into conversation. She would either stand at her window or hang over her garden gate but, apart from a brief wave, Martha hurried on, being disinclined to stop in case the extreme agitation she was feeling should be obvious and leave that arch gossip with cause to wonder.

Undeterred, Harriet waved again, this time with some emphasis and Martha wondered if something was amiss, so she stopped as Harriet, nearly out of breath, opened her gate and rushed up to her.

'You've got a visitor,' she said, her eyes glinting with excitement. 'Two.'

'*Two* visitors?' Martha said.

'I thought I'd *warn* you,' Harriet took a deep breath. 'Eliza is back.'

'Eliza!' Martha gasped.

'You won't recognise her. Just you wait and see.'

'Eliza,' Martha repeated. 'What does she want?'

'She is with a man,' Harriet grimaced. 'Not young, but rich I would say. They came in a small carriage and Eliza looked very pretty and *smart*. My, you should see her bonnet,' Harriet rolled her eyes. 'Her outfit must have cost a fortune.'

'And where are they now? I saw no carriage in the road.'

'They found the shop shut and I said I didn't know where you were, but that you would not be far so they set off to look for you. Hurry or you may miss them.'

'I'm not sure I want to see Eliza,' Martha said slowly. 'She may want her son back.'

'*That's* why I thought I should warn you.' Harriet could scarcely contain her excitement. 'In case you want to hide him.'

'Hide him! Why should I hide him? Besides, I have no right. He is not mine to hide. I left him playing in the garden knowing I would not be gone long.' Martha put her hand to her mouth. 'Perhaps Eliza is there with him now.'

Without saying goodbye Martha hurried along to her house and rushed through and out to the back where, as she feared, Eliza was sitting on the grass holding out her hand towards the little boy. But Seth, who had no idea who she was, held back, his finger in his mouth and at the sight of Martha he ran over to her and hid his face in her skirt.

Eliza wore a dress of light green taffeta with a full skirt and dark green flounces, a mauve pelisse and a straw bonnet edged with green velvet and with roses at each side. Her rich brown hair was arranged in large puffs over each ear, trailing ringlets hanging on her neck. Her shoes were of kid with side buttons. She got up, carefully brushing the back of her skirt, while Martha stared at her almost unable to believe the transformation and grateful that, at least, she had been partly warned by Harriet Knight.

'You did not expect to see me, Martha.' Eliza gave her a slightly nervous smile.

'Harriet Knight told me you were here. I was delivering groceries.'

'Seth doesn't know me.' Eliza sounded wounded.

'That's not surprising. We have not seen you, or heard from you for, I think, nearly three years.'

'He looks very well, though.' Eliza looked at him anxiously, almost diffidently.

'He is very well, but subject to coughs in winter time. He is chesty like your father.'

'And so tall.'

'I hope you haven't come to ask for him back,' Martha said. 'I regard him as my son.'

'Well,' Eliza gave her that shy, slightly nervous smile. 'He *is* my son.'

Martha bit her lip, her worst fears realised.

'Martha, I'm able to provide for Seth. I am now married to a rich merchant from Dorchester, Joshua Coombes. Mr Coombes is somewhat older than me. He was a widower and has a grown-up family.'

'I'm very pleased for you, Eliza,' Martha said formally. 'I hope you and Mr Coombes will be very happy.'

'My husband knows about Seth. I have told him the truth about my past life and he was very understanding. There is as much difference in our ages as there was between you and my father or,' she hesitated, 'you and John.'

'Twenty years?' Martha said stiffly.

'Thereabouts. He is sixty and I am thirty-four.'

'Quite a big gap. How did you come to meet him?'

'I worked for his daughter as a parlour maid. My stay in Long Bredy didn't last long. My father's brother was dead too, so I went to Dorchester. Needless to say, my husband's family were not best pleased at the marriage as they had hoped for his money. Instead,' Eliza smiled, 'it will all go to me.'

'Congratulations, Eliza.' With difficulty Martha kept the tone of her voice even. 'You have done very well.'

'But I don't want you to think I married Mr Coombes solely for his money,' Eliza said with an earnest expression, 'though I confess that, after a life of hardship, it was an attraction. I also valued the security he offered me. I sincerely appreciated him for his good qualities, and I still do. You know, Martha, you may not have a lot of sympathy for me, but my life hasn't been an easy one. I was headstrong and difficult as a young girl and, believe me, I regretted it.'

'You gave me a hard time,' Martha said, but her manner was softening. At first inclined to doubt Eliza's sincerity, she now began to believe it. There certainly was something very different about her manner: a wisdom, a maturity, as though marriage had helped to strengthen and settle her. And after all, she, Martha, had scarcely been out of her teens when she married Bernard and was ill-equipped to understand his motherless daughter.

As if to confirm her thoughts Eliza went on hurriedly: 'I admit I was difficult and I resented you because you took the place of my mother.' She held up a hand. 'Oh, I know it wasn't fair and many is the time I've regretted that relations between us weren't better.'

'Partly my fault,' Martha made a gesture towards her. 'I didn't make much of an effort to understand you either. You were always referring to me as a servant and instead of ignoring it I allowed it to rile me.'

Eliza blushed. 'I was horrible. But I did not intend what happened to James to happen. I want you to believe that, Martha. I was jealous of him but I loved him. I never forgave myself for his death, and the guilt made me troublesome so that even Sarah Crocker, who was good to me, came to dislike me.'

'If I'd have been a good stepmother,' Martha confessed, 'you could have turned to me. Instead, I suppose my devotion to my own two babies put your nose out of joint even further.'

'Now that we're being frank with each other, there is one other thing,' Eliza lowered her eyes. 'I might have flirted with your husband, for which I humbly beg your pardon, but nothing else. I did not deserve to be sent away the way you sent me. That, too, hardened my heart against you.'

'I behaved badly.' Martha's expression was remorseful. 'I confess I am an impulsive woman. I find it hard to change. I have done many things in my life that I regret. I am jealous of a man I love but who is so much younger than I. I am so sorry, Eliza.' Impulsively she held out her arms to her stepdaughter. 'We've left it rather late in the day but shall we try and let bygones be bygones?'

And for the first time since she had known Eliza as a young, unhappy and rebellious child the two embraced, each controlling with difficulty their pent-up emotions, close to tears.

When Martha finally looked up she saw a portly elderly gentleman standing in the doorway.

Mr Coombes, who appeared extremely amiable, advanced towards Martha with his hand outstretched, but his eyes rested on the child whose face was still hidden in Martha's skirts.

'How do you do, Mrs Brown?'

'How do you do, Mr Coombes?' Martha said politely, shaking hands.

'And I deduce this,' Mr Coombes put a hand on Seth's head, 'is my wife's little boy?'

'Yes.' Martha took one of Seth's hands and tried gently to turn him round.

'Seth, say hello to your mother and . . . stepfather.'

But Seth wouldn't budge and Martha could feel his little face pressed up against her thigh.

'Naturally the little boy is very shy,' Mr Coombes said indulgently. 'How old is he now, Mrs Brown?'

'He will be four this summer. Eliza brought him to me in August 1853. I love him dearly.'

'I'm sure you do, Mrs Brown,' Mr Coombes went on, rubbing Seth's head with a thoughtful expression on his face. 'I'm sure you do.'

'Three years ago Eliza was content to leave the baby. Has she now changed her mind?'

Martha, aware of her rapidly beating heart, aimed her question at Mr Coombes almost as though Eliza was not there. She liked what she saw and imagined that he was a kind and experienced man – a father, perhaps a grandfather too.

'Mrs Brown . . .' Mr Coombes rested his other hand on a cane he was carrying and looked at her as if he didn't know how to continue. He was a little shorter than Eliza, much shorter than Martha, with a rubicund face, bright, shrewd-looking blue eyes over which there were pince-nez, and grey mutton chop whiskers. He looked his age. He wore a grey suit with a plum-coloured waistcoat and a grey cravat and on his head was a top hat which he had doffed when he saw Martha. He looked like a countryman, with a rich Dorset accent, obviously not a gentleman but someone who had made his money – and lots of it – in trade. Martha rather took to him.

'Would you like to come in and have a cup of tea, Mr Coombes? And Eliza too, of course.'

'Thank you, Mrs Brown. After you,' Mr Coombes stood aside to let her pass as she struggled to get Seth to take his head out of her skirts, and half pulled, half dragged him into the house where she set about making tea with great difficulty as Seth remained clinging onto her.

Eliza sat and watched her, a wistful expression on her face, but Mr Coombes was the soul of amiability and when Martha came back with a tray he rose to help her arrange the cups and saucers and took the first cup of tea across to Eliza.

'There you are, my dear. You will be glad of it. It is quite a long way from Dorchester, Mrs Brown. I had not realised the distance.'

'Hilly, a lot of ups and downs,' Martha said. 'It makes the journey seem longer.'

She gave Mr Coombes his cup and then handed round a plate on which were pieces of cut cake. 'I baked this myself,' she said. 'It is very popular in my shop.'

'It seems a nice little place you have here,' Mr Coombes looked round appreciatively. 'Have you been here long?'

'Since January 1852 when I married Mr Brown.'

'And how is Mr Brown?'

'Very well, thank you.'

'I hope I shall have the pleasure one day of meeting him.'

'I hope you will.'

'I am in your line of business, as a matter of fact. I make

sweets and biscuits, mainly for the London market and abroad. Coombes Dorset Nuggets. You may have heard of them.'

'I have heard of them, but they are too expensive to stock in my shop.'

'I will send you some as a gift. Now, to the point, Mrs Brown.' Mr Coombes finished his tea and moved a little nearer to the edge of his chair. 'As you can see I am considerably older than my dear Eliza, and my children, with the exception of my youngest son, are older than she.

'I must tell you that at my age and having raised a family I am reluctant to embark on another and I think Eliza shares my feelings, don't you, my dear?'

Eliza nodded, her eyes still on Seth.

'My wife may have been content to leave her son, but the circumstances, as I understand them, were very different from the ones in which she finds herself today. She was then unable to support a child. Now she is.'

'Then you do want him back?' Martha gulped and her eyes suddenly filled with tears.

'In time . . .' Mr Coombes paused and then nodded. 'We may. I think it is only fair to warn you that that might happen but,' he held up a hand, 'it will not happen immediately. You have been very good to Seth, both Eliza and I realise that, and I can understand how attached you have become to him. Neither of us would wish to deprive you of him instantly.'

'Then what do you propose?' Feeling a little calmer, Martha joined her hands neatly together in her lap and looked at him.

'I am going to suggest that in a month or two he pays us a visit. See how we get on. He has to become used to his mother and me. My children have children his age and there will be plenty of friends for him to play with. We shall engage a nursemaid for him. I am guessing that, if all goes well, Seth will make a home with us, with his rightful mother. You must agree, Mrs Brown, that much as you love him the opportunities here for him are limited. I can offer him the best education and good prospects. There would always be an opening for him in my business, but he may become a professional man, who knows? One of my sons is a barrister in London.

'But you, of course, will always be welcome to visit and, in time, I am quite sure he will not forget you and will wish to visit you too. Frankly, I shall enjoy having a child of his age – he is handsome and looks very bright – about the place again.'

When John got home just after eight it was to find the house in darkness, the candles not yet lit. There was no welcoming smell of cooking, no fire in the hearth.

He called 'Martha' but there was no reply. After he had stumbled about and lit a candle at first he thought the place was empty and then called her name again.

Slumped in a chair in the corner Martha stirred herself.

'I'm here, John.'

He walked over to her, holding the candle aloft, and then stooped to look at her.

'What ails you, Martha? Are you ill?'

'They're going to take Seth away,' Martha murmured, slumping back in the chair again.

'Who is going to take Seth?' John demanded, putting the candle in a holder and lighting another.

'Eliza was here. She is married to a rich man and wants her child back.'

'Oh, is that all?' John said dismissively, turning his back on her. 'Is that why the fire is unlit and my supper isn't ready?'

'Don't you *care* about Seth, John?'

'Of course I care about him,' John spun round angrily, 'but he is not our child and never was. Your relationship with him is unnatural, Martha. Sometimes I think you imagine you bore him.'

'I confess he is to me like my own child and I don't want to lose him. Eliza is a changed person, it is true, but it came as a shock to me. They are going to leave him here for a while, then suggest a visit.'

'It seems they have behaved very well,' John said. 'And I can tell you there is nothing you can do about it. The child does not belong to you. Now please go and get my supper.'

'Get it yourself,' Martha retorted. 'You are a most unfeeling man, John Brown.'

'I *beg* your pardon?' John paused in the act of going upstairs, and looked at her.

'I said get it yourself. Or perhaps get Mary Davis to get it. I know you were with her today.'

'Oh!' John came back into the room his arms crossed, a leer on his lips. 'This is what this is all about, is it?'

'No, it is about losing Seth, and also your infidelity. Two things that make me grieve.'

'I said,' John bawled, reaching for her arm and trying to pull her out of the chair, 'go and get my supper!'

'And I *won't*,' Martha shrugged him off again and, instead of sitting back in the chair, walked behind it so that it stood as a barrier between her and her husband. 'You are always flirting openly with Mary Davis. I've seen you several times chatting to her outside the shop door.'

'Well, what is wrong with that? I was being neighbourly, that's all.'

'Today I saw your cart up the hill along the Painsdown road and Mary Davis waiting for you.'

'How did you know she was waiting for me?'

'Who else would she be waiting for? Did you lend your cart to someone?'

'George Fooks maybe,' he said slyly.

'Oh, you lent it to George Fooks?'

'Well, I might have done and gone for a drink at the Rose and Crown.'

'Well, as it happens,' Martha retorted, by now thoroughly roused, 'I was talking to Mrs Staunton at the back door of the Rose and Crown a few minutes before, and she didn't mention you were inside.'

'What I did today is my business and nothing to do with you. Now if you don't get my supper, I'll beat you, Martha.'

'And I'll scream and raise the roof,' she said defiantly.

'You can scream as much as you like. Everyone will understand that a disobedient wife should be beaten.'

'Tell me you are not Mary Davis's lover,' Martha implored, her voice suddenly breaking.

'I am *not* Mary Davis's lover,' John replied.

'I don't believe you.'

'So, why do you ask if you don't believe me? Why do you provoke me, Martha? Why don't you do as I say? If you ask me you're losing your mind. What reasonable woman would cling to a child that is not her own? And isn't it the duty of a wife to be obedient and to get a man's supper when he has worked hard all day and is hungry?'

'And did you lend your cart to George Fooks?' Martha persisted.

'No, I did *not* lend my cart to George Fooks,' John snapped. 'And yes, I gave a lift to Mary Davis who was walking back all the way from Painsdown with some washing. I felt sorry for her. That is all. That is all that happened.'

'And why did you stop on the road then? Why didn't you tell me that in the first place if it was all so innocent?'

'Because you are so jealous and, besides, it is none of your business,' John roared, his patience finally snapping, and, grabbing her by her mop of curls, he pulled her from behind the chair and administered a series of such sharp blows across her face that they made her nose bleed.

'And don't think I am going to buy you a new horse,' Martha managed to gasp, holding her nose, 'there is nothing wrong with the one you have. He stood there peacefully eating from his bag. You want the money to spend on Mary Davis!'

Enraged by her words, John threw her across the chair, drew up her skirt and began to beat her about the legs and backside, preventing her from screaming by brutally gagging her with one hand pressed over her mouth.

When he had finished he let her go and she fell back on the chair like a rag doll, whimpering.

'Now get up and get my supper,' he commanded. 'I'm going to the Rose and Crown and if it's not ready by the time I get back you will get another sound thrashing. This time with the whip.'

Martha lay where she was, slumped over the chair, her hands clasped to her bleeding nose, and listened for the outside door to shut. There was a drumming in her ears and she found it difficult to focus her eyes. She sat up and pulled her dress as best as she could down over her knees. She held her head back and could feel the blood running down her throat. Then, still with her head back, she went into the kitchen and poured some water into a bowl and with a cloth dabbed at her face and head.

When the bleeding stopped she washed her face and tried to stop the trembling that seemed to shake her whole body. She had a bottle of brandy that, unknown to John, she kept hidden in a cupboard for medical emergencies. This was such an emergency, she decided, and she poured some into a cup and drank it at a gulp. She was tempted to have another but as the fire shot down into her belly her head also began to swim from the effects of the strong liquor taken too quickly, so she tottered back to the chair and sat down again. After a while the brandy appeared to be doing its job; she felt stronger and returned, still a little shaky, to the kitchen and began unsteadily to peel the potatoes and chop the cabbage for her husband's supper.

Pausing, she looked out of the window into the night sky and swore silently to herself that, if this went on, one day she would kill her husband before he killed her.

John and Martha didn't speak to each other for several days after the beating. She went about her tasks docilely, washed his clothes and prepared his meals but with never a word. He would look at her, scowling, and ask for things or tell her what to do, but otherwise he didn't attempt to converse with her either. It didn't seem that he was ashamed, but still angry. As usual he demanded his marital rights in the bedroom, but these were also conducted without words being spoken. Martha gave in because she had no choice, and also she was dearly afraid of the whip and of what the consequences might be, above all of what terrible forces might be unleashed in herself, if he once again attempted violence on her.

Not unnaturally little Seth seemed to sense the strained atmosphere and be subdued and frightened by it. He was by nature rather a withdrawn and nervous child, very dependent on Martha for reassurance. He had been upstairs when the beating had taken place and had, surely, been aware of it? The following day he had clung even more to Martha, watching her apprehensively, his finger firmly in his mouth. He did not want to let her out of his sight and followed her everywhere. When John was around he was silent, and watched him with fear clearly showing on his face.

Martha wondered if he had crept downstairs and seen what was going on. She had never known him like this.

She began to think that, unless the situation between John and herself improved, the very best thing for Seth would be that he should go, at least temporarily, and stay with his mother. She could never see that nice Mr Coombes turning on Eliza as John turned on her.

Susan Damon, who was a regular visitor to the shop, and indeed to the house, as Richard and John were so close, visited Martha a few days later and the first thing she asked Martha was how she came by her black eye. Martha replied that she had bumped into the door. She'd put a piece of beefsteak on it but it was slow to heal.

She was making up a pound of sugar for Susan to complete her grocery order but, by the way Susan was looking at her, she knew she didn't believe her.

'There,' Martha said, fastening the top of the packet and tying a piece of string around it. 'Anything else you need?'

'That eye looks awfully sore.' Susan persisted with her questioning and, before she could prevent herself, before she even knew what was happening, Martha burst into tears.

'Oh, I'm so sorry . . .' Susan came round the counter to try and comfort her. 'I didn't think . . . It's John isn't it? He beats you?'

Martha nodded and, releasing herself from Susan, went over to the door to lock it. 'I don't want anyone to see me like this,' she said apologetically. 'I am sorry you did.'

'Let me make you a cup of tea,' Susan suggested, leading her from the shop into the house and noticing how concerned Seth looked, and how he clung onto Martha's skirts.

'I'm so afraid,' Martha said, sitting down and blowing her nose. 'I think he will kill me.'

'Is it about Mary Davis?' Susan enquired, lifting the kettle from the hob and pouring water into the teapot.

'You *know* about Mary Davis?'

'I think the whole village does.'

'I wish someone had told me.'

'Well, it hasn't been going on for long. At least I don't think so. And I don't think it's so very serious, Martha. I mean . . .' Susan finished brewing the tea and brought a cup across to Martha. 'I know how upset you must feel, but she *has* a reputation. Her husband is old and bad-tempered and she is an unhappy woman. She gets comfort where she can in the admiration of other men.'

'That's no excuse for making eyes at my husband!' Martha said angrily, blowing her nose again. 'It is an added humiliation for me, and besides,' once more she started weeping, 'I fear I am going to lose Seth.'

'Why should you lose Seth?' Susan brought her own cup of tea and sat down next to Martha.

'Because Eliza wants him. She has married a wealthy man and is able to keep him and, do you know . . . I am so afraid of what John might do that I think it will be best for Seth. I think he saw John beating me the other night and, who knows, but that one day John might turn on him?'

'Oh, I don't think John would do that.' Susan looked shocked.

'He is a man of violence,' Martha insisted. 'Not as nice as everyone thinks. You'd think he wouldn't harm a fly.' Martha drew up her skirt and showed Susan the bruises on her leg. The whole of one side was black and purple. 'My bottom too,' she said, shifting uncomfortably in her chair. 'I can hardly sit on it.'

'I'd no idea it was so bad.' Susan began to stroke Martha's back in an effort to comfort her.

'The thing is,' Martha faltered, 'I still love John. I try so hard to please him, to do everything he wants. Yet I can't seem to do anything right by him, and then I saw his cart on the Painsdown road and Mary Davis coming out of the wood as cocky as you please, with John surely close behind her, though I didn't see him. Truly I felt that I was going mad. I went down the road and saw Harriet Knight who told me, as if I hadn't enough on my plate, that Eliza was in my home, and then when I met with her and her new husband I heard that they wanted little Seth,' Martha gazed fondly down at the child wondering how much he understood of what was going on, 'and that was more than I could bear. But, instead of sympathy that night from my husband I got a beating when I mentioned Mary Davis's name.' Martha started weeping into her handkerchief again. 'I really don't know what will become of us. I really don't.'

'I don't know how you could continue to love a man who beats you,' Susan murmured.

'There is, despite everything, a lot of good in John,' Martha sniffed. 'He is well liked, you know that.'

'Yes, by everyone,' Susan agreed.

'Things go well between us, sometimes for weeks on end. The trouble is, I suppose, that my jealous nature gets the better of me. But in all truth, Susan, I can't help myself because I love my husband. I suppose I should be glad I have a roof over my head and enough to eat. I suppose I should turn a blind eye, but when I see him flirting with another woman, especially someone as young and pretty as Mary Davis, it becomes intolerable for me. She sets her cap at John deliberately because it vexes me so. And people have no sympathy for me because I am so much older than he is.'

At this Susan said nothing because it was partly true. 'What can she expect,' people said, 'if she goes and marries such a young man?'

But then there was no sympathy for Mary Davis either. In this male-dominated society, unfair as it was, it seemed that the women could do no right and men could do no wrong.

But was it not ever thus?

Chapter Seventeen

June 1856

'I'm sure you're doing the right thing, Mrs Brown,' Mr Coombes said, attempting to take Seth's hand as Martha, struggling to keep back her tears, urged the little boy towards him, 'and if the lad is in any way unhappy, or fails to settle, you can be sure we shall send him straight back to you.'

But Seth refused to take Mr Coombes's hand and resolutely clung to Martha, bawling his eyes out.

It had been a very difficult, distressing forty-eight hours after Martha had contacted Mr Coombes. He had sent word that he would come with a nursemaid to pick Seth up. She had tried to explain what was happening to the little boy, but he was scarcely able to comprehend what she was saying until, freshly washed and scrubbed and dressed in his best clothes, he was reintroduced to Mr Coombes.

These few days before he left had been most precious to Martha. The weather had been kind and she had spent much time with Seth in the garden, or walking in the lanes inspecting the hedgerows full of red rosebay willow-herb, fragrant white meadow-sweet and purple mallow. Not knowing what was in store for him Seth had seemed happy too, prattling non-stop in his excited childish talk, the bond between them stronger than ever. Then, neither John nor Mary Davis seemed to matter to Martha, forgotten in a temporary happiness, an outpouring of joy that was all the stronger because it would soon end.

But that morning, as Martha had dressed him, she had tried to explain that what was happening was for his own good. That they would see each other again and even if they didn't they would always remember each other and love each other. She was sure he didn't understand a word of it but, because of the expression on her face and the tears never far away from her eyes, he probably divined in his childish way what was going on.

Seth clung even more tightly to Martha, wrapping his face in her skirts and refusing to budge, his sobs now great, uneven heaves as if he could cry no more. As Mr Coombes, beginning to perspire, attempted once more to take him he bawled the louder until Jemima, the nursemaid, who looked a kindly soul, took charge, gently detaching his hand and taking it in her own as she smiled down at him. Desperate for reassurance he looked up at her, then at Martha who also smiled encouragingly, then again at Jemima. She was a woman possibly of about Martha's age, and her manner with the child was gentle. Suddenly his tears abated and, as if accepting the inevitable, he seemed inclined to trust her, gripping her hand tightly in his.

'I only wish the best for him,' Martha said, as Seth's tears stopped. 'He has more opportunities with you. Mr Brown and I are not very well off and you can give him everything we can't give him, an education which I and my husband never had.'

'I'm glad it was your decision.' Mr Coombes was also watching the growing accord between Seth and Jemima. 'I think you're very wise. Very wise, Mrs Brown.'

Martha looked towards the carriage where Eliza, who had not got out, sat watching the proceedings with an anxious expression.

'Will Mrs Coombes not come in and say goodbye to me?'

'I think,' Mr Coombes replied, 'she thought it would be too painful for you. Eliza realises how fond you are of the child and wanted to allow you the last few moments together.'

Martha bowed her head. 'It is very kind of your wife. In the past, I have misunderstood her. I think she will be a good mother to Seth, and it is fitting that he goes to her.'

'I am sure she will. She loves him so much. The poor lady has led an unfortunate life, as you know. She regrets much of the past and is most anxious to give the child a good home, as I am, and make him feel loved and wanted. After he has settled we want you to come and visit us, like a well-loved aunt. I am sure Seth will never forget you.'

Martha found herself once more on the brink of tears and merely nodded whereupon Mr Coombes seized her hand and kissed it in an awkward gesture because, after all, he was not a gentleman and not practised in the art.

With one hand in Jemima's, the other clutching Mr Coombes's, Seth walked to the door and across to the carriage where Eliza waited to receive him, arms extended. He appeared to hesitate but, suddenly and unexpectedly, her anxious features were transformed into a brilliant smile, the sort of smile that had undoubtedly captivated the ageing biscuit manufacturer. It now appeared to have the same effect on her son because, almost with alacrity, he jumped into the carriage and sat down next to her.

Then taking Seth on her lap she held up his hand so that he could wave to Martha who waved frantically back.

Jemima got in on the other side of Seth and Mr Coombes took up the reins of the horse. Doffing his hat to Martha he then clicked his tongue, shook the reins and as the horse set off Eliza leaned out of the window, waving energetically.

'Come and see us soon, Martha!' she cried. 'We will never let little Seth forget you.'

And she blew her kisses until the carriage disappeared out of sight.

Martha stood there for a long time, long after the carriage had disappeared. Then slowly she went back inside to an empty house. No more would she delight in the sound of his little footsteps, no more would she cuddle him before putting him to bed.

She realised that Seth had been her life and, without that life, what now was left for her?

When John came home that night he seemed to sense that Seth had gone, even without going up the stairs. Martha stood at the sink preparing supper and didn't look up at her husband.

'Well,' he said after a while, 'has the boy gone?'

'Yes.'

'I expected to find you all weepy again, Martha, because you'd lost your child.'

'I hope to have more dignity,' Martha said, still without turning round.

'Pah!' John gave an exclamation of disgust. 'You didn't show much dignity last time. I expected my supper not to be ready and was preparing to give you another beating.'

Stung, Martha turned round and faced him. 'John, why are you always so unkind to me? What more can I do to please you? I do all I can.'

'You can't turn the clock back,' John said. 'Unfortunately.'

'I don't know what you mean by that. If it's my age, you knew that when you married me.'

As he didn't reply she went across to the range and inspected the pot simmering on top.

'Your supper is nearly ready, John. We need more wood for the fire. Tomorrow you must go out and chop some.'

'My hatchet is blunt,' John said.

'Then you'll have to borrow Richard's.' Martha glanced over her shoulder. 'Your hatchet has been blunt for so long you should take it to Beaminster next time you go to get it sharpened if you can't sharpen it yourself.'

Martha spooned the contents of the pot onto a plate she was holding and, taking it to the table, set it before him.

John looked at her with surprise. 'Aren't you eating, Martha?'

'I'm not hungry,' she said, and she went upstairs to tidy Seth's room so that no trace of him remained. After that she stood looking for a long time out of the window as night fell and the landscape gradually merged with the darkness. Birdsmoorgate was a beautiful place, with its own kind of grandeur, but she felt that she had never really been happy here. One day perhaps she would leave John and find work again as a housekeeper.

But then, again, perhaps she wouldn't. She thought of the little boy who had brought such joy and consolation to her life and, somehow, in her bones she felt she would never see him again. He would become spoilt and pampered and even if she did go and see him he would probably not recognise her, having quickly forgotten the woman who looked after him so well in his tender years when his mother had been forced to abandon him.

She looked over at the Davis's house and saw no light in the downstairs room. She wondered if the old man and young boy were in bed and if Mary Davis had gone up to the pub and was waiting there for John.

She knew she was obsessed by Mary Davis and, in her unhappiness, growing daily more so. Somehow she was always there just below the surface, taunting Martha.

In the same way that Mary used to stare in through the shop window, so Martha these days now spent a lot of time at her own window looking across, waiting for a glimpse of her or, maybe, trying to catch John going into the house or coming out, but she never did.

After a while she heard the door shut and knew that John had gone up to the Rose and Crown. The change of atmosphere in the house was immediate. The brooding sense of doom and unease had gone. Somehow the house seemed so much nicer, calmer, more friendly when John was out of it.

She went downstairs and, after clearing the dishes and washing up, still not hungry, she went out into the garden where she sat for a long time inhaling the scents of summer and trying to find a place for peace and hope within her troubled soul.

Saturday 5 July and Sunday 6 July 1856

George Fooks, who lived along the road at Blackdown, was one of John's drinking cronies. He also frequently accompanied John on his trips to Beaminster or Broadwindsor to help carry poles or logs or anything that needed transporting in the area. Martha had little time for him. He was rather older than John but the sort of person who was easily led, and where John led George invariably followed, aiding and abetting.

When George came to help John with a load he liked to have breakfast because he got a better one from Martha than he got at home. This particular morning was no exception and as Martha set his plate before him he tucked in with hog-like greed until it was clean. Even then he looked up hopefully for more.

'When will you be back, John?' Martha asked her husband as he rose from the table and made for the door, ready to load the carts.

'I won't be late,' he replied, putting on his cap.

'I'll have something nice for your supper,' Martha promised with a smile and, for once, John smiled back.

Things, Martha thought, were on the mend. Ever since Seth had left John seemed to have gone out of his way to be nicer to her, and that morning his lovemaking had been almost as tender and as thoughtful as in the heyday of their love affair. Maybe there was, after all, the chance of a new beginning? She accompanied them to the door to open the shop and stood on the threshold watching them set off on the road towards Beaminster with the load of poles John had stacked up the night before.

Conscious of a feeling of wellbeing Martha busied herself about the shop for a while and then went back to the kitchen to wash the breakfast dishes, tidy up and prepare for the evening meal. To mark this new beginning she decided to add a fresh piece of lace to the collar of her dress, and in the afternoon she would wash her hair and pretty herself for what, possibly, could be a romantic evening if the mood of that early morning lovemaking continued.

Between serving customers she made a steak pie, prepared the vegetables and put some ale to cool in the larder. She felt in a curiously happy, relaxed mood and hummed under her breath as she went about her business.

Maybe John did love her after all? Perhaps he had been jealous of Seth all the time, and she had given him cause because of all the attention she had lavished on that little boy? She had been unfair to John who, in many ways, was like a child himself. He had wanted her attention and she hadn't given it to him. No wonder he'd made a pass or two at Mary Davis. And how seriously she'd taken *that*! Why, Mary Davis had come to obsess her almost to the point of derangement, so much so that she had sometimes imagined she had seen her when she wasn't there at all.

Hopefully now all this would change.

In the afternoon Martha washed her hair and sat out in the sun drying it. She heard the shop bell and went indoors shaking her head as her curls were still wet.

Behind the counter was Thomas Smith, a thatcher, still with his leggings on, who was eagerly inspecting the jars of tobacco as if he was in urgent need of a smoke.

'Afternoon, Tom,' Martha said cheerily, unfastening the lid of one of the jars. 'Your usual?'

'Yes please, Mrs Brown. I'm right out of baccy and desperate for a smoke.'

'You finished now for the day, Tom?'

'Aye. I finished the ridge and I'll clean up and collect my money Monday. Oh, by the way, Mrs Brown,' Tom chuckled mischievously, 'I seed Mrs Davis riding along of your husband this morning. They was on their way to Beaminster. Reckon he was giving her a lift.' He gave a broad wink and reached for the twist of tobacco she handed him. Then, seeing the expression on her face, doubt seemed to set in. 'Maybe I didn't ought to have mentioned it, Mrs Brown. George Fooks was close behind him, so no harm done.'

'You can say what you like, Tom,' Martha said off-handedly. 'Nothing wrong in giving a lift to a neighbour. Mrs Davis was probably on her way to collect some washing.'

'That's 'zactly what I thought,' Tom mumbled, pocketing the change she'd given him and ambling out of the shop. 'Meant no offence.'

'None taken,' Martha said, following him to the door and shutting it firmly behind him. Then she leaned against it breathing heavily, and closed her eyes, fighting the tormenting visions of John and Mary together.

Suddenly she opened the door again and ran across the road to Mary Davis's house and knocked frenziedly on the door. There was no reply, so she knocked again and after a few moments it opened and William Davis stood blinking into the sunlight.

'Is your wife in by any chance, Mr Davis?'

'Wife gone out,' Davis said abruptly, preparing to close the door again.

'Do you know where?'

'Attisham, to get some washing.'

'What time did she go?'

''Bout nine. Don't know what business it is of yours.' And this time William Davis succeeded in shutting the door in her face.

He knows, Martha thought with dreadful certainty, he knows she is carrying on with my husband.

Martha returned to the shop trying hard to regain control of her emotions. The sunny, optimistic mood of the morning had gone completely. What a wicked old gossip Tom Smith was, as bad as any woman. She was quite sure she'd seen a malicious gleam in his eye as he unburdened himself of his news.

But supposing it was true? Well, it *was* true. John had gone to Beaminster and George Fooks had travelled behind him. What, then, could have taken place but a little harmless flirtation?

Harmless! Martha banged the door of her shop shut and locked it. Then she went into the living room and slumped into a chair. This time when he came home she would really have it out with him, whip or no whip. She looked up to where it hung on the wall and considered removing it. But John might regard that as a provocation. He could still give her a good thrashing, with the whip or without it. She lowered her eyes towards the fender where lay the blunt hatchet that he still hadn't sharpened. She thought she'd take it out to the shed and try to sharpen it herself and chop some wood. But an awful inertia had taken hold of her, a sense of desolation and futility, a feeling that she'd been deceiving herself all along, emotions she hadn't felt since Seth had gone.

She went upstairs and instead of putting lace on her green dress she decided she would keep on the black dress she always wore in the shop, just to show John what she thought of him. Why should she titivate herself for such a worthless man?

She went into Seth's room, but there was no sense of him there now. She had not heard from Mr Coombes and she had to assume all was well. She remembered how she'd gone into the boys' room before she left Powerstock and how any feeling that they had been there no longer remained.

It was the same now with Seth. All trace of him had gone. She stood for a while at the window, looking across to Mary Davis's house, but she saw no movement, no sign that she had returned with the washing. Maybe she had gone into Beaminster with John and maybe . . . she put her head in her hands and threw herself on the bed. Was there no end to this torment? This frenzy of jealousy over a completely worthless woman like Mary Davis?

Towards evening Martha went upstairs to wash her face and brush her hair. Afterwards she looked at herself steadily in the mirror and decided that, for her age, she had worn quite well. She was not bad looking. Her figure was neat, her skin was good and there were no streaks of grey in her hair. But . . . compared to flighty, flirtatious and utterly unscrupulous Mary Davis she was old.

The hour at which she had been expecting John came and went. Seven, then eight. She kept on going to the window and looking across at the Davis house, or for a sight of his cart. Her obsession with the wretched woman had returned and was worse than ever. She paced up and down like a soul in torment.

Just after eight o'clock Mary Davis appeared at the door of her house looking rather agitated. As she crossed the road she began removing her bonnet before disappearing into the Turners' house next door without even stopping to glance in at the Browns'. This in itself was unusual and Martha's agitation increased, also her sense of outrage. She felt like accosting Mary Davis on her way back but, before she could, she saw the door of the Damons' cottage open and Susan ran across the road with an empty bottle in her hand also going into her brother's house.

All this was too much for Martha who put a sinister connotation on the whole thing and wondered what on earth was going on. She hurried through the shop, opened the door and waited for one or the other to reappear. After what seemed an age she heard Susan's voice saying goodbye to her sister-in-law and then, as Susan started to cross the road, Martha called out to her. Susan stopped.

'Martha . . . I can't stop. I went to my brother for some water. My husband is in bed and I have a bad cold . . .'

'Come in, come in,' Martha urged, standing back from the door as Susan, with a show of reluctance, went inside. 'Mary Davis has gone into your brother's. What's she gone there for?'

'She's gone for some beefsteaks.'

'She took off her bonnet. What's that for?'

'Martha, calm down,' Susan said gently. 'I think my sister-in-law wants one like it.' Suddenly Susan's expression changed to one of excitement. 'Martha, what do you think? I just heard Mary tell my sister-in-law that she is expecting again.'

'Mary *expecting*?' Martha cried out in astonishment. 'With that old husband of hers?'

'Who knows?' Susan suggestively raised her eyebrows. 'I did hear that old William was no longer capable, but . . .' she shrugged her shoulders. 'I must go or Richard will wonder where I am.'

'Old bitch,' Martha muttered savagely as she accompanied Susan to the door and then, seeing her expression, 'no, not you. *Her*. Expecting again is she? Bitch.'

Martha returned to the kitchen and took the pie she'd cooked for her husband out of the oven. The crust was all brown and it smelt delicious. She had imagined they would have it sitting down together, all lovey dovey, accompanied by a few glasses of beer, have some cold stewed apple left over from the day before and go upstairs to bed. It would have been a new beginning, the past behind them.

Well, what a fool she had been to deceive herself. As for Mary expecting . . . words quite failed her.

Well, he would still have his pie, cabbage and potatoes, but for herself she could eat nothing. She put the plate with her husband's supper on the stove and bent down to stoke the fire, breaking up the lumps of coal with the hatchet which still lay in the grate. Then she slumped into the chair and, completely exhausted, still fully dressed, she slept.

Martha awoke with a start and looked at the clock above the fire which was now out. It was nearly two o'clock and what had awakened her was a noise in the shop. She jumped up and went to the door and as she opened it John, who must have slumped against it, fell headlong onto the living-room floor. He stank of liquor, had no hat on and his clothes were dishevelled as if he'd had to crawl home on his hands and knees.

'John!' Martha cried. 'What a *state* you're in! Get up at once! Where is your hat?'

'My *hat*,' John gasped, rolling his eyes to the ceiling, 'is that all you're bothered about – my hat?' He laughed tipsily and tried to stagger to his feet. Coupled with all she'd heard, or conjectured, about him during the day the sight of his inebriated state now filled her with rage and, reaching out, she grabbed him by his collar and helped drag him upright.

Once on his feet he hit out at her. 'Damn you, woman. Take your hands off me. Get me some cold tea. I am terribly thirsty.'

'I'll warm it for you, John,' Martha muttered, going to the stove, 'it might help sober you up.'

'Then you can drink it yourself and be damned.' John lurched across to the table, holding onto it with both hands to steady himself. Supported by it he looked at her with a stupid expression on his face. 'I'm going to bed.'

'At least eat your supper.' Martha took the plate of congealed food from the stove and slapped it down in front of him.

'Eat it yourself,' John said contemptuously and with a single movement swept the contents of the plate onto the floor. He then turned and hit her across the side of the face so hard that it made her dizzy and she fell onto a chair, clasping her face.

This gesture enraged Martha all the more when she thought of the hopes she'd entertained about the evening meal, and the care with which she'd prepared it, now lying on the floor not fit for a dog. Once more she tried to keep her emotions, almost running wild, under control. She rose to her feet grasping the mantelpiece for support.

'What makes you so cross, John, and so rude?' she said. 'I know you've been drinking and . . . I suppose you've also been with Mary Davis?'

John aimed a kick at her which missed and, instead, hit the chair on which she'd been sitting, almost breaking it in half.

'You *know* I have been with Mary Davis,' he roared. 'You do nothing but look for her out of the window, you jealous cow.'

'I hear she is expecting.'

'Oh, did you? How did you hear that?'

'Susan told me. She said William is past it, so . . . I suppose it is your child, John?'

'Aye, it must be. She can at least give me a child which is more than you can.' John's voice rose to a crescendo and it seemed as though his wrath had started to sober him up because he stood square on his two feet. 'She's going to leave her old man and come away with me.'

'And what about me, John?'

'You can go where you like. I don't want to have anything more to do with you – you, you, you . . .'

'I hope she's got money,' Martha said acidly, 'for you have none.'

John lurched towards the wall and, wrenching the whip away, struck Martha three times with it on the shoulders. With every blow she screamed with pain.

'If you do that again I will cry "murder" and everyone in the village will hear me.'

'If you do, I'll knock your brains through the window and hope I will find you dead in the morning. Do you think anyone in the village cares what happens to you? They don't, and they never did, with your uppity ways, your airs and your graces.'

'That is not true.'

'It is true. They wondered how I could marry someone like you.' He scratched his chin reflectively. 'Sometimes I have wondered too.'

'Did you tell them it was for my money?' Martha shouted. 'Did you tell them the truth? You married *me* for my money because you hadn't got a penny of your own? You took me away from a good job, a place where I was happy, pretending to love me . . .'

John now aimed a kick at her side which nearly took her breath away and she cried out again in pain.

'Shut up!' he bawled, seizing her by the shoulders and shaking her so hard that her teeth chattered. Suddenly he let go and shook his head as though he too felt dizzy. He sat on the chair and bent down as if to unfasten his boots and Martha's first thought was that he was going to throttle her with the laces. He looked up at her with a malevolent leer and, at that instant, Martha's eyes fell on the hatchet lying in the grate. Seizing it, she raised it in the air threateningly towards him. For a fraction of a second their eyes met and she saw his hatred turn to fear as, before he could rise again, and with both hands holding it steady she smashed the hatchet down on his head and as he attempted to struggle up she did it again, and again. John crashed like a stone onto the floor and Martha stood over him in case he attempted to rise, the hatchet at the ready. But John didn't move, blood slowly beginning to ooze from the terrible wound she had inflicted on the back of his head.

Martha stared uncomprehendingly at the body of her husband as if she didn't understand what she'd done. The force with which she'd hit him made her wrists ache and, in panic, she threw down the hatchet and knelt beside his inert form.

'John,' she said, touching him timidly. 'Get up, John.'

But John didn't move, and suddenly feeling very frightened she made an attempt to put the little pieces of broken bone together again, rather as a child might try to mend a toy, trying to pull the flesh to cover them. She knew it was a futile gesture, but then she wasn't herself but someone else, someone who had done something she would never do, someone who acted stupidly trying to save herself from harm.

She sat staring at the wound for some time, her hands covered in blood, and then she crossed to the sink, rinsed her hands and soaked a cloth in water. Hurrying back she tied it carefully round John's head in an attempt to staunch the flow of blood.

'John,' she said again, pleadingly. 'John, I'm sorry. Please open your eyes. *Please*, John.'

She realised she was crying hysterically and she lay down beside him. His eyes were open wide, staring at her with that very frightened expression she'd last seen.

She sat up, managing to lift his head onto her lap and, stroking his face, she started to croon to him as if he had been her baby.

'John, my poor John. Don't die. *Please* don't. I didn't intend to hit you so hard, John. I didn't know my own strength. I thought you would kill me, and I think you would have. But I never meant to harm you, really, John. I love you, I truly do. But you shouldn't have said you would leave me. John . . .' she touched his cheek and tapped it sharply. 'Do speak to me, John. Now it will be all right. Oh, John, John.' Realising the futility of her efforts she began to cry again and leaning down put her cheek against his. Already it seemed to her it was cold. She pulled his eyelids over his eyes so that he wouldn't stare so. But they only half shut so that they still seemed to gleam accusingly at her.

For a long time Martha sat holding him, wishing so much, so very much, that she could undo what she had done and bring him back to life. She would have given the world for it not to have happened.

Perhaps she slept for a short while because when she looked at the clock again it was four. Two hours had passed since he'd come home. She looked down at him and saw nothing had changed. She'd hoped it had been a bad dream and that she would wake up and find herself in bed with him snoring beside her.

The blood had formed a small pool on the floor, and a little rivulet was making its way towards the hatchet which lay by the grate, covered with blood and hair.

It was then that reality struck home. John was dead, killed by her. Her hand stole round her throat and she recalled that choking feeling and now she knew what it had meant. How she wished that she had been able to control her temper, as she had so many times in the past, and not unleashed that rage within her. She should have heeded the warning – people *had* warned her. Now she could be hanged for killing her husband.

Then she thought of the horse. That vicious horse. Everyone knew it was vicious. The horse could quite well have kicked her husband, causing that wound. Carefully laying John's head on the floor she put a green cushion under it. As she knelt beside him she kissed him, placing her hand against his heart, praying that she might feel it flutter.

'Remember, you did love me once, John,' she said in

a broken voice. 'I'm sure you did, and I never stopped loving you.'

She went again to the sink and, filling a bucket, began to wash the spots of blood off the walls. With the broken chair the place looked in a terrible mess. She scooped the supper from the floor and washed that too, straightened the table, tried to put the pieces of the broken chair together.

She had to tell someone about this, but she didn't want it to look like murder . . . because it wasn't. It was an accident. She hadn't *meant* to kill John. She had tried to save herself from him killing her. Only no one would believe her. John was right. The people of Birdsmoorgate had never taken her to their hearts in the way they had taken him.

She took the hatchet and wiped it carefully. Then she went upstairs to change her apron which was covered with blood and stuffed it into a drawer.

She put on a fresh apron, tidied her hair and, taking the hatchet, went out into the garden, tucking it away behind some logs in the garden shed.

Then she ran across the road and beat a tattoo on Richard Damon's door. After a moment the upper window flew open and, as his head appeared, she called out.

'Richard, come quick. John's horse has nearly killed him.'

She stood back and in a few seconds the front door opened and John's cousin emerged still fastening up his trousers.

'Quick, Richard,' she urged, and hurried ahead of him, entering the house first.

*   *   *

Richard Damon was appalled at the scene in front of him. His cousin was stretched out on the floor lying on his right side, his head on a cushion, his face towards the grate. The cloth that had been tied around his head was stained bright red and the blood was still oozing from it onto the floor where it had half congealed into a little pool. Richard knelt by John and took his left arm which hung limply and flopped back onto the floor as he let it go.

He looked up at Martha who was gazing anxiously at him.

'John is dead, Martha.'

'Is he?' she said, and covered her face with her hands.

'Yes.' Richard rose to his feet. 'How long has he been here and where did you find him?'

'I found him slumped outside the door at around two o'clock. It took me a fair time to drag him in, I can tell you. He was bleeding from his head. All he said to me was "horse". You know what a vicious brute it is and it nearly killed him. It will have to be shot.'

'It *has* killed him, Martha,' Richard said gently. 'John is quite dead.'

'Oh, my God!' Martha covered her face with her hands again and sank into the chair which Richard noticed was partly broken.

'Why did you not call me before?' he asked, looking around, puzzled by the disorder in the room.

Martha stuck a finger in her chest. 'He caught hold of my dress as he fell and I could not get away. His grip was so tight, he was so heavy. Oh please, please, Richard, go and get Harriet Knight. Ask her to help me.'

And as Martha slumped back into the chair, almost in

a swoon, Richard hurried out and ran up the road to do as she asked.

But by dawn it seemed as though the whole village was awake and converging on the house of death.

Harriet Knight, breathless with exertion, arrived just after five and was followed at eight-thirty by Hannah Smith who helped her lay out the corpse which they inspected carefully. Harriet voiced to Martha her disbelief that his horse could have killed him and Martha rounded on her and said it most certainly did. After that Harriet kept her opinion to herself, at least for a while. Francis Turner from next door went with Richard Damon and Joseph Davis to inspect the field and the road leading to the house. They found John's hat by the side of the gate and a pool of vomit, but they found no traces of blood either there or, later, in the passageway where Martha went to elaborate pains to show them how she had found her husband on his knees, his head resting on his hands.

George Fooks was summoned by Mr Staunton's boy and Susan Damon also came to view the corpse and hear how Martha had found him.

Monday 7 July
In the morning, Martha went with George Fooks to Crewkerne to buy a new black satin dress to wear for the funeral. Schooled by now at least to appear calm and in control, she chatted to George about his family and then what should be done with John's horse and how quickly it could be shot, the wicked evil beast. George said he had never known it to be *that* vicious and thought perhaps John exaggerated because it was old and slow and he wanted a new one. Martha kept her eyes firmly on the

road, her lips pursed and said it *was* a most evil horse and the sooner it was shot the better. George, who was a weak man easily dominated and impressed by Martha's firmness, said that if indeed it had killed his friend he would like to shoot it himself.

When Martha got home she found Henry Jeffery, a constable from Broadwindsor, waiting for her. He said she would be wanted for an inquest that evening, and he was followed by the coroner from Bridport who came to view the body.

Martha began to be alarmed by all this formality for what, after all, was an accident. But she changed into her new black dress, stuffed her other bloodstained one in a bag and put it in the wash house.

Then, just before five in the afternoon – still in a trance-like state as if nothing was real – and feeling desperately tired, for she had not slept for forty-eight hours, she went up to the Rose and Crown where a jury had convened and was the first to make her deposition, after being sworn, speaking in a firm resolute voice:

'My name is Martha Brown. My husband is twenty-six years of age – last Saturday he went to Beaminster with a load of poles, and was absent the whole of the day. George Fooks went with him. I did not see or hear anything of him until two o'clock on Sunday morning, when hearing a scuffle under the window, I went out, and found him lying on his face, with both arms and hands under his face; he appeared to be insensible. He groaned out "horse", as I thought. I got him into the house with great difficulty; he caught hold of my dress and tore it. I got him into an armchair, and in that position I remained until five o'clock, when he appeared to be exhausted. I could not go away to call anyone, but knocked at the wall as well as I could. No one came. I found blood flowing from his head, but did not know it was so bad as it proved to be. As soon as I could I went for Richard Damon, his cousin, who lives about a hundred yards from my house, and asked him to come directly, as my husband was nearly dead – I did not wait, but returned immediately; he breathed but twice after I got back. The horse he drove was his own, it was a very vicious one; no one could manage it but himself. I have often seen it attempt to strike my husband with its forefeet, and I once saw it strike his hat off. When the horse was shut in, it always made work, stamping and kicking. At first I considered my husband was in liquor, but when I saw the blood, I thought the horse must have struck him, which I still believe. No one but myself was in the house until after the death – I could not leave him to call any one, because he was so far gone and had my dress firmly clenched. He died at five o'clock on Sunday morning. Damon came just after he died.'

The room at the Rose and Crown was packed with onlookers who maintained a somewhat sceptical silence as Martha finished her testimony and took her place in the front row. She looked hopefully at those around her for agreement, searched the faces of the jury, but all had their eyes on the next witness, Richard Damon, who gave his account of seeing the body and being unable to find evidence of blood anywhere but in the house. He concluded by saying that he saw a lot of John and Martha and for the last three months they had lived 'comfortable and happy'. Inwardly Martha smiled to herself, as the last three months had been anything but; however she maintained an air of calm indifference although she smiled encouragingly at Richard as he sat down next to her.

Hannah Smith provided some grizzly details about the state of John's body prior to its being laid out.

'He had several wounds on his head, four or five, or more, and from some of them the brains were oozing out.'

She added that the deceased had very little dirt on his hands or his clothes. As his hat had been found by the gate she had supposed that he crawled home on his hands and knees. In contradiction of Richard Damon she added:

'Mrs Brown has complained to me of the conduct of her husband, that he had struck her. She intimated she was jealous of him, and her speaking to him on the subject caused him to strike her.'

A Bridport surgeon, Mr Hounsell, followed with his evidence about the state of the body when he examined it, adding ominously:

'The wounds appear to have been inflicted by some blunt instrument. I think it possible, but not probable, that the wounds on the deceased's head could have been caused by the feet of a horse . . . I am firmly of the opinion that if John Brown had received these injuries on his head at the gate where his hat was found he could not have possibly walked to his own house, a distance of some hundred and fifty to two hundred yards. I think Mrs Brown might have dragged her husband from the door to the room where the body now lies, but I should then have expected to see marks of blood in the passage.'

Martha lowered her eyes and bit her lip as the surgeon stood down, but was then surprised to hear Elizabeth

Sampson called. She owned the field where John kept his horse, but they scarcely had anything to do with her. Mrs Sampson said that at about two o'clock on the Sunday morning she had heard loud screams or groans which appeared to come from the direction of the Browns' house. She could not say whether they were male or female and added: 'I was not much acquainted with John Brown and his wife and do not know in what terms they lived.'

The last witness was George Fooks, who gave an account of John Brown's actions until they parted, just after eleven on the night of 5 July, after calling in at several public houses on the way home from Beaminster.

Then, after discussion among themselves, the jury passed a verdict that surprised no one but Martha, namely one of wilful murder committed by a person or persons unknown. This produced a reaction among the crowd as a buzz of excited conversation broke out.

'But it was an accident . . .' Martha said to Richard Damon as everyone rose to leave. To her surprise he didn't reply but seemed anxious to get away, and she was shocked to find that, as she made her way outside, everyone seemed similarly intent on shunning her instead of gathering round in support, and she was left to walk home alone.

Martha's state of mind was very confused as she realised she was alone in the house with John's body and that no one had attempted to accompany her or offer her comfort.

She made herself a cup of tea and then went out into the garden, reluctant to remain alone in the house where John's body lay as if a silent witness to what she had done.

Then the awful truth, at last, seemed to sink in. John was there upstairs, killed by her own hand, however provoked.

And, what was worse, the rest of the village seemed to know the truth too. They might have understood better if only they could see the marks on her body, but even they were fading.

Martha spent a long time in the garden gazing at the scenery around her, the sheep grazing on the hill rising up in front of her, the flowers and shrubs she had so lovingly planted in the garden. A blackbird was singing brilliantly in the top of one of the trees and his pure, beautiful tone uplifted her. She might not believe in God but she believed in the restorative powers of nature to soothe and to heal.

She went inside and up the stairs to where John lay. He had been dressed in clean clothes and his head was covered by a cap. His eyes, though, were still only partly closed and this unnerved her, as though he were looking at her and asking her how she could have done this to him.

She fled from the room in terror at the thought of those dead, accusing eyes following her.

Martha slept fitfully, waking every hour. Finally she rose with the dawn and busied herself about the house, uncertain whether or not to maintain normality and open the shop, or when they would come for John's body. And, then, what was her own situation with a verdict of murder, the finger of suspicion surely pointing at her?

In the end she decided against opening the shop. She thought it would be more decorous to leave it closed until the body had been removed.

She was busy about some mundane household tasks

when there was a knock on the door and hastening to it, thinking it was the undertaker, she was disconcerted to see a face at the other side that she hadn't seen for a long time, and didn't particularly want to see now.

Frances Brown, John's mother, was accompanied by her nephew, Richard Damon, whose expression was apologetic.

'Aunt has come to see John's body, Martha. Is it all right?'

'Of course it's all right,' Martha said, standing aside. 'How are you, Frances? It is terrible, I know, about John.'

But Frances Brown didn't reply and looked past her daughter-in-law as if she were looking for something.

'Where is he?' she asked and then, gazing straight at her, 'I know you killed him, Martha.'

'That is simply not true,' Martha said angrily, following the pair into the living room. 'Everyone knows it was the horse did it.'

'Everyone thinks it was *you* did it,' Frances said accusingly. 'Don't they, Richard?'

Richard looked nervously at Martha who pointed to the stairs.

'You know where to go.'

And as they went up and entered the room Frances gave a hysterical scream and Martha could hear Richard trying to comfort her.

Martha now was at a loss as to what to do. She put the kettle on the hob and decided to make tea, despite the hostility of her mother-in-law who would clearly do her a lot of harm if she talked this way before the whole village.

However, she was spared further speculation by the

arrival, a few minutes later, of a clergyman who introduced himself as Augustus de la Fosse, curate of Broadwindsor, and politely shook hands with her. 'I offer you my profound condolences, Mrs Brown, on your sad loss,' he said. 'I only heard of this sad event late yesterday afternoon and I am here to offer you what spiritual comfort I can.'

'Thank you, Reverend. My husband's mother and cousin are in with my husband's body at the moment but please come in. Would you like a cup of tea?'

As Frances had done, the clergyman stood looking round and Martha wondered what they had expected to see. Then he found what he was looking for and pointed to the floor where there was still a large bloodstain in the middle of the flagstone which Martha, scrub as she might, had not yet been able to remove.

'In the midst of life we are in death,' he intoned gloomily. 'I am profoundly sorry, Mrs Brown. It must have been a terrible shock for you.'

At that moment Frances came down the stairs in tears and paused when she saw the clergyman.

'This is Mr de la Fosse, Frances,' Martha said, 'curate of Broadwindsor.'

'Oh sir,' Frances cried, 'will you come up and pray by the body of my son?'

'Certainly, madam.' The curate looked questioningly at Martha who waved a hand. 'Please go up.'

'Perhaps you will join us in our prayers?' he enquired.

Martha shook her head. 'I am not a person of prayer, Reverend. I do not think there is anyone to hear us, certainly not after what happened to my husband. I have now lost two husbands and two children, and they still tell me that God is good.'

Shrugging his shoulders, the clergyman took Frances's arm and accompanied her up the stairs, and Martha soon heard the low murmur of voices from John's room. She knew it was important to be calm, to show resolution in the face of all this emotion and Frances's hysterical outburst, so she made tea and put the cups and saucers on the table and got out the cake that she would normally have been selling in her shop. Would that that normality could return.

When they came down, the curate was supporting Frances on one side, Richard on the other.

'Mrs Brown fainted in my arms,' the curate said. 'Have you water for her?'

'Certainly,' Martha said. 'Maybe a cup of hot tea would help revive her? I have some fresh just brewed.'

'I will not take tea in this house,' Frances said with a shudder, 'from the woman who murdered my son.'

Martha, upset by this outburst, now showed some emotion.

'You see,' she cried, 'I am accused of murdering my husband, yet I am as innocent as the angels in heaven.'

'*I* have not accused you, Mrs Brown,' the curate said thoughtfully, 'but the absence of blood everywhere but in this room seems to show he was not killed by the horse. He must have been killed in this room.'

'They will find another pool of blood somewhere and the thing it was done with,' Martha said with a toss of her head and looked defiantly at the curate whose expression showed quite plainly that now he had joined the swelling numbers of those who did not believe her.

Then, throwing her arms towards him, she cried despairingly:

'Why should I kill him and lose my home and have to lie under a hedge?'

'Everyone says you did it,' Frances muttered. 'They know you didn't get on. You were jealous of the woman across the road. Susan Damon told me.'

'Oh, did she?' Martha retorted. 'And what did you say to her?'

'*I* said, quite rightly, that you should never have married him. He was too young for you. I always said no good would come of it and it hasn't. It was your vanity that made you do it.'

'And his *greed* that made him ask me,' Martha said, shaking with anger. 'Did you tell everyone he was after my money, what little I had? And he used up every penny.'

At that Frances put her hand to her head and swayed, much to the concern of Richard who caught her, and the curate who had been distressed by the conversation between the women.

'I can't stay in this house for a moment longer,' Frances murmured. 'Please take me away, Richard.'

The curate appeared to hesitate as the others left the room.

'Is there anything you would like to say to me, Mrs Brown? I promise you it will be in confidence.'

'What should I say to you?' Martha looked puzzled. 'That I am guilty? Is that what you believe? Well, I am not. It was the horse that did it. No one wants to believe it because they do not like me.'

'I will pray for you, Mrs Brown,' the Reverend de la Fosse said piously. 'I am always there if you need me.'

As Martha walked to the door with him she was aware of a commotion outside. A small crowd had gathered to watch a constable in uniform walk down the road from the Rose and Crown where the magistrate had been examining more witnesses.

As the curate turned to her the constable, Mr Hull, asked if he could speak to Martha inside.

'Would you like me to stay, Mrs Brown?' Mr de la Fosse asked, but Martha shook her head and asked the constable to accompany her to the living room where she stood and faced him.

'What is it you want of me, Mr Hull?'

The constable cleared his throat. 'Martha Brown, on the instruction of the magistrate I am here to arrest you for the wilful murder of your husband, John Anthony Brown, and am charged to convey you to gaol in Dorchester where you will face trial.'

Martha Brown looked neither to right nor left as the carriage containing her and Mr Hull made its way slowly from her house along the Broadwindsor road which was lined with people, many of whom seem to have been alerted from remote farms and hamlets to watch her go. The carriage passed John Brown's cart which he had left at the side of the road some time after midnight in the early hours of Sunday morning. It looked very forlorn standing there, the harness thrown carelessly upon it as if at any moment he would come along with his horse, attach it and be off on another errand.

The sight made Martha feel emotional and she wiped tears from her eyes.

She had on her black dress and black bonnet. A small bundle lay at her feet and her face was as white as chalk. She couldn't believe that this was happening, yet, in her heart, she had known it was bound to happen. She couldn't bear to look at the faces of her neighbours who had never taken to her, few of whom, despite her efforts, had offered her friendship. She had done her best to please the villagers of Birdsmoorgate and yet they had not trusted her.

This sad little journey with her small bundle of possessions took her back to the many times she had set off as a child with her parents in search of another job to another temporary home, of the trip she and Bernard had made when they left Powerstock. Of the long journey to Steeple with John Symes, bringing fresh hope of a new life, and the fateful journey back to the Marshwood Vale as a bride desperately in love with her young, handsome husband.

It was a wretched plight for a woman whose ambition had always been to better herself, to escape from the poverty and rootlessness of her early life, who had always sought ways of escape towards a brighter future. Now that future seemed to lie in a gaol and the prospect of the hangman's rope.

Martha suddenly shivered despite the warmth and beauty of a midsummer's day. The carriage, pulled by a single horse, trudged through the wooded lanes of the Marshwood Vale, past the hedgerows with the pink-starred centaury, the great hairy willow-herb, the tall spires of agrimony, the blue meadow cranesbill and, as an omen filling her with dread, its red relation, bloody cranesbill.

Some workers gathering hay in the fields rested on their forks as the carriage passed by, doubtless alerted by the fast winds of gossip as to its occupants. She would have given much for a wave, or a friendly smile, but all she saw was stony faces. She felt so alone, utterly alone. There were few people left to care and who knew what her relations would say when they heard the news? Charles and Thomas, Ann and Mary? Eliza Coombes would doubtless express regret, but would say that she always knew that Martha, with her ungovernable temper, had it in her to kill. And perhaps she always had. She had nearly killed Eliza, but for Bernard's intervention. If only someone had been there to restrain her on Sunday morning last, as Bernard did then. If only John could have defended himself, big strong man that he was, but he was too drunk.

Well, she had denied it and she would go on denying it. In some ways she was beginning to believe her story herself.

'I hope they shoot that horse,' she said to Mr Hull, 'the horse, I mean, that did it.' She stared for some time fixedly at him but he ignored her and remained looking out of the window. So she herself turned to look again at the beautiful countryside where she had been born, not far away at Whitechurch Canonicorum. This was where she had lived all her life except for the ten years at Steeple.

In that instant Martha Brown felt, with a peculiar intensity, that she loved it, that it was beautiful and vibrant and meant so much to her; that she was like a daughter rooted in its soil. And as the horse clip-clopped along, maintaining a steady gait on its way to Dorchester, she wondered sadly when, if ever, she would see it again.

Chapter Eighteen

Monday 21 July 1856
Martha Brown sat in a small dark cell with no window and little other illumination beneath the crown court in Dorchester. She could scarcely believe the number of people who had gathered in the streets to see her. There had been such a crowd as she arrived that she was bundled, surrounded by policemen, into the court and down to the cells. The buzz from the courtroom above was now clearly audible to her. She had thought in the past about making something of her life and she had achieved it in an unexpected, and entirely unwelcome, way.

It was scarcely two weeks since John's death and events had occurred with astonishing rapidity.

She was guarded day and night by women warders. She was visited by the Governor of the prison, the Deputy Governor, the magistrate who had committed her, and the prison chaplain, the Reverend Dacre Clemetson, to whom she gave a piece of her mind when he started talking to her about the goodness of God and His mercy, so that he quickly left. She had been visited by a solicitor to whom she told her story, and learned counsel, Mr Edwards, who would defend her today. He had appeared to have little grasp of the case, and said it had been arranged in too much of a hurry to fit in with the Summer Assizes and that he had been inadequately briefed.

Their attitudes made Martha feel that these important men didn't care very much about her. The outlook, it was true, wasn't too good but nevertheless her optimism seemed unshakeable.

She had by now almost convinced herself that the story she had told so often was true, so that she was again able to trot it out with great conviction to anyone who asked. It was almost as though she *had* seen John's hat falling by the gate; John being sick next to it because of his intake of liquor, and then crawling all the way home to the passage from where she dragged him inside and tried to bathe his wound.

It was really the only explanation for what had happened, because she knew she was incapable of murder. Had she not been a virtuous woman all her life, cursed with a bit of a temper, it was true, but not a killer?

Thus it was important for her to maintain the firm control over her emotions that she had practised since John's death. She knew that her calm, her air of detachment, above all her dignity had impressed everybody. After all, had she not been housekeeper at Blackmanston Farm for over ten years? She'd been looked up to and respected for her hard work and diligence, her irreproachably chaste and worthy life. How she wished she'd stayed that way and not lost her heart and her head to a good-looking youth, who played havoc with her emotions and deceived her with other women while pretending to love her.

Sudden silence fell in the courtroom above her. A warder opened the door of her cell and, outwardly perfectly in control but inwardly trembling a little, she followed him up the stairs and into the courtroom which was so crowded that momentarily she paused, swallowed hard and closed her eyes. Opening them she followed the warder into the dock and stood there, every face in the courtroom turned towards her, appraising, examining, perhaps already condemning. To her right sat a row of grim-faced men dressed in their best – the jury, among whom she thought she recognised one or two faces.

The voice of the usher rang out, 'All Stand' and as the whole courtroom rose to its feet the majestic figure of the judge, robed and bewigged, entered from a door behind the bench, bowed and as he sat down glared fixedly at Martha who instinctively quailed.

His name, she had been told, was Serjeant Channell. She didn't think he looked a kindly man; he undoubtedly came from a class she neither knew nor understood and, for sure, they did not understand someone like her. He was of the ilk of the Walbridges, the Cooksons or the pious Mr de la Fosse with his fancy name who got on so well with her mother-in-law.

Mr Edwards, also in a wig and flowing gown, sat in front of her with two other men similarly dressed, one of whom, Mr Stock, after the clerk read out the charge and the court settled down, rose to present the Crown's evidence which, he said, was largely circumstantial.

'No human being beheld the prisoner strike the blow; to no one had she before her husband's death ever expressed any intention or desire of taking away his life; and to no one since his death has she made any statement as to the admission of guilt.'

However, they were, he said, an ill-assorted couple, 'he being twenty-one and she nearly fifty, the natural consequence of which was that there was no great harmony between them. The deceased was a mild man of moderate temper and tolerably good habits, but he was sometimes intemperate in drinking when he was out late at night and on occasions it did not infrequently happen that on his return home he passed the night on the floor of the room instead of going to bed.'

Martha nodded vigorously at this and leaned forward so that she would not miss a word.

'The strongest feeling, however, entertained by the prisoner towards her husband was one of jealousy, which had reference to a person named Mary Davis.'

Mary Davis. Martha, quivering at the very mention of her name, looked round the court and decided that had she seen Mary, that bitch, she would have stood up and shaken her fist at her. Mr Stock then went on to give what he considered were the facts of the case. He concluded with the statement that John's wound could not have been produced by a horse but by some blunt instrument such as the back of a hatchet which had been seen in the house but which could not now be found.

Martha suddenly remembered putting the hatchet in the shed and felt a moment of panic wondering if she'd hidden it well enough.

It was at that moment that she realised that fact alternated with fiction in her mind, and that this story was true and the one she had told was made up. There had been a hatchet. She had used it on John and then had hidden it. But she knew for certain, having seen them, she could have expected no mercy from these people if she confessed. She would stick to her story and she would believe in it, because she did not deserve to die.

Martha, who could not give evidence, listened with growing incredulity to all the people from Birdsmoorgate who were called and stood in the dock to testify against her. Some of them she had considered her friends but now proved themselves otherwise. In they came one after the other: George Fooks, Harriet Knight, Mrs Sampson, Joseph Davis, Francis Turner, Hannah Smith, Richard Damon and Susan who, in recounting their conversation the night before the killing and what she had said about Mary Davis, broke down and could hardly continue.

To her great indignation even Mr de la Fosse was called to repeat what he'd said and seen when visiting her, ostensibly to offer her words of spiritual comfort, thus lowering even further her estimation of the clergy.

Not one of them looked at her until they completed their testimony and sat in the well of the court where one or two glanced up at her surreptitiously, but she pretended not to see.

Martha shifted uneasily in the dock. It was very hot, and she glanced at the perspiring faces of the crowd to see how they reacted to the evidence. Hard to tell. They seemed enthralled, caught up in the drama that had been enacted one July in the small hours of the morning in the tiny hamlet of Birdsmoorgate. She knew Ann was there somewhere. Maybe Charles, maybe others that she knew, but they were lost in the sea of faces which sometimes, as the day went on, became blurred especially as the medical evidence was given, though she couldn't understand half of what was said with all the long names used to describe John's injuries.

Everyone seemed pretty certain that the horse couldn't have done it.

However, when finally at the end of a long day, during which she only had bread and water in her cell, her counsel stood up she thought he made an overwhelming case for her innocence. She leaned forward with her arm resting on the dock, listening intently.

Why, he asked, should she kill her husband? She had no motive and the idea of jealousy was ridiculous. There was no evidence that John Brown and Mary Davis were even known to each other. (Here Martha averted her eyes and gazed at the floor.)

'If Mrs Brown had been guilty, she would have fled like Cain from the scene of so diabolical a crime; but instead of this she was found remaining in her house, summoning her friends and going before the coroner to give evidence.'

He even put forward the hypothesis that, as it was improbable Brown's injuries could have been caused by a horse, he might have been waylaid on his way home and robbed of his wages. Mrs Brown appeared to corroborate this when she suggested to the Reverend de la Fosse that a pool of blood might still be found elsewhere. If he had been attacked close to home that would explain the absence of blood on the road.

Having concluded his address Mr Edwards called a single witness to Martha's character and, although she had suggested his name, she still received a shock when John Symes entered the witness box and stood there looking bewildered. She hadn't seen him since Blackmanston Farm and wished he would look at her so that she could give him a smile of encouragement, but he took no notice of her and in response to Mr Edwards's question said: 'I have known Mrs Brown for fourteen years and she lived with me and my brother for ten as housekeeper. She was as kind and as inoffensive a woman as ever lived and I was sorry to lose her.'

Martha would have liked John to proceed with his flattering testimony but he was stood down and passed by the dock without so much as glancing at her. She gazed after him, disappointed. She wanted a friend, someone to give her a kindly smile. She didn't seem to have any at all, not even John who came all the way from Steeple to testify for her. She had known him for such a long time and served him well. Perhaps he was ashamed of her, seeing her in the dock accused of murdering a man she had met at his farm? Maybe he wished now that he'd never heard of her? Would she were still at Blackmanston Farm, soberly and industriously carrying out her duties with nothing to distract her, and not in this awful place.

John's testimony gave her a little hope, but the instructions the judge gave to the jury dashed it again. She thought, in his summing up, that he unfairly relied almost entirely on the medical evidence: John could not have uttered a word, never mind walked, after the terrible wounds he had received from several blows to the head.

The judge felt that if John had been killed in his home then she was the only one who could have done it because, on her own admission, the only person in the house that night was his wife.

It was just after six o'clock when the judge sent the jury to consider their verdict and Martha back to the cells where she was given a hot meal and some tea and then left to her own thoughts.

These fluctuated from hope to despair, optimism to terror. She felt she was damned by the evidence, but the judge had stressed that the jury must have no reasonable doubt. Her hope was that one or two of them were honest men and might have just a little doubt.

Her hope seemed justified, her spirits soared, when she was called to the courtroom again just after ten to learn that the jury disagreed, and were not likely to agree.

The judge then told them he would have to retain them for the night and they could reconsider their verdict in the morning. But then the foreman asked if they could question one of the medical witnesses again, to which the judge consented. Martha's elation turned to dismay when Dr Gilbert, who had provided the medical evidence, was sent for and asked if the post-mortem examination, which had taken place several days after John's death, would have altered the state of his injuries. Could the way the corpse was handled have driven the bones further into the skull and made the wounds look much worse?

The doctor seemed incensed by this question – perhaps because it was so late at night – and said it was ridiculous. With that Martha's fate was sealed. After consulting among themselves in court the jury returned a verdict of guilty. Solemnly Serjeant Channell placed the black cap on his head and leaned towards the prisoner in the dock, addressing her directly.

'You have been found guilty of the wilful murder of John Anthony Brown.'

'I am not guilty, my lord!' Martha exclaimed and was

immediately cautioned by an usher. The judge paused, frowned at her and then went on to say that, in his opinion, Martha's crime was greatly aggravated by the fact that the victim was her husband.

'The nature of their verdict shows that it was in that room (in the house) that your husband met his death and by the verdict of guilty they have come to the conclusion that it was from your hands he met his untimely end.'

Martha interrupted again, this time stabbing her finger repeatedly at the judge.

'I never lifted a hand against him or any mortal.'

Once again she was restrained, the judge continuing by saying that Martha took advantage of the fact that her husband was drunk and could not defend himself.

'And you have sent to his account without any opportunity of preparation, and in a state of insensibility I think from what he had been drinking, not only a fellow creature but him whom you had solemnly promised to love, honour and obey. Whether or not you were influenced by feelings of jealousy with respect to the person to whom reference has been made . . .'

'No sir!' Martha shouted, clinging to the side of the dock, but the judge didn't even pause, 'or whether or not you inflicted these wounds with a blunt hatchet . . .'

'I am not guilty!' Martha cried in rage, but the judge continued as though he had not heard her, '. . . on him is known only to yourself and to that "being to whom all hearts are open and from whom no secrets are hid".'

He concurred with the verdict and concluded with the awful words as ordained by law, 'That you be taken back to the place from whence you came and on a certain day taken to a place of execution, there to be hanged by the neck until you are dead; and that your body be afterwards buried within the precincts of the gaol. May the Lord have mercy on your soul.'

As he pronounced sentence Martha raised her eyes upwards, lifted her hands and cried with great emphasis, 'I am *not* guilty!'

There was an uproar as she was seized by two prison officers and led out through the crowd that had formed in the court, in the vestibule and in the street outside. For a moment their way was blocked and Martha was disconcerted when the Reverend de la Fosse approached her and hissed:

'My dear woman, now that your fate is sealed, for God's sake tell the truth!'

Irritated and angered by his impertinence Martha facetiously, and somewhat unwisely, only had time to hiss back: 'The horse did not do it, Mr Fosse, he fell downstairs,' before she was hurried on to a fly waiting in the street outside. As the unruly crowd attempted to mob her she was bundled inside, police officers gathered round to clear a way for the carriage which was then driven rapidly the few hundred yards to the prison which was around the corner. From this she emerged and was taken to her cell where she collapsed on her bed weeping.

A few hours later Martha, still fully clothed, sat on the edge of her bed staring in front of her. The noise of the crowd's taunts after she had been convicted of murder still resounded in her ears. Hands had clawed at her and she thought she would have been hung there and then if they could have got hold of her.

She hardly slept at all and now from the window high

up in the wall of her cell she could glimpse dawn lighting up the sky.

In the opposite corner, sitting in a chair, was Emelia, one of her warders, who kept glancing at her. Finally she rose and put a hand on Martha's shoulder.

'Will you not try and sleep, Mrs Brown? Sitting up brooding does you no good.'

'I never thought I should be condemned.' Martha looked up at her. 'I am innocent. Why does no one believe me?'

Emelia was a sensible countrywoman from a village near Dorchester and had known many female prisoners but never one condemned to be hanged.

At first she had considered the prisoner remote and arrogant but, in the short time she had known her, she came to realise that it was her way of holding on, of not giving in. She was still doing it, acting a part.

'All is not lost, Mrs Brown. There is time for a reprieve. They do not like to hang women. There now.' She gently but unsuccessfully attempted to lower Martha onto the bed.

'Leave me be, Emelia. I have tried but I cannot sleep.'

'Then lie quietly, Mrs Brown. You will soon go off.'

'What? With my thoughts? You think I am to be left to lie with my terrible memories? The crowds that surged about me, trying to paw me with their hands, the people staring up at me, all believing I was guilty?'

'I do not believe you are guilty, Mrs Brown. There,' Emelia sat on the edge of the bed and took her hand. 'I am sure there are many like me and you will soon hear you are reprieved.'

'Oh Emelia!' Martha turned to her, eyes brimming over. 'Thank you. If you believe that, it gives me hope.'

'Now, you lie down,' Emelia succeeded in her task, 'and think sweet thoughts.'

'Of my children.'

'Yes, and the good times you had. There must have been many of those, Mrs Brown?'

'A few,' Martha admitted. 'Not many. I have had a sad life, Emelia, and nothing sadder than my years in Birdsmoorgate and my life with John Brown who did not treat me well, much as I loved him. I should never have married him, but I did not kill him. If it was not the horse it was someone else, a thief who waylaid him and stole his money, for he had none on him when he came home. Now, isn't that a strange fact, Emelia?'

'Very strange,' Emelia agreed, drawing up a blanket over her charge. 'So you see, when they find the real culprit you will get a pardon and be a free woman again.'

Martha managed to get a few hours' sleep but as soon as she woke her position seemed all the more frightening. The shadow of the gallows loomed, a fact she found impossible to contemplate. Her hand stole around her throat but Emelia appeared with a cup of tea and some bread and Martha broke her fast and even managed to enjoy what she ate.

She then washed and brushed her hair and sat down again, this time with Betty, another wardress who did not share Emelia's belief in Martha's innocence and showed it by her brusque behaviour towards her. Betty didn't attempt to converse with her or comfort her, whereas Emelia did. Betty considered her a convicted murderess; Emelia a person who might be innocent.

So Martha sat in one corner of the room with her grim thoughts and Betty knitted in the other, not encouraging conversation. Martha thought that at this rate time would pass very slowly and all she would have to think about would be the wretchedness of her condition.

At about three in the afternoon the cell door swung open and the Reverend Clemetson, the prison chaplain, stood hesitantly on the threshold as if unsure of his welcome. His previous brief interviews with Martha had not been promising. Mr Clemetson was a tall, lean man of about fifty-five with thinning grey hair and an earnest expression, the light of a fierce faith burning behind his steel-rimmed spectacles.

'Mrs Brown?'

She looked up, her expression apathetic.

'Would it be all right now if I came in?'

Martha nodded and Betty came over with a seat for the clergyman who sat down and put the Bible he carried on the table next to him.

'I am condemned to death, Mr Clemetson.'

'So I heard.' The clergyman cleared his throat. 'I am here to offer you what comfort I can and, believe me, that comfort comes from hope in the Lord.'

'How can I hope in the Lord if He allows such things to happen? An innocent woman to be sent to the scaffold?'

'Mrs Brown,' the clergyman moved his chair forward so that their knees almost touched. 'You must never give in to the sin of despair. Never. The good Lord is there to comfort, not condemn.'

'I really do not believe that,' Martha said firmly. 'If

there is a God, circumstances have meant that I don't believe in His goodness.'

'Why is it that you reject God, Mrs Brown?' he asked gently.

'Because God rejected me. I had two dear little boys and they were taken away from me in infancy, one after the other. I had a good husband who died searching for his daughter. Then I married a man who said he loved me and he did not.'

'Were you married in church, Mrs Brown?'

Martha shook her head. 'My last husband was much younger than I was. Neither of our families approved. We were married in a register office in Wareham.'

'You see, Mrs Brown, did you not think that a marriage not blessed by God was bound to fail? We all need help in our married lives. I have a daughter but I lost my dear wife and God has given me such strength to bear my loss. Without Him I would never have managed.'

'The first time I did marry in church, and it made no difference.' She gazed at him defiantly.

'I see.' Nonplussed, the Reverend Clemetson reconsidered his situation.

'I must tell you, Mr Clemetson,' Martha said, pressing her advantage, 'I don't have a high opinion of the clergy. Explain to me, if you can, why God sends us bad things if He is good?'

Mr Clemetson shook his head. 'It is a mystery. I must be truthful with you, as you have been with me. We don't know. But all will be revealed in the next world.'

Martha looked at him dubiously. 'Are you sure?'

'Quite sure.'

'And will I see my children there?'

'Undoubtedly.'

'And Bernard?'

'Of course . . . and John too,' he added, but noticed that Martha's expression changed at the mention of her late husband's name.

Rather more hopeful about her outlook, sensing a possible change of heart, he took up his Bible and opened it. 'May I read to you from the good book?'

'If you wish,' Martha said politely, adding, 'It will help pass the time.'

'This is from the book of Isaiah.' Mr Clemetson opened it at a page he had already marked. 'I think it will be of comfort to you:

'"Oh Lord thou art my God: I will exalt thee. I will praise Thy name: for thou hast done wonderful things: thy counsels of old are faithfulness and truth . . . For thou hast been a strength to the poor, a strength to the needy in his distress, a refuge from the storm, a shadow from the heat, when the blast of the terrible ones is as a storm against the wall . . .

He will swallow up death in victory; and the Lord God will wipe away tears from off all faces and the rebuke of his people shall he take away from off all the earth; for the Lord hath spoken it. And it shall be said in that day, Lo, this is our God; we have waited for him, and he will save us; this is the Lord; we have waited for him, we will be glad and rejoice in his salvation."'

When the minister had finished reading he noticed that Martha had been listening to him attentively.

'Those words are very beautiful,' she said. 'To tell

you the truth I have never understood the Bible. I am an uneducated woman, my parents were simple farm workers and I was until I married my first husband. I knew about dairykeeping but not much more. So it always seemed to me that the clergy thought themselves better than me and my kind. As I told you, I don't have much time for them. I don't respect them. Mr de la Fosse came to my home to offer me comfort and then appeared in court to give evidence against me. Is that a very Christian thing to do, I ask you?'

Mr Clemetson mumbled something and shook his head.

'So when I saw the judge and the lawyers in the courtroom they reminded me of people like Mr de la Fosse and Mr Cookson the vicar at Powerstock whom I considered most stuck-up. He was not very nice to my husband who so wanted to be a churchwarden, and was little comfort to me when my children died. We were not poor. We had bettered ourselves and my husband rented a lot of land and also owned some. But the vicar didn't treat us with the respect that he treated others with, who were better educated, though my husband could read and write. I thought that Mr Cookson and people like him didn't understand us at all, us simple folk, just like the lawyers in the court. So they never explained the Bible properly and it meant nothing to me. Some children attended Bible classes but I and my brothers and sisters never did because we had to help our parents on the farm. We had to work from an early age. But I can see now, from the way you read from the Bible just now, that it is indeed beautiful.'

Mr Clemetson's sallow features glowed with pleasure.

'Oh, Mrs Brown, I am so happy to hear you say that.'
He closed his book and placed his hand on her forehead.
'May God's blessing be upon you.'

Impulsively she clasped his hand and for a moment
they sat like that, looking at each other.

'I will come again,' he said and as he left the cell his
heart felt uplifted because he thought that, not for the
first time, he had seen a soul in extremity touched by
God which, to him, was proof of His existence.

The following day Martha, having slept a little better,
felt more cheerful and she sat talking to Emelia when
the cell door opened and the warder announced that
she had two visitors.

'Who are they?' she asked.

'Mr Brown and his daughter.'

'My husband's father!' she exclaimed, looking triumphantly at Emelia. 'You see, Emelia, I could not have
killed my husband, or his father and sister would never
have come to see me.'

And she hastened out, accompanied by the warder
who led her to a small room furnished with chairs and
a plain deal table at one side of which sat Robert Brown
and Christiana who both rose as Martha entered. Robert
Brown's manner seemed awkward, rather as if he had
been dragged here by his daughter, but she ran over to
Martha and embraced her.

'Oh Martha, I never thought to see you in this terrible
situation.'

'I never thought to be here,' Martha said, sombrely,
turning to Robert.

'It is good of you to come, Robert.'

'We could do no less,' he said, sitting down and

mopping his brow as though this was an ordeal he had not relished. 'You know, Martha, that I never shared my wife's feelings about you. I thought if you and John chose to wed that was your affair.'

'I'm glad you thought that, Robert.'

'And we certainly don't believe you killed John,' Christiana spoke excitedly. 'We, Father and I, that is, don't believe you capable of such a thing.'

'Your mother came to see John's body. She accused me of killing him.'

'Mother was upset. She had a mother's tenderness for her only son. She did not want to lose him to you, and now he has gone forever.'

'A nicer man never existed.' Robert had tears in his eyes. 'You loved him, Martha, didn't you?'

'I did. So why should I kill him? Your wife thought I did and made much mischief. I was friendly with the Damons and they both testified against me, influenced by *her*.'

'You should take no notice of her. Don't upset yourself.'

'I am upset because Frances, to whom I never did any harm, helped to turn the villagers against me by saying cruel and untrue things about me. She was befriended by the Reverend de la Fosse who later testified in court against me. He came to offer me comfort and ended by accusing me. But I can tell you this: if the horse didn't kill him someone else certainly did.'

'You don't think the horse killed him?' Robert looked surprised.

'I did think it, but as they found no blood it looks as though he was waylaid outside our door and hit with a stone or some such. He had no money in his

366

pockets. I didn't think to question that until it was too late.'

'Many people are trying to get you a reprieve, Martha,' Christiana said. 'Petitions are going round Dorset seeking signatures. There is quite a lot of steam got up about the whole affair.'

'I never thought to be so well known,' Martha said. 'Would that it was from some other cause than that my name is on everyone's tongue as a murderess.'

'The trial was unjust, with witnesses being called who were not examined by the magistrate. I was sitting at the back and heard every word,' Christiana said indignantly.

'My counsel said the same. He had inadequate time to prepare. I only saw him once myself. He did his best, poor man, but the fact is it was all rushed through to get a verdict against me. But, do you know,' she sat back with a little half smile, 'I am convinced I will not hang. I have friends, even in prison, who believe the same thing. Now,' she leaned across to her sister-in-law, 'let's be more cheerful. How is your little girl, Fanny?'

'She is so sweet, and good,' Christiana affirmed with proper mother's pride. 'You will soon be able to see her, Martha. When all the world knows you are innocent and you are released you must come and stay with us.'

Martha felt cheered by the visit of John's father and sister but that evening the prison Governor, Mr Lawrence, entered her cell, accompanied by his Deputy Governor. Mr Lawrence, who clearly had no doubts about the prisoner's guilt, didn't mince his words.

'Mrs Brown, it is my duty to inform you that the date

of your execution has been fixed for Saturday week, 9 August, at eight o'clock in the morning.'

The blood drained from Martha's face. 'I am told there are petitions going round for my reprieve.'

'That is not the same thing as a judicial reprieve. Until the Home Secretary decides otherwise, this sentence will stand. I tell you now so that you have time to prepare to meet your Maker, and you might consider if a confession will give you an easier conscience for that awesome encounter when you will be judged.'

'I have nothing to confess,' Martha said stubbornly. 'As I said in court, I am innocent.'

The Governor said no more but, with the Deputy Governor, left the room whereupon Martha abandoned pretence and fell into Emelia's arms and wept.

'There, there,' Emelia led her to a chair. 'He is obeying orders. It is the law.'

'But it will not happen will it, Emelia?' Wild-eyed, Martha clutched at her. 'You promised me?'

'I am sure it will not happen,' Emelia said soothingly. 'Now, would you like to play cards to take your mind off it?'

And getting out the pack she began to shuffle it distractedly as if she was unsure herself.

Chapter Nineteen

30 July—6 August 1856

It was a beautiful summer's day, warm and temperate. The apricot-coloured roses that climbed up the wall of Meadways were interspersed with purple clematis and yellow waxy honeysuckle whose heady perfume intermingled with that of the massed lavender, white phlox, lilies and pink dianthus wafting up from the herbaceous border of the garden in front of the house. Martha had spread a rug out on the grass, and sat there clutching Thomas who, flinging out his chubby arms with glee, was chuckling at the antics of his brother William playing 'tig' in the field with Joanna and James. William giggled so much he kept on falling over and being caught and the air was full of laughter. Beyond them, making their way slowly alongside the river, the fat cattle grazed contentedly in the field while a few reckless hens, their brown feathers ruffled, scurried about agitatedly pecking at the grass, scouring it for tit-bits.

The trees in their full summer finery provided a thick, interlocking green canopy, casting deep shadows on the ground, and under which the cattle, mechanically chewing the cud, finally paused to rest.

Martha, with a sense of complete fulfilment, thought that she would never have such a perfect day as this. She lightly kissed the top of little Thomas's head, inhaling his sweet baby smell. Then she closed her eyes savouring the scents and sounds of summer: birdsong and the drone of bees, the sheer happiness of Thomas clasped in her arms, and children playing.

Martha woke abruptly and, as a contrast to her dream, felt engulfed, smothered by the darkness. She blinked her eyes rapidly and then closed them again, hoping against hope that this was the dream and the world she'd just woken from, reality. In her mind's eye she could still see so vividly the scene on that perfect summer's day in the year 1834, could smell the fragrances and hear the happy sound of children playing as she tightly hugged the precious baby in her arms.

Tears sprang to her eyes and she turned and buried her face in her pillow, sobbing wildly.

For onto that vision of a summer's day long ago had fallen the tall shadow of the gallows, very real and very near.

During the days that followed the Governor's announcement, most of the women who looked after her did their best to keep Martha's spirits up. Mr Clemetson came daily, but, despite his initial optimism, he could get no further with her spiritual progress: her acceptance of her fate and trust in the final mercy and goodness of God.

He would read to her from the Bible but she liked nothing better than the verses from Isaiah which had

370

marked the beginning of her trust in him. He also told her that the MP for Dorchester, Mr Sheridan, had taken an interest in her case on the grounds that she killed her husband in a fit of jealousy, and therefore it was not a premeditated act, to which she stonily replied:

'I did not kill my husband, Mr Clemetson. How many times do I have to tell you?'

'They also say that your demeanour is not one of an innocent person.'

'How do you mean my "demeanour"?' she demanded.

'That you appear too calm.'

'That is because I am innocent.'

'Nevertheless they seem to think it tells against you.'

'That I can do nothing about. I am calm and controlled because I am innocent. If I were to start having hysterics and tearing my clothes would that make me less guilty? I think not.'

However, as the days passed and the day set for her execution drew nearer Martha became less calm and more agitated, inwardly at least. Despite all the efforts being made on her behalf the hours were ticking by. She was again playing cards with Emelia and Betty when she was told that her brother and sister were waiting to see her.

'Ann!' she cried, throwing down her cards and running after the warder as he left the room. 'My sister has come!'

When Martha entered the room Ann burst into tears and Charles stood stoically by, biting his lip. Martha immediately folded Ann into her arms.

'There, there, my dearest sister,' she said. 'Don't cry, I am going to be reprieved.'

'Oh, have you heard?' Ann cried, her face lighting up as she brushed away her tears.

'Not yet, but I feel it. I am told there is a big movement to save me.'

Ann's face fell. 'Yes, but comments from some of the papers are not so helpful.'

'Oh, no one takes any notice of them!' Martha said airily, going across to Charles and taking him by the arm. 'How are you, dear brother?'

'As well as I can be, Martha.'

'And Sophia and the children?'

'They are . . .' Charles began, then he put his hands over his face and burst into tears. 'Oh Martha, this is a terrible thing to happen.'

'Charles, Charles, you must not weep. I am not going to die . . . I cannot die because I did not kill John. I tell you we will all be united again one day under one roof . . . and I do not mean in heaven.' She attempted a smile but it was not easy. Charles, as the baby, had always been a particular favourite and she tenderly put her arms round him now as she had when he was small. She could recall the screams of her mother when Charles was being born, vowing never to have another child, and she never did; she had had enough, after twenty years of childbearing.

Charles seemed to recover his composure and perhaps the memories of childhood, the warmth of that sisterly embrace, helped.

Martha looked into his eyes and brushed away his tears.

'You must be brave, as I am,' she whispered and she took his hand as they joined Ann at the table.

But Ann, once the tears had dried, continued to look

troubled. Leaning towards Martha she lowered her voice so that the warder standing in the corner should not hear.

'Martha,' she whispered, 'I must speak. No one believes that you did not kill John. Not even me. That *is* the truth.'

'I cannot believe my own sister,' Martha began furiously, but Ann held up a warning hand.

'I love you, Martha, you know that. I believe that what you did, you did out of provocation. I know that John beat you. I saw the marks. I tried so hard not to think you did it but the evidence is against you. And I know you have such a temper! I am sure it was an act you immediately regretted, and probably you have blotted it from your mind, or tried to. But why don't you tell the truth? You have very little time left and it might save your life.'

'How do you mean it might save my life?'

'If you were provoked, acted rashly, and now repent of what you did it might persuade the Home Secretary to save you. That is what I have heard. You also did yourself no good by shouting at the judge. It did not make a favourable impression. People thought you a wild woman, an ill-tempered harridan.' Ann began to weep again. 'I can see I've upset you, Martha. But it is only because I love you that I want to see you reprieved.'

'How can they reprieve me if I say I am guilty, that I have lied all along?'

'Because your husband beat you and provoked you into that rash action for which you do not deserve to lose your life.' Ann held out her arms pleadingly towards her sister. 'Please, Martha. I beg you. You have so little time.'

*   *   *

Martha was so distressed by the visit of her brother and sister that she requested that there should be no more visitors. But Ann's words had made a great impression on her and, as more days passed and there was no news of a reprieve she began to consider Ann's advice as a last resort, harsh but meant lovingly she knew that. Her thoughts were concentrated all the more when she heard that they were constructing the scaffold outside the new gate of the prison, and that the town's population were already making plans for a day out, a hang-fair, as it was twenty-three years since there had last been a public execution in Dorchester.

One morning a few days before the appointed day, when she awoke she could actually hear the sound of banging. She lay still in her bed while a chill crept all along her body from her toes to her head, and she wished then that she was able to pray.

She got up, washed and dressed, and when Emelia brought her breakfast she said: 'Do you believe in God, Emelia?'

'Oh yes,' Emelia said, fervently, 'and if you did, Martha, it would bring great comfort to you.' The two women then fell upon each other and wept.

'Please ask Mr Clemetson to come to me,' Martha said when she recovered, 'and bring his book.'

Mr Clemetson came to her that morning at about eleven o'clock and noticed at once a change in her attitude.

'You asked to see me, Martha?'

Martha pointed to a chair.

'Will you read to me from the Bible?'

'Of course.' As Mr Clemetson opened his book he looked across at her.

'You know, Martha, that you are very near death?'

'I don't believe it,' she said robustly. 'I am told petitions are going round for my reprieve and if there is a God and He is good, as you say, I don't think He will let me hang.'

'Why cannot I get you to believe in the goodness of God when there is so much evidence?'

'What evidence?' she said rudely.

'All around us. The beauty of the earth. The majesty of the heavens.'

'Well then, if there *is* a God He has not been very good to me. He took my first husband and children away, my second husband ill-treated me . . .'

'But Martha, why didn't you tell that to the lawyers?'

'They wouldn't have believed me.'

'But you had scars?'

'They've faded.' Martha rolled up her sleeve. 'Though I believe one of the marks remained.' She pointed to a red weal left by the whip which the clergyman inspected intently.

'Martha, I have good reason to believe that if you told the truth – and no one believes you so far, I'm afraid – we might be able to win you a pardon. Despite the petitions going around, the papers now are saying that you are a hard-hearted murderess, but if the truth were known, that you *were* severely provoked, I think the Home Secretary might intervene. Now, Martha, I do not wish to trivialise the nature of this crime. Murder is a very evil thing, even if you were provoked, murder of a husband above all. But if you repent, even if you are not reprieved, God will forgive you and take you to His bosom and you will see your loved ones again.'

'Do you *really* think so?' Martha asked as if she had a sudden moment of illumination.

'Yes I do. With all my heart.'

'You are a good man,' Martha said softly. 'As good as Bernard ever was, perhaps better.'

'Will you pray with me, Martha?' he asked gently and as she nodded he knelt on the floor and so did she and together they bent their heads in prayer:

'Lord God,' Mr Clemetson intoned, 'listen to the prayers of Your servant, Martha Brown, and, if it be Your will, Lord, grant her a reprieve. If not, grant her peace of mind in the knowledge that You will take her to Your bosom and unite her with her loved ones again.'

Thursday 7 August 1856

The magistrate who had committed Martha in Birdsmoorgate, Mr Tatchell Bullen, and the Governor together with the Reverend Mr Clemetson, stood before Martha who, looking pale but composed, rose from the table at which she had been sitting.

'I hear you have something you wish to tell us, Mrs Brown?' the Governor asked stiffly.

Martha nodded.

Mr Clemetson came eagerly forward. 'Martha, if you tell the truth about what really happened I myself will go to London with Mr Sheridan and present the case for a reprieve to the Home Secretary in person.'

'You promise?'

'I promise. This very day. Everyone wants to save you, but you must first save yourself.'

Martha nodded again as if she understood. Then, as a piece of paper was placed before her, she said:

'I was never a scholar, but I had a little shop and learned to manage. Despite my first husband's efforts, I am poor at reading or writing other than my name.' She handed back the paper, 'So you must do this for me.'

'Then you must tell me what to say, Martha,' and, looking at the Governor and the magistrate, the Reverend Clemetson took his seat beside the prisoner.

'My husband, John Anthony Brown, came home on Sunday morning, 6 July, at two o'clock, in liquor, and was sick. He had no hat on. I asked him what he had done with his hat. He abused me, and said "What is that to you? Damn you!" He then asked for some cold tea. I said I had none, but would make him some warm. His answer was: – "Drink it yourself, and be d——d." I then said, "What makes you so cross? Have you been to Mary Davis's?"

'He then kicked out the bottom of the chair on which I had been sitting, and we continued quarrelling until three o'clock, when he struck me a severe blow on the side of the head, which confused me so much that I was obliged to sit down. He then said (supper being on the table at the time), "Eat it yourself and be d——d", and reached down from the mantelpiece a heavy hand-whip, with a plaited head, and struck me across the shoulders with it three times, and every time I screamed out I said, "If you strike me again, I will cry murder." He replied, "If you do, I will knock your brains through the window," and said he hoped he should find me dead in the morning, and then kicked me on the left side, which caused me much pain. He immediately stooped down to unlace his boots, and being much enraged, and in an ungovernable passion at being so abused and struck, I seized a hatchet that was lying close to where I sat, and which I had been making use of to break the coal for keeping up the fire to keep his supper warm, and struck him several violent blows on the head — I could not say how many — and he fell at the first blow on his side, with his face to the fireplace and he never spoke or moved afterwards.

'As soon as I had done it I would have given the world not to have done it. I had never struck him before after all this ill-treatment; but when he hit me so hard at this time I was almost out of my senses, and hardly knew what I was doing.'

Friday 8 August 1856
Twenty-four hours passed during which time Martha heard nothing except that Mr Clemetson had hurried to London with the Member of Parliament, but time was running out. She knew the scaffold was in place and the townsfolk were already eagerly anticipating the spectacle.

Martha woke on the morning of the day that might be her last but one on earth and contemplated the ceiling. To her surprise she felt no fear. There was even a sense of optimism but, above all, of peace now that her conscience was clear. She had stopped deceiving herself and pretending that something had happened which had not.

She was sorry she had deceived the Browns and lied to her sister, but now she had done what she had to and there was nothing more to do.

She had told the truth and if there was a God and He was good, as Mr Clemetson assured her, then she had also made her peace with Him. She wanted to believe in

God's goodness because now she realised that this was the only hope she had; otherwise, if a reprieve was not granted, there was only emptiness.

Time that day seemed to pass very slowly. Martha was on edge as were Emelia and Betty, and cards didn't take their mind off what was in their hearts. Just before noon, however, the door opened and as Mr Lawrence entered Martha immediately knew her fate.

'I am sorry to tell you, Mrs Brown, that despite the efforts of Mr Clemetson and Mr Sheridan you have not been reprieved. The Home Secretary is out of the country and the official acting in his place is unable to grant one, and says the law must take its course.'

'Then could we not wait until the Home Secretary returns?' Martha said desperately, looking from her attendants to the Governor who shook his head.

'I am sorry to have to give you this news.' With that he hastily left the room as if to spare himself further recriminations.

Martha remained where she was for a long time. Then Emelia stealthily approached her and, standing by her side, took her hand.

'It is done,' Martha said. 'It is just. I accept it, Emelia, because if there is a God, and I hope there is, Mr Clemetson says I will be united with my children and my first husband, and perhaps poor John if he can find it in his heart to forgive me for what I did, for I have forgiven him for what he did to me.'

Emelia began to weep softly and Martha took her in her arms. 'Don't weep for me, Emelia. I lied to you and I'm sorry, but I almost believed for a time that the story I told was true. I wanted to, because I was afraid to hang. But now, after so much fear, I am resigned. You know, for many years I sometimes awoke in the night with the sensation that I was choking. Now I know what it meant. I had a temper and I was not always able to control it. People warned me that one day I would do something I regretted, and it happened just as they said it would. If John had not been drunk he would have been able to save himself, and thus me, from the consequences of my behaviour.

'But God meant that it was not to be. I did not mean to kill John, but I think if I had not he would have killed me. He said as much. After he was dead I would have given *anything* for it not to have happened. I scarcely knew what I was doing. But now I have to face the consequences and I'm glad because this life has ceased to matter very much to me, after all.'

Martha did not sleep well. Often she awoke and her courage failed her. She trembled with fear. This time tomorrow she would be no more. It was a concept that was almost impossible to contemplate. She was comparatively young and, normally, would have relished many more years of life. A small consolation was that she would never grow old as her parents had and sink into decrepitude.

Emelia spent the night with her in her cell and came to her when she cried out to her for comfort.

'You will be strong,' she said to Martha, 'I know you will.'

Martha welcomed the dawn as much as she dreaded it, and Emelia brought her a cup of tea. Then Martha rose, washed herself carefully and dressed with the help of Emelia whose fingers trembled as she endeavoured to do up the buttons on her black dress.

'This is the dress I bought for John's funeral,' Martha said sadly. 'Now it will be for mine.' This made Emelia cry again and she was unable to complete her task which was taken over by Betty whose temperament was a little stronger.

'Mr Clemetson is back and will come and see you,' she murmured. 'He told me to say when you were ready.'

'Tell him I am ready,' Martha said robustly, taking a brush to her hair. 'I want to look my best.'

'There are hundreds of people out there,' Betty said with awe, 'maybe thousands.'

Martha's chin trembled but she composed herself as Betty left to fetch the chaplain. He came in with the Reverend Henry Moule who had visited Martha the previous evening when, in the chaplain's absence, they had prayed together and he had read to her from the Bible.

Martha greeted them both politely.

'I am very sorry, Martha, I did all I could.' Mr Clemetson himself seemed close to tears.

'You did your best,' she smiled. 'I am resigned to my fate.'

'Mr Moule has brought you Communion,' Mr Clemetson said. 'He told me you asked for it last night.'

It was many years since Martha had received the sacrament and as the priest held aloft the host she regretted that she had rejected God all these years for if she had not she might not be in the present situation. He would have helped and strengthened her and, when tempted, she could have prayed.

She closed her eyes fervently as the wafer was laid on her tongue. She felt then an extraordinary sense of peace, and knew that God existed and was with her. She remained for some time on her knees, praying with Mr Clemetson, and then she rose and embraced him.

'I shall miss you very much, Martha,' he said, trembling a little. 'You have been an inspiration to me.'

Martha seemed surprised. 'But how could I, a poor almost illiterate countrywoman, inspire you, Mr Clemetson, a man of learning and so close to God?'

'You have. You have taught me humility and strengthened my faith, for I have witnessed the power of God in your conversion.'

She impulsively clutched his hand. 'And I *will* see my beloved ones?'

'This very day. As Christ said on the cross to the good thief who died next to him, "This day thou shalt be with me in Paradise." So shall you, Martha Brown, rest in God's bosom together with the ones you have loved on this earth.'

At that moment, as the door opened to admit the Governor and prison officials, the prison bell started solemnly tolling. It was just eight o'clock. Martha began to tremble again and clutched Mr Clemetson by the hand.

Then, as the procession formed to leave the cell, Emelia broke into wild sobs. Her grief gave Martha the strength she needed and she took her hand, murmuring, 'Only think, Emelia, this day I will be with my children in Paradise.'

At the same time as the procession moved off and wended its way through the gloomy prison corridors Mr Clemetson began intoning the comforting words from the Gospel of St John:

'"I am the resurrection, and the life; he that believeth

in me though he were dead, shall live. And whoever liveth and believeth in me shall never die."'

At the entrance to the gaol the prison van awaited her.

'Is it all right if we walk?' Martha asked, looking at the sky, though it was starting to rain. 'I would so like a breath of fresh air.'

'If you wish.'

Martha then turned and shook hands with the warders who had accompanied her so far.

'Thank you for looking after me,' she said and was rewarded by the expressions on their faces as they grasped her hand before hurriedly looking away.

The procession then continued round the walls of the prison towards the new gate where the scaffold had been erected.

'I'm sorry it's such a dismal day,' the Reverend Moule, who was less close to the prisoner and therefore less affected by emotion than Mr Clemetson, remarked chattily.

'That can't be helped,' Martha replied. 'I am glad of the fresh air. I like to feel the rain on my face.'

'You are remarkably composed, Mrs Brown.'

'Thanks to Mr Clemetson I have made my peace with God,' Martha replied, 'and with myself.'

'It is a pity that for so long you rejected Christ and His comfort was denied you.'

'But Mr Moule, Mr Clemetson assures me that God has forgiven me. That He welcomes a sinner that repents.'

Mr Moule looked anxiously across at the Reverend Clemetson who, listening to this conversation, seemed on the verge of breaking down.

'Would you like to stand aside, Mr Clemetson,' he enquired solicitously, 'and allow me to accompany the prisoner?'

'No, I cannot leave her,' Mr Clemetson murmured, wiping his eyes. 'I promised I would be with her at the end.'

As they turned the corner of the prison Martha now saw the great wooden scaffold outlined against the sky and she started to tremble. She now had very few moments left of life and she needed to savour every one. But she had promised herself she would not lose heart and glanced at Emelia, still near her, for support.

She now became aware of the vast crowd gathered in North Square to watch her die. They leaned out of the windows of the surrounding houses, and youths perched perilously on the branches of the trees, gaping at her, all agog for the merriment of the hang-fair to begin.

They were ghouls, she thought, all ghouls. At the bottom of the scaffold the procession stopped. Martha turned and shook hands with the Governor and Deputy Governor and thanked them for their courtesy towards her.

She then embraced Emelia who clung pitifully to her. She was finally pulled away by Betty whom Martha kissed warmly on the cheek. 'Thank you, thank you,' she murmured.

'God bless you, Martha,' Emelia sobbed.

'Pray for me,' she murmured, looking afraid, then, with a nod to the clergymen who remained with her, she walked firmly up the first flight of steps to the pinioning room where William Calcraft, the public executioner, confronted her.

'Good morning,' she said, a greeting Calcraft was certainly not used to hearing from those he was about to hang, so he ignored her, producing a rope ready to tie her hands behind her back.

'Let me first say goodbye to this good clergyman,' she said, turning to Mr Clemetson who was too overcome to speak and, as she grasped his hands, he finally broke down.

'You told me to think of Paradise,' she whispered. 'I am. Thank you for sustaining me. Now you go back and let Mr Moule stay with me. It is too upsetting for you. Besides, I know we shall meet again,' she glanced briefly at the sky and gave him a gentle push, sadly watching him walk down the steps, still weeping.

Martha then presented her hands to Calcraft.

'Though it is not necessary,' Martha murmured, 'I am not going to run away.'

Martha, feeling clumsy with her hands tied, took deep breaths as she followed the executioner up the second flight of steps, nineteen in all. Mr Moule put out a hand to assist her.

'I am very frightened,' she whispered. 'Pray for me.'

'I am,' Mr Moule said firmly, 'and you are doing very well.'

'Oh, that I had told the truth in the first place and then I would not be brought to this.'

When she got to the top she was breathless and as her heart was beating so rapidly she was afraid that her courage would finally fail her.

Mr Moule smiled encouragingly. 'I am praying,' he said, 'and you will not weaken.'

Martha looked down at the crowd gazing up at her, from which still there was scarcely a sound. This now was the end and, perhaps, in her end she might be remembered. She felt that sudden constriction of the throat that she had felt so many times before. Then she had been afraid, but now it would be real. Only she had never considered that the rope closing round her neck would be a welcome release from this world which had not treated her well.

The executioner approached her with a white cap which he attempted to put over her face.

'It is not necessary,' she said.

'It is necessary,' Calcraft insisted.

'Then let me say goodbye to the chaplain.' Martha turned to the chaplain.

'You have been most kind. Thank you, Reverend Moule.'

'God be with you,' Mr Moule said, displaying for the first time some emotion and, turning, he hurried down the steps.

'I am ready,' Martha said as Calcraft positioned her over the drop. Looking down she saw the trapdoor but, just before he placed the cap over her face, she cast a brief glance at the dark grey clouds and she knew that beyond them the sky was a clear blue, the sun was shining and her children, in all their young loveliness, and Bernard were waiting for her. If even half of what Mr Clemetson had promised her was true she would now soon be joining them.

A youth of sixteen was among those standing in the dense crowd outside the prison watching Martha Brown hang. He never forgot her and in time he would make her name immortal so that, as she had hoped, people would indeed remember her.

'I remember what a fine figure she showed against the sky as she hung in the misty rain, and how the tight black silk gown set off her shape as she wheeled half-round and back.'

Thomas Hardy, writing as an old man in 1926.

Postscript

It is with some trepidation that one approaches a fictional reconstruction of the life of a rather obscure if notorious woman who perished on the scaffold nearly one hundred and fifty years ago.

Martha Brown was a real person whose tragic life and grim death seem to have been of perpetual fascination to Thomas Hardy, who made frequent references to her in letters during his long life. As late as 1925, when he was eighty-five, he asked Lady Pinney, who lived not far from where Martha spent her final years, to find out more about her.

'I am ashamed to say I saw her hanged, my only excuse being that I was but a youth, and had to be in the town at the time for other reasons.'

It may be that Hardy had something of Martha in mind with the fate, if not the character, of Tess.

So little is known about Martha's life that it has had to be invented. When I began my research in the Record Office in Dorchester just a few facts were known, mostly gleaned from the very full newspaper accounts of her trial: her age, that she had been housekeeper to John

Symes, 'a farmer in Purbeck', and that there she had met and married John Brown who was twenty years her junior and whom she is alleged to have killed.

I did not then know who her parents were or about her first marriage or where she had lived. It was a very interesting journey of discovery. Also, it must be confessed, very tedious as one scanned old parish registers looking for clues, and searched through the census returns of 1841 and 1851, frequently getting nowhere. A breakthrough was a cause for great rejoicing, almost euphoria. This made the whole thing worthwhile, although in the course of research one gleaned fascinating insights into rural lives of the period – for instance, the extent of infant mortality and the frequency of illegitimate births at a time when so much stigma was attached to them.

Whereas there is a lot on record about noble, middle-class or affluent people in the years I was concerned with, the fact is that Martha came from a humble peasant family and was probably illiterate. Very little is known or recorded about the lives of the vast agricultural working classes besides the fact that they were tough and often short.

Eventually many more facts about Martha were unearthed – about her parentage, her first marriage and where she lived – and these I have tried to incorporate in my novel as faithfully as I can but, of course, most of it is fiction. We even identified exactly where the Bearn house was in Powerstock. This was some feat of detection involving the 1839 Tithe Map and old account books of the Bolton Estates which owned much of the land.

In writing my novel, being able to identify so many locations known to be connected with Martha was very useful, enabling me, as it were, to inhabit them with my characters. I travelled extensively through Bridport, Askerswell, Netherbury, Powerstock and then over to the Marshwood Vale where she was probably born (the 1851 census gives her birthplace as Whitechurch – undoubtedly Whitechurch Canonicorum). Marshalsea, where her mother died, and the church where she was buried are not far from the tiny hamlet of Birdsmoorgate where Martha lived with John Brown. It has hardly changed and though the Browns' house is no longer there we know the precise spot where it stood.

Blackmanston Farm in Steeple in the beautiful Purbeck Hills can have changed little since Martha was house-keeper there. One could even imagine what might have been her room high up under the eaves. Bob and Enda Braisby who live there now were most kind and hospitable and gave us free run of the place. Bob's family have been farming at Blackmanston for a hundred years and may well have taken over from the Symes brothers who disappear from the census after 1871.

The Old Crown Court in Dorchester has been pre-served, mostly, it must be said, because of its association with the Tolpuddle Martyrs, but Martha was tried there too years later and she was a real martyr, meeting death on the scaffold and in public outside the prison which stands today where it was originally, but greatly changed. Again, we know exactly where the scaffold stood on that occasion overlooking North Square, before a crowd of about four thousand people.

There is no known likeness of Martha and no record of her day-to-day life before her arrest for murder in 1856. We were told by a court reporter that she was a 'rather wild looking woman with short black curls' so

I have made her spirited with a bit of a temper, partly to help explain and understand that awful final act if, indeed, she did kill John; and, sadly, I have little doubt that she did.

No official record of her trial even exists, but we were fortunate in having a very full account of that and her last days in the local press.

However, there remains something tantalising and enigmatic about Martha and she exercises a curious fascination for many people. I was introduced to her by Nick Gilbey, cameraman and director, who wanted to make a film about her. Nick had been researching her on and off for years. Once I started to delve into her life I became completely obsessed. Then we met Graham Chester, a young scholar and writer living in Swanage who also had done some very thorough research into Martha's life. Much of the material was extremely hard to unearth and we went down many avenues that ultimately led to nowhere. Cracking the first marriage was very difficult because we were given the wrong surname by official authorities! That held us up for months – and Graham probably for years – as we were told Martha's first married name had been Barnes (as it appears on the 1851 census) whereas it was Bearn. There are not many Bearns in Dorset but an awful lot of people with the name of Barnes, and I think Graham had found every one!

It often seemed as though Martha was determined to remain mysterious even from the grave. We have never found her birth record so we don't know exactly where or when she was born. We have, however, found out a lot about her family, the Clarks, and from this have been able to deduce much about her life before her first marriage.

I want particularly to pay tribute to Graham Chester's generosity in sharing so much of his research with Nick and me.

I also want to thank film-producer Angela Howard-Bent who was a vital part of the team delving into Martha's life and a terrific morale-booster when spirits sank, as they so often did.

Finally, grateful thanks too to family archivist Jane Ferentzi-Sheppard who helped us with much valuable research early on in our investigations, particularly by finding John Brown's and Martha's marriage certificate, and to Jo Draper who kindly let me see the typescript before publication of her book, *Regency: Riot and Reform*, which deals with life in early nineteenth-century Dorset.

Nicola Thorne
December 1999

A Knight Two-in-One Special Edition

FIVE GO OFF IN A CARAVAN
FIVE ON KIRRIN ISLAND AGAIN

The Famous Five are Julian, Dick,
George (Georgina by rights), Anne and
Timmy the dog.

This book brings together their fifth
and sixth exciting adventures.

Join the Famous Five . . .

ENID BLYTON

FIVE GO OFF IN
A CARAVAN

Illustrated by Betty Maxey

KNIGHT BOOKS
Hodder and Stoughton

This Famous Five Two-in-One Special Edition
was first published by Knight Books 1988

Copyright © Darrell Waters Ltd
Illustrations copyright © 1974 Hodder
& Stoughton Ltd
All rights reserved

First published in a single volume 1946
First Knight Books single volume edition 1967

*The characters and situations in this
book are entirely imaginary and bear
no relation to any real person
or actual happening.*

British Library C.I.P.

Blyton, Enid
    Five go off in a caravan; Five on
Kirrin Island again.——(A Knight
two in one special edition.——(The
Famous Five; 5 and 6).
    I. Title   II. Series
823'.912[J]   PZ7

ISBN 0 340 42599 7

Printed and bound in Great Britain
for Hodder and Stoughton
Paperbacks, a division of Hodder and
Stoughton Ltd., Mill Road,
Dunton Green, Sevenoaks, Kent
TN13 2YA.
(Editorial Office: 47 Bedford Square,
London WC1B 3DP) by
Cox & Wyman Ltd., Reading

FIVE GO OFF IN
A CARAVAN

CONTENTS

Chapter One

THE BEGINNING OF THE HOLIDAYS

'I DO love the beginning of the summer hols,' said
Julian. 'They always seem to stretch out ahead for ages
and ages.'

'They go so nice and slowly at first,' said Anne, his
little sister. 'Then they start to gallop.'

The others laughed. They knew exactly what Anne
meant. 'Woof,' said a deep voice, as if someone else
thoroughly agreed too.

'Timmy thinks you're right, Anne,' said George, and
patted the big dog lying panting beside them. Dick
patted him, too, and Timmy licked them both.

The four children were lying in a sunny garden in the
first week of the holidays. Usually they went to their
cousin Georgina's home for holidays, at Kirrin – but this
time, for a change, they were all at the home of Julian,
Dick and Anne.

Julian was the oldest, a tall, sturdy boy with a strong
and pleasant face. Dick and Georgina came next.
Georgina looked more like a curly-headed boy than a
girl, and she insisted on being called George. Even the
teachers at school called her George. Anne was the
youngest, though, much to her delight, she was really
growing taller now.

'Daddy said this morning that if we didn't want to
stay here all the hols we could choose what we wanted
to do,' said Anne. 'I vote for staying here.'

'We could go off somewhere just for two weeks, perhaps,' said Dick. 'For a change.'

'Shall we go to Kirrin, and stay with George's mother and father for a bit?' said Julian, thinking that perhaps George would like this.

'No,' said George at once. 'I went home at half-term, and Mother said Father was just beginning one of his experiments in something or other – and you know what *that* means. If we go there we'd have to walk about on tiptoe, and talk in whispers, and keep out of his way the whole time.'

'That's the worst of having a scientist for a father,' said Dick, lying down on his back and shutting his eyes. 'Well, your mother couldn't cope with us and with your father, too, in the middle of one of his experiments at the same time. Sparks would fly.'

'I like Uncle Quentin, but I'm afraid of him when he's in one of his tempers,' said Anne. 'He shouts so.'

'It's decided that we won't go to Kirrin, then,' said Julian, yawning. 'Not these hols, anyhow. You can always go and see Mother for a week or so, George, when you want to. What shall we do, then? Stay here all the time?'

They were now all lying down on their backs in the sun, their eyes shut. What a hot afternoon! Timmy sat up by George, his pink tongue hanging out, panting loudly.

'Don't, Timmy,' said Anne. 'You sound as if you have been running for miles, and you make me feel hotter than ever.'

Timmy put a friendly paw on Anne's middle and she squealed. 'Oh, Timmy – your paw's heavy. Take it off.'

'You know, I think if we were allowed to go off by ourselves somewhere, it would be rather fun,' said George, biting a blade of grass and squinting up into the deep blue sky. 'The biggest fun we've ever had was when we were alone on Kirrin Island, for instance. Couldn't we go off somewhere all by ourselves?'

'But where?' said Dick. 'And how? I mean we aren't old enough to take a car – though I bet I could drive one. It wouldn't be much fun going on bicycles, because Anne can't ride as fast as we can.'

'And somebody always gets a puncture,' said Julian.

'It would be jolly good fun to go off on horses,' said George. 'Only we haven't got even one.'

'Yes, we have – there's old Dobby down in the field,' said Dick. 'He is ours. He used to draw the pony-cart, but we don't use it any more now he's turned out to grass.'

'Well, one horse wouldn't take four of us, silly,' said George. 'Dobby's no good.'

There was a silence, and everyone thought lazily about holidays. Timmy snapped at a fly, and his teeth came together with a loud click.

'Wish I could catch flies like that,' said Dick, flapping away a blue-bottle. 'Come and catch this one, Timmy, old thing.'

'What about a walking tour?' said Julian after a pause. There was a chorus of groans.

'What! In this weather! You're mad!'

'We shouldn't be allowed to.'

'All right, all right,' said Julian. 'Think of a better idea, then.'

'I'd like to go somewhere where we could bathe,' said

Anne. 'In a lake, for instance, if we can't go to the sea.'

'Sounds nice,' said Dick. 'My goodness, I'm sleepy. Let's hurry up and settle this matter, or I shall be snoring hard.'

But it wasn't easy to settle. Nobody wanted to go off to an hotel, or to rooms. Grown-ups would want to go with them and look after them. And nobody wanted to go walking or cycling in the hot August weather.

'Looks as if we'll have to stay at home all the hols, then,' said Julian. 'Well – I'm going to have a snooze.'

In two minutes they were all asleep on the grass except Timmy. If his family fell asleep like this, Timmy considered himself on guard. The big dog gave his mistress George a soft lick and sat up firmly beside her, his ears cocked, and his eyes bright. He panted hard, but nobody heard him. They were all snoozing deliciously in the sun, getting browner and browner.

The garden sloped up a hillside. From where he sat Timmy could see quite a long way, both up and down the road that ran by the house. It was a wide road, but not a very busy one, for it was a country district.

Timmy heard a dog barking in the distance, and his ears twitched in that direction. He heard people walking down the road and his ears twitched again. He missed nothing, not even the robin that flew down to get a caterpillar on a bush not far off. He growled softly in his throat at the robin – just to tell it that he was on guard, so beware.

Then something came down the wide road, something that made Timmy shake with excitement, and sniff at the strange smells that came floating up to the garden. A big procession came winding up the road, with a

rumble and clatter of wheels – a slow procession, headed
by a very strange thing.

Timmy had no idea what it was that headed the
procession. Actually it was a big elephant, and Timmy
smelt its smell, strange and strong, and didn't like it. He
smelt the scent of the monkeys in their travelling cage,
too, and he heard the barking of the performing dogs in
their van.

He answered them defiantly. 'WOOF, WOOF, WOOF.'

The loud barking awoke all four children at once.
'Shut up, Timmy,' said George crossly. 'What a row to
make when we're all having a nap.'

'WOOF,' said Timmy obstinately, and pawed at his
mistress to make her sit up and take notice. George sat
up. She saw the procession at once and gave a yell.

'Hey, you others. There's a circus procession going by.
Look.'

They all sat up, wide awake now. They stared down at
the caravans going slowly along, and listened to an
animal howling, and the dogs barking.

'Look at that elephant, pulling the caravan along,'
said Anne. 'He must be jolly strong.'

'Let's go down to the gate of the drive and watch,' said
Dick. So they all got up and ran down the garden, then
round the house and into the drive that led to the road.
The procession was just passing the gates.

It was a gay sight. The caravans were painted in
brilliant colours, and looked spick and span from the
outside. Little flowery curtains hung at the windows.
At the front of each caravan sat the man or woman who
owned it, driving the horse that pulled it. Only the front
caravan was pulled by an elephant.

'Golly – doesn't it look exciting?' said George. 'I wish I belonged to a circus that went wandering all over the place all the year. That's just the sort of life I'd like.'

'Fat lot of good you'd be in the circus,' said Dick rudely. 'You can't even turn a cart-wheel.'

'What's a cart-wheel?' said Anne.

'What that boy's doing over there,' said Dick. 'Look.'

He pointed to a boy who was turning cart-wheels very quickly, going over and over on his hands and feet, turning himself like a wheel. It looked so easy, but it wasn't, as Dick very well knew.

'Oh, is he turning a cart-wheel?' said Anne admiringly. 'I wish I could do that.'

The boy came up to them and grinned. He had two

terrier dogs with him. Timmy growled and George put
her hand on his collar.

'Don't come too near,' she called. 'Timmy isn't quite
sure about you.'

'We won't hurt him!' said the boy, and grinned again.
He had an ugly, freckled face, with a shock of untidy
hair. 'I won't let my dogs eat your Timmy.'

'As if they could!' began George scornfully, and then
laughed. The terriers kept close to the boy's heels. He
clicked and both dogs rose at once on their hind legs and
walked sedately behind him with funny little steps.

'Oh – are they performing dogs?' said Anne. 'Are they
yours?'

'These two are,' said, the boy. This is Barker and this

is Growler. I've had them from pups – clever as paint they are!'

'Woof,' said Timmy, apparently disgusted at seeing dogs walk in such a peculiar way. It had never occurred to him that a dog could get up on his hind legs.

'Where are you giving your next show?' asked George eagerly. 'We'd like to see it.'

'We're off for a rest,' said the boy. 'Up in the hills, where there's a blue lake at the bottom. We're allowed to camp there with our animals – it's wild and lonely and we don't disturb nobody. We just camp there with our caravans.'

'It sounds fine,' said Dick. 'Which is your caravan?'

'This one, just coming ' said the boy, and he pointed to a brightly painted van, whose sides were blue and yellow, and whose wheels were red. 'I live in it with my Uncle Dan. He's the chief clown of the circus. There he is, sitting on the front, driving the horse.'

The children stared at the chief clown, and thought that they had never seen anyone less like a clown. He was dressed in dirty grey flannel trousers and a dirty red shirt open at an equally dirty neck.

He didn't look as if he could make a single joke, or do anything in the least funny. In fact, he looked really bad-tempered, the children thought, and he scowled so fiercely as he chewed on an old pipe that Anne felt quite scared. He didn't look at the children at all, but called in a sharp voice to the boy:

'Nobby! You come on along of us. Get in the caravan and make me a cup of tea.'

The boy Nobby winked at the children and ran to the caravan. It was plain that Uncle Dan kept him in order all right! He poked his head out of the little window in the side of the caravan nearest to the children.

'Sorry I can't ask you to tea too!' he called. 'And the dog. Barker and Growler wouldn't half like to know him!'

The caravan passed on, taking the scowling clown with it, and the grinning Nobby. The children watched the others going by, too; it was quite a big circus. There was a cage of monkeys, a chimpanzee sitting in a corner of a dark cage, asleep, a string of beautiful horses, sleek and shining, a great wagon carrying benches and forms and tents, caravans for the circus folk to live in, and a host of interesting people to see, sitting on the steps of their vans or walking together outside to stretch their legs.

At last the procession was gone and the children went slowly back to their sunny corner in the garden. They sat down – and then George announced something that made them sit up straight.

'*I* know what we'll do these hols! We'll hire a caravan and go off in it by ourselves. Do let's! Oh, do let's!'

Chapter Two

GEORGE'S GREAT IDEA

THE others stared at George's excited face. She had gone quite red. Dick thumped on the ground.

'A jolly good idea! Why didn't we think of it before?'

'Oh, *yes*! A caravan to ourselves! It sounds too good to be true!' said Anne, and her eyes shone.

'Well, I must say it would be something we've never done before,' said Julian, wondering if it was really possible. 'I say – wouldn't it be gorgeous if we could go off into the hills – where that lake is that the boy spoke about? We could bathe there – and we could perhaps get to know the circus folk. I've always wanted to know about circuses.'

'Oh, *Julian*! That's a better idea still!' said George, rubbing her hands together in delight. 'I liked that boy Nobby, didn't you?'

'Yes,' said everyone.

'But I didn't like his uncle,' said Dick. 'He looked a nasty bit of work. I bet he makes Nobby toe the mark and do what he's told.'

'Julian, do you think we'd be allowed to go caravanning by ourselves?' asked Anne earnestly. 'It does seem to me to be the most marvellous idea we've ever had.'

'Well – we can ask and see,' said Julian. 'I'm old enough to look after you all.'

'Pooh!' said George. 'I don't want any looking after, thank you. And anyway, if we want looking after, Timmy can do that. I bet the grown-ups will be glad to be rid of us for a week or two. They always think the summer hols are too long.'

'We'll take Dobby with us to pull the caravan!' said Anne suddenly, looking down at the field where Dobby stood, patiently flicking away the flies with his long tail. 'Dobby would love that! I always think he must be lonely, living in that field all by himself, just being borrowed by people occasionally.'

'Of course – Dobby could come,' said Dick. 'That would be fine. Where could we get the caravan from? Are they easy to hire?'

'Don't know,' said Julian. 'I knew a chap at school – you remember him, Dick, that big fellow called Perry – he used to go caravanning every hols with his people. They used to hire caravans, I know. I might find out from him where he got them from.'

'Daddy will know,' said Anne. 'Or Mummy. Grownups always know things like that. I'd like a nice large caravan – red and blue – with a little chimney, and windows each side, and a door at the back, and steps to go up into the caravan, and . . .'

The others interrupted with their own ideas, and soon they were all talking excitedly about it – so loudly that they didn't see someone walking up and standing near by, laughing at the excitement.

'Woof,' said Timmy politely. He was the only one who had ears and eyes for anything else at the moment. The children looked up.

'Oh, hallo, Mother!' said Julian. 'You've just come at the right moment. We want to tell you about an idea we've got.'

His mother sat down, smiling. 'You seem very excited about something,' she said. 'What is it?'

'Well, it's like this, Mummy,' said Anne, before anyone else could get a word in, 'we've made up our minds that we'd like to go off in a caravan for a holiday by ourselves! Oh, Mummy – it would be such fun!'

'By yourselves?' said her mother doubtfully. 'Well, I don't know about that.'

'Julian can look after us,' said Anne.

'So can Timmy,' put in George at once, and Timmy thumped the ground with his tail. Of course he could look after them! Hadn't he done it for years, and shared all their adventures? Thump, thump, thump!

'I'll have to talk it over with Daddy,' said Mother. 'Now don't look so disappointed – I can't decide a thing like this all by myself in a hurry. But it may fit in quite well because I know Daddy has to go up north for a little while, and he would like me to go with him. So he might think a little caravanning quite a good idea. I'll talk to him tonight.'

'We could have Dobby to pull the caravan, Mummy,' said Anne, her eyes bright. 'Couldn't we? He'd love to come. He has such a dull life now.'

'We'll see, we'll see,' said her mother, getting up. 'Now you'd better all come in and wash. It's nearly tea-time. Your hair is terrible, Anne. What *have* you been doing?'

Everyone rushed indoors to wash, feeling distinctly cheerful. Mother hadn't said NO. She had even thought it might fit in quite well. Golly, to go off in a caravan all alone – doing their own cooking and washing – having Dobby for company, and Timmy as well, of course. How simply gorgeous.

The children's father did not come home until late that evening, which was a nuisance, for nobody felt that they could wait for very long to know whether they might or might not go. Everyone but Julian was in bed when he came home, and even when he, too, came to bed he had nothing to report.

He stuck his head into the girls' bedroom. 'Daddy's tired and he's having a late supper, and Mother won't bother him till he's feeling better. So we shan't know till morning, worse luck!'

The girls groaned. How could they possibly go to sleep with thoughts of caravans floating deliciously in their heads – not knowing whether or not they would be allowed to go!

'Blow!' said George. 'I shan't go to sleep for ages. Get off my feet, Timmy. Honestly, it's too hot to have you anywhere near me this weather.'

In the morning good news awaited the four children. They sat down at the breakfast-table, all very punctual for once, and Julian looked expectantly at his mother. She smiled at him and nodded.

'Yes, we've talked it over,' she said. 'And Daddy says he doesn't see why you shouldn't have a caravan holiday. He thinks it would be good for you to go off and rough it a bit. But you will have to have two caravans, not one. We couldn't have all four of you, and Timmy too, living in one caravan.'

'Oh – but Dobby couldn't pull *two* caravans, Mummy,' said Anne.

'We can borrow another horse,' said Julian. 'Can't we, Mother? Thanks awfully, Daddy, for saying we can go. It's jolly sporting of you.'

'Absolutely super,' said Dick.

'Wizard!' said George, her fingers scratching Timmy's head excitedly. 'When can we go? Tomorrow?'

'Of course not!' said Julian. 'We've got to get the caravans – and borrow a horse – and pack – and all sorts of things.'

'You can go next week, when I take your mother up north with me,' said his father. 'That will suit us very well. We can give Cook a holiday, too, then. You will have to send us a card every single day to tell us how you are and where you are.'

'It does sound thrilling,' said Anne. 'I really don't feel as if I can eat any breakfast, Mummy.'

'Well, if that's the effect the idea of caravanning has on you, I don't think you'd better go,' said her mother. Anne hastily began to eat her shredded wheat, and her appetite soon came back. It was too good to be true – to have *two* caravans – and *two* horses – and sleep in bunks perhaps – and cook meals outside in the open air – and ...

'You will be in complete charge, you understand, Julian,' said the boy's father. 'You are old enough now to be really responsible. The others must realise that you are in charge and they must do as you say.'

'Yes, sir,' said Julian, feeling proud. 'I'll see to things all right.'

'And Timmy will be in charge, too,' said George. 'He's just as responsible as Julian.'

'Woof,' said Timmy, hearing his name, and thumping the floor with his tail.

'You're a darling, Timmy,' said Anne. 'I'll always do what *you* say, as well as what Julian says!'

'Idiot!' said Dick. He patted Timmy's head. 'I bet we wouldn't be allowed to go without you, Timothy. You are a jolly good guard for anyone.'

'You certainly wouldn't be allowed to go without Timmy,' said his mother. 'We know you'll be safe with him.'

It was all most exciting. The children went off to talk things over by themselves when breakfast was finished.

'I vote we go caravanning up into the hills that boy spoke of, where the lake lies at the bottom – and camp there,' said Julian. 'We'd have company then – jolly exciting company, too. We wouldn't live *too* near the circus camp – they might not like strangers butting in – but we'll live near enough to see the elephant going for his daily walk, and the dogs being exercised . . .'

'And we'll make friends with Nobby, won't we?' said Anne eagerly. 'I liked him. We won't go near his uncle, though. I think it's queer that such a bad-tempered looking man should be the chief clown in a circus.'

'I wonder when and where Mother will get the caravans!' said Julian. 'Gosh, won't it be fun when we see them for the first time!'

'Let's go and tell Dobby!' said Anne. 'He is sure to be excited, too!'

'Baby! He won't understand a word you tell him!' said George. But off she went with Anne just the same, and soon Dobby was hearing all about the wonderful holiday plan. Hrrrrumph! So long as it included him, too, he was happy!

Chapter Three

THE CARAVANS ARRIVE

At last the great day came when the two caravans were due to arrive. The children stood at the end of the drive for hours, watching for them.

Mother had managed to borrow them from an old friend of hers. The children had promised faithfully to look after them well, and not to damage anything. Now they stood at the end of the drive, watching eagerly for the caravans to arrive.

'They are being drawn by cars today,' said Julian. 'But they are fitted up to be horse-drawn, too. I wonder what they are like – and what colour they are?'

'Will they be like gypsy caravans, on high wheels, do you think?' asked Anne. Julian shook his head.

'No, they're modern, Mother says. Streamlined and all that. Not too big either, because a horse can't draw too heavy a van.'

'They're coming, they're coming! I can see them!' suddenly yelled George, making them all jump. 'Look, isn't that them, far down the road?'

They all looked hard into the distance. No one had such good eyes as George, and all they could see was a blotch, a moving speck far away on the road. But George's eyes saw two caravans, one behind the other.

'George is right,' said Julian, straining his eyes. 'It's our caravans. They're each drawn by a small car.'

'One's red and the other's green,' said Anne. 'Bags I the red one. Oh, hurry up, caravans!'

At last they were near enough to see properly. The children ran to meet them. They certainly were very nice ones, quite modern and 'streamlined', as Julian had said, well built and comfortable.

'They almost reach the ground!' said Anne. 'And look at the wheels, set so neatly into the side of the vans. I do like the red one, bags I the red one.'

Each van had a little chimney, long, narrow windows down the two sides, and tiny ones in front by the driver's seat. There was a broad door at the back and two steps down. Pretty curtains fluttered at the open windows.

'Red curtains for the green caravan, and green ones for the red caravan!' said Anne. 'Oh, I want to go inside!'

But she couldn't because the doors were locked. So she had to be content to run with the others up the drive after the two caravans, shouting loudly:

'Mummy! They're here, the caravans are here.'

Her mother came running down the steps to see. Soon the doors were unlocked and the children went inside the caravans. Delighted shouts came from both vans.

'Bunks along one side – is that where we sleep? How gorgeous!'

'Look at this little sink – we can really wash up. And golly, water comes out of these taps!'

'There's a proper stove to cook on – but I vote we cook out of doors on a camp fire. I say, look at the bright frying-pans – and all the cups and saucers hanging up!'

'It's like a proper little house inside. Doesn't it seem nice and *big*? Mother, isn't it beautifully planned? Don't you wish you were coming with us?'

'Hey, you girls! Do you see where the water comes from? Out of that tank on the roof. It must collect rainwater. And look at this gadget for heating water. Isn't it all super?'

The children spent hours examining their caravans and finding out all the secrets. They certainly were very well fitted, spotlessly clean, and very roomy. George felt as if she couldn't wait to start out. She really must get Dobby and set out at once!

'No, you must wait, silly,' said Julian. 'You know we've to get the other horse. He's not coming till tomorrow.'

The other horse was a sturdy little black fellow called Trotter. He belonged to the milkman, who often lent him out. He was a sensible little horse, and the children knew him very well and liked him. They all learnt riding at school, and knew how to groom and look after a horse, so there would be no difficulty over their managing Dobby and Trotter.

Mother was thrilled over the caravans, too, and looked very longingly at them. 'If I wasn't going with Daddy I should be most tempted to come with you,' she said. 'Don't look so startled, Anne dear – I'm not really coming!'

'We're jolly lucky to get such decent caravans,' said Julian. 'We'd better pack our things today, hadn't we, Mother – and start off tomorrow, now we've got the caravans.'

'You won't need to pack,' said his mother. 'All you have to do is to pop your things straight into the cupboards and drawers – you will only want clothes and books and a few games to play in case it's rainy.'

'We don't need any clothes except our night things, do

we?' said George, who would have lived in a jersey and jeans all day and every day if she had been allowed to.

'You must take plenty of jerseys, another pair of jeans each, in case you get wet, your rain-coats, bathing-things, towels, a change of shoes, night things, and some cool shirts or blouses,' said Mother. Everyone groaned.

'What a frightful lot of things!' said Dick. 'There'll never be room for all those.'

'Oh yes there will,' said Mother. 'You will be sorry if you take too few clothes, get soaked through, have nothing to change into, and catch fearful colds that will stop you from enjoying a lovely holiday like this.'

'Come on, let's get the things,' said Dick. 'Once Mother starts off about catching cold there's no knowing what else she'll make us take – is there, Mother?'

'You're a cheeky boy,' said his mother, smiling. 'Yes, go and collect your things. I'll help you to put them into the cupboards and drawers. Isn't it marvellous how everything folds so neatly into the walls of the caravans – there seems to be room for everything, and you don't notice the cupboards.'

'I shall keep everything very clean,' said Anne. 'You know how I like *playing* at keeping house, don't you, Mother – well, it will be real this time. I shall have two caravans to keep clean, all by myself.'

'All by yourself!' said her mother. 'Well, surely the boys will help you – and certainly George must.'

'Pooh, the boys!' said Anne. 'They won't know how to wash and dry a cup properly – and George never bothers about things like that. If I don't make the bunks and wash the crockery, they would never be made or washed, I know that!'

'Well, it's a good thing that one of you is sensible!' said her mother. 'You'll find that everyone will share in the work, Anne. Now off you go and get your things. Bring all the rain-coats, to start with.'

It was fun taking things down to the caravans and packing them all in. There were shelves for a few books and games, so Julian brought down snap cards, ludo, lexicon, happy families and dominoes, as well as four or five books for each of them. He also brought down some maps of the district, because he meant to plan out where they were to go, and the best roads to follow.

Daddy had given him a useful little book in which were the names of farms that would give permission to caravanners to camp in fields for the night. 'You must always choose a field where there is a stream, if possible,' said his father, 'because Dobby and Trotter will want water.'

'Remember to boil every drop of water you drink,' said the children's mother. 'That's very important. Get as much milk from the farms as they will let you have. And remember that there is plenty of ginger-beer in the locker under the second caravan.'

'It's all so thrilling,' said Anne, peering down to look at the locker into which Julian had put the bottles of ginger-beer. 'I can't believe we're really going tomorrow.'

But it was true. Dobby and Trotter were to be taken to the caravans the next day and harnessed. How exciting for them, too, Anne thought.

Timmy couldn't quite understand all the excitement, but he shared in it, of course, and kept his tail on the wag all day long. He examined the caravans thoroughly from end to end, found a rug he liked the smell of, and lay down on it. 'This is *my* corner,' he seemed to say. 'If you go off in these peculiar houses on wheels, this is my own little corner.'

'We'll have the red caravan, George,' said Anne. 'The boys can have the green one. They don't care what colour they have – but I love red. I say, won't it be sport to sleep in those bunks? They look jolly comfortable.'

At last tomorrow came – and the milkman brought the sturdy little black horse, Trotter, up the drive. Julian fetched Dobby from the field. The horses nuzzled one another and Dobby said 'Hrrrumph' in a very civil horsey voice.

'They're going to like each other,' said Anne. 'Look at them nuzzling. Trotter, you're going to draw *my* caravan.'

The two horses stood patiently while they were harnessed. Dobby jerked his head once or twice as if he was impatient to be off and stamped a little.

'Oh, Dobby, I feel like that, too!' said Anne. 'Don't you, Dick, don't you, Julian?'

'I do rather,' said Dick with a grin. 'Get up there, Dobby – that's right. Who's going to drive, Julian – take it in turns, shall we?'

'I'm going to drive *our* caravan,' said George. 'Anne wouldn't be any good at it, though I'll let her have a turn at it sometimes. Driving is a man's job.'

'Well, you're only a girl!' said Anne indignantly. 'You're not a man, nor even a boy!'

George put on one of her scowls. She always wanted to be a boy, and even thought of herself as one. She didn't like to be reminded that she was only a girl. But not even George could scowl for long that exciting morning! She soon began to caper round and about again, laughing and calling out with the others:

'We're ready! Surely we're ready!'

'Yes. Do let's go! JULIAN! He's gone indoors, the idiot, just when we want to start.'

'He's gone to get the cakes that Cook has baked this morning for us. We've heaps of food in the larder. I feel hungry already.'

'Here's Julian. Do come on, Julian. We'll drive off without you. Good-bye, Mother! We'll send you a card every single day, we faithfully promise.'

Julian got up on the front of the green caravan. He clicked to Dobby. 'Get on, Dobby! We're off! Good-bye, Mother!'

Dick sat beside him, grinning with pure happiness. The caravans moved off down the drive. George pulled at Trotter's reins and the little horse followed the caravan in front. Anne, sitting beside George, waved wildly.

'Good-bye, Mother! We're off at last on another adventure. Hurrah! Three cheers! Hurrah!'

Chapter Four

AWAY THEY GO!

THE caravans went slowly down the wide road. Julian was so happy that he sang at the top of his voice, and the others joined in the choruses. Timmy barked excitedly. He was sitting on one side of George and as Anne was on the other George was decidedly squashed. But little things like that did not bother her at all.

Dobby plodded on slowly, enjoying the sunshine and the little breeze that raised the hairs on his mane. Trotter followed at a short distance. He was very much interested in Timmy, and always turned his head when the dog barked or got down for a run. It was fun to have two horses and a dog to travel with.

It had been decided that they should make their way towards the hills where they hoped to find the circus. Julian had traced the place in his map. He was sure it must be right because of the lake that lay in the valley at the foot of the hills.

'See?' he said to the others, pointing. 'There it is – Lake Merran. I bet we'll find the circus camp somewhere near it. It would be a very good place for all their animals – no one to interfere with the camp, plenty of water for both animals and men, and probably good farms to supply them with food.'

'We'll have to find a good farm ourselves tonight,' said Dick. 'And ask permission to camp. Lucky we've got that little book telling us where to go and ask.'

Anne thought with delight of the coming evening, when they would stop and camp, cook a meal, drowse over a camp fire, and go to sleep in the little bunks. She didn't know which was nicer – ambling along down country lanes with the caravans – or preparing to settle in for the night. She was sure it was going to be the nicest holiday they had ever had.

'Don't you think so?' she asked George as they sat together on the driving-seat, with Timmy, for once, trotting beside the caravan, and leaving them a little more room than usual. 'You know, most of our hols have been packed with adventures – awfully exciting, I know – but I'd like an *ordinary* holiday now, wouldn't you – not *too* exciting.'

'Oh, I like adventures,' said George, shaking the reins and making Trotter do a little trot. 'I wouldn't a bit mind having another one. But we shan't this time, Anne. No such luck!'

They stopped for a meal at half-past twelve, all of them feeling very hungry. Dobby and Trotter moved towards a ditch in which long, juicy grass grew, and munched away happily.

The children lay on a sunny bank and ate and drank. Anne looked at George. 'You've got more freckles these hols, George, than you ever had in your life before.'

'That doesn't worry *me*!' said George, who never cared in the least how she looked, and was even angry with her hair for being too curly, and making her look too much like a girl. 'Pass the sandwiches, Anne – the tomato ones – golly, if we always feel as hungry as this we'll have to buy eggs and bacon and butter and milk at every farm we pass!'

They set off again. Dick took his turn at driving Dobby, and Julian walked to stretch his legs. George still wanted to drive, but Anne felt too sleepy to sit beside her with safety.

'If I shut my eyes and sleep I shall fall off the seat,' she said. 'I'd better go into the caravan and sleep there.'

So in she went, all by herself. It was cool and dim inside the caravan, for the curtains had been pulled across the window to keep the inside cool. Anne climbed on to one of the bunks and lay down. She shut her eyes. The caravan rumbled slowly on, and the little girl fell asleep.

Julian peeped in at her and grinned. Timmy came and looked, too, but Julian wouldn't let him go in and wake Anne by licking her.

'You come and walk with me, Tim,' he said. 'You're getting fat. Exercise will do you good.'

'He's *not* getting fat!' called George, indignantly. 'He's a very nice shape. Don't you listen to him, Timothy.'

'Woof,' said Timmy, and trotted along at Julian's heels.

The two caravans covered quite a good distance that day, even though they went slowly. Julian did not miss the way once. He was very good indeed at map-reading. Anne was disappointed that they could not see the hills they were making for, at the end of the day.

'Goodness, they're miles and miles away!' said Julian. 'We shan't arrive for at least four or five days, silly! Now, look out for a farm, kids. There should be one near here, where we can ask permission to camp for the night.'

'There's one, surely,' said George, after a few minutes. She pointed to where a red-roofed building with moss-covered barns, stood glowing in the evening sun. Hens clucked about it, and a dog or two watched them from a gateway.

'Yes, that's the one,' said Julian, examining his map. 'Longman's Farm. There should be a stream near it. There it is, look – in that field. Now, if we could get permission to camp just here, it would be lovely.'

Julian went to the farm to see the farmer, and Anne went with him to ask for eggs. The farmer was not there, but the farmer's wife, who liked the look of the tall, well-spoken Julian very much, gave them permission at once to spend the night in the field by the stream.

'I know you won't leave a lot of litter, or go chasing the farm animals,' she said. 'Or leave the gates open like some ill-bred campers do. And what's that you want, Missy – some new-laid eggs. Yes, of course, you can have some – and you can pick the ripe plums off that tree, too, to go with your supper!'

There was bacon in the larder of the caravans, and Anne said she would fry that and an egg each for everyone. She was very proud of being able to cook them. She had taken a few lessons from Cook in the last few days, and was very anxious to show the others what she had learnt.

Julian said it was too hot to cook in the caravan, and he built her a fine fire in the field. Dick set the two horses free and they wandered off to the stream, where they stood knee-high in the cool water, enjoying it immensely. Trotter muzzled against Dobby, and then tried to nuzzle down to Timmy, too, when the big dog came to drink beside him.

'Doesn't the bacon smell lovely?' called Anne to George,

who was busy getting plates and mugs out of the red
caravan. 'Let's have ginger-beer to drink, George. I'm
jolly thirsty. Watch me crack these eggs on the edge of
this cup, everybody, so that I can get out the yolk and
white and fry them.'

Crack! The egg broke against the edge of the cup – but
its contents unfortunately fell outside the cup instead of
inside. Anne went red when everyone roared with
laughter.

Timmy came and licked up the mess. He was very
useful for that sort of thing. 'You'd make a good dust-bin,
Timmy,' said Anne. 'Here's a bit of bacon-rind, too.
Catch!'

Anne fried the bacon and eggs really well. The others
were most admiring, even George, and they all cleared
their plates well, wiping the last bit of fat off with bread,
so that they would be easy to wash.

'Do you think Timmy would like me to fry him a few
dog-biscuits, instead of having them cold?' said Anne,
suddenly. 'Fried things are so nice. I'm sure Timmy
would like fried biscuits better than ordinary ones.'

'Well, he wouldn't,' said George. 'They would just
make him sick.'

'How do you know?' said Anne. 'You can't possibly
tell.'

'I always know what Timmy would really like and
what he wouldn't,' said George. 'And he wouldn't like
his biscuits fried. Pass the plums, Dick. They look super.'

They lingered over the little camp-fire for a long time,
and then Julian said it was time for bed. Nobody
minded, because they all wanted to try sleeping on the
comfortable-looking bunks.

'Shall I wash at the stream or in the little sink where I washed the plates?' said Anne. 'I don't know which would be nicer.'

'There's more water to spare in the stream,' said Julian. 'Hurry up, won't you, because I want to lock your caravan door so that you'll be safe.'

'Lock our door!' said George, indignantly. 'You jolly well won't! Nobody's going to lock *me* in! I might think I'd like to take a walk in the moonlight or something.'

'Yes, but a tramp or somebody might . . .' began Julian. George interrupted him scornfully.

'What about Timmy? You know jolly well he'd never let anyone come *near* our caravans, let alone into them! I won't be locked in, Julian. I couldn't bear it. Timmy's better than any locked door.'

'Well, I suppose he is,' said Julian. 'All right, don't look so furious, George. Walk half the night in moonlight if you want to – though there won't be any moon tonight, I'm sure. Golly, I'm sleepy!'

They climbed into the two caravans, after washing in the stream. They all undressed, and got into the inviting bunks. There was a sheet, one blanket and a rug – but all the children threw off both blanket and rug and kept only a sheet over them that hot night.

At first Anne tried sleeping in the lower bunk, beneath George – but Timmy would keep on trying to clamber up to get to George. He wanted to lie on her feet as usual. Anne got cross.

'George! You'd better change places with me. Timmy keeps jumping on me and walking all over me trying to get up to your bunk. I'll never get to sleep.'

So George changed places, and after that Timmy made no more noise, but lay contentedly at the end of George's bunk on the rolled-up blanket, while Anne lay in the bunk above, trying not to go to sleep because it was such a lovely feeling to be inside a caravan that stood by a stream in a field.

Owls hooted to one another, and Timmy growled softly. The voice of the stream, contented and babbling, could be quite clearly heard now that everything was so quiet. Anne felt her eyes closing. Oh dear – she would simply *have* to go to sleep.

But something suddenly awoke her with a jump, and Timmy barked so loudly that both Anne and George almost fell out of their bunks in fright. Something bumped violently against the caravan, and shook it from end to end! Was somebody trying to get in?

Timmy leapt to the floor and ran to the door, which George had left open a little because of the heat. Then the voices of Dick and Julian were heard.

'What's up? Are you girls all right? We're coming!' And over the wet grass raced the two boys in their dressing-gowns. Julian ran straight into something hard and warm and solid. He yelled.

Dick switched on his torch and began to laugh helplessly. 'You ran straight into Dobby. Look at him staring at you! He must have lumbered all round our caravans making the bumps we heard. It's all right, girls. It's only Dobby.'

So back they all went again to sleep, and this time they slept till the morning, not even stirring when Trotter, too, came to nuzzle round the caravan and snort softly in the night.

Chapter Five

THE WAY TO MERRAN LAKE

THE next three or four days were absolutely perfect, the children thought. Blue skies, blazing sun, wayside streams to paddle or bathe in, and two houses on wheels that went rumbling for miles down roads and lanes quite new to them – what could be lovelier for four children all on their own?

Timmy seemed to enjoy everything thoroughly, too, and had made firm friends with Trotter, the little black horse. Trotter was always looking for Timmy to run beside him, and he whinnied to Timmy whenever he wanted him. The two horses were friends, too, and when they were set free at night they made for the stream together, and stood in the water side by side, nuzzling one another happily.

'I like this holiday better than any we've ever had,' said Anne, busily cooking something in a pan. 'It's exciting without being adventurous. And although Julian thinks he's in charge of us, *I* am really! You'd never get your bunks made, or your meals cooked, or the caravans kept clean if it wasn't for me!'

'Don't boast!' said George, feeling rather guilty because she let Anne do so much.

'I'm not boasting!' said Anne, indignantly. 'I'm just telling the truth. Why, you've never even made your own bunk once, George. Not that I mind doing it. I love having two houses on wheels to look after.'

'You're a very good little housekeeper,' said Julian. 'We couldn't possibly do without you!'

Anne blushed with pride. She took the pan off the camp-fire and put the contents on to four plates. 'Come along!' she called, in a voice just like her mother's. 'Have your meal while it's hot.'

'I'd rather have mine when it's cold, thank you,' said George. 'It doesn't seem to have got a bit cooler, even though it's evening-time.'

They had been on the road four days now, and Anne had given up looking for the hills where they hoped to find the circus folk camping. In fact she secretly hoped they wouldn't find them, because she was so much enjoying the daily wanderings over the lovely countryside.

Timmy came to lick the plates. The children always let him do that now because it made them so much easier to wash. Anne and George took the things down to a little brown brook to rinse, and Julian took out his map.

He and Dick pored over it. 'We're just about here,' said Julian, pointing. 'And if so, it looks as if tomorrow we ought to come to those hills above the lake. Then we should see the circus.'

'Good!' said Dick. 'I hope Nobby will be there. He would love to show us round, I'm sure. He would show us a good place to camp, too, perhaps.'

'Oh, we can find that ourselves,' said Julian, who now rather prided himself on picking excellent camping-sites. 'Anyway, I don't want to be *too* near the circus. It might be a bit smelly. I'd rather be up in the hills some way above it. We'll get a place with a lovely view.'

'Right,' said Dick, and Julian folded up the map. The two girls came back with the clean crockery, and Anne put it neatly back on the shelves in the red caravan. Trotter came to look for Timmy, who was lying panting under George's caravan.

Timmy wouldn't budge, so Trotter tried to get under the caravan too. But he couldn't possibly, of course, for he was much too big. So he lay down on the shady side, as near to Timmy as he could get.

'Trotter's really a comic horse,' said Dick. 'He'd be quite good in a circus, I should think! Did you see him chasing Timmy yesterday – just as if they were playing "He"?'

The word 'circus' reminded them of Nobby and his circus, and they began to talk eagerly of all the animals there.

'I liked the look of the elephant,' said George. 'I wonder what his name is. And wouldn't I like to hold a monkey!'

'I bet that chimpanzee's clever,' said Dick. 'I wonder what Timmy will think of him. I hope he'll get on all right with all the animals, especially the other dogs.'

'I hope we don't see much of Nobby's uncle,' said Anne. 'He looked as if he'd like to box anybody's ears if they so much as answered him back.'

'Well, he won't box *mine*,' said Julian. 'We'll keep out of his way. He doesn't look a very pleasant chap, I must say. Perhaps he won't be there.'

'Timmy, come out from under the caravan!' called George. 'It's quite cool and shady where we are. Come on!'

He came, panting. Trotter immediately got up and came with him. The little horse lay down beside Timmy and nuzzled him. Timmy gave his nose a lick and then turned away, looking bored.

'Isn't Trotter funny?' said Anne. 'Timmy, what *will* you think of all the circus animals, I wonder! I do hope we see the circus tomorrow. Shall we get as far as the hills, Julian? Though really I shan't mind a bit if we don't; it's so nice being on our own like this.'

They all looked out for the hills the next day as the caravans rumbled slowly down the lanes, pulled by Trotter and Dobby. And, in the afternoon, they saw them, blue in the distance.

'There they are!' said Julian. 'Those must be the Merran Hills – and Merran Lake must lie at the foot. I say, I hope the two horses are strong enough to pull the caravans a good way up. There should be an absolutely marvellous view over the lake if we get up high enough.'

The hills came nearer and nearer. They were high ones, and looked lovely in the evening light. Julian looked at his watch.

'We shan't have time to climb them and find a camping site there tonight, I'm afraid,' he said. 'We'd better camp a little way on this evening, and then make our way up into the hills tomorrow morning.'

'All right,' said Dick. 'Anything you say, Captain! There should be a farm about two miles on, according to the book. We'll camp there.'

They came to the farm, which was set by a wide stream that ran swiftly along. Julian went as usual to ask permission to camp, and Dick went with him, leaving the two girls to prepare a meal.

Julian easily got permission, and the farmer's daughter,

a plump jolly girl, sold the boys eggs, bacon, milk, and butter, besides a little crock of yellow cream. She also offered them raspberries from the garden if they liked to pick them and have them with the cream.

'Oh, I say, thanks awfully,' said Julian. 'Could you tell me if there's a circus camping in those hills? Somewhere by the lake.'

'Yes, it went by about a week ago,' said the girl. 'It goes camping there every year, for a rest. I always watch the caravans go by – quite a treat in a quiet place like this! One year they had lions, and at nights I could hear them roaring away. That fair frizzled my spine!'

The boys said good-bye and went off, chuckling to think of the farm-girl's spine being 'fair frizzled' by the roars of the distant lions.

'Well, it looks as if we'll pass the circus camp tomorrow all right,' said Julian. 'I shall enjoy camping up in the hills, won't you, Dick? It will be cooler up there, I expect – usually there's a breeze on the hills.'

'I hope we shan't get our spines fair frizzled by the noise of the circus animals at night,' grinned Dick. 'I feel fair frizzled up by the sun today, I must say!'

The next morning the caravans set off again on what the children hoped would be the last lap of their journey. They would find a lovely camping-place and stay there till they had to go home.

Julian had remembered to send a post-card each day to his parents, telling them where he was, and that everything was fine. He had found out from the farm-girl the right address for that district, and he planned to arrange with the nearest post office to take in any letters for them that came. They had not been able to receive any post, of course, when they were wandering about in their caravans.

Dobby and Trotter walked sedately down the narrow country lane that led towards the hills. Suddenly George caught sight of something flashing blue between the trees.

'Look! There's the lake! Merran Lake!' she shouted. 'Make Dobby go more quickly, Ju. I'm longing to come out into the open and see the lake.'

Soon the lane ended in a broad cart-track that led over a heathery common. The common sloped right down to the edge of an enormous blue lake that lay glittering in the August sunshine.

'I say! Isn't it magnificent?' said Dick, stopping Dobby with a pull. 'Come on, let's get down and go to the edge, Julian. Come on, girls!'

'It's lovely!' said Anne, jumping down from the driving-seat of the red caravan. 'Oh, do let's bathe straight away!'

'Yes, let's,' said Julian, and they all dived into their caravans, stripped off jeans and blouses and pulled on bathing-things. Then, without even a towel to dry themselves on, they tore down to the lake-side, eager to plunge into its blue coolness.

It was very warm at the edge of the water, but further in, where it was deep, the lake was deliciously cold. All the children could swim strongly, and they splashed and yelled in delight. The bottom of the lake was sandy, so the water was as clear as crystal.

When they were tired they all came out and lay on the warm sandy bank of the lake. They dried at once in the sun. Then as soon as they felt too hot in they went again, squealing with joy at the cold water.

'What gorgeous fun to come down here every day and bathe!' said Dick. 'Get away, Timmy, when I'm swimming on my back. Timmy's enjoying the bathe as much as we are, George.'

'Yes, and old Trotter wants to come in, too,' shouted Julian. 'Look at him – he's brought the red caravan right down to the edge of the lake. He'll be in the water with it if we don't stop him!'

They decided to have a picnic by the lake, and to set the horses free to have a bathe if they wanted one. But all they wanted was to drink and to stand knee-high in the water, swishing their tails to keep away the flies that worried them all day long.

'Where's the circus camp?' said George suddenly as they sat munching ham and tomato sandwiches. 'I can't see it.'

The children looked all round the edge of the lake, which stretched as far as they could see. At last George's sharp eyes saw a small spire of smoke rising in the air about a mile or so round the lake.

'The camp must be in that hollow at the foot of the hills over there,' she said. 'I expect the road leads round to it. We'll go that way, shall we, and then go up into the hills behind?'

'Yes,' agreed Julian. 'We shall have plenty of time to have a word with Nobby, and to find a good camping-place before night comes – and to find a farm, too, that will let us have food. Won't Nobby be surprised to see us?'

They cleared up, put the horses into their harness again and set off for the circus camp. Now for a bit of excitement!

Chapter Six

THE CIRCUS CAMP AND NOBBY

IT did not take the caravans very long to come in sight of
the circus camp. As George had said, it was in a comfortable hollow, set at the foot of the hills – a quiet spot, well
away from any dwelling-places, where the circus animals
could enjoy a certain amount of freedom and be exercised
in peace.

The caravans were set round in a wide circle. Tents
had been put up here and there. The big elephant was
tied by a thick rope to a stout tree. Dogs ran about everywhere, and a string of shining horses was being paraded
round a large field nearby.

'There they all are!' said Anne, excitedly, standing up
on the driving-seat to see better. 'Golly, the chimpanzee
is loose, isn't he? No, he isn't – someone has got him on a
rope. Is it Nobby with him?'

'Yes, it is. I say, fancy walking about with a live
chimp like that!' said Julian.

The children looked at everything with the greatest
interest as their caravans came nearer to the circus
camp. Few people seemed to be about that hot afternoon.
Nobby was there with the chimpanzee, and one or two
women were stirring pots over small fires – but that
seemed to be all.

The circus dogs set up a great barking as the red and
green caravans drew nearer. One or two men came out
of the tents and looked up the track that led to the camp.

They pointed to the children's caravans and seemed astonished.

Nobby, with the chimpanzee held firmly by the paw, came out of the camp in curiosity to meet the strange caravans. Julian hailed him.

'Hi, Nobby! You didn't think you'd see *us* here, did you?'

Nobby was amazed to hear his name called. At first he did not remember the children at all. Then he gave a yell.

'Jumping Jiminy, it's you kids I saw away back on the road! What are *you* doing here?'

Timmy growled ominously and George called to Nobby. 'He's never seen a chimpanzee before. Do you think they'll be friends?'

'Don't know,' said Nobby doubtfully. 'Old Pongo likes the circus dogs all right. Anyway, don't you let your dog fly at Pongo, or he'll be eaten alive! A chimp is very strong, you know.'

'Could I make friends with Pongo, do you think?' asked George. 'If he would shake hands with me, or something, Timmy would know I was friends with him and he'd be all right. Would Pongo make friends with me?'

' 'Course he will!' said Nobby. 'He's the sweetest-tempered chimp alive – ain't you, Pongo? Now, shake hands with the lady.'

Anne didn't feel at all inclined to go near the chimpanzee, but George was quite fearless. She walked up to the big animal and held out her hand. The chimpanzee took it at once, raised it to his mouth and pretended to nibble it, making friendly noises all the time.

George laughed. 'He's nice, isn't he?' she said. 'Timmy, this is Pongo, a friend. Nice Pongo, good Pongo!'

She patted Pongo on the shoulder to show Timmy that she liked the chimpanzee, and Pongo at once patted her on the shoulder, too, grinning amiably. He then patted her on the head and pulled one of her curls.

Timmy wagged his tail a little. He looked very doubtful indeed. What was this strange creature that his mistress appeared to like so much. He took a step towards Pongo.

'Come on, Timmy, say how do you do to Pongo,' said George. 'Like this.' And she shook hands with the chimpanzee again. This time he wouldn't let her hand go, but went on shaking it up and down as if he was pumping water with a pump-handle.

'He won't let go,' said George.

'Don't be naughty, Pongo,' said Nobby in a stern voice. Pongo at once dropped George's hand and covered his face with a hairy paw as if he was ashamed. But the children saw that he was peeping through his fingers with wicked eyes that twinkled with fun.

'He's a real monkey!' said George, laughing.

'You're wrong – he's an ape!' said Nobby. 'Ah, here comes Timmy to make friends. Jumping Jiminy, they're shaking paws!'

So they were. Timmy, having once made up his mind that Pongo was to be a friend, remembered his manners and held out his right paw as he had been taught. Pongo seized it and shook it vigorously. Then he walked round to the back of Timmy and shook hands with his tail. Timmy didn't know what to make of it all.

The children yelled with laughter, and Timmy sat down firmly on his tail. Then he stood up again, his tail wagging, for Barker and Growler had come rushing up. Timmy remembered them, and they remembered him.

'Well, *they're* making friends all right,' said Nobby, pleased. 'Now they'll introduce Timmy to all the other dogs, and there'll be no trouble. Hey, look out for Pongo, there!'

The chimpanzee had stolen round to the back of Julian and was slipping his hand into the boy's pocket.

Nobby went to him and slapped the chimpanzee's paw hard.

'Naughty! Bad boy! Pickpocket!'

The children laughed again when the chimpanzee covered his face with his paws, pretending to be ashamed.

'You'll have to watch out when Pongo's about,' said Nobby. 'He loves to take things out of people's pockets. I say – do tell me – are those your caravans? Aren't they posh?'

'They've been lent to us,' said Dick. 'As a matter of fact, it was seeing your circus go by, with all its gay caravans, that made us think of borrowing caravans, too, and coming away for a holiday.'

'And as you'd told us where you were going we thought we'd follow you and find you out, and get you to show us round the camp,' said Julian. 'Hope you don't mind.'

'I'm proud,' said Nobby, going a bright red. ' 'Tisn't often folks want to make friends with a circus fellow like me – not gentlefolk like you, I mean. I'll be proud to show you round – and you can make friends with every blessed monkey, dog and horse on the place!'

'Oh, thanks!' said all four at once.

'Jolly decent of you,' said Dick. 'Gosh, look at that chimp – he's trying to shake hands with Timmy's tail again. I bet he's funny in the circus ring, ·isn't he, Nobby?'

'He's a scream,' said Nobby. 'Brings the house down. You should see him act with my Uncle Dan. He's the chief clown, you know. Pongo is just as big a clown as my uncle is – it's a fair scream to see them act the fool together.'

'I wish we *could* see them,' said Anne. 'Acting in the

ring, I mean. Will your uncle mind you showing us all
the animals and everything?'

'Why should he?' said Nobby. 'Shan't ask him! But
you'll mind and act polite to him, won't you? He's worse
than a tiger when he's in a temper. They call him Tiger
Dan because of his rages.'

Anne didn't like the sound of that at all – Tiger Dan!
It sounded very fierce and savage.

'I hope he isn't about anywhere now,' she said nervously, looking round.

'No. He's gone off somewhere,' said Nobby. 'He's a
lonesome sort of chap – got no friends much in the circus,
except Lou, the acrobat. That's Lou over there.'

Lou was a long-limbed, loose-jointed fellow with an
ugly face, and a crop of black shining hair that curled
tightly. He sat on the steps of a caravan, smoking a pipe
and reading a paper. The children thought that he and
Tiger Dan would make a good pair – bad-tempered,
scowling and unfriendly. They all made up their minds
that they would have as little as possible to do with Lou
the acrobat and Tiger Dan the clown.

'Is he a very good acrobat?' said Anne in a low voice,
though Lou was much too far away to hear her.

'Fine. First class,' said Nobby with admiration in his
voice. 'He can climb anything anywhere – he could go up
that tree there like a monkey – and I've seen him climb a
drainpipe straight up the side of a tall building just like a
cat. He's a marvel. You should see him on the tight-rope,
too. He can dance on it!'

The children gazed at Lou with awe. He felt their
glances, looked up and scowled. 'Well,' thought Julian,
'he may be the finest acrobat that ever lived – but he's a

jolly nasty-looking fellow. There's not much to choose between him and Tiger Dan!'

Lou got up, uncurling his long body like a cat. He moved easily and softly. He loped to Nobby, still with the ugly scowl on his face.

'Who are these kids?' he said. 'What are they doing messing about here?'

'We're not messing about,' said Julian politely. 'We came to see Nobby. We've seen him before.'

Lou looked at Julian as if he was something that smelt nasty. 'Them your caravans?' he asked jerking his head towards them.

'Yes,' said Julian.

'Posh, aren't you?' said Lou sneeringly.

'Not particularly,' said Julian, still polite.

'Any grown-ups with you?' asked Lou.

'No. I'm in charge,' said Julian, 'and we've got a dog that flies at people he doesn't like.'

Timmy clearly didn't like Lou. He stood near him, growling in his throat. Lou kicked out at him.

George caught hold of Timmy's collar just in time. 'Down Tim, down!' she cried. Then she turned on Lou, her eyes blazing.

'Don't you dare kick my dog!' she shouted. 'He'll have you down on the ground if you do. You keep out of his way, or he'll go for you now.'

Lou spat on the ground in contempt and turned to go. 'You clear out,' he said. 'We don't want no kids messing about here. And I ain't afraid of no dog. I got ways of dealing with bad dogs.'

'What do you mean by that?' yelled George, still in a furious temper. But Lou did not bother to reply. He went up the steps of his caravan and slammed the door shut. Timmy barked angrily and tugged at his collar, which George was still holding firmly.

'Now you've torn it!' said Nobby dismally. 'If Lou catches you about anywhere he'll hoof you out. And you be careful of that dog of yours, or he'll disappear.'

George was angry and alarmed. 'Disappear! What do you mean? If you think Timmy would let anyone steal him, you're wrong.'

'All right, all right. I'm only telling you. Don't fly at me like that!' said Nobby. 'Jumping Jiminy, look at that chimp. He's gone inside one of your caravans!'

The sudden storm was forgotten as everyone rushed to the green caravan. Pongo was inside, helping himself liberally from a tin of sweets. As soon as he saw the children he groaned and covered his face with his paws – but he sucked hard at the sweets all the time.

'Pongo! Bad boy! Come here!' scolded Nobby. 'Shall I whip you?'

'Oh, no, don't,' begged Anne. 'He's a scamp, but I do like him. We've plenty of sweets to spare. You have some, too, Nobby.'

'Well, thank you.' said Nobby, and helped himself. He grinned round at everyone. 'Nice to have friends like you,' he said. 'Ain't it, Pongo?'

Chapter Seven

A TEA-PARTY – AND A VISIT IN THE NIGHT

NOBODY particularly wanted to see round the camp just then, as Lou had been so unpleasant. So instead they showed the admiring Nobby over the two caravans. He had never seen such beauties.

'Jumping Jiminy, they're like palaces!' he said. 'Do you mean to say them taps turn on and water comes out? Can I turn on a tap? I've never turned a tap in my life!'

He turned the taps on and off a dozen times, exclaiming in wonder to see the water come gushing out. He thumped the bunks to see how soft they were. He admired the gay soft rugs and the shining crockery. He was, in fact, a very nice guest to have, and the children liked him more and more. They liked Barker and Growler, too, who were both well-behaved, obedient, merry dogs.

Pongo, of course, wanted to turn the taps on and off, too, and he threw all the coverings off the two bunks to see what was underneath. He also took the kettle off the stove put the spout to his thick lips and drank all the water out of it very noisily indeed.

'You're forgetting your manners, Pongo!' said Nobby in horror, and snatched the kettle away from him. Anne squealed with laughter. She loved the chimpanzee, and he seemed to have taken a great fancy to Anne, too. He followed her about and stroked her hair and made funny affectionate noises.

'Would you like to stay and have tea here with us?'

54

asked Julian, looking at his watch. 'It's about time.'

'Coo – I don't have tea as a rule,' said Nobby. 'Yes, I'd like to. Sure you don't mind me staying, though? I ain't got your manners, I know, and I'm a bit dirty, and not your sort at all. But you're real kind.'

'We'd love to have you stay,' said Anne in delight. 'I'll cut some bread and butter and make some sandwiches. Do you like potted meat sandwiches, Nobby?'

'Don't I just!' said Nobby. 'And Pongo does, too. Don't you let him get near them or he'll finish up the lot.'

It was a pleasant and amusing little tea-party. They all sat out on the heather, on the shady side of the caravan. Barker and Growler sat with Timmy. Pongo sat beside Anne, taking bits of sandwich from her most politely. Nobby enjoyed his tea immensely, eating more sandwiches than anyone and talking all the time with his mouth full.

He made the four children yell with laughter. He imitated his Uncle Dan doing some of his clown tricks. He turned cart-wheels all round the caravan while he was waiting for Anne to cut more sandwiches. He stood solemnly on his head and ate a sandwich like that, much to Timmy's amazement. Timmy walked round and round him, and sniffed at his face as if to say: 'Strange! No legs! Something's gone wrong.'

At last nobody could eat any more. Nobby stood up to go, suddenly wondering if he had stayed too long.

'I was enjoying myself so much I forgot the time,' he said awkwardly. 'Bet I've stayed too long and you've been too polite to tell me to get out. Coo, that wasn't half a good tea! Thanks, Miss, awfully, for all them delicious sandwiches. 'Fraid my manners aren't like yours, kids, but thanks for a very good time.'

'You've got very good manners indeed,' said Anne, warmly. 'You've been a splendid guest. Come again, won't you?'

'Well, thanks, I will,' said Nobby, forgetting his sudden awkwardness, and beaming round. 'Where's Pongo? Look at that chimp! He's got one of your hankies, and he's blowing his nose!'

Anne squealed in delight. 'He can keep it!' she said. 'It's only an old one.'

'Will you be here camping for long?' asked Nobby.

'Well, not just exactly *here*,' said Julian. 'We thought of going up higher into the hills. It will be cooler there. But we might camp here just for tonight. We meant to go up higher this evening, but we might as well stay here and go tomorrow morning now. Perhaps we could see round the camp tomorrow morning.'

'Not if Lou's there you can't,' said Nobby. 'Once he's told people to clear out he means it. But it will be all right if he's not. I'll come and tell you.'

'All right,' said Julian. 'I'm not afraid of Lou – but we don't want to get *you* into any trouble, Nobby. If Lou's there tomorrow morning, we'll go on up into the hills, and you can always signal to us if he's out of the camp, and we can come down any time. And mind you come up and see us when you want to.'

'And bring Pongo,' said Anne.

'You bet!' said Nobby. 'Well – so long!'

He went off with Barker and Growler at his heels and with Pongo held firmly by the paw. Pongo didn't want to go at all. He kept pulling back like a naughty child.

'I do like Nobby and Pongo,' said Anne. 'I wonder what Mummy would say if she knew we'd made friends with a chimpanzee. She'd have a fit.'

Julian suddenly looked rather doubtful. He was wondering if he had done right to follow the circus and let

Anne and the others make friends with such queer folk and even queerer animals. But Nobby was so nice. He was sure his mother would like Nobby. And they could easily keep away from Tiger Dan and Lou the acrobat.

'Have we got enough to eat for supper tonight and breakfast tomorrow?' he asked Anne. 'Because there doesn't seem to be a farm near enough to go to just here. But Nobby says there's one up on the hill up there – the circus folk get their supplies from it, too – what they don't get from the nearest town. Apparently somebody goes in each day to shop.'

'I'll just see what we've got in the larder, Julian,' said Anne, getting up. She knew perfectly well what there was in the larder – but it made her feel grown-up and important to go and look. It was nice to feel like that when she so often felt small and young, and the others were big and knew so much.

She called back to them: 'I've got eggs and tomatoes and potted meat, and plenty of bread, and a cake we bought today, and a pound of butter.'

'That's all right then,' said Julian. 'We won't bother about going to the farm tonight.'

When darkness fell that night, there were clouds across the sky for the first time. Not a star showed and there was no moon. It was pitch-black, and Julian, looking out of the window of his caravan, before clambering into his bunk, could not even see a shimmer of water from the lake.

He got into his bunk and pulled the covers up. In the other caravan George and Anne were asleep. Timmy was, as usual, on George's feet. She had pushed him off them once or twice, but now that she was asleep he was undisturbed, and lay heavily across her ankles, his head on his paws.

Suddenly his ears cocked up. He raised his head cautiously. Then he growled softly in his throat. He had heard something. He sat there stiffly, listening. He could hear footsteps from two different directions. Then he heard voices – cautious voices, low and muffled.

Timmy growled again, more loudly. George awoke and reached for his collar. 'What's the matter?' she whispered. Timmy listened and so did she. They both heard the voices.

George slipped quietly out of the bunk and went to the half-open door of the caravan. She could not see anything outside at all because it was so dark. 'Don't make a noise, Tim,' she whispered.

Timmy understood. He did not growl again, but George could feel the hairs rising all along the back of his neck.

The voices seemed to come from not very far away. Two men must be talking together, George thought. Then she heard a match struck, and in its light she saw two men lighting their cigarettes from the same match. She recognised them at once – they were Nobby's Uncle Dan and Lou the acrobat.

What were they doing there? Had they got a meeting-place there – or had they come to steal something from the caravans? George wished she could tell Julian and Dick – but she did not like to go out of her caravan in case the men heard her.

At first she could not hear anything the men said. They were discussing something very earnestly. Then one raised his voice.

'Okay, then – that's settled.' Then came the sound of footsteps again, this time towards George's caravan. The men walked straight into the side of it, exclaimed in surprise and pain, and began to feel about to find out what they had walked into.

'It's those posh caravans!' George heard Lou exclaim. 'Still here! I told those kids to clear out!'

'What kids?' asked Tiger Dan, in surprise. Evidently he had come back in the dark and did not know they had arrived.

'Some kids Nobby knows,' said Lou in an angry voice. He rapped loudly on the walls of the caravan, and Anne woke up with a jump. George, just inside the caravan with Timmy, jumped in fright, too. Timmy barked in rage.

Julian and Dick woke up. Julian flashed on his torch and went to his door. The light picked out the two men standing by George's caravan.

'What are you doing here at this time of night?' said Julian. 'Making a row like that! Clear off!'

This was quite the wrong thing to have said to Dan and Lou, both bad-tempered men who felt that the whole of the camping-ground around belonged to them and the circus.

'Who do you think you're talking to?' shouted Dan angrily. 'You're the ones to clear off! Do you hear?'

'Didn't I tell you to clear out this afternoon?' yelled Lou, losing his temper, too. 'You do as you're told, you young rogue, or I'll set the dogs on you and have you chased for miles.'

Anne began to cry. George trembled with rage. Timmy growled. Julian spoke calmly but determinedly.

'We're going in the morning, as we meant. But if you're suggesting we should go now, you can think again. This is as much our camping-ground as yours. Now get off, and don't come disturbing us again.'

'I'll give you a leathering, you young cockerel!' cried Lou, and began to unfasten the leather belt from round his waist.

George let go her hold of Timmy's collar. 'Go for them, Timmy,' she said. 'But don't bite. Just worry them!'

Timmy sprang down to the ground with a joyful bark. He flung himself at the two men. He knew what George wanted him to do, and although he longed to snap at the two rogues with his sharp teeth, he didn't. He pretended to, though, and growled so fiercely that they were scared out of their wits.

Lou hit out at Timmy, threatening to kill him. But Timmy cared for no threats of that kind. He got hold of Lou's right trouser-leg, pulled, and ripped it open from knee to ankle.

'Come on – the dog's mad!' cried Dan. 'He'll have us by the throat if we don't go. Call him off, you kids. We're going. But mind you clear out in the morning, or we'll see you do! We'll pay you out one day.'

Seeing that the men really meant to go, George whistled to Timmy. 'Come here, Tim. Stand on guard till they're really gone. Fly at them if they come back.'

But the men soon disappeared – and nothing would have made either of them come back and face Timmy again that night!

Chapter Eight

UP IN THE HILLS

THE four children were upset and puzzled by the behaviour of the two men. George told how Timmy had wakened her by growling and how she had heard the men talking together in low voices.

'I don't really think they had come to steal anything,' she said. 'I think they were just meeting near here for a secret talk. They didn't know the caravans were here and walked straight into ours.'

'They're bad-tempered brutes,' said Julian. 'And I don't care what you say, George, I'm going to lock your caravan door tonight. I know you've got Timmy – but I'm not running any risk of these men coming back, Timmy or no Timmy.'

Anne was so scared that George consented to let Julian lock the red caravan door. Timmy was locked in with them. The boys went back to their own caravan, and Julian locked his door, too, from the inside. He wanted to be on the safe side.

'I'll be glad to get away from here up into the hills,' he said. 'I shan't feel safe as long as we are quite so near the camp. We'll be all right up in the hills.'

'We'll go first thing after breakfast,' said Dick, settling down to his bunk again. 'Gosh, it's a good thing the girls had Timmy tonight. Those fellows looked as if they meant to go for you properly, Ju.'

'Yes. I shouldn't have had much chance against the

two of them either,' said Julian. 'They are both hefty, strong fellows.'

The next morning all the four awoke early. Nobody felt inclined to lie and snooze – all of them were anxious to get off before Lou and Dan appeared again.

'You get the breakfast, Anne and George, and Dick and I will catch the horses and put them in the caravan shafts,' said Julian. 'Then we shall be ready to go off immediately after breakfast.'

They had breakfast and cleared up. They got up on to the driving-seats and were just about to drive away when Lou and Dan came down the track towards them.

'Oh, you're going, are you?' said Dan, with an ugly grin on his face. 'That's right. Nice to see kids so obedient. Where you going?'

'Up into the hills,' said Julian. 'Not that it's anything to do with you where we go.'

'Why don't you go round the foot of the hills, instead of over the top?' said Lou. 'Silly way to go – up there, with the caravans dragging them horses back all the way.'

Julian was just about to say that he didn't intend to go right up to the top of the hills and over to the other side, when he stopped himself. No – just as well not to let these fellows know that he meant to camp up there, or they might come and worry them all again.

He clicked to Dobby. 'We're going the way we want to go,' he said to Lou in a curt voice. 'And that's up the hill. Get out of the way, please.'

As Dobby was walking straight at them, the men had to jump to one side. They scowled at the four children. Then they all heard the sound of running footsteps and

along came Nobby, with Barker and Growler at his heels
as usual.

'Hey, what you going so early for?' he yelled. 'Let me
come part of the way with you.'

'No, you don't,' said his uncle, and gave the surprised
boy an unexpected cuff. 'I've told these kids to clear out,
and they're going. I won't have no meddling strangers
round this camp. And don't you kid yourself they want
to make friends with you, see! You go and get out those
dogs and exercise them, or I'll give you another box on
the ears that'll make you see all the stars in the sky.'

Nobby stared at him, angry and afraid. He knew his
uncle too well to defy him. He turned on his heel sullenly
and went off back to the camp. The caravans overtook
him on the way. Julian called to him in a low voice:

'Cheer up, Nobby. We'll be waiting for you up in the
hills – don't tell Lou and your uncle about it. Let them
think we've gone right away. Bring Pongo up sometime!'

Nobby grinned. 'Right you are!' he said. 'I can bring
the dogs up to exercise them, too – but not today. I
dursent today. And as soon as them two are safely out
for the day I'll bring you down to the camp and show
you round, see? That all right?'

'Fine,' said Julian, and drove on. Neither Lou nor
Dan had heard a word, or even guessed that this conversation was going on, for Nobby had been careful to
walk on all the time and not even turn his face towards
the children.

The road wound upwards into the hills. At first it was
not very steep, but wound to and fro across the side of the
hill. Half-way up the caravans crossed a stone bridge
under which a very swift stream flowed.

'That stream's in a hurry!' said George, watching it bubble and gurgle downwards. 'Look – is that where it starts from – just there in the hillside?'

She pointed some way up the hill, and it seemed as if the stream really did suddenly start just where she pointed.

'But it can't suddenly start there – not such a big fast stream as this!' said Julian, stopping Dobby on the other side of the bridge. 'Let's go and see, I'm thirsty, and if there's a spring there, it will be very cold and clear – lovely to drink from. Come on, we'll go and see.'

But there was no spring. The stream did not 'begin' just there, but flowed out of a hole in the hillside, as big and as fast as it was just under the stone bridge. The children bent down and peered into the water-filled hole.

'It comes out from inside the hill,' said Anne, surprised. 'Fancy it running around in the hill itself. It must be glad to find a way out!'

They didn't like to drink it as it was not the clear, fresh spring they had hoped to find. But, wandering a little farther on, they came to a real spring that gushed out from beneath a stone, cold and crystal clear. They drank from this and voted that it was the nicest drink they had ever had in their lives. Dick followed the spring-water downwards and saw that it joined the little rushing stream.

'I suppose it flows into the lake,' he said. 'Come on. Let's get on and find a farm, Julian. I'm sure I heard the crowing of a cock just then, so one can't be far away.'

They went round a bend of the hill and saw the farm, a rambling collection of old buildings sprawling down the hillside. Hens ran about, clucking. Sheep grazed above the farm, and cows chewed the cud in fields nearby. A man was working not far off, and Julian hailed him. 'Good morning! Are you the farmer?'

'No. Farmer's over yonder,' said the man, pointing to a barn near the farm house. 'Be careful of the dogs.'

The two caravans went on towards the farm. The farmer heard them coming and came out with his dogs. When he saw that there were only children driving the two caravans he looked surprised.

Julian had a polite, well-mannered way with him that all the grown-ups liked. Soon he was deep in a talk with the man, with most satisfactory results. The farmer was willing to supply them with any farm produce they wanted, and they could have as much milk as they liked at any time. His wife, he was sure, would cook them anything they asked her to, and bake them cakes, too.

'Perhaps I could arrange payment with her?' said Julian. 'I'd like to pay for everything as I buy it.'

'That's right, son,' said the farmer. 'Always pay your way as you go along, and you won't come to any harm. You go and see my old woman. She likes children and she'll make you right welcome. Where are you going to camp?'

'I'd like to camp somewhere with a fine view over the lake,' said Julian. 'We can't see it from just here. Maybe a bit farther on we'll get just the view I want.'

'Yes, you go on about half a mile,' said the farmer. 'The track goes that far – and when you come to a clump of fine birch trees you'll see a sheltered hollow, set right in the hillside, with a wonderful fine view over the lake. You can pull your caravans in there, son, and you'll be sheltered from the winds.'

'Thanks awfully,' said all the children together, thinking what a nice man this old farmer was. How different from Lou and Dan, with their threats and rages!

'We'll go and see your wife first, sir,' said Julian. 'Then we'll go on and pull into the hollow you suggest. We'll be seeing you again some time, I expect.'

They went to see the farmer's wife, a fat, round-cheeked old woman, whose little curranty eyes twinkled with good humour. She made them very welcome, gave them hot buns from the oven and told them to help themselves to the little purple plums on the tree outside the old farm house.

Julian arranged to pay on the spot for anything they bought each day. The prices the farmer's wife asked seemed very low indeed, but she would not hear of taking any more money for her goods.

'It'll be a pleasure to see your bonny faces at my door!' she said. 'That'll be part of my payment, see? I can tell you're well-brought-up children by your nice manners and ways. You'll not be doing any damage or foolishness on the farm, *I* know.'

The children came away laden with all kinds of food, from eggs and ham to scones and ginger cakes. She pushed a bottle of raspberry syrup into Anne's hand when the little girl said good-bye. But when Julian turned back to pay her for it she was quite annoyed.

'If I want to make a present to somebody I'll do it!' she said. 'Go on with you . . . paying for this and paying for that. I'll have a little something extra for you each time, and don't you dare to ask to pay for it, or I'll be after you with my rolling pin!'

'Isn't she awfully nice?' said Anne as they made their

way back to the caravans. 'Even Timmy offered to shake hands with her without you telling him to, George – and he hardly ever does that to anyone, does he?'

They packed the things away into the larder, got up into the driving-seats, clicked to Dobby and Trotter and set off up the track again.

Just over half a mile away was a clump of birch trees. 'We'll find that sheltered hollow near them,' said Julian.

'Yes, look – there it is – set back into the hill, a really cosy place! Just right for camping in – and oh, what a magnificent view!'

It certainly was. They could see right down the steep hillside to the lake. It lay spread out, flat and smooth, like an enchanted mirror. From where they were they could now see right to the opposite banks of the lake – and it was indeed a big stretch of water.

'Isn't it blue?' said Anne, staring. 'Bluer even than the sky. Oh, won't it be lovely to see this marvellous view every single day we're here?'

Julian backed the caravans into the hollow. Heather grew there, like a springy purple carpet. Harebells, pale as an evening sky, grew in clumps in crevices of the hill behind. It was a lovely spot for camping in.

George's sharp ears caught the sound of water and she went to look for it. She called back to the others. 'What do you think? There's another spring here, coming out of the hill. Drinking and washing water laid on! Aren't we lucky?'

'We certainly are,' said Julian. 'It's a lovely place – and nobody will disturb us here!'

But he spoke too soon!

Chapter Nine

AN UNPLEASANT MEETING

It really was fun settling into that cosy hollow. The two
caravans were backed in side by side. The horses were
taken out and led to a big field where the farmer's horses
were kept when they had done their day's work. Trotter
and Dobby seemed very pleased with the green, sloping
field. It had a spring of its own that ran into a stone
trough and out of it, keeping it always filled with fresh
cold water. Both horses went to take a long drink.

'Well, that settles the two horses all right,' said Julian.
'We'll tell the farmer he can borrow them if he wants to
– he'll be harvesting soon and may like to have Dobby
and Trotter for a few days. They will enjoy hobnobbing
with other horses again.'

At the front of the hollow was a rocky ledge, hung with
heathery tufts. 'This is the front seat for Lake View!'
said Anne. 'Oh, it's warm from the sun! How lovely!'

'I vote we have all our meals on this ledge,' said
George, sitting down too. 'It's comfortable and roomy –
and flat enough to take our cups and plates without
spilling anything – and honestly the view from here is too
gorgeous for words. Can anyone see anything of the
circus from up here?'

'There's a spire or two of smoke over yonder,' said
Dick, pointing. 'I should think that's where the camp is.
And look – there's a boat pushing out on the lake –
doesn't it look tiny?'

'Perhaps Nobby is in it,' said Anne. 'Haven't we brought any field-glasses, Julian? I thought we had.'

'Yes – we have,' said Julian, remembering. 'I'll get them.' He went to the green caravan, rummaged about in the drawers, and came out with his field-glasses swinging on the end of their straps.

'Here we are!' he said, and set them to his eyes. 'Yes – I can see the boat clearly now – and it *is* Nobby in it – but who's with him? Golly, it's Pongo!'

Everyone had to look through the glasses to see Nobby and Pongo in the boat. 'You know, we could always get Nobby to signal to us somehow from his boat when he wanted to tell us that Lou and his uncle were away,' said Dick. 'Then we should know it was safe, and we could pop down to the camp and see round it.'

'Yes. Good idea,' said George. 'Give me the glasses, Dick. Timmy wants to have a turn at seeing, too.'

'He can't see through glasses like these, idiot,' said Dick, handing them to George. But Timmy most solemnly glued his eyes to the glasses, and appeared to be looking through them very earnestly indeed.

'Woof,' he remarked, when he took his eyes away at last.

'He says he's seen Nobby and Pongo, too,' said George, and the others laughed. Anne half-believed that he had. Timmy was such an extraordinary dog, she thought, as she patted his smooth head.

It was a terribly hot day. Too hot to do anything – even to walk down to the lake and bathe! The children were glad they were up in the hills, for at least there was a little breeze that fanned them now and again. They did not expect to see Nobby again that day, but they hoped

he would come up the next day. If not they would go
down and bathe in the lake and hope to see him somewhere about there.

Soon the rocky ledge got too hot to sit on. The children
retreated to the clump of birch trees, which at least cast
some shade. They took books with them, and Timmy
came along, too, panting as if he had run for miles. He
kept going off to the little spring to drink. Anne filled a
big bowl with the cold water, and stood it in a breezy
place near by, with a cup to dip into it. They were
thirsty all day long, and it was pleasant to dip a cup into
the bowl of spring-water and drink.

The lake was unbelievably blue that day, and lay as
still as a mirror. Nobby's boat was no longer in the water.
He and Pongo had gone. There was not a single movement to be seen down by the lake.

'Shall we go down to the lake this evening, when it's
cooler, and bathe there?' said Julian, at tea-time. 'We
haven't had much exercise today, and it would do us
good to walk down and have a swim. We won't take
Timmy in case we happen to come across Lou or Dan.
He'd certainly fly at them today. We can always keep an
eye open for those two and avoid them ourselves – but
Timmy would go for them as soon as he spotted them.
We might be in the water and unable to stop him.'

'Anyway, he'll guard the caravans for us,' said Anne.
'Well, I'll just take these cups and plates and rinse them
in the stream. Nobody wants any more to eat, do they?'

'Too hot,' said Dick, rolling over on to his back. 'I
wish we were by the lake at this moment – I'd go straight
into the water now!'

At half-past six it was cooler, and the four children set

off down the hill. Timmy was angry and hurt at being left behind.

'You're to be on guard, Timmy,' said George firmly. 'See? Don't let anyone come near our caravans. On guard, Timmy!'

'Woof,' said Timmy dismally, and put his tail down. On guard! Didn't George know that the caravans wouldn't walk off by themselves, and that he wanted a good splash in the lake?

Still, he stayed behind, standing on the rocky ledge to see the last of the children, his ears cocked to hear their voices and his tail still down in disgust. Then he went and lay down beneath George's caravan, and waited patiently for his friends to return.

The children went down the hill with their bathing-things, taking short cuts, and leaping like goats over the steep bits. It had seemed quite a long way up when they had gone so slowly in the caravans with Dobby and Trotter – but it wasn't nearly so far when they could go on their own legs, and take rabbit-paths and short cuts whenever they liked.

There was one steep bit that forced them back on to the track. They went along it to where the track turned a sharp corner round a cliff-like bend – and to their surprise and dismay they walked almost straight into Lou and Tiger Dan!

'Take no notice,' said Julian, in a low voice. 'Keep together and walk straight on. Pretend that Timmy is somewhere just behind us.'

'Tim, Tim!' called George, at once.

Lou and Dan seemed just as surprised to see the children, as they had been to see the two men. They stopped and looked hard at them, but Julian hurried the others on.

'Hey, wait a minute!' called Dan. 'I thought you had gone off – over the hill-top!'

'Sorry we can't stop!' called back Julian. 'We're in rather a hurry!'

Lou looked round for Timmy. He wasn't going to lose his temper and start shouting in case that mad dog came at him again. He spoke to the children loudly, forcing himself to appear good-tempered.

'Where are your caravans? Are you camping up here anywhere?'

But the children still walked on, and the men had to go after them to make them hear.

'Hey! What's the matter? We shan't hurt you! We only want to know if you're camping here. It's better down below, you know.'

'Keep on walking,' muttered Julian. 'Don't tell them anything. Why do they tell us it's better to camp down below when they were so anxious for us to clear out yesterday? They're mad!'

'Timmy, Timmy!' called George, again, hoping that the men would stop following them if they heard her calling for her dog.

It did stop them. They gave up going after the children, and didn't shout any more. They turned angrily and went on up the track.

'Well, we've thrown them off all right,' said Dick, with relief. 'Don't look so scared, Anne. I wonder what they want up in the hills. They don't look the sort that would go walking for pleasure.'

'Dick – we're not going to have another adventure, are

we?' said Anne suddenly, looking very woebegone. 'I don't want one. I just want a nice ordinary, peaceful holiday.'

' 'Course we're not going to have an adventure!' said Dick, scornfully. 'Just because we meet two bad-tempered fellows from a circus camp you think we're in for an adventure, Anne! Well, *I* jolly well wish we were! Every hols we've been together so far we've had adventures – and you must admit that you love talking about them and remembering them.'

'Yes, I do. But I don't like it much when I'm in the *middle* of one,' said Anne. 'I don't think I'm a very adventurous person, really.'

'No, you're not,' said Julian, pulling Anne over a very steep bit. 'But you're a very nice little person, Anne, so don't worry about it. And, anyway, you wouldn't like to be left out of any of our adventures, would you?'

'Oh *no*,' said Anne. 'I couldn't bear it. Oh, look – we're at the bottom of the hill – and there's the lake, looking icy-cold!'

It wasn't long before they were all in the water – and suddenly there was Nobby too, waving and yelling. 'I'm coming in! Lou and my uncle have gone off somewhere. Hurray!'

Barker and Growler were with Nobby, but not Pongo the chimpanzee. Nobby was soon in the water, swimming like a dog, and splashing George as soon as he got up to her.

'We met Lou and your uncle as we came down,' called George. 'Shut up, Nobby, and let me talk to you. I said, we met Lou and your uncle just now – going up into the hills.'

'Up into the hills?' said Nobby, astonished. 'Whatever for? They don't go and fetch things from the farm. The women do that, early each morning.'

'Well, we met those two,' said Dick swimming up. 'They seemed jolly surprised to see us. I hope they aren't going to bother us any more.'

'I've had a bad day,' said Nobby, and he showed black bruises on his arms. 'My uncle hit me like anything for making friends with you. He says I'm not to go talking to strangers no more.'

'Why ever not?' said Dick. 'What a surly, selfish fellow he is! Well, you don't seem to be taking much notice of him now!'

' 'Course not!' said Nobby. 'He's safe up in the hills, isn't he? I'll have to be careful he doesn't see me with you, that's all. Nobody else at the camp will split on me – they all hate Lou and Tiger Dan.'

'We saw you out in your boat with Pongo,' said Julian, swimming up to join in the conversation. 'We thought that if ever you wanted to signal to us you could easily do it by going out in your boat, and waving a handkerchief or something. We've got field-glasses, and we can easily see you. We could come along down if you signalled. We'd know it would be safe.'

'Right,' said Nobby. 'Come on, let's have a race. Bet you I'm on the shore first!'

He wasn't, of course, because he didn't swim properly. Even Anne could race him. Soon they were all drying themselves vigorously.

'Golly, I'm hungry!' said Julian. 'Come on up the hill with us, Nobby, and share our supper!'

Chapter Ten

A CURIOUS CHANGE OF MIND

NOBBY felt very much tempted to go and have a meal up in the hills with the children. But he was afraid of meeting Lou and his uncle coming back from their walk.

'We can easily look out for them and warn you if we see or hear them,' said Dick, 'and you can flop under a bush and hide till they go past. You may be sure we'll be on the look-out for them ourselves, because *we* don't want to meet them either!'

'Well, I'll come,' said Nobby. 'I'll take Barker and Growler too. They'll like to see Timmy.'

So all five of them, with the two dogs, set off up the hill. They climbed up short cuts at first, but they were soon panting, and decided to take the track, which, although longer, was easier to follow.

They all kept a sharp look-out for the two men, but they could see no sign of them. 'We shall be at our caravans soon,' said Julian. Then he heard Timmy barking in the distance. 'Hallo! What's old Tim barking for? I wonder if those fellows have been up to our caravans?'

'Good thing we left Timmy on guard if so,' said Dick. 'We might have missed something if not.'

Then he went red, remembering that it was Nobby's uncle he had been talking of. Nobby might feel upset and offended to hear someone speaking as if he thought Tiger Dan would commit a little robbery.

But Nobby wasn't at all offended. 'Don't you worry

about what you say of my uncle,' he said, cheerfully. 'He's a bad lot. I know that. Anyway, he's not really my uncle, you know. When my father and mother died, they left a little money for me – and it turned out that they had asked Tiger Dan to look after me. So he took the money, called himself my uncle, and I've had to be with him ever since.'

'Was he in the same circus, then?' asked Julian.

'Oh yes. He and my father were both clowns,' said Nobby. 'Always have been clowns, in my family. But wait till I'm old enough, and I'll do a bunk – clear off and join another circus, where they'll let me look after the horses. I'm mad on horses. But the fellow at our circus won't often let me go near them. Jealous because I can handle them, I suppose!'

The children gazed at Nobby in wonder. He seemed an extraordinary boy to them – one who walked about with a tame chimpanzee, exercised hordes of performing dogs, lived with the chief clown in the circus, could turn the most marvellous cart-wheels, and whose only ambition was to work with horses! What a boy! Dick half-envied him.

'Haven't you ever been to school?' he asked Nobby.

The boy shook his head. 'Never! I can't write. And I can only read a bit. Most circus folk are like that, so nobody minds. Jumping Jiminy, I bet *you're* all clever, though! I bet even little Anne can read a book!'

'I've been able to read for *years*,' said Anne. 'And I'm up to fractions now in numbers.'

'Coo! What's fractions?' said Nobby, impressed.

'Well – quarters and halves and seven-eighths, and things like that,' said Anne. 'But I'd rather be able to turn a cart-wheel like you can, Nobby, than know how to do fractions.'

'Whatever *is* Timmy barking for?' said George as they came near the clump of birch trees. Then she stopped suddenly, for she had seen two figures lying down in the grass below the trees. Lou – and Tiger Dan!

It was too late for Nobby to hide. The men saw him at once. They got up and waited for the children to come near. George felt thankful that Timmy was within whistling distance. He would come at the first call or whistle, she knew.

Julian looked at the men. To his surprise they appeared to be quite amiable. A faint scowl came over Tiger Dan's face when he caught sight of Nobby, but it passed at once.

'Good evening,' said Julian curtly, and would have passed on without another word, but Lou stepped up to him.

'We see you're camping up by here,' said Lou, and smiled showing yellow teeth. 'Ain't you going over the hill?'

'I don't need to discuss my affairs with either you or your friend,' said Julian, sounding extremely grown-up. 'You told us to clear out from down below, and we have. What we do now is nothing to do with you.'

'Ho yes, it is,' said Tiger Dan, sounding as if he was being polite with great difficulty. 'We come up here to-night to plan a place for some of our animals, see? And we don't want you to be in no danger.'

'We shan't be,' said Julian, scornfully. 'And there is plenty of room on these hills for you and your animals and for us, too. You won't scare us off, so don't think it.

We shall stay here as long as we want to – and if we want help there's the farmer and his men quite near by – to say nothing of our dog.'

'Did you leave that there dog on guard?' asked Lou, as he heard Timmy barking again. 'He ought to be destroyed, that dog of yours. He's dangerous.'

'He's only dangerous to rogues and scamps,' said George, joining in at once. 'You keep away from our caravans when Timmy's on guard. He'll maul you if you go near.'

Lou began to lose his temper. 'Well, are you going or ain't you?' he said. 'We've told you we want this here bit of the hill. You can come down and camp by the lake again if you want to.'

'Yes – you come,' said Tiger Dan to the children's growing astonishment. 'You come, see? You can bathe in the lake every day, then – and Nobby here can show you round the camp, and you can make friends with all the animals, see?'

Now it was Nobby's turn to look amazed.

'Jumping Jiminy! Didn't you beat me black and blue for making friends with these kids?' he demanded. 'What's the game, now? You've never had animals up in the hills before. You've . . .'

'Shut up,' said Tiger Dan in such a fierce voice that all the children were shocked. Lou nudged Dan, and he made an effort to appear pleasant again.

'We didn't want Nobby to make friends with posh folk like you,' he began again. 'But it seems as if you want to pal up with him – so it's okay with us. You come on down and camp by the lake, and Nobby'll show you everything in the circus. Can't say fairer than that.'

'You've got other reasons for making all these suggestions,' said Julian, scornfully. 'I'm sorry – but our plans are made, and I am not going to discuss them with you.'

'Come on,' said Dick. 'Let's go and find Timmy. He's barking his head off because he can hear us, and it won't be long before he comes flying along here. Then we shall find it difficult to keep him off these two fellows.'

The four children began to move off. Nobby looked doubtfully at his uncle. He didn't know whether to go with them or not. Lou nudged Dan again.

'You go, too, if you want to,' said Tiger Dan, trying to grin amiably at the surprised Nobby. 'Keep your fine friends, see! Much good may they do you!' The grin vanished into a scowl, and Nobby skipped smartly out of reach of his uncle's hand. He was puzzled and wondered what was behind his uncle's change of mind.

He tore after the children. Timmy came to meet them, barking his head off, waving his plumy tail wildly in joy.

'Good dog, good dog!' said George, patting him. 'You keep on guard beautifully. You know I would have whistled for you if I'd wanted you, didn't you, Timmy? Good dog!'

'I'll get you some supper,' said Anne to everyone. 'We're all famishing. We can talk while we eat. George, come and help. Julian, can you get some ginger-beer? And, Dick, do fill up the water-bowl for me.'

The boys winked at one another. They always thought that Anne was very funny when she took command like this, and gave her orders. But everyone went obediently to work.

Nobby went to help Anne. Together they boiled ten eggs hard in the little saucepan. Then Anne made

tomato sandwiches with potted meat and got out the cake
the farmer's wife had given them. She remembered the
raspberry syrup, too – how lovely!

Soon they were all sitting on the rocky ledge, which
was still warm, watching the sun go down into the lake.
It was a most beautiful evening, with the lake as blue
as a cornflower and the sky flecked with rosy clouds.
They held their hard-boiled eggs in one hand and a
piece of bread and butter in the other, munching happily. There was a dish of salt for everyone to dip their
eggs into.

'I don't know why, but the meals we have on picnics
always taste so much nicer than the ones we have
indoors,' said George. 'For instance, even if we had hard-
boiled eggs and bread and butter indoors, they wouldn't
taste as nice as these.'

'Can everyone eat two eggs?' asked Anne. 'I did two
each. And there's plenty of cake – and more sandwiches and some plums we picked this morning.'

'Best meal I've ever had in my life,' said Nobby, and
picked up his second egg. 'Best company I've ever been
in, too!'

'Thank you,' said Anne, and everyone looked pleased.
Nobby might not have their good manners, but he always
seemed to say just the right thing.

'It's a good thing your uncle didn't make you go back
with him and Lou,' said Dick. 'Funny business –
changing his mind like that!'

They began to talk about it. Julian was very puzzled
indeed, and had even begun to wonder if he hadn't
better find another camping site and go over the hill.

The others raised their voices scornfully.

'JULIAN! We're not cowards. We'll jolly well stay here!'

'What, leave now – why should we? We're in nobody's way, whatever those men say!'

'*I'm* not moving *my* caravan, whatever *anyone* says!' That was George, of course.

'No, don't you go,' said Nobby. 'Don't you take no notice of Lou and my uncle. They can't do nothing to you at all. They're just trying to make trouble for you. You stay and let me show you over the camp, see?'

'It isn't that I *want* to give in to those fellows' ideas,' said Julian. 'It's just that – well, I'm in charge of us all – and I *don't* like the look of Lou and Tiger Dan – and, well . . .'

'Oh, have another egg and forget about it,' said Dick. 'We're going to stay here in this hollow, however much Dan and Lou want us out of it. And, what's more, I'd like to find out why they're so keen to push us off. It seems jolly queer to me.'

The sun went down in a blaze of orange and red, and the lake shimmered with its fiery reflection. Nobby got up regretfully, and Barker and Growler, who had been hobnobbing with Timmy, got up, too.

'I'll have to go,' said Nobby. 'Still got some jobs to do down there. What about you coming down tomorrow to see the animals? You'll like Old Lady, the elephant. She's a pet. And Pongo will be pleased to see you again.'

'Your uncle may have changed his mind again by tomorrow, and not want us near the camp,' said Dick.

'Well – I'll signal to you,' said Nobby. 'I'll go out in the boat, see? And wave a hanky. Then you'll know it's all right. Well – so long! I'll be seeing you.'

Chapter Eleven

FUN AT THE CIRCUS CAMP

Next morning, while Anne cleared up the breakfast things with George, and Dick went off to the farm to buy whatever the farmer's wife had ready for him, Julian took the field-glasses and sat on the ledge to watch for Nobby to go out on the lake in his boat.

Dick sauntered along, whistling. The farmer's wife was delighted to see him, and showed him two big baskets full of delicious food.

'Slices of ham I've cured myself,' she said, lifting up the white cloth that covered one of the baskets. 'And a pot of brawn I've made. Keep it in a cool place. And some fresh lettuces and radishes I pulled myself this morning early. And some more tomatoes.'

'How gorgeous!' said Dick, eyeing the food in delight. 'Just the kind of things we love! Thanks awfully, Mrs Mackie. What's in the other basket?'

'Eggs, butter, milk, and a tin of shortbread I've baked,' said Mrs Mackie. 'You should do all right till tomorrow, the four of you! And in that paper there is a bone for the dog.'

'How much do I owe you?' asked Dick. He paid his bill and took up the baskets. Mrs Mackie slipped a bag into his pocket.

'Just a few home-made sweets,' she said. That was her little present. Dick grinned at her.

'Well, I won't offer to pay you for them because I'm

afraid of that rolling-pin of yours,' he said. 'But thank you very, very much.'

He went off delighted. He thought of Anne's pleasure when she came to unpack the baskets. How she would love to put the things in the little larder – and pop the butter in a dish set in a bowl of cold water – and set the eggs in the little rack!

When he got back Julian called to him: 'Nobby's out in his boat. Come and look. He's waving something that can't possibly be a hanky. It must be the sheet off his bed!'

'Nobby doesn't sleep in sheets,' said Anne. 'He didn't know what they were when he saw them in our bunks. Perhaps it's a table-cloth.'

'Anyway, it's something big, to tell us that it's absolutely all right to come down to the camp,' said Julian. 'Are we ready?'

'Not quite,' said Anne, unpacking the baskets Dick had brought. 'I must put away these things – and do you want to take a picnic lunch with you? Because if so I must prepare it. Oh – look at all these gorgeous things!'

They all came back to look. 'Mrs Mackie is a darling,' said Anne. 'Honestly, these things are super – look at this gorgeous ham. It smells heavenly.'

'Here's her little present – home-made sweets,' said Dick, remembering them and taking them out of his pocket. 'Have one?'

Anne had everything ready in half an hour. They had decided to take a picnic lunch with them for themselves and for Nobby as well. They took their bathing-things and towels, too.

'Are we going to take Timmy or not?' said George. 'I

want to. But as these two men seem rather interested in our caravans, perhaps we had better leave him on guard again. We don't want to come back and find the caravans damaged or half the things stolen.'

'I should think not!' said Dick. 'They're not our things, nor our caravans. They belong to somebody else and we've got to take extra good care of them. I think we ought to leave Timmy on guard, don't you, Ju?'

'Yes, I do,' said Julian at once. 'These caravans are too valuable to leave at the mercy of any passing tramp – though I suppose we could lock them up. Anyway – we'll leave Timmy on guard today – poor old Timmy, it's a shame, isn't it?'

Timmy didn't answer. He looked gloomy and miserable. What! They were all going off without him again? He knew what 'on guard' meant – he was to stay here with these houses on wheels till the children chose to come back. He badly wanted to see Pongo again. He stood with his ears and tail drooping, the picture of misery.

But there was no help for it. The children felt that they couldn't leave the caravans unguarded while they were still so uncertain about Lou and Tiger Dan. So they all patted poor Timmy and fondled him, and then said good-bye. He sat down on the rocky ledge with his back to them and wouldn't even watch them go.

'He's sulking,' said George. 'Poor Timothy!'

It didn't take them very long to get down to the camp, and they found Nobby, Pongo, Barker and Growler waiting for them. Nobby was grinning from ear to ear.

'You saw my signal all right?' he said. 'Uncle hasn't changed his mind – in fact, he seems quite to have taken to you, and says I'm to show you all round and let you see anything you want to. That was his shirt I waved. I thought if I waved something enormous you'd know things were absolutely safe.'

'Where shall we put the bathing-things and the picnic baskets while we see round the camp?' asked Anne. 'Somewhere cool, if possible.'

'Put them in my caravan,' said Nobby, and led them to a caravan painted blue and yellow, with red wheels. The children remembered having seen it when the procession passed by their house a week or two before.

They peeped inside. It wasn't nearly so nice as theirs. It was much smaller, for one thing, and very untidy. It looked dirty, too, and had a nasty smell. Anne didn't like it very much.

'Not so good as yours!' said Nobby. 'I wish I had a caravan like yours. I'd feel like a prince. Now what do you want to see first? The elephant? Come on, then.'

They went to the tree to which Old Lady the elephant was tied. She curled her trunk round Nobby and looked at the children out of small, intelligent eyes.

'Well, Old Lady!' said Nobby. 'Want a bathe?'

The elephant trumpeted and made the children jump. 'I'll take you later on,' promised Nobby. 'Now then – hup, hup, hup!'

At these words the elephant curled her trunk tightly round Nobby's waist and lifted him bodily into the air, placing him gently on her big head!

Anne gasped.

'Oh! Did he hurt you, Nobby?'

' 'Course not!' said Nobby. 'Old Lady wouldn't hurt anyone, would you, big one?'

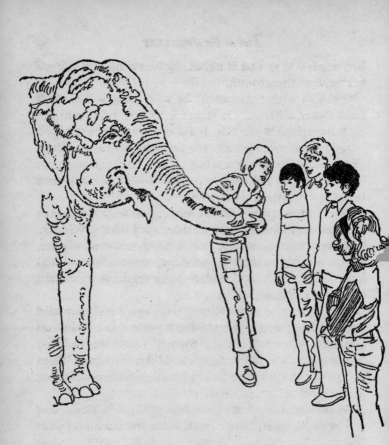

A small man came up. He had bright eyes that shone as if they had been polished, and a very wide grin. 'Good morning,' he said. 'How do you like my Old Lady? Like to see her play cricket?'

'Oh, *yes*!' said everyone, and the small man produced a cricket bat and held it out to Old Lady. She took it in her trunk and waved it about. Nobby slipped deftly off her head to the ground.

'I'll play with her, Larry,' he said, and took the ball from the small man. He threw it to Old Lady and she hit it smartly with the bat. It sailed over their heads!

Julian fetched the ball. He threw it at the elephant, and again the great creature hit the ball with a bang. Soon all the children were playing with Old Lady and enjoying the game very much.

Some small camp children came up to watch. But they were as scared as rabbits as soon as Julian or George spoke to them and scuttled off to their caravans at once. They were dirty and ragged, but most of them had beautiful eyes and thick curly hair, though it wanted brushing and washing.

Nobby went to fetch Pongo, who was dancing to and fro in his cage, making anguished sounds, thinking he was forgotten. He was simply delighted to see the children again, and put his arm right round Anne at once. Then he pulled George's hair and hid his face behind his paws, peeping out mischievously.

'He's a caution, aren't you, Pongo?' said Nobby. 'Now you keep with me, Pongo, or I'll put you back into your cage, see?'

They went to see the dogs and let them all out. They were mostly terrier dogs, or mongrels, smart, well-kept little things who jumped up eagerly at Nobby, and made a great fuss of him. It was clear that they loved him and trusted him.

'Like to see them play football?' asked Nobby. 'Here, Barker – fetch the ball. Go on, quick!'

Barker darted off to Nobby's caravan. The door was

shut, but the clever little dog stood on his hind legs and jerked the handle with his nose. The door opened and in went Barker. He came out dribbling a football with his nose. Down the steps it went and into the camp field. All the dogs leapt on it with howls of delight.

'Yap-yap-yap! Yap-yap!' They dribbled that football to and fro, while Nobby stood with his legs open to make a goal for them.

It was Barker's job and Growler's to score the goals, and the task of the other dogs to stop them. So it was a most amusing game to watch. Once, when Barker scored a goal by hurling himself on the ball and sending it rolling fast between Nobby's arched legs, Pongo leapt into the fray, picked up the ball and ran off with it.

'Foul, foul!' yelled Nobby and all the dogs rushed after the mischievous chimpanzee. He leapt on to the top of a caravan and began to bounce the ball there, grinning down at the furious dogs.

'Oh, this is such fun!' said Anne, wiping the tears of laughter from her eyes. 'Oh, dear! I've got such a pain in my side from laughing.'

Nobby had to climb up to the roof of the caravan to get the ball. Pongo jumped down the other side, but left the ball balanced neatly on the chimney. He was really a most mischievous chimpanzee.

Then they went to see the beautiful horses. All of them had shining satiny coats. They were being trotted round a big field by a slim, tall young fellow called Rossy, and they obeyed his slightest word.

'Can I ride Black Queen, Rossy?' asked Nobby eagerly. 'Do let me!'

'Okay,' said Rossy, his black hair shining like the horses'

coats. Then Nobby amazed the watching children, for he leapt on to a great black horse, stood up on her back and trotted all round the field like that!

'He'll fall!' cried Anne. But he didn't, of course. Then he suddenly swung himself down on to his hands and rode Black Queen standing upside down.

'Good, good!' cried Rossy. 'You are good with horses, young one! Now ride Fury!'

Fury was a small, fiery-looking little horse, whose gleaming eyes showed a temper. Nobby ran to her and leapt on her bare-backed. She rose up, snorting and tried to throw him off. But he wouldn't be thrown off. No matter what she did, Nobby clung on like a limpet to a rock.

At last Fury tired of it and began to canter round the field. Then she galloped – and suddenly she stopped absolutely dead, meaning to fling Nobby over her head!

But the boy was waiting for that trick and threw himself backwards at once. 'Good, good!' cried Rossy. 'She will soon eat out of your hand, Nobby! Good boy.'

'Nobby, Nobby, you're terribly clever!' yelled Anne. 'Oh, I wish I could do the things you do! I wish I could.'

Nobby slid off Fury's back, looking pleased. It was nice to show off a little to his 'posh' friends. Then he looked round and about. 'I say – where's that chimp? Up to some mischief, I'll be bound! Let's go and find him.'

Chapter Twelve

A LOVELY DAY – WITH A HORRID END

THEY soon saw Pongo. He was coming round one of the caravans, looking exceedingly pleased with himself. He went to Anne and held out his paw to her, making little affectionate noises.

Anne took what he held. She looked at it. 'It's a hard-boiled egg! Oh, Nobby, he's been at the picnic baskets!'

So he had! Two of the eggs were gone, and some of the tomatoes! Nobby smacked the chimpanzee and took him back to his cage. He was very sad and made a noise as if he was crying, hiding his face in his paws. Anne was upset.

'Is he really crying? Oh, do forgive him, Nobby. He didn't mean to be naughty.'

'He's not crying. He's only pretending,' said Nobby. 'And he *did* mean to be naughty. I know him!'

The morning soon went in visiting the circus animals. It was dinner-time before they had had time to see the monkeys. 'We'll see them afterwards,' said Nobby. 'Let's have a meal now. Come on. We'll go and have it by the lake.'

The children hadn't seen Lou or Tiger Dan at all, much to their joy. 'Where are they?' asked Julian. 'Gone out for the day?'

'Yes, thank goodness,' said Nobby. 'Gone out on one of their mysterious jaunts. You know, when we're on the road, going from place to place, my uncle sometimes disappears at night. I wake up – and he's not there.'

'Where does he go?' asked George.

'I wouldn't dare to ask,' said Nobby. 'Anyway, he and Lou are out of the way today. I don't expect they'll be back till night.'

They had their meal by the lake. It glittered at their feet, calm and blue, and looked very inviting.

'What about a swim?' asked Dick when they had eaten as much as they could. Julian looked at his watch.

'Can't swim directly after a good meal,' he said. 'You know that, Dick. We'll have to wait a bit.'

'Right,' said Dick, and lay down. 'I'll have a snooze – or shall we go and see the monkeys?'

They all had a short nap and then got up to go and see the monkeys. When they got back to the camp they found it alive with people, all excited and yelling.

'What's up?' said Nobby. 'Jumping Jiminy, the monkeys are all loose!'

So they were. Wherever they looked the children saw a small brown monkey, chattering to itself, on the roof of a caravan or tent!

A brown-faced woman with sharp eyes came up to Nobby. She caught him by the shoulder and shook him. 'See what that chimp of yours has done!' she said. 'You put him in his cage and couldn't have locked it properly. He got out and let all the monkeys loose. Drat that chimp – I'll take a broomstick to him if ever I catch him!'

'Where's Lucilla then?' asked Nobby, dragging himself away from the cross woman. 'Can't she get them in?'

'Lucilla's gone to the town,' scolded the woman. 'And fine and pleased she'll be to hear this when she comes back!'

'Aw, let the monkeys be!' said Nobby. 'They won't

come to any harm. They'll wait for Lucilla all right!'

'Who's Lucilla?' asked Anne, thinking that life in a circus camp was very exciting.

'She owns the monkeys,' said Nobby. 'Hi, look – there's Lucilla coming back! Now we'll be all right!'

A little wizened old woman was hurrying towards the camp. She really looked rather like a monkey herself, Anne thought. Her eyes were bright and sharp, and her tiny hands clutched a red shawl round her. They looked like brown paws.

'Your monkeys are out!' yelled the camp children. 'LUCILLA! Your monkeys are out.'

Lucilla heard and, raising her voice, she scolded everyone in sight fully and shrilly. Then she stood still and held out her arms. She spoke some soft words in a language the children didn't know – magic words, Anne said afterwards.

One by one the wandering monkeys came scampering over to her, flinging themselves down from the caravan roofs, making little chattering sounds of love and welcome. They leapt on to Lucilla's shoulders and into her arms, cuddling against her like tiny brown children. Not one monkey was left out – all went to Lucilla as if drawn by some enchantment.

She walked slowly towards their cage, murmuring her soft words as she went. Everyone watched in silence.

'She's a queer one,' said the brown-faced woman to Nobby. 'She don't love nobody but her monkeys – and there's nobody loves her but them. You mind out she doesn't go for that chimp of yours, letting out her precious monkeys!'

'I'll take him and Old Lady down to bathe,' said

Nobby, hastily. 'By the time we're back, Lucilla will have forgotten.'

They fetched Old Lady and discovered where naughty Pongo was hiding under a caravan. As quickly as possible they went back to the lake, Old Lady stepping out well, looking forward to her bathe.

'I suppose things like that are always happening in a circus camp,' said Anne. 'It's not a bit like real life.'

'Isn't it?' said Nobby, surprised. 'It's real life all right to *me*!'

It was cool in the lake and they all enjoyed themselves very much, swimming and splashing. Pongo wouldn't go in very far, but splashed everyone who came within reach, laughing and cackling loudly. He gave Old Lady a shock by leaping up on to her back, and pulling one of her big ears.

She dipped her trunk into the lake, sucked up a lot of water, turned her trunk over her back, and squirted the water all over the startled chimpanzee! The children yelled with laughter, and roared again to see Pongo falling in fright off Old Lady's back. Splash! He went right in and got himself wet from head to foot – a thing he hated doing.

'Serves you right, you scamp!' shouted Nobby. 'Hey, Old Lady, stop it! Don't squirt at me!'

The elephant, pleased with her little joke, didn't want to stop it. So the children had to keep well away from her, for her aim was very good.

'I've never had such a lovely time in my life!' said Anne, as she dried herself. 'I shall dream all night of monkeys and elephants, horses, dogs and chimpanzees!'

Nobby turned about twenty cart-wheels by the edge of

the lake from sheer good spirits – and Pongo at once did
the same. He was even better at it than Nobby. Anne
tried and fell down flop immediately.

They went back to the camp. 'Sorry I can't offer you
any tea,' said Nobby, 'but we never seem to have tea, you
know – we circus folk, I mean. Anyway, I'm not hungry
after that enormous lunch. Are you?'

Nobody was. They shared out Mrs Mackie's home-
made toffees, and gave one to Pongo. It stuck his teeth
together, and he looked so comically alarmed when he
found that he couldn't open his mouth that the children
roared at him.

He sat down, swayed from side to side, and began to
groan dismally. But the toffee soon melted away, and he
found that he could open his mouth after all. He sucked
the rest of the sweet noisily, but wouldn't have another.

They wandered round the camp, looking at the different caravans. Nobody took much notice of them now.
They were just Nobby's 'posh' friends – that was all.
Some of the smaller children peeped out and stuck out
their little red tongues – but at Nobby's roar they
vanished.

'Got no manners at all!' said Nobby. 'But they're all
right really.'

They came to where big wagons stood, stored with all
kinds of circus things. 'We don't bother to unpack these
when we're resting in camp like this,' said Nobby. 'Don't
need them here. One of my jobs is to help to unpack this
stuff when we're camping to give a show. Have to get out
all them benches and set them up in the big top – that's
the circus tent, you know. We're pretty busy then, I can
tell you!'

'What's in *this* cart?' asked Anne, coming to a small wagon with a tightly-fitting hood of tarpaulin.

'Don't know,' said Nobby. 'That cart belongs to my uncle. He won't never let me unpack it. I don't know what he keeps there. I've wondered if it was things belonging to my Dad and Mum. I told you they were dead. Anyway, I thought I'd peep and see one day; but Uncle Dan caught me and half-killed me!'

'But if they belonged to your parents, they ought to be yours!' said George.

'Funny thing is, sometimes that cart's crammed full,' said Nobby. 'And sometimes it isn't. Maybe Lou puts some of his things there too.'

'Well, nobody could get anything else in there at the moment!' said Julian. 'It's full to bursting!'

They lost interest in the little wagon and wandered round to see the 'props' as Nobby called them. Anne pictured these as clothes-props, but they turned out to be gilt chairs and tables, the shining poles used for the tight-rope, gaily-painted stools for the performing dogs to sit on, and circus 'props' of that kind.

'*Pro*perties, Anne,' said Julian. 'Circus *pro*perties. Props for short. Look here, isn't it about time we went back? My watch has stopped. Whatever time is it?'

'Golly, it's quite late!' said Dick, looking at his watch. 'Seven o' clock. No wonder I feel jolly hungry. Time we went back. Coming with us, Nobby? You can have supper up there if you like. I bet you could find your way back in the dark.'

'I'll take Pongo with me, and Barker and Growler,' said Nobby, delighted at the invitation. 'If *I* lose the way back, *they* won't!'

So they all set off up the hill, tired with their long and exciting day. Anne began to plan what she would give the little company for supper. Ham, certainly – and tomatoes – and some of that raspberry syrup diluted with icy-cold spring-water.

They all heard Timmy barking excitedly as soon as they came near the caravans. He barked without ceasing, loudly and determinedly.

'He sounds cross,' said Dick. 'Poor old Tim! He must think we've quite deserted him.'

They came to the caravans and Timmy flung himself on George as if he hadn't seen her for a year. He pawed her and licked her, then pawed her again.

Barker and Growler were pleased to see him too, and as for Pongo, he was delighted. He shook hands with Timmy's tail several times, and was disappointed that Timmy took no notice of him.

'Hallo! What's Barker gnawing at?' suddenly said Dick. 'Raw meat! How did it come here? Do you suppose the farmer has been by and given Timmy some? Well, why didn't he eat it, then?'

They all looked at Barker, who was gnawing some meat on the ground. Growler ran to it too. But Timmy would not go near it. Nor would Pongo. Timmy put his tail down and Pongo hid his furry face behind his paws.

'Funny,' said the children, puzzled at the queer behaviour of the two animals. Then suddenly they understood – for poor Barker suddenly gave a terrible whine, shivered from head to foot, and rolled over on his side.

'Jiminy – it's poisoned!' yelled Nobby, and kicked Growler away from the meat. He picked Barker up, and to the children's utter dismay they saw that Nobby was crying.

'He's done for,' said the boy, in a choking voice. 'Poor old Barker.'

Carrying Barker in his arms, with Growler and Pongo behind him, poor Nobby stumbled down the hill. No one liked to follow him. Poisoned meat! What a terrible thing.

Chapter Thirteen

JULIAN THINKS OF A PLAN

GEORGE was trembling. Her legs felt as if they wouldn't hold her up, and she sank down on the ledge. She put her arms round Timmy.

'Oh, Timmy! That meat was meant for you! Oh, thank goodness, thank goodness you were clever enough not to touch it! Timmy, you might have been poisoned!'

Timmy licked his mistress soberly. The others stood round, staring, not knowing what to think. Poor Barker! Would he die? Suppose it had been old Timmy? They had left him all alone, and he might have eaten the meat and died.

'I'll never, never leave you up here alone again!' said George.

'Who threw him the poisoned meat, do you think?' said Anne, in a small voice.

'Who do you suppose?' said George, in a hard, scornful voice. 'Lou and Tiger Dan!'

'They want to get us away from here, that's plain,' said Dick. 'But again – why?'

'What can there be about this place that makes the men want to get rid of us all?' wondered Julian. 'They're real rogues. Poor Nobby. He must have an awful life with them. And now they've gone and poisoned his dog.'

Nobody felt like eating very much that evening. Anne got out the bread and the butter and a pot of jam. George wouldn't eat anything. What a horrid end to a lovely day!

They all went to bed early, and nobody objected when Julian said he was going to lock both the caravans. 'Not that I think either Lou or Dan will be up here tonight,' he said. 'But you never know!'

Whether they came or not the children didn't know, for although Timmy began to bark loudly in the middle of the night, and scraped frantically at the shut door of George's caravan, there was nothing to be seen or heard when Julian opened his door and flashed on his torch.

Timmy didn't bark any more. He lay quite quietly sleeping with one ear cocked. Julian lay in bed and thought hard. Probably Lou and Dan had come creeping up in the dark, hoping that Timmy had taken the meat and been poisoned. But when they heard him bark, they knew he was all right, and they must have gone away again. What plan would they make next?

'There's something behind all this,' Julian thought, again and again. 'But what can it be? Why do they want us out of this particular spot?'

He couldn't imagine. He fell asleep at last with a vague plan in his mind. He would tell it to the others tomorrow. Perhaps if he could make Lou and Dan think they had all gone off for the day – with Timmy – but really, he, Julian, would be left behind, in hiding – maybe he could find out something, if Lou and Dan came along . . .

Julian fell asleep in the middle of thinking out his plan. Like the others, he dreamt of elephants squirting him with water, of Pongo chasing the monkeys, of the dogs playing football with excited yaps – and then into the dream came lumps of poisoned meat! Horrid.

Anne woke with a jump, having dreamt that someone had put poison into the hard-boiled eggs they were going to eat. She lay trembling in her bunk, and called to George in a small voice.

'George! I've been having an awful dream!'

George woke up, and Timmy stirred and stretched himself. George switched on her torch.

'I've been having beastly dreams, too,' she said. 'I dreamt that those men were after Timmy. I'll leave my torch on for a bit and we'll talk. I expect that with all the excitement we've had today, and the horrid end to it this evening, we're just in the mood for horrid dreams! Still – they are only dreams.'

'Woof,' said Timmy, and scratched himself.

'Don't,' said George. 'You shake the whole caravan when you do that, Timmy. Stop it.'

Timmy stopped. He sighed and lay down heavily. He put his head on his paws and looked sleepily at George, as if to say, 'put that torch out. I want to go to sleep.'

The next morning was not so warm, and the sky was cloudy. Nobody felt very cheerful, because they kept thinking of Nobby and poor Barker. They ate their breakfast almost in silence, and then Anne and George began to stack the plates, ready to take them to the spring to rinse.

'*I'll* go to the farm this morning,' said Julian. 'You sit on the ledge and take the field-glasses, Dick. We'll see if Nobby goes out in his boat and waves. I've an idea that he won't want us down in the camp this morning. If he suspects his Uncle Dan and Lou of putting down the meat that poisoned Barker, he'll probably have had a frightful row with them.'

He went off to the farm with two empty baskets. Mrs Mackie was ready for him, and he bought a further supply of delicious-looking food. Her present this time was a round ginger cake, warm from the oven!

'Do the circus folk come up here often to buy food?' asked Julian, as he paid Mrs Mackie.

'They come sometimes,' said Mrs Mackie. 'I don't mind the women or the children – dirty though they are, and not above taking one of my chickens now and again – but it's the men I can't abide. There were two here last year, messing about in the hills, that my husband had to send off quick.'

Julian pricked up his ears. 'Two men? What were they like?'

'Ugly fellows,' said Mrs Mackie. 'And one had the yellowest teeth I ever saw. Bad-tempered chaps, both of them. They came up here at night, and we were afraid our chickens would go. They swore they weren't after our chickens – but what else would they be up here at night for?'

'I can't imagine,' said Julian. He was sure that the two men Mrs Mackie spoke of were Lou and Tiger Dan. Why did they wander about in the hills at night?

He went off with the food. When he got near the camping-place, Dick called to him excitedly.

'Hey, Julian! Come and look through the glasses. Nobby's out in his boat with Pongo, and I simply can't make out what it is they're both waving.'

Julian took the glasses and looked through them. Far down the hill, on the surface of the lake, floated Nobby's little boat. In it was Nobby, and with him was Pongo. Both of them were waving something bright red.

'Can't see what they're waving – but that doesn't matter,' said Julian. 'The thing is – what they're waving is red, not white. Red for danger. He's warning us.'

'Golly – I didn't think of that. What an idiot I am!' said Dick. 'Yes – red for danger. What's up, I wonder?'

'Well, it's clear we'd better not go down to the camp today,' said Julian. 'And it's also clear that whatever danger there is, is pretty bad – because both he *and* Pongo are waving red cloths – doubly dangerous!'

'Julian, you're jolly sharp,' said George, who was listening. 'You're the only one of us who tumbled to all that. Double-danger. What can it be?'

'Perhaps it means danger down at the camp, and danger here too,' said Julian, thoughtfully. 'I hope poor old Nobby is all right. Tiger Dan is so jolly beastly to him. I bet he's had a beating or two since last night.'

'It's a shame!' said Dick.

'Don't tell Anne we think there is double-danger about,' said Julian, seeing Anne coming back from the spring. 'She'll be scared. She was hoping we wouldn't have an adventure these hols – and now we seem to be plunged into the middle of one. Golly I really think we ought to leave these hills and go on somewhere else.'

But he only said this half-heartedly, because he was burning to solve the curious mystery behind Lou's behaviour and Dan's. The others pounced on him at once.

'We can't leave! Don't be a coward, Ju!'

'I *won't* leave. Nor will Timmy.'

'Shut up,' said Julian. 'Here comes Anne.'

They said no more. Julian watched Nobby for a little while longer. Then the boy and the chimpanzee drew in to the shore and disappeared.

When they were all sitting together on the ledge,

Julian proposed the plan he had been thinking out the night before.

'I'd like to find out what there is about this place that attracts Lou and Dan,' he said. 'There is *something* not far from here that makes the men want to get rid of us. Now suppose we four and Timmy go off down the hill and pass the camp, and yell out to Nobby that we're *all* – *all* of us – going to the town for the day – and you three do go, but I slip back up the hill – maybe Lou and Dan will come up here, and if I'm in hiding I shall see what they're up to!'

'You mean, we'll all four pretend to go to town – but really only three of us go, and you get back and hide,' said Dick. 'I see. It's a good idea.'

'And you'll hide somewhere and watch for the men to come,' said George. 'Well, for goodness sake don't let them see you, Julian. You won't have Timmy, you know! Those men could make mincemeat of you if they wanted to.'

'Oh, they'd want to all right. I know that,' said Julian grimly. 'But you can be sure I'll be jolly well hidden.'

'I don't see why we can't have a good look round and see if we can't find the cave or whatever it is the men want to come to,' said Dick. 'If they can find it, we can, too!'

'We don't know that it *is* a cave,' said Julian. 'We haven't any idea at all what attracts the men up here. Mrs Mackie said they were up here last year, too, and the farmer had to drive them away. They thought the men were after the chickens – but I don't think so. There's *something* in these hills that makes the men want to get us away.'

'Let's have a good look round,' said George, feeling suddenly thrilled. 'I've gone all adventurous again!'

'Oh dear!' said Anne. But she couldn't help feeling rather thrilled, too. They all got up and Timmy followed, wagging his tail. He was pleased that his friends hadn't gone off and left him on guard by himself that morning.

'We'll all go different ways,' said Julian. 'Up, down and sideways. I'll go up.'

They separated and went off, George and Timmy together, of course. They hunted in the hillside for possible caves, or even for some kind of hiding-place. Timmy put his head down every rabbit-hole and felt very busy indeed.

After about half an hour the others heard Julian yelling. They ran back to the caravans, sure that he had found something exciting.

But he hadn't. He had simply got tired of hunting and decided to give it up. He shook his head when they rushed up to him, shouting to know what he had found.

'Nothing,' he said. 'I'm fed up with looking. There's not a cave anywhere here. I'm sure of that! Anyone else found anything?'

'Not a thing,' said everyone in disappointment. 'What shall we do now?'

'Put our plan into action,' said Julian, promptly. 'Let the men themselves show us what they're after. Off we go down the hills, and we'll yell out to Nobby that we're off for the day – and we'll hope that Lou and Tiger Dan will hear us!'

Chapter Fourteen

A VERY GOOD HIDING-PLACE

THEY went down the hill with Timmy. Julian gave Dick some instructions. 'Have a meal in the town,' he said. 'Keep away for the day, so as to give the men a chance to come up the hill. Go to the post office and see if there are any letters for us – and buy some tins of fruit. They'll make a nice change.'

'Right, Captain!' said Dick. 'And just you be careful, old boy. These men will stick at nothing – bad-tempered brutes they are.'

'Look after the girls,' said Julian. 'Don't let George do anything mad!'

Dick grinned. 'Who can stop George doing what she wants to? Not me!'

They were now at the bottom of the hill. The circus camp lay nearby. The children could hear the barking of the dogs and the shrill trumpeting of Old Lady.

They looked about for Nobby. He was nowhere to be seen. Blow! It wouldn't be any good setting off to the town and laying such a good plan if they couldn't tell Nobby they were going!

Nobody dared to go into the camp. Julian thought of the two red cloths that Nobby and Pongo had waved. Double-danger! It would be wise not to go into the camp that morning. He stood still, undecided what to do.

Then he opened his mouth and yelled:

'Nobby! NOBBY!'

No answer and no Nobby. The elephant man heard him shouting and came up. 'Do you want Nobby? I'll fetch him.'

'Thanks,' said Julian.

The little man went off, whistling. Soon Nobby appeared from behind a caravan, looking rather scared. He didn't come near Julian, but stood a good way away, looking pale and troubled.

'Nobby! We're going into the town for the day,' yelled Julian at the top of his voice. 'We're . . .'

Tiger Dan suddenly appeared behind Nobby and grabbed his arm fiercely. Nobby put up a hand to protect his face, as if he expected a blow. Julian yelled again:

'We're going into the town, Nobby! We shan't be back till evening. Can you hear me? WE'RE GOING TO THE TOWN!'

The whole camp must have heard Julian. But he was quite determined that, whoever else didn't hear, Tiger Dan certainly should.

Nobby tried to shake off his uncle's hand, and opened his mouth to yell back something. But Dan roughly put his hand across Nobby's mouth and hauled him away, shaking him as a dog shakes a rat.

'HOW'S BARKER?' yelled Julian. But Nobby had disappeared, dragged into his uncle's caravan by Dan. The little elephant man heard, however.

'Barker's bad,' he said. 'Not dead yet. But nearly. Never saw a dog so sick in my life. Nobby's fair upset!'

The children walked off with Timmy. George had had to hold his collar all the time, for once he saw Dan he growled without stopping, and tried to get away from George.

'Thank goodness Barker isn't dead,' said Anne. 'I do hope he'll get better.'

'Not much chance,' said Julian. 'That meat must have been chockful of poison. Poor old Nobby. How awful to be under the thumb of a fellow like Tiger Dan.'

'I just simply can't *imagine* him as a clown – Tiger Dan, I mean,' said Anne. 'Clowns are always so merry and gay and jolly.'

'Well, that's just acting,' said Dick. 'A clown needn't be the same out of the ring as he has to be when he's in it. If you look at photographs of clowns when they're just being ordinary men, they've got quite sad faces.'

'Well, Tiger Dan hasn't got a sad face. He's got a nasty, ugly, savage, cruel, fierce one,' said Anne, looking quite fierce herself.

That made the others laugh. Dick turned round to see if anyone was watching them walking towards the bus-stop, where the buses turned to go to the town.

'Lou the acrobat is watching us,' he said. 'Good! Can he see the bus-stop from where he is, Ju?'

Julian turned round. 'Yes, he can. He'll watch to see us all get into the bus – so I'd better climb in, too, and I'll get out at the first stop, double back, and get into the hills by some path he won't be able to see.'

'Right,' said Dick, enjoying the thought of playing a trick on Lou. 'Come on. There's the bus. We'll have to run for it.'

They all got into the bus. Lou was still watching, a small figure very far away. Dick felt inclined to wave cheekily to him, but didn't.

The bus set off. They took three tickets for the town and one for the nearest stop. Timmy had a ticket, too, which he wore proudly in his collar. He loved going in a bus.

Julian got out at the first stop. 'Well, see you this evening!' he said. 'Send Timmy on ahead to the caravans when you come back – just in case the men are anywhere about. I may not be able to warn you.'

'Right,' said Dick. 'Good-bye – and good luck!'

Julian waved and set off back down the road he had come. He saw a little lane leading off up into the hills and decided to take it. It led him not very far from Mrs Mackie's farm, so he soon knew where he was. He went back to the caravans, and quickly made himself some sandwiches and cut some cake to take to his hiding-place. He might have a long wait!

'Now – where shall I hide?' thought the boy. 'I want somewhere that will give me a view of the track so that I can see when the men come up it. And yet it must be somewhere that gives me a good view of their doings, too. What would be the best place?'

A tree? No, there wasn't one that was near enough or thick enough. Behind a bush? No, the men might easily come round it and see him. What about the middle of a thick gorse bush? That might be a good idea.

But Julian gave that up very quickly, for he found the bush far too prickly to force his way into the middle. He scratched his arms and legs terribly.

'Blow!' he said. 'I really must make up my mind, or the men may be here before I'm in hiding!'

And then he suddenly had a real brainwave, and he crowed in delight. Of course! The very place!

'I'll climb up on to the roof of one of the caravans!' thought Julian. 'Nobody will see me there – and certainly

nobody would guess I was there! That really is a fine
idea. I shall have a fine view of the track and a first-rate
view of the men and where they go!'

It wasn't very easy to climb up on to the high roof. He
had to get a rope, loop it at the end, and try to lasso the
chimney in order to climb up.

He managed to lasso the chimney, and the rope hung
down over the side of the caravan, ready for him to
swarm up. He threw his packet of food up on to the roof
and then climbed up himself. He pulled up the rope and
coiled it beside him.

Then he lay down flat. He was certain that nobody
could see him from below. Of course, if the men went
higher up the hill and looked down on the caravans, he
could easily be spotted – but he would have to chance
that.

He lay there quite still, watching the lake, and keeping
eyes and ears open for anyone coming up the hillside.
He was glad that it was not a very hot sunny day, or he
would have been cooked up on the roof. He wished he
had thought of filling a bottle with water in case he was
thirsty.

He saw spires of smoke rising from where the circus
camp lay, far below. He saw a couple of boats on the
lake, a good way round the water – people fishing, he
supposed. He watched a couple of rabbits come out and
play on the hillside just below.

The sun came out from behind the clouds for about ten
minutes and Julian began to feel uncomfortably hot.
Then it went in again and he felt better.

He suddenly heard somebody whistling and stiffened
himself in expectation – but it was only someone belong-

ing to the farm, going down the hill some distance away. The whistle had carried clearly in the still air.

Then he got bored. The rabbits went in, and not even a butterfly sailed by. He could see no birds except a yellow-hammer that sat on the topmost spray of a bush and sang: 'Little-bit-of-bread-and-no-cheese', over and over again in a most maddening manner.

Then it gave a cry of alarm and flew off. It had heard something that frightened it.

Julian heard something, too, and glued his eyes to the track that led up the hill. His heart began to beat. He could see two men. Were they Lou and Dan?

He did not dare to raise his head to see them when they came nearer in case they spotted him. But he knew their voices when they came near enough!

Yes – it was Lou and Tiger Dan all right. There was no mistaking those two harsh, coarse voices. The men came right into the hollow, and Julian heard them talking.

'Yes, there's nobody here. Those kids have really gone off for the day at least – and taken that wretched dog with them!'

'I saw them get on the bus, dog and all, I told you,' growled Lou. 'There'll be nobody here for the day. We can get what we want to.'

'Let's go and get it, then,' said Dan.

Julian waited to see where they would go to. But they didn't go out of the hollow. They stayed there, apparently beside the caravans. Julian did not dare to look over the edge of the roof to see what they were up to. He was glad he had fastened all the windows and locked the doors.

Then there began some curious scuffling sounds, and

the men panted. The caravan on which Julian was lying
began to shake a little.

'What *are* they doing?' thought Julian in bewilder-
ment. In intense curiosity he slid quietly to the edge of
the caravan roof and cautiously peeped over, though he
had firmly made up his mind not to do this on any
account.

He looked down on the ground. There was nobody
there at all. Perhaps the men were the other side. He
slid carefully across and peeped over the opposite side
of the caravan, which was still shaking a little, as if the
men were bumping against it.

There was nobody the other side either! How very
extraordinary! 'Golly! They must be underneath the
caravan!' thought Julian, going back to the middle of
the roof. 'Underneath! What in the wide world for?'

It was quite impossible to see underneath the caravan
from where he was, so he had to lie quietly and wonder
about the men's doings. They grunted and groaned, and
seemed to be scraping and scrabbling about, but nothing
happened. Then Julian heard them scrambling out
from underneath, angry and disappointed.

'Give us a cigarette,' said Lou in a disagreeable voice.
'I'm fed up with this. Have to shift this van. Those tiresome brats! What did they want to choose this spot for?'

Julian heard a match struck and smelt cigarette
smoke. Then he got a shock. The caravan he was on
began to move! Heavens! Were the men going to push
it over the ledge and send it rolling down the hillside?

Chapter Fifteen

SEVERAL THINGS HAPPEN

JULIAN was suddenly very scared. He wondered if he had better slide off the roof and run. He wouldn't have much chance if the caravan went hurtling down the hill! But he didn't move. He clung to the chimney with both hands, whilst the men shoved hard against the caravan.

It ran a few feet to the rocky ledge, and then stopped. Julian felt his forehead getting very damp, and he saw that his hands were trembling. He felt ashamed of being so scared, but he couldn't help it.

'Hey! Don't send it down the hill!' said Lou in alarm, and Julian's heart felt lighter. So they didn't mean to destroy the caravan in that way! They had just moved it to get at something underneath. But what could it be? Julian racked his brains to try and think what the floor of the hollow had been like when Dobby and Trotter pulled their caravans into it. As far as he could remember it was just an ordinary heathery hollow.

The men were now scrabbling away again by the back steps of the caravan. Julian was absolutely eaten up with curiosity, but he did not dare even to move. He could find out the secret when the men had gone. Meantime he really must be patient or he would spoil everything.

There was some muttered talking, but Julian couldn't catch a word. Then, quite suddenly, there was complete and utter silence. Not a word. Not a bump against the caravan. Not a pant or even a grunt. Nothing at all.

Julian lay still. Maybe the men were still there. He wasn't going to give himself away. He lay for quite a long time, waiting and wondering. But he heard nothing.

Then he saw a robin fly to a nearby bramble spray. It flicked its wings and looked about for crumbs. It was a robin that came around when the children were having a meal – but it was not as tame as most robins, and would not fly down until the children had left the hollow.

Then a rabbit popped out of a hole on the hillside and capered about, running suddenly up to the hollow.

'Well,' thought Julian, 'it's plain the men aren't here now, or the birds and animals wouldn't be about like this. There's another rabbit. Those men have gone somewhere – though goodness knows where. I can peep over now and have a look, quite safely, I should think.'

He slid himself round and peered over the roof at the back end of the caravan. He looked down at the ground. There was absolutely nothing to be seen to tell him what the men had been doing, or where they had gone! The heather grew luxuriantly there as it did everywhere else. There was nothing to show what the men had been making such a disturbance about.

'This is really very queer,' thought Julian, beginning to wonder if he had been dreaming. 'The men are certainly gone – vanished into thin air, apparently! Dare I get down and explore a bit? No, I daren't. The men may appear at any moment, and it's quite on the cards they'll lose their temper if they find me here, and chuck both me and the caravans down the hill! It's pretty steep just here, too.'

He lay there, thinking. He suddenly felt very hungry and thirsty. Thank goodness he had been sensible enough to take food up to the roof! He could at least have a meal while he was waiting for the men to come back – if they ever did!

He began to eat his sandwiches. They tasted very good indeed. He finished them all and began on the cake. That was good, too. He had brought a few plums up as well, and was very glad of them because he was thirsty. He flicked the plum stones from the roof before he thought what he was doing.

'Dash! Why did I do that? If the men notice them they may remember they weren't there before. Still, they've most of them gone into the heather!'

The sun came out a little and Julian felt hot. He wished the men would come again and go down the hill. He was tired of lying flat on the hard roof. Also he was terribly sleepy. He yawned silently and shut his eyes.

How long he slept he had no idea – but he was suddenly awakened by feeling the caravan being moved again! He clutched the chimney in alarm, listening to the low voices of the two men.

They were pulling the caravan back into place again. Soon it was in the same position as before. Then Julian heard a match struck and smelt smoke again.

The men went and sat on the rocky ledge and took out food they had brought. Julian did not dare to peep at them, though he felt sure they had their backs to him. The men ate, and talked in low voices, and then, to Julian's dismay, they lay down and went to sleep! He knew that they were asleep because he could hear them snoring.

'Am I going to stay on this awful roof all day long?' he

thought. 'I'm getting so cramped, lying flat like this. I want to sit up!'

'R-r-r-r-r-r!' snored Lou and Dan. Julian felt that surely it would be all right to sit up now that the men were obviously asleep. So he sat up cautiously, stretching himself with pleasure.

He looked down on the two men, who were lying on their backs with their mouths open. Beside them were two neat sacks, strong and thick. Julian wondered what was inside them. They certainly had not had them when they came up the track.

The boy gazed down the hillside, frowning, trying to probe the mystery of where the men had been, and what they were doing up here – and suddenly he jumped violently. He stared as if he could not believe his eyes.

A squat and ugly face was peering out from a bramble bush there. There was almost no nose, and an enormous mouth. Who could it be? Was it someone spying on Lou and Dan? But what a face! It didn't seem human.

A hand came up to rub the face – and Julian saw that it was hairy. With a start he knew who the face belonged to – Pongo the chimpanzee! No wonder he had thought it such an ugly, inhuman face. It was all right on a chimp, of course – quite a nice face – but not on a man.

Pongo stared at Julian solemnly, and Julian stared back, his mind in a whirl. What was Pongo doing there? Was Nobby with him? If so, Nobby was in danger, for at any moment the men might wake up. He couldn't think what to do. If he called out to warn Nobby, he would wake the men.

Pongo was pleased to see Julian, and did not seem to think the roof of a caravan a curious place to be in at all.

After all, *he* often went up on the roofs of caravans. He nodded and blinked at the boy, and then scratched his head for a long time.

Then beside him appeared Nobby's face – a tear-stained face, bruised and swollen. He suddenly saw Julian looking over the roof of the caravan, and his mouth fell open in surprise. He seemed about to call out, and Julian shook his head frantically to stop him, pointing downwards to try and warn Nobby that somebody was there.

But Nobby didn't understand. He grinned and, to Julian's horror, began to climb up the hillside to the rocky ledge! The men were sleeping there, and Julian saw with dismay that Nobby would probably heave himself up right on top of them.

'Look out!' he said, in a low, urgent voice. 'Look out, you fathead!'

But it was too late. Nobby heaved himself up on to the ledge, and, to his utmost horror, found himself sprawling on top of Tiger Dan! He gave a yell and tried to slide away – but Dan, rousing suddenly, shot out a hand and gripped him.

Lou woke up, too. The men glared at poor Nobby, and the boy began to tremble, and to beg for mercy.

'I didn't know you were here, I swear it! Let me go, let me go! I only came up to look for my knife that I lost yesterday!'

Dan shook him savagely. 'How long have you been here? You been spying?'

'No, no! I've only just come! I've been at the camp all morning – you ask Larry and Rossy. I been helping them!'

'You been spying on us, that's what you've been doing!' said Lou, in a cold, hard voice that filled the listening Julian with dread. 'You've had plenty of beatings this week, but seemingly they ain't enough. Well, up here, there's nobody to hear your yells, see? So we'll show you what a real beating is! And if you can walk down to the camp after it, I'll be surprised.'

Nobby was terrified. He begged for mercy, he promised to do anything the men asked him, and tried to jerk his poor swollen face away from Dan's hard hands.

Julian couldn't bear it. He didn't want to give away the fact that it was he who had been spying, nor did he want to fight the men at all, for he was pretty certain he would get the worst of it. But nobody could lie in silence, watching two men treat a young boy in such a way. He made up his mind to leap off the roof right on to the men, and to rescue poor Nobby if he could.

Nobby gave an anguished yell as Lou gave him a flick with his leather belt – but before Julian could jump down to help him, somebody else bounded up! Somebody who bared his teeth and made ugly animal noises of rage, somebody whose arms were far stronger than either Lou's or Dan's – somebody who loved poor Nobby, and wasn't going to let him be beaten any more!

It was Pongo. The chimpanzee had been watching the scene with his sharp little eyes. He had still hidden himself in the bush, for he was afraid of Lou and Dan – but now, hearing Nobby's cries, he leapt out of the brambles and flung himself on the astonished men.

He bit Lou's arm hard. Then he bit Dan's leg. The men yelled loudly, much more loudly than poor Nobby had. Lou lashed out with his leather belt, and it caught

Pongo on the shoulder. The chimpanzee made a shrill chattering noise, and leapt on Lou with his arms open, clasping the man to him, trying to bite his throat.

Tiger Dan rushed down the hill at top speed, terrified of the angry chimpanzee. Lou yelled to Nobby.

'Call him off! He'll kill me!'

'Pongo!' shouted Nobby. 'Stop it! Pongo! Come here.'

Pongo gave Nobby a look of the greatest surprise. 'What!' he seemed to say, 'you won't let me punish this bad man who beat you? Well, well – whatever you say must be right!'

And the chimpanzee, giving Lou one last vicious nip, let the man go. Lou followed Dan down the hill at top speed, and Julian heard him crashing through the bushes as if a hundred chimpanzees were after him.

Nobby sat down, trembling. Pongo, not quite sure if his beloved friend was angry with him or not, crept up to him putting a paw on the boy's knee. Nobby put his arm round the anxious animal, and Pongo chattered with joy.

Julian slid down from the roof of the caravan and went to Nobby. He, too, sat down beside him. He put his arm round the trembling boy and gave him a hug.

'I was just coming to give you a hand, when Pongo shot up the hill,' he said.

'Were you really?' said Nobby, his face lighting up. 'You're a real friend, you are. Good as Pongo, here.'

And Julian felt quite proud to be ranked in bravery with the chimpanzee!

Chapter Sixteen

A SURPRISING DISCOVERY

'LISTEN – somebody's coming!' said Nobby, and Pongo gave an ugly growl. The sound of voices could be heard coming up the hill. Then a dog barked.

'It's all right. It's Timmy – and the others,' said Julian, unspeakably glad to welcome them back. He stood up and yelled.

'All right! Come along!'

George, Timmy, Dick and Anne came running up the track. 'Hallo!' shouted Dick. 'We thought it would be safe, because we saw Lou and Dan in the distance, running along at the bottom of the hill. I say – there's Pongo!'

Pongo shook hands with Dick, and then went to the back of Timmy, to shake hands with his tail. But Timmy was ready for him, and backing round, he held out his paw to Pongo instead. It was very funny to see the two animals solemnly shaking hands with one another.

'Hallo, Nobby!' said Dick. 'Goodness – what have you been doing to yourself? You look as if you've been in the wars.'

'Well, I have, rather,' said Nobby, with a feeble grin. He was very much shaken, and did not get up. Pongo ran to Anne and tried to put his arms round her.

'Oh, Pongo – you squeeze too hard,' said Anne. 'Julian, did anything happen? Did the men come? Have you any news?'

'Plenty,' said Julian. 'But what I want first is a jolly good drink. I've had none all day. Ginger-beer, I think.'

'We're all thirsty. I'll get five bottles – no, six, because I expect Pongo would like some.'

Pongo loved ginger-beer. He sat down with the children on the rocky ledge, and took his glass from Anne just like a child. Timmy was a little jealous, but as he didn't like ginger-beer he couldn't make a fuss.

Julian began to tell the others about his day, and how he had hidden on the caravan roof. He described how the men had come – and had gone under the caravan – and then moved it. They all listened with wide eyes. What a story!

Then Nobby told his part. 'I butted in and almost gave the game away,' he said, when Julian had got as far as the men falling asleep and snoring. 'But, you see, I had to come and warn you. Lou and Dan swear they'll poison Timmy somehow, even if they have to dope him, put him into a sack and take him down to the camp to do it. Or they might knock him on the head.'

'Let them try!' said George, in her fiercest voice, and put her arm round Timmy. Pongo at once put his arm round Timmy too.

'And they said they'd damage your caravans too – maybe put a fire underneath and burn them up,' went on Nobby.

The four children stared at him in horror. 'But they wouldn't do a thing like that, surely?' said Julian, at last. 'They'd get into trouble with the police if they did.'

'Well, I'm just telling you what they said,' Nobby went on. 'You don't know Lou and Tiger Dan like I do. They'll stick at nothing to get their way – or to get anybody *out* of their way. They tried to poison Timmy, didn't they? And poor old Barker got it instead.'

'Is – is Barker – all right?' asked Anne.

'No,' said Nobby. 'He's dying, I think. I've given him to Lucilla to dose. She's a marvel with sick animals. I've put Growler with the other dogs. He's safe with them.'

He stared round at the other children, his mouth trembling, sniffing as if he had a bad cold.

'I dursent go back,' he said, in a low voice, 'I dursent. They'll half-kill me.'

'You're not going back, so that's settled,' said Julian, in a brisk voice. 'You're staying here with us. We shall love to have you. It was jolly decent of you to come up and warn us – and bad luck to have got caught like that. You're our friend now – and we'll stick together.'

Nobby couldn't say a word, but his face shone. He rubbed a dirty hand across his eyes, then grinned his old grin. He nodded his head, not trusting himself to speak, and the children all thought how nice he was. Poor old Nobby.

They finished their ginger-beer and then Julian got up. 'And now,' he said, 'we will do a little exploring and find out where those men went, shall we?'

'Oh yes!' cried George, who had sat still quite long enough. 'We *must* find out! Do we have to get under the caravan, Julian?'

' 'Fraid so,' said Julian. 'You sit there quietly, Nobby, and keep guard in case Lou or Dan come back.'

He didn't think for a moment that they would, but he could see that Nobby needed to sit quietly for a while. Nobby, however, had different ideas. He was going to share this adventure!

'Timmy's guard enough, and so is Pongo,' he said 'They'll hear anyone coming half a mile away. I'm in on this!'

And he was. He went scrabbling underneath the low-swung base of the caravan with the others, eager to find out anything he could.

But it was impossible to explore down in the heather, with the caravan base just over their heads. They had no room at all. Like Dan and Lou they soon felt that they would have to move the van.

It took all five of them, with Pongo giving a shove, too, to move the caravan a few feet away. Then down they dropped to the thick carpet of heather again.

The tufts came up easily by the roots, because the men had already pulled them up once that day and then re-planted them. The children dragged up a patch of heather about five feet square, and then gave an exclamation.

'Look! Boards under the heather!'

'Laid neatly across and across. What for?'

'Pull them up!'

The boys pulled up the planks one by one and piled them on one side. Then they saw that the boards had closed up the entrance of a deep hole. 'I'll get my torch,' said Julian. He fetched it and flashed it on.

The light showed them a dark hole, going down into the hillside, with footholds sticking out of one side. They all sat and gazed down in excitement.

'To think we went and put our caravan *exactly* over the entrance of the men's hiding-place!' said Dick. 'No wonder they were wild! No wonder they changed their minds and told us we could go down to the lake and camp there instead of here!'

'Gosh!' said Julian, staring into the hole. 'So that's where the men went! Where does it lead to? They were down there a mighty long time. They were clever enough to replace the planks and drag some of the heather over them, too, to hide them when they went down.'

Pongo suddenly took it into his head to go down the hole. Down he went, feeling for the footholds with his hairy feet, grinning up at the others. He disappeared at the bottom. Julian's torch could not pick him out at all.

'Hey, Pongo! Don't lose yourself down there!' called Nobby, anxiously. But Pongo had gone.

'Blow him!' said Nobby. 'He'll never find his way back,

if he goes wandering about underground. I'll have to go after him. Can I have your torch, Julian?'

'I'll come too,' said Julian. 'George, get me your torch as well, will you?'

'It's broken,' said George. 'I dropped it last night. And nobody else has got one.'

'What an awful nuisance!' said Julian. 'I want us to go and explore down there – but we can't with only one torch. Well, I'll just go down with Nobby and get Pongo – have a quick look round and come back. I may see something worth seeing!'

Nobby went down first, and Julian followed, the others all kneeling round the hole, watching them enviously. They disappeared.

'Pongo!' yelled Nobby. 'Pongo! Come here, you idiot!'

Pongo had not gone very far. He didn't like the dark down there very much, and he came to Nobby as soon as he saw the light of the torch. The boys found themselves in a narrow passage at the bottom of the hole, which widened as they went further into the hill.

'Must be caves somewhere,' said Julian, flashing his torch round. 'We know that a lot of springs run out of this hill. I daresay that through the centuries the water has eaten away the softer stuff and made caves and tunnels everywhere in the hill. And somewhere in a cave Lou and Dan store away things they don't want anyone to know about. Stolen goods, probably.'

The passage ended in a small cave that seemed to have no other opening out of it at all. There was nothing in it. Julian flashed his torch up and down the walls.

He saw footholds up one part, and traced them to a hole in the roof, which must have been made, years before, by running water. 'That's the way we go!' he said. 'Come on.'

'Wait!' said Nobby. 'Isn't your torch getting rather faint?'

'Goodness – yes!' said Julian in alarm, and shook his torch violently to make the light brighter. But the battery had almost worn out, and no better light came. Instead the light grew even fainter, until it was just a pin-prick in the torch.

'Come on – we'd better get back at once,' said Julian, feeling a bit scared. 'I don't want to wander about here in the pitch dark. Not my idea of fun at all.'

Nobby took firm hold of Pongo's hairy paw and equally firm hold of Julian's jersey. He didn't mean to lose either of them! The light in the torch went out completely. Now they must find their way back in black darkness.

Julian felt round for the beginning of the passage that led back to the hole. He found it and made his way up it, feeling the sides with his hands. It wasn't a pleasant experience at all, and Julian was thankful that he and Nobby had only gone a little way into the hill. It would have been like a nightmare if they had gone well in, and then found themselves unable to see the way back.

They saw a faint light shining further on and guessed it was the daylight shining down the entrance-hole. They stumbled thankfully towards it. They looked up and saw the anxious faces of the other three peering down at them, unable to see them.

'We're back!' called Julian, beginning to climb up. 'My torch went out, and we daren't go very far. We've got Pongo, though.'

The others helped to pull them out at the top of the hole. Julian told them about the hole in the roof of the little cave.

'That's were the men went,' he said. 'And tomorrow, when we've all bought torches, and matches and candles, that's where we're going, too! We'll go down to the town and buy what we want, and come back and do a Really Good Exploration!'

'We're going to have an adventure after all,' said Anne, in rather a small voice.

' 'Fraid so,' said Julian. 'But you can stay at the farm with Mrs Mackie for the day, Anne dear. Don't you come with us.'

'If you're going on an adventure, I'm coming, too,' said Anne. 'So there! I wouldn't *dream* of not coming.'

'All right,' said Julian. 'We'll all go together. Golly, things are getting exciting!'

Chapter Seventeen

ANOTHER VISIT FROM LOU AND DAN

NOBODY disturbed the children that night, and Timmy did not bark once. Nobby slept on a pile of rugs in the boy's caravan, and Pongo cuddled up to him. The chimpanzee seemed delighted at staying with the caravanners. Timmy was rather jealous that another animal should be with them, and wouldn't take any notice of Pongo at all.

The next morning, after breakfast, the children discussed who was to go down to the town. 'Not Nobby and Pongo, because they wouldn't be allowed in the bus together,' said Julian. 'They had better stay behind.'

'Not by ourselves?' said Nobby, looking alarmed. 'Suppose Lou and Uncle Dan come up? Even if I've got Pongo I'd be scared.'

'Well, I'll stay here, too,' said Dick. 'We don't all need to go to buy torches. Don't forget to post that letter to Daddy and Mother, Julian.'

They had written a long letter to their parents, telling them of the exciting happenings. Julian put it into his pocket. 'I'll post it all right,' he said. 'Well, I suppose we might as well go now. Come on, girls. Keep a look-out, Dick, in case those rogues come back.'

George, Timmy, Anne and Julian went down the hill together, Timmy running on in front, his tail wagging nineteen to the dozen. Pongo climbed up to the roof of the red caravan to watch them go. Nobby and Dick sat down in the warm sun on the ledge, their heads resting on springy clumps of heather.

'It's nice up here,' said Nobby. 'Much nicer than down below. I wonder what everyone is thinking about Pongo and me. I bet Mr Gorgio, the head of the circus, is wild that the chimpanzee's gone. I bet he'll send up to fetch us.'

Nobby was right. Two people were sent up to get him — Lou and Tiger Dan. They came creeping up through the bracken and heather, keeping a sharp eye for Timmy or Pongo.

Pongo sensed them long before they could be seen and warned Nobby. Nobby went very pale. He was terrified of the two scoundrels.

'Get into one of the caravans,' said Dick in a low voice. 'Go on. I'll deal with those fellows — if it *is* them. Pongo will help me if necessary.'

Nobby scuttled into the green caravan and shut the door. Dick sat where he was. Pongo squatted on the roof of the caravan, watching.

Lou and Dan suddenly appeared. They saw Dick, but did not see Pongo. They looked all round for the others.

'What do you want?' said Dick.

'Nobby and Pongo,' said Lou with a scowl. 'Where are they?'

'They're going to stay on with us,' said Dick.

'Oh, no, they're not!' said Tiger Dan. 'Nobby's in my charge, see? I'm his uncle.'

'Funny sort of uncle,' remarked Dick. 'How's that dog you poisoned, by the way?'

Tiger Dan went purple in the face. He looked as if he

would willingly have thrown Dick down the hill.

'You be careful what you say to me!' he said, beginning to shout.

Nobby, hidden in the caravan, trembled when he heard his uncle's angry yell. Pongo kept quite still, his face set and ugly.

'Well, you may as well say good-bye and go,' said Dick in a calm voice to Dan. 'I've told you that Nobby and Pongo are staying with us for the present.'

'Where *is* Nobby?' demanded Tiger Dan, looking as if he would burst with rage at any moment. 'Wait till I get my hands on him. Wait . . .'

He began to walk towards the caravans – but Pongo was not having any of that! He leapt straight off the roof on to the horrified man, and flung him to the ground. He made such a terrible snarling noise that Dan was terrified.

'Call him off!' he yelled. 'Lou, come and help.'

'Pongo won't obey *me*,' said Dick still sitting down looking quite undisturbed. 'You'd better go before he bites big pieces out of you.'

Dan staggered to the rock ledge, looking as if he would box Dick's ears. But the boy did not move, and somehow Dan did not dare to touch him. Pongo let him go and stood glowering at him, his great hairy arms hanging down his sides, ready to fly at either of the men if they came near.

Tiger Dan picked up a stone – and as quick as lightning Pongo flung himself on him again and sent the man rolling down the hill. Lou fled in terror. Dan got up and fled, too, yelling furiously as he went. Pongo chased them in delight. He, too, picked up stones and flung them

with a very accurate aim, so that Dick kept hearing yells of pain.

Pongo came back, looking extremely pleased with himself. He went to the green caravan, as Dick shouted to Nobby.

'All right, Nobby. They've gone. Pongo and I won the battle!'

Nobby came out. Pongo put his arm round him at once and chattered nonsense in his ear. Nobby looked rather ashamed of himself.

'Bit of a coward, aren't I?' he said. 'Leaving you out here all alone.'

'I enjoyed it,' said Dick truthfully. 'And I'm sure Pongo did!'

'You don't know what dangerous fellows Lou and Dan are,' said Nobby, looking down the hillside to make sure the men were really gone. 'I tell you they'd stick at nothing. They'd burn your caravans, hurl them down the hill, poison your dog, and do what harm they could to you, too. You don't know them like I do!'

'Well, as a matter of fact, we've had some pretty exciting adventures with men just as tough as Dan and Lou,' said Dick. 'We always seem to be falling into the middle of some adventure or other. Now, last hols we went to a place called Smuggler's Top – and, my word, the adventures we had there! You wouldn't believe them!'

'You tell me and Pongo,' said Nobby, sitting down beside Dick. 'We've plenty of time before the others come back.'

So Dick began to tell the tale of all the other thrilling adventures that the five of them had had, and the time flew. Both boys were surprised when they heard Timmy barking down the track, and knew that the others were back.

George came tearing up with Timmy at her heels. 'Are you all right? Did anything happen while we were away? Do you know, we saw Lou and Tiger Dan getting on the bus when we got off it! They were carrying bags as if they meant to go away and stay somewhere.'

Nobby brightened up at once. 'Did you really? Good! They came up here, you know, and Pongo chased them down the hill. They must have gone back to the camp, collected their bags, and gone to catch the bus. Hurrah!'

'We've got fine torches,' said Julian, and showed Dick his. 'Powerful ones. Here's one for you, Dick – and one for you, Nobby.'

'Oooh – thanks,' said Nobby. Then he went red. 'I haven't got enough money to pay you for such a grand torch,' he said awkwardly.

'It's a present for you,' said Anne at once, 'a present for a friend of ours, Nobby!'

'Coo! Thanks awfully,' said Nobby, looking quite overcome. 'I've never had a present before. You're decent kids, you are.'

Pongo held out his hand to Anne and made a chattering noise as if to say: 'What about one for me, too?'

'Oh – we didn't bring one for Pongo!' said Anne. 'Why ever didn't we?'

'Good thing you didn't,' said Nobby. 'He would have put it on and off all day long and wasted the battery in no time!'

'I'll give him my old torch,' said George. 'It's broken, but he won't mind that!'

Pongo was delighted with it. He kept pressing down the knob that should make the light flash – and when there was no light he looked all about on the ground as if the light must have dropped out! The children roared at him. He liked them to laugh at him. He did a little dance all round them to show how pleased he was.

'Look here – wouldn't it be a jolly good time to explore underground now that we know Lou and Dan are safely out of the way?' asked Julian suddenly. 'If they've got bags with them, surely that means they're going to spend the night somewhere and won't be back till tomorrow at least. We'd be quite safe to go down and explore.'

'Yes, we would,' said George eagerly. 'I'm longing to get down there and Make Discoveries!'

'Well, let's have something to eat first,' said Dick. 'It's long past our dinner-time. It must be about half-past one. Yes, it is!'

'George and I will get you a meal,' said Anne. 'We called at the farm on our way up and got a lovely lot of food. Come on, George.'

George got up unwillingly. Timmy followed her, sniffing expectantly. Soon the two girls were busy getting a fine meal ready, and they all sat on the rocky ledge to eat it.

'Mrs Mackie gave us this enormous bar of chocolate for a present today,' said Anne, showing a great slab to Dick and Nobby. 'Isn't it lovely? No, Pongo, it's not for you. Eat your sandwiches properly, and don't grab.'

'I vote we take some food down into the hill with us,' said Julian. 'We may be quite a long time down there, and we shan't want to come back at tea-time.'

'Oooh – a picnic inside the hill!' said Anne. 'That would be thrilling. I'll soon pack up some food in the kit-bag. I won't bother to make sandwiches. We'll take a new loaf, butter, ham and a cake, and cut what we want. What about something to drink?'

'Oh, we can last out till we get back,' said Julian. 'Just take something to eat to keep us going till we have finished exploring.'

George and Nobby cleared up and rinsed the plates. Anne wrapped up some food in greased paper, and packed it carefully into the kitbag for Julian to carry. She popped the big bar of chocolate into the bag, too. It would be nice to eat at odd moments.

At last they were all ready. Timmy wagged his tail. He knew they were going somewhere.

The five of them pushed the caravan back a few feet to expose the hole. They had all tugged the van back into place the night before, in case Lou and Dan came to go down the hole again. No one could get down it if the caravan was over it.

The boards had been laid roughly across the hole and the boys took them off, tossing them to one side. As soon as Pongo saw the hole he drew back, frightened.

'He's remembered the darkness down there,' said George. 'He doesn't like it. Come on, Pongo. You'll be all right. We've all got torches!'

But nothing would persuade Pongo to go down that hole again. He cried like a baby when Nobby tried to make him.

'It's no good,' said Julian. 'You'll have to stop up here with him.'

'What – and miss all the excitement!' cried Nobby indignantly. 'I jolly well won't. We can tie old Pongo up to a wheel of the van so that he won't wander off. Lou and Dan are away somewhere, and no one else is likely to tackle a big chimp like Pongo. We'll tie him up.'

So Pongo was tied firmly to one of the caravan wheels. 'You stay there like a good chimp till we come back,' said Nobby, putting a pail of water beside him in case he should want a drink. 'We'll be back soon!'

Pongo was sad to see them go – but nothing would have made him go down that hole again! So he sat watching the children disappear one by one. Timmy jumped down, too, and then they were all gone. Gone on another adventure. What would happen now?

Chapter Eighteen

INSIDE THE HILL

THE children had all put on extra jerseys, by Julian's orders, for he knew it would be cold inside the dark hill. Nobby had been lent an old one of Dick's. They were glad of them as soon as they were walking down the dark passage that led to the first cave, for the air was very chilly.

They came to the small cave and Julian flashed his torch to show them where the footholds went up the wall to a hole in the roof.

'It's exciting,' said George, thrilled. 'I like this sort of thing. Where does that hole in the roof lead to, I wonder? I'll go first, Ju.'

'No, you won't,' said Julian firmly. 'I go first. You don't know what might be at the top!'

Up he went, his torch held in his mouth, for he needed both hands to climb. The footholds were strong nails driven into the rock of the cave-wall, and were fairly easy to climb.

He got to the hole in the roof and popped his head through. He gave a cry of astonishment.

'I say! There's a most ENORMOUS cavern here – bigger than six dance-halls – and the walls are all glittering with something – phosphorescence, I should think.'

He scrambled out of the hole and stood on the floor of the immense cave. Its walls twinkled in their queer light, and Julian shut off his torch. There was almost enough phosphorescent light in the cavern to see by!

One by one the others came up and stared in wonder. 'It's like Aladdin's cave!' said Anne. 'Isn't that a queer light shining from the walls – and from the roof, too, Julian?'

Dick and George had rather a difficulty in getting Timmy up to the cavern, but they managed it at last. Timmy put his tail down at once when he saw the curious light gleaming everywhere. But it went up again when George patted him.

'What an enormous place!' said Dick. 'Do you suppose this is where the men hide their stuff, whatever it is?'

Julian flashed his torch on again and swung it round and about, picking out the dark, rocky corners. 'Can't see anything hidden,' he said. 'But we'd better explore the cave properly before we go on.'

So the five children explored every nook and cranny of the gleaming cave, but could find nothing at all. Julian gave a sudden exclamation and picked something up from the floor.

'A cigarette end!' he said. 'That shows that Lou and Dan have been here. Come on, let's see if there's a way out of this great cave.'

Right at the far end, half-way up the gleaming wall, was a large hole, rather like a tunnel. Julian climbed up to it and called to the others. 'This is the way they went. There's a dead match just at the entrance to the tunnel or whatever this is.'

It was a curious tunnel, no higher than their shoulders in some places, and it wound about as it went further into the hill. Julian thought that at one time water must

have run through it. But it was quite dry now. The floor
of the tunnel was worn very smooth, as if a stream had
hollowed it out through many, many years.

'I hope the stream won't take it into its head to begin
running suddenly again!' said George. 'We should get
jolly wet!'

The tunnel went on for some way, and Anne was beginning to feel it must go on for ever. Then the wall at one side widened out and made a big rocky shelf. Julian, who was first, flashed his torch into the hollow.

'I say!' he shouted. 'Here's where those fellows keep their stores! There's a whole pile of things here!'

The others crowded up as closely as they could, each of them flashing their torch brightly. On the wide, rocky shelf lay boxes and packages, sacks and cases. The children stared at them. 'What's in them?' said Nobby, full of intense curiosity. 'Let's see!'

He put down his torch and undid a sack. He slid in his hand – and brought it out holding a piece of shining gold plate!

'Coo!' said Nobby. 'So that's what the police were after last year when they came and searched the camp! And it was hidden safely here. Coo, look at all these things. Jumping Jiminy, they must have robbed the Queen herself!'

The sack was full of exquisite pieces of gold plate – cups, dishes, small trays. The childen set them all out on the ledge. How they gleamed in the light of their torches!

'They're thieves in a very big way,' said Julian. 'No doubt about that. Let's look in this box.'

The box was not locked, and the lid opened easily. Inside was a piece of china, a vase so fragile that it looked as if it might break at a breath!

'Well, I don't know anything about china,' said Julian, 'but I suppose this is a very precious piece, worth thousands of pounds. A collector of china would probably give a very large sum for it. What rogues Lou and Dan are!'

'Look here!' suddenly said George, and she pulled leather boxes out of a bag. 'Jewellery!'

She opened the boxes. The children exclaimed in awe. Diamonds flashed brilliantly, rubies glowed, emeralds shone green. Necklaces, bracelets, rings, brooches – the beautiful things gleamed in the light of the five torches.

There was a tiara in one box that seemed to be made only of big diamonds. Anne picked it out of its box gently. Then she put it on her hair.

'I'm a princess! It's my crown!' she said.

'You look lovely,' said Nobby admiringly. 'You look as grand as Delphine the Bareback Rider when she goes into the ring on her horse, with jewels shining all over her!'

Anne put on necklaces and bracelets and sat there on the ledge like a little princess, shining brightly in the magnificent jewels. Then she took them off and put them carefully back into their satin-lined boxes.

'Well – what a haul those two rogues have made!' said Julian, pulling out some gleaming silver plate from another package. 'They must be very fine burglars!'

'*I* know how they work,' said Dick. 'Lou's a wonderful acrobat, isn't he? I bet he does all the climbing about up walls and over roofs and into windows – and Tiger Dan stands below and catches everything he throws down.'

'You're about right,' said Nobby, handling a beautiful silver cup. 'Lou could climb anywhere – up ivy, up pipes – even up the bare wall of a house, I shouldn't wonder! And jump! He can jump like a cat. He and Tiger Dan have been in this business for a long time, I expect. That's where Uncle Dan went at night, of course, when we were on tour, and I woke up and found him gone out of the caravan!'

'And I expect he stores the stolen goods in that wagon of his you showed us,' said Julian, remembering. 'You told us how angry he was with you once when you went and rummaged about in it. He probably stored it there, and then he and Lou came up here each year and hid the stuff underground – waiting till the police had given up the search for the stolen things – and then they come and get it and sell it somewhere safe.'

'A jolly clever plan,' said Dick. 'What a fine chance they've got – wandering about from place to place like that hearing of famous jewels or plate – slipping out at night – and Lou climbing up to bedrooms like a cat. I wonder how they found this place – it's a most wonderful hidey-hole!'

'Yes. Nobody would ever dream of it!' said George.

'And then we go and put our caravan bang on the top of the entrance – just when they want to put something in and take something out!' said Julian. 'I *must* have annoyed them.'

'What are we going to do about it?' said Dick.

'Tell the police, of course,' said Julian, promptly. 'What do you suppose? My word, I'd like to see the face of the policeman who first sees this little haul.'

They put everything back carefully. Julian shone his torch up the tunnel. 'Shall we explore a bit further, or not?' he said. 'It still goes on. Look!'

'Better get back,' said Nobby. 'Now we've found this we'd better do something about it.'

'Oh, let's just see where the tunnel goes to,' said George. 'It won't take a minute!'

'All right,' said Julian, who wanted to go up the tunnel as much as she did. He led the way, his torch shining brightly.

The tunnel came out into another cave, not nearly as big as the one they had left behind. At one end something gleamed like silver, and seemed to move. There was a curious sound there, too.

'What is it?' said Anne, alarmed. They stood and listened.

'Water!' said Julian, suddenly. 'Of course! Can't you hear it flowing along? It's an underground stream, flowing through the hill to find an opening where it can rush out.'

'Like that stream we saw before we came to our caravan camping-place,' said George. 'It rushed out of the hill. Do you remember? This may be the very one!'

'I expect it is!' said Dick. They went over to it and watched it. It rushed along in its own hollowed out channel, close to the side of the cave-wall.

'Maybe at one time it ran across this cave and down the tunnel we came up by,' said Julian. 'Yes, look – there's a big kind of groove in the floor of the cave here – the stream must have run there once. Then for some reason it went a different way.'

'Let's get back,' said Nobby. 'I want to know if Pongo's all right. I don't somehow feel very comfortable about him. And I'm jolly cold, too. Let's go back to the sunshine and have something to eat. I don't want a picnic down here, after all.'

'All right,' said Julian, and they made their way back through the tunnel. They passed the rock shelf on which lay the treasure, and came at last to the enormous gleaming cavern. They went across it to the hole that led down into the small cave. Down they went, Julian and George trying to manage Timmy between them. But it was very awkward, for he was a big dog.

Then along the passage to the entrance-hole. They all felt quite pleased at the idea of going up into the sunshine again.

'Can't see any daylight shining down the hole,' said Julian puzzled. 'It would be near here.'

He came up against a blank wall, and was surprised. Where was the hole? Had they missed their way? Then he flashed his torch above him and saw the hole there – but there was no daylight shining in!

'I say!' said Julian, in horror. 'I say! What do you think's happened?'

'What?' asked everyone, in panic.

'The hole is closed!' said Julian. 'We can't get out! Somebody's been along and put those planks across – and I bet they've put the caravan over them, too. We can't get out!'

Everyone stared up at the closed entrance in dismay. They were prisoners.

'Whatever are we to do?' said George. 'Julian – what *are* we going to do?'

Chapter Nineteen

PRISONERS UNDERGROUND

JULIAN didn't answer. He was angry with himself for not thinking that this might happen! Although Lou and Dan had been seen getting on the bus with bags, they might easily not have been spending the night away – the bags might contain things they wanted to sell – stolen goods of some kind.

'They came back quickly – and came up the hill, I suppose, to have another try at getting Nobby and Pongo back,' said Julian, out loud. 'What an idiot I am to leave things to chance like that. Well – I'll have a try at shifting these planks. I should be able to, with luck.'

He did his best, and did shift them to a certain extent – but, as he feared, the caravan had been run back over the hole, and even if he managed to shift some of the planks it was impossible to make a way out.

'Perhaps Pongo can help,' he said suddenly. He shouted loudly: 'Pongo! Pongo! Come and help!'

Everyone stood still, hoping that they would hear Pongo chattering somewhere near, or scraping at the planks above. But there was no sign or sound of Pongo.

Everyone called, but it was no use. Pongo didn't come. What had happened to him? Poor Nobby felt very worried.

'I wish I knew what has happened,' he kept saying. 'I feel as if something horrid has happened to poor old Pongo. Where can he be?'

Pongo was not very far away. He was lying on his side,

his head bleeding. He was quite unconscious, and could not hear the frantic calls of the children at all. Poor Pongo!

What Julian had feared had actually happened. Lou and Dan had come back up the hill, bringing money with them to tempt Nobby and Pongo back. When they had got near to the hollow, they had stood still and called loudly.

'Nobby! Nobby! We've come to make friends, not to hurt you! We've got money for you. Be a sensible boy and come back to the camp. Mr Gorgio is asking for you.'

When there had been no reply at all, the men had gone nearer. Then they had seen Pongo and had stopped. The chimpanzee could not get at them because he was tied up. He sat there snarling.

'Where have those kids gone?' asked Lou. Then he saw that the caravan had been moved back a little, and he at once guessed.

'They've found the way underground! The interfering little brutes! See, they've moved one of the caravans off the hole. What do we do *now*!'

'This first,' said Tiger Dan, in a brutal voice, and he picked up an enormous stone. He threw it with all his force at poor Pongo, who tried to leap out of the way. But the rope prevented him, and the stone hit him full on the head.

He gave a loud scream and fell down at once, lying quite still.

'You've gone and killed him,' said Lou.

'So much the better!' said Tiger Dan. 'Now let's go and see if the entrance-hole is open. Those kids want their necks wringing!'

They went to the hollow and saw at once that the hole

had been discovered, opened, and that the children must have gone down it.

'They're down there now,' said Tiger Dan, almost choking with rage. 'Shall we go down and deal with them – and get our stuff and clear off? We meant to clear off tomorrow, anyway. We might as well get the stuff out now.'

'What – in the daylight – with any of the farm men about to see us!' said Lou with a sneer. 'Clever, aren't you?'

'Well, have you got a better idea?' asked Tiger Dan.

'Why not follow our plan?' said Lou. 'Go down when it's dark and collect the stuff. We can bring our wagon up as we planned to do tonight. We don't need to bother about forcing the children to go now – they're underground – and we can make them prisoners till we're ready to clear off!'

'I see,' said Dan, and he grinned suddenly, showing his ugly teeth. 'Yes – we'll close up the hole and run the caravan back over it – and come up tonight in the dark with the wagon – go down – collect everything – and shut up the hole again with the children in it. We'll send a card to Gorgio when we're safe and tell him to go up and set the kids free.'

'Why bother to do that?' said Lou, in a cruel voice. 'Let 'em starve underground, the interfering little beasts. Serve 'em right.'

'Can't do that,' said Dan. 'Have the police after us worse than ever. We'll have to chuck some food down the hole, to keep them going till they're set free. No good starving them, Lou. There'd be an awful outcry if we do anything like that.'

The two men carefully put back the boards over the top of the hole and replaced the heather tufts. Then they ran the caravan back over the place. They looked at Pongo. The chimpanzee was still lying on his side, and the men could see what a nasty wound he had on his head.

'He ain't dead,' said Lou, and gave him a kick. 'He'll come round all right. Better leave him here. He might come to himself if we carried him back to camp, and fight us. He can't do us any harm tonight, tied up like that.'

They went away down the track. Not ten minutes afterwards the children came to the hole and found it blocked up! If only they hadn't stopped to explore that tunnel a bit further, they would have been able to get out and set Timmy on the two men.

But it was too late now. The hole was well and truly closed. No one could get out. No one could find poor Pongo and bathe his head. They were real prisoners.

They didn't like it at all. Anne began to cry, though she tried not to let the others see her. Nobby saw that she was upset, and put his arm round her.

'Don't cry, little Anne,' he said. 'We'll be all right.'

'It's no good staying here,' said Julian, at last. 'We might as well go somewhere more comfortable, and sit down and talk and eat. I'm hungry.'

They all went back down the passage, up through the hole in the roof, and into the enormous cavern. They found a sandy corner and sat down. Julian handed Anne the kitbag and she undid it to get the food inside.

'Better only have one torch going,' said Julian. 'We don't know how long we'll be here. We don't want to be left in the dark!'

Everybody immediately switched off their torches.

The idea of being lost in the dark inside the hill wasn't at all nice! Anne handed out slices of bread and butter, and the children put thin slices of Mrs Mackie's delicious ham on them.

They felt distinctly better when they had all eaten a good meal. 'That was jolly good,' said Dick. 'No, we won't eat that chocolate, Anne. We may want it later on. Golly, I'm thirsty!'

'So am I,' said Nobby. 'My tongue's hanging out like old Timmy's. Let's go and get a drink.'

'Well, there was a stream in that other cave beyond the tunnel, wasn't there?' said Nobby. 'We can drink from that. It'll be all right.'

'Well, I hope it will,' said Julian. 'We were told not to drink water that wasn't boiled while we were caravanning – but we didn't know this sort of thing was going to happen! We'll go through the tunnel and get some water to drink from the stream.'

They made their way through the long, winding tunnel, and passed the shelf of stolen goods. Then on they went and came out into the cave through which the stream rushed so quickly. They dipped in their hands and drank thirstily. The water tasted lovely – so clear and cold.

Timmy drank too. He was puzzled at this adventure, but so long as he was with George he was happy. If his mistress suddenly took it into her head to live underground like a worm, that was all right – so long as Timmy was with her!

'I wonder if this stream *does* go to that hole in the hillside, and pours out there,' said Julian, suddenly. 'If it does, and we could follow it, we might be able to squeeze out.'

'We'd get terribly wet,' said George, 'but that wouldn't matter. Let's see if we can follow the water.'

They went to where the stream disappeared into a tunnel rather like the dry one they had come along. Julian shone his torch into it.

'We could wade along, I think,' he said. 'It is very fast but not very deep. I know – I'll go along it myself and see where it goes, and come back and tell you.'

'No,' said George, at once. 'If you go, we all go. You might get separated from us. That would be awful.'

'All right,' said Julian. 'I thought there was no sense in us all getting wet, that's all. Come on, we'll try now.'

One by one they waded into the stream. The current tugged at their legs, for the water ran very fast. But it was only just above their knees there. They waded along by the light of their torches, wondering where the tunnel would lead to.

Timmy half-waded, half-swam. He didn't like this water-business very much. It seemed silly to him. He pushed ahead of Julian and then a little further down, jumped up to a ledge that ran beside the water.

'Good idea, Tim,' said Julian, and he got up on to it too. He had to crouch down rather as he walked because his head touched the roof of the tunnel if he didn't – but at least his legs were out of the icy-cold water! All the others did the same, and as long as the ledge ran along beside the stream they all walked along it.

But at times it disappeared and then they had to wade in the water again, which now suddenly got deeper. 'Gracious! It's almost to my waist,' said Anne. 'I hope it doesn't get any deeper. I'm holding my clothes up as high as I can, but they'll get soaked soon.'

Fortunately the water got no deeper, but it seemed to go faster. 'We're going down hill a bit,' said Julian at last. 'Perhaps we are getting near to where it pours out of the hill.'

They were! Some distance ahead of him Julian suddenly saw a dim light, and wondered whatever it could be. He soon knew! It was daylight creeping in through the water that poured out of the hole in the hillside – poured out in a torrent into the sunshine.

'We're almost there!' cried Julian. 'Come on.'

With light hearts the children waded along in the water. Now they would soon be out in the warm sunshine. They would find Pongo, and race down the hill in the warmth, catch the first bus, and go to the police station.

But nothing like that happened at all. To their enormous disappointment the water got far too deep to wade through, and Nobby stopped in fright. 'I dursent go no further,' he said. 'I'm almost off my feet now with the water rushing by.'

'I am, too,' said Anne, frightened.

'Perhaps I can swim out,' said Julian, and he struck out. But he gave it up in dismay, for the torrent of water was too much for him, and he was afraid of being hurled against the rocky sides and having his head cracked.

'It's no good,' he said, gloomily. 'No good at all. All that wading for nothing. It's far too dangerous to go any further – and yet daylight is only a few yards ahead. It's too sickening for words.'

'We must go back,' said George. 'I'm afraid Timmy will be drowned if we don't. Oh, dear – we must go all that way back!'

Chapter Twenty

MORE EXCITEMENT

IT was a very sad and disappointed little company that made their way back to the cave. Along the tunnel they went, painfully and slowly, for it was not so easy against the current. Julian shivered; he was wet through with trying to swim.

At last they were back in the cave through which the stream flowed so swiftly. 'Let's run round and round it to get warm,' said Julian. 'I'm frozen. Dick, let me have one of your dry jerseys. I must take off these wet ones.'

The children ran round and round the cave, pretending to race one another, trying to get warm. They did get warm in the end, and sank down in a heap on some soft sand in a corner, panting. They sat there for a little while to get their breath.

Then they heard something. Timmy heard it first and growled. 'Jumping Jiminy, what's up with Timmy?' said Nobby, in fright. He was the most easily scared of the children, probably because of the frights he had had the last few days.

They all listened, George with her hand on Timmy's collar. He growled again, softly. The noise they all heard was a loud panting coming from the stream over at the other side of the cave!

'Someone is wading up the stream,' whispered Dick, in astonishment. 'Did they get in at the place where we couldn't get out? They must have!'

'But who is it?' asked Julian. 'Can't be Lou or Dan. They wouldn't come that way when they could come the right way. Sh! Whoever it is, is arriving in the cave. I'll shut off my torch.'

Darkness fell in the cave as the light from Julian's torch was clicked off. They all sat and listened, and poor Nobby shook and shivered. Timmy didn't growl any more, which was surprising. In fact, he even wagged his tail!

There was a sneeze from the other end of the cave — and then soft footsteps padded towards them. Anne felt as if she must scream. WHO was it?

Julian switched on his torch suddenly, and its light fell on a squat, hairy figure, halting in the bright glare. It was Pongo!

'It's *Pongo*!' everyone yelled, and leapt up at once. Timmy ran over to the surprised chimpanzee and sniffed round him in delight. Pongo put his arms round Nobby and Anne.

'Pongo! You've escaped! You must have bitten through your rope!' said Julian. 'How clever you are to find your way through that hole where the stream pours out. How did you know you would find us here! Clever Pongo.'

Then he saw the big wound on poor Pongo's head. 'Oh look!' said Julian. 'He's been hurt! I expect those brutes threw a stone at him. Poor old Pongo.'

'Let's bathe his head,' said Anne. 'I'll use my hanky.'

But Pongo wouldn't let anyone touch his wound, not even Nobby. He didn't snap or snarl at them, but simply held their hands away from him, and refused to leave go. So nobody could bathe his head or bind it up.

'Never mind,' said Nobby at last, 'Animals' wounds often heal up very quickly without any attention at all. He won't let us touch it, that's certain. I expect Lou and Dan hit him with a stone, and knocked him unconscious when they came. They then shut up the hole and made us prisoners. Beasts!'

'I say,' suddenly said Dick. 'I say! I've got an idea. I don't know if it will work – but it really *is* an idea.'

'What?' asked everyone, thrilled.

'Well – what about tying a letter round Pongo's neck and sending him out of the hole again, to take the letter to the camp?' said Dick. 'He won't go to Lou or Dan because he's scared of them – but he'd go to any of the others all right, wouldn't he? Larry would be the best one. He seems to be a good fellow.'

'Would Pongo understand enough to do all that, though?' asked Julian, doubtfully.

'We could try him,' said Nobby. 'I do send him here and there sometimes, just for fun – to take the elephant's bat to Larry, for instance – or to put my coat away in my caravan.'

'Well, we could certainly try,' said Dick. 'I've got a notebook and a pencil. I'll write a note and wrap it up in another sheet, pin it together and tie it round Pongo's neck with a bit of string.'

So he wrote a note. It said:

'*To whoever gets this note – please come up the hill to the hollow where there are two caravans. Under the red one is the entrance to an underground passage. We are prisoners inside the hill. Please rescue us soon.*

Julian, Dick, George, Anne and Nobby.'

He read it out to the others. Then he tied the note round Pongo's neck. Pongo was surprised, but fortunately did not try to pull it off.

'Now, you give him his orders,' said Dick to Nobby. So Nobby spoke slowly and importantly to the listening chimpanzee.

'Where's Larry? Go to Larry, Pongo. Fetch Larry. Go. GO!'

Pongo blinked at him and made a funny little noise as if he was saying: 'Please, Nobby, I don't want to go.'

Nobby repeated everything again. 'Understand Pongo? I think you do. GO, then, GO. GO!'

And Pongo turned and went! He disappeared into the stream, splashing along by himself. The children watched him as far as they could by the light of their torches.

'He really is clever,' said Anne. 'He didn't want to go a bit, did he? Oh, I do hope he finds Larry, and that Larry sees the note and reads it and sends someone to rescue us.'

'I hope the note doesn't get all soaked and pulpy in the water,' said Julian, rather gloomily. 'Gosh, I wish I wasn't so cold. Let's run round a bit again, then have a piece of chocolate.'

They ran about and played 'he' for a time till they all felt warm again. Then they decided to sit down and have some chocolate, and play some sort of guessing game to while away the time. Timmy sat close to Julian, and the boy was very glad.

'He's like a big hot-water bottle,' he said. 'Sit closer, Tim. That's right. You'll soon warm me up!'

It was dull after a time, sitting in the light of one torch, for they dared not use them all. Already it seemed

as if Julian's torch was getting a little dim. They played
all the games they could think of and then yawned.

'What's the time? I suppose it must be getting dark
outside now. I feel quite sleepy.'

'It's nine o'clock almost,' said Julian. 'I hope Pongo
has got down to the camp all right and found someone.
We could expect help quite soon, if so.'

'Well, then, we'd better get along to the passage that
leads to the hole,' said Dick, getting up. 'It's quite likely
that if Larry or anyone else comes they'll not see the
foot-holds leading up the wall out of that first little cave.
They might not know where we were!'

This seemed very likely. They all made their way down
the tunnel that led past the hidden store of valuables,
and came out into the enormous cave. There was a nice
sandy corner just by the hole that led down into the first
small cave, and the children decided to sit there, rather
than in the passage or in the first rocky and uncomfortable little cave. They cuddled up together for warmth,
and felt hungry.

Anne and Nobby dozed off to sleep. George almost
fell asleep, too. But the boys and Timmy kept awake, and
talked in low voices. At least, Timmy didn't talk, but
wagged his tail whenever either Dick or Julian said anything. That was his way of joining in their conversation.

After what seemed a long while Timmy growled, and
the two boys sat up straight. Whatever it was that
Timmy's sharp ears had heard, they had heard nothing
at all. And they continued to hear nothing. But Timmy
went on growling.

Julian shook the others awake. 'I believe help has
come,' he said. 'But we'd better not go and see in case it's

Dan and Lou come back. So wake up and look lively!'

They were all wide awake at once. Was it Larry come in answer to their note – or was it those horrid men, Tiger Dan and Lou the acrobat?

They soon knew! A head suddenly poked out of the hole nearby, and a torch shone on them. Timmy growled ferociously and struggled to fly at the head, but George held on firmly to his collar, thinking it might be Larry.

But it wasn't! It was Lou the acrobat, as the children knew only too well when they heard his voice. Julian shone his torch on to him.

'I hope you've enjoyed your little selves,' came Lou's harsh voice. 'And you keep that dog under control, boy, or I'll shoot him. See? I'm not standing no nonsense from that dog this time. Have a look at this here gun!'

To George's horror she saw that Lou was pointing a gun at poor Timmy. She gave a scream and flung herself in front of him. 'Don't you dare to shoot my dog! I'll – I'll – I'll . . .'

She couldn't think of anything bad enough to do to the man who could shoot Timmy, and she stopped, choked by tears of rage and fear. Timmy, not knowing what the gun was, couldn't for the life of him understand why George wouldn't let him get at his enemy – such a nice position, too, with his head poking through a hole like that. Timmy felt he could deal with that head very quickly.

'Now, you kids, get up and go into that tunnel,' said Lou. 'Go on – go right ahead of me, and don't dare to stop. We've got work to do here tonight, and we're not going to have any more interference from kids like you. See?'

The children saw quite well. They began to walk towards the entrance of the tunnel. One by one they
climbed into it. George first with Timmy. She dared not
let his collar go for an instant. A few paces behind them
came Lou with his revolver, and Dan with a couple of
big sacks.

The children were made to walk right past the shelf on
which were the hidden goods.

Then Lou sat down in the tunnel, his torch switched
on fully so that he could pick out each child. He still
pointed his revolver at Timmy.

'Now we'll get on,' he said to Tiger Dan. 'You know
what to do. Get on with it.'

Tiger Dan began to stuff the things into one of the big
sacks he had brought. He staggered off with it. He came
back in about ten minutes and filled the other sack. It was

plain that the men meant to take everything away this time.

'Thought you'd made a very fine discovery, didn't you?' said Lou, mockingly, to the children. 'Ho, yes – very smart you were! See what happens to little smarties like you – you're prisoners – and here you'll stay for two or three days!'

'What do you mean?' said Julian, in alarm. 'Surely you wouldn't leave us here to starve?'

'Not to starve. We're too fond of you,' grinned Lou. 'We'll chuck you down some food into the tunnel. And in two or three days maybe someone will come and rescue you.'

Julian wished desperately that Pongo would bring help before Lou and Dan finished their business in the tunnel and went, leaving them prisoners. He watched

Tiger Dan, working quickly, packing everything, carrying it off, coming back again, and packing feverishly once more. Lou sat still with his torch and revolver, enjoying the scared faces of the girls and Nobby. Julian and Dick put on a brave show which they were far from feeling.

Tiger Dan staggered away with another sackful. But he hadn't been gone for more than half a minute before a wail echoed through the tunnel.

'Lou! Help! Help! Something's attacking me! HELP.'

Lou rose up and went swiftly down the tunnel. 'It's Pongo, I bet it's old Pongo,' said Julian thrilled.

Chapter Twenty-one

DICK HAS A GREAT IDEA!

'Listen,' said Dick, in an urgent voice. 'It may be Pongo by himself – he may not have gone back to the camp at all – he may have wandered about and at last gone down the entrance-hole by the caravans, and come up behind Tiger Dan. If so he won't have much chance because Lou's got a gun and will shoot him. And we shan't be rescued. So I'm going to slip down the tunnel while there's a chance and hide in the big cave.'

'What good will that do?' said Julian.

'Well, idiot, I may be able to slip down into the passage that leads to the entrance hole and hop out without the others seeing me,' said Dick, getting up. 'Then I can fetch help, see? You'd better all clear off somewhere and hide – find a good place, Julian, in case the men come after you when they find one of us is gone. Go on.'

Without another word the boy began to walk down the tunnel, past the rocky shelf on which now very few goods were left, and then came to the enormous cave.

Here there was a great noise going on, for Pongo appeared to have got hold of both men at once! Their torches were out, and Lou did not dare to shoot for fear of hurting Dan. Dick could see very little of this; he could only hear snarlings and shouting. He took a wide course round the heaving heap on the floor and made his way as quickly as he could in the dark to where he thought the hole was that led down into the first passage. He had to go carefully for fear of falling down it. He found it at last and let himself down into the cave below, and then, thinking it safe to switch on his torch in the passage he flashed it in front of him to show him the way.

It wasn't long before he was out of the hole and was speeding round the caravans. Then he stopped. A thought struck him. He could fetch help all right – but the men would be gone by then! They had laid their plans for a getaway with all the goods; there was no doubt about that.

Suppose he put the boards over the hole, ramming them in with all his strength, and then rolled some heavy stones on top? He couldn't move the caravan over the boards, for it was far too heavy for a boy to push. But heavy stones would probably do the trick. The men would imagine that it was the caravan overhead again!

In great excitement Dick put back the boards, lugging them into place, panting and puffing. Then he flashed his torch round for stones. There were several small rocks nearby. He could not lift them, but he managed to roll them to the boards. Plonk! They went on to them one by one. Now nobody could move the boards at all.

'I know I've shut the others in with the men,' thought Dick. 'But I hope Julian will find a very safe hiding-place just for a time. Gosh, I'm hot! Now, down the hill I go – and I hope I don't lose my way in the darkness!'

Down below, the two men had at last freed themselves from the angry chimpanzee. They were badly bitten and mauled, but Pongo was not as strong and savage as usual because of his bad head-wound. The men were able to drive him off at last, and he went limping in the direction of the tunnel, sniffing out the children.

He would certainly have been shot if Lou could have found his revolver quickly enough. But he could not find it in the dark. He felt about for his torch, and found that although it was damaged, he could still put on the light by knocking it once or twice on the ground. He shone it on to Dan.

'We ought to have looked out for that ape when we saw he was gone,' growled Dan. 'He had bitten his rope through. We might have known he was somewhere about. He nearly did for me, leaping on me like that out of the darkness. It was lucky he flung himself on to my sack and not me.'

'Let's get the last of the things and clear out,' said Lou, who was badly shaken up. 'There's only one more load. We'll get back to the tunnel, scare the life out of those kids once more, shoot Pongo if we can, and then clear out. We'll chuck a few tins of food down the hole and then close it up.'

'I'm not going to risk meeting that chimp again,' said Dan. 'We'll leave the rest of the things. Come on. Let's go.'

Lou was not particularly anxious to see Pongo again either. Keeping his torch carefully switched on and his revolver ready, he followed Dan to the hole that led down to the first cave. Down they went, and then along the passage, eager to get out into the night and go with their wagon down the track.

They got a terrible shock when they found that the hole was closed. Lou shone his torch upwards, and gazed in amazement at the underside of the boards. Someone had put them back into place again. *They* were prisoners now!

Tiger Dan went mad. One of his furious rages overtook him, and he hammered against those boards like a
mad-man. But the heavy stones held them down, and the
raging man dropped down beside Lou.

'Can't budge the boards! Someone must have put the
caravan overhead again. We're prisoners!'

'But who's made us prisoners? Who's put back those
boards?' shouted Lou, almost beside himself with fury.
'Could those kids have slipped by us when we were
having that fight with the chimp?'

'We'll go and see if the kids are still there,' said Tiger
Dan, grimly. 'We'll find out. We'll make them very,
very sorry for themselves. Come on.'

The two men went back again to the tunnel. The
children were not there. Julian had taken Dick's advice
and had gone off to try and find a good hiding-place.
He had suddenly thought that perhaps Dick might get
the idea of shutting up the entrance-hole – in which case
the two men would certainly be furious!

So up the tunnel the children went, and into the cave
with the stream. It seemed impossible to find any hiding-
place there at all.

'I don't see where we can hide,' said Julian, feeling
rather desperate. 'It's no good wading down that stream
again – we shall only get wet and cold – and we have no
escape from there at all if the men should come after us!'

'I can hear something,' said George, suddenly. 'Put
your light out, Julian – quick!'

The torch was snapped off, and the children waited in
the darkness. Timmy didn't growl. Instead George felt
that he was wagging his tail.

'It's someone friendly,' she whispered. 'Over there.

Perhaps it's Pongo. Put the torch on again.'

The light flashed out, and picked out the chimpanzee, who was coming towards them across the cave. Nobby gave a cry of joy.

'Here's old Pongo again!' he said. 'Pongo, did you go to the camp? Did you bring help?'

'No – he hasn't been down to the camp,' said Julian, his eyes catching sight of the note still tied round the chimpanzee's neck. 'There's our letter still on him. Blow!'

'He's clever – but not clever enough to understand a difficult errand like that,' said George.

'Oh, Pongo – and we were depending on you! Never mind – perhaps Dick will escape and bring help. Julian, where *shall* we hide?'

'*Up* the stream?' suddenly said Anne. 'We've tried going *down* it. But we haven't tried going up it. Do you think it would be any good?'

'We could see,' said Julian, doubtfully. He didn't like this business of wading through water that might suddenly get deep. 'I'll shine my torch up the stream and see what it looks like.'

He went to the stream and shone his light up the tunnel from which it came. 'It seems as if we might walk along the ledge beside it,' he said. 'But we'd have to bend almost double – and the water runs so fast just here we must be careful not to slip and fall in.'

'I'll go first,' said Nobby. 'You go last, Julian. The girls can go in the middle with Pongo and Timmy.'

He stepped on to the narrow ledge inside the rocky tunnel, just above the rushing water. Then came Pongo. Then Anne, then George and Timmy – and last of all Julian.

But just as Julian was disappearing, the two men came into the cave, and by chance Lou's torch shone right on to the vanishing Julian. He gave a yell.

'There's one of them – look, over there! Come on!'

The men ran to where the stream came out of the tunnel, and Lou shone his torch up it. He saw the line of children, with Julian last of all. He grabbed hold of the boy and pulled him back.

Anne yelled when she saw Julian being pulled back. Nobby had a dreadful shock. Timmy growled ferociously, and Pongo made a most peculiar noise.

'Now look here,' came Lou's voice, 'I've got a gun, and I'm going to shoot that dog and that chimp if they so much as put their noses out of here. So hang on to them if you want to save their lives!'

He passed Julian to Tiger Dan, who gripped the boy firmly by the collar. Lou shone his torch up the tunnel again to count the children. 'Ho, there's Nobby,' he said. 'You come on out here, Nobby.'

'If I do, the chimp will come out too,' said Nobby. 'You know that. And he may get *you* before you get him!'

Lou thought about that. He was afraid of the big chimpanzee. 'You stay up there with him, then,' he said. 'And the girl can stay with you, holding the dog. But the other boy can come out here.'

He thought that George was a boy. George didn't mind. She liked people to think she was a boy. She answered at once.

'I can't come. If I do the dog will follow me, and I'm not going to have him shot.'

'You come on out,' said Lou, threateningly. 'I'm going to show you two boys what happens to kids who keep spying and interfering. Nobby knows what happens, don't you, Nobby? He's had his lesson. And you two boys are going to have yours, too.'

Dan called to him. 'There ought to be another girl there, Lou. I thought Nobby said there were two boys and two girls. Where's the other girl?'

'Gone further up the tunnel, I suppose,' said Lou, trying to see. 'Now, you boy – come on out!'

Anne began to cry. 'Don't go, George; don't go. They'll hurt you. Tell them you're a . . .'

'Shut up,' said George, fiercely. She added, in a whisper: 'If I say I'm a girl they'll know Dick is missing, and will be all the angrier. Hang on to Timmy.'

Anne clutched Timmy's collar in her trembling hand. George began to walk back to the cave. But Julian was not going to let George be hurt. She might like to think of herself as a boy, but he wasn't going to let her be treated like one. He began to struggle.

Lou caught hold of George as she came out of the tunnel – and at the same moment Julian managed to kick high in the air, and knocked Lou's torch right out of his hand. It flew up into the roof of the cave and fell somewhere with a crash. It went out. Now the cave was in darkness.

'Get back into the tunnel, George, with Anne,' yelled Julian. 'Timmy, Timmy, come on! Pongo, come here!'

'I don't want Timmy to be shot!' cried out George, in terror, as the dog shot past her into the cave.

Even as she spoke a shot rang out. It was Lou, shooting blindly at where he thought Timmy was. George screamed.

'Oh, Timmy, Timmy! You're not hurt, are you?'

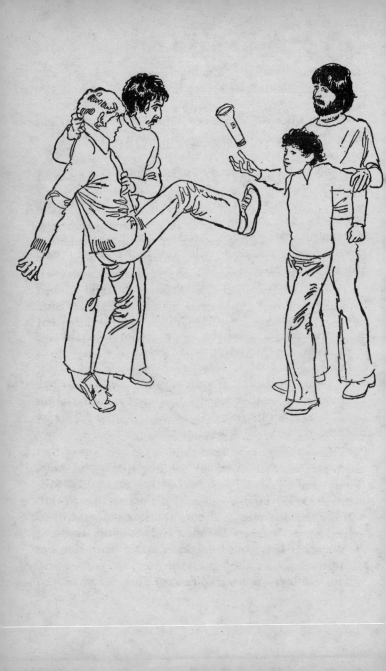

Chapter Twenty-two

THE END OF THE ADVENTURE

No, Timmy wasn't hurt. The bullet zipped past his head and struck the wall of the cave. Timmy went for Lou's legs. Down went the man with a crash and a yell, and the revolver flew out of his hand. Julian heard it slithering across the floor of the cave, and he was very thankful.

'Put on your torch, George, quickly!' he yelled. 'We must see what we're doing. Goodness, here's Pongo now!'

Tiger Dan gave a yell of fright when the torch flashed on and he saw the chimpanzee making straight for him. He dealt the ape a smashing blow on the face that knocked him down, and then turned to run. Lou was trying to keep Timmy off his throat, kicking frantically at the excited dog.

Dan ran to the tunnel – and then stopped in astonishment. Four burly policemen were pushing their way out of the tunnel, led by Dick! One of them carried a revolver in his hand. Dan put his hands up at once.

'Timmy! Come off!' commanded George, seeing that there was now no need for the dog's delighted help. Timmy gave her a reproachful glance that said: 'Mistress! I'm really enjoying myself! Let me eat him all up!'

Then the dog caught sight of the four policemen and yelped furiously. More enemies! He would eat the lot.

'What's all this going on?' said the first man, who was an Inspector. 'Get up, you on the floor. Go on, get up!'

Lou got up with great difficulty. Timmy had nipped

him in various places. His hair was over his eyes, his clothes were torn. He stared at the policemen, his mouth open in the utmost surprise. How had they come here? Then he saw Dick.

'So one of you kids slipped out – and shut the boards on us!' he said, savagely. 'I might have guessed. You . . .'

'Hold your tongue, Lewis Allburg,' rapped out the Inspector. 'You can talk when we tell you. You'll have quite a lot of talking to do, to explain some of the things we've heard about you.'

'Dick! How did you get here so soon?' cried Julian, going over to his brother. 'I didn't expect you for hours! Surely you didn't go all the way to the town and back?'

'No. I shot off to the farm, woke up the Mackies, used their telephone and got the police up here double-quick in their car,' said Dick, grinning. 'Everyone all right? Where's Anne? And Nobby?'

'There they are – just coming out of the tunnel, up-stream,' said Julian, and swung his torch round. Dick saw Anne's white, scared face, and went over to her.

'It's all right,' he said. 'The adventure is over, Anne! You can smile again!'

Anne gave a watery sort of smile. Pongo took her hand and made little affectionate noises, and that made her smile a little more. George called Timmy to her, afraid that he might take a last nip at Lou.

Lou swung round and stared at her. Then he looked at Dick and Julian. Then at Anne.

'So there *was* only one girl!' he said. 'What did you want to tell me there were two boys and two girls for?' he said to Nobby.

'Because there were,' answered Nobby. He pointed to

George. 'She's a girl, though she looks like a boy. And she's as good as a boy any day.'

George felt proud. She stared defiantly at Lou. He was now in the grip of a stout policeman, and Tiger Dan was being hustled off by two more.

'I think we'll leave this rather gloomy place,' said the Inspector, putting away the notebook he had been hastily scribbling in. 'Quick march!'

Julian led the way down the tunnel. He pointed out the shelf where the men had stored their things, and the Inspector collected the few things that were still left. Then on they went, Tiger Dan muttering and growling to himself.

'Will they go to prison?' whispered Anne to Dick.

'You bet,' said Dick. 'That's where they ought to have gone long ago. Their burglaries have been worrying the police for four years!'

Out of the tunnel and into the cave with gleaming walls. Then down the hole and into the small cave and along the narrow passage to the entrance-hole. Stars glittered over the black hole, and the children were very thankful to see them. They were tired of being underground!

Lou and Dan did not have a very comfortable journey along the tunnels and passages, for their guards had a very firm hold of them indeed. Once out in the open they were handcuffed and put into the large police car that stood a little way down the track.

'What are you children going to do?' asked the big Inspector, who was now at the wheel of the car. 'Hadn't you better come down into the town with us after this disturbing adventure?'

'Oh, no thanks,' said Julian politely. 'We're quite used to adventures. We've had plenty, you know. We shall be all right here with Timmy and Pongo.'

'Well, I can't say I'd like a chimpanzee for company myself,' said the Inspector. 'We'll be up here in the morning, looking round and asking a few questions, which I'm sure you'll be pleased to answer. And many thanks for your help in capturing two dangerous thieves!'

'What about the wagon of goods?' asked Dick. 'Are you going to leave it up here? It's got lots of valuables in it.'

'Oh, one of the men is driving down,' said the Inspector, nodding towards a policeman, who stood near by. 'He'll follow us. He can drive a horse all right. Well, look after yourselves. See you tomorrow!'

The car started up suddenly. The Inspector put her into gear, took off the brake and the car slid quietly down the hill, following the winding track. The policeman with the wagon followed slowly, clicking to the horse, which didn't seem at all surprised to have a new driver.

'Well, that's that!' said Julian thankfully. 'I must say we were well out of that. Gosh, Dick, I was glad to see you back with those bobbies so quickly. That was a brain wave of yours to telephone from the farm.'

Dick suddenly yawned. 'It must be frightfully late!' he said. 'Long past the middle of the night. But I'm so fearfully hungry that I simply must have something to eat before I fall into my bunk!'

'Got anything, Anne?' asked Julian.

Anne brightened up at once. 'I'll see,' she said. 'I can find something, I'm sure!'

And she did, of course. She opened two tins of sardines and made sandwiches, and she opened two tins of peaches, so they had a very nice meal in the middle of the night! They ate it sitting on the floor of George's caravan. Pongo had as good a meal as anyone, and Timmy crunched at one of his bones.

It didn't take them long to go to sleep that night. In fact they were all so sleepy when they had finished their meal that nobody undressed! They clambered into the bunks just as they were and fell asleep at once. Nobby curled up with Pongo, and Timmy, as usual, was on George's feet. Peace reigned in the caravans – and tonight no one came to disturb them!

All the children slept very late the next morning. They were awakened by a loud knocking on Julian's caravan. He woke up with a jump and yelled out:

'Yes! Who is it?'

'It's us,' said a familiar voice, and the door opened. Farmer Mackie and his wife peeped in, looking rather anxious.

'We wondered what had happened,' said the farmer. 'You rushed out of the farmhouse when you had used the 'phone last night and didn't come back.'

'I ought to have slipped back and told you,' said Dick, sitting up with his hair over his eyes. He pushed it back. 'But I forgot. The police went down into the hills with us and got the two men. They're well-known burglars. The police got all the goods, too. It was a very thrilling night. Thanks most awfully for letting me use the 'phone.'

'You're very welcome,' said Mrs Mackie. 'And look – I've brought you some food.'

She had two baskets stacked with good things. Dick felt wide awake and very hungry when he saw them. 'Oh, thanks,' he said gratefully. 'You *are* a good sort!'

Nobby and Pongo suddenly uncurled themselves from their pile of rugs, and Mrs Mackie gave a squeal.

'Land-snakes, what's that? A monkey?'

'No, an ape, Mam,' said Nobby politely. 'He won't hurt you. Hi, take your hand out of that basket!'

Pongo, who had been hoping to find a little titbit unnoticed, covered his face with his hairy paw and looked through his fingers at Mrs Mackie.

'Look at that now – he's like a naughty child!' said Mrs Mackie. 'Isn't he, Ted?'

'He is that,' said the farmer. 'Queer sort of bedfellow, I must say!'

'Well, I must be getting along,' said Mrs Mackie, nodding and smiling at George and Anne, who had now come out of their caravan with Timmy to see who the visitors were. 'You come along to the farm if you want anything. We'll be right pleased to see you.'

'Aren't they nice?' said Anne as the two farm-folk went down the cart-track. 'And oh, my goodness – what a breakfast we're going to have! Cold bacon – tomatoes – fresh radishes – curly lettuces – and who wants new honey?'

'Marvellous!' said Julian. 'Come on – let us have it now, before we clean up.'

But Anne made them wash and tidy themselves first! 'You'll enjoy it much more if you're clean,' she said. 'We all look as black as sweeps! I'll give you five minutes – then you can come to a perfectly wonderful breakfast!'

'All right, Ma!' grinned Nobby, and he went off with the others to wash at the spring. Then back they all went to the sunny ledge to feast on the good things kind Mrs Mackie had provided.

Chapter Twenty-three

GOOD-BYE, NOBBY – GOOD-BYE, CARAVANNERS!

BEFORE they had finished their breakfast the Inspector came roaring up the track in his powerful police car. There was one sharp-eyed policeman with him to take down notes.

'Hallo, hallo!' said the Inspector, eyeing the good things set out on the ledge. 'You seem to do yourselves well, I must say!'

'Have some new bread and honey?' said Anne in her best manner. 'Do! There's plenty!'

'Thanks,' said the Inspector, and sat down with the children. The other policeman wandered round the caravans, examining everything. The Inspector munched away at honey and bread, and the children talked to him, telling him all about their extraordinary adventure.

'It must have been a most unpleasant shock for those two fellows when they found that your caravan was immediately over the entrance to the place where they hid their stolen goods.' said the Inspector. 'Most unpleasant.'

'Have you examined the goods?' asked Dick eagerly. 'Are they very valuable?'

'Priceless,' answered the Inspector, taking another bit of bread and dabbing it thickly with honey. 'Quite priceless. Those rogues apparently stole goods they knew to be of great value, hid them here for a year or two till the hue and cry had died down, then got them out and quietly disposed of them to friends in Holland and Belgium.'

'Tiger Dan used to act in circuses in Holland,' said Nobby. 'He often told me about them. He had friends all over Europe – people in the circus line, you know.'

'Yes. It was easy for him to dispose of his goods abroad,' said the Inspector. 'He planned to go across to Holland today, you know – got everything ready with Lou – or, to give him the right name, Lewis Allburg – and was going to sell most of those things. You just saved them in time!'

'What a bit of luck!' said George. 'They almost got away with it. If Dick hadn't managed to slip out when Pongo was attacking them, we'd still have been prisoners down in the hill, and Lou and Dan would have been half-way to Holland!'

'Smart bit of work you children did,' said the Inspector approvingly, and looked longingly at the honey-pot. 'That's fine honey, I must buy some from Mrs Mackie.'

'Have some more,' said Anne, remembering her manners. 'Do. We've got another loaf.'

'Well, I will,' said the Inspector, and took another slice of bread, spreading it with the yellow honey. It looked as if there wouldn't even be enough left for Pongo to lick out! Anne thought it was nice to see a grown-up enjoying bread and honey as much as children did.

'You know, that fellow Lou did some very remarkable burglaries,' said the Inspector. 'Once he got across from the third floor of one house to the third floor of another *across the street* – and nobody knows how!'

'That would be easy for Lou,' said Nobby, suddenly losing his fear of the big Inspector. 'He'd just throw a wire rope across, lasso something with the end of it, top of a gutter-pipe, perhaps, draw tight, and walk across!

He's wonderful on the tight-rope. There ain't nothing he can't do on the tight-rope.'

'Yes – that's probably what he did,' said the Inspector. 'Never thought of that! No, thanks, I really won't have any more honey. That chimpanzee will eat me if I don't leave some for him to lick out!'

Pongo took away the jar, sat himself down behind one of the caravans, and put a large pink tongue into the remains of the honey. When Timmy came running up to see what he had got, Pongo held the jar high above his head and chattered at him.

'Yarra-yarra-yarra-yarra!' he said. Timmy looked rather surprised and went back to George. She was listening with great interest to what the Inspector had to tell them about the underground caves.

'They're very old,' he said. 'The entrance to them used to be some way down the hill, but there was a landslide and it was blocked up. Nobody bothered to unblock it because the caves were not particularly interesting.'

'Oh, but they *are*,' said Anne, 'especially the one with the gleaming walls.'

'Well, I imagine that quite by accident one day Dan and Lou found another way in,' said the Inspector. 'The way you know – a hole going down into the hill. They must have thought what a fine hiding-place it would make for any stolen goods – perfectly safe, perfectly dry, and quite near the camping-place here each year. What could be better?'

'And I suppose they would have gone on burgling for years and hiding the stuff if we hadn't just happened to put our caravan over the very spot!' said Julian. 'What a bit of bad luck for them!'

'And what a bit of good luck for us!' said the Inspector. 'We did suspect those two, you know, and once or twice we raided the circus to try and find the goods – but they must always have got warning of our coming and got them away in time – up here!'

'Have you been down to the camp, mister?' asked Nobby suddenly.

The Inspector nodded. 'Oh, yes. We've been down already this morning – seen everyone and questioned them. We created quite a stir!'

Nobby looked gloomy.

'What's the matter, Nobby?' said Anne.

'I shan't half cop it when I get back to the camp,' said Nobby. 'They'll say it's all my fault the coppers going there. We don't like the bobbies round the camp. I shall get into a whole lot of trouble when I go back. I don't want to go back.'

Nobody said anything. They all wondered what would happen to poor Nobby now his Uncle Dan was in prison.

Then Anne asked him: 'Who will you live with now in the camp, Nobby?'

'Oh, somebody will take me in and work me hard,' said Nobby. 'I wouldn't mind if I could be with the horses – but Rossy won't let me. I know that. If I could be with horses I'd be happy. I love them and they understand me all right.'

'How old are you, Nobby?' asked the Inspector, joining in the talk. 'Oughtn't you to be going to school?'

'Never been in my life, mister,' said Nobby. 'I'm just over fourteen, so I reckon I never will go now!'

He grinned. He didn't look fourteen. He seemed more like twelve by his size. Then he looked solemn again.

'Reckon I won't go down to the camp today,' he said. 'I'll be proper set on by them all – about you going there and snooping round like. And Mr Gorgio, he won't like losing his best clown and best acrobat!'

'You can stay with us as long as you like,' said Julian. 'We'll be here a bit longer, anyway.'

But he was wrong. Just after the Inspector had left, taking his policeman with him, Mrs Mackie came hurrying up to them with a little orange envelope in her hand.

'The telegraph boy's just been up,' she said. 'He was looking for you. He left this telegram for you. I hope it's not bad news.'

Julian tore the envelope open and read the telegram out loud.

'AMAZED TO GET YOUR LETTER ABOUT THE EXTRA-ORDINARY HAPPENINGS YOU DESCRIBE. THEY SOUND DANGEROUS. COME HOME AT ONCE.   DADDY.'

'Oh dear,' said Anne. 'Now we shall have to leave. What a pity!'

'I'd better go down to the town and telephone Daddy and tell him we're all right,' said Julian.

'You can 'phone from my house,' said Mrs Mackie, so Julian thought he would. They talked as they went along and suddenly a bright idea struck Julian.

'I say – I suppose Farmer Mackie doesn't want anyone to help him with his horses, does he?' he asked. 'He wouldn't want a boy who really loves and understands them and would work hard and well?'

'Well, now, I dare say he would,' said Mrs Mackie. 'He's a bit short-handed now. He was saying the other day he could do with a good lad, just leaving school.'

'Oh, *do* you think he'd try our friend Nobby from the

circus camp?' said Julian. 'He's mad on horses. He can do anything with them. And he's been used to working very hard. I'm sure he'd do well.'

Before Julian had left the farmhouse after telephoning to his amazed parents, he had had a long talk with Farmer Mackie – and now he was running back with the good news to the caravans.

'Nobby!' he shouted as he got near. 'Nobby! How would you like to go and work for Farmer Mackie and help with the horses? He says you can start tomorrow if you like – and live at the farm!'

'Jumping Jiminy!' said Nobby, looking startled and disbelieving. 'At the farm? Work with the horses? Coo – I wouldn't half like that. But Farmer Mackie wouldn't have the likes of me.'

'He will. He says he'll try you,' said Julian. 'We've got to start back home tomorrow, and you can be with us till then. You don't need to go back to the camp at all.'

'Well – but what about Growler?' said Nobby. 'I'd have to have him with me. He's my dog. I expect poor old Barker's dead. Would the farmer mind me having a dog?'

'I shouldn't think so,' said Julian. 'Well, you'll have to go down to the camp, I suppose, to collect your few things – and to get Growler. Better go now, Nobby, and then you'll have the rest of the day with us.'

Nobby went off, his face shining with delight. 'Well, I never!' he kept saying to himself. 'Well, I never did! Dan and Lou gone, so they'll never hurt me again – and me not going to live in the camp any more – and going to have charge of them fine farm horses. Well, I never!'

The children had said good-bye to Pongo because he

had to go back with Nobby to the camp. He belonged to Mr Gorgio, and Nobby could not possibly keep him. Anyway, it was certain that even if he could have kept him, Mrs Mackie wouldn't have let him live at the farm.

Pongo shook hands gravely with each one of them, even with Timmy. He seemed to know it was good-bye. The children were really sorry to see the comical chimpanzee go. He had shared in their adventure with them and seemed much more like a human being than an animal.

When he had gone down the hill a little way he ran back to Anne. He put his arms round her and gave her a gentle squeeze, as if to say: 'You're all nice, the lot of you, but little Anne's the nicest!'

'Oh, Pongo, you're really a dear!' said Anne, and gave him a tomato. He ran off with it, leaping high for joy.

The children cleared up everything, put the breakfast things away, and cleaned the caravans, ready for starting off the next day. At dinner-time they looked out for Nobby. Surely he should be back soon?

They heard him whistling as he came up the track. He carried a bundle on his back. Round his feet ran two dogs. Two!

'Why – one of them is Barker!' shouted George in delight. 'He must have got better! How simply marvellous!'

Nobby came up, grinning. They all crowded round him, asking about Barker.

'Yes, it's fine, isn't it?' said Nobby, putting down his bundle of belongings. 'Lucilla dosed him all right. He almost died – then he started to wriggle a bit, she said, and the next she knew he was as lively as could be – bit weak on his legs at first – but he's fine this morning.'

Certainly there didn't seem anything wrong with

Barker. He and Growler sniffed round Timmy, their tails wagging fast. Timmy stood towering above them, but his tail wagged, too, so Barker and Growler knew he was friendly.

'I was lucky,' said Nobby. 'I only spoke to Lucilla and Larry. Mr Gorgio has gone off to answer some questions at the police station, and so have some of the others. So I just told Larry to tell Mr Gorgio I was leaving, and I got my things and hopped it.'

'Well, now we can really enjoy our last day,' said Julian. 'Everybody's happy!'

And they did enjoy that last day. They went down to the lake and bathed. They had a fine farmhouse tea at Mrs Mackie's, by special invitation. They had a picnic supper on the rocky ledge, with the three dogs rolling over and over in play. Nobby felt sad to think he would so soon say good-bye to his 'posh' friends – but he couldn't help feeling proud and pleased to have a fine job of his own on the farm – with the horses he loved so much.

Nobby, Barker, Growler, Farmer Mackie and his wife all stood on the cart-track to wave good-bye to the two caravans the next morning.

'Good-bye!' yelled Nobby. 'Good luck! See you again some time!'

'Good-bye!' shouted the others. 'Give our love to Pongo when you see him.'

'Woof! woof!' barked Timmy, but only Barker and Growler knew what *that* meant. It meant, 'Shake paws with Pongo for me!'

Good-bye, five caravanners . . . till your next exciting adventure!

ENID BLYTON

FIVE ON KIRRIN ISLAND AGAIN

Illustrated by Betty Maxey

KNIGHT BOOKS
Hodder and Stoughton

Printed and bound in Great Britain
for Hodder and Stoughton
Paperbacks, a division of Hodder and
Stoughton Ltd., Mill Road,
Dunton Green, Sevenoaks, Kent
TN13 2YA.
(Editorial Office: 47 Bedford Square,
London WC1B 3DP) by
Cox & Wyman Ltd., Reading

FIVE ON KIRRIN ISLAND
AGAIN

CONTENTS

Chapter One

A LETTER FOR GEORGE

ANNE was trying to do some of her prep. in a corner of the common-room when her cousin George came bursting in.

George was not a boy; she was a girl called Georgina, but because she had always wanted to be a boy she insisted on being called George. So George she was. She wore her curly hair cut short, and her bright blue eyes gleamed angrily now as she came towards Anne.

'Anne! I've just had a letter from home – and what do you think? Father wants to go and live on my island to do some special work – and he wants to build a sort of tower or something in the castle yard!'

The other girls looked up in amusement, and Anne held out her hand for the letter that George was waving at her. Everyone knew about the little island off Kirrin Bay that belonged to George. Kirrin Island was a tiny place with an old ruined castle in the middle of it: the home of rabbits and gulls and jackdaws.

It had underground dungeons in which George and her cousins had had one or two amazing adventures. It had once belonged to George's mother, and she had given it to George – and George was very fierce where her precious Kirrin Island was concerned! It was *hers*.

Nobody else must live there, or even land there without her permission.

And now, dear me, here was her father proposing to go to her island, and even build some sort of workshop there! George was red with exasperation.

'It's just like grown-ups; they go and give you things and then act as though the things were theirs all the time. I don't *want* Father living on my island, and building nasty messy sheds and things there.'

'Oh George – you know your father is a very famous scientist, who needs to work in peace,' said Anne, taking the letter. 'Surely you can lend him your island for a bit?'

'There are plenty of other places where he can work in peace,' said George. 'Oh dear – I was so hoping we could go and stay there in the Easter hols – take our boat there, and food and everything, just like we've done before. Now we shan't be able to if Father really does go there.'

Anne read the letter. It was from George's mother.
'*My darling George,*

'*I think I must tell you at once that your father proposes to live on Kirrin Island for some little time in order to finish some very important experiments he is making. He will have to have some kind of building erected there – a sort of tower, I believe. Apparently he needs a place where he can have absolute peace and isolation, and also, for some reason, where there is water all around him. The fact of being surrounded by water is necessary to his experiment.*

'*Now, dear, don't be upset about this. I know that you consider Kirrin Island is your very own, but you must allow your family to share it, especially when it is for something as important as your father's scientific work. Father thinks you will be very pleased indeed to lend him Kirrin Island, but I know your funny feelings about it, so I thought I had better write and tell you, before you arrive home and see him installed there, complete with his tower.'*

The letter then went on about other things, but Anne did not bother to read these. She looked at George.

'Oh, George! I don't see why you mind your father borrowing Kirrin Island for a bit! I wouldn't mind *my* father borrowing an island from me – if I was lucky enough to have one!'

'*Your* father would talk to you about it first, and ask your permission, and see if you minded,' said George, sulkily. 'My father never does anything like that. He just does exactly as he likes without asking anybody anything. I really do think he might have written to me himself. He just puts my back up.'

'You've got a back that is very easily put up, George,' said Anne, laughing. 'Don't scowl at me like that. *I'm* not borrowing your island without your gracious permission.'

But George wouldn't smile back. She took her letter and read it again gloomily. 'To think that all my lovely holiday plans are spoilt!' she said. 'You know how super Kirrin Island is at Eastertime – all primroses and gorse and baby rabbits. And you and Julian and Dick were coming to stay, and we haven't stayed together since last summer when we went caravanning.'

'I know. It *is* hard luck!' said Anne. 'It would have

been wizard to go and stay on the island these hols. But perhaps your father wouldn't mind if we did? We needn't disturb him.'

'As if living on Kirrin Island with Father there would be the same as living there all by ourselves,' said George, scornfully. 'You know it would be horrid.'

Well yes – Anne didn't think on the whole that Kirrin Island would be much fun with Uncle Quentin there. George's father was such a hot-tempered, impatient man, and when he was in the middle of one of his experiments he was quite unbearable. The least noise upset him.

'Oh dear – how he will yell at the jackdaws to keep quiet, and shout at the noisy gulls!' said Anne, beginning to giggle. 'He won't find Kirrin quite so peaceful as he imagines!'

George gave a watery sort of smile. She folded up the letter and turned away. 'Well, I think it's just the limit,' she said. 'I wouldn't have felt so bad if only Father had asked my permission.'

'He'd never do that!' said Anne. 'It just wouldn't occur to him. Now George, don't spend the rest of the day brooding over your wrongs, for goodness' sake. Go down to the kennels and fetch Timmy. He'll soon cheer you up.'

Timothy was George's dog, whom she loved with all her heart. He was a big brown mongrel dog, with a ridiculously long tail, and a wide mouth that really seemed to smile. All the four cousins loved him. He was so friendly and loving, so lively and amusing, and he had shared so very many adventures with them all.

The five of them had had many happy times together.

George went to get Timmy. Her school allowed the children to keep their own pets. If it hadn't allowed this, it is quite certain that George would not have gone to boarding-school! She could not bear to be parted from Timmy for even a day.

Timmy began to bark excitedly as soon as she came near. George lost her sulky look and smiled. Dear Timmy, dear trustable Timmy – he was better than any person! He was always on her side, always her friend whatever she did, and to Timmy there was no one in the world so wonderful as George.

They were soon going through the fields together, and George talked to Timmy as she always did. She told him about her father borrowing Kirrin Island. Timmy agreed with every word she said. He listened as if he understood everything, and not even when a rabbit shot across his path did he leave his mistress's side. Timmy always knew when George was upset.

He gave her hand a few little licks every now and again. By the time that George was back at school again she felt much better. She took Timmy into school with her smuggling him in at a side door. Dogs were not allowed in the school building, but George, like her father, often did exactly as she liked.

She hurried Timmy up to her dormitory. He scuttled under her bed quickly and lay down. His tail thumped the floor gently. He knew what this meant. George wanted the comfort of his nearness that night! He would be able to jump on her bed, when lights were out, and snuggle into the crook of

her knees. His brown eyes gleamed with delight.

'Now, lie quiet,' said George, and went out of the room to join the other girls. She found Anne, who was busy writing a letter to her brothers, Julian and Dick, at their boarding-school.

'I've told them about Kirrin Island, and your father wanting to borrow it,' she said. 'Would you like to come and stay with *us*, George, these hols, instead of us coming to Kirrin? Then you won't feel cross all the time because your father is on your island.'

'No thanks,' said George, at once. 'I'm going home. I want to keep an eye on Father! I don't want him blowing up Kirrin Island with one of his experiments. You know he's messing about with explosives now, don't you?'

'Ooooh – atom bombs, or things like that?' said Anne.

'I don't know,' said George. 'Anyway, quite apart from keeping an eye on Father and my island, we ought to go and stay at Kirrin to keep Mother company. She'll be all alone if Father's on the island. I suppose he'll take food and everything there.'

'Well, there's one thing, we shan't have to creep about on tiptoe and whisper, if your father isn't at Kirrin Cottage!' said Anne. 'We can be as noisy as we like. Do cheer up, George!'

But it took George quite a long time to get over the fit of gloom caused by her mother's letter. Even having Timmy on her bed each night, till he was discovered by an angry teacher, did not quite make up for her disappointment.

The term ran swiftly on to its end. April came in, with sunshine and showers. Holidays came nearer and nearer! Anne thought joyfully of Kirrin, with its lovely sandy beach, its blue sea, its fishing-boats and its lovely cliffside walks.

Julian and Dick thought longingly of them too. This term both they and the girls broke up on the same day. They could meet in London and travel down to Kirrin together. Hurrah!

The day came at last. Trunks were piled in the hall. Cars arrived to fetch some of the children who lived fairly near. The school coaches drew up to take the others down to the station. There was a terrific noise of yelling and shouting everywhere. The teachers could not make themselves heard in the din.

'Anyone would think that every single child had gone completely mad,' said one of them to another. 'Oh, thank goodness, they're getting into the coaches. George! *Must* you rush along the corridor at sixty miles an hour, with Timmy barking his head off all the time!'

'Yes, I must, I must!' cried George. 'Anne, where are you? Do come and get into the coach. I've got Timmy. He knows it's holidays now. Come on, Tim!'

Down to the station went the singing crowd of children. They piled into the train. 'Bags I this seat! Who's taken my bag? Get out, Hetty, you know you can't bring your dog in here with mine. They fight like anything. Hurrah, the guard's blowing his whistle! We're off!'

The engine pulled slowly out of the station, its long

train of carriages behind it, filled to bursting with girls off for their holidays. Through the quiet country-side it went, through small towns and villages, and at last ran through the smoky outskirts of London.

'The boys' train is due in two minutes before ours,' said Anne, leaning out of the window, as the train drew slowly into the London station. 'If it was punctual, they might be on our platform to meet us. Oh look, George, look – there they are!'

George hung out of the window too. 'Hi, Julian!' she yelled. 'Here we are! Hi, Dick, Julian!'

Chapter Two

BACK AT KIRRIN COTTAGE

JULIAN, Dick, Anne, George and Timmy went straight-away to have buns and ginger-beer at the station tea-room. It was good to be all together again. Timmy went nearly mad with joy at seeing the two boys. He kept trying to get on to their knees.

'Look here, Timmy, old thing, I love you very much and I'm jolly glad to see you,' said Dick, 'but that's twice you've upset my ginger-beer all over me. Has he behaved himself this term, George?'

'Fairly well,' said George, considering. 'Hasn't he, Anne? I mean – he only got the joint out of the larder once – and he didn't do so *much* harm to that cushion he chewed – and if people *will* leave their goloshes all over the place nobody can blame Timmy for having a good old game with them.'

'And that was the end of the goloshes, I suppose,' said Julian, with a grin. 'On the whole, Timmy, you have a rather poor report. I'm afraid our Uncle Quentin will not award you the usual twenty-five pence we get for good reports.'

At the mention of her father, George scowled. 'I see George has not lost her pretty scowl,' said Dick, in a teasing voice. 'Dear old George! We shouldn't know her unless she put on that fearsome scowl half a dozen times a day!'

'Oh, she's better than she was,' said Anne hurrying to George's defence at once. George was not so touchy as she had once been, when she was being teased. All the same, Anne knew that there might be sparks flying over her father taking Kirrin Island these holidays, and she didn't want George to fly into a temper too soon!

Julian looked at his cousin. 'I say, old thing, you're not going to take this business of Kirrin Island too much to heart, are you?' he said. 'You've just got to realise that your father's a remarkably clever man, one of the finest scientists we've got – and *I* think that those kind of fellows ought to be allowed as much freedom as they like, for their work. I mean – if Uncle Quentin wants to work on Kirrin Island for some peculiar reason of his own, then you ought to be pleased to say "Go ahead, Father!"'

George looked a little mutinous after this rather long speech; but she thought a great deal of Julian, and usually went by what he said. He was older than any of them, a tall, good-looking boy, with determined eyes and a strong chin. George scratched Timmy's head, and spoke in a low voice.

'All right. I won't go up in smoke about it, Julian. But I'm frightfully disappointed. I'd planned to go to Kirrin Island ourselves these hols.'

'Well, we're all disappointed,' said Julian. 'Buck up with your bun, old thing. We've got to get across

London and catch the train for Kirrin. We shall miss it if we don't look out.'

Soon they were in the train for Kirrin. Julian was very good at getting porters and taxis. Anne gazed admiringly at her big brother as he found them all corner-seats in a carriage. Julian did know how to tackle things!

'Do you think I've grown, Julian?' she asked him. 'I did hope I'd be as tall as George by the end of this term, but she grew too!'

'Well, I should think you might be a quarter of an inch taller than last term,' said Julian. 'You can't catch us up, Anne – you'll always be the smallest! But I like you small.'

'Look at Timmy, putting his head out of the window as usual!' said Dick. 'Timmy you'll get a grit in your eye. Then George will go quite mad with grief and think you're going blind!'

'Woof,' said Timmy, and wagged his tail. That was the nice part about Timmy. He always knew when he was being spoken to, even if his name was not mentioned, and he answered at once.

Aunt Fanny was at the station to meet them in the pony-trap. The children flung themselves on her, for they were very fond of her. She was kind and gentle, and did her best to keep her clever, impatient husband from finding too much fault with the children.

'How's Uncle Quentin?' asked Julian, politely, when they were setting off in the trap.

'He's very well,' said his aunt. 'And terribly excited. Really, I've never known him to be so thrilled as he has been lately. His work has been coming along very successfully.'

'I suppose you don't know what his latest experiment is?' said Dick.

'Oh no. He never tells me a word,' said Aunt Fanny. 'He never tells anyone anything while he is at work, except his colleagues, of course. But I do know it's very important – and I know, of course, that the last part of the experiment has to be made in a place where there is deep water all around. Don't ask me why! I don't know.'

'Look! There's Kirrin Island!' said Anne, suddenly. They had rounded a corner, and had come in sight of the bay. Guarding the entrance to it was the curious little island topped by the old ruined castle. The sun shone down on the blue sea, and the island looked most enchanting.

George looked earnestly at it. She was looking for the building, whatever it was, that her father said he needed for his work. Everyone looked at the island, seeking the same thing.

They saw it easily enough! Rising from the centre of the castle, probably from the castle yard, was a tall thin tower, rather like a lighthouse. At the top was a glass-enclosed room, which glittered in the sun.

'Oh Mother! I don't like it! It spoils Kirrin Island,' said George, in dismay.

'Darling, it can come down when your father has finished his work,' said her mother. 'It's a very flimsy, temporary thing. It can easily be pulled down. Father promised me he would scrap it as soon as his work was done. He says you can go across and see it, if you like. It's really rather interesting.'

'Ooooh – I'd *love* to go and see it,' said Anne, at once. 'It looks so queer. Is Uncle Quentin all alone on Kirrin Island, Aunt Fanny?'

'Yes, I don't like him to be alone,' said her aunt. 'For one thing I am sure he doesn't get his meals properly, and for another, I'm always afraid some harm might come to him when he's experimenting – and if he's alone, how would I know if anything happened to him?'

'Well, Aunt Fanny, you could always arrange for him to signal to you each morning and night, couldn't you?' said Julian, sensibly. 'He could use that tower easily. He could flash a signal to you in the morning, using a mirror, you know – heliographing that he was all right – and at night he could signal with a lamp. Easy!'

'Yes. I did suggest that sort of thing,' said his aunt. 'I said I'd go over with you all tomorrow, to see him and perhaps, Julian dear, you could arrange something of the sort with your uncle? He seems to listen to you now.'

'Gracious! Do you mean to say Father wants us to invade his secret lair, and actually to see his strange tower?' asked George, surprised. 'Well – I don't think I want to go. After all, it's *my* island – and it's horrid to see someone else taking possession of it.'

'Oh, George, don't begin all that again,' said Anne, with a sigh. 'You and your island! Can't you even *lend* it to your own father! Aunt Fanny, you should have seen George when your letter came. She looked so fierce that I was quite scared!'

Everyone laughed except George and Aunt Fanny. She looked distressed. George was always so difficult! She found fault with her father, and got up against him time after time – but dear me, how very, very like him she was, with her scowls, her sudden temper, and her fierceness! If only George was as sweet-tempered and as easy-going as these three cousins of hers!

George looked at her mother's troubled face, and felt ashamed of herself. She put her hand on her knee. 'It's all right Mother! I won't make a fuss. I'll try and keep my feelings to myself, really I will. I know Father's work is important. I'll go with you to the island tomorrow.'

Julian gave George a gentle clap on the back. 'Good old George! She's actually learned, not only to give in, but to give in gracefully! George, you're more like a boy than ever when you act like that.'

George glowed. She liked Julian to say she was like a boy. She didn't want to be petty and catty and bear malice as so many girls did. But Anne looked a little indignant.

'It isn't *only* boys that can learn to give in decently, and things like that,' she said. 'Heaps of girls do. Well, I jolly well hope I do myself!'

'My goodness, here's another fire-brand!' said Aunt Fanny, smiling. 'Stop arguing now, all of you – here's Kirrin Cottage. Doesn't it look sweet with all the primroses in the garden, and the wallflowers coming out, and the daffodils peeping everywhere?'

It certainly did. The four children and Timmy tore
in at the front gate, delighted to be back. They clat-
tered into the house, and, to their great delight, found
Joanna, the old cook there. She had come back to help
for the holidays. She beamed at the children, and
fondled Timmy when he leapt round her barking.

'Well, there now! Haven't you all grown again?
How big you are, Master Julian – taller than I am, I
declare. And little Miss Anne, why, she's getting quite
big.'

That pleased Anne, of course. Julian went back to
the front door to help his aunt with the small bags in
the trap. The trunks were coming later. Julian and
Dick took everything upstairs.

Anne joined them, eager to see her old bedroom
again. Oh, how good it was to be in Kirrin Cottage
once more! She looked out of the windows. One looked
on to the moor at the back. The other looked sideways on to the sea. Lovely! Lovely! She began to sing
a little song as she undid her bag.

'You know,' she said to Dick, when he brought
George's bag in, 'you know, Dick, I'm really quite
pleased that Uncle Quentin has gone to Kirrin Island,
even if it means we won't be able to go there much! I
feel much freer in the house when he's away. He's a
very clever man and he can be awfully nice – but I
always feel a bit afraid of him.'

Dick laughed. 'I'm not afraid of him – but he's a bit
of a wet blanket in a house, I must say, when we're
here for the holidays. Funny to think of him on Kirrin
Island all alone.'

A voice came up the stairs. 'Come down to tea, children, because there are hot scones for you, just out of the oven.'

'Coming, Aunt Fanny!' called Dick. 'Hurry, Anne. I'm awfully hungry. Julian, did you hear Aunt Fanny calling?'

George came up the stairs to fetch Anne. She was pleased to be home, and as for Timmy, he was engaged in going round every single corner of the house, sniffing vigorously.

'He always does that!' said George. 'As if he thought that there *might* be a chair or a table that didn't smell quite the same as it always did. Come on, Tim. Tea-time! Mother, as Father isn't here, can Timmy sit beside me on the floor? He's awfully well-behaved now.'

'Very well,' said her mother, and tea began. What a tea! It looked as if it was a spread for a party of twenty. Good old Joanna! She must have baked all day. Well, there wouldn't be much left when the Five had finished!

Chapter Three

OFF TO KIRRIN ISLAND

NEXT day was fine and warm. 'We can go across to the island this morning,' said Aunt Fanny. 'We'll take our own food, because I'm sure Uncle Quentin will have forgotten we're coming.'

'Has he a boat there?' asked George. 'Mother – he hasn't taken *my* boat, has he?'

'No, dear,' said her mother. 'He's got another boat. I was afraid he would never be able to get it in and out of all those dangerous rocks round the island, but he got one of the fishermen to take him, and had his own boat towed behind, with all its stuff in.'

'Who built the tower?' asked Julian.

'Oh, he made out the plans himself and some men were sent down from the Ministry of Research to put the tower up for him,' said Aunt Fanny. 'It was all rather hush-hush really. The people here were most curious about it, but they don't know any more than I do! No local man helped in the building, but one or two fishermen were hired to take the material to the island, and to land the men and so on.'

'It's all very mysterious,' said Julian. 'Uncle Quentin leads rather an exciting life, really, doesn't he? I wouldn't mind being a scientist myself. I want to be something really worthwhile when I grow up – I'm not just going into somebody's office. I'm going to be on my own.'

'I think I shall be a doctor,' said Dick.

'I'm off to get my boat,' said George, rather bored with this talk. She knew what *she* was going to do when she was grown-up – live on Kirrin Island with Timmy!

Aunt Fanny had got ready plenty of food to take across to the island. She was quite looking forward to the trip. She had not seen her husband for some days, and was anxious to know that he was all right.

They all went down to the beach, Julian carrying the bag of food. George was already there with her boat. James, a fisher-boy friend of George's, was there too, ready to push the boat out for them.

He grinned at the children. He knew them all well. In the old days he had looked after Timmy for George when her father had said the dog must be given away. George had never forgotten James's kindness to Timmy, and always went to see him every holiday.

'Going off to the island?' said James. 'That's a queer thing in the middle of it, isn't it? Kind of lighthouse, it looks. Take my hand, Miss, and let me help you in.'

Anne took his hand and jumped into the boat. George was already there with Timmy. Soon they were all in. Julian and George took the oars. James gave them a shove and off they went on the calm, clear water. Anne could see every stone on the bottom!

Julian and George rowed strongly. They sent the boat along swiftly. George began to sing a rowing song and they all took it up. It was lovely to be on the sea in a boat again. Oh holidays, go slowly, don't rush away too fast!

'George,' said her mother nervously, as they came near to Kirrin Island, 'you *will* be careful of these awful rocks, won't you? The water's so clear today that I can see them all – and some of them are only just below the water.'

'Oh Mother! You know I've rowed hundreds of times to Kirrin Island!' laughed George. 'I simply *couldn't* go on a rock! I know them all, really I do. I could almost row blindfold to the island now.'

There was only one place to land on the island in safety. This was a little cove, a natural little harbour running up to a stretch of sand. It was sheltered by high rocks all round. George and Julian worked their way to the east side of the island, rounded a low wall of very sharp rocks, and there lay the cove, a smooth inlet of water running into the shore!

Anne had been looking at the island as the others rowed. There was the old ruined Kirrin Castle in the centre, just the same as ever. Its tumbledown towers were full of jackdaws as usual. Its old walls were gripped by ivy.

'It's a lovely place!' said Anne, with a sigh. Then she gazed at the curious tower that now rose from the centre of the castle yard. It was not built of brick but some smooth, shiny material, that was fitted together in sections. Evidently the tower had been made in that way so that it might be brought to the island easily, and set up there quickly.

'Isn't it queer?' said Dick. 'Look at that little glass

room at the top – like a look-out room! I wonder what it's for?'

'Can anyone climb up inside the tower?' asked Dick, turning to Aunt Fanny.

'Oh yes. There is a narrow spiral staircase inside,' said his aunt. 'That's about all there is inside the tower itself. It's the little room at the top that is important. It has got some extraordinary wiring there, essential to your uncle's experiments. I don't think he *does* anything with the tower – it just has to be there, doing something on its own, which has a certain effect on the experiments he is making.'

Anne couldn't follow this. It sounded too complicated. 'I should like to go up the tower,' she said.

'Well, perhaps your uncle will let you,' said her aunt.

'If he's in a good temper,' said George.

'Now George – you're not to say things like that,' said her mother.

The boat ran into the little harbour, and grounded softly. There was another boat there already – Uncle Quentin's.

George leapt out with Julian and they pulled it up a little further, so that the others could get out without wetting their feet. Out they all got, and Timmy ran up the beach in delight.

'Now, Timmy!' said George, warningly, and Timmy turned a despairing eye on his mistress. Surely she wasn't going to stop him looking to see if there were any rabbits? Only just *looking*! What harm was there in that?

Ah – there was a rabbit! And another and another!
They sat all about, looking at the little company coming up from the shore. They flicked their ears and
twitched their noses, keeping quite still.

'Oh, they're as tame as ever!' said Anne in delight.
'Aunty Fanny, aren't they lovely? Do look at the baby
one over there. He's washing his face!'

They stopped to look at the rabbits. They really
were astonishingly tame. But then very few people
came to Kirrin Island, and the rabbits multiplied in
peace, running about where they liked, quite unafraid.

'Oh, that one is . . .' began Dick, but then the picture was spoilt. Timmy, quite unable to do nothing
but look, had suddenly lost his self-control and was
bounding on the surprised rabbits. In a trice nothing
could be seen but white bobtails flashing up and down
as rabbit after rabbit rushed to its burrow.

'*Timmy!*' called George, crossly, and poor Timmy
put his tail down, looking round at George miserably.
'What!' he seemed to say. 'Not even a scamper after
the rabbits? What a hard-hearted mistress!'

'Where's Uncle Quentin?' asked Anne, as they
walked to the great broken archway that was the entrance to the old castle. Behind it were the stone steps
that led towards the centre. They were broken and
irregular now. Aunt Fanny went across them carefully,
afraid of stumbling, but the children, who were wearing rubber shoes, ran over them quickly.

They passed through an old ruined doorway
into what looked like a great yard. Once there had
been a stone-paved floor, but now most of it was

covered by sand, and by close-growing weeds or grass.

The castle had had two towers. One was almost a complete ruin. The other was in better shape. Jackdaws circled round it, and flew above the children's heads, crying 'chack, chack, chack'.

'I suppose your father lives in the little old room with the two slit-like windows,' said Dick to George. 'That's the only place in the castle that would give him any shelter. Everywhere else is in ruins except that one room. Do you remember we once spent a night there?'

'Yes,' said George. 'It was fun. I suppose that's where Father lives. There's nowhere else – unless he's down in the dungeons!'

'Oh, no one would live in the dungeons surely, unless they simply *had* to!' said Julian. 'They're so dark and cold. Where *is* your father, George? I can't see him anywhere.'

'Mother, where would Father be?' asked George. 'Where's his workshop – in that old room there?' She pointed to the dark, stone-walled, stone-roofed room, which was really all that was left of the part in which people had long ago lived. It jutted out from what had once been the wall of the castle.

'Well, really, I don't exactly know,' said her mother. 'I suppose he works over there. He's always met me down at the cove, and we've just sat on the sand and had a picnic and talked. He didn't seem to want me to poke round much.'

'Let's call him,' said Dick. So they shouted loudly.

'Uncle QUEN-tin! Uncle QUEN-tin! Where are you?'

The jackdaws flew up in fright, and a few gulls, who had been sitting on part of the ruined wall, joined in the noise, crying 'ee-oo, ee-oo, ee-oo' over and over again. Every rabbit disappeared in a trice.

No Uncle Quentin appeared. They shouted again. 'UNCLE QUENTIN! WHERE ARE YOU?'

'What a noise!' said Aunt Fanny, covering her ears. 'I should think that Joanna must have heard that at home. Oh dear – where is your uncle? This is most annoying of him. I *told* him I'd bring you across today.'

'Oh well – he must be somewhere about,' said Julian, cheerfully. 'If Mahomet won't come to the mountain, then the mountain must go to Mahomet. I expect he's deep in some book or other. We'll hunt for him.'

'We'll look in that little dark room,' said Anne. So they all went through the stone doorway, and found themselves in a little dark room, lit only by two slits of windows. At one end was a space, or recess, where a fireplace had once been, going back into the thick stone wall.

'He's not here' said Julian in surprise. 'And what's more – there's nothing here at all! No food, no clothes, no books, no stores of any sort. This is not his work-room, nor even his store!'

'Then he must be down in the dungeons,' said Dick. 'Perhaps it's necessary to his work to be underground – and with water all round! Let's go and find the entrance. We know where it is – not far from the old well in the middle of the yard.'

'Yes. He must be down in the dungeons. Mustn't he,

Aunt Fanny?' said Anne. 'Are you coming down?'

'Oh no,' said her aunt. 'I can't bear those dungeons. I'll sit out here in the sun, in this sheltered corner, and unpack the sandwiches. It's almost lunch-time.'

'Oh good,' said everyone. They went towards the dungeon entrance. They expected to see the big flat stone that covered the entrance, standing upright, so that they might go down the steps underground.

But the stone was lying flat. Julian was just about to pull on the iron ring to lift it up when he noticed something peculiar.

'Look,' he said. 'There are weeds growing round the edges of the stone. Nobody has lifted it for a long time. Uncle Quentin isn't down in the dungeons!'

'Then where *is* he?' said Dick. 'Wherever *can* he be?'

Chapter Four

WHERE IS UNCLE QUENTIN?

THE four of them, with Timmy nosing round their legs, stood staring down at the big stone that hid the entrance to the dungeons. Julian was perfectly right. The stone could not have been lifted for months, because weeds had grown closely round the edges, sending their small roots into every crack.

'No one is down there,' said Julian. 'We need not even bother to pull up the stone and go down to see. If it had been lifted lately, those weeds would have been torn up as it was raised.'

'And anyway, we know that no one can get *out* of the dungeon once the entrance stone is closing it,' said Dick. 'It's too heavy. Uncle Quentin wouldn't be silly enough to shut himself in! He'd leave it open.'

'Of course he would,' said Anne. 'Well – he's not there, then. He must be somewhere else.'

'But *where*?' said George. 'This is only a small island, and we know every corner of it. Oh – would he be in that cave we hid in once? The only cave on the island.'

'Oh yes – he might be,' said Julian. 'But I doubt it. I can't see Uncle Quentin dropping down through the hole in the cave's roof – and that's the only way of getting into it unless you're going to clamber and slide

215

about the rocks on the shore for ages. I can't see him doing that, either.'

They made their way beyond the castle to the other side of the island. Here there was a cave they had once lived in. It could be entered with difficulty on the seaward side, as Julian had said, by clambering over slippery rocks, or it could be entered by dropping down a rope through a hole in the roof to the floor some way below.

They found the hole, half hidden in old heather. Julian felt about. The rope was still there. 'I'll slide down and have a look,' he said.

He went down the rope. It was knotted at intervals so that his feet found holding-places and he did not slide down too quickly and scorch his hands.

He was soon in the cave. A dim light came in from the seaward side. Julian took a quick look round. There was absolutely nothing there at all, except for an old box that they must have left behind when they were last here themselves.

He climbed up the rope again, his head appearing suddenly out of the hole. Dick gave him a hand.

'Well?' he said. 'Any sign of Uncle Quentin?'

'No,' said Julian. 'He's not there, and hasn't been there either, I should think. It's a mystery! Where is he, and if he's really doing important work where is all his stuff? I mean, we know that plenty of stuff was brought here, because Aunt Fanny told us so.'

'Do you think he's in the tower?' said Anne, suddenly. 'He might be in that glass room at the top.'

'Well, he'd see us at once, if he were!' said Julian,

scornfully. '*And* hear our yells too! Still, we might as well have a look.'

So back to the castle they went and walked to the queer tower. Their aunt saw them and called to them. 'Your lunch is ready. Come and have it. Your uncle will turn up, I expect.'

'But Aunt Fanny where is he?' said Anne, with a puzzled face. 'We've looked simply *every*where!'

Her aunt did not know the island as well as the children did. She imagined that there were plenty of places to shelter in, or to work in. 'Never mind,' she said, looking quite undisturbed. 'He'll turn up later. You come along and have your meal.'

'We think we'll go up the tower,' said Julian. 'Just in case he's up there working.'

The four children and Timmy went to where the tower rose up from the castle yard. They ran their hands over the smooth, shining sections, which were fitted together in curving rows. 'What's this stuff it's built of?' said Dick.

'Some kind of new plastic material, I should think,' said Julian. 'Very light and strong, and easily put together.'

'I should be afraid it would blow down in a gale,' said George.

'Yes, so should I,' said Dick. 'Look – here is the door.'

The door was small, and rounded at the top. A key was in the keyhole. Julian turned it and unlocked the door. It opened outwards not inwards. Julian put his head inside and looked round.

There was not much room in the tower. A spiral staircase, made of the same shiny stuff as the tower itself, wound up and up and up. There was a space at one side of it, into which projected curious hook-like objects made of what looked like steel. Wire ran from one to the other.

'Better not touch them,' said Julian, looking curiously at them. 'Goodness, this is like a tower out of a fairy-tale. Come on – I'm going up the stairs to the top.'

He began to climb the steep, spiral stairway. It made him quite giddy to go up and round, up and round so many, many times.

The others followed him. Tiny, slit-like windows, set sideways not downwards, were let into the side of the tower here and there, and gave a little light to the stairway. Julian looked through one, and had a wonderful view of the sea and the mainland.

He went on up to the top. When he got there he found himself in a small round room, whose sides were of thick, gleaming glass. Wires ran right into the glass itself, and then pierced through it, the free ends waving and glittering in the strong wind that blew round the tower.

There was nothing in the little room at all! Certainly Uncle Quentin was not there. It was clearly only a tower meant to take the wires up on the hook-like things, and to run them through the strange, thick glass at the top, and set them free in the air. What for? Were they catching some kind of wireless waves? Was it to do with Radar? Julian wondered, frowning, what was the meaning of the tower and the thin, shining wires?

The others crowded into the little room. Timmy came too, having managed the spiral stairs with difficulty.

'Gracious! What a queer place!' said George. 'My goodness, what a view we've got from here. We can see miles and miles out to sea – and on this other side we can see miles and miles across the bay, over the mainland to the hills beyond.'

'Yes. It's lovely,' said Anne. 'But – *where* is Uncle Quentin? We still haven't found him. I suppose he *is* on the island.'

'Well, his boat was pulled up in the cove,' said George. 'We saw it.'

'Then he must be here somewhere,' said Dick. 'But he's not in the castle, he's not in the dungeons, he's not in the cave and he's not up here. It's a first-class mystery.'

'The Missing Uncle. Where is he?' said Julian. 'Look there's poor Aunt Fanny still down there, waiting with the lunch. We'd better go down. She's signalling to us.'

'I should like to,' said Anne. 'It's an awful squash·in this tiny glass room. I say – did you feel the tower sway then, when that gust of wind shook it? I'm going down quickly, before the whole thing blows over!'

She began to go down the spiral stairs, holding on to a little hand-rail that ran down beside them. The stairs were so steep that she was afraid of falling. She nearly *did* fall when Timmy pushed his way past her, and disappeared below at a remarkably fast pace.

Soon they were all down at the bottom. Julian locked the door again. 'Not much good locking a door if you leave the key in,' he said. 'Still – I'd better.'

They walked over to Aunt Fanny. 'Well, I thought you were never coming!' she said. 'Did you see anything interesting up there?'

'Only a lovely view,' said Anne. 'Simply magnificent. But we didn't find Uncle Quentin. It's very mysterious, Aunt Fanny – we really have looked everywere on the island – but he's just not here.'

'And yet his boat is in the cove,' said Dick. 'So he can't have gone.'

'Yes, it does sound queer,' said Aunt Fanny, handing round the sandwiches. 'But you don't know your uncle as well as I do. He always turns up all right. He's forgotten I was bringing you, or he would be here. As it is, we may not see him, if he's quite forgotten about your coming. If he remembers, he'll suddenly turn up.'

'But where from?' asked Dick, munching a potted meat sandwich. 'He's done a jolly good disappearing trick, Aunt Fanny.'

'Well, you'll see where he comes from, I've no doubt, when he arrives,' said Aunt Fanny. 'Another sandwich, George? No, *not* you, Timmy. You've had three already. Oh George, do keep Timmy's head out of that plate.'

'He's hungry too, Mother,' said George.

'Well, I've brought dog-biscuits for him,' said her mother.

'Oh, Mother! As if Timmy would eat *dog* biscuits

when he can have sandwiches,' said George. 'He only eats dog biscuits when there's absolutely nothing else and he's so ravenous he can't help eating them.'

They sat in the warm April sunshine, eating hungrily. There was orangeade to drink, cool and delicious. Timmy wandered over to a rock pool he knew, where rain-water collected, and he could be heard lapping there.

'Hasn't he got a good memory?' said George proudly. 'It's ages since he was here – and yet he remembered that pool at once, when he felt thirsty.'

'It's funny Timmy hasn't found Uncle Quentin, isn't it?' said Dick, suddenly. 'I mean – when we were hunting for him, and got "Warm" you'd think Timmy would bark or scrape about or something. But he didn't.'

'I think it's jolly funny that Father can't be found anywhere,' said George. 'I do really. I can't think how you can take it so calmly, Mother.'

'Well, dear, as I said before, I know your father better than you do,' said her mother. 'He'll turn up in his own good time. Why, I remember once when he was doing some sort of work in the stalactite caves at Cheddar, he disappeared in them for over a week – but he wandered out all right when he had finished his experiments.'

'It's very queer,' began Anne, and then stopped suddenly. A curious noise came to their ears – a rumbling grumbling, angry noise, like a giant hidden dog, growling in fury. Then there was a hissing noise from the tower, and all the wires that waved at the top were suddenly lit up as if by lightning.

'There now – I knew your father was somewhere about,' said George's mother. 'I heard that noise when I was here before – but I couldn't make out where it came from.'

'Where *did* it come from?' said Dick. 'It sounded almost as if it was underneath us, but it couldn't have been. Gracious, this is most mysterious.'

No more noises came. They each helped themselves to buns with jam in the middle. And then Anne gave a squeal that made them all jump violently.

'Look! *There's* Uncle Quentin! Standing over there, near the tower. He's watching the jackdaws! Wherever *did* he come from?'

Chapter Five

A MYSTERY

EVERYONE stared at Uncle Quentin. There he was, intently watching the jackdaws, his hands in his pockets. He hadn't seen the children or his wife.

Timmy leapt to his feet, and gambolled over to George's father. He barked loudly. Uncle Quentin jumped and turned round. He saw Timmy – and then he saw all the others, staring at him in real astonishment.

Uncle Quentin did not look particularly pleased to see anyone. He walked slowly over to them, a slight frown on his face. 'This *is* a surprise,' he said. 'I had no idea you were all coming today.'

'Oh *Quentin*!' said his wife, reproachfully. 'I wrote it down for you in your diary. You know I did.'

'Did you! Well, I haven't looked at my diary since, so it's no wonder I forgot,' said Uncle Quentin, a little peevishly. He kissed his wife, George and Anne, and shook hands with the boys.

'Uncle Quentin – where did you come from?' asked Dick, who was eaten up with curiosity. 'We've looked for you for ages.'

'Oh, I was in my workroom,' said Uncle Quentin, vaguely.

'Well, but where's that?' demanded Dick. 'Honestly, Uncle, we can't imagine where you hide yourself.

We even went up the tower to see if you were in that funny glass room at the top.'

'*What!*' exploded his uncle, in a sudden surprising fury. 'You dared to go up there? You might have been in great danger. I've just finished an experiment, and all those wires in there were connected with it.'

'Yes, we saw them acting a bit queerly,' said Julian.

'You've no business to come over here, and interfere with my work,' said his uncle, still looking furious. 'How did you get into that tower? I locked it.'

'Yes, it was locked all right,' said Julian. 'But you left the key in, you see, Uncle – so I thought it wouldn't matter if . . .'

'Oh, that's where the key is, is it?' said his uncle. 'I thought I'd lost it. Well, don't you ever go into that tower again. I tell you, it's dangerous.'

'Uncle Quentin, you haven't told us yet where your workroom is,' said Dick, who was quite determined to know. 'We can't imagine where you suddenly came from.'

'I told them you would turn up, Quentin,' said his wife. 'You look a bit thin, dear. Have you been having regular meals. You know, I left you plenty of good soup to heat up.'

'Did you?' said her husband. 'Well, I don't know if I've had it or not. I don't worry about meals when I'm working. I'll have some of those sandwiches now, though, if nobody else wants them.'

He began to devour the sandwiches, one after another, as if he was ravenous. Aunt Fanny watched him in distress.

'Oh Quentin – you're starving. I shall come over here and stay and look after you!'

Her husband looked alarmed. 'Oh no! Nobody is to come here. I can't have my work interfered with. I'm working on an extremely important discovery.'

'Is it a discovery that nobody else knows about?' asked Anne, her eyes wide with admiration. How clever Uncle Quentin was!

'Well – I'm not sure about that,' said Uncle Quentin, taking two sandwiches at once. 'That's partly why I came over here – besides the fact that I wanted water round me and above me. I have a feeling that somebody knows a bit more than I want them to know. But there's one thing – they can't come here unless they're shown the way through all those rocks that lie round the island. Only a few of the fishermen know that, and they've been given orders not to bring anyone here at all. I think you're the only other person that knows the way, George.'

'Uncle Quentin – please do tell us where your workroom is,' begged Dick, feeling that he could not wait a single moment more to solve the mystery.

'Don't keep bothering your uncle,' said his aunt, annoyingly. 'Let him eat his lunch. He can't have had anything for ages!'

'Yes, but Aunt Fanny, I . . .' began Dick and was interrupted by his uncle.

'You obey your aunt, young man. I don't want to be pestered by any of you. What does it matter where I work?'

'Oh, it doesn't really matter a bit, sir,' said Dick,

hurriedly. 'It's only that I'm awfully curious to know. You see, we looked for you simply everywhere.'

'Well, you're not quite so clever as you thought you were then,' said Uncle Quentin, and reached for a jammy bun. 'George, take this dog of yours away from me. He keeps breathing down my neck, hoping I shall give him a tit-bit. I don't approve of tit-bits at meal-times.'

George pulled Timmy away. Her mother watched her father gobbling up the rest of the food. Most of the sandwiches she had saved for tea-time had gone already. Poor Quentin! How very hungry he must be.

'Quentin, you don't think there's any danger for you here, do you?' she said. 'I mean – you don't think any-one would try to come spying on you, as they did once before?'

'No. How could they?' said her husband. 'No plane can land on this island. No boat can get through the rocks unless the way through is known, and the sea's too rough round the rocks for any swimmer.'

'Julian, see if you can make him promise to signal to me night and morning,' said Aunt Fanny, turning to her nephew. 'I feel worried about him somehow.'

Julian tackled his uncle manfully. 'Uncle, it wouldn't be too much of a bother to you to signal to Aunt Fanny twice a day, would it?'

'If you don't, Quentin, I shall come over every single day to see you,' said his wife.

'And we might come too,' said Anne mischievously. Her uncle looked most dismayed at the idea.

'Well, I could signal in the morning and in the

evening when I go up to the top of the tower,' he said, 'I have to go up once every twelve hours to re-adjust the wires. I'll signal then. Half past ten in the morning and half past ten at night.'

'How will you signal?' asked Julian. 'Will you flash with a mirror in the morning?'

'Yes – that would be quite a good idea,' said his uncle. 'I could do that easily. And I'll use a lantern at night. I'll shine it out six times at half past ten. Then perhaps you'll all know I'm all right and will leave me alone! But don't look for the signal tonight. I'll start tomorrow morning.'

'Oh Quentin dear, you do sound cross,' said his wife. 'I don't like you being all alone here, that's all. You look thin and tired. I'm sure you're not . . .'

Uncle Quentin put on a scowl exactly like George sometimes put on. He looked at his wrist-watch. 'Well, I must go,' he said. 'Time to get to work again. I'll see you to your boat.'

'We're going to stay to tea here, Father,' said George.

'No, I'd rather you didn't,' said her father, getting up. 'Come on – I'll take you to your boat.'

'But Father – I haven't been on my island for ages!' said George, indignantly. 'I want to stay here a bit longer. I don't see why I shouldn't.'

'Well, I've had enough interruption to my work,' said her father. 'I want to get on.'

'We shan't disturb you, Uncle Quentin,' said Dick, who was still terribly curious to know where his uncle had his workroom. Why wouldn't he tell them! Was he just being annoying? Or didn't he want them to know?

Uncle Quentin led them all firmly towards the little cove. It was plain that he meant them to go and to go quickly.

'When shall we come over and see you again, Quentin?' asked his wife.

'Not till I say so,' said her husband. 'It won't take me long now to finish what I'm on. My word, that dog's got a rabbit at last!'

'Oh *Timmy*!' yelled George in distress. Timmy dropped the rabbit he had actually managed to grab. It scampered away unhurt. Timmy came to his mistress looking very sheepish.

'You're a very bad dog. Just because I took my eye off you for half a second! No, it's no good licking my hand like that. I'm cross.'

They all came to the boat. 'I'll push her off,' said Julian. 'Get in, all of you. Well, good-bye, Uncle Quentin. I hope your work goes well.'

Everyone got into the boat. Timmy tried to put his head on George's knee, but she pushed it away.

'Oh, be kind to him and forgive him,' begged Anne. 'He looks as if he's going to cry.'

'Are you ready?' cried Julian. 'Got the oars, George? Dick, take the other pair.'

He shoved the boat off and leapt in himself. He cupped his hands round his mouth. 'Don't forget to signal, sir! We'll be watching out morning and evening!'

'And if you forget, I shall come over the very next day!' called his wife.

The boat slid away down the little inlet of water, and Uncle Quentin was lost to sight. Then round the low wall of rocks went the boat, and was soon on the open sea.

'Ju, watch and see if you can make out where Uncle Quentin is, when we're round these rocks,' said Dick. 'See what direction he goes in.'

Julian tried to see his uncle, but the rocks just there hid the cove from sight, and there was no sign of him at all.

'*Why* didn't he want us to stay? Because he didn't want us to know his hiding-place!' said Dick. 'And *why* doesn't he want us to know? Because it's somewhere *we* don't know, either!'

'But I thought we knew every single corner of my island,' said George. 'I think it's mean of Father not to tell me, if it's somewhere I don't know. I can't think *where* it can be!'

Timmy put his head on her knee again. George was so absorbed in trying to think where her father's hiding place could be that she absent-mindedly stroked Timmy's head. He was almost beside himself with delight. He licked her fingers lovingly.

'Oh Timmy – I didn't mean to pet you for ages,' said George. 'Stop licking my hands. You make them feel wet and horrid. Dick, it's very mysterious, isn't it – where *can* Father be hiding?'

'I can't imagine,' said Dick. He looked back at the island. A cloud of jackdaws rose up into the air calling loudly, 'Chack, chack, chack!'

The boy watched them. What had disturbed them?

Was it Uncle Quentin? Perhaps his hiding-place was somewhere about that old tower then, the one the jackdaws nested in? On the other hand, the jackdaws often rose into the air together for no reason at all.

'Those jackdaws are making a bit of fuss,' he said. 'Perhaps Uncle's hiding-place is not far from where they roost together, by that tower.'

'Can't be,' said Julian. 'We went all round there to-day.'

'Well, it's a mystery,' said George, gloomily, 'and I think it's horrible having a mystery about my very own island – and to be forbidden to go to it, and solve it. It's really *too* bad!'

Chapter Six

UP ON THE CLIFF

THE next day was rainy. The four children put on their macintoshes and sou'-westers and went out for a walk with Timmy. They never minded the weather. In fact Julian said that he really *liked* the feel of the wind and rain buffeting against his face.

'We forgot that Uncle Quentin couldn't flash to us if the weather wasn't sunny!' said Dick. 'Do you suppose he'll find some way to signal instead?'

'No,' said George. 'He just won't bother. He thinks we're awful fussers anyway, I'm sure. We'll have to watch at half past ten tonight to see if he signals.'

'I say! Shall I be able to stay up till then?' said Anne pleased.

'I shouldn't think so,' said Dick. 'I expect Julian and I will stay up – but you kids will have to buzz off to bed!'

George gave him a punch. 'Don't call us "*kids*"! I'm almost as tall as you are now.'

'It's not much use waiting about till half past ten now to see if Uncle signals to us in an any way, is it?' said Anne. 'Let's go up on the cliff – it'll be lovely and blowy. Timmy will like that. I love to see him racing along in the wind, with his ears blown back straight!'

'Woof,' said Timmy.

'He says he likes to see you with yours blown back too,' said Julian, gravely. Anne gave a squeal of laughter.

'You really are an idiot, Ju! Come on – let's take the cliff-path!'

They went up the cliff. At the top it was very windy indeed. Anne's sou'-wester was blown to the back of her head. The rain stung their cheeks and made them gasp.

'I should think we must be about the only people out this morning!' gasped George.

'Well, you're wrong,' said Julian. 'There are two people coming towards us!'

So there was. They were a man and a boy, both well wrapped up in macintoshes and sou'-westers. Like the children, they too wore high rubber boots.

The children took a look at them as they passed. The man was tall and well built, with shaggy eyebrows and a determined mouth. The boy was about sixteen, also tall and well built. He was not a bad-looking boy, but he had rather a sullen expression.

'Good morning,' said the man, and nodded. 'Good morning,' chorused the children, politely. The man looked them over keenly, and then he and the boy went on.

'Wonder who they are?' said George. 'Mother didn't say there were any new people here.'

'Just walked over from the next village, I expect,' said Dick.

They went on for some way. 'We'll walk to the coast-guard's cottage and then go back,' said Julian. 'Hi, Tim, don't go so near the cliff!'

The coastguard lived in a little whitewashed cottage on the cliff, facing the sea. Two other cottages stood beside it, also whitewashed. The children knew the coastguard well. He was a red-faced, barrel-shaped man, fond of joking.

He was nowhere to be seen when they came to his cottage. Then they heard his enormous voice singing a sea-shanty in the little shed behind. They went to find him.

'Hallo, coastguard,' said Anne.

He looked up and grinned at the children. He was busy making something. 'Hallo to you!' he said. 'So you're back again are you? Bad pennies, the lot of you – always turning up when you're not wanted!'

'What are you making?' asked Anne.

'A windmill for my young grandson,' said the coastguard, showing it to Anne. He was very clever at making toys.

'Oh, it's *lovely*,' said Anne, taking it in her hands. 'Does the windmill part go round – oh yes – it's super, coastguard!'

'I've been making quite a bit of money out of my toys,' said the old fellow, proudly. 'I've got some new neighbours in the next cottage – man and a boy – and the man's been buying all the toys I make. Seems to have a lot of nephews and nieces! He gives me good prices too.'

'Oh – would that be the man and the boy we met, I

wonder?' said Dick. 'Both tall, and well built – and the man had shaggy eyebrows.'

'That's right,' said the coastguard, trimming a bit of his windmill. 'Mr Curton and his son. They came here some weeks ago. You ought to get to know the son, Master Julian. He's about your age, I should think. Must be pretty lonely for him up here?'

'Doesn't he go to any school?' asked Julian.

'No. He's been ill, so his father said. Got to have plenty of sea-air and that sort of thing. Not a bad sort of boy. He comes and helps me with my toys sometimes. And he likes to mess about with my telescope.'

'I do too,' said George. 'I love looking through your telescope. Can I look through now? I'd like to see if I can spot Kirrin Island.'

'Well, you won't see much this weather,' said the coastguard. 'You wait a few minutes. See that break in the clouds? Well, it'll clear in a few minutes, and you'll be able to see your island easily. That's a funny thing your father's built there, Miss. Part of his work, I suppose.'

'Yes,' said George. 'Oh Timmy – look what he's done, coastguard – he's upset that tin of paint. Bad boy, Timmy!'

'It's not my tin,' said the coastguard. 'It's a tin belonging to that young fellow next door. I told you he comes in to help me sometimes. He brought in that tin to help paint a little dolls' house I made for his father.'

'Oh dear,' said George, in dismay. 'Do you think he'll be cross when he knows Timmy spilt it?'

'Shouldn't think so,' said the coastguard. 'He's a

queer boy though – quiet and a bit sulky. Not a bad boy, but doesn't seem very friendly like.'

George tried to clear up the mess of paint. Timmy had some on his paws, and made a little pattern of green paw-marks as he pattered about the shed.

'I'll tell the boy I'm sorry, if I meet him on the way back,' she said. 'Timmy if you dare to go near any more tins of paint you shan't sleep on my bed tonight.'

'The weather's a bit clearer now,' said Dick. 'Can we have a squint through the telescope, coastguard?'

'Let *me* see my island first,' said George at once. She tilted the telescope in the direction of Kirrin Island. She looked through it earnestly, and a smile came over her face.

'Yes, I can see it clearly. There's the tower Father has had built. I can even see the glass room quite clearly, and there's nobody in it. No sign of Father anywhere.'

Everyone had a turn at looking through the telescope. It was fascinating to see the island appearing so close. On a clear day it would be even easier to see all the details. 'I can see a rabbit scampering,' said Anne, when her turn came.

'Don't you let that dog of yours squint through the telescope then,' said the coastguard at once. 'He'll try to get down it after that rabbit!'

Timmy cocked his ears up at the mention of the word rabbit. He looked all round and sniffed. No, there was no rabbit. Then why did people mention them?

'We'd better go now,' said Julian. 'We'll be up here again sometime, and we'll come and see what toys

you've done. Thanks for letting us look through the telescope.'

'You're welcome!' said the old fellow. 'You're not likely to wear it out through looking! Come along any time you want to use it.'

They said good-bye and went off, Timmy capering round them. 'Couldn't we see Kirrin Island well!' said Anne. 'I wished I could see where your father was, George. Wouldn't it be fun if we spotted him just coming out of his hiding-place?'

The four children had discussed this problem a good deal since they had left the island. It puzzled them very much indeed. How did it happen that George's father knew a hiding-place that they didn't know? Why, they had been over every inch of the island! It must be quite a big hiding-place too, if he had got all his stuff for his experiments with him. According to George's mother, there had been quite a lot of this, to say nothing of stores of food.

'If Father knew a place I didn't know, and never told me about it, I think he's jolly mean,' George said half a dozen times. 'I do really. It's *my* island?'

'Well, he'll probably tell you when he's finished the work he's on,' said Julian. 'Then you'll know. We can all go and explore it then, wherever it is.'

After they left the coastguard's cottage they turned their steps home. They made their way along the cliff, and then saw the boy they had met before. He was standing on the path looking out to sea. The man was not with him.

He turned as they came up and gave them a pale kind of smile. 'Hallo! Been up to see the coastguard?'

'Yes,' said Julian. 'Nice old fellow, isn't he?'

'I say,' said George, 'I'm so sorry but my dog upset a tin of green paint, and the coastguard said it was yours. Can I pay you for it, please?'

'Goodness, no!' said the boy. 'I don't mind. There wasn't much of it left anyway. That's a nice dog of yours.'

'Yes, he is,' said George, warmly. 'Best dog in the world. I've had him for years, but he's still as young as ever. Do you like dogs?'

'Oh yes,' said the boy, but he made no move to pat Timmy or fuss him, as most people did. And Timmy did not run round the boy and sniff at him as he usually did when he met anyone new. He just stood by George, his tail neither up nor down.

'That's an interesting little island,' said the boy, pointing to Kirrin. 'I wish I could go there.'

'It's *my* island,' said George, proudly. 'My very own.'

'Really?' said the boy, politely. 'Could you let me go over one day then?'

'Well – not just at present,' said George. 'You see, my father's there – working – he's a scientist.'

'Really?' said the boy again. 'Er – has he got some new experiment on hand, then?'

'Yes,' said George.

'Ah – and that queer tower is something to do with it, I suppose,' said the boy, looking interested for the first time. 'When will his experiment be finished?'

'What's that to do with you?' said Dick, suddenly. The others stared at him in surprise. Dick sounded rather rude, and it was not like him.

'Oh nothing!' said the boy, hastily. 'I only thought that if his work will soon be finished, perhaps your brother would take me over to his island!'

George couldn't help feeling pleased. This boy thought *she* was a boy! George was always gracious to people who made the mistake of thinking she was a boy.

'Of *course* I'll take you!' she said. 'It shouldn't be long before I do – the experiment is nearly done.'

Chapter Seven

A LITTLE SQUABBLE

A SOUND made them turn. It was the boy's father coming up. He nodded to the children. 'Making friends?' he said, amiably. 'That's right. My boy's pretty lonely here. I hope you'll come up and see us some time. Finished your conversation, son?'

'Yes,' said the boy. 'This boy here says that island is his, and he's going to take me over it when his father has finished his work there – and that won't be long.'

'And do you know the way through all those wicked rocks?' said the man. '*I* shouldn't care to try it. I was talking to the fishermen the other day, and not one of them appeared to know the way!'

This was rather astonishing. Some of the fishermen *did* know it. Then the children remembered that the men had all been forbidden to take anyone to the island while Uncle Quentin was at work there. It was clear that they had pretended not to know the way, in loyalty to their orders.

'Did you want to go to the island then?' asked Dick, suddenly.

'Oh no! But my boy here would love to go,' said the man. '*I* don't want to be seasick, bobbing up and down on those waves near the island. I'm a poor sailor. I never go on the sea if I can help it!'

'Well, we must go,' said Julian. 'We've got to do some shopping for my aunt. Good-bye!'

'Come and see us as soon as you can,' said the man. 'I've a fine television set that Martin here would like to show you. Any afternoon you like!'

'Oh thanks!' said George. She seldom saw television. 'We'll come!'

They parted, and the four children and Timmy went on down the cliff-path.

'Whatever made you sound so rude, Dick?' said George. 'The way you said "What's that to do with you?" sounded quite insulting.'

'Well – I just felt suspicious, that's all,' said Dick. 'That boy seemed to be so jolly interested in the island and in your father's work, and when it would be finished.'

'Why shouldn't he be?' demanded George. 'Everyone in the village is interested. They all know about the tower. And all the boy wanted to know was when he could go to my island – that's why he asked when Father's work would be finished. I liked him.'

'You only liked him because he was ass enough to think you were a boy,' said Dick. 'Jolly girlish-looking boy you are, that's all I can say.'

George flared up at once. 'Don't be mean! I'm *not* girlish-looking. I've far more freckles than you have, for one thing, and better eyebrows. *And* I can make my voice go deep.'

'You're just silly,' said Dick, in disgust. 'As if freckles

are boyish! Girls have them just as much as boys. I don't believe that boy thought you were a boy at all. He was just sucking up to you. He must have heard how much you like playing at being what you aren't.'

George walked up to Dick with such a furious look on her face that Julian hastily put himself in between them. 'Now, no brawls,' he said. 'You're both too old to begin slapping each other like kids in the nursery. Let me tell you, you're both behaving like babies, not like boys *or* girls!'

Anne was looking on with scared eyes. George didn't. go off the deep end like this usually. And it *was* funny of Dick to have spoken so rudely to the boy on the cliff. Timmy gave a sudden little whine. His tail was down, and he looked very miserable.

'Oh George – Timmy can't *bear* you to quarrel with Dick!' said Anne. 'Look at him! He's just miserable!'

'He didn't like that boy a bit,' said Dick. 'That was another thing I thought was funny. If Timmy doesn't like a person, *I* don't like him either.'

'Timmy doesn't *always* rush round new people,' said George. 'He didn't growl or snarl, anyway. All right, all right, Julian; I'm not going to start brawling. But I do think Dick is being silly. Making a mountain out of a molehill – just because someone was interested in Kirrin Island and Father's work, and just because Timmy didn't caper all round him. He was such a solemn sort of boy that I'm not surprised Timmy wasn't all over him. He probably knew the boy wouldn't like it. Timmy's clever like that.'

'Oh, do stop,' said Dick. 'I give in – gracefully! I

may be making a fuss. Probably am. I couldn't help my feelings, though.'

Anne gave a sigh of relief. The squabble was over. She hoped it wouldn't crop up again. George had been very touchy since she had been home. If only Uncle Quentin would hurry up and finish his work, and they could all go to the island as much as they liked, things would be all right.

'I'd rather like to see that television set,' said George. 'We might go up some afternoon.'

'Right,' said Julian. 'But on the whole, I think it would be best if we steered clear of any talk about your father's work. Not that we know much. Still, we do know that once before there were people after one of his theories. The secrets of the scientists are very, very important these days, you know, George. Scientists are V I P!'

'What's V I P?' asked Anne.

'Very Important People, baby!' said Julian, with a laugh. 'What did you think it meant? Violet, Indigo, Purple? I guess those are the colours Uncle Quentin would go if he knew anyone was trying to snoop into his secrets!'

Everyone laughed, even George. She looked affectionately at Julian. He was always so sensible and good-tempered. She really would go by what he said.

The day passed swiftly. The weather cleared and the sun came out strongly. The air smelt of gorse and primroses and the salt of the sea. Lovely! They went shopping for Aunt Fanny, and stopped to talk with James, the fisher-boy.

'Your father's got the island, I see,' he said to George with a grin. 'Bad luck, Miss. You'll not be going over there so often. And nobody else will, either, so I've heard.'

'That's right,' said George. 'Nobody is allowed to go over there for some time. Did you help to take some of the stuff over, James?'

'Yes. I know the way, you see, because I've been with you,' said James. 'Well, Miss, how did you find your boat when you went across yesterday? I got her all ship-shape for you, didn't I?'

'Yes, you did, James,' said George, warmly. 'You made her look beautiful. You must come across to the island with us next time we go.'

'Thanks,' said James, his ready grin showing all his white teeth. 'Like to leave Timmy with me for a week or two? See how he wants to stay!'

George laughed. She knew James was only joking. He was very fond of Timmy, though, and Timmy adored James. He was now pushing himself hard against the fisher-boy's knees, and trying to put his nose into his brown hand. Timmy had never forgotten the time when James looked after him so well.

The evening came, and the bay was softly blue. Little white horses flecked it here and there. The four gazed across to Kirrin Island. It always looked so lovely at this time of the evening.

The glass top of the tower winked and blinked in the sun. It looked almost as if someone was signalling. But there was no one in the little glass room. As the children watched they heard a faint rumbling sound, and suddenly the top of the tower was ablaze with a curious glare.

'Look! That's what happened yesterday!' said Julian, in excitement. 'Your father's at work all right, George. I do wonder what he's doing!'

Then there came a throbbing sound, almost like the noise of an aeroplane, and once more the glass top of the tower shone and blazed, as the wires became full of some curious power.

'Weird,' said Dick. 'A bit frightening too. Where's your father at this very moment, I wonder, George. How I'd like to know!'

'I bet he's forgotten all about meals again,' said George. 'Didn't he wolf our sandwiches – he must have been starving. I wish he'd let Mother go over there and look after him.'

Her mother came in at that moment. 'Did you hear the noise?' she said. 'I suppose that was your father at work again. Oh dear, I hope he doesn't blow himself up one of these days!'

'Aunt Fanny, can I stay up till half past ten tonight?' asked Anne, hopefully. 'To see Uncle Quentin's signal, you know?'

'Good gracious, no!' said her aunt. 'No one needs to stay up. I am quite capable of watching for it myself!'

'Oh Aunt Fanny! Surely I and Dick can stay up!' said Julian. 'After all, we're not in bed till ten at school.'

'Yes – but this is *half past* ten, and you wouldn't even be in bed then,' said his aunt. 'There's no reason why you shouldn't lie in bed and watch for it though, if you want to – providing you haven't fallen asleep!'

'Oh yes – I can do that,' said Julian. 'My window looks across to Kirrin Island. Six flashes with a lantern? I shall count them carefully.'

So the four went to bed at the usual time. Anne was asleep long before half past ten, and George was so drowsy that she could not make herself get up and go into the boys' room. But Dick and Julian were both wide awake. They lay in their beds and looked out of the window. There was no moon, but the sky was clear, and the stars shone down, giving a faint light. The sea looked very black. There was no sign of Kirrin Island. It was lost in the darkness of the night.

'Almost half past ten,' said Julian, looking at his watch which had luminous hands. 'Now then, Uncle Quentin, what about it?'

Almost as if his uncle was answering him, a light shone out in the glass top of the tower. It was a clear, small light, like the light of a lantern.

Julian began to count. 'One flash.' There was a pause. 'Two flashes.' Another pause 'Three . . . four . . . five . . . six!'

The flashes stopped. Julian snuggled down into bed. 'Well, that's that. Uncle Quentin's all right. I say, it's weird to think of him climbing that spiral stairway right to the top of the tower, in the dark of night, isn't it? – just to mess about with those wires.'

'Mmmmm,' said Dick sleepily. 'I'd rather he did it, than I! You can be a scientist if you like, Ju – but *I* don't want to climb towers in the dead of night on a lonely island. I'd like Timmy there, at least!'

Someone knocked on their door and it opened. Julian sat up at once. It was Aunt Fanny.

'Oh Julian dear – did you see the flashes? I forgot to count them. Were there six?'

'Oh yes, Aunt Fanny! I'd have rushed down to tell

you if anything was wrong. Uncle's all right. Don't you worry!'

'I wish I'd told him to do an *extra* flash to tell me if he's had some of that nice soup,' said his aunt. 'Well, good night, Julian. Sleep well!'

Chapter Eight

DOWN IN THE QUARRY

THE next day dawned bright and sunny. The four tore down to breakfast, full of high spirits. 'Can we bathe? Aunt Fanny, it's *really* warm enough! Oh do say we can!'

'Of course not! Whoever heard of bathing in April!' said Aunt Fanny. 'Why, the sea is terribly cold. Do you want to be in bed for the rest of the holiday with a chill?'

'Well, let's go for a walk on the moors at the back of Kirrin Cottage,' said George. 'Timmy would love that. Wouldn't you, Tim?'

'Woof,' said Timmy, thumping his tail hard on the ground.

'Take your lunch with you if you like,' said her mother. 'I'll pack some for you.'

'You'll be glad to be rid of us for a little while, I expect, Aunt Fanny,' said Dick, with a grin. 'I know what we'll do. We'll go to the old quarry and look for prehistoric weapons! We've got a jolly good museum at school, and I'd like to take back some stone arrowheads or something like that.'

They all liked hunting for things. It would be fun to go to the old quarry, and it would be lovely and warm in the hollow there.

'I hope we shan't find a poor dead sheep there, as we once did,' said Anne, with a shudder. 'Poor thing! It must have fallen down and baa-ed for help for ages.'

'Of course we shan't,' said Julian. 'We shall find stacks of primroses and violets though, growing down the sides of the quarry. They are always early there because it's sheltered from every wind.'

'I should love to have bunches of primroses,' said his aunt. 'Nice big ones! Enough to put all over the house.'

'Well, while the boys are looking for arrow-heads we'll look for primroses,' said Anne, pleased. 'I like picking flowers.'

'And Timmy, of course, will hunt for rabbits, and will hope to bring home enough for you to decorate the larder from top to bottom,' said Dick, solemnly. Timmy looked thrilled and gave an excited little woof.

They waited for Uncle Quentin's signal at half past ten. It came – six flashes of a mirror in the sun. The flashes were quite blinding.

'Nice little bit of heliographing!' said Dick. 'Good morning and good-bye, Uncle! We'll watch for you to-night. Now, everybody ready?'

'Yes! Come on, Tim! Who's got the sandwiches? I say, isn't the sun hot!'

Off they all went. It was going to be a really lovely day!

The quarry was not really very far – only about a quarter of a mile. The children went for a walk beforehand, for Timmy's sake. Then they made for the quarry.

It was a queer place. At some time or other it had been deeply quarried for stone, and then left to itself. Now the sides were covered with small bushes and grass and plants of all kinds. In the sandy places heather grew.

The sides were very steep, and as few people came there, there were no paths to follow. It was like a huge rough bowl, irregular in places, and full of colour now where primroses opened their pale petals to the sky. Violets grew there by the thousand, both white and purple. Cowslips were opening too, the earliest anywhere.

'Oh, it's lovely!' said Anne, stopping at the top and looking down. 'Simply super! I never in my life saw so many primroses – nor such huge ones!'

'Be careful how you go, Anne,' said Julian. 'These sides are very steep. If you lose your footing you'll roll right down to the bottom – and find yourself with a broken arm or leg!'

'I'll be careful,' said Anne. 'I'll throw my basket down to the bottom, so that I can have two hands to cling to bushes with, if I want to. I shall be able to fill that basket cramful of primroses and violets!'

She flung the basket down, and it bounced all the way to the bottom of the quarry. The children climbed down to where they wanted to go – the girls to a great patch of big primroses, the boys to a place where they thought they might find stone weapons.

'Hallo!' said a voice, suddenly, from much lower

down. The four stopped in surprise, and Timmy
growled.

'Why – it's you!' said George, recognizing the boy
they had met the day before.

'Yes. I don't know if you know my name. It's Martin
Curton,' said the boy.

Julian told him their names too. 'We've come to
picnic here,' he said. 'And to see if we can find stone
weapons. What have you come for?'

'Oh – to see if I can find stone weapons too,' said the
boy.

'Have you found any?' asked George.

'No. Not yet.'

'Well, you won't find any just there,' said Dick. 'Not
in heather! You want to come over here, where the
ground is bare and gravelly.'

Dick was trying to be friendly, to make up for the
day before. Martin came over and began to scrape
about with the boys. They had trowels with them, but
he had only his hands.

'Isn't it hot down here?' called Anne. 'I'm going to
take off my coat.'

Timmy had his head and shoulders down a rabbit-
hole. He was scraping violently, sending up heaps of
soil behind him in a shower.

'Don't go near Timmy unless you want to be buried
in earth!' said Dick. 'Hey, Timmy – is a rabbit really
worth all that hard work?'

Apparently it was, for Timmy, panting loudly, went
on digging for all he was worth. A stone flew high in
the air and hit Julian. He rubbed his cheek. Then he

looked at the stone that lay beside him. He gave a
shout. 'Look at this – a jolly fine arrow-head! Thanks,
Timmy, old fellow. Very good of you to go digging for
me. What about a hammer-head next?'

The others came to see the stone arrow-head. Anne
thought she would never have known what it was – but
Julian and Dick exclaimed over it in admiration.

'Jolly good specimen,' said Dick. 'See how it's been
shaped, George? To think that this was used thousands of years ago to kill the enemies of a cave-man!'
Martin did not say much. He just looked at the arrow-
head, which certainly was a very fine unspoilt specimen, and then turned away. Dick thought he was a
queer fellow. A bit dull and boring. He wondered if
they ought to ask him to their picnic. He didn't want
to in the least.

But George did! 'Are you having a picnic here too?'
she said. Martin shook his head.

'No. I've not brought any sandwiches.'

'Well, we've plenty. Stay and have some with us
when we eat them,' said George, generously.

'Thanks. It's very nice of you,' said the boy. 'And
will you come and see my television set this afternoon
in return! I'd like you to.'

'Yes, we will,' said George. 'It would be something
to do! Oh Anne – just look at those violets! I've never
seen such big white ones before. Won't Mother be
pleased?'

The boys went deeper down, scraping about with
their trowels in any likely place. They came to where a
shelf of stone projected out a good way. It would be a

nice place to have their lunch. The stone would be warm to sit on, and was flat enough to take ginger-beer bottles and cups in safety.

At half past twelve they all had their lunch. They were very hungry. Martin shared their sandwiches, and became quite friendly over them.

'Best sandwiches I've ever tasted,' he said. 'I do like those sardine ones. Does your mother make them for you? I wish I had a mother. Mine died ages ago.'

There was a sympathetic silence. The four could not think of any worse thing to happen to a boy or girl. They offered Martin the nicest buns, and the biggest piece of cake immediately.

'I saw your father flashing his signals last night,' said Martin, munching a bun.

Dick looked up at once. 'How do you know he was signalling?' he asked. 'Who told you?'

'Nobody,' said the boy. 'I just saw the six flashes, and I thought it must be George's father.' He looked surprised at Dick's sharp tone. Julian gave Dick a nudge, to warn him not to go off the deep end again.

George scowled at Dick. 'I suppose you saw my father signalling this morning too,' she said to Martin. 'I bet scores of people saw the flashes. He just helio-graphs with a mirror at half past ten to signal that he's all right – and flashes a lantern at the same time at night.'

Now it was Dick's turn to scowl at George. Why give away all this information? It wasn't necessary. Dick felt sure she was doing it just to pay him out for his sharp question. He tried to change the subject.

'Where do you go to school?' he asked.

'I don't,' said the boy. 'I've been ill.'

'Well, where did you go to school before you were ill?' asked Dick.

'I – I had a tutor,' said Martin. 'I didn't go to school.'

'Bad luck!' said Julian. He thought it must be terrible not to go to school and have all the fun, the work and the games of school-life. He looked curiously at Martin. Was he one of these rather stupid boys who did no good at school, but had to have a tutor at home? Still he didn't *look* stupid. He just looked rather sullen and dull.

Timmy was sitting on the warm stone with the others. He had his share of the sandwiches, but had to be rationed, as Martin had to have some too.

He was funny with Martin. He took absolutely no notice of him at all. Martin might not have been there!

And Martin took no notice of Timmy. He did not talk to him, or pat him. Anne was sure he didn't really like dogs, as he had said. How could anyone be with Timmy and not give him even *one* pat?

Timmy did not even look at Martin, but sat with his back to him, leaning against George. It was really rather amusing, if it wasn't so odd. After all, George was talking in a friendly way to Martin; they were all sharing their food with him – and Timmy behaved as if Martin simply wasn't there at all!

Anne was just about to remark on Timmy's odd behaviour when he yawned, shook himself, and leapt down from the rock. 'He's going rabbiting again,' said

Julian. 'Hey, Tim – find me another arrow-head will you, old fellow?'

Timmy wagged his tail. He disappeared under the shelf of rock, and there came the sound of digging. A shower of stones and soil flew into the air.

The children lay back on the stone and felt sleepy. They talked for some minutes, and then Anne felt her eyes closing. She was awakened by George's voice.

'Where's Timmy? Timmy! Timmy! Come here! Where have you got to?'

But no Timmy came. There was not even an answering bark. 'Oh blow, said George. 'Now he's gone down some extra-deep rabbit hole, I suppose. I must get him. Timmy! Wherever are you?'

Chapter Nine

GEORGE MAKES A DISCOVERY – AND LOSES HER TEMPER

GEORGE slipped down from the rock. She peered under it. There was a large opening there, scattered with stones that Timmy had loosened in his digging.

'Surely you haven't at last found a rabbit hole big enough to go down!' said George. 'TIMMY! Where are you?'

Not a bark, not a whine came from the hole. George wriggled under the shelf of rock, and peered down the burrow. Timmy had certainly made it very big. George called up to Julian.

'Julian! Throw me down your trowel, will you?'

The trowel landed by her foot. George took it and began to make the hole bigger. It might be big enough for Timmy, but it wasn't big enough for her!

She dug hard and soon got very hot. She crawled out and looked over on to the rock to see if she could get one of the others to help her. They were all asleep.

'Lazy things!' thought George, quite forgetting that she too would have been dozing if she hadn't wondered where Timmy had gone.

She slipped down under the rock again and began to dig hard with her trowel. Soon she had made the hole big enough to get through. She was surprised to find

quite a large passage, once she had made the entrance
big enough to take her. She could crawl along on hands
and knees!

'I say – I wonder if this is just some animal's run-
way – or leads somewhere!' thought George. 'TIMMY!
Where *are* you?'

From somewhere deep in the quarry side there came
a faint whine. George felt thankful. So Timmy *was*
there, after all. She crawled along, and then quite
suddenly the tunnel became high and wide and she
realized that she must be in a passage. It was perfectly
dark, so she could not see anything, she could only
feel.

Then she heard the sound of pattering feet, and
Timmy pressed affectionately against her legs, whining.
'Oh Timmy – you gave me a bit of a fright!' said
George. 'Where have you been? Is this a real passage –
or just a tunnel in the quarry, made by the old miners,
and now used by animals?'

'Woof,' said Timmy, and pulled at George's jeans
to make her go back to the daylight.

'All right, I'm coming!' said George. 'Don't imagine
I want to wander alone in the dark! I only came to
look for you.'

She made her way back to the shelf of rock. By this
time Dick was awake, and wondered where George
had gone. He waited a few minutes, blinking up into
the deep blue sky, and then sat up.

'George!' There was no answer. So, in his turn Dick
slipped down from the rock and looked around. And,
to his very great astonishment he saw first Timmy, and

then George on hands and knees, appearing out of the hole under the rock. He stared open-mouthed, and George began to giggle.

'It's all right. I've only been rabbiting with Timmy!'

She stood beside him, shaking and brushing soil from her jersey and trousers. 'There's a passage behind the entrance to the hole under the rock,' she said. 'At first it's just a narrow tunnel, like an animal's hole – then it gets wider – and then it becomes a proper high wide passage! I couldn't see if it went on, of course, because it was dark. Timmy was a long way in.'

'Good gracious!' said Dick. 'It sounds exciting.'

'Let's explore it, shall we?' said George. 'I expect Julian's got a torch.'

'No,' said Dick. 'We won't explore today.'

The others were now awake, and listening with interest. 'Is it a secret passage?' said Anne, thrilled. 'Oh do let's explore it!'

'No, not today,' said Dick again. He looked at Julian. Julian guessed that Dick did not want Martin to share this secret. Why should he? He was not a real friend of theirs, and they had only just got to know him. He nodded back to Dick.

'No, we won't explore today. Anyway, it may be nothing – just an old tunnel made by the quarrymen.'

Martin was listening with great interest. He went and looked into the hole. 'I wish we could explore,' he said. 'Maybe we could plan to meet again with torches and see if there really is a passage there.'

Julian looked at his watch. 'Nearly two o'clock. Well, Martin, if we're going to see that half past two programme of yours, we'd better be getting on.'

Carrying baskets of primroses and violets, the girls began to climb up the steep side of the quarry. Julian took Anne's basket from her, afraid she might slip and fall. Soon they were all at the top. The air felt quite cool there after the warmth of the quarry.

They made their way to the cliff path and before long were passing the coastguard's cottage. He was out in his garden, and he waved to them.

They went in the gateway of the next-door cottage. Martin pushed the door open. His father was sitting at the window of the room inside, reading. He got up with a broad, welcoming smile.

'Well, well, well! This *is* nice! Come along in, do. Yes, the dog as well. I don't mind dogs a bit. I like them.'

It seemed rather a crowd in the small room. They all shook hands politely. Martin explained hurriedly that he had brought the children to see a television programme.

'A good idea,' said Mr Curton, still beaming. Anne stared at his great eyebrows. They were very long and thick. She wondered why he didn't have them trimmed – but perhaps he liked them like that. They made him look very fierce, she thought.

The four looked round the little room. There was a television set standing at the far end, on a table. There was also a magnificent wireless – and something else that made the boys stare with interest.

'Hallo! You've got a transmitting set, as well as a receiving set,' said Julian.

'Yes,' said Mr Curton. 'It's a hobby of mine. I made that set.'

'Well! You must be brainy!' said Dick.

'What's a transmitting set?' asked Anne. 'I haven't heard of one before.'

'Oh, it just means a set to send out messages by wireless – like police-cars have, when they send back messages to the police stations,' said Dick. 'This is a very powerful one, though.'

Martin was fiddling about with the television switches. Then the programme began.

It was great fun seeing the television programme. When it was over Mr Curton asked them to stay to tea.

'Now don't say no,' he said. 'I'll ring up and ask your aunt, if you like, if you're afraid she might be worried.'

'Well – if you'd do that, sir,' said Julian. 'I think she *would* wonder where we'd gone!'

Mr Curton rang up Aunt Fanny. Yes, it was quite all right for them to stay, but they mustn't be too late back. So they settled down to an unexpectedly good tea. Martin was not very talkative, but Mr Curton made up for it. He laughed and joked and was altogether very good company.

The talk came round to Kirrin Island. Mr Curton said how beautiful it looked each evening. George looked pleased.

'Yes,' she said. '*I* always think that. I do wish Father hadn't chosen this particular time to work on my island. I'd planned to go and stay there.'

'I suppose you know every inch of it!' said Mr Curton.

'Oh yes!' said George. 'We all do. There are dungeons there, you know – real dungeons that go deep down – where we once found gold ingots.'

'Yes – I remember reading about that,' said Mr Curton. 'That must have been exciting. Fancy *finding* the dungeons too! And there's an old well too you once got down, isn't there?'

'Yes,' said Anne, remembering. 'And there is a cave where we once lived – it's got an entrance through the roof, as well as from the sea.'

'And I suppose your father is conducting his marvellous experiments down in the dungeons?' said Mr Curton. 'Well, what a strange place to work in!'

'No – we don't . . .' began George, when she got a kick on the ankle from Dick. She screwed up her face in pain. It had been a very sharp kick indeed.

'What were you going to say?' said Mr Curton, looking surprised.

'Er – I was just going to say that – er – er – we don't know which place Father has chosen,' said George, keeping her legs well out of the way of Dick's feet.

Timmy gave a sudden sharp whine. George looked down at him in surprise. He was looking up at Dick, with a very hurt expression.

'What's the matter, Timmy!' said George anxiously.

'He's finding the room too hot, I think,' said Dick. 'Better take him out, George.'

George, feeling quite anxious, took him out. Dick joined her. She scowled at him. 'What did you want to kick me for like that? I shall have a frightful bruise.'

'You know jolly well why I did,' said Dick. 'Giving away everything like that! Can't you see the chap's very interested in your father being on the island? There may be nothing in it at all, but you might at least keep your mouth shut. Just like a girl, can't help blabbing. I had to stop you somehow. I don't mind telling you I trod jolly hard on poor old Timmy's tail too, to make him yelp, so that you'd stop talking!'

'Oh – you beast!' said George, indignantly. 'How *could* you hurt Timmy?'

'I didn't want to. It was a shame,' said Dick, stopping to fondle Timmy's ears. 'Poor old Tim. I didn't want to hurt you, old fellow.'

'I'm going home,' said George, her face scarlet with anger. 'I hate you for talking to me like that – telling me I blab like a girl – and stamping on poor Timmy's tail. You can go back and say I'm taking Timmy home.'

'Right,' said Dick. 'And a jolly good thing too. The less you talk to Mr Curton the better. *I'm* going back to find out exactly what he is and what he does. I'm getting jolly suspicious. You'd better go before you give anything else away!'

Almost choking with rage, George went off with Timmy. Dick went back to make her apologies. Julian and Anne, sure that something was up, felt most uncomfortable. They rose to go, but to their surprise, Dick became very talkative and appeared to be suddenly very much interested in Mr Curton and what he did.

But at last they said good-bye and went. 'Come again, do,' said Mr Curton, beaming at the three of them. 'And tell the other boy – what's his name, George – that I hope his dog is quite all right again now. Such a nice, well-behaved dog! Well good-bye! See you again soon, I hope!'

Chapter Ten

A SURPRISING SIGNAL

'WHAT's up with George?' demanded Julian, as soon as they were safely out of earshot. 'I know you kicked her at tea-time, for talking too much about the island – that was idiotic of her – but why has she gone home in a huff?'

Dick told them how he had trodden on poor Timmy's tail to make him whine, so that George would turn her attention to him and stop talking. Julian laughed, but Anne was indignant.

'That was *horrid* of you, Dick.'

'Yes, it was,' said Dick. 'But I couldn't think of any other way to head George off the island. I really honestly thought she was giving away to that fellow all the things he badly wanted to know. But now I think he wanted to know them for quite another reason.'

'What do you mean?' said Julian puzzled.

'Well, I thought at first he must be after Uncle Quentin's secret, whatever it is,' said Dick, 'and that was why he wanted to know all the ins and outs of everything. But now that he's told me he's a journalist – that's a man who writes for the newspapers, Anne – I think after all he only wants the information so that he can use it for his paper, and make a splash when Uncle has finished his work.'

'Yes, I think that too,' said Julian thoughtfully; 'in

fact, I'm pretty sure of it. Well, there's no harm in that but I don't see why we should sit there and be pumped all the time. He could easily say, "Look here, I'd be obliged if you'd spill the beans about Kirrin Island – I want to use it in a newspaper story." But he didn't say that.'

'No. So I was suspicious,' said Dick. 'But I see now he'd want all sorts of tit-bits about Kirrin Island to put in his newspaper, whatever it is. Blow! Now I shall have to explain to George I was wrong – and she really is in a temper!'

'Let's take the road to Kirrin Village and go to get some bones for Timmy at the butcher's,' said Julian. 'A sort of apology to Tim!'

This seemed a good idea. They bought two large meaty bones at the butcher's, and then went to Kirrin Cottage. George was up in her bedroom with Timmy. The three went up to find her.

She was sitting on the floor with a book. She looked up sulkily as they came in.

'George, sorry I was such a beast,' said Dick. 'I did it in a good cause, if you only knew it. But I've discovered that Mr Curton isn't a spy, seeking out your father's secret – he's only a journalist, smelling out a story for his paper! Look – I've brought these for Timmy – I apologize to him too.'

George was in a very bad temper, but she tried to respond to Dick's friendliness. She gave him a small smile.

'All right. Thanks for the bones. Don't talk to me tonight anybody. I feel mad, but I'll get over it.'

They left her sitting on the floor. It was always best to leave George severely alone when she was in one of her tempers. As long as Timmy was with her, she was all right, and he certainly would not leave her while she was cross and unhappy.

George did not come down to supper. Dick explained. 'We had a bit of a row, Aunt Fanny, but we've made it up. George still feels sore about it though. Shall I take her supper up?'

'No, I will,' said Anne, and she took up a tray of food.

'I'm not hungry,' said George, so Anne prepared to take it away again. 'Well, you can leave it,' said George hurriedly. 'I expect Timmy will like it.'

So Anne, with a secret smile to herself left the tray. All the dishes were empty by the time she climbed the stairs to fetch the tray again!

'Dear me – Timmy *was* hungry!' she said to George, and her cousin smiled sheepishly. 'Aren't you coming down now? We're going to play monopoly.'

'No thanks. You leave me alone this evening, and I'll be all right tomorrow,' said George. 'Really I will.'

So Julian, Dick, Anne and Aunt Fanny played monopoly without George. They went up to bed at the usual time and found George in bed, fast asleep, with Timmy curled up on her toes.

'I'll look out for Uncle Quentin's signal,' said Julian, as he got into bed. 'Gosh, it's a dark night tonight.'

He lay in bed and looked out of the window towards Kirrin Island. Then, at exactly half past ten the six flashes came – flash, flash, flash, through the darkness. Julian buried his head in his pillow. Now for a good sleep!

He was awakened by a throbbing noise some time later. He sat up and looked out of the window, expecting to see the top of the tower ablaze with light, as it sometimes was when his uncle conducted a special experiment. But nothing happened. There was no flare of light. The throbbing died away and Julian lay down again.

'I saw Uncle's signals all right last night, Aunt Fanny,' he said next morning. 'Did you?'

'Yes,' said his aunt. 'Julian, do you think you would watch for them this morning, dear? I have to go and see the vicar about something, and I don't believe I should be able to see the tower from the vicarage.'

'Yes, of course I will, Aunt Fanny,' said Julian. 'What's the time now? Half past nine. Right. I'll

write some letters sitting by the window in my room –
and at half past ten I'll watch for the signals.'

He wrote his letters interrupted first by Dick, then
by George, Anne and Timmy, who wanted him to go
on the beach with them. George had quite recovered
herself now, and was trying to be specially nice to
make up for yesterday's temper.

'I'll come at half past ten,' said Julian. 'After I've
seen the signals from the tower. They're due in ten
minutes.'

At half past ten he looked at the glass top of the
tower. Ah – there was the first signal, blazing brightly
as the sun caught the mirror held by his uncle in the
tower.

'One flash,' counted Julian. 'Two – three – four –
five – six. He's all right.'

He was just about to turn away when another flash
caught his eyes. 'Seven!' Then another came. Eight.
Nine. Ten. Eleven. Twelve.

'How queer,' said Julian. 'Why twelve flashes? Hallo
here we go again!'

Another six flashes came from the tower, then no
more at all. Julian wished he had a telescope, then he
could see right into the tower! He sat and thought for a
moment, puzzled. Then he heard the others come
pounding up the stairs. They burst into the room.

'Julian! Father flashed eighteen times instead of six!

'Did you count them, Ju?'

'Why did he do that? Is he in danger of some sort?'

'No. If he was he'd flash the SOS signal,' said
Julian.

'He doesn't know Morse!' said George.

'Well, I expect he just wants to let us know that he needs something,' said Julian. 'We must go over today and find out what it is. More food perhaps.'

So, when Aunt Fanny came home they suggested they should all go over to the island. Aunt Fanny was pleased.

'Oh yes! That would be nice. I expect your uncle wants a message sent off somewhere. We'll go this morning.'

George flew off to tell James she wanted her boat. Aunt Fanny packed up plenty of food with Joanna's help. Then they set off to Kirrin Island in George's boat.

As they rounded the low wall of rocks and came into the little cove, they saw Uncle Quentin waiting for them. He waved his hand, and helped to pull in the boat when it ran gently on to the sand.

'We saw your treble signal,' said Aunt Fanny. 'Did you want something, dear?'

'Yes, I did,' said Uncle Quentin. 'What's that you've got in your basket, Fanny? More of those delicious sandwiches. I'll have some!'

'Oh Quentin – haven't you been having your meals properly again?' said Aunt Fanny. 'What about that lovely soup?'

'What soup?' said Uncle Quentin, looking surprised. 'I wish I'd known about it. I could have done with some last night.'

'But *Quentin*! I told you about it before,' said Aunt Fanny. 'It will be bad by now. You must pour it away.

Now don't forget – pour it away! Where is it? Perhaps I had better pour it away myself.'

'No. I'll do it,' said Uncle Quentin. 'Let's sit down and have our lunch.'

It was much too early for lunch, but Aunt Fanny at once sat down and began to unpack the food. The children were always ready for a meal at any time, so they didn't in the least mind lunch being so early.

'Well, dear – how is your work getting on?' asked Aunt Fanny, watching her husband devour sandwich after sandwich. She began to wonder if he had had anything at all to eat since she had left him two days ago.

'Oh very well indeed,' said her husband. 'Couldn't be better. Just got to a most tricky and interesting point. I'll have another sandwich, please.'

'Why did you signal eighteen times, Uncle Quentin?' asked Anne.

'Ah, well – it's difficult to explain, really,' said her uncle. 'The fact is – I can't help feeling there's somebody else on this island besides myself!'

'*Quentin!* What in the world do you mean?' cried Aunt Fanny, in alarm. She looked over her shoulder as if she half expected to see somebody there. All the children stared in amazement at Uncle Quentin.

He took another sandwich. 'Yes, I know it sounds mad. Nobody else could possibly have got here. But I know there *is* someone!'

'Oh don't Uncle!' said Anne, with a shiver. 'It sounds horrid. And you're all alone at night too!'

'Ah, that's just it! I wouldn't mind a bit if I *was* all

alone at night!' said her uncle. 'What worries me is that I don't think I *shall* be all alone.'

'Uncle, what makes you think there's somebody here?' asked Julian.

'Well, when I had finished the experiment I was doing last night – about half past three in the early morning it would be – but pitch dark, of course,' said Uncle Quentin, 'I came into the open for a breath of fresh air. And I could swear I heard somebody cough – yes, cough twice?'

'Good gracious!' said Aunt Fanny, startled. 'But Quentin – you might have been mistaken. You do imagine things sometimes, you know, when you're tired.'

'Yes, I know,' said her husband. 'But I couldn't imagine *this*, could I?'

He put his hand into his pocket and took something out. He showed it to the others. It was a cigarette end, quite crisp and fresh.

'Now, I don't smoke cigarettes. Nor do any of you! Well then – who smoked that cigarette? And how did he come here? No one would bring him by boat – and that's the only way here.'

There was a silence. Anne felt scared. George stared at her father, puzzled. Who could be here? And why? And how had they got there?

'Well, Quentin – what are you going to do?' said his wife. 'What would be best?'

'I'll be all right if George will give her consent to something,' said Uncle Quentin. 'I want Timmy here, George! Will you leave him behind with me?'

Chapter Eleven

GEORGE MAKES A HARD CHOICE

THERE was a horrified silence. George stared at her father in complete dismay. Everyone waited to see what she would say.

'But Father – Timmy and I have never been separated once,' she said at last, in a pleading voice. 'I do see you want him to guard you – and you *can* have him – but I'll have to stay here too!'

'Oh no!' said her father at once. 'You can't possibly stay, George. That's out of the question. As for never being separated from Timmy, well surely you wouldn't mind that for once? If it was to ensure my safety?'

George swallowed hard. This was the most difficult decision she had ever had to make in her life. Leave Timmy behind on the island – where there was some unknown hidden enemy, likely to harm him if he possibly could!

And yet there was Father too – he might be in danger if there was no one to guard him.

'I shall just *have* to stay here, Father,' she said. 'I can't leave Timmy behind unless I stay too. It's no good.'

Her father began to lose his temper. He was like

George – he wanted his own way, and if he didn't have it he was going to make a fuss!

'If I'd asked Julian or Dick or Anne this same thing, and they'd had a dog, they would all have said yes, at once!' he raged. 'But you, George, you must always make things difficult if you can! You and that dog – anyone would think he was worth a thousand pounds!'

'He's worth much more than that to me,' said George, in a trembling voice. Timmy crept nearer to her and pushed his nose into her hand. She held his collar as if she would not let him go for a moment.

'Yes. That dog's worth more to you than your father or mother or anyone,' said her father, in disgust.

'No, Quentin, I can't have you saying things like that,' said his wife, firmly. 'That's just silly. A mother and father are quite different from a dog – they're loved in different ways. But you are perfectly right, of course – Timmy *must* stay behind with you – and I shall certainly not allow George to stay with him. I'm not going to have *both* of you exposed to danger. It's bad enough to worry about *you*, as it is.'

George looked at her mother in dismay.

'Mother! Do tell Father I must stay here with Timmy.'

'Certainly not,' said her mother. 'Now George, be unselfish. If it were left to Tim to decide, you know perfectly well that he would stay here – and stay *without* you. He would say to himself, "I'm needed here – my eyes are needed to spy out enemies, my ears to hear a quiet footfall – and maybe my teeth to protect my master. I shall be parted from George for a few days –

but she, like me, is big enough to put up with that!"
That's what Timmy would say, George, if it were left
to him.'

Everyone had been listening to this unexpected
speech with great attention. It was about the only one
that could persuade George to give in willingly!

She looked at Timmy. He looked back at her, wagging his tail. Then he did an extraordinary thing – he
got up, walked over to George's father, and lay down
beside him, looking at George as if to say 'There you
are! Now you know what *I* think is right!'

'You see?' said her mother. 'He agrees with me.
You've always said that Timmy was a good dog, and
this proves it. He knows what his duty is. You ought to
be proud of him.'

'I am,' said George, in a choky voice. She got up
and walked off. 'All right,' she said over her shoulder.
'I'll leave him on the island with Father. I'll come back
in a minute.'

Anne got up to go after poor George, but Julian
pulled her down again. 'Leave her alone! She'll be all
right. Good old Timmy – you know what's right and
what's wrong, don't you? Good dog, splendid dog!'

Timmy wagged his tail. He did not attempt to follow George. No – he meant to stay by her father now,
even though he would much rather be with his mistress.
He was sorry that George was unhappy – but sometimes it was better to do a hard thing and be unhappy
about it, than try to be happy without doing it.

'Oh Quentin dear, I don't like this business of you
being here and somebody else spying on you,' said his

wife, 'I really don't. How long will you be before you've finished your work?'

'A few days more,' said her husband. He looked at Timmy admiringly. 'That dog might almost have known what you were saying, Fanny, just now. It was remarkable the way he walked straight over to me.'

'He's a very clever dog,' said Anne warmly. 'Aren't you, Tim? You'll be quite safe with him, Uncle Quentin. He's terribly fierce when he wants to be!'

'Yes. I shouldn't care to have him leaping at *my* throat,' said her uncle. 'He's so big and powerful. Are there any more pieces of cake?'

'Quentin, it's really too bad of you to go without your meals,' said his wife. 'It's no good telling me you haven't, because you wouldn't be as ravenous as this if you had had your food regularly.'

Her husband took no notice of what she was saying. He was looking up at his tower. 'Do you ever see those wires at the top blaze out?' he asked. 'Wonderful sight, isn't it?'

'Uncle, you're not inventing a new atom bomb, or anything are you?' asked Anne.

Her uncle looked at her scornfully. 'I wouldn't waste my time inventing things that will be used to kill and maim people! No – I'm inventing something that will be of the greatest use to mankind. You wait and see!'

George came back. 'Father,' she said, 'I'm leaving Timmy behind for you – but please will you do something for me?'

'What?' asked her father. 'No silly conditions now! I shall feed Timmy regularly, and look after him, if that's what you want to ask me. I may forget my own meals, but you ought to know me well enough to know I shouldn't neglect any animal dependent on me.'

'Yes – I know, Father,' said George, looking a bit doubtful all the same. 'What I wanted to ask you was this – when you go up in the tower to signal each morning, will you please take Timmy with you? I shall be up at the coastguard's cottage, looking through his telescope at the glass room in the tower – and I shall be able to see Timmy then. If I catch just a glimpse of him each day and know he's all right, I shan't worry so much.'

'Very well,' said her father. 'But I don't suppose for a moment that Timmy will be able to climb up the spiral stairway.'

'Oh, he can, Father – he's been up it once already,' said George.

'Good heavens!' said her father. 'Has the dog been up there too? All right, George – I promise I'll take him up with me each morning that I signal, and get him to wag his tail at you. There! Will that satisfy you?'

'Yes. Thank you,' said George. 'And you'll give him a few kind words and a pat occasionally, Father, won't you . . . and . . .?'

'And put his bib on for him at meal-times, I suppose, and clean his teeth for him at night!' said her father, looking cross again. 'I shall treat Timmy like a proper grown-up dog, a friend of mine, George – and believe me, that's the way he wants me to treat him. Isn't it, Timmy? You like all those frills to be kept for your mistress, don't you, not for me?'

'Woof,' said Timmy, and thumped his tail. The children looked at him admiringly. He really was a very sensible clever dog. He seemed somehow much more grown-up than George.

'Uncle, if anything goes wrong, or you want help or anything, flash eighteen times again,' said Julian. 'You ought to be all right with Timmy. He's better than a dozen policemen – but you never know.'

'Right. Eighteen flashes if I want you over here for anything,' said his uncle. 'I'll remember. Now you'd better all go. It's time I got on with my work.'

'You'll pour that soup away, won't you, Quentin?' said his wife, anxiously. 'You don't want to make yourself ill by eating bad soup. It must be green by now! It would be so like you to forget all about it while it was fresh and good – and only remember when it was bad!'

'What a thing to say!' said her husband, getting up. 'Anyone would think I was five years old, without a brain in my head, the way you talk to me!'

'You've plenty of brains dear, we all know that,' said his wife. 'But you don't seem very old sometimes! Now look after yourself – and keep Timmy by you all the time.'

'Father won't need to bother about *that*,' said George. 'Timmy will keep by *him*! You're on guard, Timmy, aren't you? And you know what *that* means!'

'Woof,' said Timmy, solemnly. He went with them all to the boat, but he did not attempt to get in. He stood by George's father and watched the boat bob away over the water. 'Good-bye, Timmy!' shouted

George, in a funny fierce voice. 'Look after yourself!'

Her father waved, and Timmy wagged his tail. George took one of the pairs of oars from Dick and began to row furiously, her face red with the hard work.

Julian looked at her in amusement. It was hard work for him, too, to keep up with the furious rowing, but he didn't say anything. He knew all this fury in rowing was George's way of hiding her grief at parting with Timmy. Funny old George! She was always so intense about things – furiously happy or furiously unhappy, in the seventh heaven of delight or down in the very depths of despair or anger.

Everyone talked hard so that George would think they were not noticing her feelings at parting with Timmy. The talk, of course, was mostly about the unknown man on the island. It seemed very mysterious indeed that he should suddenly have arrived.

'How did he get there? I'm sure not one of the fishermen would have taken him,' said Dick. 'He must have gone at night, of course, and I doubt if there is anyone but George who would know the way in the dark – or even dare to try and find it. These rocks are so close together, and so near the surface; one yard out of the right course and any boat would have a hole in the bottom!'

'No one could reach the island by swimming from the shore,' said Anne. 'It's too far, and the sea is too rough over these rocks. I honestly do wonder if there *is* anyone on the island after all. Perhaps that cigarette end was an old one.'

'It didn't look it ' said Julian. 'Well, it just beats me how anyone got there?'

He fell into thought, puzzling out all the possible and impossible ways. Then he gave an exclamation. The others looked at him.

'I've just thought – would it be possible for an aeroplane to parachute anyone down on the island? I did hear a throbbing noise one night – was it last night? It must have been a plane's engine, of course! *Could* anyone be dropped on the island?'

'Easily,' said Dick. 'I believe you've hit on the explanation, Ju! Good for you! But I say – whoever it is must be in deadly earnest, to risk being dropped on a small island like that in the dark of night!'

In deadly earnest! That didn't sound at all nice. A little shiver went down Anne's back. 'I *am* glad Timmy's there,' she said. And everyone felt the same – yes even George!

Chapter Twelve

THE OLD MAP AGAIN

IT was only about half past one when they arrived back, because they had had lunch so very early, and had not stayed long on the island. Joanna was most surprised to see them.

'Well, here you are again!' she said. 'I hope you don't all want another lunch, because there's nothing in the house till I go to the butcher's!'

'Oh no, Joanna – we've had our picnic lunch,' said her mistress, 'and it was a good thing we packed so much, because the master ate quite half of the lunch! He still hasn't had that nice soup we made for him. Now it will be bad of course.'

'Oh, the men! They're as bad as children!' said Joanna.

'*Well*!' said George. 'Do you really think any of *us* would let your good soup go bad, Joanna? You know jolly well we'd probably eat it up before we ought to!'

'That's true – I wouldn't accuse any of you four – or Timmy either – of playing about with your food,' said Joanna. 'You make good work of it, the lot of you. But where is Timmy?'

'I left him behind to look after Father,' said George. Joanna stared at her in surprise. She knew how passionately fond of Timmy George was.

'You're a very good girl – sometimes!' she said. 'See now – if you're still hungry because your father has eaten most of your lunch, you go and look in the biscuit tin. I made you some of your favourite ginger biscuits this morning. You go and find them.'

That was always Joanna's way! If she thought anyone was upset, she offered them her best and freshest food. George went off to find the biscuits.

'You're a kind soul, Joanna,' said George's mother. 'I'm so thankful we left Timmy there. I feel happier about the master now.'

'What shall we do this afternoon?' said Dick, when they had finished munching the delicious ginger biscuits. 'I say, aren't these good? You know, I do think good cooks deserve some kind of decoration, just as much as good soldiers or scientists, or writers. I should give Joanna the OBCBE.'

'Whatever's that?' said Julian.

'Order of the Best Cooks of the British Empire,' said Dick grinning. 'What did you think it was? "Oh, Be Careful Before Eating"?'

'You really are an absolute donkey,' said Julian. 'Now, what *shall* we do this afternoon?'

'Go and explore the passage in the quarry,' said George.

Julian cocked an eye at the window. 'It's about to pour with rain,' he said. 'I don't think that clambering up and down the steep sides of that quarry in the wet would be very easy. No – we'll leave that till a fine day.'

'I'll tell you what we'll do,' said Anne suddenly. 'Do you remember that old map of Kirrin Castle we once found in a box? It had plans of the castle in it – a plan of the dungeons, and of the ground floor, and of the top part. Well, let's have it out and study it? Now we know there is another hiding-place somewhere, we might be able to trace it on that old map. It's sure to be on it somewhere – but perhaps we didn't notice it before!'

The others looked at her, thrilled. 'Now that really is a brilliant idea of yours, Anne,' said Julian, and Anne glowed with pleasure at his praise. 'A very fine idea indeed. Just the thing for a wet afternoon. Where's the map? I suppose you've got it somewhere safe, George?'

'Oh yes,' said George. 'It's still in that old wooden box, inside the tin lining. I'll get it.'

She disappeared upstairs and came down again with the map. It was made of thick parchment, and was yellow with age. She laid it out on the table. The others bent over it, eager to look at it once more.

'Do you remember how frightfully excited we were when we first found the box?' said Dick.

'Yes, and we couldn't open it, so we threw it out of the top window down to the ground below, hoping it would burst open!' said George.

'And the crash woke up Uncle Quentin,' said Anne, with a giggle. 'And he came out and got the box and wouldn't let us have it!'

'Oh dear yes – and poor Julian had to wait till Uncle

Quentin was alseep, and creep in and get the box to see what was in it!' finished Dick. 'And we found this map – and how we pored over it!'

They all pored over it again. It was in three parts, as Anne had said – a plan of the dungeons, a plan of the ground floor and a plan of the top part.

'It's no good bothering about the top part of the castle,' said Dick. 'It's all fallen down and ruined. There's practically none of it left except for that one tower.'

'I say!' said Julian, suddenly putting his finger on a certain spot in the map, 'do you remember there were

two entrances to the dungeons? One that seemed to start somewhere about that little stone room – and the other that started where we did at last find the entrance? Well – we never found the other entrance, did we?'

'No! We didn't!' said George, in excitement. She pushed Julian's finger away from the map. 'Look –. there are steps shown here – somewhere where that little room is – so there *must* be an entrance there! Here's the *other* flight of steps – the ones we did find, near the well.'

'I remember that we hunted pretty hard for the entrance in the little room,' said Dick. 'We scraped away the weeds from every single stone, and gave it up at last. Then we found the other entrance, and forgot all about this one.'

'And *I* think Father has found the entrance we *didn't* find!' said George, triumphantly. 'It leads underground, obviously. Whether or not it joins up with the dungeons we know I can't make out from this map. It's a bit blurred here. But it's quite plain that there *is* an entrance here, with stone steps leading underground somewhere! See, there's some sort of passage or tunnel marked, leading from the steps. Goodness knows where it goes, it's so smeared.'

'It joins up with the dungeons, I expect,' said Julian. 'We never explored the whole of them, you know – they're so vast and weird. If we explored the whole place, we should probably come across the stone steps leading from somewhere near that little room. Still, they may be ruined or fallen in now.'

'No, they can't be,' said George. 'I'm perfectly *sure*

that's the entrance Father has found. And I'll tell you something that seems to prove it, too.'

'What?' said everyone.

'Well, do you remember the other day when we first went to see Father?' said George. 'He didn't let us stay long, and he came to see us off at the boat. Well, we tried to see where he went, but we couldn't – but Dick said he saw the jackdaws rising up in a flock, as if they had been suddenly disturbed – and he wondered if Father had gone somewhere in that direction.'

Julian whistled. 'Yes – the jackdaws build in the tower, which is by the little room – and anyone going into the room would disturb them. I believe you're right, George.'

'It's been puzzling me awfully where Uncle Quentin could be doing his work,' said Dick. 'I simply could *not* solve the mystery – but now I think we have!'

'I wonder how Father found his hiding-place,' said George, thoughtfully. 'I still think it was mean of him not to tell me.'

'There must have been some reason,' said Dick, sensibly. 'Don't start brooding again!'

'I'm not,' said George. 'I'm puzzled, that's all. I wish we could take the boat and go over to the island at once, and explore!'

'Yes. I bet we'd find the entrance all right now,' said Dick. 'Your father is sure to have left some trace of where it is – a stone a bit cleaner than the rest – or weeds scraped off – or something.'

'Do you suppose the unknown enemy on the island knows Uncle Quentin's hiding-place?' said Anne, suddenly. 'Oh, I do hope he doesn't! He could so easily shut him in if he did.'

'Well, he hasn't gone there to shut Uncle up – he's gone there to steal his secret, or find it out,' said Julian. 'Golly, I'm thankful he's got Timmy. Timmy could tackle a dozen enemies.'

'Not if they had guns,' said George, in a small voice. There was a silence. It was not a nice thought to think of Timmy at the wrong end of a gun. This had happened once or twice before in their adventures, and they didn't want to think of it happening again.

'Well, it's no good thinking silly things like that,' said Dick, getting up. 'We've had a jolly interesting half-hour. I think we've solved *that* mystery. But I suppose we shan't know for certain till your father's finished his experiment, George, and left the island – then we can go over and have a good snoop round.'

'It's still raining,' said Anne, looking out of the window. 'But it's a bit clearer. It looks as if the sun will be out soon. Let's go for a walk.'

'I shall go up to the coastguard's cottage,' said George, at once. 'I want to look through his telescope to see if I can just get a glimpse of Timmy.'

'Try the field-glasses,' suggested Julian. 'Go up to the top of the house with them.'

'Yes, I will,' said George. 'Thanks for the idea.'

She fetched the field-glasses, where they hung in the hall, and took them out of their leather case. She ran upstairs with them. But she soon came down again, looking disappointed.

'The house isn't high enough for me to see much of

the island properly. I can see the glass top of the tower easily, of course – but the telescope would show it much better. It's more powerful. I think I'll go up and have a squint. You don't need to come if you don't want to.' She put the glasses back into their case.

'Oh, we'll all come and have a squint for old Timmy dog,' said Dick, getting up. 'And I don't mind telling you what we'll see!'

'What?' said George, in surprise.

'We'll see Timmy having a perfectly wonderful time, chasing every single rabbit on the island!' said Dick with a grin. 'My word – you needn't worry about Timmy not having his food regularly! He'll have rabbit for breakfast, rabbit for dinner, rabbit for tea – and rain-water from his favourite pool. Not a bad life for old Timmy!'

'You know perfectly well he'll do nothing of the sort,' said George. 'He'll keep close to Father and not think of rabbits once!'

'You don't know Timmy if you think that,' said Dick dodging out of George's way. She was turning red with exasperation. 'I bet that's why he wanted to stay. *Just* for the rabbits!'

George threw a book at him. It crashed to the floor. Anne giggled. 'Oh stop it, you two. We'll never get out. Come on Ju – we won't wait for the squabblers!'

Chapter Thirteen

AFTERNOON WITH MARTIN

By the time they reached the coastguard's cottage the
sun was out. It was a real April day, with sudden
showers and then the sun sweeping out, smiling.
Everything glittered, especially the sea. It was wet
underfoot, but the children had on their rubber boots.

They looked for the coastguard. As usual he was in
his shed, singing and hammering.

'Good-day to you,' he said, beaming all over his
red face. 'I was wondering when you'd come and see
me again. How do you like this railway station I'm
making?'

'It's better than any I've ever seen in the shops,' said
Anne in great admiration. The coastguard certainly
had made it well, down to the smallest detail.

He nodded his head towards some small wooden
figures of porters and guards and passengers. 'Those
are waiting to be painted,' he said. 'That boy Martin
said he'd come in and do them for me – very handy
with his paints he is, a proper artist – but he's had an
accident.'

'*Has* he? What happened?' said Julian.

'I don't quite know. He was half-carried home this
morning by his father,' said the coastguard. 'Must have

slipped and fallen somewhere. I went out to ask, but Mr Curton was in a hurry to get the boy on a couch. Why don't you go in and ask after him? He's a queer sort of boy – but he's not a bad boy.'

'Yes, we will go and ask,' said Julian. 'I say, coast-guard – would you mind if we looked through your telescope again?'

'Now you go and look at all you want to!' said the old fellow. 'I tell you, you won't wear it out by looking! I saw the signal from your father's tower last night, Miss George – just happened to be looking that way. He went on flashing for a long time, didn't he?'

'Yes,' said George. 'Thank you. I'll go and have a look now.'

She went to the telescope and trained it on her island. But no matter where she looked she could not see Timmy, or her father. They must be down in his workroom, wherever it was. She looked at the glass room in the top of the tower. That was empty too, of course. She sighed. It would have been nice to see Timmy.

The others had a look through as well. But nobody saw Timmy. It was plain that he was keeping close to his master – a proper little guard!

'Well – shall we go in and see what's happened to Martin?' said Julian, when they had finished with the telescope. 'It's just about to pour with rain again – another April shower! We could wait next door till it's over.'

'Right, Let's go,' said Dick. He looked at George 'Don't be afraid I shall be rude, George. Now that I know Mr Curton is a journalist, I shan't bother about him.'

'All the same – I'm not "blabbing" any more,' said George, with a grin. 'I see your point now – even if it doesn't matter, I still shan't "blab" any more.'

'Good for you!' said Dick, pleased. 'Spoken like a boy!'

'Ass!' said George, but she was pleased all the same. They went through the front gateway of the next cottage. As they filed in, they heard an angry voice.

'Well, you can't! Always wanting to mess about with a brush and paint. I thought I'd knocked that idea out of your head. You lie still and get that ankle better. Spraining it just when I want your help!'

Anne stopped, feeling frightened. It was Mr Curton's voice they could hear through the open window. He was giving Martin a good talking to about something, that was plain. The others stopped too, wondering whether to go in or not.

Then they heard a bang, and saw Mr Curton leaving the cottage from the back entrance. He walked rapidly down the garden, and made for the path, that led to the back of the cliff. There was a road there that went to the village.

'Good. He's gone. *And* he didn't see us!' said Dick. 'Who would have thought that such a genial, smiling fellow could have such a rough brutal voice when he loses his temper? Come on – let's pop in and see poor Martin while there's a chance.'

They knocked on the door. 'It's us!' called Julian, cheerfully. 'Can we come in?'

'Oh yes!' shouted Martin from indoors, sounding pleased. Julian opened the door and they all went in.

'I say! We heard you'd had an accident,' said Julian. 'What's up? Are you hurt much?'

'No. It's just that I twisted my ankle, and it was so painful to walk on that I had to be half-carried up here,' said Martin. 'Silly thing to do!'

'Oh – it'll soon be right if it's just a twist,' said Dick. 'I've often done that. The thing is to walk on it as soon as you can. Where were you when you fell?'

Martin went suddenly red, to everyone's surprise. 'Well – I was walking on the edge of the quarry with my father – and I slipped and rolled a good way down,' he said.

There was a silence. Then George spoke. 'I say,' she said, 'I hope you didn't go and give away our little secret to your father? I mean – it's not so much fun when grown-ups share a secret. They want to go snooping about themselves – and it's much more fun to discover things by ourselves. You didn't tell him about that hole under the shelf of rock, did you?'

Martin hesitated. 'I'm afraid I did,' he said at last. 'I didn't think it would matter. I'm sorry.'

'Blow!' said Dick. 'That was our own little discovery. We wanted to go and explore it this afternoon, but we thought it would be so wet we'd fall down the steep slope.'

Julian looked at Martin sharply. 'I suppose that's what happened to *you?*' he said. 'You tried clambering down and slipped!'

'Yes,' said Martin. 'I'm really sorry if you thought it

was your secret. I just mentioned it to my father out of interest – you know – something to say – and he wanted to go down and see for himself.'

'I suppose journalists are always like that,' said Dick. 'Wanting to be on the spot if there's anything to be ferreted out. It's their job. All right, Martin – forget it. But do try and head your father off the quarry. We *would* like to do a bit of exploring, before he butts in. Though there may be nothing to be found at all!'

There was a pause. Nobody knew quite what to say. Martin was rather difficult to talk to. He didn't talk like any ordinary boy – he never made a joke, or said anything silly.

'Aren't you bored, lying here?' said Anne feeling sorry for him.

'Yes, awfully. I wanted my father to go in and ask the coastguard to bring in some little figures I said I'd paint for him,' said Martin. 'But he wouldn't let me. You know I simply love painting – even doing a little thing like that – painting clothes on toy porters and guards – so long as I can have a brush in my hand and colours to choose from!'

This was the longest speech Martin had ever made to the four children! His face lost its dull, bored look as he spoke, and became bright and cheerful.

'O – you want to be an artist, I suppose?' said Anne. 'I would like that too!'

'Anne! you can't even draw a cat that looks like one!' said Dick, scornfully. 'And when you drew a cow I thought it was an elephant.'

Martin smiled at Anne's indignant face. 'I'll show

you some of my pictures,' he said. 'I have to keep them hidden away, because my father can't bear me to want to be an artist!'

'Don't get up if you don't want to,' said Julian. 'I'll get them for you.'

'It's all right. If it's good for me to try and walk, I will,' said Martin, and got off the couch. He put his right foot gingerly to the floor and then stood up. 'Not so bad after all!' he said. He limped across the room to a bookcase. He put his hand behind the second row of books and brought out a cardboard case, big and flat. He took it to the table. He opened it and spread out some pictures.

'Gracious!' said Anne. 'They're *beautiful*! Did you really do these?'

They were queer pictures for a boy to draw, for they were of flowers and trees, birds and butterflies — all drawn and coloured most perfectly, every detail put in lovingly.

Julian looked at them in surprise. This boy was certainly gifted. Why, these drawings were as good as any he had ever seen in exhibitions! He picked a few up and took them to the window.

'Do you mean to say your father doesn't think these are good — doesn't think it's worth while to let you train as an artist?' he said, in surprise.

'He hates my pictures,' said Martin, bitterly. 'I ran away from school, and went to an art-school to train — but he found me and forbade me to think of drawing any more. He thinks it's a weak, feeble thing for a man to do. So I only do it in secret now.'

The children looked at Martin with sympathy. It seemed an awful thing to them that a boy who had no mother, should have a father who hated the thing his son most loved. No wonder he always looked dull and miserable and sullen!

'It's very bad luck,' said Julian at last. 'I wish we could do something to help.'

'Well – get me those figures and the paint tins from the coastguard,' said Martin, eagerly. 'Will you? Father won't be back till six. I'll have time to do them. And do stay and have tea with me. It's so dull up here. I hate it.'

'Yes, I'll get the things for you,' said Julian. 'I can't for the life of me see why you shouldn't have something to amuse yourself with if you want to. And we'll ring up my aunt and tell her we're staying here to tea – so long as we don't eat everything you've got!'

'Oh, that's all right,' said Martin, looking very cheerful indeed. 'There's plenty of food in the house. My father has an enormous appetite. I say, thanks most awfully.'

Julian rang up his aunt. The girls and Dick went to fetch the figures and the paint from the coastguard. They brought them back and arranged them on a table beside Martin. His eyes brightened at once. He seemed quite different.

'This is grand,' he said. 'Now I can get on! It's a silly little job, this, but it will help the old man next door, and I'm always happy when I'm messing about with a brush and paints!'

Martin was very, very clever at painting the little

figures. He was quick and deft, and Anne sat watching him, quite fascinated. George went to hunt in the larder for the tea-things. There was certainly plenty of food! She cut some bread and butter, found some new honey, brought out a huge chocolate cake and some ginger buns, and put the kettle on to boil.

'I say, this is really grand,' said Martin again. 'I wish my father wasn't coming back till eight. By the way – where's the dog? I thought he always went everywhere with you! Where's Timmy?'

Chapter Fourteen

A SHOCK FOR GEORGE

Dick looked at George. He didn't think it would matter telling Martin where Timmy was, so long as George didn't give the *reason* why he had been left on the island.

But George was going to hold her tongue now. She looked at Martin and spoke quite airily. 'Oh, Timmy? We left him behind today. He's all right.'

'Gone out shopping with your mother, I suppose, hoping for a visit to the butcher's!' said Martin. This was the first joke he had ever made to the children, and though it was rather a feeble one they laughed heartily. Martin looked pleased. He began to try and think of another little joke, while his deft hands put reds and blues and greens on the little wooden figures.

They all had a huge tea. Then, when the clock said a quarter to six the girls carried the painted figures carefully back to the coastguard, who was delighted with them. Dick took back the little tins of paint, and the brush stuck in a jar of turpentine.

'Well now, he's clever that boy, isn't he?' said the coastguard, eyeing the figures in delight. 'Looks sort of miserable and sulky – but he's not a bad sort of boy!'

'I'll just have one more squint through your

telescope,' said George, 'before it gets too dark.'

She tilted it towards her island. But once more there was no sign of Timmy, or of her father either. She looked for some time, and then went to join the others. She shook her head as they raised their eyebrows inquiringly.

The girls washed up the tea-things, and cleared away neatly. Nobody felt as if they wanted to wait and see Mr Curton. They didn't feel as if they liked him very much, now they knew how hard he was on Martin.

'Thanks for a lovely afternoon,' said Martin, limping to the door with them. 'I enjoyed my spot of painting, to say nothing of your company.'

'You stick out for your painting,' said Julian. 'If it's the thing you've *got* to do, and you know it, you must go all out for it. See?'

'Yes,' said Martin, and his face went sullen again. 'But there are things that make it difficult – things I can't very well tell you. Oh well – never mind! I dare say it will all come right one day, and I'll be a famous artist with pictures in the academy!'

'Come on, quickly,' said Dick, in a low voice to Julian. 'There's his father coming back!'

They hurried off down the cliff-path, seeing Mr Curton out of the corner of their eyes, coming up the other path.

'Horrid man!' said Anne. 'Forbidding Martin to do what he really longs to do. And he seemed so nice and jolly and all-over-us, didn't he?'

'Very all-over-us,' said Dick, smiling at Anne's new

word. 'But there are a lot of people like thàt – one thing at home and quite another outside!'

'I hope Mr Curton hasn't been trying to explore that passage in the side of the quarry,' said George, looking back, and watching the man walk up to his back door. 'It would be too bad if he butted in and spoilt our fun. I mean – there may be nothing to discover at all – but it will be fun even finding there *is* nothing.'

'Very involved!' said Dick, with a grin. 'But I gather what you mean. I say, that was a good tea, wasn't it?'

'Yes,' said George, looking all round her in an absent-minded manner.

'What's up?' said Dick. 'What are you looking like that for?'

'Oh – how silly of me – I was just looking for Timmy,' said George. 'You know, I'm so used to him always being at my heels or somewhere near that I just can't get used to him not being here.'

'Yes, I feel a bit like that too,' said Julian. 'As if there was something missing all the time. Good old Tim! We shall miss him awfully, all of us – but you most of all, George.'

'Yes. Especially on my bed at night,' said George. 'I shan't be able to go to sleep for ages and ages.'

'I'll wrap a cushion up in a rug and plonk it down on your feet when you're in bed,' said Dick. 'Then it will feel like Timmy!'

'It won't! Don't be silly,' said George, rather crossly. 'And anyway it wouldn't *smell* like him. He's got a lovely smell.'

'Yes, a Timmy-smell,' agreed Anne. 'I like it too.'

The evening went very quickly, playing the endless game of monopoly again. Julian lay in bed later, watching for his uncle's signal. Needless to say, George was at the window too! They waited for half past ten.

'Now!' said Julian. And just as he spoke there came the first flash from the lantern in the tower.

'One,' counted George, 'two – three – four – five – six!' She waited anxiously to see if there were any more, but there weren't.

'Now you can go to bed in peace,' said Julian to George. 'Your father is all right, and that means that Timmy is all right too. Probably he has remembered to give Timmy a good supper and has had some himself as well!'

'Well, Timmy would soon remind him, if he forgot to feed him, that's one thing,' said George, slipping out of the room. 'Good night, Dick; good night, Ju! See you in the morning.'

And back she went to her own bed and snuggled down under the sheets. It was queer not to have Timmy on her feet. She tossed about for a while, missing him, and then fell asleep quite suddenly. She dreamed of her island. She was there with Timmy – and they were discovering ingots of gold down in the dungeon. What a lovely dream!

Next morning dawned bright and sunny again. The April sky was as blue as the forget-me-nots coming out in the garden. George gazed out of the dining-room window at breakfast time wondering if Timmy was running about her island.

'Dreaming about Tim?' said Julian, with a laugh. 'Never mind – you'll soon see him, George. Another hour or so and you'll feast your eyes on him through the coastguard's telescope!'

'Do you really think you'll be able to make out Tim, if he's in the tower with your father at half past ten?' asked her mother. 'I shouldn't have thought you would be able to.'

'Yes, I shall, Mother,' said George. 'It's a very powerful telescope, you know. I'll just go up and make my bed, then I'll go up the cliff-path. Anyone else coming?'

'I want Anne to help me with some turning out,' said her mother. 'I'm looking out some old clothes to give to the vicar's wife for her jumble sale. You don't mind helping me, Anne, do you?'

'No, I'd like to,' said Anne at once. 'What are the boys going to do?'

'I think I must do a bit of my holiday work this morning,' said Julian, with a sigh. 'I don't want to – but I've kept on putting it off. You'd better do some too, Dick. You know what you are – you'll leave it all to the last day if you're not careful!'

'All right. I'll do some too,' said Dick. 'You won't mind scooting up to the coastguard's cottage alone, will you, George?'

'Not a bit,' said George. 'I'll come back just after half past ten, as soon as I've spotted Timmy and Father.'

She disappeared to make her bed. Julian and Dick went to fetch some books. Anne went to make her bed too, and then came down to help her aunt. In a few minutes George yelled good-bye and rushed out of the house.

'What a hurricane!' said her mother. 'It seems as if George never walks if she can possibly run. Now Anne – put the clothes in three piles – the very old – the not so old – and the quite nice.'

Just before half past ten Julian went up to his window to watch for the signal from his uncle. He waited patiently. A few seconds after the half-hour the flashes came – one, two, three, four, five, six – good! Now George would settle down for the day. Perhaps they could go to the quarry in the afternoon. Julian went back to his books and was soon buried in them, with Dick grunting by his side.

At about five minutes to eleven there was the sound of running feet and panting breath. George appeared at the door of the sitting-room where the two boys were doing their work. They looked up.

George was red in the face, and her hair was windblown. She fought to get her breath enough to speak. 'Julian! Dick! Something's happened – Timmy wasn't there!'

'What do you mean?' said Julian in surprise. George slumped down on a chair, still panting. The boys could see that she was trembling too.

'It's serious, Julian! I tell you Timmy wasn't in the tower when the signals came!'

'Well – it only means that your absent-minded father forgot to take him up with him,' said Julian, in his most sensible voice. 'What *did* you see?'

'I had my eye glued to the telescope,' said George, 'and suddenly I saw someone come into the little glass room at the top. I looked for Timmy, of course, at once – but I tell you, he wasn't there! The six flashes came, the man disappeared – and that was all. No Timmy! Oh I do feel so dreadfully worried, Julian.'

'Well, don't be,' said Julian, soothingly. 'Honestly, I'm sure that's what happened. Your father forgot about Timmy. Anyway, if you saw *him*, obviously things are all right.'

'I'm not thinking about Father!' cried George. 'He must be all right if he flashed his signals – I'm thinking about Timmy. Why, even if Father forgot to take him, he'd go with him. You know that!'

'Your father might have shut the door at the bottom and prevented Timmy from going up,' said Dick.

'He might,' said George, frowning. She hadn't thought of that. 'Oh dear – now I shall worry all day long. *Why* didn't I stay with Timmy? What shall I do now?'

'Wait till tomorrow morning,' said Dick. 'Then probably you'll see old Tim all right.'

'Tomorrow morning! Why, that's *ages* away!' said poor George. She put her head in her hands and groaned. 'Oh, nobody understands how much I love Timmy. You would perhaps if you had a dog of your own, Julian. It's an awful feeling, really. Oh Timmy, are you all right?'

'Of course he's all right,' said Julian, impatiently. 'Do pull yourself together, George.'

'I *feel* as if something's wrong,' said George, looking obstinate. 'Julian – I think I'd better go across to the island.'

'No,' said Julian at once. 'Don't be idiotic, George. Nothing is wrong, except that your father's been forgetful. He's sent his O K signal. That's enough! You're not to go and create a scene over there with him. That would be disgraceful!'

'Well – I'll try and be patient,' said George, unexpectedly meek. She got up, looking worried. Julian spoke in a kinder voice.

'Cheer up, old thing! You do like to go off the deep end, don't you?'

Chapter Fifteen

IN THE MIDDLE OF THE NIGHT

GEORGE did not moan any more about her worries. She went about with an anxious look in her blue eyes, but she had the sense not to tell her mother how worried she was at not seeing Timmy in the glass room, when her father signalled.

She mentioned it, of course, but her mother took the same view as Julian did. 'There! I knew he'd forget to take Timmy up! He's so very forgetful when he's at work.'

The children decided to go to the quarry that afternoon and explore the tunnel under the shelf of rock. So they set off after their lunch. But when they came to the quarry, they did not dare to climb down the steep sides. The heavy rain of the day before had made them far too dangerous.

'Look,' said Julian, pointing to where the bushes and smaller plants were ripped up and crushed. 'I bet that's where old Martin fell down yesterday! He might have broken his neck!'

'Yes. I vote we don't attempt to go down till it's as dry as it was the other day,' said Dick.

It was very disappointing. They had brought torches, and a rope, and had looked forward to a little excitement. 'Well, what shall we do?' asked Julian.

'I'm going back home,' said George, unexpectedly. 'I'm tired. You others go for a walk.'

Anne looked at George. She did seem rather pale. 'I'll come back with you, George,' said Anne slipping her hand through her cousin's arm. But George shook it off.

'No thanks, Anne. I want to be alone.'

'Well – we'll go over to the cliff then,' said Julian. 'It'll be nice and blowy up there. See you later, George!'

They went off. George turned and sped back to Kirrin Cottage. Her mother was out. Joanna was upstairs in her bedroom. George went to the larder and took several things from it. She bundled them into a bag and then fled out of the house.

She found James the fisher-boy. 'James! You're not to tell a soul. I'm going over to Kirrin Island tonight – because I'm worried about Timmy. We left him there. Have my boat ready at ten o'clock.'

James was always ready to do anything in the world for George. He nodded and asked no questions at all. 'Right, Miss. It'll be ready. Anything you want put in it?'

'Yes, this bag,' said George. 'Now don't split on me, James. I'll be back tomorrow if I find Tim's all right.'

She fled back to the house. She hoped Joanna would not notice the things she had taken from the larder shelf.

'I can't help it if what I'm doing is wrong,' she kept whispering to herself. 'I know something isn't right with Timmy. And I'm not at all sure about Father,

either. He *wouldn't* have forgotten his solemn promise
to me about taking Timmy up with him. I'll have to go
across to the island. I can't help it if it's wrong!'

The others wondered what was up with George
when they came back from their walk. She was so
fidgety and restless. They had tea and then did some
gardening for Aunt Fanny. George did some too, but
her thoughts were far away, and twice her mother had
to stop her pulling up seedlings instead of weeds.

Bedtime came. The girls got into bed at about a
quarter to ten. Anne was tired and fell asleep at once.
As soon as George heard her regular breathing she
crept quietly out of bed and dressed again. She pulled
on her warmest jersey, got her raincoat, rubber boots
and a thick rug, and tiptoed downstairs.

Out of the side door she went and into the night.
There was a bit of a moon in the sky, so it was not as
dark as usual. George was glad. She would be able to
see her way through the rocks a little now – though
she was sure she could guide the boat even in the dark!

James was waiting for her. Her boat was ready.
'Everything's in,' said James. 'I'll push off. Now you
be careful, Miss – and if you do scrape a rock, row
like anything in case she fills and sinks. Ready?'

Off went George, hearing the lap-lap of the water
against the sides of the boat. She heaved a sigh of relief, and began to row strongly away from the shore.
She frowned as she rowed. Had she brought everything she might want? Two torches. Plenty of food. A
tin-opener. Something to drink. A rug to wrap herself
in tonight.

Back at Kirrin Cottage Julian lay in bed watching
for his uncle's signal. Half past ten. Now for the signal.
Ah, here they were! One – two – three – four – five –
six! Good. Six and no more!

He wondered why George hadn't come into his and
Dick's room to watch for them. She had last night. He
got up, padded to the door of George's room and put
his head in 'George!' he said softly. 'It's OK. Your
father's signals have just come again.'

There was no reply. Julian heard regular breathing
and turned to go back to bed. The girls must be
asleep already! Well, George couldn't really be worrying much about Timmy now, then! Julian got into his
bed and soon fell asleep himself. He had no idea that
George's bed was empty – no idea that even now

George was battling with the waves that guarded Kirrin Island!

It was more difficult than she had expected, for the moon did not really give very much light, and had an annoying way of going behind a cloud just when she badly needed every scrap of light she could get. But, deftly and cleverly, she managed to make her way through the passage between the hidden rocks. Thank goodness the tide was high so that most of them were well below the surface!

At last she swung her boat into the little cove. Here the water was perfectly calm. Panting a little, George pulled her boat up as far as she could. Then she stood in the darkness and thought hard.

What was she going to do? She did not know where her father's hiding-place was – but she felt certain the entrance to it must be somewhere in or near the little stone room. Should she make her way to that?

Yes, she would. It would be the only place to shelter in for the night, anyway. She would put on her torch when she got there, and hunt round for any likely entrance to the hiding-place. If she found it, she would go in – and what a surprise she would give her father! If old Timmy was there he would go mad with delight.

She took the heavy bag, draped the rug over her arm, and set off. She did not dare to put on her torch yet, in case the unknown enemy was lurking near. After all, her father had heard him cough at night!

George was not frightened. She did not even think about being frightened. All her thoughts were set on finding Timmy and making sure he was safe.

She came to the little stone room. It was pitch-dark in there, of course – not even the faint light of the moon pierced into its blackness. George had to put on her torch.

She put down her bundle by the wall at the back, near the old fireplace recess. She draped the rug over it and sat down to have a rest, switching off her torch.

After a while she got up cautiously and switched on her torch again. She began to search for the hiding-place. Where *could* the entrance be? She flashed her torch on to every flagstone in the floor of the room. But not one looked as if it had been moved or lifted. There was nothing to show where there might be an entrance underground.

She moved round the walls, examining those too in the light of her torch. No – there was no sign that a hidden way lay behind any of those stones either. It was most tantalising. If she only knew!

She went to wrap the rug round her, and to sit and think. It was cold now. She was shivering, as she sat there in the dark, trying to puzzle out where the hidden entrance could be.

And then she heard a sound! She jumped and then stiffened all over, holding her breath painfully. What was it?

There was a curious grating noise. Then a slight thud. It came from the recess where people long ago had built their big log fires! George sat perfectly still, straining her eyes and ears.

She saw a beam of light in the fireplace recess. Then she heard a man's cough!

Was it her father? He had a cough at times. She listened hard. The beam of light grew brighter. Then she heard another noise – it sounded as if someone had jumped down from somewhere! And then – a voice!

'Come on!'

It was not her father's voice! George grew cold with fear then. Not her father's voice! Then what had happened to him – and to Timmy?

Someone else jumped down into the recess, grumbling. 'I'm not used to this crawling about!'

That wasn't her father's voice either. So there were *two* unknown enemies! Not one. And they knew her father's secret workroom. George felt almost faint with horror. Whatever had happened to him and Timmy?

The men walked out of the little stone room without seeing George at all. She guessed they were going to the tower. How long would they be? Long enough for her to search for the place they had appeared from?

She strained her ears again. She heard their footsteps going into the great yard. She tiptoed to the doorway and looked out. Yes – there was the light of their torch near the tower! If they were going up, there would be plenty of time to look round.

She went back into the little stone room. Her hands were trembling and she found it difficult to switch on her torch. She went to the fireplace recess and flashed the light in it.

She gave a gasp! Half way up the recess at the back was a black opening! She flashed the light up there. Evidently there was a movable stone half way up that swung back and revealed an entrance behind. An entrance to what? Were there steps such as were shown in the old map?

Feeling quite breathless, George stood on tip-toe and flashed her light into the hole. Yes – there were steps! They went down into the wall at the back. She remembered that the little stone room backed on to one of the immensely thick old walls still left.

She stood there, uncertain what to do. Had she better go down and see if she could find Timmy and her father? But if she did, she might be made a prisoner too. On the other hand, if she stayed outside, and the men came back and shut up the entrance, she might not be able to open it. She would be worse off than ever!

'I'll go down!' she suddenly decided. 'But I'd better take my bag and the rug, in case the men come back and see them. I don't want them to know I'm on the island if I can help it! I could hide them somewhere down there, I expect. I wonder if this entrance leads to the dungeons.'

She lifted up the rug and the bag and pushed them into the hole. She heard the bag roll down the steps, the tins inside making a muffled noise.

Then she climbed up herself. Gracious, what a long dark flight of steps! Wherever did they lead to?

Chapter Sixteen

DOWN TO THE CAVES

GEORGE went cautiously down the stone steps. They were steep and narrow. 'I should think they run right down in the middle of the stone wall,' thought George 'Goodness, here's a narrow bit!'

It was so narrow that she had to go sideways. 'A fat man would never get through there!' she thought to herself. 'Hallo – the steps have ended!'

She had got the rug round her shoulders, and had picked up her bag on the way down. In her other hand she held her torch. It was terribly dark and quiet down there. George did not feel scared because she was hoping to see Timmy at any moment. No one could feel afraid with Timmy just round the corner, ready to welcome them!

She stood at the bottom of the steps, her torch showing her a narrow tunnel. It curved sharply to the left. 'Now will it join the dungeons from here?' she wondered, trying to get her sense of direction to help her. 'They can't be far off. But there's no sign of them at the moment.'

She went on down the narrow tunnel. Once the roof

came down so low she almost had to crawl. She flashed her torch on it. She saw black rock there, which had evidently been too hard to be removed by the tunnel-builders long ago.

The tunnel went on and on and on. George was puzzled. Surely by now she must have gone by all the dungeons! Why – she must be heading towards the shore of the island! How very queer! Didn't this tunnel join the dungeons then? A little further and she would be under the bed of the sea itself.

The tunnel took a deep slope downwards. More steps appeared, cut roughly from rock. George climbed down them cautiously. Where in the world was she going?

At the bottom of the steps the tunnel seemed to be cut out of solid rock – or else it was a natural passage, not made by man at all. George didn't know. Her torch showed her black, rocky walls and roof, and her feet stumbled over an irregular rocky path. How she longed for Timmy beside her!

'I must be very deep down,' she thought, pausing to flash her torch round her once more. 'Very deep down and very far from the castle! Good gracious – whatever's that awful noise?'

She listened. She heard a muffled booming and moaning. Was it her father doing one of his experiments? The noise went on and on, a deep, never-ending boom.

'Why – I believe it's the sea!' said George, amazed. She stood and listened again. 'Yes – it *is* the sea – over my head! I'm under the rocky bed of Kirrin Bay!'

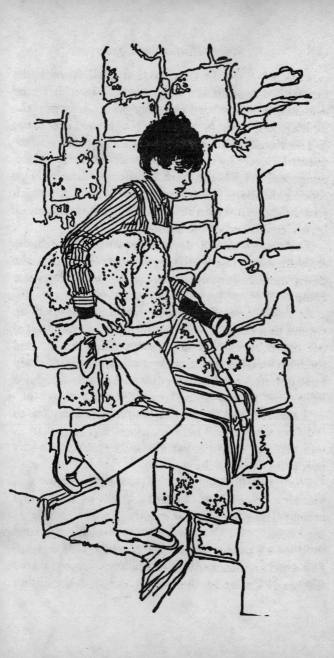

And now poor George did feel a bit scared! She thought of the great waves surging above her, she thought of the restless, moving water scouring the rocky bed over her head, and felt frightened in case the sea should find a way to leak down into her narrow tunnel!

'Now don't be silly,' she told herself sternly. 'This tunnel has been here under the sea-bed for hundreds of years – why should it suddenly become unsafe just when *you* are in it, George?'

Talking to herself like this, to keep up her spirits, she went on again. It was very queer indeed to think she was walking under the sea. So this was where her father was at work! Under the sea itself.

And then George suddenly remembered something he had said to them all, the first time they had visited him on the island. What was it now? 'Oh yes! He said he had to have water *above* and *around* him!' said George. '*Now* I see what he meant! His workroom is somewhere down here – so the sea-water is *above* him – and it's all *round* the tower, because it's built on an island!'

Water above and water around – so that was why her father had chosen Kirrin Island for his experiment. How had he found the secret passage under the sea, though? 'Why, even I didn't know of that,' said George. 'Hallo – what am I coming to?'

She stopped. The passage had suddenly widened out into an enormous dark cave, whose roof was unexpectedly high, lost in dark shadows. George stared round. She saw queer things there that she didn't

understand at all – wires, glass boxes, little machines
that seemed to be at work without a sound, whose
centres were alive with queer, gleaming, shivering
light.

Sudden sparks shot up now and again, and when
that happened a funny smell crept round the cave.
'How weird all this is!' thought George. 'However can
Father understand all these machines and things! I
wonder where he is. I do hope those men haven't
made him prisoner somewhere!'

From this queer, Aladdin's cave another tunnel led.
George switched on her torch again and went into it.
It was much like the other one, but the roof was higher.

She came to another cave, smaller this time, and
crammed with wires of all kinds. There was a curious
humming sound here, like thousands of bees in a hive.
George half-expected to see some flying round.

'It must be these wires making the noise,' she said.
There was nobody in the cave at all, but it led into an-
other one, and George hoped that soon she would find
Timmy and her father.

She went into the next cave, which was perfectly
empty and very cold. She shivered. Then down another passage, and into a small cave. The first thing
she saw beyond this tiny cave was a light!

A light! Then perhaps she was coming to the cave
her father must be in! She flashed her torch round the
little cave she was now standing in and saw tins of
food, bottles of beer, tins of sweets, and a pile of clothes
of some sort. Ah, this was where her father kept his
stores. She went on to the next cave, wondering why

Timmy had not heard her and come to greet her.

She looked cautiously into the cave where the light came from. Sitting at a table, his head in his hands, perfectly still, was her father! There was no sign of Timmy.

'Father!' said George. The man at the table jumped

violently and turned round. He stared at George as if he really could not believe his eyes. Then he turned back again, and buried his face in his hands.

'*Father*!' said George again, quite frightened because he did not say anything to her.

He looked round again, and this time he got up. He stared at George once more, and then sat down heavily. George ran to him 'What's the matter? Oh Father, what's the matter? Where's Timmy?'

'George! Is it *really* you, George? I thought I must be dreaming when I looked up and saw you!' said her father. 'How did you get here? Good gracious, it's impossible that you should be here!'

'Father, are you all right? What's happened – and where's Timmy?' said George, urgently. She looked all round, but could see no sign of him. Her heart went cold. Surely nothing awful had happened to Timmy?

'Did you see two men?' asked her father. 'Where were they?'

'Oh Father – we keep asking each other questions and not answering them!' said George. 'Tell me first – where is Timmy?'

'I don't know,' said her father. 'Did those two men go to the tower?'

'Yes,' said George. 'Father, what's happened?'

'Well, if they've gone to the tower, we've got about an hour in peace,' said her father. 'Now listen to me, George, very carefully. This is terribly important.'

'I'm listening,' said George. 'But do hurry up and tell me about Timmy.'

'These two men were parachuted down on to the

island, to try and find out my secret,' said her father. 'I'll tell you what my experiments are for, George – they are to find a way of replacing all coal, coke and oil – an idea to give the world all the heat and power it wants, and to do away with mines and miners.'

'Good gracious!' said George. 'It would be one of the most wonderful things the world has ever known.'

'Yes,' said her father. 'And I should *give* it to the whole world – it shall not be in the power of any one country, or collection of men. It shall be a gift to the whole of mankind – but, George, there are men who want my secret for themselves, so that they may make colossal fortunes out of it.'

'How hateful!' cried George. 'Go on, Father – how did they hear of it?'

'Well, I was at work on this idea with some of my colleagues, my fellow-workers,' said her father. 'And one of them betrayed us, and went to some powerful business men to tell them of my idea. So when I knew this I decided to come away in secret and finish my experiments by myself. Then nobody could betray me.'

'And you came here!' said George. 'To my island.'

'Yes – because I needed water over me and water around me,' said her father. 'Quite by chance I looked at a copy of that old map, and thought that if the passage shown there – the one leading from the little stone room, I mean – if the passage there *really* did lead under the sea, as it seemed to show, that would be the ideal place to finish my experiments.'

'Oh Father – and I made such a fuss!' said George,

ashamed now, to remember how cross she had been.

'Did you?' said her father, as if he had forgotten all
about that. 'Well, I got all my stuff and came here.
And now these fellows have found me, and got hold of
me!'

'Poor Father! Can't I help?' said George. 'I could
go back and bring help over here, couldn't I?'

'Yes, you could!' said her father. 'But you mustn't
let those men see you, George.'

'I'll do anything you want me to, Father, anything!'
said George. 'But first do tell me what's happened to
Timmy?'

'Well, he kept by me all the time,' said her father.
'Really, he's a wonderful dog, George. And then,
this morning, just as I was coming out of the entrance
in that little room to go up into the tower with Timmy
to signal, the two men pounced on me and forced me
back here.'

'But what happened to Timmy?' asked George, impatiently. Would her father *never* tell her what she
wanted to know?

'He flew at the men, of course,' said her father. 'But
somehow or other one of them lassoed him with a
noose of rope and caught him. They pulled the rope
so tight round his neck that he almost choked.'

'Oh poor, poor Timmy,' said George, and the tears
ran down her cheeks. 'Is he – do you think – he's all
right, Father?'

'Yes. From what I heard the men saying afterwards
I think they've taken him to some cave and shut him
in there,' said her father. 'Anyway, I saw one of them

getting some dog-biscuits out of a bag this evening – so that looks as if he's alive and kicking — and hungry!'

George heaved a great sigh of relief. So long as Timmy was alive and all right! She took a few steps towards what she thought must be another cave. 'I'm going to find Timmy, Father,' she said. 'I *must* find him!'

Chapter Seventeen

TIMMY AT LAST

'No, George!' called her father sharply. 'Come back. There is something very important I want to say. Come here!'

George went over to him, filled with impatience to get to Timmy, wherever he was. She *must* find him!

'Now listen,' said her father. 'I have a book in which I have made all my notes of this great experiment. The men haven't found it! I want you to take it safely to the mainland, George. Don't let it out of your sight! If the men get hold of it they would have all the information they needed!'

'But don't they know everything just by looking at your wires and machines and things?' asked George.

'They know a very great deal,' said her father, 'and they've found out a lot more since they've been here – but not quite enough. I daren't destroy my book of notes, because if anything should happen to me, my great idea would be completely lost. So, George, I must entrust it to you and you must take it to an address I will give you, and hand it to the person there.'

'It's an awful responsibility,' said George, a little scared of handling a book which meant so much, not only to her father, but possibly to the whole of the world. 'But I'll do my best, Father. I'll hide in one of the caves till the men come back, and then I'll slip back up the passage to the hidden entrance, get out, go to my boat and row back to the mainland. Then I'll deliver your book of notes without fail, and get help sent over here to you.'

'Good girl,' said her father, and gave her a hug. 'Honestly, George, you do behave as bravely as any boy. I'm proud of you.'

George thought that was the nicest thing her father had ever said to her. She smiled at him. 'Well, Father, I'll go and see if I can find Timmy now. I simply must see that he's all right before I go to hide in one of the other caves.'

'Very well,' said her father. 'The man who took the biscuits went in that direction – still further under the sea, George. Oh – by the way – how is it you're here, in the middle of the night?'

It seemed to strike her father for the first time that George also might have a story to tell. But George felt that she really couldn't waste any more time – she *must* find Timmy!

'I'll tell you later, Father,' she said. 'Oh – where's that book of notes?'

Her father rose and went to the back of the cave. He took a box and stood on it. He ran his hand along a dark ridge of rock, and felt about until he had found what he wanted.

He brought down a slim book, whose pages were of very thin paper. He opened the book and George saw many beautifully drawn diagrams, and pages of notes in her father's small neat handwriting.

'Here you are,' said her father, handing her the book 'do the best you can. If anything happens to me, this book will still enable my fellow-workers to give my idea to the world. If I come through this all right, I shall be glad to have the book, because it will mean I shall not have to work out all my experiments again.'

George took the precious book. She stuffed it into her macintosh pocket, which was a big one. 'I'll keep it safe, Father. Now I must go and find Timmy, or those two men will be back before I can hide in one of the other caves.'

She left her father's cave and went into the next one. There was nothing there at all. Then on she went down a passage that twisted and turned in the rock.

And then she heard a sound she longed to hear. A whine! Yes, really a whine!

'Timmy!' shouted George, eagerly. 'Oh Timmy! I'm coming!'

Timmy's whine stopped suddenly. Then he barked joyously. 'Woof, woof, woof, woof!' George almost fell as she tried to run down the narrow tunnel. Her torch showed her a big boulder that seemed to be blocking up a small cave in the side of the tunnel. Behind the boulder Timmy barked, and scraped frantically!

George tugged at the stone with all her strength. 'Timmy!' she panted. 'Timmy! I'll get you out! I'm coming! Oh, Timmy!'

The stone moved a little. George tugged again. It was almost too heavy for her to move at all, but despair

made her stronger than she had ever been in her life.
The stone quite suddenly swung to one side, and
George just got one of her feet out of its way in time,
or it would have been crushed.

Timmy squeezed out of the space left. He flung himself on George, who fell on the ground with her arms
tight round him. He licked her face and whined, and
she buried her nose in his thick fur in joy. 'Timmy!
What have they done to you? Timmy, I came as soon
as I could!'

Timmy whined again and again in joy, and tried to
paw and lick George as if he couldn't have enough of
her. It would have been difficult to say which of the
two was the happier.

At last George pushed Timmy away firmly. 'Timmy
we've got work to do! We've got to escape from here
and get across to the mainland and bring help.'

'Woof,' said Timmy. George stood up and flashed
her torch into the tiny cave where Timmy had been.
She saw that there was a bowl of water there and some
biscuits. The men had not ill-treated him, then, except
to lasso him and half-choke him when they caught
him. She felt round his neck tenderly, but except for a
swollen ridge there, he seemed none the worse.

'Now hurry up – we'll go back to Father's cave –
and then find another cave beyond his to hide in till
the two men come back from the tower. Then we'll
creep out into the little stone room and row back to the
mainland,' said George. 'I've got a very, very important book here in my pocket, Timmy.'

Timmy growled suddenly, and the hairs on the

back of his neck rose up. George stiffened, and stood listening.

A stern voice came down the passage. 'I don't know who you are or where you've come from – but if you have dared to let that dog loose he'll be shot! And, to show you that I mean what I say, here's something to let you know I've a revolver!'

Then there came a deafening crash, as the man pulled the trigger, and a bullet hit the roof somewhere in the passage. Timmy and George almost jumped out of their skins. Timmy would have leapt up the passage at once, but George had her hand on his collar. She was very frightened, and tried hard to think what was best to do.

The echoes of the shot went on and on. It was horrid. Timmy stopped growling, and George stayed absolutely still.

'Well?' said the voice, 'Did you hear what I said? If that dog is loose, he'll be shot. I'm not having my plans spoilt now. And you, whoever you are, will please come up the tunnel and let me see you. But I warn you – if the dog's with you, that's the end of him!'

'Timmy! Timmy, run away and hide somewhere!' whispered George suddenly. And then she remembered something else that filled her with despair. She had her father's precious book of notes with her – in her pocket! Suppose the man found it on her? It would break her father's heart to know that his wonderful secret had been stolen from him after all.

George hurriedly took the thin, flat little book from

her pocket. She pushed it at Timmy. 'Put it in your mouth. Take it with you, Tim. And go and hide till it's safe to come. Quick! Go, Timmy, go! I'll be all right.'

To her great relief Timmy, with the book in his mouth, turned and disappeared down the tunnel that led further under the sea. How she hoped he would find a safe hiding place! The tunnel must end soon – but maybe before it did, Timmy would settle down in some dark corner and wait for her to call him again.

'Will you come up the passage or not?' shouted the voice angrily. 'You'll be sorry if I have to come and fetch you – because I shall shoot all the way along!'

'I'm coming!' called George, in a small voice, and she went up the passage. She soon saw a beam of light, and in a moment she was in the flash of a powerful torch. There was a surprised exclamation.

'Good heavens! A boy! What are *you* doing here, and where did you come from?'

George's short curly hair made the man with the torch think she was a boy, and George did not tell him he was wrong. The man held a revolver, but he let it drop as he saw George.

'I only came to rescue my dog, and to find my father,' said George, in a meek voice.

'Well, you can't move that heavy stone!' said the man. 'A kid like you wouldn't have the strength. And you can't rescue your father either! We've got him prisoner, as you no doubt saw.'

'Yes,' said George, delighted to think that the man

was sure she had not been strong enough to move the big stone. She wasn't going to say a word about Timmy! If the man thought he was still shut up in that tiny cave, well and good!

Then she heard her father's voice, anxiously calling from somewhere beyond the man. 'George! Is that you? Are you all right?'

'Yes, Father!' shouted back George, hoping that he would not ask anything about Timmy. The man beckoned her to come to him. Then he pushed her in front of him and they walked to her father's cave.

'I've brought your boy back,' said the man. 'Silly little idiot – thinking he could set that savage dog free! We've got him penned up in a cave with a big boulder in front!'

Another man came in from the opposite end of the cave. He was amazed to see George. The other man explained.

'When I got down here, I heard a noise out beyond this cave, the dog barking and someone talking to him – and found this kid there, trying to set the dog free. I'd have shot the dog, of course, if he *had* been freed.'

'But – how did this boy get here?' asked the other man, still amazed.

'Maybe *he* can tell us that!' said the other. And then, for the first time, George's father heard how George had got there and why.

She told them how she had watched for Timmy in the glass room of the tower and hadn't seen him – and that had worried her and made her suspicious. So she had come across to the island in her boat at night, and had seen where the men came from. She had gone down the tunnel, and kept on till she came to the cave, where she had found her father.

The three men listened in silence. 'Well, you're a tiresome nuisance,' one of the men said to George, 'but my word, you're a son to be proud of. It's not many boys would have been brave enough to run so much risk for anyone.'

'Yes. I'm really proud of you, George,' said her father. He looked at her anxiously. She knew what he was thinking – what about his precious book? Had she been sensible enough to hide it? She did not dare to let him know anything while the men were there.

'Now, this complicates matters,' said the other man, looking at George. 'If you don't go back home you'll soon be missed, and there will be all kinds of search-parties going on – and maybe someone will send over to the island here to tell your father you have dis-appeared! We don't want anyone here at present – not till we know what we want to know!'

He turned to George's father. 'If you will tell us what we want to know, and give us all your notes, we will set you free, give you whatever sum of money you ask us for, and disappear ourselves.'

'And if I still say I won't?' said George's father.

'Then I am afraid we shall blow up the whole of your machines and the tower – and possibly you will never be found again because you will be buried down here,' said the man, in a voice that was suddenly very hard.

There was a dead silence. George looked at her

father. 'You couldn't do a thing like that,' he said at last. 'You would gain nothing by it at all!'

'It's all or nothing with us,' said the man. 'All or nothing. Make up your mind. We'll give you till half past ten tomorrow morning – about seven hours. Then either you tell us everything, or we blow the island sky-high!'

They went out of the cave and left George and her father together. Only seven hours! And then, perhaps, the end of Kirrin Island!

Chapter Eighteen

HALF PAST FOUR IN THE MORNING

As soon as the men were out of earshot, George's father spoke in a low voice.

'It's no good. I'll have to let them have my book of notes. I can't risk having you buried down here, George. I don't mind anything for myself – workers of my sort have to be ready to take risks all their lives – but it's different now you're here!'

'Father, I haven't got the book of notes,' whispered George, thankfully. 'I gave them to Timmy. I *did* manage to get that stone away from the entrance to his little prison – though the men think I didn't! I gave the book to Timmy and told him to go and hide till I fetched him.'

'Fine work, George!' said her father. 'Well – perhaps if you got Timmy now and brought him here – he could deal with these two men before they suspect he is free! He is quite capable of getting them both down on the ground at once.'

'Oh yes! It's our only chance,' said George. 'I'll go and get him now. I'll go a little way along the passage and whistle. Father – why didn't *you* go and try and rescue Timmy?'

334

'I didn't want to leave my book,' said her father. 'I dared not take it with me, in case the men came after me and found it. They've been looking in all the caves for it. I couldn't bear to leave it here, and go and look for the dog. I was sure he was all right, when I saw the men taking biscuits out of the bag. Now do go, George, and whistle to Timmy. The men may be back at any moment.'

George took her torch and went into the passage that led to the little cave where Timmy had been. She whistled loudly, and then waited. But no Timmy came. She whistled again, and then went farther along the passage. Still no Timmy.

She called him loudly. 'TIMMY! TIMMY! COME HERE!' But Timmy did not come. There was no sound of scampering feet, no joyful bark.

'Oh bother!' thought George. 'I hope he hasn't gone so far away that he can't hear me. I'll go a little farther.'

So she made her way along the tunnel, past the cave where Timmy had been, and then on down the tunnel again. Still no Timmy.

George rounded a corner and then saw that the tunnel split into three. Three different passages, all dark, silent and cold. Oh dear! She didn't in the least know which to take. She took the one on the left.

But that also split into three a little way on! George stopped. 'I shall get absolutely lost in this maze of passages under the sea if I go on,' she thought. 'I simply daren't. It's too frightening. TIMMY! TIMMY!'

Her voice went echoing along the passage and sounded very queer indeed. She retraced her steps and went right back to her father's cave, feeling miserable.

'Father, there's no sign of Timmy at all. He must have gone along one of the passages and got lost! Oh dear, this is awful. There are lots of tunnels beyond this cave. It seems as if the whole rocky bed of the sea is mined with tunnels!' George sat down and looked very downhearted.

'Quite likely,' said her father. 'Well – that's a perfectly good plan gone wrong. We must try and think of another.'

'I do wonder what Julian and the others will think when they wake up and find me gone,' said George, suddenly. 'They might even come and try to find me here.'

'That wouldn't be much good,' said her father. 'These men will simply come down here and wait, and nobody will know where we are. The others don't know of the entrance in the little stone room, do they?'

'No,' said George. 'If they came over here I'm sure they'd never find it! We've looked before. And that would mean they'd be blown up with the island. Father, this is simply dreadful.'

'If only we knew where Timmy was!' said her father, 'or if we could get a message to Julian to tell him not to come. What's the time? My word, it's half past three in the early morning! I suppose Julian and the others are fast asleep.'

Julian *was* fast asleep. So was Anne. Dick was in a deep sleep as well, so nobody guessed that George's bed was empty.

But, about half past four Anne awoke, feeling very hot. 'I really must open the window!' she thought. 'I'm boiling!'

She got up and went to the window. She opened it, and stood looking out. The stars were out and the bay shone faintly.

'George,' whispered Anne. 'Are you awake?'

She listened for a reply. But none came. Then she listened more intently. Why, she couldn't even hear George's breathing! Surely George was there?

She felt over George's bed. It was flat and empty. She switched on the light and looked at it. George's pyjamas were still on the bed. Her clothes were gone.

'George has gone to the island!' said Anne, in a fright. 'All in the dark by herself!'

She went to the boys' room. She felt about Julian's bed for his shoulder, and shook him hard. He woke up with a jump. 'What is it? What's up?'

'Julian! George is gone. Her bed's not been slept in,' whispered Anne. Her whisper awoke Dick, and soon both boys were sitting up wide awake.

'Blow! I might have guessed she'd do a fool thing like that,' said Julian. 'In the middle of the night too – and all those dangerous rocks to row round. *Now* what are we going to do about it? I *told* her she wasn't to go to the island – Timmy would be quite all right! I expect Uncle Quentin forgot to take him up to the tower with him yesterday, that's all. She might have waited till half past ten this morning – then she would probably have seen him.'

'Well – we can't do anything now, I suppose, can we?' said Anne, anxiously.

'Not a thing,' said Julian. 'I've no doubt she's safely on Kirrin Island by now, making a fuss of Timmy, and having a good old row with Uncle Quentin. Really George is the limit!'

They talked for half an hour and then Julian looked at his watch. 'Five o'clock. We'd better try and get a bit more sleep. Aunt Fanny will be worried in the morning when she hears of George's latest escapade!'

Anne went back to her room. She got into bed and fell asleep. Julian could not sleep – he kept thinking of George and wondering where exactly she was. Wouldn't he give her a talking-to when she came back!

He suddenly heard a peculiar noise downstairs. Whatever could it be? It sounded like someone climbing in at a window. Was there one open? Yes, the window of the little wash-place might be open. Crash! What in the world was that? It couldn't be a burglar – no burglar would be foolish enough to make such a noise.

There was a sound on the stairs, and then the bedroom door was pushed open. In alarm Julian put out his hand to switch on the light, but before he could do something heavy jumped right on top of him!

He yelled and Dick woke up with a jump. He put on the light – then Julian saw what was on his bed – Timmy!

'Timmy! How did you get here? Where's George! Timmy, is it really you?'

'Timmy!' echoed Dick, amazed. 'Has George brought him back then? Is she here too?'

Anne came in, wakened by the noise. 'Why, *Timmy*! Oh Julian, is George back too, then?'

'No, apparently not,' said Julian, puzzled. 'I say, Tim, what's this you've got in your mouth? Drop it, old chap, drop it!'

Timmy dropped it. Julian picked it up from the bed.

'It's a book of notes – all in Uncle's handwriting! What *does* this mean? How did Timmy get hold of it – and why did he bring it here? It's most extraordinary!'

Nobody could imagine why Timmy had suddenly appeared with the book of notes – and no George.

'It's very queer,' said Julian. 'There's something I don't understand here. Let's go and wake Aunt Fanny.'

So they went and woke her up, telling her all they knew. She was very worried indeed to hear that George was gone. She picked up the book of notes and knew at once that it was very important.

'I must put this into the safe,' she said. 'I know this is valuable. How *did* Timmy get hold of it?'

Timmy was acting queerly. He kept pawing at Julian and whining. He had been very pleased to see everyone, but he seemed to have something on his mind.

'What is it, old boy?' asked Dick. 'How did you get here? You didn't swim, because you're not wet. If you came in a boat, it must have been with George – and yet you've left her behind!'

'*I* think something's happened to George,' said Anne, suddenly. 'I think Timmy keeps pawing you to tell you to go with him and find her. Perhaps she brought him back in the boat, and then was terribly tired and fell asleep on the beach or something. We ought to go and see.'

'Yes, I think we ought,' said Julian. 'Aunt Fanny, would you like to wake Joanna and get something hot ready, in case we find George is tired out and cold?

We'll go down to the beach and look. It will soon be daylight now. The eastern sky is just beginning to show its first light.'

'Well go and dress then,' said Aunt Fanny, still looking very worried indeed. 'Oh, what a dreadful family I've got – always in some scrape or other!'

The three children began to dress. Timmy watched them, waiting patiently till they were ready. Then they all went downstairs and out of doors. Julian turned towards the beach, but Timmy stood still. He pawed at Dick and then ran a few steps in the opposite direction.

'Why – he doesn't *want* us to go to the beach! He wants us to go another way!' cried Julian, in surprise. 'All right, Timmy – you lead the way and we'll follow!'

Chapter Nineteen

A MEETING WITH MARTIN

TIMMY ran round the house and made for the moor behind. It was most extraordinary. Wherever was he going?

'This is awfully queer,' said Julian. 'I'm sure George can't be anywhere in this direction.'

Timmy went on swiftly, occasionally turning his head to make sure everyone was following him. He led the way to the quarry!

'The quarry! Did George come here then?' said Dick. 'But why?'

The dog disappeared down into the middle of the quarry, slipping and sliding down the steep sides as he went. The others followed as best they could. Luckily it was not as slippery as before, and they reached the bottom without accident.

Timmy went straight to the shelf of rock and disappeared underneath it. They heard him give a short sharp bark as if to say 'Come on! This is the way! Hurry up!'

'He's gone into the tunnel under there,' said Dick. 'Where we thought we might explore and didn't.

There must be a passage or something there, then. But is George there?'

'I'll go first,' said Julian, and wriggled through the hole. He was soon in the wider bit and then came out into the part where he could almost stand. He walked a little way in the dark, hearing Timmy bark impatiently now and then. But in a moment or two Julian stopped.

'It's no good trying to follow you in the dark,

Timmy!' he called. 'We'll have to go back and get torches. I can't see a foot in front of me!'

Dick was just wriggling through the first part of the hole. Julian called to him to go back.

'It's too dark,' he said. 'We must go and get torches. If George for some reason is up this passage, she must have had an accident, and we'd better get a rope, and some brandy.'

Anne began to cry. She didn't like the idea of George lying hurt in that dark passage. Julian put his arm round her as soon as he was in the open air again. He helped her up the sides of the quarry, followed by Dick.

'Now don't worry. We'll get her all right. But it beats me why she went there – and I still can't imagine how Tim and she came from the island, if they are here, instead of on the beach!'

'Look – there's Martin!' suddenly said Dick in surprise. So there was! He was standing at the top of the quarry, and seemed just as surprised to see them as they were to see him!

'You're up early,' called Dick. 'And goodness me – are you going gardening or something? Why the spades?'

Martin looked sheepish and didn't seem to know what to say. Julian suddenly walked up to him and caught hold of his shoulder. 'Look here, Martin! There's some funny business going on here! What are you going to do with those spades? Have you seen George? Do you know where she is, or anything about her? Come on, tell me!'

Martin shook his shoulder away from Julian's grip looking extremely surprised.

'George? No! What's happened to him?'

'George isn't a him – she's a her,' said Anne, still crying. 'She's disappeared. We thought she'd gone to the island to find her dog – and Timmy suddenly appeared at Kirrin Cottage, and brought us here!'

'So it looks as if George might be somewhere near here,' said Julian. 'And I want to know if you've seen her or know anything of her whereabouts?'

'No, Julian. I swear I don't!' said Martin.

'Well, tell me what you're doing here so early in the morning, with spades,' said Julian, roughly. 'Who are you waiting for? Your father?'

'Yes,' said Martin.

'And what are you going to do?' asked Dick. 'Going exploring up the hole there?'

'Yes,' said Màrtin again, sullen and worried. 'No harm in that, is there?'

'It's all – very – queer?' said Julian, eyeing him and speaking slowly and loudly. 'But – let me tell you this – *we're* going exploring – not you! If there's anything queer up that hole, *we'll* find it! We shall not allow you or your father to get through the hole. So go and find him and tell him that!'

Martin didn't move. He went very white, and stared at Julian miserably. Anne went up to him, tears still on her face and put her hand on his arm.

'Martin, what is it? Why do you look like that? What's the mystery?'

And then, to the dismay and horror of everyone,

Martin turned away with a noise that sounded very like a sob! He stood with his back to them, his shoulders shaking.

'Good gracious! What *is* up?' said Julian, in exasperation. 'Pull yourself together, Martin! Tell us what's worrying you.'

'Everything, everything!' said Martin, in a muffled voice. Then he swung round to face them. 'You don't know what it is to have no mother and no father – nobody who cares about you – and then . . .'

'But you *have* got a father!' said Dick at once.

'I haven't. He's not my father, that man. He's only my guardian, but he makes me call him father whenever we're on a job together.'

'A job? What sort of job?' said Julian.

'Oh any kind – all beastly,' said Martin. 'Snooping round and finding things out about people, and then getting money from them if we promise to say nothing – and receiving stolen goods and selling them – and helping people like the men who are after your uncle's secret . . .'

'*Oho!*' said Dick at once. 'Now we're coming to it. I *thought* you and Mr Curton were both suspiciously interested in Kirrin Island. What's this present job, then?'

'My guardian will half-kill me for telling all this,' said Martin. 'But, you see, they're planning to blow up the island – and it's about the worst thing I've ever been mixed up in – and I know your uncle is there – and perhaps George too now, you say. I can't go on with it!'

A few more tears ran down his cheeks. It was awful to see a boy crying like that, and the three felt sorry for Martin now. They were also full of horror when they heard him say that the island was to be blown up!

'How do you know this?' asked Julian.

'Well, Mr Curton's got a wireless receiver and transmitter as you know,' explained Martin, 'and so have the fellows on the island – the ones who are after your uncle's secret – so they can easily keep in touch with one another. They mean to get the secret if they can – if not they are going to blow the whole place sky-high so that *nobody* can get the secret. But they can't get away by boat because they don't know the way through those rocks . . .'

'Well, how will they get away then?' demanded Julian.

'We feel sure this hole that Timmy found the other day, leads down to the sea, and under the sea-bed to Kirrin Island,' said Martin. 'Yes, I know it sounds too mad to be true – but Mr Curton's got an old map which clearly shows there was once a passage under the sea-bed. If there is – well, the fellows across on the island can escape down it, after making all preparations for the island to be blown up. See?'

'Yes,' said Julian, taking a long breath. 'I *do* see. I see it all very clearly now. I see something else too! *Timmy* has found his way from the island, using that same passage you have just told us about – and *that's* why he's led us back here – to take us to the island and rescue Uncle Quentin and George.'

There was a deep silence. Martin stared at the

ground. Dick and Julian thought hard. Anne sobbed a little. It all seemed quite unbelievable to her. Then Julian put his hand on Martin's arm.

'Martin! You did right to tell us. We may be able to prevent something dreadful. But you must help. We may need those spades of yours – and I expect you've got torches too. We haven't. We don't want to waste time going back and getting them – so will you come with us and help us? Will you lend us those spades and torches?'

'Would you trust me?' said Martin, in a low voice. 'Yes, I want to come and help you. And if we get in now, my guardian won't be able to follow, because he won't have a torch. We can get to the island and bring your uncle and George safely back.'

'Good for you!' said Dick. 'Well, come on then. We've been talking far too long. Come on down again, Ju. Hand him a spade and torch, Martin.'

'Anne you're not to come,' said Julian to his little sister. 'You're to go back and tell Aunt Fanny what's happened. Will you do that?'

'Yes. I don't want to come,' said Anne. 'I'll go back now. Do be careful, Julian!'

She climbed down with the boys and then stood and watched till all three had disappeared into the hole. Timmy, who had been waiting impatiently during the talking, barking now and again, was glad to find that at last they were going to make a move. He ran ahead in the tunnel, his eyes gleaming green every time he turned to see if they were following.

Anne began to climb up the steep side of the quarry

again. Then, thinking she heard a cough, she stopped and crouched under a bush. She peered through the leaves and saw Mr Curton. Then she heard his voice:

'Martin! Where on earth are you?'

So he had come to look for Martin and go up the tunnel with him! Anne hardly dared to breathe. Mr Curton called again and again, then made an impatient noise and began to climb down the side of the quarry.

Suddenly he slipped! He clutched at a bush as he passed, but it gave way. He rolled quite near Anne, and caught sight of her. He looked astonished, but then his look became one of fear as he rolled more and more quickly to the bottom of the deep quarry. Anne heard him give a deep groan as at last he came to a stop.

Anne peered down in fright. Mr Curton was sitting up, holding one of his legs and groaning. He looked up to see if he could spy Anne.

'Anne!' he called. 'I've broken my leg, I think. Can you fetch help? What are you doing here so early? Have you seen Martin?'

Anne did not answer. If he had broken his leg, then he couldn't go after the others! And Anne could get away quickly. She climbed carefully, afraid of rolling down to the bottom, and having to lie beside the horrid Mr Curton.

'Anne! Have you seen Martin? Look for him and get help for me, will you?' shouted Mr Curton, and then groaned again.

Anne climbed to the top of the quarry and looked

down. She cupped her hands round her mouth and shouted loudly:

'You're a very wicked man. I shan't fetch help for you. I simply can't *bear* you!'

And, having got all that off her chest, the little girl shot off at top speed over the moor.

'I must tell Aunt Fanny. She'll know what to do! Oh I hope the others are safe. What shall we do if the island blows up? I'm glad, glad, glad I told Mr Curton he was a very wicked man.'

And on she ran, panting. Aunt Fanny would know what to do!

Chapter Twenty

EVERYTHING BOILS UP

MEANWHILE the three boys and Timmy were having a strange journey underground. Timmy led the way without faltering, stopping every now and again for the others to catch up with him.

The tunnel at first had a very low roof and the boys had to walk along in a stooping position, which was very tiring indeed. But after a bit the roof became higher and Julian, flashing his torch round, saw that the walls and floor, instead of being made of soil, were now made of rock. He tried to reckon out where they were.

'We've come practically straight towards the cliff,' he said to Dick. 'That's allowing for a few turns and twists. The tunnel has sloped down so steeply the last few hundred yards that I think we must be very far underground indeed.'

It was not until the boys heard the curious booming noise that George had heard in the caves, that they knew they must be under the rocky bed of the sea. They were walking under the sea to Kirrin Island. How strange, how unbelievably astonishing!

'It's like a peculiarly vivid dream,' said Julian. 'I'm

not sure I like it very much! All right Tim – we're coming. Hallo – what's this?'

They all stopped. Julian flashed his torch ahead and saw a pile of fallen rocks. Timmy had managed to squeeze himself through a hole in them and go through to the other side, but the boys couldn't.

'This is where the spades come in, Martin!' said Dick, cheerfully. 'Take a hand!'

By dint of pushing and shovelling, the boys at last managed to move the pile of fallen rocks enough to make a way past. 'Thank goodness for the spades!' said Julian.

They went on, and were soon very glad of the spades again, to move another heap of rock. Timmy barked impatiently when they kept him waiting. He was very anxious to get back to George.

Soon they came to where the tunnel forked into two. But Timmy took the right-hand passage without hesitation, and when that one forked into three, he again chose one without stopping to think for a moment.

'Marvellous, isn't he?' said Julian. 'All done by smell! He's been this way once, so he knows it again. We should be completely lost under here if we came by ourselves.'

Martin was not enjoying this adventure at all. He said very little, but laboured on after the others. Dick guessed he was worrying about what was going to happen when the adventure was over. Poor Martin. All he wanted to do was to draw – and instead of that he had been dragged into one horrible job after another, and used as a cat's-paw by his evil guardian.

'Do you think we're anywhere near the island?' said Dick, at last. 'I'm getting tired of this!'

'Yes, we must be,' said Julian. 'In fact I think we'd better be as quiet as we can, in case we come suddenly on the enemy!'

So, without speaking again, they went as quietly as they could – and then suddenly they saw a faint light ahead of them. Julian put out his hand to stop the others.

They were nearing the cave where George's father had his books and papers – where George had found him the night before. Timmy stood in front of them, listening too. He was not going to run headlong into danger!

They heard voices, and listened intently to see whose they were. 'George's – and Uncle Quentin's,' said Julian at last. And as if Timmy had also satisfied himself that those were indeed the two voices, the dog ran ahead and went into the lighted cave, barking joyfully.

'Timmy!' came George's voice, and they heard something overturn as she sprang up. 'Where have you been?'

'Woof,' said Timmy, trying to explain. 'Woof!'

And then Julian and Dick ran into the cave followed by Martin! Uncle Quentin and George stared in the very greatest amazement.

'Julian! Dick! And *Martin*! How did *you* get here?' cried George, while Timmy jumped and capered round her.

'I'll explain,' said Julian. 'It was Timmy that

fetched us!' And he related the whole story of how Timmy had come into Kirrin Cottage in the early morning and had jumped on his bed, and all that had happened since.

And then, in their turn, Uncle Quentin and George told all that had happened to *them*!

'Where are the two men?' asked Julian.

'Somewhere on the island,' said George. 'I went scouting after them some time ago, and followed them up to where they get out into the little stone room. I think they're there until half past ten, when they'll go up and signal, so that people will think everything is all right.'

'Well, what are our plans?' said Julian. 'Will you come back down the passage under the sea with us? Or what shall we do?'

'Better not do that,' said Martin, quickly. 'My guardian may be coming – and he's in touch with other men. If he wonders where I am, and thinks something is up, he may call in two or three others, and we might meet them making their way up the passage.'

They did not know, of course, that Mr Curton was even then lying with a broken leg at the bottom of the quarry. Uncle Quentin considered.

'I've been given seven hours to say whether or not I will give the fellows my secret,' he said. 'That time will be up just after half past ten. Then the men will come down again to see me. I think between us we ought to be able to capture them – especially as we've got Timmy with us!'

'Yes – that's a good idea,' said Julian. 'We could hide somewhere till they come – and then set Timmy on them before they suspect anything!'

Almost before he had finished these words the light in the cave went out! Then a voice spoke out of the blackness.

'Keep still! One movement and I'll shoot.'

George gasped. What was happening? Had the men come back unexpectedly? Oh, why hadn't Timmy given them warning? She had been fondling his ears, so probably he had been unable to hear anything!

She held Timmy's collar, afraid that he would fly at the man in the darkness and be shot. The voice spoke again.

'Will you or will you not give us your secret?'

'Not,' said Uncle Quentin in a low voice.

'You will have this whole island, and all your work blown up then, and yourself too and the others?'

'Yes! You can do what you like!' suddenly yelled George. 'You'll be blown up yourself too. You'll never be able to get away in a boat – you'll go on the rocks!'

The man in the darkness laughed. 'We shall be safe.' he said. 'Now keep at the back of the cave. I have you covered with my revolver.'

They all crouched at the back. Timmy growled, but George made him stop at once. She did not know if the men knew he was free or not.

Quiet footsteps passed across the cave in the darkness. George listened, straining her ears. Two pairs of footsteps! Both men were passing through the cave. She knew where they were going! They were going to escape by the undersea passage – and leave the island to be blown up behind them!

As soon as the footsteps had died away, George switched on her torch. 'Father! Those men are escaping now, down the sea-tunnel. We must escape too – but not that way, My boat is on the shore. Let's get there quickly and get away before there's any explosion.'

'Yes, come along,' said her father. 'But if only I could get up into my tower, I could stop any wicked plan of theirs! They mean to use the power there. I know – but if I could get up to the glass room, I could undo all their plans!'

'Oh do be quick then, Father!' cried George, getting in quite a panic now. 'Save my island if you can!'

They all made their way through the cave up to the passage that led to the stone flight of steps from the little stone room. And there they had a shock!

The stone could not be opened from the inside! The men had altered the mechanism so that it could now only be opened from the outside.

In vain Uncle Quentin swung the lever to and fro. Nothing happened. The stone would not move.

'It's only from outside it can be opened,' he said in despair. 'We're trapped!'

They sat down on the stone steps in a row, one above the other. They were cold, hungry and miserable. What could they do now? Make their way back to the cave, and then go on down the under-sea tunnel?

'I don't want to do that,' said Uncle Quentin. 'I'm

so afraid that if there is an explosion, it may crack the
rocky bed of the sea, which is the roof of the tunnel –
and then water would pour in. It wouldn't be pleasant
if we happened to be there at that moment.'

'Oh no. Don't let's be trapped like that,' said George
with a shudder. 'I couldn't bear it.'

'Perhaps I could get something to explode this stone
away,' said her father, after a while. 'I've got plenty of
stuff if only I've time to put it together.'

'Listen!' said Julian, suddenly. 'I can hear something outside this wall. Sh!'

They all listened intently. Timmy whined and
scratched at the stone that would not move.

'It's voices!' cried Dick. 'Lots of them. Who can it
be?'

'Be *quiet*,' said Julian, fiercely. 'We *must* find out!'

'I know, I know!' said George, suddenly. 'It's the
fishermen who have come over in their boats! *That's*
why the men didn't wait till half past ten! *That's* why
they've gone in such a hurry! They saw the fisher-
boats coming!'

'Then Anne must have brought them!' cried Dick.
'She must have run home to Aunt Fanny, told her
everything and given the news to the fishermen – and
they've come to rescue us! Anne! ANNE! WE'RE
HERE!'

Timmy began to bark deafeningly. The others encouraged him, because they felt certain that Timmy's
bark was louder than their shouts!

'WOOF! WOOF! WOOF!'

Anne heard the barking and the shouting as soon as

she ran into the little stone room. 'Where are you? Where are you?' she yelled.

'HERE! HERE! MOVE THE STONE!' yelled Julian, shouting so loudly that everyone near him jumped violently.

'Move aside, Miss – I can see which stone it is,' said a man's deep voice. It was one of the fishermen. He felt round and about the stone in the recess, sure it was the right one because it was cleaner than the others through being used as an entrance.

Suddenly he touched the right place, and found a tiny iron spike. He pulled it down – and the lever swung back behind it, and pulled the stone aside!

Everyone hurried out, one on top of the other! The six fishermen standing in the little room stared in astonishment. Aunt Fanny was there too, and Anne. Aunt Fanny ran to her husband as soon as he appeared – but to her surprise he pushed her away quite roughly.

He ran out of the room, and hurried to the tower. Was he in time to save the island and everyone on it? Oh hurry, hurry!

Chapter Twenty-one

THE END OF THE ADVENTURE

'WHERE's he gone?' said Aunt Fanny, quite hurt. Nobody answered. Julian, George and Martin were
watching the tower with anxious intensity. If only
Uncle Quentin would appear at the top. Ah – there he
was!

He had taken up with him a big stone. As everyone
watched he smashed the glass round the tower with the
stone. Crash! Crash! Crash!

The wires that ran through the glass were broken
and split as the glass crashed into pieces. No power
could race through them now. Uncle Quentin leaned
out of the broken glass room and shouted exultantly.

'It's all right! I was in time! I've destroyed the
power that might have blown up the island – you're
safe!'

George found that her knees were suddenly shaking.
She had to sit down on the floor. Timmy came and
licked her face wonderingly. Then he too sat down.

'What's he doing, smashing the tower up?' asked a
burly fisherman. 'I don't understand all this.'

Uncle Quentin came down the tower and rejoined
them. 'Another ten minutes and I should have been

too late,' he said. 'Thank goodness, Anne, you all arrived when you did.'

'I ran all the way home, told Aunt Fanny, and we got the fishermen to come over as soon as they could get out their boats,' explained Anne. 'We couldn't think of any other way of rescuing you. Where are the wicked men?'

'Trying to escape down the under-sea tunnel,' said Julian. 'Oh – you don't know about that, Anne!' And he told her, while the fishermen listened open-mouthed.

'Look here,' said Uncle Quentin, when he had finished. 'As the boats are here, the men might as well take all my gear back with them. I've finished my job here. I shan't want the island any more.'

'Oh! Then *we* can have it!' said George, delighted. 'And there's plenty of the holidays left. We'll help to bring up what you want, Father.'

'We ought to get back as quickly as we can, so as to catch those fellows at the other end of the tunnel, sir,' said one of the fishermen.

'Yes. We ought,' said Aunt Fanny.

'Gracious! They'll find Mr Curton there with a broken leg,' said Anne, suddenly remembering.

The others looked at her in surprise. This was the first they had heard of Mr Curton being in the quarry. Anne explained.

'And I told him he was a very wicked man,' she ended triumphantly.

'Quite right,' said Uncle Quentin, with a laugh. 'Well, perhaps we'd better get my gear another time.'

'Oh, two of us can see to that for you now,' said the

burly fisherman. 'Miss George here, she's got her boat in the cove, and you've got yours, sir. The others can go back with you, if you like – and Tom and me, we'll fix up your things and bring them across to the mainland later on. Save us coming over again, sir.'

'Right,' said Uncle Quentin, pleased. 'You do that then. It's down in the caves through that tunnel behind the stone.'

They all went down to the cove. It was a beautiful day and the sea was very calm, except just round the island where the waters were always rough. Soon the boats were being sailed or rowed to the mainland.

'The adventure is over!' said Anne. 'How queer – I didn't think it was one while it was happening – but now I see it was!'

'Another to add to our long list of adventures,' said Julian. 'Cheer up, Martin – don't look so blue. Whatever happens, we'll see you don't come out badly over this. You helped us, and you threw in your lot with us. We'll see that you don't suffer – won't we, Uncle Quentin? We'd never have got through those falls of rock if we hadn't had Martin and his spades!'

'Well – thanks,' said Martin. 'If you can get me away from my guardian – and never let me see him again – I'd be happy!'

'It's quite likely that Mr Curton will be put somewhere safe where he won't be able to see his friends for quite a long time,' said Uncle Quentin dryly. 'So I don't think you need worry.'

As soon as the boats reached shore, Julian, Dick, Timmy and Uncle Quentin went off to the quarry to see if Mr Curton was still there – and to wait for the other two men to come out of the tunnel!

Mr Curton was there all right, still groaning and calling for help. Uncle Quentin spoke to him sternly.

'We know your part in this matter, Curton. You will be dealt with by the police. They will be along in a short while.'

Timmy sniffed round Mr Curton, and then walked away, nose in air, as if to say 'What a nasty bit of work!' The others arranged themselves at the mouth of the hole and waited.

But nobody came. An hour went by – two hours. Still nobody. 'I'm glad Martin and Anne didn't come,' said Uncle Quentin. 'I do wish we'd brought sand-wiches.'

At that moment the police arrived, scrambling down the steep sides of the quarry. The police doctor was with them and he saw to Mr Curton's leg. Then, with the help of the others, he got the man to the top with great difficulty.

'Julian, go back and get sandwiches,' said Uncle Quentin at last. 'It looks as if we've got a long wait!'

Julian went back, and was soon down the quarry with neat packets of ham sandwiches and a thermos of hot coffee. The two policemen who were still left offer-ed to stay and watch, if Uncle Quentin wanted to go home.

'Dear me, no!' he said. 'I want to see the faces of these two fellows when they come out. It's going to be one of the nicest moments of my life! The island is not blown up. My secret is safe. My book is safe. My work is finished. And I just want to tell these things to my two dear friends!'

'You know, Father, I believe they've lost their way underground,' said George. 'Julian said there were many different passages. Timmy took the boys through the right ones, of course – but they would have been quite lost if they hadn't had him with them!'

Her father's face fell at the thought of the men being lost underground. He did so badly want to see their dismayed faces when they arrived in the quarry!

'We could send Timmy in,' said Julian. 'He would soon find them and bring them out. Wouldn't you, Tim?'

'Woof,' said Timmy, agreeing.

'Oh yes – that's a good idea,' said George. 'They won't hurt him if they think he can show them the way out! Go on in, Timmy. Find them boy; find them! Bring them here!'

'Woof,' said Timmy, obligingly, and disappeared under the shelf of rock.

Everyone waited, munching sandwiches and sipping coffee. And then they heard Timmy's bark again, from underground!

There was a panting noise, then a scraping sound as somebody came wriggling out from under the rock. He stood up – and then he saw the silent group watching him. He gasped.

'Good morning, Johnson,' said Uncle Quentin, in an amiable voice. 'How are you?'

Johnson went white. He sat down on the nearby heather. 'You win!' he said.

'I do,' said Uncle Quentin. 'In fact, I win hand-somely. Your little plan went wrong. My secret is still safe – and next year it will be given to the whole world!'

There was another scraping sound and the second man arrived. He stood up too – and then he saw the quietly watching group.

'Good morning, Peters,' said Uncle Quentin. 'So nice to see you again. How did you like your underground walk? We found it better to come by sea.'

Peters looked at Johnson, and he too sat down suddenly. 'What's happened?' he said to Johnson.

'It's all up,' said Johnson. Then Timmy appeared, wagging his tail, and went to George.

'I bet they were glad when Timmy came up to them!' said Julian.

Johnson looked at him. 'Yes. We were lost in those hateful tunnels. Curton said he'd come to meet us, but he never came.'

'No. He's probably in the prison hospital by now, with a broken leg,' said Uncle Quentin. 'Well, constable – do your duty.'

Both men were at once arrested. Then the whole company made their way back over the moor. The two men were put into a police car and driven off. The rest of the company went into Kirrin Cottage to have a good meal.

'I'm most terribly hungry,' said George. 'Joanna, have you got anything nice for breakfast?'

'Not much,' said Joanna, from the kitchen. 'Only bacon and eggs and mushrooms!'

'Oooh!' said Anne, 'Joanna, you shall have the OBCBE!'

'And what may that be?' cried Joanna, but Anne couldn't remember.

'It's a decoration!' she cried.

'Well, I'm not a Christmas tree!' shouted back Joanna. 'You come and help with the breakfast!'

It was a very jolly breakfast that the seven of them – no eight, for Timmy must certainly be counted – sat down to. Martin, now that he was free of his guardian, became quite a different boy.

The children made plans for him. 'You can stay with the coastguard, because he likes you – he kept on and on saying you weren't a bad boy! And you can come and play with us and go to the island. And Uncle Quentin will see if he can get you into an art-school. He says you deserve a reward for helping to save his wonderful secret!'

Martin glowed with pleasure. It seemed as if a load had fallen away from his shoulders. 'I've never had a chance till now,' he said, 'I'll make good. You see if I don't!'

'Mother! Can we go and stay on Kirrin Island and watch the tower being taken down tomorrow?' begged George. 'Do say yes! And can we stay there a whole week? We can sleep in that little room as we did before.'

'Well – I suppose you can!' said her mother, smiling at George's eager face. 'I'd rather like to have your father to myself for a few days and feed him up a bit.'

'Oh – that reminds me, Fanny,' said her husband,

suddenly. 'I tried some soup you left for me, the night before last. And my dear, it was horrible! Quite bad!'

'Oh *Quentin*! I told you to pour it away! You know I did,' said his wife, distressed. 'It must have been completely bad. You really are dreadful.'

They all finished their breakfast at last, and went out into the garden. They looked across Kirrin Bay to Kirrin Island. It looked lovely in the morning sun.

'We've had a lot of adventures together,' said Julian. 'More than most children. They *have* been exciting, haven't they?'

Yes – they have, but now we must say good-bye to the Five, and to Kirrin Island too. Good-bye, Julian, Dick, George, Anne – and Timmy. But only Timmy hears our good-bye, for he has such sharp ears.

A *complete list of the* FAMOUS FIVE ADVENTURES *by Enid Blyton*

Do YOU belong to the FAMOUS FIVE CLUB?

Have you got the FAMOUS FIVE BADGE?

There are friends of the FAMOUS FIVE all over the world.

Wear the FAMOUS FIVE badge and you will know each other at once.

If you would like to join the club, send a 25p postal order or postage stamps, but no coins please, with a stamped envelope addressed to yourself, inside an envelope addressed to:

FAMOUS FIVE CLUB
c/o Darrell Waters Ltd
International House
1, St Katharine's Way
London
E1 9UN

You shall have your badge and a membership card as soon as possible, and your gifts will be used to help and comfort children in hospital.